AYLUN

THE EVER-BRANCHING TREE

EPISODE TWO

THE EVER-BRANCHING TREE

AYLUN

DAVID SCIDMORE

Meerdon Publishing
Verona, Wisconsin

David Scidmore / Meerdon Publishing, Inc.
P.O. Box 1234
Verona, WI 53593
meerdon.com

Publisher's Note: This is a work of fiction. Names, characters, places, and incidents are a product of the author's imagination. Locales and public names are sometimes used for atmospheric purposes. Any resemblance to actual people, living or dead, or to businesses, companies, events, institutions, or locales is completely coincidental.

Front cover image by Elena Dudina
Front cover layout by JD Smith
Book layout by David Scidmore

Aylun (The Ever-Branching Tree, Episode Two) – 1st Edition
Library of Congress Control Number: 2019908155
ISBN 978-1-64571-006-6

To Sophie, who was happy just to lie in the grass at my side, basking in the sun and watching the world go by as I wrote.

Acknowledgments

There isn't a single page of this book that has not benefited, in ways big and small, from the professionalism, kindness, skill, knowledge, and diligence of Christopher Noel, Susannah Noel, and Megan Zinn at Noel Editorial.

Thanks again to the amazing Elena Dudina for her fantastic cover artwork and other beautiful images she has crafted for this story. Once again, Jane Dixon-Smith's brilliant layout ensured the cover captures the true spirit of the book.

Lastly, thanks to the musicians in U.K., Knight Area, Spock's Beard, Pat Metheny Group, The Flower Kings, The Moody Blues, Noel, Mystery, The Alan Parsons Project, and many others whose work, once again, became the soundtrack to the story in my mind.

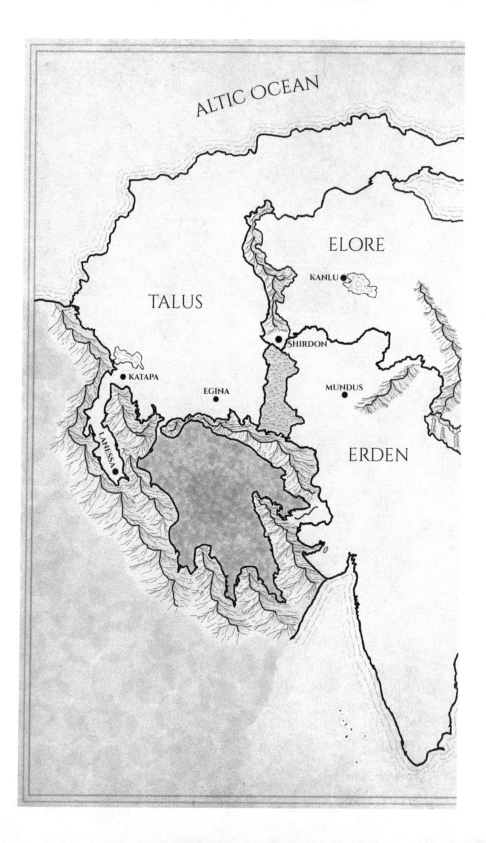

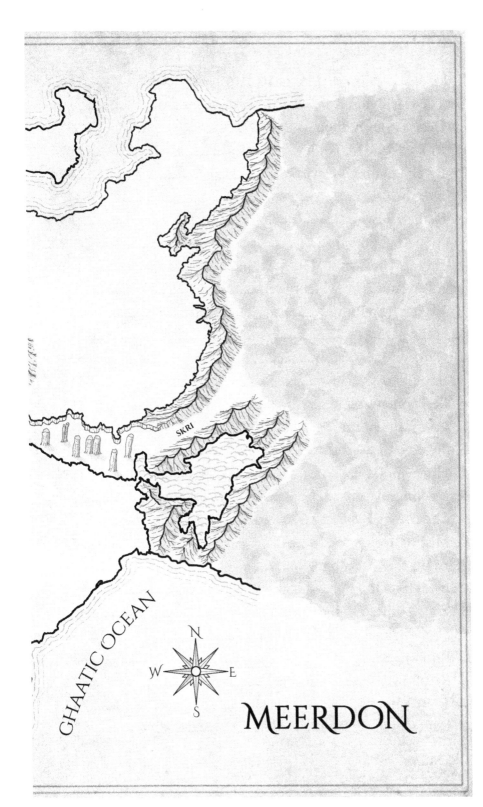

SKRI

GHAATIC OCEAN

MEERDON

Contents

PART ONE

THE LOST CITY

Chapter One

THE DAY BEFORE

Megan stared through the streaks of rain drizzling down the picture window of the second-story break room. Far out in the distance, lightning flashed through gloomy gray skies. Across the storm-soaked yard, a sleek white Mercedes approached on the dark street. It splashed past the glowing glass-and-aluminum Delas Labs sign that stood at the corner. Thunder boomed, then rumbled outward. The wave of sound crashed across the suburban rooftops as the vehicle rounded the corner and headed down the drive to the facility.

Megan tilted her head. It was an S-Class, the fifth such expensive car to arrive in the last fifteen minutes. In general, a vehicle like that was out of reach for those on the lower rungs of the corporate ladder. Employee parking stalls at the research facility seldom sported such a status-flaunting symbol. It was the caliber of car more at home in the parking lot of the downtown central offices.

The squeal of a noisy cart echoed from the hallway outside the room, interrupting her rumination and raising her ire. Chances were good it was another lab assistant, like her, absconding with a piece of equipment. Some measurement devices were rare and had to be shared, so they were in constant demand. How many times had she spent a chunk of her day searching for an electronic gizmo she and Jon needed for an experiment? She would lug it back to the lab and take great pains to set it up. Then, she'd go on break or to lunch and come back to find it had been "borrowed." Even Post-it Notes with "IN USE—DO NOT TAKE" scribbled on them had, on occasion, gone unheeded. Thieving varmints!

1

Megan sighed, then pulled her gaze from the Mercedes and took a deep breath, the air heavy with the scent of coffee from the nearby brewing monstrosity. She fished in her pocket and found the antique black-and-red key chain with its single key. On her way to the break room, she had stumbled across it, lying outside the closed door to Robin's office. She held it up in front of her, examining the worn image of a large jungle cat that stared back from its surface. It was a puzzle, to be sure. In many ways, it was yet another sign of an expensive car—only it fit one that was in an altogether different league, the kind of car that was beyond the reach of all but the very highest rungs of the corporate ladder.

She pocketed the key chain and headed for the door. It was time to return to the lab. Not only because her break was over, but also because she had something she needed to discuss with Jon. It was a decision she had struggled with for some time because it held the potential to damage a treasured relationship. Yet how the future might unfold was not a mystery she could ever solve, so the time had come to act.

Her hard shoes clacked against the bright white linoleum as she marched down the hall. When she whipped around the next corner, Megan caught sight of Jon's longish blond hair and colorful shirt passing by. She turned back and grabbed his arm from behind. "Hey, hey, hey." She tugged, and he skidded to a stop.

He gaped at her over his shoulder, appearing to be in a hurry. "I have a meeting. I—"

"It'll just take a second."

Jon gave a small chuckle as he turned to face her.

Megan looked down at the reflections of the hallway lights on the shiny flooring and scuffed her feet as she searched for the most diplomatic way to broach the topic. Above the rumble of rain came the crackle of distant thunder. It was followed by a low, rumbling boom as she hemmed and hawed, her mind drawing a total blank. Eventually, forced by awkwardness, she chickened out.

"Uh … you were going to come over tonight, right?"

Jon gave a firm nod.

"Um, I thought we could watch that movie about that girl with the thing."

He gave a startled shake of his head. "The scary part is I know exactly which movie you're talking about."

"But you're still coming, right?"

He appeared a bit befuddled. "... Yeah?"

"Okay, good, good."

He eyed her with suspicion. "You stopped me in the hall, on the way to a meeting, to talk about something we just planned an hour ago?"

Megan lowered her head, and after a couple of seconds of strained silence, she spoke with reluctance. "Well, no. Not really."

"Then what is it?" He checked his watch.

She delayed for another few seconds, then the words came on their own. "Can I ask you something?"

He shot her a sly smile. "If I say no, you're going to ask anyway."

She looked up and smiled back. "You know me so well."

"Okay, what is it?"

Megan glanced away, trying once again to summon the right words. Somewhere in the distance, a pair of muffled voices burst into laughter, then hushed again as their footsteps shuffled away down the hall. From the sound, it seemed to be Ashley and Sarah gossiping again or making jokes. The pair took great glee in entertaining themselves at the expense of their coworkers and boss.

She had once even overheard them making fun of her ginger hair. Her parents had emigrated from China when they were students. Being of Asian descent did make her natural red hair an unheard-of rarity. No doubt, there had to be some European heritage some-where in her family tree, but she had never done a DNA test to verify that hypothesis. Anyway, it wasn't like people didn't dye their hair these days.

Megan returned her attention to the conversation. She looked into Jon's soft blue eyes and began with reluctance. "Have you ever thought about being a manager? I mean, being in charge, organizing people's work, drawing up schedules, making important decisions?" Her own words encouraged her, so she let her enthusiasm take over. "You could learn new skills, invest in your future, make more money. Who knows, maybe even go out someday and start your own company."

As she rambled on, Jon's eyes widened, and his body stiffened. "Oh jeez, being in charge, that's the last thing I'd ever want." He shuddered. "You know I dread that sort of thing. Did you really just stop me in the hallway to posit nightmare scenarios?"

Megan placed a hand on his shoulder. "Okay, okay. Don't panic. I wasn't really talking about you." She mimicked Jon's wide-eyed expression and panted, as if having a panic attack. "Do I need to put a bag over your head to keep you from hyperventilating?"

He laughed. "Maybe."

She paused for another moment as the waves of rain roaring against the building rose and fell. Jon was here, and she had his full attention. If she was ever going to ask, now would be the time. So she gathered her courage, then chose each word with care. "Look, I know it's not your thing, but … what if while you're passing up opportunities, I took one? What if I got promoted?" Megan pointed to herself. "You could end up working for me someday."

Jon took a step back, seeming surprised. "I suppose … it's possible, I guess … I mean, I never really thought about it."

She glanced at him sideways. "That'd be too weird, right?"

His response was almost instantaneous. "No. No, not at all."

She shook her head. "Nah, you're just saying that. You'd be uncomfortable, I can tell."

Jon seemed to consider her query for a long while, then he became quiet and serious. "No, you'd be a great boss. In fact, I've had two different managers since I started working here, and I think you'd be as good as either of them." He lowered his voice further and moved closer. "Better even. In fact, I think I'd like working for you more than either of them."

Relief spread, and she broke out in a smile. "Thanks. You always know the right thing to say. I was worried you'd freak out."

His manner took on a sudden businesslike air. "Now, if you're done giving me nightmares about being in charge of other people, I'm late for a meeting."

Megan grabbed his shoulders, twirled him around, and pushed him down the hall as though he were a shopping cart. "Then why the heck are you standing around talking to *me*?"

The clomping of their footsteps echoed down the hallway as Jon turned his head and a mischievous glint appeared in his eyes. He said over his shoulder, "Hey, boss?"

Megan put on her most pompous expression and spoke in a deep and authoritative voice. "Yes."

"Can I have a raise?"

"No."

"More vacation time?"

"No."

"A company car?"

"No." Megan shook her head. "*I* get the company car."

"Then I should get the day off."

"No. You have to cover for me." She jutted her chin in the air. "I'm going golfing."

"But … you don't golf."

"Don't be ridiculous. All managers golf."

"What?"

Megan giggled. "It's a rule."

Jon shook his head in confusion. "Can I at least skip this meeting?"

"No." She gave a last strong shove.

He scowled and mumbled, loud enough for her to hear, "I take it all back. You're a crummy boss."

She laughed as she spun around and marched off down the hall.

Doorways leading to well-lit rooms sped by. Each housed diligent workers with their heads buried in papers and screens. Beyond them were dark and gloomy windows streaked with rain. As Megan hurried along, buoyed by a new sense of optimism, she again slipped the red key chain from her pocket. She looked down at its shiny metallic surface, and her newfound enthusiasm became tinged with anxiety. Jon's encouraging words had cleared the way, but they also meant the time had come to push for what she wanted.

Megan hurried through the door to Robin's sterile, uninspired office. Seated behind her spotless desk, Robin stared at an undersized screen as she hammered away at an old keyboard whose letters she'd almost worn off. Rain poured down outside her picture window, blurring the view of the modest yard and small wooded area beyond. The darkness only served to magnify the room's barren white walls and empty shelves, making it seem all the more bleak in the bright fluorescent light.

At the sound of Megan entering, Robin raised her head and followed her movements, her eyes impassive behind a pair of heavy black glasses. Her drab, businesslike attire and short black hair suited someone whose job it was to be the face of the company to its employees. Manager of human resources was a position that granted little in the way of direct power, yet she played a crucial role in all hiring and firing and every promotion or demotion.

A knot of anxiety formed in Megan's stomach as she strolled over and stopped at the desk. "You're hiring to staff a new project, right?"

Robin sent her an annoyed glare. "Good morning to you too."

Megan kept on staring as she plopped down in the white rolling chair across the uncluttered desk.

Robin made no attempt to mask her exasperation. "What makes you think I'm hiring?"

Megan shrugged. "A few different things."

"Like what?"

"I don't know. ..." She paused to gather her thoughts. "Well, a couple months ago, a copy of the development road map got left up on a screen in a conference room. It listed some projects starting around now with code names I'd never heard before. On its own, that's not noteworthy"—she pointed out the enormous picture window—"but visits from the corporate offices have almost doubled recently." She placed the red key chain she had found on Robin's desk. "And the other day, I found this outside your office when you were having a closed-door meeting."

"It's a key. I don't get it."

"That's a key chain for a classic Jaguar. My bet is it belongs to that director of research guy, Daniel. A classic Jaguar is worth hundreds of thousands, maybe even millions, of dollars. No one except top management could afford one, and I remember his profile in the company newsletter a few years ago. It mentioned he restores classic cars."

"I still don't get it. What's your point?"

Megan leaned forward. "The director of research never gets involved in human resources unless he needs people to staff a project."

Robin sighed again. "Look, even if you were right, and I'm not saying you are, I couldn't talk about it."

Megan gave a small, slow nod of her head. "Well, that's not really why I came here anyway."

Robin rolled her eyes. "Just tell me what's on your mind."

Megan stared for a moment, then turned her gaze to the window. The roar of the rain rose, the storm turning into a torrential downpour as her small knot grew and she struggled to find the most diplomatic way to voice her desire. "I work in a basement, assisting Jon … and he's great and all, but I just wanted, you know, to do something a little more … exciting."

"Like what?"

Her attention whipped back to Robin as she leaned forward and blurted out, "Project management."

Robin stared for a second, seeming surprised, then shook her head. "I'm sorry, but you're not qualified."

Megan remained animated. "Why? Because a job description says I'm not?"

"Well, yeah."

"You know as well as I do, a master's degree in physics doesn't teach you how to manage people or schedule a project."

"That's true, but—"

Megan jabbed her finger at Robin. "Besides, you wrote the job descriptions. You decided what it means to be qualified in the first place. You can just change it and decide I'm qualified."

Robin stammered, "It's—it's not that simple."

"You've made other exceptions in the past."

"Okay, sure, when it made sense, but—"

"How does it not make sense with me? I took almost all the same physics courses as Jon. The only difference is he went on to take a few more advanced classes and did a research project to finish his doctorate. How does that make him more qualified than me to manage resources or motivate a team to meet a deadline?"

Robin gave an exasperated shake of her head. "What happens if you're on a conference call with a client and they start asking questions about the theories behind the research?"

"You don't think I could answer a few questions? My job for the last two years has been setting up and running experiments to prove those theories. I write summary reports, for crying out loud. How do you think I can summarize the results of an experiment without understanding the theory behind it?"

Robin remained mute, her face frozen in a skeptical stare.

"And if a customer had a question I didn't feel qualified to handle, I could get the lead researcher on the call with me." Megan pointed in the direction of Jon's lab. "Like suppose I was in charge of Jon's project. I could bring him in on the call."

"Doesn't that just tell you that Jon should be a ... project ..." Robin trailed off, and her face lit up as if some epiphany had interrupted her train of thought.

8

Thunder boomed, and the echo shuddered through the building as Megan smiled. "Jon should be a project?" She gave a vigorous nod. "Oh, trust me, Jon is definitely a project. But I don't get what you're—"

"No, no … don't you see? You're right. It's the perfect answer. *Jon* should be a project manager."

"What?" Megan jerked herself forward in the chair. "We were talking about me."

"No. No, Jon needs to be a project manager."

"No. No, he doesn't."

Robin ticked off points on her fingers. "He's passionate and brilliant—"

"And articulate and personable and focused … and totally not suited." Megan crossed her arms. "Besides, he'll never do it."

Robin flashed a smug grin. "I can be very persuasive. In fact, I have an idea."

An awful sinking feeling wormed its way into the pit of Megan's stomach. "Please don't put him in an awkward posit—"

The phone rang, and Robin glanced down as she thrust out her palm to halt Megan. After a quick breath, she raised the handset to her mouth. "I'll be with you in just a second." She stabbed a button on the phone and hung up the receiver. In a great rush, she rose, and as she hurried around the desk, she babbled at Megan. "Sorry, but I have a call I have to take."

As Robin ushered her up from her chair, Megan scooped up the red key chain from the desk with a sharp jangle. Robin continued her one-sided conversation as she escorted Megan to the door as if she were shooing a crazy person out of her domain. "Look, just leave everything to me. I'll handle it." She put on a fake smile. "I might even be able to figure out some kind of assistant project manager position for you."

Having scooted her into the hall, Robin began to close the door. As she did, Megan tried to fit in a few last words. "How is assisting Jon different from what I'm already do—" The door shut in her face.

She slumped and stood for a second, staring at the drab gray of the door's painted metal surface. Then she stomped her feet and groaned in frustration. The roar of the rain eased, but the pit in her stomach remained. She had entered the office infused with a sense of resolve, but here she was standing in the hall afterward with an awful feeling of trepidation gnawing at her. Robin may have seemed a bit unhinged, but one thing was clear: she had some half-baked plan, and it wasn't going to be pleasant for Jon. Megan closed her eyes and shook her head as she muttered to herself, "Unbelievable."

The rustling of papers and clicking of keys drifted over the cubicle walls as Megan focused on the screen before her. Upon it was her latest "masterpiece," yet another in an endless stream of test reports. For every experiment, it was her job to list each piece of test and measurement equipment used to monitor conditions and record results, give its inventory tag and calibration status, describe the conditions of the test, including pictures of the entire setup, and summarize the results. It was one of those tasks that seemed interesting the first couple of times you did it but soon grew tedious. Still, like many jobs, it was all in your attitude. As routine as composing reports might be, it required a level of knowledge, insight, and attention to detail that allowed for a sense of pride in a job well done.

The rustling and key clicks stopped, replaced by the squeaking of chairs being rolled back as her coworkers rose and headed for the door. Megan hit save on the final draft and looked at the clock. It was just past three thirty, time for her afternoon break. That awful sinking feeling from her encounter with Robin had eased some, but the whole situation had made things seem awkward with Jon. She didn't feel right hiding their conversation from him, yet she didn't quite know how she'd let it swerve so far off-track, much less how to explain it. So she decided to drag her feet, checking her email before she ventured into the hallway and risked bumping into him. She found a new message from Robin titled "EMPLOYEE NEWSLETTER."

AYLUN

She began scanning the attached document, and it had the usual dull ramblings. There was an update about ongoing projects and an announcement of a couple of new customers. That was followed by a short, useless spiel on workers' compensation insurance. Then, about halfway through, she found a section titled "PLANS FOR THE FUTURE." In it was a chart whose caption read, "*Development Road Map.*" The last of her coworkers shuffled across the carpet and down the hard tile of the hallway as she stared at the screen in bewilderment.

It was like the chart she had recently seen in the conference room weeks ago, except in this version, the two projects that had been slated to begin soon were absent. She cocked her head and stared. It seemed odd that a company of this size would scrap its long-term development plans so close to the launch of the projects.

She scrolled farther down to an announcement titled "CONGRATULATIONS." Her chair creaked as she leaned forward and stared at the screen in surprise. There, in black and white, was the news that Jon had been promoted to project manager. It went on to say he would be starting soon on a new initiative. It was to focus on "reproduction of hypersonic flight conditions in a next-generation wind tunnel." Jon could do it, of course, but it wasn't his area of interest or expertise. Confusion reigned, and she mumbled under her breath, "No way. Jon *agreed?*"

She turned her head toward the handful of pictures she kept pinned to the fabric walls of her cubicle. Her mind raced as her gaze rested on one of her and Jon. They were standing together on a sunny street. It was the day she had arrived at Delas Labs, and he was giving her a tour of the city that was to be her new home. Then, she recalled their conversation in the hallway earlier today. He had been in a near panic at the mere mention of a promotion. "A nightmare," he had called it. She shook her head and whispered to herself, "No. He would never agree to this."

Suddenly, she remembered Robin's insistence that Jon should be a project manager, and when she had objected, the unhinged woman assured her she had a plan and should leave everything to her.

Megan slumped in her chair as it came to her that this *was* the plan. Robin was ambushing Jon by announcing the promotion without discussing it with him first. Her eyes returned to the screen, and she mumbled under her breath, "Is she out of her ever-loving mind?"

Then she made the most distressing connection of all. That awful feeling in her stomach exploded into full-blown guilt as her hand flew to her mouth. "Oh, no. I caused this."

A chime rang out from her screen. Megan clicked, and a window titled DELAS LABS CHAT came to the front. It was a message from Nichole, a nosy coworker and sometime lunch mate, suggesting a location for tomorrow's meal. As she was firing off a response, another message came in, this time from Jon. It read, "Sorry, something came up. I have to cancel tonight." Her guilt doubled. Sitting in the stillness and quiet of an empty office, she let her head fall forward and closed her eyes. This was classic Jon. Nothing had come up. He was embarrassed and hiding in the lab, most likely to avoid his coworkers' inquiries about a promotion he had no intention of allowing to happen. She shook her head in dismay.

She stayed at her desk and fretted the rest of the afternoon as she worked on preparations for tomorrow's experiment. It became harder to concentrate as the day wore on, and she agonized over how to fix the mess she'd made.

The moment her day was done, Megan yanked the drawer of her desk open and grabbed a pair of chopsticks. She sprang from her seat with a sharp creak. The red key chain gave a rattle as she scooped it up and another as she dropped it into her pocket. Then she hurried out into the sterile white hall and down to the lower-level break room.

She had been on her own since she was sixteen, supporting herself through the end of high school and, later, college by waiting tables. Trying to pay tuition and living expenses on meager wages and tips meant she had adopted many habits to save money. Rising early to sling together a meal she could bring to school or work was one of them. Today, she was thankful she still made her own lunch from time to time. From the small white refrigerator, she snatched her translucent plastic lunch box containing the leftovers of her lunch and headed to Jon's lab.

She brought herself to an abrupt halt outside the door and stared at its gray metal surface as she calmed her uneasy heart. After donning a forced smile, she pulled the door open and slipped inside. Jon was too preoccupied with something on his computer screen to notice her arrival or the hallway sounds falling silent as she eased the door closed.

She crept across the neat, well-organized lab, passing the giant metal table full of mirrors and brackets that lay in the center. It wasn't just a marvel of intricate electronics and precision machinery. It was also an extension of the research to which Jon had dedicated the last four years of his life. Its roots went all the way back to a time before she'd met him.

Since childhood, he had been an avid fan of science fiction, but his curious mind never rested. It compelled him to find out which of the things he saw on screen were possible and which were mere flights of fancy. So, he studied them and learned the theories behind them.

When she watched a show with him, he was always respectful, never wanting to burst her bubble. However, if she asked, he would become animated and explain in detail what was and was not possible and why. Even though he never seemed aware of it, his reaction betrayed a deep fascination for warp drives and wormholes. So, when faced with choosing his doctoral thesis, she suggested he focus on methods for creating negative energy. Proving it could be done was a small step toward creating the warp drives and wormholes that seemed to fascinate him. He seized upon the idea, and the table of lasers and mirrors next to her was the result.

The lithium niobate laser at one end emitted alternating pulses of positive and negative energy, each around ten femtoseconds in duration. His goal was to use mirrors to split that beam, sending all the positive pulses in one direction and all the negative to a target. In theory, the cumulative effect of the negative pulses would be a measurable warping of space-time.

Given that the experiment didn't do anything other than prove it was possible to create negative energy, it was hard to guess who the customer could be. Still, Delas Labs did a lot of leading-edge research for big names in the aerospace industry. Some of it was undoubtedly for applications like hypersonic missiles or surveillance satellites, but it was impossible to know for sure. Customers were adept at hiding the details of the larger project. The team at Delas Labs was given a task and seldom knew the whys and wherefores of its application.

As her shadow crossed the screen, Jon looked up. "Oh." His expression fell. "I just sent you—"

"I got your message." Megan halted before him and shot him a stern expression. "So you're really going to skip out on me?"

"It's just ... I ..."

She let her expression melt into a warm smile as she pulled up a nearby chair. "You don't have to explain. It's okay. I understand."

"Honestly, I was looking forward to it."

She put on a mischievous grin. "You did seem excited about seeing that movie about the girl with the thing."

Jon flashed a broad grin of his own. "I am a big fan of the whole 'girl with the thing' genre." His expression softened as he peered into her eyes. "But what I was really looking forward to was seeing it with you."

Megan froze at the sincerity of his confession. It was a throwback to an older version of Jon. The one who'd pursued her with dogged determination throughout their college years. From the day they first met to his last day at school, he was always hanging around her. When he wasn't asking her out point-blank, he was joking about it or hinting at how they would make the perfect couple.

In so many ways, he *was* the perfect guy, except that he spent most of his time sitting in his dorm studying. At the time, she just wanted to cut loose, to go out and party and have a good time. The bottom line was, they didn't fit together. So she rejected him over and over.

Eventually, his crushed expression became too much. In a very real sense, he was her best friend. She liked having him around and couldn't bear the idea of him vanishing out of her life, so she resorted to white lies. She would claim she was dating some random guy she had danced with at a bar or chatted with over a drink. It worked, and he would lay off for a while so they could just hang out and be friends. That whole phase of their relationship ended in a spectacular and unexpected blowup when he left for this job at Delas Labs.

Since that day, he had been different. Oh, he was still the same great guy he had always been. He even went out of his way to get her a job as his lab assistant. But his attitude toward her seemed to have forever changed. Even now, they would go to concerts together, hang out in the park, or even go to each other's houses to share a meal and a movie. Yet, there was a conspicuous care with which he chose each action and every word. There was a line he refused to cross. He never said or did things that might be taken as romantic advances.

The moment dragged on, the quiet whir of fans and soft chittering of disk drives the only sounds as she gazed into his blue eyes, frozen in surprise and confusion. Then she snapped out of it. She was overthinking it. It was obvious he liked watching movies with her, or he wouldn't do it. It was a simple statement of preference, and it wouldn't do to make a bigger deal out of it than that.

She glanced down at her chopsticks as she fidgeted with them, still feeling conspicuous and uncomfortable. "It's fine. You can leave me in the lurch. You have to work late, it's okay." She looked back into his face and held up the plastic lunch box where he could see it. "But it's not okay if you skip dinner." She set the translucent container on the desk near Jon.

His face adopted a peculiar look. "What is it?"

She laughed. "It's a lunch box, silly."

"That's not a lunch box. A lunch box is a square metal thing with pictures of Scooby-Doo or Batman."

"Sure, if you're, like, twelve. This is my lunch box." She popped open the lid with a soft click of the plastic.

Jon stared down at the contents. On one side sat a couple of remaining meatballs. On the other lay a leftover portion of fried rice with egg and shrimp, while in the middle were a few last cherry tomatoes.

He lowered his head over it and inhaled a deep breath, taking in the rich, savory scent. "Honestly, I am pretty hungry, and that smells pretty good." He reached for a meatball, but Megan slapped his hand. He glanced up at her in surprise as she positioned the chopsticks.

Jon looked down at them. "Chopsticks?"

"You know my family originally came from China. My parents were very traditional. This is how we ate meals."

"Yeah, but you always use a fork and knife."

"This was what was handy." Megan clicked the end of the two sticks together, then adroitly lifted one of the meatballs. She held it between the tips of the sticks with the palm of her other hand under it to catch any drips as she ferried it up to her friend's face.

He stared at it with a bewildered expression, then glanced at Megan. She nodded at the meatball, and, with reluctance, Jon opened his mouth. She placed it on his tongue and watched in anticipation as he closed his mouth and chewed. After a moment, he shut his eyes as if enjoying it immensely.

As he swallowed, Jon looked up at her in surprise. "Did you make that? It's really good?"

She scowled. "Don't act so surprised. You know I've been on my own since before college. Of course I can cook."

"But 'it's really, really good?"

Megan beamed. "They're spicy meatballs, one of my favorites." She handed the chopsticks over.

He eyed them as if they were some strange alien artifact. He tried to hold them in the correct position but failed miserably.

"Then finish it. I have to go." Megan stood.

Jon halted his fumbling and glanced up at her in surprise and disappointment. "Go?"

16

She nodded. "Yeah, I have to fix a mistake."

"A mistake?"

"Yeah, I did something to hurt a friend, and now I have to make it right."

Jon's expression remained bewildered as he nodded.

As Megan turned to go, he set the chopsticks on the lunch box and sprang from his chair. He raced around the table to the door and lifted a folded black umbrella off a hook. He laid it on the palms of his outstretched hands, then presented it to her. "Take this. It's cold and rainy out."

"But you'll get wet."

"My weather app says it will stop by the time I leave."

"But—"

"Please." Jon took on a look of concern.

Megan regarded it for a second before accepting it. She looked up at him and smiled.

He waved goodbye. "See you tomorrow?"

She nodded and rushed out the door.

As she headed down the hall with the umbrella in hand, Megan pulled the key chain out of her pocket. Apprehension filled her as she looked down at it. The world she needed to enter now was not one she had visited before, and she had no idea what to expect. Her discussion with Robin had created this disaster, and now it seemed her best chance of fixing it was to confront the owner of the key.

The rain had stopped, but the streets were still wet and the air crisp and clean on the drive to the Delas Labs downtown headquarters. Rush-hour traffic was heavy, so it wasn't until a little after six that Megan arrived at the almost deserted offices. After a short elevator ride, she stepped out onto the thirty-seventh floor. Chances were good that Daniel had gone home for the evening, but she had to try. So she poked around the empty offices until she found a standoffish man in a navy-blue suit to ask for directions. With an uncomfortable economy of words, he ushered her to an office and instructed her to wait.

She knew she had found the right place because the nameplate on the oversized desk announced its occupant as "DANIEL HOBBS, DIRECTOR OF RESEARCH." Megan drummed her fingers on the soft cream-colored leather of a plush easy chair. It was one of a pair around a glass coffee table to the side and in back of the sleek, modern-looking desk. Giant glass windows made up the two outside walls of the spacious corner office. Outside them, dark clouds rolled out to the distance, where infrequent sprays of lightning lit up the horizon. Below them, punctuated by the occasional sign or streetlight, lay a crisscross of darkened streets that stretched out, block upon block, until they vanished behind a curtain of distant rain.

Daniel's high status and power within the company, his sleek office, and the imposing view made her mission seem all the more daunting. It wore on her confidence, and she wondered if she had just blithely cast *herself* into a lion's den. Then, as she looked around, anxiety tugged at her and her chest tightened. Every item in the well-appointed office was pristine and arranged with the utmost care. Each piece of art was placed to create the perfect aesthetic, and not a speck of dust or a single smudge was to be found anywhere. It was an instant reminder of her father's obsessive and tyrannical nature.

All of a sudden, everything seemed oppressive, and her mind slipped away from her. Memories came rushing back of a frightened child's bitter punishment from a loveless father. Torturous hours of sitting in a corner, her arms held over her head until her fingers went numb and her muscles failed. All because she had left a dirty handprint on a wall or chipped a plate. Nights of gnawing hunger as she lay in bed, sent there early with no dinner because her grades weren't good enough or she'd stayed out a few minutes too late. Most traumatic of all were the hours spent trembling in a dark closet, imagining ghosts and ghouls hungering for her from every shelf and corner because she had "talked back," when all she had done was try to make her father understand she wasn't at fault. She had tried her best.

18

Her gaze shot over and her grip on the overstuffed chair tightened as a middle-aged man entered. She stared at his well-groomed short black hair and graying sideburns as he closed the door behind him. With his appearance, the oversized room began to feel claustrophobic. His navy-blue suit was well fitted, and as he marched over to her, he had the same sense of urgency about him that her father always had. It brought back fresh memories of his tyranny and how it had led to the death of her mother and sister.

But as he crossed the room, it became clear that the two men were not the same. Where her father had been rigid, unforgiving, and tightly wound, this man seemed confident and self-assured. Despite this, she tensed as he unbuttoned his suit jacket and seated himself near her. Frozen by intimidation and uncertainty, Megan waited, half expecting an unrelenting scolding for wasting his valuable time.

The man simply leaned forward in his chair, and when he spoke, his voice carried a cordial note. "I hope you didn't wait long." He reached out to shake her hand. "Megan, isn't it?" Without thinking, she shot her hand out and shook his. The man's grip was firm, and he smiled. "You work with Jon on the negative energy project, right?"

Megan nodded.

Daniel leaned back in the plush cream-colored chair. "Mind if I ask how it's going?"

She was nervous and distracted, and her mind froze for a moment. Then she heard herself say, "Pretty good, I guess. Jon is doing component-level checks now."

Daniel gave an approving nod. "Then he must be getting ready for the first full-system test."

Megan stared at him and nodded again. "Yeah, in about two or three weeks." Suddenly, the peculiarity of the situation struck her. Here she was, a nobody in the company, and yet someone of Daniel's position knew of her and Jon. Not to mention, he seemed well versed in their project and its general methodology.

He seemed to sense her confusion and gave a disarming smile. "Don't be so surprised. The whole thing was my idea. A Skunk Works project of sorts. You know, off the books, outside of normal channels, no deadlines or pressure for results. I liked Jon's thesis. I wanted to see where he could take it. I know all about you and him and the project."

Megan sat up straighter and said, "Really?"

He raised himself up taller, too, and gave a confident nod.

She paused a second as she considered the novel implications. "Well, that explains a lot." She cocked her head and eyed him. "But why all the interest in his research?"

Daniel gave a casual shrug. "You know better than I do. Negative energy could be the key to faster-than-light travel and wormholes. It could allow for instantaneous transport. Imagine being able to deliver goods and resources over vast distances in seconds. The possibilities are staggering."

"Not without inconceivable amounts of power."

He leaned forward, his interest appearing even more keen. "But that's how technology advances. You can't get bogged down by all the hurdles in your way. You have to focus on overcoming one obstacle at a time. In this case, the first step is to prove you can create an energy density less than zero."

As she peered into his face, a feeling came over her, an instinct that pursuing his interest in their project was the key to broaching the topic she had come here to discuss. Megan leaned back in her overstuffed chair. "Then, can I ask you a question?"

"Shoot."

"Jon's experiment is a mere proof of concept. It has no practical application. Why fund a project that will never make any money?"

" 'Never' is a strong word." Daniel gave another slight shrug. "The benefits might not be direct. Instead, we may gain notoriety or make countless new discoveries along the way. Some of them could give us crucial competitive advantages in ways we cannot envision."

"But surely there have to be more lucrative projects you could invest in."

He seemed to think for a moment, then looked her in the eye. "Ever hear of the Coyote Hill Research Center?"

The change of subject threw her for a second, and Megan stared as she tried to puzzle out the relevance.

He continued, "They developed one of the first object-oriented programming languages. They used it to create the first desktop operating system, for which they invented the computer mouse. They pioneered laser printing and even theorized tablet computers decades before they were practical."

"Then why has no one ever heard of them?"

Daniel gave a disapproving scowl. "The company that owned them didn't know what to do with them, so they didn't see it through. They didn't stick with it until their inventions could be monetized."

The myriad questions his discourse had raised spun through her mind as Megan lowered her head and said, "Huh."

"Sorry, I didn't mean to derail the conversation. I'm sure you didn't come here just to give me a report on Jon's project."

She looked up and gave a single nod of acknowledgment.

"My door is always open. What can I do for you?"

She took a deep breath. This was her chance to fix what she had done and put an end to all this promotion talk—but first, she needed to understand the situation. Megan fished in her pocket and found the faded red key chain. With a quiet clacking of metal on glass, she set it on the crystal clear surface of the coffee table. "I wanted to return your key."

It jangled as Daniel picked it up and held it in front of his face. Light flashed far out across the distant wall of rain as he examined it. "This isn't mine." He handed it back to her, then settled into the creamy leather of his overstuffed chair.

She cocked her head and stared as the low rumble of thunder lingered around them. "But it's a key to a classic Jaguar and you—"

"Collect classic cars. Yes. And if that key chain matches the car I'm thinking of, I'd love to own one, but it's way above my pay grade."

"Huh, I was sure ..."

Daniel eyed her with suspicion. "You could have just emailed me to ask about the key. You didn't need to come all the way down here."

"That's true." Megan looked into his eyes. "Truth is, I came because I wanted to discuss Jon."

"What about him?"

"Are you aware Robin announced his promotion to project manager?"

Daniel brought himself up a little straighter in the chair again as he stared at the key in her hand. "No, I wasn't." He pondered for a moment as if the news were a revelation of some kind, then looked up into her face. "But I have to admit, I'm not surprised."

"He won't accept it."

"Wait." He straightened even more. "Are you saying she promoted him without discussing it with him first?"

"Yes."

"No." He shook his head. "There has to be some misunderstanding."

"I don't think so. It was quite deliberate."

Daniel lifted one eyebrow. "Well, that's a new one." He stared for a moment, seeming immersed in thought, then cocked his head. "Then Robin must know him pretty well?"

"Not well enough to know he won't accept it."

"Huh?" He pondered for another long moment, then looked her in the eye again and responded with a firm nod. "I think he should."

The statement seemed totally out of left field. "What?" Megan averted her gaze, staring out the window in stunned silence, scanning the stormy skyline. "That's ... that's confusing."

"How so?"

Her attention returned to Daniel. "Earlier, you implied it would be a mistake not to stick with Jon's negative energy research. But now you're saying he should take a promotion that would put an end to his project."

Daniel smiled in what looked like admiration. Then, he leaned back in the chair again as he pressed his fingertips together. For a short while, he gazed out the window at the lights of traffic far below. Then he leaned forward. "I understand being worried about Jon's research. Honestly, so am I, but there are other factors at work here that might make Robin's choice a wise one."

A sudden sinking feeling hit her. One explanation fit all the facts. "Like what? Layoffs?"

Daniel shot upright in his chair and stared at her, seeming shocked. "What? No!"

"The increase in visits from corporate, the recent scaling back of the company development road map, and frequent meetings with Robin in HR. Isn't it all just a prelude to layoffs?"

He seemed flustered. "You're overthinking things."

"If not layoffs, then what?"

"I'm not in a position to discuss these kinds of things with you."

His admission that there was something deeper behind it all struck with unexpected force.

Daniel leaned back in his chair again and took a deep breath. "However, in this case, I assure you, you have misread the situation."

Then it came to her that he had just handed her another opening, one last chance to help herself and fix what she had done to Jon at the same time. Megan sat up, prim and proper. "Then why put Jon's project at risk? If you need a project manager, promote me. That way, you can keep his negative energy experiment, and whatever project you need to manage, I can do it."

"Look, I appreciate your enthusiasm, but—"

"Then give me a chance to prove myself."

Daniel scrutinized her as if sizing her up, then gazed into her face with an earnest expression. "I like you, Megan, and based on our discussion here, I'd recommend you for a promotion in a heartbeat. You're obviously smart, outspoken, perceptive, and ambitious, and I know you have a great work ethic. But it's not possible."

"I don't understand."

"And I can't explain. But I will give you a piece of advice: Talk Jon into accepting the promotion. I think it will be best for both of you."

"But what about—"

"Now, if you'll excuse me, my wife is expecting me home for dinner, and I'm already running late." Daniel stood and motioned to the door.

Megan rose from her seat. He grabbed his coat and whisked her out of his office.

On the ride down in the elevator, the stroll to her car, and even the drive home, one thought would not leave her mind: Daniel had as much as admitted there was something big and secret going on. And that it somehow affected her and Jon and their project.

With her mind still drifting in a groggy haze of sleep, lights of various colors flashed through Megan's eyelids. She drifted up from sleep, and her eyes crept open to pinpoints of glowing color swirling across the ceiling of her bedroom. They scattered across the soft-peach walls and sparkled along the plum-bough wall hanging over her bed, diving in and out of its branches laden with oversized blossoms of delicate pink. Megan closed her eyes again. It was all wrong; her bedroom should be in complete darkness.

She propped herself up on her elbows. Disoriented, she blinked and squinted as she looked down at the multicolored light flittering across her covers' quilted surface. Her mind cleared to a point, and she looked up.

Confusion hit, and she gasped. There, in front of her, stood the source of the light. Watching from the corner of the room stood a glimmering, translucent image of her own thin frame and familiar face. She shook her head in disbelief, but the likeness remained, staring at her with her own unmistakable Chinese features, ginger hair, and dark eyes.

AYLUN

The image smiled and waved. "Don't be afraid. It's just me." Its face adopted a peculiar look. "Um, future me." It appeared thoughtful for a few seconds. "Or I guess it's future you."

Megan gawked, her thoughts mired in a fog of shock. Then, her quiet words drifted through the still air. "I'm asleep. I have to be asleep."

The image rolled its eyes. "You know, you really have to work on this whole denial thing. It doesn't suit us at all."

"No. This is impossible." Megan shook her head and stared some more, but the image just smiled. This couldn't be real. The technology didn't exist to send a 3D likeness through solid walls and render it in the middle of thin air. You needed a medium over which to send it and a screen or glass plate to project it onto. This was impossible, and she would prove it. "All right. Answer me this. Wha—"

"Tuesday. And how exactly does that prove this isn't a dream?"

"Whoa." The answer was correct. It was the day of the week she had pictured in her mind. She lifted her hand and stared down at it, then back at the image. "Wait. How do I know—"

"I'm really you. Hmm, let me think." After the briefest of moments, a look of satisfaction came over the image's face. "Oh. Right. You go to the King Chi every Friday for lunch. Somehow you always wind up with that hot and sour soup you dislike. Last week it was particularly awful. You thought it was burning the skin off your tongue."

Megan scoffed. "That doesn't prove anything. Everyone knows King Chi's hot and sour soup tastes like battery acid."

"I know, right? What do they put in that stuff, furniture stripper?"

"Hey, that's what I was going to say."

Her likeness giggled as Megan paused, taken aback at the words she was about to speak coming from the mouth of an impossible phenomenon. Unable to conjure a rational explanation, she granted the image a slow nod. "Okay. So, maybe you *are* me. So what?"

25

Pinpoints of light twinkled and flickered across her flowered covers as she waited for an answer.

The image adopted a somber expression. "There's something I need you to do."

Alarm spread in Megan at the image's sudden change of mood. "Why? What's wrong?"

"Nothing, now. It's just ... tomorrow, in the lab, Jon is going to ask you out."

Megan sat up straight in bed. "Really?" Then the absurdity of it hit. "Wait, you visited me from the future to talk about a date?"

"What? No. ... Well, yes." Her image scrunched up her face. "Kinda? ... Hey, it's complicated." The likeness planted her fists on her hips. "Besides, that's not the point." She sighed and let her arms drop to her sides. "Look, I don't have time to explain, it's just ... the thing is ..." She turned her head and stared at something behind her. The shimmering lights sparkled across the walls and ceiling as she froze there for a long moment. Then she faced Megan again, and her voice seemed more resolute. "I need you to turn him down."

Megan slumped back down in the bed. "What?"

The glimmering image cocked her head and gazed with sudden sympathy. "And you need to be emphatic."

She slumped even further. "You mean, like, really turn him down hard?"

Her likeness nodded. "Yes."

"I can't do that. He'll be crushed."

The image gave a scant nod, and her voice took on a sympathetic tone that made it all the harder to disbelieve. "I know, but you have to. The next day, you can take it back. You can tell him anything you want. You can say I made you do it, but you have to do this."

"But why?"

Her likeness pondered for a long moment as if searching for the right words. "Sometimes, to get what you want, you have to give it up."

AYLUN

Wracked by a sudden sorrow, Megan' let her head fall, and she peered down at the soft pink covers on her cozy bed. "How can I take you seriously when you sound like a fortune cookie?"

The image gazed with affection. "Megan, I know you, every thought, every feeling. And I know how hard this is—but this is important."

"But you're asking me to—"

"I know what I'm asking." The image averted its gaze as a look of profound sorrow crossed its face. "I've lived through it. ... Trust me. I know."

Megan's eyes drifted across the room as her mind rebelled. "But to do it so cruelly. How can I hurt him like that?"

The image shook her head, and her eyes took on a faraway expression. "You've hurt him dozens of times already. Every time you rejected him."

Megan slumped yet further.

Her likeness stared with an earnest expression. "Promise me you'll do this."

"But I've waited so long, and I ... and I ..." Megan stared at the covers again as an unbearable sadness sank into her soul. "I love him." Tears came to her eyes as she looked back up into the image's face.

The image tilted her head and, in a quavering voice, said, "I know." She lowered her head, and as she began to fade, she repeated, "I know."

Then, the image vanished, leaving Megan staring into a dark corner of her room as tears ran down her cheeks.

Chapter Two

DECISION OF A SHOU

Surrounded by darkness, Aylun slashed with his staff. The blade at its tip caught a dark shadowy figure, and his stomach lurched as something fetid and wet splattered his face. A jarring weight crashed into him, sending him flying through the blackness. The scream of a desperate woman tore at his insides He slammed into the cold, hard ground, as imaginings of his hurt sister sent him into a panic. He leaped to his feet, hurtling after the only sign he could see, the fading light of her flamestone. Half-crazed, stumbling in the dark, he tripped and crashed to the ground. Confusion struck as he watched the light disappear in front of him while the sound of his sister's frantic voice came from behind him, in the opposite direction.

Disoriented and terrified, he shot to his feet and flew back toward her. As he neared, the lighted faces of his sister and closest friend flashed through the cracks in the cloud of dark figures swirling around them. He hacked and stabbed, his blade catching over and over. Dark liquid drenched the earth, but there were too many. Something yanked his friend off the ground and tossed him through the air to land some distance away with the sickening crunch of bones breaking. Frozen and torn between the two, he stared in horror as a swarm of dark creatures enveloped his oldest friend until his cries grew muffled, then ceased. Surrounded and overwhelmed by the massive black forms, Ayrue locked her eyes on to his. Again and again, razor claws slashed her small body, the stench of blood thick in the air as she cried out, "Elder brother, please—"

Aylun bolted awake, gasping for breath through the tightness in his chest. Drenched in a cold sweat, he pounded his breast with a tight fist and waited for the morbid terror and anxiety to pass. Even after four years, the nightmares were as sharp and agonizing as ever.

Still trembling, he stared out across a peaceful pond, struggling to find a focus so he could clear his mind and regain control. His eyes fixed on the carpet of rounded stones that spread across its bottom. Curved and smooth, their well-worn shapes seemed magnified by the crystal clear surface. The sight was a comforting reminder that he was still in the Augury, the secretive heart of all prophecy. It was the home of Chenyu, the Great Oracle, and the place in which all those with the Gift of Prophecy belonged. This spot within its walls was his customary refuge, an island of still water in an ocean of emerald grass. This time, he had sought it out to calm himself from the night terrors, but his sleepless state had caught up with him, and the horrid dreams had returned with a vengeance.

He raised his eyes to the small rock cliff, studying it as he endeavored to banish all thoughts and calm himself. His eyes followed the graceful arc of an evergreen that swooped down from the top of the bluff, wandering along the rocky face only to wind out across the pond's calm surface.

Beyond the tree, a small waterfall masked the sounds of the busy streets of Kanlu outside the Augury. Water from it splashed across the rocks, then spilled into a quiet stream that meandered down to empty into the motionless water.

There, on a large boulder where the stream met the pond, sat Ruahn, eyes closed and cross-legged. Aylun could recognize her countenance with ease by her small eyes and dull black hair, parted in the middle and plastered to her head by a too-tight braid that ran down her back. She had a frustrating habit of being present in places he had sought out for privacy, and today was no exception.

The Augury had selected her to be Shou, or, to be more precise, Shou in training. She was preparing to be like him, an unseen hand that carried out the will of the greatest oracles that ever lived. Though she claimed to have no prophetic gift, he always seemed to encounter her in meditation, as if pretending to be an oracle. What's more, she always did so with the same creepy piece of jewelry in her lap. Smooth, round, and dark, the jewelry had a bright inlay of indigo stone shaped like the iris of an eye. Three red scratches branched out from it like bloodshot veins. She claimed it was a mere focal point for her meditation. Yet resting in her lap and pointed up at her face, it had the appearance of a disembodied, gangrenous eye, watching Ruahn as she sat in deep concentration.

Aylun startled at the sudden appearance of Yaolin coming to rest beside him. As stealthy as the most accomplished Shou, she didn't need the low rumble of the waterfall to mask her approach. She turned her bright brown eyes to his and brushed her silky long black hair over her shoulder, then paused as if waiting for a sign of acknowledgment.

Still wrestling with guilt and anxiety, he wasn't yet in a fit state for discussion. And since conversations with Yaolin tended to resemble sparring matches, his compromised state would make it all the more difficult. Still, it would be wrong to let his discordant emotions affect their exchange. If there was one thing he had learned in this place, it was the importance of remaining detached and professional.

Aylun glanced over at her and, in a deliberate monotone, conceded, "You found me."

Yaolin smiled as she held up her hand and wiggled her fingers, showing off the dark metallic ring with a dashed line of jade inlaid around the middle.

He turned his eyes downward to a similar ring on his own finger, only his had a single, continuous line of jade. "The rings are not toys."

Upon his parents' death, the Rings of Pairing had been passed down to him and his sister, Ayrue. It had happened at such a young age that they never had a chance to reveal anything about the rings other than their name. That, and the prominent dashed and solid lines that made them female and male, dark and bright, yin and yang, each essential to the other, each defined by the other.

Only later, through his parents' colleagues, had he learned of their usefulness. As partners in the Shou, they employed the rings as a tool to find each other, regardless of the distance between them. He and his sister had continued to use them in that way after they became a working team. When she died and Yaolin was assigned to be his partner, it seemed only natural to lend her the ring so he could use it as he always had. Unfortunately, that also meant she could always find him.

Yaolin folded her arms and scowled. "Why do you assume my intent is frivolous?"

Finding it hard not to be amused by the lively manner in which she delivered her indignant response, he smiled and gave a small shrug. "Excessive experience?"

She brought herself up taller, appearing quite incensed. "You are wrong. I came because Father has a mission for us."

Aylun breathed a heavy sigh as his gaze drifted out across the surface of the peaceful pond. She wasn't here merely to chat. This was business. He bowed his head in solemn acknowledgment.

"It is very critical and very dangerous. Chenyu was reluctant, and Father refused outright." She jutted her chin out as if defiant and proud of it. "But I talked them into it."

He gave a quiet chuckle, then turned to face her. "I see. I can imagine how that conversation must have gone."

Her manner took on a sudden petulance. "Father can be so stubborn."

This time, he couldn't suppress a full-throated laugh. "You do not see the irony at all, do you?"

She grinned. "Hey. Are you calling me stubborn?"

Aylun bowed his head to her once again. "I would never do that." Under his breath and yet loud enough for her to hear, he added, "At least not to your face."

Her eyes widened. "Hey, you are supposed to be on my side." She thrust out her chin again. "We are partners. It is your duty."

"Oh, I see." He looked away again.

AYLUN

His unease had been growing as the discussion had become more casual. In matters such as this purported "dangerous mission," he of all people should be keeping things professional. After all, Yaolin seemed incapable. Aylun straightened, endeavoring to take on an efficient and businesslike air. "It might not have occurred to you, with him being your father and all, but he is in charge of the Shou. We are Shou. That makes it his job to object when a mission is too risky."

"No, this mission needs to happen, and soon. Because it is his daughter and son-in-law, he is not being objective."

Though annoyed by the reference, he strived to remain dispassionate, eyeing her with a blank stare. "Stop calling me that. I am not his son-in-law."

"Because you are too stubborn to admit we were meant to be together."

The words touched a part of him he struggled hard not to entertain, but they also filled him with anxiety. He had seen firsthand how dangerous those feelings could be. Aylun stiffened and steeled himself. "No, I am trying to keep this professional."

At his cold, unemotional words, her countenance turned taut and angry. "Fine. Be that way." Then she muttered, "As if I would marry a coldhearted rascal like you anyway."

He paused for a moment to collect himself, then let out another deep sigh. "So, should I be afraid to ask what this very dangerous mission is that you have talked them into?"

Yaolin gave a slight turn of her head and winced as if expecting a rebuke. "The Dead of Night?"

Aylun froze. His reason for seeking this calming place of refuge had been a conversation he'd overheard between Yaolin and Ruahn where Ruahn had insisted one of Wistra's journals was in Lanessa. Of course, it was preposterous that a clueless new recruit would possess such well-guarded information, but the talk of Wistra's journal had triggered memories of the Dead of Night and his sister's demise there. The mere thought of Yaolin in that place threw him into a panic. Fear and anger swept through his veins, and he lost composure. "What?" he almost shouted.

She batted her eyes. "It is just the Dead of Night."

"I knew I should be afraid when I overheard you and Ruahn spouting nonsense about a second Wistra journal in Lanessa."

Yaolin shook her head. "What are you talking about? One has nothing to do with the other."

"Really? So it is just coincidence that after talking to her about it, you are here now trying to con me into a mission to the Dead of Night?"

"Yes, it is."

Aylun scoffed.

Yaolin threw her hands up. "Why would I believe Ruahn? It is obvious she is only parroting some mindless rumor or speculation she heard."

"Oh, and this mysterious information of yours about a journal in the Dead of Night is not just rumor and speculation?"

She crossed her arms. "No, it is not, and we *are* doing this."

At her intransigence, his chest began to tighten again, and a growing heaviness crushed out his breath. "Do you have holes in your brain? I am not going back there. Especially not with you."

As if to comfort him, Yaolin reached out to take his hand.

Aylun yanked it away. "Your father approved of this? Where is Chenyu? I am going to talk to him right away and put a stop to this lunacy."

He rose and began to walk away from the deep blue pond and tumbling waterfall, but Yaolin clutched his wrist with both of her slender hands and yanked him to a stop. "You cannot do that."

"Oh, really?" He scoffed. "Watch me."

She cringed as she blurted out, "I told them both it was your idea."

All thoughts of remaining businesslike flew from his head, and his manner became hard and sharp. "And they believed that? After what happened?"

She looked away and cowered even further. "I told them you wanted to. I told them it was to honor their memory."

"Do you have any idea what you are asking?" Aylun glared. "No. You are just planning to use my feelings for—"

"Oh, feelings? *Now* you have feelings?"

Aylun growled under his breath, "See, this is exactly why I should have never let myself ..."

"Let yourself what? Look at you. You cannot even say it."

"No. I refuse." With great effort, he mastered some small portion of his turmoil. He folded his arms, but his manner remained harsh and brusque. "Whatever you feel for me, do not. It is a liability. It will get us both killed."

Anger flashed on Yaolin's face. "Yes, I have heard it all before." She planted her fists on her hips and mocked him in a deep voice. "Feelings cloud your judgment. They can be used against you. Blah blah blah."

All semblance of control disappeared as anger and frustration took over. Aylun folded his arms. "What are you? A child? You think the appropriate response right now is to mock my affect— I mean, my concern for you?"

Yaolin folded her arms and glared back, mocking him once again.

He stepped back and pointed at her. "This kind of unprofessional behavior is precisely why we are not going." He spun around and stormed away. His footfalls thudded through the lush grass as he headed toward a path that led to a row of dark buildings at the edge of the garden. He had to put an end to this lunacy before it went a single step further.

Once the sparkling lights had vanished, Megan spent what seemed like an eternity staring into the darkness of her cozy room. Her thoughts drifted in a muddled haze as she tried to make sense of the impossible visit from her future self. After a while, she lay back down and pulled the blankets close, huddling alone in the unbroken silence. As the hours passed, the unreality of it grew, and she began to question whether she had been awake or perhaps half-asleep and dreaming. She stayed that way until slumber overtook her. When she awoke to the morning sun pouring through her small bedroom window, her skepticism had turned to certainty. What she had imagined happening last night couldn't be real.

She arrived at work half in a daze from lack of sleep. The well-lit white hallway drifted along, its passersby unnoticed as she pondered her strange dream. She rounded a corner and halted in her tracks as there, before her, stood Jon. His face had the look of a startled deer as Nichole interrogated him. The sight of him flustered and stammering in front of Nichole's piercing dark gaze banished all thoughts of her future self.

Megan pulled back and hid around the corner. She had almost forgotten the whole promotion mess. Jon was still faced with an unwanted project manager position that had sprung from her discussion with Robin.

For a moment, she was uncertain what to do. She had always strived to be a source of strength to him. In school, when he was faced with job interviews, it had been her words of encouragement that had convinced him to consider positions far away, that he could handle life on his own in a city where he knew nobody. What he needed now was not a friend who sympathized with his traumatic plight, but someone who acted like the news was no big deal. Sure, she had been instrumental in creating this whole mess, and she had to find a way to make that right. But in the meantime, what Jon needed was for the person who knew him best to treat it lightly, as if it were yet another simple choice that he could handle.

She pushed off from the wall and rounded the corner again.

An embarrassed and uncomfortable Jon looked over from his conversation as she neared. She endeavored to put on a relaxed and encouraging face, and he brightened as she stepped up to him.

She set her hand on his shoulder and sent him a crisp nod. "Hey, congrats on the—"

"He turned it down," Nichole interrupted.

Megan gave a shake of her head. "Typical."

"Wimped out. Didn't want to do performance reviews."

Jon looked over at Nichole with surprise. "That's what you got out of—"

"Oh, performance reviews," Megan chirped, trying to distract her friend from the comment and put a positive spin on the situation. "That's the good part. Other people's, not mine, of course. And planning and budgeting and being in control."

Nichole leaned closer and lowered her voice as if speaking in confidence. "Hey, what is Jon's deal?"

Megan stumbled on the question. She wasn't even sure herself what his problem was, just that Jon had some aversion to being in charge of anything, no matter how trivial. Though to call it an aversion was an understatement. It was more like a fear that verged on a phobia. From the few comments he had made over the years, it seemed as if it was tied up in some past school trauma. Something had happened to make him dread being in any position of responsibility, convinced that people would get hurt if he was in charge.

Not wanting to embarrass Jon further by dwelling on the subject, she just made light of it. "I don't think he's real comfortable being in charge."

"I've heard that," Nichole responded with a solemn nod.

Jon straightened, seeming incredulous. "Yeah, just now, from me."

Megan lowered her voice and leaned a little closer, just as Nichole had done with her. "I think it's because of something that happened when he was a kid." She scrunched up her nose and gave a quick shake of her head. "He doesn't really talk about it." She turned to Jon, then smiled and gave him a firm hug. "Well, congratulations anyway."

He seemed to dally in her embrace, not wanting to let go, so she indulged him for a moment. Then he stepped back. "Thanks, but I have stuff to do. Besides, I should leave so you don't have to talk about me behind my back, to my face." He smiled, then hurried off along the hallway, head down and avoiding his coworkers as if they were hungry predators ready to pounce.

No sooner had he left than Nichole inquired about their lunch plans. After agreeing on a time to meet, Megan left, eager to get a start on her list of morning duties. Those tasks would keep her away from the lab but couldn't distract her from fretting over Jon's obvious distress at the difficult position in which she had put him.

By the time the lunch hour arrived, it was a welcome break. Nichole drove, allowing Megan to unwind and enjoy the trip along the lively city streets on a warm, sunny day. Their destination was King Chi, a small but clean establishment situated across from a large hill. It was also where Megan usually went for Friday lunch. After a short walk from their parking spot, they arrived and were seated at a table on the side near a broad, sunlit window. It wasn't long before a waitress in a red cheongsam came and took their orders and they could relax and chat as they waited for plates of savory food to be ferried to them.

The murmur of customers conversing blended with the clanking of dishes and rattling of utensils as Megan's lunch companion sat with chopsticks in hand. She closed and opened them in eager anticipation as an unobtrusive waiter slid a plate with three dumplings and a saucer of thin dark sauce in front of her. She stared down at them, her black cornrow braids falling over her dusky face as she inhaled the rich aroma.

The pungent smell of hot and sour soup assaulted Megan's nostrils as a bowl appeared in front of her. She sighed as she looked down at it. How did this always happen? It was way too harsh and way too sour. It was like they used hydrochloric peppers and military-grade vinegar or something. But it came with the lunch special, and she always forgot to ask for a substitution.

She scooped up a spoonful of the wretched substance and lifted it to her lips. As it hit her tongue, she grimaced. It was as caustic as ever. It couldn't have been her prettiest face, that's for sure, but Nichole never noticed. She was too busy scrutinizing her fried dumplings. With chopsticks in hand, she plucked one of the bundles from the plate and dunked it in the small saucer of dipping sauce. She lifted it to her face but paused before consuming it.

Nichole leaned closer and eyed Megan. "So, what's the deal with you and Jon?" She popped the dumpling in her mouth and stared as she chewed.

Megan cocked her head. "What do you mean 'deal'?"

Nichole swallowed, then set the chopsticks on her plate. "Come on." With a theatrical flair, she reached across the table and rested a hand on Megan's shoulder. Then she donned a caricature of a coy expression and batted her eyelashes. "Hey, Jon, want to go to a movie?" She batted them a few more times.

Megan smiled and suppressed a laugh as she picked up Nichole's wrist from her shoulder and dropped it. "You're exaggerating."

"Oh, come on. You're always touching him, smiling at him, making goo-goo eyes at him, being way friendly."

Megan covered her mouth and stifled a laugh. "Goo-goo eyes?"

Nichole stared with a serious expression and nodded with enthusiasm. "Absolutely."

When her stare didn't relent, Megan threw her a nonchalant shrug. "He's my best friend."

Nichole lowered her head and sent an even more skeptical stare, one that expected an explanation.

Megan returned her own coy look. "Okay, so maybe I might flirt a little."

Nichole perked up. "But why?"

Embarrassed and self-conscious about the trajectory of the conversation, Megan glanced out the large plate glass window. Beyond it, sunlight rained down on the black wire-frame tables and chairs scattered across the small brick patio of the open-air seating area. After a moment, she shrugged. "Because I like him, okay?"

Nichole perked up even more and leaned in closer. "And he's never caught on? He's never taken an interest in you, never asked you out? For ten years?"

Megan's gaze shot over to Nichole, and she smiled as she recalled those early days. Jon was smart and funny and kind. He was generous and open with his feelings where her father was cruel and miserly. He was soft and gentle where her father was hard and unfeeling. More than anything, he was respectful and considerate where her father was dismissive and hurtful.

From the time they first met, she had liked him. She began spending time with him because she was drawn to him. And he was certainly eager to be with her. But she had just freed herself from the tyranny of her father's oppression. She had escaped from the despot who had taken away everything that mattered to her. The last thing she wanted was to find herself under the thumb of anyone. So, even as she found herself going out of her way to meet him, to get him out of his dorm and spend time with him, she hated the idea of a serious relationship with any man.

Megan rolled her eyes. "Are you kidding me? I can't count the number of times he asked me out. It got to the point where I'd make up guys I was seeing just to get him to stop."

"I don't get it. If you like him, why would you do that?"

Megan glanced down again. "Well, you know, he isn't very exciting, is he?" She returned her gaze to Nichole. "Well, at least that's how I thought about him before. I mean, back when we first met, I just wanted to go out and have fun, not get married."

A look of shock crossed Nichole's face. "Married? Jon?" She leaned in again with a look of suspicion. "Are we talking about *Jon*?"

"Hey. He's a great guy."

"But, marriage?"

Megan stared down again, reluctant to say the words. "Well, yeah. I always thought that if I were to get married, he would be the kind of guy I'd want as a husband." She mumbled to herself, "The exact opposite of my father."

Nichole looked at her sideways. "The *kind* of guy? Or *the* guy?"

Megan stared into the bowl and stirred her soup in slow, lazy circles, stalling as the drone of quiet conversations filled the awkward silence. She raised her head and nodded. "Okay. Yeah. *The* guy."

Nichole leaned back in her chair, appearing stunned. "Okay, now I'm totally confused."

Megan shrugged again, making light of it. "Well, it just wasn't part of the plan, you know?"

Nichole's stunned look turned to bewilderment. "The plan?"

Megan set her spoon down and began counting off on her fingers. "I wanted to get a degree at twenty-three, then get settled in a new job by twenty-five, build up a little savings, then I figured maybe when I got to around twenty-eight, I'd get married."

Nichole puzzled for a moment. "And Jon is the one you want to marry?"

"Well, yeah. Sort of … someday … when I'm ready."

Nichole gave her head a small shake. "So let me see if I've got this straight. Jon is the guy you want to marry, but he wasn't part of the plan. So, you said no to him while you led him on and went out and had a good time with a bunch of other guys."

Megan stared in shock and embarrassment. "Hey. Don't say it like that. It makes it sound so bad."

Nichole's eyes flew wide. "Because it is."

"Look, it's not like I didn't spend time with him." Megan gave a casual shrug. "Jon and I have always spent a lot of time together."

Nichole's eyes widened even more. "You do realize that's worse, right?"

Flustered, all Megan could do was continue to stare.

Nichole threw her hands up and shook her head. "You know what? I don't even want to know what goes on in that twisted little head of yours." A broad smile spread across her face as she raised an index finger to Megan's skull and pretended to drill into it.

Megan tried to squirm away, then they both laughed.

The laughter subsided, replaced by the clanking of dishes and the clatter of cooking from the kitchen. Megan returned to stirring her soup. This time, the circles were no longer slow and lazy. With all the talk of marriage, images had crept into her mind of her father and the cold, heartless things he had done to her mother. He would forbid her from going anywhere or seeing anyone he had not pre-approved. On more than one occasion, she made the mistake of smiling at a man or laughing at his jokes and was later treated to a furious tirade about flirting, behaving shamelessly, and dishonoring him. Mother loved him and tried hard to please him, yet he never granted her the slightest sliver of praise. All he ever dished out was anger and recrimination at anything that was not perfect.

She shoved the memories out of her mind. Despite the way it had all ended, despite the fact it had killed her mother and sister, she knew that was not what real marriage was about. Besides, she had left all that behind. That chapter of her life was over now.

Her nervous stirring jerked to a stop, and she took a deep breath. Then she smiled, determined not to let the past decide who she was. She filled her mind with happy memories of going sailing with Jon, camping in the hills, watching Shakespeare in an outdoor theater. With a forced sense of optimism, she scooped up more soup in her ceramic spoon, but as soon as the caustic liquid hit her tongue, she regretted it … again.

While Megan suppressed another grimace, Nichole snatched a dumpling, dipped it in sauce, and tossed it into her mouth. As she chewed, her face adopted a perplexed expression. She swallowed and set her chopsticks down. As her demeanor became more curious, she leaned closer. "Okay, just answer me this. You have a degree. You've been settled in this job for a while now, and you'll be twenty-eight in a few months. …" Nichole shot her another one of those looks that demanded an explanation.

Sadness filled Megan as she lowered her head and set her spoon down, gazing into her bowl of soup. "He stopped asking."

42

Nichole shook her head. "Oh, girl." She sighed as she looked Megan in the face. "How long?"

Megan drew a long, deep breath. "A couple years. Not since he got me this job. I think he gave up on me, after college, when he moved away."

Nichole grabbed the last dumpling with her chopsticks and dunked it in what remained of the dark liquid. Then she held it near her face as she leaned even closer. "You should ask him out." She lobbed it into her mouth and nodded as she chewed.

"I'm afraid I might have said 'no' one too many times."

Nichole shook her head as she swallowed. "I don't buy it. You're not the shy type."

A vague anxiety clutched at Megan as she tried to put her ambivalent feelings into words. "Honestly, I guess I'm just a little scared. I mean, I like being independent. I like going where I want to go, doing what I want to do. I'm my own person. I don't answer to anyone. Jon"—she shook her head—"I don't think he's capable of being easygoing in a relationship. He would be all-in, you know? He would be intense. I don't know if I could do that. I mean, if I get that serious with him, what happens to me?"

Nichole froze for a moment, then her manner adopted a serious tone as she pushed her plate away. "Woman, you need to make up your mind what you want, because if you don't, fate will decide for you."

She was right, of course, but Megan wasn't about to show any doubt. She pushed away her still-full bowl of soup and smiled. "I make my own fate."

Aylun crept across the simple office, passing a desk covered in ornate carvings and adorned with fittings of dark metal and jade. He stared down at its surface with its neat stacks of papers, inkwell, and official stamp of the Augury. His discussion with Yaolin had left him unsettled, and his thoughts were mired in guilt and anxiety. He had thought better of visiting the Great Oracle in that impaired state and spent the remainder of the morning trying to deal with his stress.

He had started with a visit to the Vault of Time. One of the Shou was assigned to each day of the week to perform a routine check, and this was his day. Despite its pretentious name, it was nothing more than a locked basement with a number of dusty old chests. Each had a metal plaque attached to the front on which was inscribed a list of signs that must come to pass before the chest could be opened. By Augury edict, the plaques had to be checked daily, even though the inscriptions never changed.

Once all the signs on a plaque had come to pass, the chest was opened. Whatever instructions were found inside would then be used by the Shou to carry out a previous Great Oracle's bidding. None of them had been opened in his lifetime, but it was said that they could contain anything: maps, warnings, prophecies, or even artifacts that might be needed to execute some long-ago Great Oracle's plan.

After he had completed his duties, he took to the streets outside the Augury, strolling down a lane that ran alongside the Baihu River. It was one of the more scenic places in Kanlu. He gazed across the water at the emperor's sprawling palace in the distance. It was a reminder that this was the seat of power, the capital city of Elore. Like each of the three realms that made up Meerdon, Elore had its own government, its own army, and its own laws. Yet all three were lorded over by an all-powerful ruling council in Shirdon. Aylun returned his attention to the row of arched bridges spanning the quiet water. Political matters were of little interest to him. He was Shou, the unseen hand of oracles who knew what those in power would do before they did it.

With time, the slow-moving waters and cool air had worked on his frustration, relieving much of it, but not all. So he made a stop at one of his favorite places. The streets that ran by Kianlong Square were the perfect place to unwind by watching children play. There was something about their carefree laughter and the way they ran and chased with such joyful abandon that calmed his spirit.

44

AYLUN

Afterward, with time and distance having worn away most of his frustration, he had returned to the Augury and sought out Tsaoshi's chambers.

He passed a wall composed of near-black stone with a jade inlay of a broad, heavily branched tree sprawled across most of its surface. Ahead lay Tsaoshi, the Great Oracle. Although everyone inside and outside the Augury called him that, he was quick to remind them he was not enlightened enough to deserve the title. Still, he was as close as anyone in this generation would get to having earned it. Not to mention he was called by another title, too, one he had proven he deserved. He was Chenyu, the one in charge of the Augury.

Being middle-aged, he was younger than most Great Oracles, but behind his dark eyes, there was a profound serenity. It was the earmark of those who had seen too much of what was to come and had learned to accept that which no soul should be asked to accept.

Appearing lost in thought, Tsaoshi stood staring out the window at the courtyard beyond. At its center towered a giant real-life manifestation of the emblem on the wall: a wide, heavily branched plum tree. A crystal pool lay beneath, its surface laden with lotus blossoms. Their pink and white petals partially obscured its bottom, which was lined with the same smooth round stones as those in the pond. At the water's edge ran a dark rock path that led along the backs of the buildings encircling the courtyard.

Before Aylun could reach Tsaoshi, the man spoke. "You know I cannot advise you on this matter." The Great Oracle turned to face him.

Aylun granted him a deep and respectful bow. "We are your people, Chenyu. Once already, we have bled and died for you in that place. And we will do so again if that is our fate. But I cannot take one more Shou there without knowing more."

"I can only tell you what I have told Yaolin. I cannot ask you to go, and I cannot dissuade you. This is your choice."

"But you know what we will choose. You know what will happen."

45

"Do I?" Tsaoshi shrugged. "I cannot say one way or the other."

"Not even for—"

"You know the Augury's purpose. You know we exist to thwart the danger oracles pose."

"But does that even apply to this situation?"

Tsaoshi shook his head. "Even answering that would violate our rules. Rules that exist to turn the misery oracles could spread into a force for good."

Aylun looked down at the well-worn stone floor. "But to choose in the dark like this …"

"Is that not always the role of the Shou? To act without question. To be the hand of the Augury, to protect oracles and prophecy."

"But I don't even know if this—"

"The future is an ever-branching tree of possibilities, each—"

"Each decided by free will. Yes, I know."

Tsaoshi placed a hand on his shoulder and looked him in the eyes. "But do you *really* understand?" He held up a lone finger. "It means there is no single predestined future. Even the smallest crumb of information I give you could influence your decision and this mission. What happens to you, to Yaolin, to everyone whose life is touched by that … by any event? It is only the beginning of a cascade of actions and reactions, the ripples from which may disrupt countless lives far into an almost infinite future."

Aylun lowered his head. "So there is nothing you can tell me?"

Tsaoshi turned his eyes downward and closed them, standing silent in the quiet and shade of his dark chamber. A gentle breeze rustled through the leaves of the tree. It wafted the scent of its blossoms through the open window as the oracle remained there for a time, motionless, in intense rumination. Then he opened his eyes and gave a single slow nod. "There are a few things I can point out. Things you already know. And perhaps there are a few others I could reveal without violating our rules. Things that would place your decision in its proper light."

Aylun bowed his head in solemn acknowledgment.

AYLUN

The Great Oracle motioned to the door. "Let us walk."

The pair exited the building and set out along the pathway of jade-streaked, dark stone. Sheltered by a generous overhang and the boughs of the tree, it skirted the backs of the buildings of the courtyard.

Tsaoshi seemed to consider his words with care, but when he spoke, they were gentle reminiscences of a time long past. "Do you recall a young woman who used to be a frequent visitor here? It was perhaps fifteen or twenty years ago. She spent a lot of time with the two young sisters, Yaolin and Yaomey."

It took a moment to dredge up the distant memory, and though the recollection annoyed, he strived to remain objective and unemotional. "Do you mean that woman who was always pointing at me and whispering to Yaolin and Yaomey? Then they would all giggle."

Tsaoshi laughed as he stopped near one of the rough wooden posts that supported the generous overhanging roof. "What was her name? Leenah … Lienai—"

"Leanna."

"Ah, yes." Tsaoshi nodded. "You have a good memory."

Aylun's response was deadpan. "She made an impression."

The oracle smiled as he motioned to the dark stone path, and the pair resumed their leisurely stroll. "Did you know that those two sisters were slipping Leanna journals, notes, orders, and other papers from our archives?"

Aylun gave a meager nod. "I suspected. But why did you not stop them? Is it not dangerous knowledge? Is it not forbidden?"

Tsaoshi sent him a reassuring glance. "Ordinarily, yes, but I had my reasons for allowing it."

"Still, I do not see the relevance."

"Leanna spent nearly every waking moment reading. She consumed almost every paper in our archive. Her thirst for knowledge drove her far beyond the Augury to unearth its history and secrets. She knew more about us and ancient prophecy than anyone in three hundred years."

"Still, I do not underst—"

"She spent countless days talking with Yaomey and Yaolin. Do you not suppose that some of those whispered conversations must have been about what she had discovered? She might have told them things she knew about prophecy and the Augury."

Though the Great Oracle had revealed nothing he did not already suspect, he had connected the events in a way that hadn't occurred to Aylun. Yaolin and Yaomey never gave the slightest impression of possessing ancient insights. Then again, a person cannot be judged by their appearance any more than the sea can be measured by a bucket. He found himself nodding as he walked. "I suppose it is highly likely."

The pair turned out of the quiet courtyard onto a path that meandered through the enormous Augury gardens. The area was strewn with tastefully arranged boulders intermingled with full-sized sculpted trees. A nearby brook gurgled as it ran along the path next to them. Farther down, it split off, winding between ponds, rock walls, and waterfalls.

A little way off to the left in a small open shelter, respectful students sat in neat rows and columns absorbing the lessons of a solemn teacher. Under a distant tree on the right, three oracles in training sat in cross-legged meditation, and beyond them, children ran along a row of logs that crossed a stream, jumping between them at a flat-out run. It was a lesson he remembered well, to teach young Shou to keep their balance while running and jumping.

Out across the grass ahead, Ruahn sat with her legs crossed, meditating on an enormous rock. She was close enough to the path to overhear their discussion. The possibility gave pause for concern, but he decided to leave it to the Great Oracle to object.

Tsaoshi let out a small sigh, and his calm exterior took on a sudden troubled veil. His head turned downward, and his words dripped with remorse. "Four years ago, when Yaomey came to me insisting on a mission, I could not foresee the outcome or its effect on the tree." He looked over at Aylun. "Do you understand the implication?"

AYLUN

Aylun glanced down as his mind stumbled on the question, unable to get past the inference buried within. The query itself was a reasonable one. After all, he had observed, firsthand, the startling accuracy of the Great Oracle's gift. Often, he would direct the Shou to intercept someone at a precise location. He would describe the surrounding people and unfolding events with uncanny accuracy. That the Great Oracle would have seen nothing of the outcome of such a crucial mission was strange.

Yet, the oddity of it paled in comparison to his admission that he had sent his precious few Shou to one of the deadliest places in the known world with no idea what would happen. Aylun glanced at Tsaoshi as his thoughts returned to the question: How could the Great Oracle not have seen the outcome? An urgency to respond tugged at him, so he blurted out the first answer that came to mind. "You ... you were not enlightened enough?"

"Perhaps." Tsaoshi gave a single nod. "But other, more recent signs lend credence to a more troubling possibility."

"Other signs?"

"Yes. A few weeks ago, a protector breached our walls."

Aylun straightened. "And no alarms were raised?"

"Not one. She was as skilled as any Shou at infiltration. She handed me three letters. Each appeared to be ancient and bore the seal of the Augury. The first I gave to Zhuwey, who left the next day bound for Sirra in Talus. He has not yet returned. The second I am to open in a week's time."

The Great Oracle stopped again and faced Aylun, making sure his words were clear and distinct. "Every facet of these events remained shrouded from my gift."

The notion was as unsettling as the manner in which he presented it. Few things could obscure a gift as powerful as Tsaoshi's, and far too many of these were portents of terrible events yet to come. Aylun considered the implications. "Just like Leanna and the sisters."

Tsaoshi nodded. "It feels as if we are being guided by the hand of one more enlightened than I."

Aylun drew a deep breath. Oracles were reluctant to act unless the need was existential, and for one more enlightened than Tsaoshi to do so was far more ominous than he had first estimated. He gave an absent-minded nod. "I see."

The Great Oracle motioned to the path, and the two resumed their stroll. "In recent days, I have had dreams that feel like coming events: the Recluse Tower in flames, blood in the temples of Mundus, our city under siege, and the rise of ancient and powerful enemies. Yet I can only see fragments, not times, nor places, nor how the events are connected."

A little stunned at the oracle's directness, Aylun stared down at his feet as they stepped along the stone path. "So this is far more than just the simple request of one unhinged woman."

Tsaoshi chuckled but soon regained his somber demeanor. "When I sent you to the Dead of Night, it was not on my insight. It was on the strength of Yaomey's conviction that a journal lies there that must be recovered."

"But did Yaolin not tell you that this time, it was me who wanted to go?"

"I am not a fool. I could see through her ruse."

"Then why did you not—"

"Because nothing has changed." Tsaoshi stopped a third time, under a collection of ever-blooming trees, their bright pink blossoms small and vibrant against their dark foliage and the clear blue sky. He faced Aylun again. "Those two sisters know something. If my gift truly is obscured by the work of one more enlightened than I, then my role is to let things happen as they must. The Shou must make this decision, and since you are the two Shou who will go, you and Yaolin must decide."

"So I am to decide on a course of action advocated by two giggling sisters when I have no hard information, just your feeling that the journal they claim can be found there is of significance, but no idea what it might hold?"

"If you wish to view it that way, then yes."

50

AYLUN

Aylun gave a solemn nod. "Perhaps I should uncover what it is they are after."

Tsaoshi exhaled a small sigh with just a hint of exasperation. "Do not bother. Over many years, I have tried, but they are steadfast in their refusal to say a single word, and no amount of meditation has revealed more."

"I do not even know how important it is."

"If Yaolin's request is the hand of an oracle more enlightened than I, then we must assume it is of ultimate importance."

Aylun took a deep breath and looked down at the dark path beneath him. "I have been there. I have seen how deadly that place is, how quickly life can be snuffed out. If I were to go, I would want to go alone and move quickly and quietly. More than that, every fiber of my being is telling me to keep Yaolin as far from that place as possible. But only she knows the full mission. So it is pointless to go without her." He looked over into Tsaoshi's serene face. "I need time to consider this coldly and rationally."

The Great Oracle let out the sigh of a father displeased with his child. "Do not underestimate feelings. When facts are lacking, they become even more critical. They are the only thing you have to go on."

"I understand, but if there is one lesson I learned in that place, it is that if I wish to survive, I cannot let anything cloud my judgment."

Tsaoshi scowled. "You still do not see. In the end, those feelings you shun may be all that keep you alive."

Aylun granted Chenyu a deep bow before he marched away. The Great Oracle had provided far more information than he had expected. Great Oracles were loath to speak of what they knew, even to the most trusted in their family. So the Shou were accustomed to acting in the dark, only knowing that their actions served a higher purpose. That Tsaoshi had been so forthcoming made the insights he had shared all the more troubling.

Still, Aylun's instinct was to refuse, to say no to the mission. Dead Shou could do nothing, no matter how devastating the impact of failure might be. Yet, he had been handed a heavy responsibility, and with it came an obligation to give the matter grave consideration. So he set out once again to stroll the grounds of the Augury and streets beyond as he considered with care all the Great Oracle had revealed.

Her comment about deciding her own fate still hung in the air as Megan glanced over at a group rising from the table next to theirs. Engrossed in their chatting, they wandered to the plate glass storefront and lingered there, oblivious to the fact they were blocking a new group of customers trying to enter.

Nichole leaned back in her chair as the rattle of a wok and clatter of utensils emanated from the busy restaurant kitchen. She eyed Megan for a long moment, then dropped the subject.

The rest of the meal went by with the talk focused on the latest coworker gossip, management incompetence, and other workplace drama. Not another word was spoken about Jon. Having paid for their feast, they consumed their fortune cookies and laughed over their generic fortunes. Then they gathered their belongings and prepared to leave.

A gunshot rang out from beyond the large storefront window. Megan startled and bolted up from her chair. She paused for only a moment before flying across the bright wooden floor, heading to the window. As she neared the door, the top of the hill opposite the restaurant came into view. There, at the crest of the ridge, stood a rifleman and two teenagers, with a woman filming just behind. Beyond them stood a group of spectators, crowded behind a line of yellow tape.

She stumbled to a stop, then tilted her head back, closed her eyes, and sighed in relief. "It's only somebody filming."

Nichole stepped up to her side, staring at her as if she were insane. "What the heck were you planning to do anyway?"

"I don't know exactly."

"You know, most people have the common sense to run the other way when they hear gunshots."

Megan gazed out through the plate glass as she motioned to the door. "Let's go."

Across the street, a man flew from his car and raced up the grassy hill toward the rifleman.

Nichole pointed. "Is that …"

Megan covered her mouth. "Jon," she said as empathetic mortification filled her over what she could see was coming.

Jon reached the top and leaped, slamming into the rifleman and sending him sprawling.

Chaos broke out among actors, crew, and spectators alike as the angry camerawoman berated Jon.

A deep sadness came over Megan as she could see him realize what he'd done. It was hard to watch, and she wanted to turn away. Without a word, eyes fixed on her humiliated friend, Megan led Nichole through the glass door and out onto the sidewalk. The sounds of the busy streets assaulted them as they watched Jon stumble down the hill, seeming quite traumatized.

Nichole gaped at him, then shook her head as she mumbled, "How can someone be that brave and that stupid all at the same time?"

When Jon looked up and spotted them, an expression of abject horror filled his face.

Megan motioned to the car. "You go back to work without me. I have to make sure he's okay."

Without glancing over, Nichole quietly said, "Okay, but try to slip something into the conversation. See if you can find out how he feels about you."

It seemed an inappropriate and insensitive thing to say, but she was too wrapped up in her concern to attempt a response. Right now, Jon needed her. As Nichole headed away, Megan stepped to the curb and turned her attention to the traffic, searching for an opening to cross the street.

She glanced up from the stream of vehicles, and when her eyes met Jon's, his look of dismay deepened. His head shot down, avoiding her gaze. It remained there as he walked up and seated himself on the grass near the edge of the sidewalk.

At a gap in the traffic, she hurried across the street. The patter of her shoes ceased as she hopped from the pavement onto the grass before the sidewalk. A stab of sympathy pierced her as her attention returned to her friend, head still down, breath labored, and shaking like a leaf. "What the heck, Jon? You were just going to go get a sandwich."

He never looked up, and his voice was almost too quiet to hear. "Why does this kind of thing always happen to me?"

Megan sat beside him on the grass. "Because you ran toward the gunshots, you idiot. Most people have the common sense to run the other way." She set her hand on his shoulder in the hope it would calm his trembling. "Are you okay?"

He gave an absent-minded nod. "But I don't think I should be driving."

He didn't seem up to talking either, so she sat and stared into the street with him. Nichole's car cruised past, her face watching out its window. The rumble of the engine blended with the sounds of midday city traffic, but Jon never seemed to notice either one. All Megan could do for him was remain next to him, hoping that even in his distracted state, her company would ease his discomfort.

After a while, his quiet words drifted out as if he were not even conscious he was speaking. "For a minute, I was right back there."

From bits and pieces of past conversations, she suspected this was a reference to a long-ago classroom tragedy that still haunted him. Something had happened in his childhood, but it was a topic he had never once brought up himself, much less explained. "Back where?" Megan asked.

With eyes still focused on the sidewalk before him, he shook his head. "It's nothing. ... It's just, sometimes I don't feel like I fit in to this world. Like this isn't the life I was meant to be leading."

Eager to brighten the mood, she seized on the change of topic. "I know, right? I always thought my life would be super exciting. Like I'd be a mixed martial arts fighter or a race car driver or something. Instead, I work in a dingy lab with no windows." She smiled and tried to catch his gaze.

Jon took a deep breath, then put on a brave face as he looked over at her and smiled. "I don't know where this conversation took a wrong turn, but you and I are not talking about the same thing."

Megan nodded. "I know. I know." She hesitated. The chance to draw him out on such a troubling subject was too rare to pass up. She peered into his eyes as she gave voice to her long-held concerns. "It's not nothing. Ever since I've known you, you've been running from something. You're a friendly guy. Yet you preferred to study instead of being with friends. You throw yourself into your work like it's some kind of protective shield. You're not dealing, Jon, and it's holding you back."

He inhaled a deep breath. "We should really get back to work." He was avoiding the topic, just like every other time she had alluded to it. Her question had made him uncomfortable. Making him even more so would not help him calm down or open up, so she resigned herself to dropping the subject.

Megan smiled. "Right. Look at me." She giggled. "Prying into your life like some kind of girlfriend or something."

He stared at her with a stunned expression. An expression that, in an instant, told her she had said the wrong thing. And it was all that idiotic Nichole's fault. At the time, she had thought Nichole's comment was callous and insensitive, and here was proof: she had rendered her best friend speechless.

Before she could compose a decent apology, or an explanation, or even a way to make light of it, Jon recovered and motioned to the car with his head. "Can you drive?"

Megan nodded, and they both got up and strolled down the sidewalk toward the vehicle. As they walked side by side, her thoughts were still stuck back in their conversation. Though her intent had been to encourage him, she had blundered into areas that had increased his discomfort. And now, she could only hope the awkwardness between them would be temporary.

Aylun spent the early part of the afternoon strolling the lively streets of Kanlu, mulling over all he had heard. As he wandered among the homes, shops, and open-air markets, residents drifted by. The streets echoed with their cheerful voices, broken by the occasional squabble or laughter. Not wanting to lend them any shred of his attention, he replayed in his head every detail of Yaolin's ambush and Tsaoshi's discussion. Over and over, he reviewed them. It was critical that he set aside his fear and face his decision with a calm and rational mind.

At first, the gravity of Tsaoshi's words weighed heavily in his thoughts. But as time passed, he began to realize the futility of it. If they were all merely players in some grand production of a long-deceased Great Oracle, then it was a fool's errand to second-guess the plot in order to decide what part he should play. Not to mention, it was an uncomfortable exercise.

The Shou were raised to carry out the Great Oracle's plans without question and to not second-guess the reasons behind them. It had been hammered into him countless times, using real-world examples, that Great Oracles must be tight-lipped, and how dangerous it could be to try to fathom their motives. In practice, Tsaoshi had often been forthcoming, explaining in great detail what was at risk and why they must do as he said. But if this was the hand of a more powerful oracle, then it was not just futile. It was wrong to try to understand what their plan might be.

With time, he almost convinced himself he should ignore all that Tsaoshi had said and base his decision only on the facts of which he was certain. Even so, he decided on one last visit before he made up his mind—a visit to consult the one person whose council he had always relied on. So he found himself dressed in white standing in the place to which he had been drawn so many times in the past four years.

He stared at a small wooden cubby, one of a large array that stretched from floor to ceiling and spanned the entire length of the long, high wall. Sunlight streamed from a small round window, casting a soft light on the collection of mementos arranged with care on one of the shelves: a treasured, well-worn rag doll, a crude ceramic bowl, a dark metallic necklace, and a carefully folded uniform of black and jade. Nestled in the center sat a painting of a young, smiling, brown-eyed Elorian woman with short black hair and bangs.

He had never had a childhood in the sense that many do. The Augury made sure there was little room for frivolity. His time was structured and his attention consumed with studying philosophy and battle strategy as well as performing exercises to increase agility, speed, stealth, and skill. Like all Shou, his parents would spend long stretches away from the Augury on missions. The only family he knew, throughout his childhood and into early adulthood, was his little sister, Ayrue. Her bright personality and endless optimism had a way of turning even the most arduous and boring study into play. He taught her how to do her lessons, and she taught him the importance of laughter, kindness, and affection. She'd been his family. They had leaned on each other, cared for each other, loved each other.

Heaviness enveloped his heart as he gazed upon the pastel likeness of his sister's cheerful face. One he would never see again. "I miss you, Ayrue. I miss my partner, and I miss my little sister. Especially now, when I have this impossible decision. ..."

He paused for a few moments, then took a deep breath. "She wants me to go back there. Back to the place that killed you. Back to the place where I failed to protect you." He raised his head and closed his eyes as the memories of swirling darkness, blind confusion, and mangled bodies flooded back as vivid and painful as the moment they had happened. "Every day, I must live with the memory of what I have done. Taising's screams of terror. The panic when I thought it was you. And the horror when I realized in chasing after her that I ... I had left you unprotected. I lost all reason. I let my emotions run away with me, and it killed you. How could I ever face that again?" He shook his head. "How can I return when I still do not know what we died for?"

Aylun lowered his gaze to the stone slab of the floor. "I know. I know. We are Shou. We are born and live to serve. Chenyu ordered it, and that is all we needed to know. But this time"—he looked up at his sister's picture again—"this time, it is my choice. Tsaoshi has ordered it be so, and I cannot choose to risk another cherished companion without knowing why."

He shut his eyes again and let the longing flow over him—for the lilting of her bright and bubbly laughter echoing across the serene gardens, for her pleading eyes that would tug at his heart every time she wanted something from him. He yearned for the warmth of her endearing smile. A smile his lack of discipline had ensured he would never see again. When he opened his eyes, he reached out, almost touching the surface of the painting.

"I thought if I worked hard and lived a life of purpose, I would be happy. But I feel like I never left that place. How can I take anyone back there, how can I risk one more precious life without a reason, without knowing why we were—"

The almost indiscernible sound of dust grinding beneath cloth shoes jarred him out of his mournful state. He tilted his head and stared at the beams of the ceiling as he listened to the sounds of movement from the rounded doorway behind him. It was not at all the level of stealth required of one who aspired to be Shou. He took a deep breath and grumbled as he exhaled. "Your footfalls and breathing could wake the dead. I am disappointed, Ruahn. Of all the recruits, I expected you to improve the fastest."

He glanced back over his shoulder as she turned the corner into the doorway and gave a deep, low bow of respect. "Was it not you who told me, 'Be not afraid of growing slowly, be only afraid of standing still'?"

He sighed. "Did I not also say, 'Dig the well before you become thirsty'?"

Ruahn gave a calm, slow nod.

Aylun turned to peer at her thin, angular outline in the bright light of the circular doorway. "We should be nine, but we have lost five Shou, most trained from childhood. Four is not enough. That is why we brought you and the others here from the outside, a thing not done in four hundred years. Our need is that dire. When disaster strikes, it will be too late for you to become ready." Aylun looked straight into her eyes, letting his gaze rest there for a moment. "Grow faster."

Ruahn lowered her head. "Yes, Laoshi."

"Now, why have you disturb—"

"It is Wistra. Yaolin seeks her journal. She believes it contains something crucial to coming events. She believes she knows where to find it in the Dead of Night."

Astounded, Aylun stepped back, bumping into the shelves containing mementos of countless fallen Shou. Outrage swept through his veins. He managed to control himself, yet his words still reeked of incredulity. "You are Shou. You *protect* prophecy. You cannot simply come before me and blurt out that which I was not to know."

Ruahn remained placid. "But I was only exercising my free will. I heard Yaolin discussing it with Yaomey, and I decided you must know."

"What if it was part of prophecy?"

"Then am I not also a part of the same prophecy? Have I not done as the oracle saw I would?"

Aylun crossed his arms and glared at her in deep disapproval. "That may be true, but it distresses me that one who aspires to be Shou would so badly miss the point. It was information Yaolin withheld for a reason. As a protector of prophecy, *you* of all people should honor that, but instead, you abrogated her wishes. You know as well as I do that once you spoke the words, the damage was done; they will change things. Even if I try to pretend I never heard, they will alter the future."

"Are Yaolin's wishes worth her life?"

"Do not play games with my words. You know full well Yaolin's wishes were *never* the point. She is Shou, and whatever the source of her information, she is almost certainly acting on instructions not to reveal it. For all you know, you have just blithely tampered with a prophecy from Wistra, the founder of the Augury itself." He stepped closer. "Disaster comes from careless talk. And for the Shou, that disaster can shatter civilizations. Do not ever, *ever* do that again. Do you understand?"

A repentant demeanor came over Ruahn. She placed her hands together and gave a deep bow, her voice dripping with contrition. "I am sorry. I feared she might go alone. I let that fear guide me. Please—"

"Go alone?" The thought of Yaolin in that deadly place without him threw him into a panic, and his words rushed out. "Did she say that? What have you heard?"

Ruahn cringed. "I am sorry. I cannot say."

He shook his head in astonishment. "*Now* you choose to become circumspect?" Aylun paused for a moment to compose himself, then glared at her. "If our need was not so dire, I would expel you this moment." He pointed to the door. "Do not say another word. Go to your chambers. Stay there for three days. Reflect carefully on your words and actions here, and do not appear in front of me again until you can demonstrate that you understand where you have erred."

Ruahn gave a last deep bow of respect before spinning around and marching out the door. Aylun watched the light streaming through the empty doorway for a while as he endeavored to calm himself. It would be just like that stubborn, implacable Yaolin to plan to go without him. Even as frustration seized him at his partner's bullheaded recklessness, he understood what he must do. He would find her and confirm all Ruahn had said. He would not blindly follow his partner into the unknown again. This time he would uncover exactly what information she was after and how she expected to acquire it.

AYLUN

He turned back to stare at the small collection of mementos of his lost sister as his anger flared anew. After all his agonizing and anxiety, after all his doubt and fear, after everything she had put him through, it turned out Yaolin had already made the decision for him.

Chapter Three

IN THE DEAD OF NIGHT

Megan steered the car through a slow, careful turn into an employee parking space, then brought it to a gentle stop. The drive from the restaurant was a short one, but the absence of discussion made it seem like forever. Jon's silence had begun the second she made her stupid "girlfriend" comment. On the way, she had considered trying to take it back, but in the end, she decided against it. It was an offhand remark, and dwelling on it would only deepen the awkwardness.

Megan slipped the car into park and turned off the engine. Jon stirred as she gathered her things. Both doors clicked open, and they stepped out onto the worn, aging blacktop. She squinted from the bright sunlight and looked over at Jon as the rumble of traffic from the nearby highway droned on in the background.

He seemed to come out of his daze a bit and sent her a fleeting glance. "What's with the granny driving? You usually accelerate into the parking stall at about sixty."

She chuckled. "I thought you'd had enough excitement for one day, what with the whole promotion thing and assaulting actors." In a quiet voice, below the thrum of nearby street sounds, she added, "And my scary 'girlfriend' comment."

Jon didn't appear to notice. He was too busy staring off across the cracked blacktop with a puzzled expression. "There they are again."

Megan scanned the rows of cars in the direction he was looking. "Who?" she inquired.

"Nobody, they're gone now." He pulled his eyes from the scene and turned toward the entryway, then they both began to stroll across the warm, black asphalt.

She motioned to the building. "Why don't we head to the lab? It's quiet there, and maybe focusing on work will distract you."

"Come on. It's not that bad."

"Don't act needlessly brave." Megan lowered her head and mumbled to herself, "I already know how brave you are." She looked over at him again. "Let's just work quietly in your lab, okay?"

Jon nodded.

As the sleek glass-and-metal entryway neared, he shot a glance back at the visitor spots at the front of the lot. "It's just … I saw them at the corporate offices, a couple of Asian-looking fellows getting out of expensive cars. They were talking about what it was like to live in the States. When I got into the elevator with them, they switched to some foreign language, Japanese or something. After they went into the CEO's office, I assumed they were investors, but then why are they here, at the research facility?"

"Maybe it's a tour."

"Then why are they here at this building alone?"

Megan stopped in her tracks as all the strange conversations and odd occurrences at the company over the last two days clicked into place. A small gasp escaped, and she shot a glance back at the cars in the visitor spaces. She couldn't quite make them out. A lump began to form in her throat, and she reminded herself it was a mere theory. It wasn't a certainty, no matter how well it explained everything. The only way to be sure would be to see those cars for herself, but she didn't want to let Jon know of her suspicion.

She motioned to the entrance with her head. "You go on to the lab. I just remembered I left something in your car."

Jon began to pivot. "I'll go with you."

Already on edge, she panicked and thrust out her palm, nearly shouting, "No!" He stared at her with a surprised expression, so she calmed herself and lowered her hand. "No. You go on ahead. Just unlock it for me."

He seemed bewildered but nodded as he fished in his pocket. "Just remember to lock it when you're done." The car chirped and its lights flashed as he spun around and continued toward the building.

Megan did an about-face and strolled off toward Jon's vehicle, all the while stealing glances over her shoulder. As soon as he disappeared into the reception area, she veered off and raced over to where he had been looking. As she marched up, her sinking feeling grew. There it was, confirmation that she understood with crystal clarity what was going on. Her breathing quickened as she stood over one of the cars, shiny and bright red in the midday sun. It was a classic Jaguar.

In a trance, she swung around and headed to the entryway. The lump in her throat grew as she scurried through the door and across the reception area. With a singular focus, she flew down barren hallways and up the stairs. Workers glanced up at her as she strutted past, her mind whirling as she tried to summon any other explanation.

Frustration and dread drove her onward as she yanked open the door and stormed into Robin's dull, uncluttered office. Two men with short jet-black hair sat with their backs to her, conversing with Robin. Their discussion came to an abrupt halt, and the crazy HR lady looked up from behind the desk with an annoyed expression.

Megan crossed her arms and stared. "You're selling the company, aren't you?"

Robin appeared surprised, and the two men twisted around in their seats. With their well-fitted suits of expensive-looking fabric, they peered up at her, surprise on their faces. In an instant she knew, they weren't Japanese as Jon had guessed. They were businessmen from China.

Robin's cheeks turned red. "*I'm* not doing anything."

Megan huffed as she yanked the key chain from her pocket. She marched up to one of the men and tossed it in his lap. "You're buying the company, right?"

The first man picked up the key with reluctance and stared at it with a baffled expression.

The second turned to him. "*Ta zhi dao.*"

Megan glared down at the second man. "Yes, she knows. And she speaks Mandarin. *Bu yao jia she.*"

Robin sighed, then snatched a set of neatly placed papers from her desk. She thrust them up for Megan to see. "You remember signing this agreement when you came to work here?"

"What?"

"This nondisclosure agreement. Do you recall signing it?"

Megan stared, dumbfounded. "You were ready for this?"

All business, Robin continued unabated. "What you're talking about is a trade secret. You can't say a word about it to anyone. It's grounds for immediate dismissal."

"What about Jon? His project is being terminated, isn't it?"

The first man stared up at her and, with a heavy accent, said, "Negative energy experiments are a waste. We cannot support research that will never produce anything we can sell."

The lump in her throat grew. "No, you can't. He's depending on this job. It's part of his life plan."

Robin rattled the papers, grabbing Megan's attention again. "You can't tell him."

"I can't tell him his job is going away? I can't believe this!" Tears came to her eyes, but she fought them back. "You want me to let him be blindsided?"

Robin shook her head. "No. He's been offered a promotion. If you're worried about him, then convince him to take it."

The first man nodded. "Do not be concerned about Jon. We are here to discuss two new projects. Robin has assured us Jon is the best person to manage the most critical of them."

The second man chimed in, "It is very high-profile, very good for his career."

"Now, if you'll excuse us, we were in a meeting." Robin dismissed her with a wave of her hand. "You can shut the door on your way out."

AYLUN

The two men turned their backs to her and resumed their quiet conversation.

With no one to talk to, Megan turned, trudged out the door, and closed it behind her.

Stunned, she shuffled along the hall, through a gray metal door, and down the two flights of stairs to the basement. It was over. She couldn't ask Jon to take a management job that would make him miserable. And even if she had been determined to convince him, it was impossible to imagine him agreeing. Any attempt to coerce him would undoubtedly wind up with him resentful and her feeling responsible. In the end, both of them would be unhappy, whether he accepted the position or not. Then it hit her: if his job was going away, it seemed probable that hers was as well, and there was nothing she could do to stop it.

She arrived at the bottom of the stairs and traipsed through another metal door into the basement hallway. Her heart sank further as she realized it was even worse. The only reason she got a job working with Jon was that she had been recruited while still in school where she had plenty of time to find the perfect position. The chances of finding an opening for a researcher and assistant at the same place, in the same department, at the same time were vanishingly small. So chances were this whole mess would drive them further apart. The idea of being forced to leave him behind for another job, most likely to never see him again, made her heartsick.

She halted outside the door to the lab, unable to open it and face him. This job was part of his life here and his dream, and he was about to see it shattered into a million pieces; his life's work—heck, his whole life plan—would be in shambles. Even if she wasn't forbidden to tell him, how could she do that to him? She took a deep breath, eased the door open a crack, and peeked inside.

Light from displays and equipment sitting along the periphery of the lab highlighted Jon as he bent over his heavy metal table. On it, a green-blue thread flashed from a laser then weaved its way from one shiny mirror to another, creating an eerie web of colored light that cast a soft emerald glow on his downturned face. He looked absorbed in his work as he turned and checked a nearby piece of recording equipment.

During their car ride, he'd appeared distracted, but as he toiled in front of her now, he seemed focused and at peace. How could she tell him his job was going away just as he had reclaimed some degree of his normal self?

She opened the door farther and slipped inside. At the sound of it closing, Jon glanced up from his work. He signaled her to come over. "Just starting." He motioned to the computer. "Can you check that?"

Megan slipped by and slid down into the chair in front of the screen. The keys gave out a soft clicking as she checked the digital video recording software. It was a familiar routine, and the camera setup was fine. Yet the longer she sat next to him, the more her guilt grew, and the more it felt like she was lying to him by hiding such a momentous secret.

Eventually the weight of it became too great, and she halted her typing and raised her head. "Jon?"

He stopped his work and glanced over at her, his blue eyes innocent and expectant. "Yeah?"

"Uh … never mind."

She returned to scanning the on-screen readings of the virtual monitoring equipment as her fingers tapped away softly at the keys. Struggling to concentrate, she wasn't truly paying attention when Jon's voice came.

"Hey, I was thinking."

"That is what they pay you for," Megan singsonged back.

"What I mean is, you know, maybe after work, we could go out."

"Sure" was her automatic response.

He paused, and then, with unmistakable emphasis, he added, "To a nice restaurant."

Her heart lifted, and all her troubles seemed to drift away; Jon was asking her out on a *date*. Then, in a flash, it all came crashing down. The events of the night before rushed back more sharp and clear than possible for a mere dream. She recalled her bedroom, the sparkling lights, and her own somber countenance telling her: "*It's just … tomorrow, in the lab, Jon is going to ask you out.*"

Suddenly, it became crystal clear that the events of last night, no matter how impossible, had not been some half-awake imagining. The woman had predicted an event that had not occurred once in the last couple of years, and she knew the exact place and time it would happen. That meant her entire visitation from the future had to be taken as real.

Then the words appeared in her mind's eye with sickening clarity. "*I need you to turn him down.*" Her future self had been adamant as she put her hands on her hips and stood taller. "*And you need to be emphatic.*"

Fear seized her, and she let out a tiny gasp. She struggled for a few moments, trying to pull herself together. Then her head came up, and she forced out a casual reply. "Wait, you mean like a date?"

"Not *like* a date. An *actual* date, you and me. What do you think?" There was a forced nonchalance to Jon's response that told her that, to him, this was not a simple request. He cared a great deal about her answer.

With that realization her panic grew. Why would her future self insist she turn Jon down? She had waited so long for this opportunity. What could possibly be so important? Yet future Megan had been quite clear and deadly serious. The only explanation she could conjure was that for some reason, her actions now would have far-reaching consequences in her future. With that deduction came the answer. No matter how much her current self was screaming at her to tell him "yes," she had to heed her own words.

Megan took a deep breath and composed herself as best she could. She stood and turned, staring at Jon across the table. Time seemed to slow for a second as a large screen behind them switched between the two camera views. On another, bars on a graph jumped up and down with each minute change in magnetic flux density.

She stiffened and, below the table, clenched her fists. "Yeah, that's not happening. Ever."

"What?" Bewilderment filled his face.

She clenched her fists tighter. "Look, I like you as a friend. Never as a boyfriend."

Jon's crushed expression ripped a hole in her heart. "But we're perfect for each other."

At his reaction, her mouth went dry, and the lump in her throat seemed to grow. If the events outside the King Chi had plunged a knife into his heart, here she was twisting the blade. She steeled herself further, becoming cold and emotionless. "Not even close. It's not happening."

"But whenever you were going out with another guy, you were always saying how you wish he was more like me."

She struggled out as plausible an answer as she could summon. "Yeah, nice, like you, but someone that actually wants to make something out of his life. Someone responsible. An actual grown-up who doesn't turn down a promotion because he doesn't want to do performance reviews."

He stumbled back as if her words had punched him in the gut. "Any other criticisms? Keep 'em coming. How about I'm a coward? Or too much of a geek, or maybe just a big idiot for even thinking I could ever have a chance with you?"

His lashing out made it easier to rebuke him. "God, you can be so insecure sometimes."

"Oh, excuse me, I forgot to throw in insecure."

"And don't put words in my mouth. It's infuriating."

Appearing devastated, Jon stopped and looked down for a second, shaking his head in disbelief. "Fine. So all these years, I was wrong about you sending me signals?"

Every fiber of her being shouted at her to tell him he wasn't wrong, that yes, she'd sent every signal in the book. Perhaps tomorrow, she could do as her future self had suggested. She could recant. She could claim it was momentary insanity or all some cruel joke, but she had already taken it this far, and there was no turning back.

Her mind spun as she grasped for any lame response. "Sure, I might have been nice to you. Because we're friends, and you were always helping me."

70

"So why are you being so mean now?"

Unable to explain away her obvious inconsistency, she blurted out another unconvincing lie. "Because I don't want there to be any misunderstanding."

"Well, too late for that."

Movement caught her eye, and she glanced over to her left. There, over the table, hovered a dark semi-spherical blob. As she watched, it shifted and moved, the nearby light sources dancing on its undulating surface as if it were some kind of liquid mass.

Every thought of their current discussion fled from her mind as she bolted upright and stared at him wide-eyed. "Uh, Jon, what's that?" Megan raised her finger and pointed.

He looked over and started, then stopped and stared. "I have no idea."

They both puzzled for a moment as it spun and grew to the size of a softball.

Jon straightened and eyed her. "Wait, are we recording this?"

They each flew to one of the cameras and checked it to ensure they were recording as the mass continued to expand to the size of a basketball.

Jon's gaze whipped over, and he eyed Megan. "The computer, is it logging this?"

Then it hit her. This might be the answer to everything. It was not at all expected, but it was almost certainly tied to the experiment. If Jon had just discovered something new and unexplained, it might make headlines. It might even be like the cold fusion experiments in the 1990s. In fact, a breakthrough like this might make enough of a splash to make it impossible for the new owners to fire either of them. And even if they did find themselves jobless, the publicity would make it easier to find someone willing to fund his research.

With renewed optimism, she danced over to the keyboard and began to check the video recording and readings. Every second was being recorded in perfect detail.

Then Jon's apprehensive words grabbed her attention. "Wait. Do you feel that?"

Megan swung around and let out a gasp. The shiny wet darkness had doubled again. As it whirled over the table, its growing size now seemed much more ominous. A scraping sound drew her attention, and out of the corner of her eye she spotted a set of paper clips flying into the swirling black mass.

She jumped at the sound of shattering china, and her gaze whipped over to catch a book and fragments of a mug hurtling into the blackness. A chair rumbled as it slid across the room on its own.

Jon shouted, "We need to leave. Now!"

Megan whipped around and grabbed for her purse but caught only air as it slid away. Again she lunged for it, but she was too late and it plunged into the shifting liquid ball.

Her stomach lurched as her feet began to slide across the floor. Her gaze shot over to him, and she yelled, "Jon!" Panic washed away all reason. She clutched at the desk and caught its rim. Her fingers barely hung on as she dragged herself along its edge, away from the force tugging at her. She lunged for a file cabinet and snagged a door handle. The drawer rattled open. She lost all balance, and her feet flew out from under her.

Papers fluttered into her face, pulled out of the open drawer. She ducked her head as stacks of documents swirled from the desk, flying into the air and churning into a whirlwind.

Still clutching the handle of the file cabinet drawer, she winced at a clatter and crackle of electricity from above. She hunched down, hiding her face as sparks scattered across the room.

All around her, equipment began to shake. Megan looked up to see an oscilloscope headed straight for her. She bent out of its way, then another object and another whizzed by her, hurtling into the giant undulating mass. Barely hanging on and no longer able to save herself, she looked to Jon.

His terrified face stared back as he struggled against the unrelenting force. He dragged himself toward her, dodging books as they rocketed off the shelf and hurtled by him. Hope seemed to flee from his eyes as he reached out for her.

Finger by finger, she lost her grip, and a shriek of terror forced its way out. Driven by blind hysteria, she flailed, clutching at chairs, desks, and tables until the inexorable force dragged her kicking and screaming into the swirling ball.

She tumbled into darkness and landed on her shoulder with a metallic thud and sharp pain. The surface under her clanked and crackled as she fell the rest of the way down onto her back. Her body ached, and her uncontrollable breath shot out in machine-gun bursts. Everything was fuzzy at first but came into focus as she gazed upward at the pattern of light on the glowing ball hovering above her.

She clenched her fists as lights and shapes from what appeared to be Jon's lab rippled and moved across the ball's surface. Somewhere beyond the ability to reason came the certainty that what floated above her was the other end of some kind of passage. She thrust out a shaking hand to touch it, but it was too far above her.

She let her hand drop, and her head fell to the side. Her shaking wouldn't be stopped as she watched lighted shapes from the gateway above flittering and darting across distant rock walls. Her still-heaving breath echoed around her, betraying the vast expanse of some kind of cavern. The air smelled wrong—almost metallic, with a hint of spent gunpowder. Through her trembling, she shivered, despite a warmth and humidity that seemed unusual for a cave. As the reality of her predicament sank in, so did a terrible nausea. She was alone and lost in a foreign place with no way back and no idea what might lie beyond the oppressive darkness.

Debris crunched underfoot as Aylun zigged and zagged his way down the barely visible ancient cobblestone road, trying to keep pace with the faint yellow light of the cloth-covered flamestone ahead. Hidden in the blackness, the screeching and flapping of wings grew closer. Over his shoulder, the rumble of fire could still be heard, but the flaming line of long-desiccated trees was long gone, devoured by the heavy darkness. Any other place in the world, the roaring blaze would have been visible from half a realm away, but this cursed place had an unnatural way of swallowing light as if it were consuming the burning tree line whole.

The pale golden light in front of him bounced and lurched in an erratic dance as Yaolin dodged and darted down the aging roadway. Flamestones had a natural ability to cut through the eerie darkness in a way no ordinary sunstone could. The golden rays ahead bobbed down. He ducked and rolled as a deafening shriek and roar of wings rushed around them on every side. In an instant, a burst of wind blasted debris and dust from the ground, sending it in every direction.

He sprang to his feet and tore onward through the darkness. The pillars marking the edge of a long-crumbled bridge jumped out at him from the dark. The light ahead continued past them, then halted and dropped to the ground. Aylun raced past and dove off the cliff, feet first. He reached up and snagged Yaolin's outstretched hand as he fell. She yanked him to a stop, then let go, and he dropped the rest of the way to the hard, stony ground at the base of a gully. He looked up as she plummeted down into his arms. It was a move they had used before, and only their years of working together allowed them to pull it off without a flaw in this complete darkness.

Aylun set Yaolin on the ground. The scant remains of the ancient stone bridge above had disappeared into the darkness, but even if it could no longer be seen, it would offer some protection from whatever loomed in the sky above. So the pair backed up underneath the overhang and plastered themselves against the rock face. They hunkered there, facing each other, as the fluttering of wings spread out high overhead.

Aylun glanced up at Yaolin's warm, smiling face. She withdrew the small bundle from her pocket and shoved it under the yellow, glowing orb. As she let its cloth covering drop, light spilled down onto the bundle, illuminating the leather-bound tome clutched in

74

her hand. A small gasp escaped her as she ran her fingers over the beautiful dragonfly engraved on its surface.

"This has to be it." She flipped open its pages and read for a few moments as the fluttering from far above grew less frequent. Her expression transformed into one of satisfaction and amazement. "It is in her hand." She peered up at him, breathless. "This is Wistra's journal."

"We cannot afford any mistakes. Are you certain it is what we seek?"

She looked down and examined it again. "I have seen her writing before. Her brushstrokes are distinctive. It is a match." Yaolin closed the cover and once again ran her fingers over the gorgeous engraving on the leather surface. "Yes. The dragonfly on the cover, the writing in her hand, it leaves no doubt." She glanced up at Aylun's face. "This changes everything."

He pointed back the way they came. "So, that little hovel where we found it, that was one of the places Wistra once lived?"

"Yes. Leanna knew the journal was there but could never reach it. It is one of a handful of journals and artifacts she was never able to obtain." Yaolin lowered her head and began to flip through its pages.

As he crouched in the dark watching her read, the words rolled around in his head, and his curiosity was piqued. "I do not understand. What does this change?"

She continued to scan the journal as she spoke. "Leanna believed this contained information about the Otherworlder prophecy. Information we will soon need to know." A particular page seemed to grab her interest, and she stopped. For a long moment, she scrutinized it by the light of her flamestone as the flaps and shrieks echoing across the landscape grew ever more distant.

All of a sudden, she jabbed a page with her finger. "Here. It mentions the Otherworlder. But ..." She adopted an expression of deep puzzlement, then glanced up at Aylun. "She says the Otherworlder is essential. She calls them 'the one who brings about a new age.'"

Aylun puzzled. "But that ... that is not at all what the council says."

A sudden look of realization came to Yaolin's face. "No. They would never."

"What?"

"Leanna would not lie to the council. So, either she did not know the true prophecy, or—"

"The council changed it."

A look of grave concern filled Yaolin's face. "To make the subject of prophecy an enemy of the state would be unthinkably reckless."

Aylun boggled for a moment at the very thought. She was right. They would be toying with the future of every life in the three realms. Then he realized, and a deep disgust came over him. "Of course they would. They were afraid they would lose power."

They stared at each other for a moment, then Yaolin returned her attention to the journal, scanning it in earnest, as if more deep secrets might be hidden there. Aylun returned to surveying their surroundings.

After a while, she perked up again. "Oh, this is unexpected."

"What?"

"She speaks of her time in Lanessa, of living in the back of a blacksmith's shop. She goes on to describe a journal containing insights on the Otherworlder prophecy and her plans to handle it. She describes it as being lost when they evacuated during the fall of the city."

Aylun nodded. "That time line would be consistent with her history." Then the implications hit home. "But that would mean Ruahn was right about a journal being in Lanessa." He grumbled, "I would have gone there three hundred times over rather than return to this place."

Yaolin paid little attention, her entire focus on her reading.

Aylun spoke half to himself. "Still, how did Ruahn know? Where would she get such carefully protected information? Information even Leanna didn't know."

Yaolin let out a quiet scoff. "You were the one who called it rumor and speculation." Her comment was flippant and absent-minded, and her gaze never faltered from the page.

"Now wait a minute here. Do not pretend you were not in agreement with me."

Yaolin gasped and poked the page again. "She mentions a broad, thick plum tree and how its branches remind her of how free choices create the future."

His gaze shot up and he peered into the dark at a sudden and louder flapping of wings, much closer than before. It reminded him of the need for vigilance. Aylun leaned closer and said, in a whisper, "Put it away. It is of no use if we do not survive this place."

"Do not be so dramatic. We have survived just fine so far." Yaolin rolled her eyes. "You are too cautious. We could have had the contents of that chest, too, if you were not so paranoid. Just a little more time and I would have had that lock picked."

"If it were within your ability to pick it, you would have done so ten times over."

"You do not know that."

Aylun remained calm and kept his voice flat. "Squandering time on a chest that you couldn't unlock was a needless risk, especially when we don't know its contents and already had what we came for."

"Who cares if we wasted time? We were safe enough inside Wistra's home."

"And *you* do not know that."

An even closer flapping made him jump and scan the area again. The smell of smoke from the burning tree line came to him, wafting on the stale breeze. He brought his gaze back to Yaolin, staring with disapproval. "Lighting that nest on fire. That was unnecessary. It was overkill."

She flashed him a broad smile and shoved the book back in her pocket. "I prefer to consider it a flair for the dramatic." Yaolin had an irritating way of making light of the deadliest of situations.

He sent her an even more stern look. "It is not funny."

"No, it was not. I did it to keep them busy, to buy time for our escape. And it worked."

"Busy? No, you only stirred them up, scattered them, and made them angry. It was dangerous."

She smiled as she stared away into the eerie darkness. "Then it is a good thing you are not the boss of me."

He scowled. "I'm not? Are you begging me to pull rank on you?"

Yaolin gave an enthusiastic nod of her head. "Oh. Yes, please. I love it when you pull rank. It is so cute."

He scowled even more as he grumped back, "What is it with you today?"

She appeared puzzled, or perhaps it was another childish game and she was feigning innocence.

He motioned to her. "This whole cavalier attitude."

"My attitude? My attitude is fine. What about *your* attitude?" She planted her hands on her hips and shot him an exaggerated scowl. In a husky male voice, she said, " 'Do you want me to pull rank?' "

Aylun glared. "Are you done now?" He stared for a second more before continuing. "I think we should hide out here for a while. At least until the danger passes."

His comment seemed to further aggravate her, and Yaolin's expression turned cold. "Now *you* are the one being melodramatic."

He strived to remain calm and controlled. "I am being cautious. One of us ought to be."

"No. We made it this far just fine. You are only doing this to prove a point, to make a stink about burning the nest. They are still occupied now, but the longer we remain exposed like this, the greater the danger. We need to seek shelter. We need to move now."

"It is too dangerous."

Yaolin's face softened. She peered into Aylun's eyes and took his hand.

He pulled it away.

At his withdrawal, her head dropped, and her tone became steeped in sadness. "Why does it always have to be like this?" She looked up as a sudden affection filled her face. "We have been partners for four years. We spend all our time together." She tried to make eye contact again, but he looked away. "A few days ago, we ate together. We went for a walk, just the two of us. We even laughed and joked like normal people. But now it is like you are a different person."

He stiffened. "We are on a mission. It is not the time."

Yaolin lowered her head, becoming sadder and even more serious. "Mission, no mission—it makes no difference. You always end up pulling away. And there is a part of you that you will never let me see."

He gazed into her eyes, unable to answer. They were Shou and now possessed a journal of immense importance. The future might very well rest on what they did, so one of them needed to be serious-minded about it. That meant he dared not let the situation get any more out of hand.

Yaolin looked up at him. "Do you know that you have never once said you care about me?"

Aylun hesitated. There were things in this world that could sense feelings. Demons of dangerous power. If he let his emotions run away with him, they would know and threaten her to manipulate him. They could do unspeakable things to her just to cripple him. Feelings like that were dangerous. They were a liability. He gave a slight tip of his head. "Yaolin—"

Her pleading eyes looked up at him. "No. No. Look. It is easy. I'll show you." She took his hands into hers, and her adoring face stared up at his. "I love you, Aylun."

He pulled his hands free and stared at the ground as he struggled for words to tell her without telling her that he cared.

"Fine," said Yaolin. "You feel nothing for me." She stood, still clutching her flamestone. "Then just stay here and hide out from your feelings. We are minutes from shelter in Kiarta. I am taking the journal there."

She turned and began to go.

Fear ignited at how deadly the situation had become. With her flamestone a shining beacon in her hand, Yaolin was going to walk right out there within striking range of whatever danger lurked in the dark.

He jolted upright. "No!" he shouted.

She never paused, continuing to head out away from the wall. He reached for her wrist, but she was already too far away.

"There are silent things. Things that will attack without warning. Get back here," he demanded as his breathing became short and rapid.

"What do you care?"

"It is dangerous. You will not hear them coming."

"Then admit your feelings and come protect me."

Aylun stiffened, standing even more staunchly. "Not one more step."

Yaolin turned to face him, her body glowing in the light of her flamestone against the sheer darkness beyond. "It is three simple words."

He froze, desperate to get her to come back yet sure that risking them both by following her would be a strategic mistake. "I cannot do my job if I let my feelings …" He stopped himself. This was precisely the kind of dangerous situation that needed a detached, rational mind.

As he calmed, Yaolin's face clouded, and she shook her head. "I love you so much, and you can't even say—"

A sudden rush of flapping wings broke the silence.

Aylun dove forward.

Yaolin's head jerked up, and her scream cut through the thick blackness as a gigantic claw grabbed her by the shoulder and jerked her from the ground.

Aylun reached for her, but it was too late.

AYLUN

Yaolin's desperate cries echoed across the rock face as something massive and dark carried her up along it.

Aylun turned and sprinted down the wall, chasing after her as she lurched higher and higher. He yanked his own flamestone from his pocket and jammed it into a holder on his belt. Only a few body lengths behind, he leaped and dashed up the cliffside, bouncing off ledges and cracks like they were stepping stones in a stream.

The light in her hand drifted up and over the wall.

He yanked himself above the cliff edge, rolled across the ground, and sprang to his feet. As he flew to a sprint, Aylun glanced down and concentrated on the Ring of Pairing on his finger. Ahead of him, a silver thread blinked into existence and wound its way toward her through the impenetrable blackness.

He grabbed the two poles slung over his back as he stared up into the darkness at the fading light from her flamestone. He jammed the two halves together and twisted, and they clicked into place, making a single stave as razor-sharp blades sprang from the ends.

At a flat-out run, he chased after her as creatures began to appear out of the darkness, a few at first, then more and more, lunging at him left and right. His staff hurtled through the blackness, his blade slashing at one creature after another. Their carcasses tumbled behind him, disintegrating in bursts of flame and ash as he raced across the dark ground.

A much louder flapping flew down at him from behind. He ducked and stabbed at it. His blade caught, and it jerked forward as dark blood spattered all around him, drenching his back. He wedged the staff into the rocks and dirt below his feet. It bent under the weight. Something gigantic and dark hurtled down in front of him and collided with the uneven ground. He dashed across its tail and back, stabbed it where it seemed like a heart should lie, and vaulted over its head. It disintegrated into a shower of light and glowing cinders.

Yaolin's screams and cries for help grew more distant, and every muscle burned as he raced onward, dispatching creatures at a frantic pace. They dove out of the dark, their wings becoming a rumble. On the verge of collapse, his breath heaving, he bellowed out an anguished roar and pushed still harder, tearing creatures asunder as their blood streaked his clothes and face.

Far ahead in the darkness, the cries for help turned to a piercing shriek that cut through the Dead of Night.

Aylun pushed on, controlling his desperation as he drove yet harder, racing along the silver thread into the darkness. He threw himself against the wave of dark figures pouring over him until the bursts of fluttering and screeches began to ease. Carcasses consumed themselves in sparks and embers, leaving a blazing trail behind him that lit the never-ending night.

A sick feeling grabbed hold of his stomach as a far more desperate shriek rang out and a distant light fell from the sky, landing some distance ahead.

As the last hideous beast hit the ground, he raced up to the end of the thread and stifled a crippling urge to retch as he stared down at his destination. It was the ring, dark and metallic, with a broken line of jade around it, still worn on the finger of Yaolin's severed hand.

The shrieks of pain no longer grew farther away as he jammed the end of his staff into the ground and fell to his knees. Clinging to it for support, he stared at the ground as the distant screams of agony drowned in a sickening gurgle, then fell silent. All that remained were the frenzied screeches of some distant abominations fighting over their kill.

Chapter Four

BY THE LIGHT OF DAY

Aylun stood at attention with his head bowed as he waited to face the inevitable. Yaochen stood with his back to him, his bald spot and stubbly hair the only part of him visible in the faint light. His stout frame clothed in white, he gazed out the window at rain drizzling down on the serene rock gardens of the Augury. Unable to see the bereaved father's face, Aylun could only imagine the depths of his grief.

Aylun remained still and waited. It was only a matter of time before the questions began, and much of his return trip remained a hazy and incomplete memory. He barely recalled fighting his way through the Dead of Night to Kiarta or collapsing in a cramped cupboard in a tiny stone home. It was impossible to tell how long he had lingered there in a despondent fugue, but it was long enough to consume all but a few sips of his water.

What had prompted him to leave and how he fought his way out of the perpetual darkness was a jumbled mishmash of images. Indistinct impressions lingered of stumbling through the Dead of Night, town to town, holing up in long-abandoned buildings. Gone were any memories of the road to the northwest or the monolith at its edge that signified his exit. He must have found it and traveled north through the caverns and out of that accursed place.

All he could summon were vague recollections of stumbling out into daylight and blundering north. Confused images remained of a nameless face, a soldier or merchant perhaps, stumbling across him in Talus along what must have been the Eastern Trail. Flashes came to him of a stern face and a stream of accusatory-sounding syllables, questions perhaps, shot at him while he lapsed in and out of consciousness. Then there was the scorching sun, burning down through a half-remembered haze as he rattled across endless grassy flatlands in the back of a creaking cart. Every bump jarred him out of his feverish delirium as the road through Mundus never seemed to end.

He had wanted to flee when he began to come out of his stupor and realized the gates of the Augury were drawing near, but he couldn't. He had earned whatever punishment awaited him. His report to the Great Oracle was brief and agonizing as he relayed in detail the manner of his utter failure. After a fitful night's sleep, fraught with dreams caught between horror and delusion, he awakened to the droning of raindrops and his unbearable shame and guilt.

He was in the process of dressing when a messenger arrived, summoning him to Yaochen's office. Every fiber of his being rebelled against the thought of standing before the father of the woman he had let die such a horrible death. Yet what he faced now was nothing compared to the agonizing end his partner had suffered. So, honor and duty compelled him to grant the man whatever he required.

He glanced up at the bereaved father. He was still focused on the scene outside his window, so Aylun lowered his head again and waited. Weak from the trip and stiff from standing in one place for too long, he remained motionless. Outside the door behind him, horses' hooves clomped along the paving stones and splashed through puddles on the busy Kanlu streets.

The clatter seemed to stir Yaochen from his grief. He raised himself up taller and pulled his gaze from the raindrops splashing across the stone and water outside his window. When he turned, his rounded face was drawn and his dark brown eyes were red and glassy, but when he spotted Aylun, they became afire.

He stepped up next to his small wooden desk, and although he struggled to contain them, he could not hide his grief and outrage. "You survived twice. The first time, three Shou died, including your sister. This time, my Yaolin. I want to know how it is that you lived when she died."

His head down and mired in anguish and self-loathing, Aylun' spoke in a soft and sincere voice. "I am sorry. I wish I had died in her stead."

Yaochen clenched his fists. "Your *wishes* are of no concern to me. I demand *answers*." He stepped closer. "How did you let my daughter die?"

Aylun stared at his feet. "One of the night beasts swooped down out of the darkness and carried her off. I used the Rings of Pairing to follow, but it was too late."

The man restrained himself again and spoke in sharp, biting words. "It is your first duty to protect your partner. Where precisely were you when this creature *'swooped down'*?"

Aylun gave a deep bow. "I am sorry. I was too far away."

The bereaved father's anger became too much to hold, and his bitter words spewed out. "Too far away. Too far away! It was your job to protect her. How did you let her get 'too far away'?"

"It is my fault. I am sorry, Father."

"My precious daughter is dead. How *dare* you call me Father? How *dare* you say you are sorry? As if your contrition mattered. As if it fixed anything." He hammered his fist against the polished surface of the desk. "I want *answers!*"

Aylun stood speechless. What answer could he give? There was no defense for what he'd allowed to happen. Denying his own culpability would be the act of a coward. So he offered the only thing he could. "I am so sorry."

Red-faced, Yaochen grabbed a long writing brush from the desktop and flung it at Aylun, hitting him just below his eye. "Your partner, one of the Shou, died on your watch. You know our rules: you owe me a life. And yet you lack the honor to even give me a simple explanation?"

Aylun cringed from the father's wrath. It tore at his insides to have to recount the events, but he had to. It was his duty, so he raised his head and looked Yaochen in the eye as his words struggled out. "We argued. I pushed it too far. I ... I made her doubt my sincerity. So when I said we should stay put and wait out the creatures, she thought I was being petty. She got mad, accused me of exaggerating the danger and walked away ..." He let his head drop again, and his words dripped with remorse. "And I let her."

"On a mission? You got into an *argument?*" He grumbled and fumed as he stormed across the smooth stone floor. "Of all the irresponsible, immature, dangerous ..." He stopped and pivoted to face Aylun. "I warned her. Four years ago, I warned her that you were damaged and useless. I told her to stay away from you. If only I had forced her." He marched up and shoved his face into Aylun's. "Or *thrown* you out."

Yaochen stomped up to the door and flung it open with an earsplitting bang. "Four years ago, I advised Chenyu to expel you, but he would not listen. Now he will have to. *Get out!* You are not fit to be Shou. The Augury has no use for a used-up, broken mockery of a man like you."

Aylun gave a last deep bow, then shuffled toward the door.

Yaochen lowered his head, and Aylun halted in front of him at his now-calmer words. "Out of respect for my daughter, I will break the rule. I cannot bring myself to send you to the dragon. But if you ever show up in front of me again, I will *kill* you myself." He yanked a small pack containing Aylun's belongings from the floor and pitched it into his arms.

Aylun caught the bundle, and Yaochen gave him a forceful shove out the door. Aylun stumbled into the rain, and the door slammed behind him, leaving him standing on the steps of the Augury, clutching his meager belongings in his arms. He hung his head as the drizzle ran down his face, soaking his hair and clothes.

At the stares of passing strangers, he felt the last few shreds of his dignity being washed away, flowing along the cobblestones, only to disappear down the lane. After a while, the cold and wet became more than he could bear. Clinging to the pitiful remains of his life, he splashed out into the street, heading away from the only home he had ever known.

The soft rustle of falling paper drifted on the air, the only sound breaking the tomb-like silence. Head to the side and half in a daze, Megan stared into the distance, where light from the shifting portal above sent glowing patterns rippling along the rock walls of an enormous cavern. Well beyond her feet, the same light reflected off a dark, curved wall, sending a fainter display shifting across the first.

Alone with her fears, Megan found the oppressive quiet and darkness closing in on her, carrying with it a stifling hopelessness and dread. The familiar feeling of being locked in a dark closet came with it, as did a paralyzing fear that, this time, something horrific really did lurk in that vast black expanse.

A sharp jangle made her jump as something crashed down on the pile of metal behind her. The clatter echoed along the rock walls as her eyes flew wide in alarm. In an instant, she clamped them shut and shuddered, afraid to look.

At the sound of panicked breathing, she opened them again. She rolled over, and intense relief spread throughout her being. There on his back next to her lay Jon. At the sound of her movement, his shocked white face whipped over to stare at her.

He remained still for a moment, his anxious eyes staring into hers. "Megan, are you hurt?"

She glanced down, looking herself over. "I don't think so."

Jon turned his eyes back upward. Concentration filled every line of his face as he studied the fluid, lighted mass rippling and churning above them.

Megan choked back tears of gratitude as she watched him. She felt wretched that this had happened to him, and in a bizarre and twisted way, his being here was her fault. Or at least it was her future self's fault for not warning her. It was as if future Megan wanted it to happen, and no matter how little sense it made to feel guilty about something she had not yet done, the feeling refused to yield.

All of a sudden, Jon leaped for her, his full weight careening down on top of her. He grabbed her and rolled, flinging them both to the side.

A massive object shot out of the mass and plummeted to the glittering ground with a tremendous clatter. The blob vanished, leaving only darkness as the crash reverberated around them. Then it faded away until all that remained was the gentle sound of falling paper and Jon's panicked breathing.

Already reeling in shock and feeling claustrophobic from the darkness, Megan remained still for a moment, but Jon's weight on her soon became too much. Through his rapid breaths came her weak voice. "Jon?"

"Yeah?"

"You're lying on top of me."

He pulled himself off, and Megan sat up. With dread of what lay beyond her view, she peered into the darkness. Then, as her eyes adjusted, she made out a faint light. It peeked around the short metallic wall farther down, revealing that they rested between two walls that curved gently off to the left.

She turned her focus to Jon. His eyes darted everywhere, taking in every minute detail of the place. Then his attention turned downward, apparently noticing for the first time that they were resting on an enormous mound of sparkling metal pieces of stunning variety and shape. He fished in his pocket and yanked out his phone, staring at its shiny black surface. His gaze shot over, and his anguished eyes peered into hers. "I'm so sorry about all of this."

"It's okay," she said, her thoughts still swimming in shock and guilt.

"No, it's really not," came Jon's soft words.

Her eyes having adjusted to a point, Megan turned her attention to her surroundings, and she whispered to herself, "What kind of rabbit hole have I fallen down?" Below them lay a sprawling jumble of bottles, goblets, daggers, pottery, and crowns. Yet, most of the mound was composed of countless gold and silver coins, some seeming ancient and others new. "Where are we?" She glanced at Jon again.

"I have no idea. No physics I know of can explain what just happened."

Megan nodded to herself. It was as if they had passed through a wormhole, yet the power to create one was way beyond anything Earth possessed. Even if they had somehow done so, the unimaginable gravity and warping of space and time at the event horizon would have ripped them apart. Jon was right. Whatever had just happened couldn't be explained by any science they knew.

Jon stared downward, then his gaze drifted up to survey their dark and ominous environs. "I think we're in a cave. There seems to be light coming from over there." He pointed, and Megan glanced at the dim light she had spotted earlier.

With a deep breath, she clambered to her feet and offered Jon a hand. "Well, if you're going to get us back home, then the first thing we have to do is figure out where we are, and we can't do that sitting here."

She helped him up, then followed as he staggered across the uneven floor of metallic objects. Each footfall crunched and clanked, the clatter echoing through the cavernous space. Jon led and she followed as he found his way along a wall of stone, eventually stepping off into solid ground. They continued on, more quietly now, feeling their way along the wall as it curved off to the left.

After a while, a warm yellow light peeked around the edge, washing across the worn stone floor out ahead. It appeared to have the quality of daylight, and hope sprang that it might lead out of this suffocating space. Megan halted at the impression of movement. Then she realized it was the wall around which the light shone. It had moved, blocking it. The feeling of suffocation grew as it moved back again. Walls don't move, so it could only signify one thing: It was alive, and that meant they weren't alone. Something else was in this dark space with them, and it was right next to them.

Fear ignited as she glanced at Jon, then back at the movement, and pointed. "What is that?"

His eyes widened in alarm, and he whispered, "Oh crap, I think it's breathing."

With a sudden scraping sound, the wall began to move forward beside them.

Jon froze.

Megan startled and broke into a mad sprint. She flew around him, headed for the daylight ahead. Every ounce of her energy pushed forward as the wall slid by her at a breathtaking pace.

"Megan!" Jon's hushed voice called out from behind her, but she was beyond the point of responding.

She shot across the floor, and the light loomed closer. A massive, long object hurtled out over her head in a flurry of wind and dust. It smashed down in front of her with a thunderous thud that shook the ground. The impact blasted a wall of debris and dirt into her face and body that stung where it hit. She covered her head and stumbled to a halt, inches from an enormous tail covered in dark metallic scales.

Beyond panicked, she cowered and trembled. Her heart jumped at a screeching noise shrieking in her ears, like chalk on an enormous chalkboard. Spikes at the end of the tail raked along the stone ground as the scaly appendage curved back around her. Through a cloud of dust, she peered at Jon, but he was frozen, staring at her with a look of absolute shock.

Somewhere inside the billowing cloud, the scraping and thuds of something enormous rumbled in the dark. The echoes overlapped, the cacophony growing until all she could hear was a wall of sound. Thundering footsteps and scraping claws cut through the roar, jangling her nerves. Unable to catch even a fleeting glimpse of it, she could only imagine what massive, unthinkable terror stalked them.

The air began to clear and as visibility returned, she scoured the area in vain, hoping for even the most remote means of escape. A shiver ran down her spine at the realization that there was no way out.

She glanced back toward Jon, hoping for help. Through the cloud of dust around him, the head of what appeared to be a massive lizard whipped out over him. Megan gasped as it dropped down, blocking his way.

She flew back toward him but froze again as the enormous head and razor teeth closed in on him. It was going to kill him, and she was trapped; all she could do was cower and watch.

Jon stood like a statue as the massive head stopped inches from his face. Then it snorted, blasting back his clothes and hair. Jagged teeth glistened in the dim light as it let out a plaintive moan that echoed all around.

The wing of the beast unfurled, whipping out over them, giving it the appearance of an enormous dragon. Except dragons couldn't exist. As she struggled to come to grips with the impossibility, the wing snapped back in a blast of wind, and a shimmering light raced across Jon. A similar glow flittered down over her, and she gasped at an odd burning sensation and a feeling that some profound change had come over her.

The sensation was forgotten when the head swung around and the creature glared at her with disturbing dark gray eyes. She stepped back. Her breath grew short and heavy as the beast eyed her, looking her up and down like she was a piece of raw meat. Then the head, with its enormous, jagged teeth, began to close in on her. Her gaze shot everywhere, scanning the area, searching again for any avenue of escape.

Her focus shot back to Jon as he leaped toward her, but the enormous head whipped back toward him and let out a shocking grunt that resonated throughout the cavern.

For a moment, the creature seemed to be eyeing them both. Then it released a low growl that sounded very much like a warning. The head swiveled back toward her and glared at her face. Then its eyes seemed to drift down, and Megan followed them to a dark metallic object dangling from a chain that had caught on a button of her pants. Terror gripped her, and she yanked the thing from her clothes and jammed it into her pocket in the hope the beast might lose interest.

Instead, the act seemed to anger the beast, and it let out a deafening roar, the hot breath whistling in her ears as it tossed back her hair and clothes. She cowered, afraid to move as the echoes faded. Then the tail rose, leaving a path for her to flee.

She hesitated. Every fiber of her being was screaming at her to run, but how could she leave Jon? Then the incident with the actors outside the King Chi flashed through her mind. If he did such a brave and foolish thing to save a pair of strangers, what peril would he put himself in to protect her? With that thought, she realized he was safer without her. Still, she looked back at him, trapped with the enormous head inching toward him.

Then he shouted, "Megan, run!"

At his urging, she spun around and broke into an all-out sprint. Guilt tore at her for leaving him behind, and she glanced back over her shoulder.

Jon yelled again, "Go!"

She turned all her attention forward as she hit the base of a path upward and what looked like sunlight shining down from a broad opening way up ahead. Her breathing grew labored, but Megan pushed on, racing toward the brightness. Her only hope now would be to reach the top as quickly as possible and pray she could somehow find help up there to save Jon.

Aylun stormed across the tall grass of the clearing, trying to control his frustration as he clutched Juzhi's reins in his hand. The fiery stallion pranced behind him, the reddish-brown spots on his white face flashing in the afternoon sun as he bucked his head. Aylun looked back at Yaomey barging after him, her long black braid bobbing as she ran. With reins in hand, she yanked along her own mare behind her. Her steed was similar to Aylun's, but had fewer and larger spots of all black.

AYLUN

When he had left Kanlu, the relentless woman caught up with him. When he revealed he intended to go and serve the dragon, Islong, she had become hysterical. She threw out every despicable argument imaginable to talk him out of it. When that failed, she accused him of being a horse thief and insisted she needed to come along to return his steed to the Augury afterward. As expected, it had been a mere ruse. She was using the animal as a pretext to hound him the entire trip.

Though she tried to hide it, every time she spoke, he could hear the rage in her voice. It was understandable: he hadn't protected her sister. Yet, there was another note there too, an echo of his own remorse, and a desperation to understand how a mission she and her sister had prompted could have ended in her death. It was a familiar echo of the two sisters' regret following the three deaths that had resulted from the last trip they orchestrated. Alongside her anger and regret, there was a distinct vein of distress, a frantic need, perhaps, to follow him and prevent the death toll from rising by one more life.

The endless journey would have been unbearable enough without her badgering. His nights were consumed by one harrowing nightmare after another of flames and blackness, blood-drenched hands, and shadows consuming loved ones whole. His days were plagued by horrific memories of desperate pleas for help and shrieks of pain piercing the oppressive darkness. And through it all, an unendurable grief and shame poured down on his soul like a never-ending avalanche. He yearned to escape his misery, and so he had gone, on his own, to serve the dragon in hopes she would put an end to his suffering.

Yaomey's company had turned it into sheer torture. Weary and beaten down, he lacked the will to battle her into leaving, yet he could not look at her diminutive frame, silky black hair, and bright brown eyes without being reminded of Yaolin. Even worse, on occasion, she would make a sound or gesture, and it would fool him. For a moment, he would think Yaolin was there with him. Then he would recall her demise, and remorse would rain down on him again like a torrential downpour.

To make matters worse, Yaomey had not ceased her pestering until she had dragged out of him every horrific detail of her sister's death. She didn't stop there, harassing him until he had divulged what they had found and the exact wording of the journal. Now, as they approached the lair, her ceaseless badgering had turned into a frantic tirade.

With her free hand, she reached out and seized his arm. "Talk to me."

He glared at her and wrested it free.

Yaomey continued to chase after him. "You cannot do this." She came up behind him and grabbed his arm a second time.

He spun around, and the pair faced each other. A short distance away loomed the hulking cavern entrance, like an open maw ready to swallow them. Beyond it, somewhere in the dark recesses, lurked the dragon.

"Leave!" Aylun shouted.

Her eyes wide with apprehension, Yaomey stared at the enormous dark cavity. "You do not have to go to the dragon. Father said so."

His annoyance grew, and he shouted, "Go away!"

The distant sound of scrambling feet on rock floors rose above the quiet swish of grass and rustling of leaves, but he was too focused on Yaomey to give it any notice.

"Islong will kill you," she pleaded. "That is what dragons do."

He nearly shouted, "And what if she does? I killed your sister. I am to blame."

She straightened. "Yes, you did. And I *do* blame you."

He took a step back, aghast that she would say it aloud.

The scraping footfalls grew closer.

She gave a small shake of her head. "But she would not want you to die."

"Why not?"

"Because she loved you."

"And it got her killed." Aylun lowered his head. "This way, at least, I will have restored some honor."

A red-haired woman rose up within the cavern entrance. She raced forward in apparent panic, shielding her eyes and stumbling over the ground.

At her arrival, Aylun started, and his gaze swung over. "Now what?" He froze, staring into her panic-stricken face as her breath heaved. She was a complete contradiction. The width and shape of her face, the darkness and curve of her eyes, and her single eyelid, with no crease where the eyelid opened, were all unmistakable. She had to be Elorian, like him and Yaomey. Yet every single Elorian had black hair where hers was red. Her skin was as flawless as any royalty's, but her clothes were far from regal. In fact, they were utterly foreign.

The woman's frantic words forced their way out between gasps for air as she pointed and waved like a wild woman. "It's Jon, he's in the ... and there was ... and I know it sounds crazy ... but it was big and—and real."

Aylun stared, frozen, his fascination intense. He tilted his head and reached out, almost touching her impossible wavy red hair.

The desperate stranger seized his wrist and yanked on it, dragging him through the long grass and toward the enormous entrance. Through labored breaths, she implored him, "Help me ... please. Jon, it'll kill him."

"Islong?" Yaomey asked.

The red-haired woman stopped and stared at her with a blank expression.

"The dragon?"

The stranger gave an intense and rapid series of nods and pulled harder.

Still captivated, Aylun stumbled along.

"Slow down," said Yaomey.

Aylun came out of his daze and caught himself. He planted his feet and pulled against the woman's frantic tugging. He stared at the cavernous opening as he muttered, "What kind of madwoman goes rummaging around in a dragon's lair?"

"We weren't. We were in the lab, there was a big ball … and we got sucked in … and then … and then … we were …"—she thrust her arm out, pointing to the dark opening—"*there.*"

He scanned the area. "Lab?"

Yaomey's eyes flew wide open. She took several steps back as she looked the woman up and down. "Your clothes? Where did you get them?"

"What? They're just … it was casual Friday. Please, he'll die. You have to help Jon."

Aylun stammered, "What's a fry—fry day?"

Yaomey pivoted to Aylun. "It is the prophecy." She pointed. "She is the Otherworlder." She addressed the woman directly. "You are not from this world, are you?"

Eyes still wide, the strange lady gave a vigorous shake of her head.

Aylun's annoyance deepened. "Don't be a fool. It cannot be the prophecy."

"But it is."

"No. It is not."

Yaomey folded her arms and glared at Aylun.

He folded his arms and glared back, incensed that he would even need to explain. "Look, she says there is another. Chenyu can see exact people, times, and places. Do you really imagine Wistra foresaw precisely what would happen but overlooked an entire second Otherworlder?"

"We don't have perfect information." She jutted out her chin. "You know that. Leanna only knew a tiny bit."

Aylun's response was curt and dismissive. "It's not my business."

"You are Shou."

"They kicked me out."

She pointed at him. "You yourself said the Otherworlder is destined to bring about a new age. Are you really so selfish and self-absorbed that you would let one die who is destined to bring about a new age?"

At her words, a fury welled up within him, and something snapped. He faced Yaomey and glared as he pointed toward Kanlu. "Leave me alone!"

The impossible stranger gave a deep bow and rubbed her palms together in supplication. "No, no, no ... I'm begging you. Please. You have to help."

His anger beyond the breaking point, Aylun turned and addressed the madwoman. "You want my help?"

She gave a frantic nod. "Desperately."

"And there are two of you?"

Another vigorous nod of her head.

"Fine." Gripped by an overwhelming wave of frustration, he seized the woman's wrist, yanked her over to him, and tossed her over his shoulder. What needed doing was dirty and distasteful, but he had been Shou, raised from childhood to do the dirty and distasteful when necessity called for it.

"Let go!" she yelled.

"What are you doing?" Yaomey's eyes grew wide.

"The Shou's' dirty work." He turned to mount his horse.

"You cannot just abduct her."

"Abduct?" The woman gasped. "No, no, no." She began to writhe and squirm, trying to wrest herself free.

At her resistance, his fury only grew, and Aylun clamped down tighter. He glared at Yaomey. "I told you all about Wistra's journal."

She glared back, not seeming to comprehend.

"The council changed the prophecy."

No sign of recognition showed in her scorching stare.

Aylun grumbled. Did he have to spell everything out? "They lied about the prophecy. The council is determined to make anyone suspected of being the Otherworlder into a fugitive. If these two stay together, they will be captured or more likely killed, and your precious prophecy will be undone." He swung up onto his tall spotted horse and slammed the woman down in front of him, facing forward. Yaomey mounted beside him as he clamped one arm around his captive, pinning her left arm.

The desperate woman squirmed and wriggled. "No, please. What are you doing?"

"Keeping you safe."

"But Jon—"

"Is dead, or safer without having to worry about you." Aylun ground his teeth as he kicked, and his horse flew across the waving grass of the open clearing. Hooves pounded, the wind whistled around them, and the grass whipped the horse's legs as Yaomey pulled up alongside him. He glanced back, peering through the bright sunlight at the cavernous opening, now shrinking behind them.

Suddenly, a frantic blond-haired man burst from it, spinning, squinting, and covering his eyes.

The sight only fueled Aylun's outrage. He faced forward, then kicked again, and they surged toward the surrounding forest.

The strange woman twisted her upper body around to stare backward in the direction he had been looking. She jerked and squirmed harder, then pointed with her free hand and yelled, "He's right there!"

Her plea tugged at his conscience, yet it was clear that only by doing what was required could he give these two the best chance for survival. He still didn't believe there was any prophecy in play here, but that was no longer his call. Yaomey was the only Shou here, and if she believed these two were part of a prophecy from Wistra, then this was how to protect them from a corrupt council. He shoved down the urge to return to the man and let it drown in an ocean of rage. The council wouldn't touch him so long as he was useful in getting their hands on the woman. He gripped her tighter and, through clenched teeth, said, "Good, then he will be fine."

"Fine? The dragon is still—"

"If Islong wanted him dead, he'd be dead."

AYLUN

When he failed to turn his head, the woman punched him in the arm. It was a solid blow and well aimed, but her angle made it impossible to inflict any real damage.

As their steeds flew into the forest, he glanced back again to see the man disappear behind layers of tree trunks, leaves, and branches. Hooves rumbled against the dirt, and the horses lurched and heaved as they weaved their way through the trees and underbrush. Aylun held tight, wrestling with his runaway frustration as his captive writhed and struggled.

She clawed at Aylun's arm, her nails digging into his flesh and scratching his skin.

His fury flared, and he eased his hold enough to grab her free wrist and clamp back down, harder now, pinning both arms.

She bent her head down, then flung it back into his face.

He attempted to dodge, but she still managed to catch the side of his skull with a sharp and painful clunk. His grip loosened as he reeled from the blow.

The woman squirmed free and began to slide off Juzhi. As she slipped farther out of his grasp, her head slid to the side, headed for a collision with an approaching tree.

He grabbed ahold of her arm, yanked her upright, and clamped down again with even greater strength. Her cunning and determination might be admirable, but he was in no mood to entertain them. After several more minutes of squirming, the woman went limp, helpless as he carried her farther and farther from her companion.

Chapter Five

DREAMWORLD

Megan wriggled and squirmed with every ounce of strength she could summon, yet the harder she pulled, the more he tightened his grip. She bent her head down until her chin jabbed her chest, then flung it backward with all her might. A blinding pain stabbed the side of her head as it collided with his. His arm around her went loose and her vision swam into darkness. The world spun as she lost all balance and began to slide off the horse. When her vision cleared she was hurtling face-first into the trunk of a tree.

The man yanked her back up like she was a rag doll and flung his left arm around her with startling strength. She tried to wrest her own left arm free, but his fingers clamped down on her right wrist like a vise, and his arm around her tightened even further. The force squeezed out her breath and lifted her out of the saddle, smashing her against his chest.

Fear and dread saturated her over what he intended to do to her. Helpless against these two strangers, she felt vulnerable and violated. Yet despite her own plight, much of her panic sprang from the fate of her best friend. She had left Jon lost and alone in a strange place outside a dragon's lair with no one to help him. No matter how capable he might be, he was way out of his element—so far out that it was impossible to imagine how he could survive. She summoned every last shred of her remaining strength to struggle and kick as she pulled forward against her abductor, but she couldn't budge. Exhausted and every muscle spent, she fell limp as her mind whirled into a traumatized haze.

The horse beneath her heaved and lurched as it weaved through towering sunlit trees and dodged around feathery brush. Alongside galloped the woman's horse, its hoof-falls sometimes farther and sometimes closer. The chirping of birds, the soft breeze rustling the leaves, and the patterns of light and shadow all drifted past, spun together by her shocked trance. They merged one into the other, blending with portals and dragons as Jon slipped farther and farther away.

The woman's horse swerved closer, and her voice yelled out, "Aylun … Aylun! Are you crazy? Stop this."

From behind her came the man's emotionless response. "No."

"You cannot just abduct a woman against her will."

"Watch me."

"What are you even planning to do with her?"

His disturbing coldness took on a note of annoyance. "It was not my idea to do anything." He turned his head toward the woman, his callous words bellowing in Megan's ear. "I wanted to be left alone, remember. But no, you two had to badger me into this."

The woman screamed back, "Are you out of your mind? I never asked you to take her! I only said it might be the prophecy. If I am wrong, then this—"

"It is irrelevant. It matters not if she is a great leader or an insignificant nobody. If the council comes to suspect she is the Otherworlder, she will be in grave danger. And so will her friend."

"Okay. Fine. But if this is not the prophecy after all, then what you are doing is perverse."

"What *I* am doing?" The man's fury assaulted her ears. "Since when is any of this my doing?" His body leaned toward the woman, his arm around Megan pulling her with him, as his harsh words boomed in her ear. "You want to ease your conscience? Fine. Go to Lanessa. Find Wistra's journal. Then perhaps, maybe, we will have an actual clue what is going on."

The woman's voice became quieter. "See, now you are just being petulant."

"Petulant? Really? Says the woman whose adolescent pestering goaded Chenyu into a mission that got three of her friends killed."

The uneven beat of the horses' hooves against the rough forest floor filled the lengthy silence as patterns of sun and shade floated past. Then came her sorrowful voice, barely discernible above the noise of the horses and forest. "And now you are being cruel."

After another long moment, the man's voice came again from right behind her, his tone just as chilling and yet at the same time somehow more conciliatory. "Look, our only choice now is to keep them apart."

Another long silence followed, and when the woman spoke, her voice carried a note of acquiescence. "I do not like it. I do not like it one tiny bit. But as the only real Shou here, I cannot fault your reasoning, but surely there must be another way."

They both remained silent for some time. Megan's weight shifted back against the man as the horses clambered up a large mound, then she fell forward into his iron grip again as the horses restrained themselves on the downhill side.

When the man spoke again, the distant and emotionless quality had returned to his voice. "I wanted to be left alone. If you have a way to resolve this, especially one that does not involve me, then speak."

Another silence dragged on as the horses worked their way down a small ravine. "Okay." The woman's voice sounded resolute. "So be it. But there are conditions to the prophecy. She must have a unique and powerful gift and be a leader. For now, we keep them apart and watch for signs. But as soon as we have made sure she is safe, we set her free." The woman fell silent, and her horse dropped back to follow the man's.

Time seemed meaningless and nothing real as the world around Megan wafted by for what seemed an eternity. The saddle under her grew uncomfortable, and the sun slipped farther and farther down in the sky. As darkness began to creep through the forest, the hoof-falls slowed to a stop beneath the branches of a massive gnarled tree at the edge of a calm, slow-moving river.

The man dismounted under twisted, weeping branches that formed an umbrella of brown and olive green that swished and swayed in the dwindling breeze. The burnt-orange skyline and golden-yellow orb of a setting sun peeped through long, winding boughs that reached down until they almost touched the quiet waters.

With unexpected gentleness, the man lifted Megan from his horse and lowered her to the rough, uneven ground. Her legs crumpled under her, and he caught her. With great care, he lifted her back onto her feet and half carried her over to the tree. Then he set her down on one of the giant contorted roots that wound out from its base. He walked back to the horses and began to untie his bedroll.

Free of the iron grip that had robbed her of her dignity and sovereign will, she began to tremble. Her numbness and shock faded as every moment of her abduction and the trip that followed drifted into sharp focus. She pulled herself to her feet. Still suffering under the veil of disorientation, she fixed her eyes on the man's backside. A wild fury crowded out her trauma and she stumbled a few steps forward. He had disregarded her feelings. He had violated her and terrorized her. But most of all, he had taken her from Jon, and he would pay.

She screamed as she charged at his back.

He spun around, and the bedroll tumbled from his hands.

Megan dove in to smash his face with her elbow.

He dodged her blow with effortless ease.

She brought up her knee to his groin at the same time she threw her forearm up under his chin.

He blocked her knee and arched backward so her forearm only grazed his jaw.

She unleashed her rage, jabbing again at his cold, evil face and hitting him with a satisfying blow square on his nose.

The impact twisted the man's head aside, but he whipped it back again, staring straight at her with those disturbing, emotionless eyes.

While she still teetered, off balance from her punch, he set a palm on each shoulder and gave her a small shove.

She stumbled back and almost fell.

Her blow had done nothing to disturb his unnatural calm. He continued to eye her as if she were an annoying fly buzzing in his ear. "It is probably best not to announce your surprise attack with a scream."

Megan dove forward, shoving her face within inches of his as she spat out her demand: "Take me back."

"No."

This time, she screamed at the top of her lungs, "Take me back *now!*"

Aylun remained matter-of-fact. "Are you married?"

Megan reeled as if knocked off balance by the utter incongruity of the question. "What difference does that make?"

He shrugged. "It makes all the difference. I will not take a wife from her husband."

"What?" She shook her head, trying to throw off her complete confusion. "I love him as much as any wife loves a husband." It was an exaggeration, of course, but she was way beyond caring what she said to such an inhuman thug.

Aylun gave another slight shake of his head. "No. You do not."

Megan yelled, "You can't tell me that. You don't know what's in my heart."

"Your actions tell me what is in your heart."

"Because we're not married? You think a stupid piece of paper makes a difference?"

Aylun's unruffled facade cracked, and he appeared puzzled. "What are you talking about? What piece of paper?"

"A piece of paper. A marriage license … or registration, or whatever."

He cocked his head, and his puzzled expression deepened. "What kind of madhouse do you come from?" His voice became strong and sure. "Marriage is a commitment, an oath, an unbreakable promise to one another to stay together, no matter what. It has nothing to do with a piece of paper." He pointed at Megan. "You have not taken that vow. That tells me you think you will be fine without him."

"You're insane!" she shouted back. "What good is a vow? People discard them as soon as they're inconvenient."

He shook his head again as he spoke half to himself. "Remind me to never make an agreement with you."

Megan stamped her foot and screamed, "Take … me … back!"

Aylun moved closer. "No," his unruffled voice replied.

She stepped backward as she restrained her tears. "You're nothing but a cruel tyrant like my father."

He raised one eyebrow. "First you disrespect marriage, and now your father?"

Her fury became all-consuming. "Don't you ever stand up for my father. He was a belligerent, unfeeling bully. His impossible demands and intolerance drove my sister to suicide and killed my mother. That's what your almighty marriage is really about."

He stood for a moment, eyeing her as if she were out of her mind, then responded with cool detachment. "All right then. This conversation is over." He turned his attention back to his bedroll.

She stomped her foot again. "You can't do that. You cannot just decide this conversation is over."

"It is a pointless discussion." He motioned to the orange-and-scarlet skyline, mostly shrouded behind layers of leaves, branches, and tree trunks. "There is nothing that can be done now. It will be dark soon." Aylun turned his back to her and reached out to his horse.

Her frustration with his obstinacy and dismissiveness grew until she raised a fist and slammed it into his turned back. Despite her anger, the blow was a restrained one, and the horrid man never even acknowledged it. Her sense of helplessness rushed back, and her voice eked out quieter now as her resolve crumbled. "You can't do this."

Having been discarded and ignored, she turned and shuffled away, but all she could focus on was how inhuman and awful he was, how normal people aren't like this in real life. Without willing it, she found herself repeating "can't do this" over and over as she withdrew back to the massive twisted base of the tree. There, she squatted, facing it, trying to shut out her oppressive sense of vulnerability and powerlessness. She wrapped her arms around both knees, and the trembling returned as she rocked back and forth on her heels.

Her mind swam through a sea of bizarre happenings as she stared at the ragged shadows in the crevices of the rough bark, made deeper by the dwindling light of the setting sun. The longer she stared, the more the unreality of it grew. Every bit of this was wrong: people in a foreign land speaking perfect English ... or was it perfect Mandarin ... or was it something else entirely? How was it possible that she couldn't even tell what language people were speaking? The very fact she couldn't tell was unreal, like a dream. The more she pondered, the more it became clear: none of this was possible.

Visions of her future self visiting her bedroom and of the phenomenon in the lab kept repeating in her mind. Images of being dragged through that bizarre portal into a dark cave and of Jon facing a dragon mingled with them. In a soft voice, she began to chant again, this time "can't be real," and with every repetition, her sense of certainty grew: things like this couldn't happen; none of it was real.

Too consumed with managing his frustration and resentment, Aylun ignored the stinging in his back where the infuriating woman had struck him. He returned to his work, determined not to acknowledge her blow as she trudged away—not only because it would be wrong to retaliate but also because he had deserved it. He had lost it completely. Any semblance of reason had abandoned him.

For the last four years, each day had been a struggle to rein in his overwhelming guilt, anger, and shame and remain in control. Yet in one brief moment, all logic had fled, and he had abducted a woman whose only sin was being between him and his goal when he'd reached the end of his rope. Even now, half a day after the event, it remained a battle to contain himself, and it was almost impossible not to blame that aggravating woman.

The sharp snarl of a far-off predator and despairing cry of its prey echoed through the forest. It mingled with the falling darkness, triggering a cascade of memories—the screeches of deadly terrors lurking in the dark and Yaolin's pleas for help as her flamestone grew more distant up the cliffside. They intertwined with her shrieks of panic and agony carrying across the black expanse. Grief and rage overtook him, a ravenous carnivore bringing down its wounded quarry. His anger and frustration welled into a fiery inferno, eager to consume any remaining shred of rationality. He took a stumbling step back as he struggled under the crushing burden of it all.

As if he were moving a mountainous weight, he shuddered back his fury as he struggled to banish the memories. As his mind calmed, he inhaled a deep breath and stared out across the darkened waters of the peaceful river. He emptied his mind, finding focus instead in the reflection of dark tree branches against a deep orange-and-crimson sky.

Whatever had snapped in him at Islong's lair had all but drowned out the remorse that had hounded him since Yaolin's death, burying it beneath an all-consuming rage. Quieting his mind dispelled some pitiful portion of it but brought back an even stronger wave of self-loathing. It was as if the weight of his failures were pushing against a wall of fury, threatening to flood back in and wage an even more suffocating assault. So he stared into the gentle waters and took another slow, deep breath as he tried again.

Worming their way into his calming mind came remembrances of Yaomey's simple proclamation. She was right. What he had done to this woman was unconscionable. There was no denying that simple truth, and the realization only deepened his shame and guilt. Yet it was also true that he was not wrong. If he had not taken her, she would have stayed, a prophecy might have been undone, and she and this man she claimed to love would be in mortal danger. So, he was trapped, with no choice but to continue down the path he had set.

AYLUN

Aylun turned, and there she was, squatting by the tree, trembling and hugging her knees to her chest as she rocked back and forth and mumbled to herself. A pang of worry and sympathy stabbed at his conscience, but it only seemed to fuel his bitterness. It made no difference that the rational part of his mind told him she had done nothing to earn his ire. He was stuck in a situation that was far beyond his ability to cope with, and he had no choice but to remain here and endure it because of *her*.

He strived again to shove all feelings aside, certain that if he gave in to them now, he would fall apart and join her in her debilitated state. Aylun strode over to Yaomey and spoke in a quiet voice tinged with the sharp edge of his agitation. "Find her a change of clothes. She already stands out enough with that freakish red hair of hers." He turned and stared at the woman as she rocked and mumbled.

Yaomey watched with him for a moment, then leaned closer and spoke with softness. "I don't think now is the time."

Aylun nodded. "Once she seems better."

He turned his attention to their campsite, trying to distract himself from his unbearable turmoil by focusing on immediate tasks. It was a good location, with a quiet, slow-moving stream on one side and a monstrous old weeping tree at its edge for cover. Surrounding it was a patch of barren, rocky ground that stretched back to the edge of the forest. Even though the chances of being followed were remote, the site was well situated to prevent surprise intrusion.

He went about gathering firewood, then constructed a simple fire and set it ablaze in the hope the familiar task would soothe his turmoil. Hunger soon reminded him he needed to eat, so he plopped down in front of the fluttering yellow flames with a few pieces of dried meat and a chunk of bread.

Yaomey started to join him, then glanced over beyond him. He followed her gaze to the woman. She was still squatting down, facing

109

the hulking old tree as she hugged her knees and rocked. Beyond her, dusk was almost over, and the outline of a sea of tree trunks and branches was now barely visible against the darkening sky.

Yaomey ripped off a chunk of the bread, and Aylun remained seated as she strolled over to the stranger. The woman showed no sign of recognizing the approach, so Yaomey tapped her on the shoulder and smiled as she held out the bread for her to take.

The woman didn't respond to her touch, continuing to stare into space and repeat "not real" over and over.

Aylun shook his head; it was worse than he had imagined.

Unable to penetrate her delirium, Yaomey reached down, lifted the woman's hand, and set the piece of bread in her palm.

At the tugging on her arm, the woman halted her chanting. She glanced down at the bread, then up into Yaomey's face. Tears appeared in her eyes, and in a meek voice, she said, "Thank you."

Yaomey gave a single deep nod of acknowledgment.

Still squatting, the strange woman waddled around to face Yaomey, then peered back down at the hunk of food resting in her hand. "But it's not real."

"It is. It is bread."

The woman shook her head. "No."

Yaomey lifted the woman's chin and gazed into her eyes. "Try it."

The stranger nodded, then raised it to her mouth, gnawed off a mouthful, and chewed.

"My name is Yaomey, and that is Aylun." She pointed to him.

The woman glanced over at Aylun and scowled.

He offered her a simple bow of his head.

"I'm Megan," she said as she continued to stare and chew.

Aylun nodded to himself. It was an interesting name: Mi-Gahn.

Yaomey granted a quick bow before turning away and heading back to join Aylun by the flickering fire.

After she finished consuming her handful of bread, the traumatized woman rose and shuffled over to join them. Aylun looked up at her as she thrust out her hand to Yaomey, asking for more. Yaomey tore off another chunk and placed it on her palm.

Their captive continued to squat, facing the dancing yellow flames, and ripped off another mouthful with her teeth, chewed, and swallowed.

Yaomey eyed her with sympathy. "I am so deeply sorry about all of this. You seemed frantic when you came out of the dragon's lair, and—"

"Dragons aren't real." Mi-Gahn remained focused on the chunk of bread clenched in her hand.

Yaomey tried to catch her gaze. "But they are."

The woman stopped before taking another bite. She looked up, and her response was cheerful yet adamant. "No, they are a physical impossibility."

Aylun shook his head. The woman had lost her mind. A smidgen of guilt stabbed at him again, but it couldn't break through his frustration and annoyance. All he had sought was release from his failed life of prophecies and oracles and everything else that had come with it. Yet here he was, nursing a crazy person.

Yaomey paused for a moment, then tried again. "What I was trying to say is that Aylun is right. If the council suspects this might be the prophecy, then—"

"Prophecies aren't real either."

Yaomey stopped again and cocked her head.

The deranged woman explained as she chewed, "The whole butterfly effect thing, you know? Chaos theory? You can't even predict next week's weather. Predicting the future … it's impossible."

"But I know people who can predict the weather."

"But you're not real." Mi-Gahn shrugged. "So that proves nothing."

Yaomey stared again.

"Ever since I visited myself from the future, nothing—"

"You visited yourself from the future?" Yaomey's eyes widened.

"Yeah, but it couldn't be real. Projecting 3D images through walls"—their captive gave a small shake of her head—"not real. Visits from your future self"—she closed her eyes and gave her head an even more dramatic shake—"*mega* not real."

Yaomey motioned to the outline of trees all around them, their silhouettes dark against the deep blue of late dusk. "Look at this forest." She picked up a handful of crumbly black dirt and browning leaves and placed it in Mi-Gahn's other hand. "This dirt in your hands. Feel it. Is that not real?"

"No." She tossed it aside as if it were toxic.

"Then what is it?"

The woman shrugged again as she wiped her hand on her clothes. "I must still be asleep."

"Asleep?"

She nodded. "Yeah. You, the forest, that dirt, it's all just part of my dreamworld."

"Okay, fine. But suppose it was real."

"But it's not."

"But suppose it was."

Mi-Gahn grinned and became animated as if she were playing a game. "Okay."

"The council lied to everyone about the prophecy. If they suspect you are the Otherworlder, they will send protectors, and—"

"Imaginary protectors."

"Okay, imaginary protectors, and who knows what lies they will tell them. The protectors may believe it is dangerous to talk to you, that they must kill you on sight, and they are more than capable of doing so. So, you see, you and your friend are in very—"

"Oh, you mean Jon ... well, imaginary Jon."

"Yes. Right. You and Jon are in grave danger."

"Imaginary grave danger."

"But if we hide you and protect you, then you are both safe."

"From the imaginary council."

Aylun shook his head. Tired and annoyed by the futility of trying to get through to her, he stepped over in front of the babbling woman. "This is pointless; she is clearly incoherent."

She gave him a confident lift of her chin. "I'm perfectly coherent. It's you who keeps talking about dragons and prophecies."

Aylun grumbled.

The crazy woman snubbed him. "And you are very cruel for a figment of my imagination."

For some odd reason, her characterization made him uncomfortable, so he struggled to adopt a somewhat less combative tone. "So if all of this is imaginary, then read my mind."

"Don't be silly. You are just random synapses firing in my brain. You don't have a mind."

"Snaps, huh? Well, *you* do have a mind, so if this is your dreamworld, then move that rock with your thoughts." Aylun pointed to a stone near her feet.

"That's just a stupid proof." She rolled her eyes. "For a figment of my imagination, you are remarkably dumb."

"No, you're afraid it will prove you are wrong."

Mi-Gahn waved a hand near the stone. "See, it proves nothing."

"Oh, come on. That was not a *real* try. You never believed you could move it. You never imagined it moving and assumed it would."

"If I do, will you take me back to Jon?"

"No."

"Okay. Fine. Whatever." She peered down at the stone, and her brow furrowed in apparent concentration. Then she flicked her finger, and with a puff of wind, the rock skittered across the ground to stop just behind Aylun's feet.

Aylun and Yaomey scooted backward, staring in awe.

Satisfied with herself and enthused, Mi-Gahn looked up at him. "See, I told you. Dreamworld." She cocked her head. "But it felt funky."

Yaomey looked at Aylun. "She has a gift."

His eyes met hers. "A completely unique one." He reached out and plucked the stone from the ground. "And powerful."

"It fits the prophecy."

Then fear struck at the realization that a gift like that might have untold destructive potential and it lay in the hands of an angry, unstable lady who hated him.

His concern melted away as the deranged woman began giggling and sent several more stones shooting across the campsite with a flick of her wrist and a burst of air. One skipped and hopped along the uneven ground to land in the fire with a flurry of sparks that whirled into the night sky.

Stretching out her palm, she lifted a far-off rock from the dirt and whistled an eerie ghost melody as it floated around the fire. She readied herself and tossed it into the air. Before it could fall back to the ground, she scooped up another rock with a whoosh of air and moved it so that the first fell back down on top of it.

Firelight danced in her eyes as her gaze shot up to Aylun. "Look. No hands." She grinned. "Want to play jacks?"

Aylun shook his head. A part of him was grateful she wasn't in full possession of her faculties and using newly demonstrated power against him. Still, it was thoroughly annoying to witness her trivializing such a powerful gift, treating it like a mere toy. With all the terrible things that had happened, all the horror and death he had lived through, here she was playing and laughing. It was obscene.

One by one, Mi-Gahn levitated larger stones from the riverside and giggled as she stacked them in a little rock cairn. Eventually, the pile became unstable and tumbled over. She scowled and said, "Oh, phooey."

Aylun watched her for a while longer in the flickering firelight as she rearranged the stones. The more he watched, the more his annoyance softened, and the more difficult it became to resist being drawn in by the charm of it all. There was something infectious in the sparkle in her eye and the childlike abandon with which she reveled in her newfound ability.

He motioned as if presenting her to his companion. "Yaomey of the Shou, I give you Mi-Gahn, the one who will lead us into a new age."

Mi-Gahn's gaze shot over, and she smiled. "Ooh, an imaginary new age. Will there be unicorns?" She laughed and gave an enthusiastic thumbs-up. Then she returned to her play, floating a last rock into place to form the outline of a heart. She looked up into Aylun's face. "Can I have a pet puffin? I always wanted a pet puffin."

He shook his head. This changed everything. The Otherworlder prophecy still didn't make a shred of sense, but the woman he had abducted, the one who had every reason to hate him, was now in possession of a dangerous gift. If he let his feelings get the best of him like he had earlier and angered her, she could make him skitter across the ground like one of those stones.

He strolled over to his bedroll, collapsed, and plopped his head down. For a long while, he calmed himself by clearing his mind as he stared up at the smoke curling through the firelight and into the branches and leaves that sheltered them. After a time, the draw of her laughter became too much, and he rolled onto his side and watched her.

The constant nightmares had made sleep a harrowing ordeal. So late into the night, as the flames dwindled and the embers grew cold, Aylun distracted himself by keeping watch over Mi-Gahn. As he did, she played and giggled, seemingly oblivious to the deadly reality of her situation or the magnitude of the terrible power she now possessed.

Morning light roused her, and Megan's eyes crept open to a canopy of gnarled branches laced with olive-green leaves. She lay still as her drowsy state cleared, listening to the sounds of the forest and the movements of her abductors nearby. It was real, the lumpy ground beneath her, the quiet shuffling of horses' hooves, and the murmur of the slow-moving river beyond her head. All of it was real. No matter what inexplicable change had occurred, the aura of unreality that had suffused this world a mere handful of hours ago was gone.

She stretched her arms and inhaled a deep breath as she reviewed all the impossible occurrences of the past couple of days: the visit from her future self, the portal in the lab, the dragon rumbling in the darkness, and that wretched person tearing her away from Jon. She lay still, telling herself every word she had uttered so many times the evening before. Over and over, she repeated how it was impossible, how none of this could be real, but no matter how many times she said them to herself, the words remained hollow and unconvincing.

An epiphany hit, and she tried to use her gift to flick a pebble near the river's edge. It responded in a puff of air, flying along the ground to skip and bound across the peaceful waters. Even the ability to move things with her mind, no matter how impossible, now seemed solid and real. Whatever delusion had gripped her the night before was now gone, shattered by the chill morning air and bright sunlight, and no matter how she yearned for that blissful dream-world, she could not get back to it.

A recollection of a moment in the dragon's lair came back, and she fished in her pocket until she found the object that had caught on her button. It was proof that she hadn't imagined it all. Unless, of course, she was still imagining things, but she knew with iron certainty that was not the case. She held it up, and it was beautiful and quite real, a dark metallic skeleton key. It was set with three deep-red gems, and a serpent, or perhaps a wingless dragon, wound its way around the outer edge. It sparkled in the morning sun, and there was a fascinating intricacy and delicate beauty about it. The beast in that cave had seemed angry and disturbed when she tore it from her pants and pocketed it. Perhaps that meant it unlocked something of great value, so she decided to hang on to it and slipped it back into her pocket.

She propped herself up on her elbows, looking at the enormous gnarled tree trunk and weeping branches that reached down toward the peaceful, slow-moving stream. Below them, that thug—Aylun, the woman had called him—was going through his belongings. He was

116

tall and lean, with tight, sinewy muscles and a soft face. His unkempt short black hair and sharp brown eyes gave him a wild and untamed look that seemed appropriate for his unpredictable and offensive personality. His partner in crime, Yaomey, was a different matter. Her diminutive stature and simple clothes made her appear quite tame, and the silky black hair she tied back in a single long braid enhanced the aura of a woman of simple means.

Megan arose and headed over to speak to the two of them. Jon was out there, and he needed her. It was imperative she reunite with him, but it appeared her only hope now was to talk some sense into the two cretins who seemed to have decided she had no say in the matter. She strolled over and stared down at the polished river stones strewn along the ground. They had been so entertaining the night before, and her guilt returned at the sight of them. Jon was out there alone, and who knows what might have happened to him while she had been giggling and playing games with stones.

Her two abductors looked up as she stood above them. She eyed first Yaomey, then Aylun. "This isn't a dream, is it?"

Aylun grumbled and opened his mouth to speak, but Yaomey shot out her palm to stop him. She gave Megan a soft and earnest look. "No. I am sorry, but it is very real."

"You said some stuff about a gift. A unique and powerful one. What exactly does that mean? What is a gift?"

"You were moving things without touching them. That is something other people cannot do. It is a gift, like opening portals, or blending into shadows, or sensing emotions."

Surprised at the revelation of more and varied gifts, Megan stared for a moment. "And all that is real?"

"I assure you it is real."

"And this council you told me about, they are real?"

Yaomey nodded.

"And you think prophecies are real?"

"They are as real as you and me. They are what we do."

Aylun shook his head. "But I do not see how this one—"

Yaomey shushed him.

Megan took a deep breath. It was crucial she set aside her outrage and trepidation for now. She was in a vast wooded area with no way to navigate except these two. Her need for them was apparent. Only they possessed the knowledge and skill to lead her back to Jon. She paused for a moment, searching for the best way to convince them. "Then why are you not worried about Jon? He is completely alone. What if they decide this prophecy is about him?"

Aylun seemed about to speak, but Yaomey put her hand on his shoulder. He winced as she dug her fingernails in. She removed her hand and peered into his eyes. "She has a point."

In an instant, his expression turned to one of exasperation. "Oh, for crying … she is just trying to get back to her friend."

"And you are only opposed to it because she wants it."

Aylun glared at Megan. "Because she is irritating."

Megan stuck out her tongue at him.

He was on the verge of responding, but this time Yaomey shot out both palms, one at each of them. Then, she returned her attention to Aylun. "What if the council gets to him first?"

He heaved a weary sigh. "Then he will be safe as long as we have her. They will keep him alive because he is their best hope of finding her."

"Are you really so certain?" She pointed back the way they had come. "What if this is the prophecy, and we just left the Otherworlder alone with no provisions, no weapon, and completely unprotected?"

Aylun peered off in the direction Yaomey was pointing, and for a moment, he seemed deep in thought.

Megan came to rest on one of the gnarled roots as she waited for his response.

When he replied, his voice was steady and resolute. "Okay. I will go back and find the man, and I will protect him." He pointed to Yaomey. "But then it falls to you to take Mi-Gahn away. And we cannot tell each other where we are headed. They cannot be together, or they will both be vulnerable."

Yaomey rose. "Then I will go prepare the horses." She strutted off, scooping up Megan's blanket as she passed. With it in hand, she headed for the horses, who were tied to some shrubs a short distance from the majestic old tree.

Megan watched for a moment, a bit stunned. They had done it again, so she faced Aylun. "So that's it. You two decide that it should be almost impossible for Jon and me to see each other again, and it's settled?"

He flashed a fake-looking smile. "I think your grasp of reality has greatly improved."

"So, someone is after us. So what? We will just take off and disappear, Jon and me. We'll go far away, and you'll never see us again."

Her words appeared to annoy, and his response was sharp and short. "Oh, for Adi's sake. We just covered this."

Everything about him irritated, and her sarcastic response just slipped out. "Oh. I'm sorry. Has my abduction been inconvenient for you? I would hate to think my misery is disrupting your reprehensible actions."

"Okay. Let me use small words." He lurched closer until she was uncomfortable with his face so near to hers. "The council will send protectors. They will track you. No matter where you go, they will find you. They will capture you, imprison you, and maybe even kill you."

In the face of his certainty, she hesitated. Then the image of Jon chasing after her in the clearing returned. "You're just trying to scare me."

He shook his head in disbelief. "Well, you can keep telling yourself that as they torture you to find out where your friend is."

Megan leaned away. "They can't be as bad as you say. They're people, like us. What if we let them know we only want to be left alone? What if we tell them we just want to go home? Maybe they'll—"

"Are all your people such blind fools?" He rolled his eyes. "Do you really think that if you simply ask nicely, they won't kill you?"

She crossed her arms. "I refuse to believe that we can't work something out with this council of yours."

He acted incensed. "It is not *my* council."

"Still, they can be reasoned with."

Aylun raised his eyes to the bright blue sky of morning that showed through the winding brown-and-green canopy. "What kind of world do you come from?" He faced her again. "Are there no politicians?"

"Not all politicians are bad."

"Oh sure, they only want to control your life so they can spread sunshine and happiness."

Megan glared.

Aylun shook his head. "So there are no thieves or murderers or wars where you come from. No bad people who would kill you for food or money or power."

She huffed. "Okay, fine. But if this council of yours is as ruthless as all that, what difference does it make if we're apart?"

His response was matter-of-fact. "It is not that they are ruthless. It is that your life is of no consequence to them."

It was her turn to roll her eyes, then she stared for a moment at the spaces between the contorted roots. Lying in one of them were the toppled rock cairn and heart outline of stones she had made last night. They were reminders that she did have power. A power that those who ruled might fear, and she knew firsthand how terrifying people could be when obsessed with controlling others.

She shook her head. "All this is based on a stupid prophecy." Her eyes met his. "What exactly does it say?"

He sighed. "It does not matter."

"It's about me; it matters."

He shrugged. "Who knows how much is even true?"

"What do you mean, not true?"

Aylun leaned in a little closer as if sharing a gem of wisdom. "There is an old saying: history is written by the victor, but prophecy can be written by the vanquished."

Megan threw up her hands. "What gibberish."

He stared. "You know, you are kind of a disagreeable person."

She glared back. "Says the kidnapper."

He heaved a deep sigh. "Do not worry about the prophecy. We will protect you."

"That's super great, except I'm not worried about *me*."

"You should be."

Megan crossed her arms again. "So, you're just not going to tell me?"

"I should never have even told you there was a prophecy. It could change things." Aylun shot her a stern look. "You have no idea how dangerous it is that you know."

"I see. So, I'm just going to die for it. No reason to bother my pretty little head about it?"

"Knowing will not change anything."

Megan came a little closer and, in a slow, calm voice, summarized, "So, let's see. You don't believe it's about me. And it might not be true. But you refuse to tell me because it might change the thing you don't think is about me and might not be true." She scowled. "Illogical much?"

"Fine. It says someone will come from another world with a unique and powerful gift, and they will lead us into a new age."

Megan straightened, and her eyes scanned the ground before her. Neither she nor Jon was the kind to lead anyone anywhere, much less a completely foreign people to a new age. "Wow. That … that makes no sense on any level."

Megan boggled for a moment as she finally understood her perilous position. If this council thought she or Jon was destined to lead their people, then that leading could only happen by usurping some or all of their power. She knew history pretty well. Governments in the past century had been quite willing to murder entire segments of society in order to seize or maintain power. The Jews in Nazi Germany, the Killing Fields of Cambodia, the Great Purge in Russia—the era had seen tens of millions of deaths. Countless human lives had been snuffed out. Not due to any act of the individual, but in cold, calculated moves to inflame public sentiment against a group of people and thereby solidify political power. The evil lengths to which leaders would go to preserve their rule were beyond obscene. The council wouldn't think twice about obliterating her or Jon if they were a threat to these people's authority.

A shout from the direction of the horses startled her. "A protector!"

Megan's gaze shot over, and Yaomey was pointing to a woman with thick brown hair and brown leather armor strolling toward them with her hands up. The strips of leather that made up her armored skirt bounced with each step. Gravel grated under her feet, and she possessed a chilling air of calm certainty about her. A horrible sick feeling burrowed its way into the pit of Megan's stomach as she realized this was one of those protectors they had warned her about.

Aylun sprang to his feet with catlike ease and landed in a fighting stance.

Fear grabbed ahold of Megan as she realized her life was in jeopardy. She rose and stumbled backward, almost tripping over one of the massive twisted roots.

Aylun and Yaomey charged the woman.

She seemed startled and slipped out a dagger, leaving a sword at her side. She readied herself in a stance that was disturbing in its casualness.

Aylun and Yaomey leaped for her.

As if it were the simplest thing in the world, the woman sidestepped and spun out of the way. She put out an arm and caught Aylun in the chest, then slammed Yaomey in the back, sending the pair hurtling to the ground.

Panic hit. They hadn't even slowed her down. Almost on instinct, Megan moved. Without her directing them, her muscles responded, remembering the stones of the night before. As she thrust out her arm, a strange sense of power surged through her. A violent burst of wind whirled around her, whipping through her clothes and hair as, by her will alone, she lifted the distant woman from the ground. Leaves and debris flew up into the air with the protector, and she dangled there, helpless, as, with intense concentration, Megan held her aloft.

Jon burst from behind a stand of tall pine-like trees. He stumbled to a stop a short distance from the protector and stared as he shouted, "Megan, wait. Stop. Don't hurt her."

Her chest constricted, and it was as if she couldn't breathe. She and Jon were together, and the protector was right next to him. It was the very situation that Yaomey and Aylun had warned her about. The words forced their way out. "Jon, you have no idea what is going on. Run."

He whipped around but didn't watch where he was going and ran straight into the tree. It looked excruciating as he staggered backward and nearly fell. Then he shook it off and looked over at the woman still hovering near him. They exchanged a few hurried words, but Megan couldn't catch a single syllable through the wind whistling around her, across the water, and up through the leaves of the tree.

The woman tossed Jon her knife. He reached for it but missed. It glanced off his hand and tumbled, end over end, until it plunged, tip first, into the dirt.

Panic struck again as Aylun and Yaomey regained their footing. Their eyes darted between Jon and the knife, their apprehension clear in every line of their faces.

Like an idiot, Jon reached down and grabbed the knife, then assumed the same stance the woman had moments earlier.

Aylun and Yaomey raced at him, and then leaped for him.

Megan winced and let out a small gasp in anticipation.

Then, exactly like the woman had, Jon slipped to the side and whirled out of the way. He put out his arm to catch Aylun in the chest and slammed the woman in the back. The two tumbled to the ground a second time.

Megan stared in stunned silence. Jon had no clue how to fight. It was like he had become a different person overnight. Or maybe this *was* a different person, some kind of impostor. After all, stranger things had happened in the last day, and it was impossible to tell what was real anymore.

Suddenly, he turned and raced right toward *her*.

She stiffened and dropped the woman, who plummeted to the ground.

Baffled by her friend's behavior and frightened of what might happen next, she reacted out of pure instinct. Just as she had done with the stones, she aimed the back of her hand at Jon and flicked her wrist like she was shooing away a fly.

A burst of dust and debris swept from the ground in a line that raced toward him.

She gasped again as horror and dread filled her.

The force blasted him off the ground and sent him hurtling back into one of the trees with a gut-wrenching crack.

A lump formed in her throat, and she covered her mouth as she raced toward him.

He landed on his feet and wobbled out a few halting steps before falling backward, dust and leaves blowing into the air as he hit the ground.

Having regained their footing, Aylun and Yaomey charged the woman, but she fell to her knees with her arms behind her back.

Megan dropped to the ground in front of Jon. She hesitated, afraid to touch him because he might be injured and in dread of finding out what she'd done to him. Sobs began to flow as she lifted his head with care and cradled it in her arms. He lay there, warm and still breathing but unmoving, and the only thought that consumed her was how badly she had hurt him. He was unconscious, he could even die, and it was all because of her.

Chapter Six

DELLIA'S RESCUE

Aylun leaped to his feet and spun around, almost bumping into Mi-Gahn as she flew past. He followed her for a fleeting moment as she raced for Jon, who lay sprawled on the ground at the base of a tree. With a quick glance and rapid brushing, he dusted the debris from his clothes, ignoring the stinging where he had landed on stone and rubble.

Across the rocky, uneven ground, their opponent rose to her feet, her movements casual and effortless. Yaomey had to be right. Few people could have tracked them to their campsite with such speed. The stylized moves and ease with which she had taken down a pair of Shou added to the certainty that she was indeed a protector. The dagger and sword hanging at her side, the cut and style of her brown leather armor, and the richness of her brown hair left little doubt: this was Dellia.

She faltered for a moment, seeming distracted by Jon, as Mi-Gahn dropped to her knees and huddled over his motionless body. Rumors about Dellia abounded. It was said she was an outcast among her peers due to some misdeed of her father, and that she had chosen to become a protector to flee that life and prove herself. To her, duty was everything, and her dedication to it verged on obsession. Yet she was also known to be fair, compassionate, and understanding. Still, her skill and speed made her one of the last protectors he would have chosen to face.

Aylun shot Yaomey a glance. She gave a hurried nod, and they both broke into a sprint. Gravel grated underfoot as they dashed toward a second encounter with the protector. Aylun was fluent in many martial arts: Itaamdo, Lingshu, Shunato, and a smattering of others, yet the techniques Dellia had used were not ones he'd seen before. She was good, but she had also surprised them with her unique fighting style. There was no way he would let that happen again. This time, they would prevail. They had to prevail.

As they neared, Dellia dropped to her knees, lowered her head, and clasped her hands behind her back. It was a clear act of surrender. Frustration welled within, and he realized that as unwelcome as the protector's arrival had been, it had given him something he perhaps needed: a way to unleash his pent-up anger.

He flew up to her and seized one arm while Yaomey grabbed the other. The protector didn't resist, so he let go long enough to untie his belt. He threaded it around her wrists and tied it tight, binding her hands behind her back. It was simple but effective. Still, for one as skilled as Dellia, it might only slow her down should she decide to free herself or fight back.

No sooner had he taken hold of the protector's arm again than Yaomey released hers and raced over to Jon. Mi-Gahn was still sitting with him on the sandy ground at the base of the towering tree, but she had pulled him up and was cradling his head in her lap as she sobbed. She lifted her head, and her tears abated as she watched Yaomey examine him.

With quick movements, Yaomey felt underneath him, along his spine and the back of his head. Then she set a finger under his nose to check for breath and put her ear to his chest. She looked up and breathed a sigh of relief as she peered into Mi-Gahn's red-eyed face. "I can find no blood, no apparent broken bones, and his breathing and heart are strong. He seems fine, but stay with him."

Mi-Gahn sniffled as she nodded.

Yaomey returned and grabbed Dellia's arm, and she and Aylun hauled her toward the horses, who were tied to some shrubs at the bank of the quiet, slow-moving river. Aylun glanced over at her as he considered the unexpected surrender. Protectors weren't known for giving up, least of all Dellia. Her persistence and determination were well known. Moreover, she had taken them out with relative ease, then abruptly given up. Why would she yield a fight she appeared to be winning?

His thoughts were interrupted when Dellia twisted her head around to peer at Megan over her shoulder.

The distraught woman glanced up from Jon, fear and worry reflected in her eyes.

Once Dellia had garnered her attention, her voice came soft and sympathetic. "It will be okay, Megan. Jon is simply unconscious. It wasn't a bad blow. I'm certain he'll be fine."

Annoyed, Aylun jerked her forward. Trying to quell his disquiet, he focused on the green canopy punctuated by bits of blue sky reflected on the river's rippling surface. There had been a sincerity and softness in the protector's words that had surprised. Then it came back to him. Dellia was known to possess the Gift of the Heart—by all accounts, the strongest in a generation. That meant she could sense feelings, even subtle ones, such as the slight guilt or apprehension someone might feel when they told a lie.

It was true that those with her gift were bound by a deep conviction not to misuse it. But that only meant she was unlikely to use it to hurt someone—to reveal their emotions, or to manipulate them. It would be second nature for her to know if any word they uttered was untrue.

Suddenly, the council's cleverness in sending her gained crystal clarity. Any protector could kill an unsuspecting stranger or two. But they had sent the one best able to ferret out who these two strangers were and how they fit in to the prophecy. Her gift also meant he and Yaomey needed to choose what they said with great care. And even one careless word between Mi-Gahn and Dellia could lead to disaster.

The protector turned her head, and her eyes met Aylun's. A look of deep concern flashed across her face, and all of a sudden it seemed as if she could see right into his soul, that she knew he had led his sister and friends to their deaths and lacked the honor to simply perish with them. He yanked on her arm again as he forced all that from his thoughts.

"Curiouser and curiouser." Dellia glanced over at Yaomey. "Perhaps you two could help me with a puzzle. What are two Elorians doing out here in the middle of the Illis Woods?"

Yaomey looked at Aylun with alarm.

He sent her a subtle shake of his head, then turned his attention back to Dellia. "I dishonored my people. I came here to end it."

The protector turned her gaze back to him, scrutinizing his face for only a moment before her brow furrowed and the look of sympathy returned. "I'm sorry." Her soft eyes rested there briefly before returning their focus to Yaomey. "Then why take the woman?"

Aylun sought the protector's gaze again, trying to get her attention back on him. "She begged for our help."

Dellia's focus settled on him. "You could have simply told me that. I came to talk. Why attack me?"

"We feared you were after us. So, tell me, why were you tracking us down?"

"Jon needed my help finding Megan." Dellia cocked her head and eyed him with apparent suspicion. "Now that we've cleared everything up, surely there's no reason you can't let me go."

"If we let you go, you could arrest us. After all, we did attack a protector."

"Clearly a misunderstanding."

Aylun forced a broad smile. "Good. Then you will let the four of us go?"

Dellia paused for a moment, seeming intrigued by the question. "I can't, but I will let the two of you go." She glanced between Yaomey and Aylun.

He drew a deep breath. "I might consider it if you tell me why you want the two of them."

"It is council business. My vow prohibits me from saying more." She glanced down in the direction of her hands bound behind her back. "At least tell me why I am being treated as a prisoner. I have agreed to forget the attack, so what threat do I continue to pose?"

"Perhaps we are in possession of information that you are not. Things we have taken a vow not to reveal."

Dellia appeared even more intrigued by his revelation. "Interesting." She seemed thoughtful for a moment. "Then it appears we are at an impasse. So, what do you intend to do?"

The question brought to mind the protector's surprising surrender. She yielded in a fight she was winning. That meant there was something more important to her than detaining her quarry or controlling the situation—in which case, their best strategy might be to appear to play along.

He was on the verge of deciding what to tell the protector when he recalled Mi-Gahn's gift. She had lifted the protector with an outstretched arm, then blasted her friend into a tree with a simple flick of her wrist. They didn't know precisely how her gift worked, so they had no way of knowing if physical restraint would inhibit it. That meant that any attempt to use force on her might result in giant rocks being flung into their faces.

Knocking her out was also unacceptable. It might cause permanent injury to a central figure in a crucial prophecy. Even if they had a safe way to subdue her, at some point they'd have to free her. Who knew what crazy repercussions she might inflict on them then? No, it was clear. It was now an unacceptable risk to try to force their will upon her.

In fact, she now possessed the power to force them to go along with any reckless scheme she might concoct. Even in her most lucid moments, the erratic woman seemed disconnected from the harsh reality of her situation. Her half-witted decisions could endanger them all. That left only one choice. He would have to use diplomacy and try to reason with her. If that was even possible.

Aylun pointed at Mi-Gahn, who was still sitting near the trunk of one of the tall trees, cradling Jon's head in her lap. "What happens now is entirely up to her." Mi-Gahn stared up at the finger aimed at her and wiped the wetness from her cheeks. "It involves her fate, so we will abide by whatever she decides."

Dellia nodded. "I would welcome a talk with her."

Aylun wagged his finger between Yaomey and himself. "We will talk to her." He pointed at the ground. "You will wait here."

He tied a rope from her bound hands to a nearby low-hanging limb, then he and Yaomey left the protector and sauntered over to Mi-Gahn. Her tears had ceased, but she was still seated on the stony ground, with Jon's head nestled in her lap while she caressed his face.

Yaomey crouched down, and Aylun followed her lead, both peering at her.

She looked up at them, and Yaomey smiled. "I am sorry, Megan, but the protector's arrival complicates matters, and there are decisions that must be made right now."

Still appearing shaken up and somber, Mi-Gahn nodded.

Aylun pointed to Dellia. "If we set the protector free, she will take you and Jon in, and it is doubtful anyone will see you again."

Mi-Gahn's red and swollen eyes widened. "Yeah, let's not do that."

Yaomey gave a solemn nod. "Then what do you suggest?"

Aylun considered proposing a course of action, but the contentious woman would most likely hate it because it came from him, no matter how sensible it might be.

She pondered for only a moment. "Why don't we leave the protector tied up? Then we can take Jon and find someplace to hide."

Though offered out of naivety and good intent, it was nonetheless an appalling suggestion. Yaomey leaned away with eyes wide. "You mean leave her here defenseless? Chances are no one will find her, and if no one unties her, she will die of thirst, starve, or get eaten. I wouldn't wish that kind of death on my worst enemy."

"Then what if we don't tie her up, or we just tie her up a little bit and then take—"

"Just tie her up a little bit?" Aylun gave a derisive shake of his head and rolled his eyes.

Mi-Gahn crossed her arms and scowled at him. "Yes. And take the horses and leave her here without one."

Yaomey shook her head. "She would catch us."

"How?" Mi-Gahn asked.

"Horses have to rest; she does not."

Aylun nodded agreement, then decided to elaborate. "For a while, we would outpace her, but eventually horses overheat if they do not rest. When we stopped to rest them, she would keep going, and eventually catch us."

Mi-Gahn peered at Yaomey with surprised and questioning eyes. "She could do that?"

Yaomey nodded. "Yes, without a doubt."

Aylun motioned with his head to where Dellia had taken them out. "Besides, you saw what happened. We did not capture her. She gave up a fight she was winning. I do not know what her game is, but she *wanted* to be taken."

Yaomey eyed Aylun. "But what could she gain by being captured?" She considered for only a second before answering her own question. "Maybe it was a ploy to stick close to us, or at least to Megan."

"Me?" Mi-Gahn said in surprise.

Aylun nodded again. "Yes, she saw what you can do. No doubt, she has many questions and more than a few concerns. If her plan is to stick close to you, and we try to leave her here, she will fight back."

Yaomey chimed in, "And if we manage to subdue her, the only way to stop her permanently would be to tie her up in such a way that she could never get free."

"Which brings us back to murder." Aylun added, "Now, if you want to kill her, then—"

"No!" Mi-Gahn shrank back. "No killing anyone."

Yaomey nodded. "Agreed, no killing."

Mi-Gahn seemed to ponder for a while longer. "Then, what if one of you two takes me and Jon and the other stays with her and unties her later?"

Aylun scowled. "Are you asking one of us to get ourselves arrested and thrown in prison so you can get away?" Even as the words left his mouth, he realized it would be the honorable thing to do. In fact, it might be the most fitting end to his pitiful life.

Mi-Gahn pouted. "It was just an idea."

Aylun muttered, "You are really stuck on this idea of you and Jon staying together."

Having heard every word, Mi-Gahn folded her arms and shot back, "And you are irrationally determined to break us apart."

"No, I am the one being rational here."

"No, you are the one being a jerk-face."

He knocked on his own head. "Get it through that impenetrable skull of yours. Nothing has changed. You and Jon being together was a bad idea at Islong's lair, and it is an even worse one now with a protector here."

"Says you. But it is *my* bad idea, and I'm entitled to have—"

Fingernails dug into his shoulder as Yaomey grabbed it and Mi-Gahn's and squeezed both. "What is obvious is that now is not the time to decide on a course of action. We have little time, and neither of you is being clearheaded. You are both irrationally determined to oppose the other. So how about a compromise?" She looked first at Mi-Gahn, then at Aylun.

"I am listening." He wrenched his shoulder free.

"I think moving Jon is a bad idea until he wakes. So, what if we take Dellia and the four of us leave him here and put some distance between him and the protector?" Mi-Gahn appeared to be about to object, but Yaomey leaned closer and stared her in the eye. "While you think about it. Then we will stop to rest and decide. Whatever you decide, we will abide by it. If you still want to go back to Jon, I will take you while Aylun gets Dellia as far away from here as possible."

Mi-Gahn gaped. "So just leave Jon behind?"

Yaomey remained calm, and her words clear and forceful. "Every moment that you and he and the protector are together is terribly dangerous. Leaving him behind might be the best way to protect him."

"But he's unconscious. He could have a concussion or even intracranial bleeding. If the pressure builds up, he could go into a coma or even die."

"And if you stay with him, would you be able to do anything about all that … entire … crane—*whatever* that stuff was you just said?"

Mi-Gahn answered with reluctance. "Well … no."

"He will be fine for the time it takes us to ride a short distance away, at least. That is all I am asking."

"And if I agree, will jerk-face here"—she pointed at Aylun—"leave me be?" Mi-Gahn glared at him for a moment, then seemed to have an epiphany. "Or better yet, will he do whatever I decide?"

He crossed his arms and stared back. "That depends on what you decide."

Mi-Gahn shrugged. "Fine, then I'll take Jon and your horse, and you can both stay with the protector."

"My horse? I am not giving you Juzhi."

"Then swear you'll abide by whatever I decide, and we'll do Yaomey's plan."

Mi-Gahn continued to stare as Aylun sorted through his options. The new reality was that she could force them to do anything she wanted, so perhaps agreeing to her proposal was his best chance to avoid a scenario that ended in his arrest.

He gave a crisp nod. "Okay, I swear."

All three rose, but Aylun paused to draw the other two's attention. "One last thing. That protector there"—he motioned to her with his head—"that is Dellia. She can tell if you are lying. Say nothing and let me do the talking."

The three strolled over to Dellia, still tied up at the horses.

As Mi-Gahn approached, their captive sought to make eye contact with her. "So, have you come to your senses? Have you decided to set me free?"

Mi-Gahn halted in front of her. "Is it true that you're out to capture Jon and me?"

Aylun scowled. Did he not just say to let him do the talking?

Dellia considered for a moment, then nodded. "I'm sorry. It's my duty."

Mi-Gahn stuck out her chin. "Making it your duty doesn't make it right."

"Trust me, what you're doing is a mistake. I am not the only one who will come for you. You need to reconsider before—"

"Enough talking." Aylun stepped between the two conversing women. "If you do not want me to gag you, then shut up."

Dellia peered around him, straight at Mi-Gahn. "At least tell me what you're planning to do?"

He stepped in front of her, blocking her view again, and answered himself. "We will leave Jon here and take you and Mi-Gahn with us."

Dellia peeked around his other side, staring at Mi-Gahn with a look of incredulity. "You're going to leave him here? Unconscious? You can't do that. I thought you were friends."

"Enough!" Aylun shouted. Angered and frustrated, he marched to his bag while mumbling, loud enough to be heard, "Okay, gagged it will be." He retrieved a cloth, ripped off a strip, and raised it to Dellia's face.

She shrank away. "You really don't want to do—"

As he tied it around her head and through her mouth, a sense of great satisfaction surged through him. He had finally gotten some control of the situation.

Then he noticed Mi-Gahn staring at him with startled eyes. "Wow. You're not just rude to me. You're rude to everybody."

Aylun ignored her and turned to fish through his pack. He found the small green box with a silver symbol for "hidden" on the lid. It was something Shou always carried since it could throw tracking dogs off their scent, but it did have other uses, and this was one. He handed it to Yaomey. "I'll watch Dellia. You and Mi-Gahn

134

fetch their horses." He nodded to Mi-Gahn with his head. "She can ride one of them."

Yaomey took the container and motioned Mi-Gahn to come. Aylun watched as the two strolled over to Jon and Yaomey popped open the box. She sprinkled a pinch of its green powdery contents over the area where Jon lay, then eyed Mi-Gahn. "To prevent predators from sensing him."

Aylun continued to keep a firm grip on Dellia's arm as his companions disappeared behind the trees. A sound like someone trying to mount a horse over and over issued from behind the massive trunks, and he shook his head. The woman couldn't even get up on a horse.

Soon they reappeared with Yaomey leading a pair of beautiful dapple-gray horses. Mi-Gahn sat atop one whose spots darkened and merged toward its back so that the rear legs were almost black. They gave Jon a wide berth, and when they arrived, Aylun hoisted Dellia up and planted her on the other of the dapple grays. Then he and Yaomey mounted their steeds, and all four set off, back into the depths of the bright green forest.

As time wore on, a profound sense of dismay fell over him, adding to his overwhelming guilt and frustration. Ever since his departure from the Augury, Yaomey had been with him, her presence a constant reminder that he had taken from her the most important thing in her life—her sister. Every look at her, every glance, had brought with it an unbearable longing to see those two sisters strolling happily side by side just one more time, or to hear their infectious giggling.

His existence had become unendurable, and the only thing that had allowed him to withstand it was the singular hope that it would end soon. Once he had hidden Mi-Gahn away, he would return to Islong's lair, and she would put an end to this insufferable nightmare. Yet, in the heat of the moment, he had been maneuvered into making a vow. He had promised to abide by the decisions of a simple-minded stranger with no concept of how things worked in this world. So now, there was no telling what cataclysm he had dragged himself into or how much longer he would be forced to suffer his torturous existence.

The horse under Megan heaved and jolted as it plodded along the lush green forest floor. It was her first time on a horse without an experienced rider there to steady her, and she feared the beast might jog her from its back any second. The need to manage the unfamiliar activity made it all the more difficult to focus on her decision.

She glanced up at Aylun ahead, seeming so confident of the path where none even existed. Behind her, Dellia's horse thudded along, with Yaomey riding at the rear in somber silence. The effort to keep her annoyance at bay distracted Megan, making an objective view of her choices hard to maintain. Her abductors had finally been gracious enough to allow her to decide her own fate, but only after that decision had become impossible. It seemed that four lives now hung in the balance, and all of her choices were bad ones.

She turned her attention to the endless landscape of brown and green. Layer upon layer of vegetation drifted past, intertwining into a tapestry of leaves, branches, foliage, and flowers. She regained her focus and tried once again to weigh her options. Like the last several attempts, this one lasted only a few minutes before her thoughts were drawn back to the scene of Jon bursting into view and shouting for her not to harm the protector.

His concern for the woman was an icy ache in her heart that would not go away. It was clear he thought she was helping him. It was also obvious that his concern for her was yet another manifestation of his irrational fear of hurting others. Even so, it was hard to hear him being more worried about a woman he had just met than about the brutal kidnapping of a best friend he had known for years.

Megan closed her eyes and tried to clear her mind once more, focusing on the rustling of leaves, chirping of birds, and buzzing of insects. Once her thoughts had settled some, she tried again to consider her choices. Every fiber of her being was imploring her to stay with Jon. The very idea of leaving him behind to fend for himself made her sick in her heart. He was wounded and needed help and protection. And with her gift and his cleverness, they would find a way to escape this prophecy nonsense and return home.

Yet all signs seemed to point to the reality that she and Jon being together posed a terrible risk. How could she ignore Aylun's warnings? Every prediction he had made so far had come to pass in some form. The council had sent a protector to find them and detain them, and this particular protector did not seem like the type they could reason with or stop until she had completed her mission. Also, as predicted, Dellia had kept Jon alive, even enlisting his help to find her.

At the same time, there were all too many ways this confusing mess defied all common sense. Were prophecies something you could change with such ease? And if you could change them, would they even be prophecies? Every story she'd ever heard of a leader trying to thwart a dire prediction ended with them facilitating their own demise. If this "council" thought it was as simple as eliminating her and Jon, then why had the protector not just killed him when she had a chance? Why did she surrender out of the blue, and why was she a captive while Jon was still free and alive?

Explanations spun through her mind. Yet, they all came back to a common thread. Either the council or the protector or both wanted something more than the mere elimination of a threat. The possibilities were too numerous. Maybe they wanted information or cooperation, or to somehow use her and Jon. Perhaps they wanted to usurp the prophecy, or maybe killing them wouldn't stop it from being realized. It was impossible to tell. What was certain was that whatever they wanted, it had been keeping her and Jon alive and would continue to do so as long as circumstances did not veer too far off their current course.

Around and around spun the possible scenarios and unanswerable questions until at last the group stopped to rest the horses. They dismounted near a crystal-clear brook that flowed through patches of sunlight as it meandered along the soft green forest floor. Aylun grabbed an empty bag from his pack, then he and Yaomey lifted Dellia down, and all three escorted her a short distance away. They sat her in a patch of warm sunlight at the base of a shaggy old tree.

As they leaned her against the trunk, Dellia looked up at Megan with sunlight glinting off her questioning eyes.

Aylun stepped between them. "We are stopping here to rest." He held up the empty bag. "I am sorry about this," He slipped it over her head. "But we have matters to discuss, and I would not want you reading any lips."

They retreated to the brook and came to rest on a few of the large smooth boulders at its edge where the quiet murmur of flowing water would mask their hushed voices. All three stared for a while into the glimmering stream before Aylun's soft voice broke the silence. "Have you reached a decision?"

Megan granted an earnest look to Yaomey, then Aylun. "Yes. I want you to know that I have heard everything you've said. And I know there's a big chance of being captured, but I can't leave Jon back there like this. In some ways, his being here at all, in this place, is my fault."

Yaomey appeared puzzled and whispered, "How is any of this your fault?"

"I thought visits from the future couldn't be real. But given what I've seen in this place, I have to admit, it might have actually happened."

Yaomey seemed thoughtful. "I have never heard of nor seen such a thing, but I cannot dismiss the possibility."

"My future self must have known all this would happen, that Jon and I would be stranded in this world, that we would be separated and persecuted because of this stupid prophecy. Yet, when she visited me from the future, she mentioned none of it. All she had to do was say a few simple words and she would have stopped every bit of it from happening, but she chose not to. And if all of this is my future self's fault, then, in a way, that makes it my fault."

"I see." Aylun nodded. "Taking responsibility fo—"

Yaomey put a finger in front of his mouth. "Shh. Your voice carries."

Aylun glanced over at Dellia and paused a second, then continued in a more muted tone. "Taking responsibility for your actions ... that I understand. But then what of the protector?"

Megan glanced in Dellia's direction. "This may be cruel and heartless, but I will leave that to you two." She peered into Yaomey's eyes. "Take her far away and release her. If that means she arrests you, then think of it as your way of taking responsibility for *your* actions."

A moment of silence followed, with only the rustling of the wind through the trees and the soft murmur of the stream. Aylun took a deep breath and turned his eyes to hers. "Okay. I said I would abide by your decision, and I will, but let Yaomey go. None of this is her fault."

Megan glanced at each of them. "That is up to you two."

Yaomey gave a single solemn nod. "Then it is settled. After we let the horses rest, I will escort you back to Jon and return to Aylun. Then we will both take Dellia far away." She leaned closer and spoke in an even softer whisper. "But we must leave quietly"—she motioned with her head to Dellia—"so she does not hear."

Megan nodded.

A somber stillness fell over the group, and all three sat for a long while, staring into the ripples where the stream shallowed over a collection of polished stones. Megan fretted about her decision, imagining worst-case scenarios. Would the protector somehow find a way to get free and track them both down? If she did, what would this council do to them? Could they use one of them to extort cooperation out of the other? Visions of them hurting Jon or torturing her flashed in her mind. Then came the disturbing images of Jon's mortification as they turned him into a puppet leader and executed their opponents and waged wars in his name.

Amid her storm of self-doubt came Jon's calm voice from right behind them. "Megan, we need to talk."

Startled, their three heads whipped around to face the intruder. Megan's heart leaped. There, behind her, stood Jon, alive and well. Next to him was a huge well-muscled stranger, the pair towering above them with swords aimed at their backs. This new stranger appeared older, larger, and much more imposing than Jon, and a patchwork of armor covered most of his golden-skinned body. The huge man with black hair looked down with a disposition that warned he was not one to be trifled with.

Megan and her abductors rose and turned to face the blades aimed at them. Aylun stepped back. "Whoa, whoa. I know how this looks, but we meant you no harm. We were merely trying to help Megan."

"Is kidnapping protectors a part of helping?" Jon scowled. "Go cut Dellia loose."

His words were like a dagger in her soul. After all she had been through, after all her trauma, worry, and suffering, Jon was here to rescue not her but a woman he had known only a matter of hours. How could he be so unconcerned with her plight? For that matter, how could he be so incredibly naive as to trust *that woman*?

Then a terrible realization dawned on her. It was imperative that Jon not know. Were he to learn of Dellia's true mission, his usefulness to her might end, and with it, everyone's freedom, perhaps even their lives. A chill ran through her as she realized just how dangerous Jon's demand was.

She opened her mouth to object, but Aylun beat her to it, responding with cool detachment. "I cannot do that. She will try to arrest us all, and I cannot let that happen. So, we will have to stop her, and someone will get hurt. Let us take our horses and leave, then you can cut her loose."

Jon appeared shaken by the prospect, but soon recovered. "You're bluffing." He threw his oversized partner a questioning look.

The man scrutinized Aylun. "No, he's not, and neither is she." He pointed at Yaomey. "If you cut Dellia loose, it won't be pleasant."

Jon stared at his partner in disbelief. "But they kidnapped Megan and Dellia."

Jon's mention of her caused her heart to leap again. He *did* understand that she had suffered. Then again, he had lumped her in the same category as a woman who would arrest them the moment she was freed. Megan feared for her and Jon, and images of Aylun and Yaomey being locked in a damp, dark dungeon appeared in her mind. Her abductors' methods may have been unconscionable, but their desire to protect her and Jon had been sincere. They didn't deserve to be locked up forever.

Megan eyed her oldest and dearest friend. "Please, Jon, just let them go."

He appeared thrown by her request. As if expecting advice or encouragement, he looked to his brawny partner.

The man stared back. "It's not my decision to make." With his head, he motioned to the protector. "Dellia can't let them go, but you can. Tough choice."

He considered for only a moment, then the look on Jon's face told her what he intended to do. He eyed Aylun and Yaomey. "No, it's not. I can't let anyone get hurt because of me. Okay, you can go, and I promise Dellia won't follow you. You have twenty-four hours, but Megan comes with me."

Her heart soared again, but her elation was short-lived as she pictured Yaomey and Aylun leaving and just her and Jon remaining. Only, it wouldn't be just her and Jon, it would be her and Jon *and the protector*. Those were the exact circumstances Dellia herself had said would lead to her and Jon's arrest.

Her heart sank. She had to leave, but how could she just abandon the man she loved? How could she leave him unprotected? As she stared at the huge warrior at Jon's side, a realization dawned on her. Perhaps Jon didn't need physical protection after all. In a matter of hours, he had somehow managed to find help from not one but two warriors. They would protect him from any physical danger far better than she ever could. What he really needed, what they both needed, was protection from this stupid prophecy.

With that realization came another, one that was infinitely more saddening. She couldn't go with Jon. Aylun was right. Her determination to stay with him was irrational. Being with him would mean Dellia would make good on her promise and detain both of them, and nobody would be left to prove this prophecy wasn't about them.

She looked at Jon as her voice came out sad and quiet. "I can't go with you." Guilt racked her as she watched the hope in Jon's eyes vanish, crushed by her heartless rejection.

"But why?" His voice had an almost imperceptible quiver, and the bewilderment and suffering in his eyes were heartrending. Memories of her merciless and undeserved words in the lab rushed back. She was rejecting him again. It was as if the hurt in those eyes were ripping a hole in her heart.

Worst of all, if she gave him any information about the prophecy or Dellia's intent, it might make him doubt the protector, and if he doubted her in any way, his usefulness to her would end, putting him in grave danger. A sick feeling came over her. She couldn't answer his question. She couldn't even tell him why.

Megan held back tears. "You have no idea how much I just want to grab you now and go away with you. Away from all this."

A glimmer of cruel hope rekindled in his eyes. "Then let's go."

Her composure threatened to crumble, but she managed to hold it together. "I know how confusing this must be, but I can't explain. Please, just trust me and understand that for now, my path can't be yours." She turned to hide her face and began to walk away.

From behind her came Jon's voice. "I might have a way home. If I find the parts to assemble this."

She turned back and saw he was holding up a metallic medallion with three empty spots, each in the shape of a leaf. His mention of home brought both hope and despair to her heart. What they both needed more than anything was to get home, where all this prophecy nonsense would soon become a distant memory. That Jon had already found a way was a flicker of hope in an otherwise bleak situation. Yet, at the same time, their being here somehow became her future self's fault. If she was to set that right, she couldn't hold him back. She couldn't stop him from going home.

She looked straight into his eyes, and out of the depths of her misery, she pulled all the persuasiveness she could muster. "If you want to go home, then you find a way. Don't let anyone or anything stop you, not even me. I will find a way to follow. Don't wait for me. Promise me."

Jon seemed dumbfounded but simply nodded.

Yaomey and Aylun mounted their horses, then Aylun shot his hand out to Megan. She took it, and he lifted her up in front of him on Juzhi.

She turned her face away from Jon, afraid she would break down and he would see that she was miserable.

Aylun brought his horse around and stopped, then from behind her came his strong, confident voice. "I know you have no reason to trust me. But this I promise on my life: no harm will come to Mi-Gahn, not by my hand or by any other."

With that, Aylun urged his horse forward, and they took off into the woods.

For a while, Megan shoved everything out of her mind and rode in stunned silence, afraid to even contemplate what had just happened. An eternity seemed to pass as they followed the stream, and her mind remained blank. The woods became a bit denser and the ground softer and muddier. Toppled trees began to litter the landscape, their roots torn from the thick black mud and dangling in the air.

With the change, her mood darkened, becoming as oppressive as her stifling environs. Then her resolve began to crack, as images of Jon's bewildered face forced their way back into her mind. It was the same expression that had shocked her years ago when he left for his new job at Delas Labs.

Every year, the college brought in companies to interview prospective employees. The year he graduated, Jon had participated, but he seemed determined to avoid any company far away. She knew he was being foolish. He was meant for bigger things. So, despite the growing ache in her soul, she'd put on a cheerful smile and encouraged him to go to each job interview that might take him away from her.

Then came the day when he brought news of an offer from Delas Labs. They were offering him a chance to continue his current research. Her heart shattered. It was the perfect job, so he had to take it, but it was far enough away that it was doubtful she'd ever see him again. Despite the heaviness in her heart, she remained steadfast, donning her most upbeat disposition as she convinced him to take the position.

All she had wanted was for him to be happy, but in the airport, before he left, he accused her of having always wanted to get rid of him. He had mistaken her cheerful facade for glee at the idea of him leaving. She wanted to tell him he was wrong, that she wanted him to stay, but then, just as now, she couldn't. How could she clear up the misunderstanding without encouraging him to abandon the job opportunity of a lifetime?

His face had that same hurt expression as he apologized for "always being a pest" and "forcing myself on you." Worst of all was the look of utter dejection just before he turned to board his flight. It was then that he told her, "You didn't have to go this far to get rid of me." They were words she hadn't wanted to remember, yet they were an all-too-perfect fit for the scene that had just played out. It had been a face she'd never wanted to see again, but now it was back, and the memories were haunting her anew because here she was rejecting him again.

The images of their parting in the airport mixed with those of Jon's questioning face and sorrowful eyes moments ago as she told him she couldn't go with him. They brought back memories of her harsh words in the lab and of older rejections spreading back ten years. The weight became like an anchor dragging her heart deeper and deeper into despair.

As she weakened, all the terror, anxiety, and guilt of the past few days came crashing back. It grabbed her chest and squeezed, the tightness growing with each scene that replayed in her head. The burden became unbearable. She couldn't breathe, and she called out, "Stop! I need to get down."

Aylun flew off his horse and hoisted Megan by the waist off Juzhi and down onto the soft brown dirt. Still holding her upright, he peered into her face.

As their eyes met, a surge of anger and revulsion came over her, and she shoved him away as if he were radioactive. She staggered back a short distance and bent over, gasping and clutching her chest.

Yaomey dismounted. "Are you all right?"

Aylun strode over to her. "Take a deep breath." He set a gentle hand on her back. "We must keep moving."

His touch was like fuel, feeding her anger, turning it into a raging fury. Tears came to her eyes, and she whirled around, bashing his hand away. "Don't you touch me!" she screamed, and flew up into his face. "You're to blame as much as every crazy person in this messed-up world." She struggled against the oppressive guilt. "Did you see Jon's face? *I* did that to him."

Aylun stood mute and stunned as she glared.

"This insane world, and its insane prophecies and insane believers!" she shouted into his face. "You all did this to us!"

Aylun's calm and detached voice became tinged with sympathy. "You did as you had to. You kept him apart and safe, and you didn't tell him—"

"Stop it." Megan shoved him away and lurched back from him. "I don't want to hear it. What I want to hear from you right now is that you're going to help me fix this."

Aylun stared at her, bemused. "How?"

"You don't believe this prophecy is about Jon and me, right?"

"No." Aylun shook his head. "No, I do not. Wistra's journal didn't mention two Other—"

"Then you're going to help me prove it."

"How?" Aylun asked again.

Megan stepped backward as a wave of even more intense anger swept through her, finding its focus on Aylun's placid face. He had made a promise, and there would be no discussion or debate. He would keep it, or she would make him. She raised her hand, then brought it down as she imagined the large dead limb of a nearby tree breaking off. With a puff of air, it plunged away at an unnatural speed, hurtling to the ground with a heavy thud, very close to Aylun.

She glared. "Wrong answer."

He appeared shaken for a moment but soon recovered. "The only proof I know of is in Wistra's journal, in the Dead of Night, and I will *not* go back there."

Megan glanced behind her at a large decayed log. She scrunched up her face in concentration and waved her hand. With a burst of air, it flew from the ground and hurtled right by Aylun's shoulder. Loose bits of dirt and debris spattered them both as it careened past.

He cringed and shrank away as it shattered on a tree behind him with a loud crash that echoed through the gently swaying trees.

Yaomey's concern showed in her eyes, and she spoke with a calm and gentle tone. "Megan, you—"

"Wrong answer!"

Aylun's calm began to crack. "I ... I ... can't."

She raised her hand again.

"Lanessa." There was alarm in Yaomey's voice as she nodded with vigor. "We know one of Wistra's journals was left behind in the lost city of Lanessa."

Aylun balked. "Lanessa? You can't be serious."

"Yes, you told me all about it. You said she described it as containing her notes on how to deal with this very prophecy. We even know she lived in the back of a blacksmith's shop. If it is still there ..."

AYLUN

Megan turned her eyes from Yaomey to glare at Aylun again. She wanted him to feel the same panic and terror she had when he took her by force. Her face twisted in anger and intense focus as she raised her hand, and an even larger fallen tree trunk floated from the ground. Wind whirled around her, and pieces of moss and dirt fell from the gigantic log as, by her will, she lifted it high into the air. It hovered there, threatening Aylun as she spat her furious words at him. "You made a vow to me that you would do whatever I decide."

The enormous tree trunk lurched toward him, and he stiffened, looking like a frightened deer, yet remaining resolute. "This is a bad idea. Nobody comes back fr—"

The hovering tree trunk heaved toward him again, even faster. He winced and cowered away. "Okay. Okay. I made a vow. I will keep it."

The log halted only an arm's length from caving in his wicked skull. A whirlwind whipped around Megan as she remained poised and tense. She stayed that way, waiting for a "but," waiting for some qualification or stipulation that might allow that unscrupulous tyrant to wriggle out of his promise later.

Instead, Aylun straightened and gave a firm nod. "Adi help us, I will take you to Lanessa to find the journal."

Megan relaxed and waved the enormous log to the side. It fell to earth with a heavy thud, spattering the rich, black dirt as it landed. She crouched down in a heap and cried.

Chapter Seven

A SPOTTED FRIEND

Aylun crouched on the wet, mushy ground and waited, endeavoring to remain patient as Mi-Gahn recovered. It was obvious they hadn't the time for this. The protector might catch up with them at any moment. Yet he couldn't bring himself to push Mi-Gahn further over the brink. The last thing he needed was another unnerving round of having the remains of fallen trees hurled at him. So he squatted among the shattered debris of wet and rotten old logs and waited.

He had just made two vows within minutes of each other. He had promised Jon that he would let no harm come to Mi-Gahn. Then, in a moment of weakness, he had committed to taking her into unthinkable peril. The two vows were at utter odds with each other, of course, but he couldn't go back on his word, and there was no way she would abandon her goal. So he watched and waited as his discomfort grew.

After a while, she stirred and scrubbed the tears from her cheeks. Striving to remain calm and respectful, Aylun stood and bowed as he offered his hand to help her up.

She slapped it away, then rose and staggered over to Juzhi, where she fumbled for a while until she mounted him on her own.

Still trying to remain respectful and quiet, he followed, swinging up behind Mi-Gahn. With care not to touch her, he reached around her for the reins, and for the first time, he became aware of how close she was to him. Before her outburst, he had spent an entire day riding in the saddle behind her and never given it a second thought. Now, as he settled in back of her and urged his steed forward, it became all too clear. He had been far too oblivious of his proximity to her and how much discomfort it must cause.

It had been his decision to take Mi-Gahn by force, so it had fallen to him and not Yaomey to protect her and prevent her escape. That made it necessary for her to ride with him on his horse. Now, circumstances had changed, and it would be unseemly for that arrangement to continue any longer than necessary. So he made a mental note, adding it to the growing list of things to be dealt with.

They had a destination now, so Aylun led the way north-northwest toward the Eastern Trail. The well-traveled path led east to the realm of Erden, but their course would be the opposite. They would head west across the lands of Talus to its old fallen capital, Katapa. Not only was that route in keeping with his most recent vow, the one to take Mi-Gahn to the lost city of Lanessa, but it was the last place anyone would look for them. No one would expect three fugitive Elorians to head toward the heart of the Talesh homeland on a well-traveled road.

The group remained silent as they trod north and west. The swampy terrain became more solid, then turned rocky. Megan's body jostled and heaved in front of him with each step as Juzhi meandered around trees and through underbrush. At first, he puzzled over why the sight of her, and her nearness, made him uncomfortable, but as time passed, that ceased to occupy his thoughts. What his mind continued to return to was the image of her face as she threatened him.

Ever since Yaolin's final gut-wrenching cries of desperation, he had sought release from his pitiable existence. Even now, to put an end to his shame and remorse, to stop the nightmares and memories of so many final moments of pain and terror, would be a relief. So why had he relented when Mi-Gahn had threatened him with the very death he sought? Why, in that moment of weakness, had he agreed to take her to Lanessa? And why, even now, did it seem so wrong to back out, although he must?

They traced the western edge of one of the large grassy clearings characteristic of this part of the Illis Woods. Strewn with large boulders, the lush fields of green were broken here and there by patches of rocky ground and tufts of taller grass waving in the light breeze. Much like the soggier terrain they had crossed earlier in the day, the clearing served as a landmark, telling him the Eastern Trail was not far now.

The more he considered it, the more convinced he became that any attempt to talk Mi-Gahn out of Lanessa would only result in a repeat of having giant logs hurled at him. Taking her there was a huge risk, that was clear, but with no direct experience with Katapa or Lanessa, he couldn't even describe the nature of the threat, much less argue his way out of facing it. Yet how was it keeping her safe to take her to the heart of danger? Unable to find an answer, his turmoil continued to deepen with each heaving of her body so close to his.

As sunset neared, he spent a good while scanning the emerald forest floor, searching for an ideal place to make camp, one that would keep them hidden from any following protector. After a long search, he found one at the intersection of a pair of gigantic fallen trees. Their massive trunks formed a natural V-shaped wall, shielding them and their fire from view, while a nearby cluster of shrubs hid their horses.

The absence of talk continued as they made a fire, tended the horses, and consumed a small meal of meat and stale bread. With the sunlight all but gone and the stars growing brighter, they sat in glum silence. Hidden from view by the pair of enormous moss-covered tree trunks on either side, they stared into the fluttering flames of a dwindling fire.

His thoughts mired in the dilemma of his conflicting vows, Aylun's attention drifted to Mi-Gahn and the firelight flickering across her face. There remained no shred of anger in her expression now, only sorrow.

Yaomey seemed to notice and leaned closer to him, her voice soft in his ear. "Do you think you might possibly owe her an apology?"

Weary from the day's events and his unsolvable dilemma, the idea of any kind of discussion with Mi-Gahn was more than he cared to handle. He eyed Yaomey and heaved a heavy sigh. Then he paused for a while before scooting over next to Mi-Gahn.

She glanced at him, and his tone came out more flat and forced than suitable for a genuine apology. "I am sorry about all of this."

Her brow creased. "Does it even count if you're asked to apologize?"

He nodded agreement, and his gaze returned to the fire, becoming lost in the yellow light that danced along the glowing charred remains of mostly burned logs.

After a moment, Mi-Gahn's gaze fell.

Aylun watched out of the corner of his eye as she stared down at the thick layer of crumbling bark that time had washed from the decaying trees on either side. Her eyes became glassy. "Do you really feel no remorse?"

He closed his eyes and shook his head, then let it drop. For a time, he studied the debris-strewn ground with her. When he finally spoke, his voice carried all the guilt that had haunted him for so many years. "Remorse is all I feel."

Mi-Gahn's head came up and her face held a look of surprise. "What?" She peered over at him. "What is that supposed to mean?"

He didn't answer for a while. It would be wrong to play on her sympathies or use his own problems to justify what he had done. Aylun closed his eyes. "There is no answer I can give that will not sound like an excuse."

"Risk it." Her words were as cold as her stare.

Puzzled, he glanced over at her.

She lowered her gaze. "I am so far beyond caring about excuses. I just want answers."

"I see." He took a deep breath. "Is this where I am supposed to bare my soul and tell you every terrible moment that led me to you so you can shower me with pity for my pathetic existence?"

Mi-Gahn scoffed. "You overestimate yourself." She looked him straight in the eye. "I will never feel the slightest bit of pity or sympathy for you."

AYLUN

He gave a firm nod. "Yes, as it should be."

No word was spoken for a while as the hoot of an owl echoed out from some distant perch.

Aylun glanced over at Mi-Gahn, studying her face. Her frustration and anger were long gone. Yet, there remained a raw determination in her eyes that reaffirmed his belief that she would never be dissuaded.

Then, like a sun lighting up the horizon, it dawned on him. It was her eyes. When she'd threatened him, as twisted as her face had been in anger, it had not been entirely out of fear that he had relented. In her gaze, he had found something shocking: a reflection of his own frustration and resentment. He had seen *himself*. And in that moment, it had become impossible to stand in her way any longer.

He returned his attention to her, studying her despondent face once again. His feeling of shame deepened. Here was a precious human life—two, in fact—and he had felt nothing for their plight. He had let his own anguish numb him to the weight of those two lives now resting in his hands. What he had done to them may have been necessary—it may even have been unavoidable—but it was still cruel. He had been the instrument that had torn them apart.

With that realization, he understood what he must do. A newfound sense of purpose took root, and he embraced it, letting it grow, crystallizing, clarifying, lending him a sense of resolve. He brought himself up taller and inhaled a deep breath of cool evening air.

Mi-Gahn looked up at him, appearing startled.

His eyes met hers, and he let his voice carry all the weight of his newfound resolve. "Regardless of what I may have said or done in the past, I will find a way to set this right. I give you my word. It is all I have left in this world, so it is far more precious to me than you can possibly imagine. Believe me when I say, no matter how long it takes, no matter what I must do, no matter what the cost, I will bring you and Jon back together. If I have to punch a hole in the veil back to your home world and fight my way through the eighteen levels of hell, then that is what I will do. This is my oath, my vow, and my promise."

Mi-Gahn remained motionless, seeming stunned by his out-pouring of sincerity. She blinked a couple of times like a startled deer. Then she seemed to come out of it and scoffed as she broke his gaze. "Am I supposed to forgive you because of a few pretty words?"

He continued to stare as her gaze returned to his. She had rebuffed him, but her eyes told of an earnest desire for reassurance. Yet, he had not made this promise to earn forgiveness. He did not deserve it, nor did he need it. Aylun shook his head. "No. Do not for-give me. Do not give my welfare even a passing thought. Just get some rest. The council is aware of your existence, and protectors will know where you are. I vow to give it my all, but we must rise early and travel far if we are to throw them off our trail."

Mi-Gahn remained seated for a while, then shook her head as she rose. She scoffed again, then shot him several fleeting glances as she turned away and walked to her bedroll.

No sooner had she laid down her head than he turned his attention to the details of his new plan. It was clear now what had to happen. He had vowed to bring Mi-Gahn and Jon back together, and he would. He would go to Lanessa, as he had promised, and he would find Wistra's journal. With it in hand, he would return. He would reveal the council's lie and spread the truth of the prophecy.

But he could not, in good conscience, take Mi-Gahn with him into that kind of peril. He had sworn he would keep her safe, so he would only take her as far as the outskirts of Katapa. There, he would leave her with Yaomey and go alone. Once he had revealed the coun-cil's lies and placed the true prophecy in trusted hands, he would return and bring Mi-Gahn back to her beloved Jon.

The night was still dark when Megan opened her eyes. It wasn't the complete darkness of a cloudy night because Yaomey's outline stood out against the moonlight filtering through the canopy above. It was enough light to see that there was no sense of urgency on Yaomey's face as she crouched over Megan, shaking her.

"We must go." Yaomey peered down with a half-asleep look of concern. "If the protector is tracking us, she will begin at sunrise. If we wish to evade her, then we must do the same."

Megan nodded. With a less-than-adequate amount of sleep, it was one of those mornings she would have stumbled into her bright yellow kitchen and brewed herself a large steaming cup of coffee. But that was not going to happen, so she would just have to cope. Megan rubbed her stinging eyes as she pulled herself up into a sitting position, staring into the sea of tree trunks, barely visible in the early dawn light.

Yaomey handed her a stack of clothing in shades of cinnamon and rust. "Put these on. They will be looking for an oddly dressed red-haired Elorian woman and her two companions. We cannot change our faces or your hair, so the best you can do now is to wear something less conspicuous."

Megan dragged herself up and wandered a good distance into the woods. She donned the new apparel swiftly and quietly, which proved to be a challenge. The ensemble was composed of several layers, and it required a bit of guesswork to intuit the order in which to put them on. It was a task made more difficult by her groggy, sleep-deprived state. Upon finishing, she squinted as she peered down at herself in the almost-nonexistent light. Her new clothes seemed similar to those Yaomey wore: loose pants and a simple robe with a sash that appeared to be made of hemp. The layers beneath those outer garments made the whole ensemble soft and warm, and despite being plain, it possessed a unique charm.

She emptied the pockets of her old clothes, examining each item before transferring it to her new outfit. There was her dead cellphone and the keys to her red Mazda and suburban apartment. She stared for a moment, struck by how out of place they seemed in this foreign context, and at their uselessness now when they had meant so much to her before.

She sighed and returned to emptying her pockets, but when she got to the dragon's skeleton key, it gave her pause. She held it up, wondering at the three gems, sparkling in the few patches of starlight shining down through the leafy canopy above. Why make something as simple as a key so large and ornate, and why had the dragon seemed upset that she had taken it?

After pocketing it, she began her slog back to camp. Through her sleepy haze, the events of the day before came drifting back. The agony of the decision to leave Jon remained a fresh wound on her soul. In her desperation to get back to him, she had threatened Aylun. She would like to think she wouldn't have hurt him. After all, she was in desperate need of his help. As gratifying as it might be to wound him, or incapacitate him, or even smash his unfeeling face to a pulp, doing so would not further her cause. Still, it had been liberating to witness the terror on her former abductor's face as she bent him to her will.

What came next she wasn't sure. Aylun's unexpected promise to bring her back to Jon had stirred her in ways she found intensely uncomfortable, though she wasn't sure why. Even so, it was clear now that the next move was his. He knew this land and her goal, and she needed that expertise, so she would wait and see what plan he concocted.

Their simple camp and spotted horses soon came back into view, and she sought out Yaomey. She was sitting with Aylun before a mound of ash and dying embers that was all that remained of the roaring fire of the night before. As Megan approached, Aylun glanced up from his paltry meal. With a blank expression, he gave a perfunctory bow of his head. Yaomey smiled and handed Megan a meager chunk of bread. So she sat and ate.

As soon as Aylun had downed the last few crumbs, he stood and wandered a short distance into the woods. He rummaged for a while until he found a long straight stick. Upon returning, he eyed Megan. Once he garnered her full attention, he scrawled an outline in the ashes: a teardrop shape that curved down and around to the right.

He jabbed a dot low on the right edge. "We are here." He poked another dot along the lower left curve of the outline. "And Lanessa is here, beyond the fallen city of Katapa. The most direct way to get there is to pass through Talus near the capital city of Egina." He placed a third dot between the other two, then eyed Megan. "We must proceed as if we are being tracked, and even the most inept tracker could follow our trail of trampled and broken vegetation in these woods or even on the Talus Plains. We need a well-traveled road where the hard-packed surface leaves few prints, and the tracks of other travelers can hide them. And not just any road—we need one with many branches where it will be difficult to guess our path."

Megan nodded.

Aylun waved the stick in Yaomey's direction. "Thing is, our appearance is also quite different from the Talesh, and we must assume the authorities will be asking around about us. So we must all avoid travelers and locals and hide our faces from any we meet. Do you understand?"

Megan nodded again.

"There's one more thing," he added. "I did an inventory of our supplies. We have enough food for perhaps five days for the three of us. For the reasons I just mentioned, we can't stop to purchase more. Since we also don't have time to stop and fish or hunt, we will have to ration."

Without further ceremony, he spun and walked away toward the horses.

Yaomey rose and began making preparations to leave while Megan turned her attention to her meal. The talk of heading away from here, farther from her last encounter with Jon, was both sad and unsettling. It meant her decision to part from him was all the more final. There would be no turning back now, and every step she took would carry her farther away from him—well, unless the protector dragged him along to find her, a possibility that was far less comforting than the alternative.

Still, she had made her choice when she told Jon she couldn't go with him. All she could do now was focus on the task in front of her: to follow Aylun and Yaomey, to remain free long enough to find proof that this absurd prophecy wasn't about either her or Jon.

They set out while it was still dark, traveling in sleepy silence as the light grew brighter and the forest stirred from its slumber. They splashed along a small stream and exited onto rockier ground, which Aylun explained would make them harder to track. Trees became scarcer and more gnarled as the terrain became rougher and stonier.

The sun had just risen above the horizon, peeking through leaves and branches to the east, when they broke out onto a dirt road that meandered its way through the forest. With two of them riding Juzhi, he soon grew tired. So they pulled back off the road to rest him while they watched through the vegetation for any signs of travelers.

As they reclined in withdrawn silence, Aylun eyed first Yaomey, then Megan. "Now comes the hard part. Mi-Gahn here needs a horse."

She scowled. "It's Megan, not Mi-Gahn."

Aylun showed no sign of acknowledgment. "We cannot simply wander into town and trade for one while the authorities are out looking for three Elorian travelers."

Yaomey raised her hand. "I can go alone. At least that way, it will be less obvious."

Megan shook her head. "That doesn't seem sensible. If the authorities ask about three Elorian travelers, anyone who spotted you will just say, 'No, but we saw an Elorian woman.'"

Aylun shrugged. "Obviously. But what choice do we have?"

Megan pondered for a moment, staring through the thicket at the wide dirt road beyond. If this land had horses, then perhaps some roamed free. She eyed Aylun. "Catch a wild one?" she ventured in a hesitant voice.

Despite Aylun's obvious downbeat mood, he chuckled. "Three Elorians trying to catch and break a wild horse. How could that attract attention?"

Megan pouted and grumbled, "Well, the sarcasm isn't really helpful."

"And are you to ride bareback? We need a saddle, blanket, and bridle."

She turned her pout into a scowl. "Is your only function here to poke holes in my ideas?"

"How about you come up with a decent one?"

Feeling defensive at his condescending attitude, Megan blurted out the first thing that came to mind. "Okay, why don't we just"—she winced—"steal a horse?"

Yaomey sat straighter. "Well, that is a stunningly bad idea. How is it avoiding attention for three Elorians to steal a horse?"

Megan scooted a little closer and leaned in as if explaining a dark secret. "No. No. If we do this right, they'll never even see us." She flicked a finger and sent a pebble skittering across the ground only to whack into a tree. "I can create a distraction from a distance while you sneak in and steal it."

"They will come looking for us afterward."

"They're already looking for us."

Aylun's face carried a shocked expression. "That is a ... a not-terrible idea."

Yaomey leaned away in surprise. "You cannot be serious. Horses are used for farming. Taking one could cause the farm to fail, leading to untold hardship and maybe even killing people. That is why it is a crime punishable by death."

Megan scowled. "My *existence* is punishable by death. What have I got to lose?"

Yaomey stared in disbelief. "You cannot be ..." She looked at her partner. "Aylun?"

He pointed to Megan. "No, no, she is right. We find a breeder, not a farm. Breeders abound in these grassy lands. Most communities will have one or two, so it should not take long. She can create a distraction while we take the equipment and a horse. And we can leave behind more than enough silver to turn it from a hardship into a blessing. Maybe even enough that they dare not risk the coin by reporting it as a crime."

Yaomey crossed her arms. "And you think … oh for crying out … You know how I know this is a bad idea?" Her eyes shifted back and forth between Megan and Aylun. "The two people here who have never agreed on anything—one of them with a death wish—both think it is a brilliant idea."

Megan smiled at her. "Oh, come on, it's simple. What could go wrong?"

Yaomey shook her head and fell silent.

The remainder of their rest went by in the quiet, with only one small group of travelers passing on the road. After they were long gone, Aylun rose and headed for Juzhi. "Now we go find someone who raises horses."

They made one last check of the road before striking out west along the well-trodden roadway. The trees on either side arched far up overhead, enclosing the path in perpetual shade. Even so, with room to ride abreast, the atmosphere seemed more relaxed than the closed-in environs of the forest.

After a while, Megan glanced down at her clothes. Her apparel might be less conspicuous now, but Aylun's observation was still valid. Their faces looked different. She glanced over at Yaomey, riding next to her. "Shouldn't we use a veil or something to cover our faces?"

Yaomey pointed to her eye. "I am the only one here with a double eyelid. Unless you think you can ride with your eyes covered, you and Aylun will give us away even if you cover everything else."

Megan glanced at Aylun, then Yaomey. She was right. Like every eye in the non-Asian world, Yaomey's eyelid had a fold when open. Aylun's had none, a clear giveaway of his heritage. Since Megan's eyes were the same, she would be taken as Elorian too.

From behind Megan, Aylun issued a guttural grunt of agreement. "We will have to avoid direct encounters where they can see our faces."

With that, the group fell silent once again. The straight and level path was a welcome change from the uneven forest floor and weaving through an endless world of trees and underbrush.

After a while, the road widened, and the foliage thinned. Occasional spots of sunlight appeared, shooting through the cracks in the umbrella overhead. They created beams of brilliance that painted sharp lines across the arching emerald canopy.

The forest continued to thin until a bright opening appeared in the distance. Despite it being visible for quite some time, passing through it was still a startling experience. All at once, the forest opened up to a bright grassy plain that stretched off to the horizon and greeted crystal-blue heavens splashed with wispy clouds. Here and there, a distant tree graced the panorama, while the well-worn dirt path wound its way into the distance only to disappear out of sight, a dark ribbon swallowed up in an ocean of green grasses. A light breeze cooled Megan's face, and she raised her arms and stretched, letting the warmth of the sun envelop her.

Behind her, Aylun took a deep breath and stirred in the saddle. He spurred Juzhi on, taking the lead again, this time angling away from the path. Once they were some distance from the hard-packed dirt, he set a course parallel to it, explaining it was a strategy to avoid direct encounters with travelers.

Soon, a loose line of trees and shrubs rose out of the verdant expanse, winding its way across the horizon. As they approached, flashes of cool blue appeared at their base, signs that the greenery graced the banks of a modest stream. Along with the water came the first village, a place Aylun announced as Dulfi. It was nothing more than a collection of stone-and-clay buildings mingling with giant oak-like trees that gathered at a point where the Eastern Trail crossed the stream.

Along the way, they encountered what appeared to be a small horse farm, but Aylun advised they forge ahead. It lay on the near side of the village, and he insisted that discovery would force them to escape back the way they came, risking an encounter with any possible pursuers. So they angled away from the road again and headed cross-country around the village.

The sun was still crawling its way up into the sky when they stopped at the brook to give their horses a drink. Megan wandered a short distance upstream and washed her face and hands in the cool, clear water while Aylun refilled their waterskins. After taking a drink, she returned to the group and sat staring into the rippling waters before her. After a while, she glanced at Aylun. "How do you know breeders are common here? For that matter, how can you remember the name of all these dinky backwater towns?"

At her question, the man froze, then his mood darkened beyond anything she had seen so far.

Yaomey shot him a fleeting glance and at the sight, her countenance fell as well.

Just when Megan had decided it would be a bad idea to pursue the topic, Aylun grumbled back, "I've been down this road before."

Yaomey looked up and added, "Not many days ago." She sent Megan a slight shake of her head. It told Megan what she already suspected, that her innocent question had struck some kind of major nerve, so she dropped the subject.

In the glum silence that followed, her mind wandered back to the days after Jon's departure for the job at Delas Labs. It was perhaps then, in the aftermath, that she had come to appreciate the depths of her feelings for him. For days after his departure, she fidgeted and worried as she tried to contact him, but every attempt to call and text was greeted with an ominous silence.

When she finally did get ahold of him, he seemed his old self. He claimed his phone had died and he'd been too busy with moving and the new job to dig a charger out of his bags. It was an unconvincing excuse, yet he acted like the same cheerful and friendly Jon she had always known. Still, there was something off, and it wasn't until much later that she put it together. He used to be playful, even flirty, but now he was being guarded. He had placed himself firmly in the "friend zone" and was determined to never again set foot out of it. No matter how much she flirted, hinted, or encouraged him, she never again saw that side of him.

Now, after refusing to go with him in their last encounter, she was worried that she had set back their relationship even further. Yet all she could do was find a way to end the threat of this idiotic prophecy and get back to Jon. Only when they were together again could she explain and mend fences. She sighed as she returned her attention to the crystal waters pouring over the stones at the bottom of the stream.

After a while, the group continued, once again following a course parallel to the road. It was not long before they encountered another town, Krosia. Its few dozen stone-and-rough-brick buildings were sprawled out along a half dozen dirt roads. Skirting it took longer but led to a series of homes and farms spread out some distance from one another along either side of the Eastern Trail.

One appeared to be a horse farm that offered an ideal setup. It was isolated, being some distance west of town and beyond the sight of any other farm or house. They first spotted it as they approached the back of the home. A short distance off the front and farther from the road stood a low, squat stable. Centered between the house and stable towered a massive oak tree, its long winding boughs reaching for both structures. Across the road, clusters of taller trees with broad trunks made a perfect spot to hide and watch the stable entrances while creating a distraction.

The sun had risen just past its peak. As they approached, a man came into view, working with a horse in a small paddock behind the stable. Intent on his work, he didn't seem to notice their approach, so they stopped and rested as they discussed their plan.

The three of them having agreed on a general course of action, Megan rose and continued down the broad dirt path. Once sheltered from view by the house, she ducked behind a tree. Attempting to remain hidden, she stooped over and skittered tree to shrub to tree until she had a good view of the rancher working behind the stable. She stopped there, her breath quick with excitement as she peered around a large tree trunk and waited, hoping he would soon return to his abode.

The man appeared to be quite muscular, despite being older, with a balding head and scrubby beard. His face seemed to hold a sour expression of perpetual disgruntlement as he worked with the horse. After a handful of minutes, he stopped and blotted his forehead with a cloth. For a while, he stared at the animal as if it were a puzzle to be figured out. Then he shook his head before leaving the paddock and heading back inside his home.

Heart pounding yet exhilarated by the sheer intrigue of it all, Megan snuck from tree to tree again until she had a good view of the front door of the house and the stable's wide entrances. Once in place, she huddled, hidden from view behind one of the trees, and peered back up the road at Aylun and Yaomey. They glanced her way, and she thrust both arms straight above her head, giving the signal that she was ready.

With an unhurried pace, the pair rose and mounted. As the two horses turned down the road and sauntered toward Megan, she stood again, taking care to remain hidden from the owner's view. With the apprehension of a young girl playing a prank on her friend, she peered out around the tree and flicked her finger. With a puff of wind, a small stone launched itself from the ground near the stable and clattered against the stone wall.

The horses inside obliged with uneasy, restless sounds.

The man soon stormed out of the house with a heavy sword in hand, its dull metal surface barely reflecting the bright midday sun. With piercing eyes, he scanned the yard. Then he checked out the area, first peering inside the stable, then strolling around them and the paddock. His search having yielded nothing, he marched out into the road, stopping a mere few feet from Megan, who was still crouched behind a mossy trunk.

When he spotted Aylun and Yaomey approaching from a distance, he stood for a while, staring at them as he scratched his beard. Megan was forced to suppress a giggle at the quizzical look on his face as he puzzled over the situation. Then he seemed to dismiss them, grumbling and shaking his head as he strolled back to his house and went inside.

Megan made another clatter by floating a rock over the stable roof and dropping it onto the dark wooden shingles. No sooner had it rolled off and thudded to the ground than the man emerged again, looking more puzzled and annoyed than last time. He spent another long while staring up the road, watching Aylun and Yaomey approach as he scratched his neck and blotted the sweat from his forehead. He roamed around, performing another patrol of the area, but when he once again found nothing, he marched back inside.

After another round of noises and another search, the man halted in the doorway of his house and peered out across his yard. Then he backed up out of view inside.

Megan reached out to make another noise, then paused. It could be a test or a trap. He might be standing back from the doorway watching the yard, hoping to spot something suspicious. So with her gift, she reached inside the entrance to the stable and shoved a metal bucket that was out of view from the house. It slid a short distance and rattled to a stop.

The horses stirred again, and the man burst from the doorway, once again beginning his search inside the stable.

The pattern continued, Megan making noises and stirring up the horses as Aylun and Yaomey passed the house and trotted away down the hard-packed dirt road. With each new disruption, the man's search became more cursory. Eventually, he ceased to appear at all, as Megan's partners in crime wandered off the road and into the field. Hidden from view of the house behind the stable, they led their horses up and around to the entrance, then slipped inside.

No sooner had they disappeared than whinnying, pawing, and restless sounds came from within. Megan tensed as the noises continued, then grew louder.

All of a sudden, the man stomped from the house, once again brandishing his hefty sword. He cursed as he hurled his sweat-soaked cloth to the ground and stormed off toward the building, the one where Aylun and Yaomey were now hiding.

Megan's tension exploded, and she stifled a gasp. She had to find a way to stop him. With her gift, she reached out and swayed a branch of the enormous twisted oak-like tree next to him. Dead twigs broke off and showered down, some landing on the stable roof with a clacking of wood on wood.

The man halted in his tracks, and his head turned toward the monstrous living artwork of winding limbs and lush greenery. Megan unconsciously held her breath as she watched him glance up at it with a baffled expression, then over at the roof. With distinct hesitancy, he approached it. Then he reached up and pulled down a hand-sized green leaf, scrutinizing it with intense curiosity. He peered up at the winding branches above, their foliage still in the faint breeze. He scratched his beard for a while and continued to stare as if it, too, were a puzzle he needed to solve. Then, with a look of resignation, he glanced around once more before giving a shrug and turning back toward his home.

He had only taken a few steps when a metallic clank resounded from inside the stable. It was too loud to ignore, and he halted in his tracks again. Slowly, he turned a suspicious eye toward the broad entrance. Then he spun around and marched off toward it at a good clip.

Megan stiffened. If he made it to the door, they would be discovered, and far more than a simple horse theft might be at risk. If he were to tell the authorities of their presence. ... In a panic, she reached out to sway another large branch, but in her alarmed state, her movements weren't restrained enough. There was a whoosh of wind, and the limb shook with wild and unnatural movements. Then it broke off with a loud crack and plummeted to the ground, landing with a heavy thud right behind the rancher.

Megan startled and gasped.

The man spun around, and his gaze shot over to her.

She froze. How could he not be suspicious of a strange Elorian-looking woman crouched down and peeking around his tree? But it was too late to hide now.

His angry eyes locked on to her, and an expression of deep skepticism filled his face. Then he took off straight toward her.

Megan hesitated. She pulled back behind the tree, then peeked out again, then pulled back, then peeked out again.

The furious man was still charging toward her.

She reached out again and shook another branch with a rush of wind.

He halted and peered up at the tree, then over at her as she waved an extended arm. Several more times, his glance shot back and forth between her and the tree. He had solved the puzzle. A taut, angry expression filled his face, and he stormed toward her once again.

Behind the man, Megan caught Aylun peeking out of the stable. She wanted to wave to him, or yell for help, or run away, but the rancher was between them. Aylun stared for a moment at the man marching toward her with the sword in his hand. Then, in the blink of an eye, he vanished from the entrance.

Megan froze. Was he really going to leave her to face this armed and infuriated stranger alone? What was she supposed to do now?

With a tremendous clatter, Aylun burst from the stable, thundering into the yard on Juzhi's back.

The man spun around to face him and raised his sword.

With adrenaline-fueled haste, Megan reached out and shook another low-hanging branch, desperate to get the man's attention. But the branch bent down farther than expected right as Juzhi leaped over the fallen limb on the ground.

Aylun's eyes went wide as his steed propelled him into the branch. It hit him full in the stomach and scraped him off like a spatula scraping a pancake off a hot griddle. He plunged to the ground, landing on his back with a deep *oomph*. Juzhi came down from his leap with a round of thumping hooves as his former rider lay sprawled out among the branches of the fallen limb, wheezing and gasping for breath.

His face twisted in rage, the rancher raised his sword high over-head. It glinted in the glaring noon sun as he charged Aylun.

Megan stood, then squatted, then stood again. Beyond flustered, she spun in a circle and muttered, "What do I do? What do I do?" Her mind raced.

Then it hit her. She reached out toward Aylun with her palm cupped and facing up. The air whirled around her as she scooped him from the ground. She lifted him up and floated him away just as the rancher's silvery sword whooshed through the air where he'd been lying.

The rancher chased Aylun, leaping and swinging his weapon like a wild man while Megan lifted him higher and farther away. With Aylun now well out of reach, the furious man continued to spin and jump, his sword shining in the bright sunlight as he whipped it around. Megan reversed direction, looping Aylun around and floating him across the yard toward the road.

Now recovered from his fall, Aylun glanced down. A look of astonishment filled his face as he spotted the rancher lunging for him from below.

Suddenly, the scruffy man halted and his gaze shot down. He peered right at Megan.

Uh-oh.

A look of alarm spread across Aylun's face.

The rancher looked back up at Aylun, then back down at Megan. When he looked up again, Aylun smiled at him, then pretended to swim through the air.

At the sight, a shred of confusion and doubt appeared on the rancher's scraggly face, as if considering the possibility that Aylun might be propelling himself through the heavens.

With another tremendous clatter, Yaomey flew out of the stable on horseback, leading a stolen horse decked out with a blanket, saddle, bit, and bridle.

AYLUN

The rancher glanced behind him and froze at the sight of Yaomey leading his red-spotted mare across the yard.

Relief spread as Megan realized Yaomey might just distract the man from her and Aylun.

Now fuming, the rancher spun around, held his sword high, and roared as he faced Yaomey. Relief turned to panic. Yaomey was racing toward an armed and heavily muscled man who was screaming at her in anger.

With lightning-fast movements, Aylun grabbed his coin pouch and tried to yank it open. Too quick for his own good, he fumbled, and it fell from his hands. His arm, a blur, shot out and snatched it by its drawstring midair. He yanked it back and jerked it open. He reached inside to produce a handful of coins, then tossed them at the rancher.

The man startled and winced as sparkling coinage pummeled his scalp. He halted and glanced back over his shoulder at Aylun, still floating in the air.

Aylun smiled and pointed to the coin-strewn ground.

The rancher glanced down at the shining pieces of silver scattered at his feet, then over at Yaomey, racing at him with his stolen horse in tow. He looked down at the coins, then up at Yaomey again. Then he let out a loud grumble and dove down, snatching coins from the dirt.

As Yaomey thundered past, the man glanced up at her again, seeming torn. When she reached Juzhi, she scooped up his reins, and the three bolted away, headed for the road.

The man looked up again, seeming more torn than before.

Aylun yanked an even larger handful of coins from the purse.

The rancher winced again as a new rain of glittering metal pelted his scalp. Then his gaze shot back and forth between the coins and Megan as she ran out to Yaomey and floated Aylun down to the ground next to them.

The rancher let out one last loud and frustrated groan, then lunged down, snatching coins from the dirt and grass at a furious pace.

Aylun launched himself onto the back of Juzhi. He reached down and seized Megan's hand, then yanked her from the ground as if she were a rag doll. He flung her up onto the back of the new horse, and the three spun and galloped away while the rancher continued to gather coins.

Hooves pounded the hard-packed road as Megan barely hung on. The beast heaved and rolled beneath her, threatening to launch her to the ground any moment as the three raced away. She shot fleeting glances behind them as the rancher and then the ranch itself grew smaller, then disappeared.

They reached a fork in the road and barreled down the left branch. As soon as that intersection had also vanished behind them, they galloped off the road a distance and dismounted onto the lush green grass.

The three horse thieves faced one another. There was a distinct note of tension in the air.

Still mortified by her panicky performance, Megan shrank away from their gaze as if by becoming smaller, she might shield herself from any coming rebuke.

Yaomey glared at Aylun, and though it was obvious she was restraining herself, her words came out short and biting. "What in the *heck* was that?"

Aylun tried hard not to chuckle in the face of her ire, but eventually, he couldn't hold back. Even as he laughed, he managed to get in a few words. "That was ... the worst ... horse theft ... *in history.*"

Megan's apprehension faded, and she began to giggle, yet her words remained defensive. "Hey! I had to do something."

"You mean, do something like this?" Aylun flailed his arms over his head and spun in a circle as he squealed, "What do I do? What do I do?" in an exaggeratedly high female voice.

Indignant and on the verge of laughter at the same time, Megan planted her fists on her hips. "That's how I think."

"Yeah, but all you could come up with was to dismember his tree and float me over his head?"

She let out an unrestrained laugh. "It worked, didn't it?" She pointed. "And you were the one pretending to swim through the air."

At her words, Yaomey's stern expression cracked, and her snickering wouldn't be held back. "You did look pretty stupid." She mimicked his swimming, complete with holding her nose, then broke into laughter. "You should have seen your face. And that poor rancher." She imitated the man scratching his beard in puzzlement.

After a moment, the laughter subsided, and Megan looked up at the new horse, white with reddish spots and, of all things, a ginger mane. "Ooh, red." She reached out to touch the steed's fiery tresses.

Aylun smirked. "When I saw her, I thought of you."

Megan smiled at her gorgeous new steed, then sidled up to her, petting her smooth red-dotted shoulder with long affectionate strokes. "Is she mine?"

He nodded.

She took several steps back and admired her new horse as a strange sense of wonder filled her at owning such a magnificent animal. "I'm going to name her Yuki." She waved her hand, signaling the horse to come. "Here, Yuki, Yuki, Yuki."

Aylun rolled his eyes. "You *just* gave her the name." He suppressed a laugh. "And she is not a dog. She will not come when called."

Megan yanked a handful of grass from a nearby tuft, then thrust her offering toward the red-maned equine. "Here, girl," she chirped.

Yuki strolled over and, with her huge teeth and lips, snatched the tender shoots from Megan's hand. The beast stood for a moment munching on them in contentment.

Aylun smiled. "You cheated."

Megan beamed. "You mean, I'm smart."

As if Aylun had come to his senses, his demeanor reverted, and all his joviality vanished. His face took on its usual joyless countenance and his voice its customary solemn tone. "My hope would be that the stable owner back there would not want to risk the coin. If we are arrested and tell the authorities we gave him compensation, he would be forced to return it or drop any claim we stole the horse. I gave him enough that most would be tempted to keep the money and remain quiet about the whole affair, but we cannot know for certain that he will not come after us or alert local patrols. We must keep moving."

The mood having turned somber, all three mounted. This time as they set off, Megan looked down, smiled, and patted her spanking new horse. In an animated voice she called out, "Let's go, Yuki."

It was early afternoon, and she was already beyond tired from the long day's ride, not to mention spent from the tumultuous encounter with the rancher. Yet, as they plodded across the grassy expanse to ride parallel to the road once again, Megan felt more exhilarated than she had since the day she had fallen into this world. How could she not be? Having a horse of her own wasn't just an exciting new experience, nor did it just mean she was free of Aylun's constant and intrusive presence in her personal space. It had a much more profound meaning: It meant she wasn't dependent on him or anyone else to get around. She had become just a sliver more free—one step closer to going where she wanted to go, when she wanted to go there.

The rest of the afternoon, Megan kept an eye on the ever-changing surroundings while the sun crawled through the sky. Their pace seemed to have increased, no doubt owing to Juzhi moving faster now that he was no longer burdened with two riders. Another pair of towns drifted by, then the dirt path became a cobblestone road. Stone homes, at first sparse, began to appear more often, their large tower-like chimneys poking up far above their roofs, like tiny monuments rising to meet the blue heavens.

Each new town seemed larger than the last, and with the change, the number of travelers on the road increased. Aylun began eyeing them with a distinct look of concern as he shifted restlessly in his saddle. After a while, he gave voice to his discomfort: "I think what we're doing might be a bit too obvious. If we stay parallel to the road like this, it's going to seem like we're only doing it to avoid encounters." Then he set a new course, one that was a slight zigzag. He would angle just a little away from the road until travelers had vanished in the distance. Then he would turn a tiny bit toward it and head back again until he could almost make out their faces. He seemed to think this made them less conspicuous since they were always heading away from or approaching the road rather than keeping a deliberate distance.

Near sundown, sojourners became even more abundant. They stood out against the glowing orange skyline, their outlines dark as they strolled on foot, pulled carts, or rode on horseback. As Aylun led them closer to the road again, they became more visible than mere silhouettes. Costumed in plain tunics and light-colored robes, they trudged along with bundles and bags of goods slung on their backs. Even though it was a sight unlike any Megan was accustomed to, it was not the strangeness of it that made her marvel. Just the opposite: here, on a world so foreign to her own, people were still people. Tired from a long day's work, they were struggling home, returning to friends and family, to the places they belonged.

It had taken being sent to a different world and separated from him, but it was clear now more than ever: With Jon was where she belonged. He was her home. She looked over at Aylun. Despite the length of the day and lateness of the hour, he sat tall and alert in the saddle. He had been so passionate and forceful in his proclamation the night before, and she had scoffed at him. Yet here he was, appearing to be quite serious in striving to follow through on his vow. It was difficult not to let it nurture the seed of hope that he might bring her and Jon back together after all, that he might return her to where she belonged.

As the last sliver of the sun disappeared over the distant horizon, all travelers on the road vanished. Aylun explained that most were loath to travel at night, and the rest would carry lamps or torches, which the trio could spot from quite a distance, allowing them to be avoided with ease. So, he led them back to the road where the group carried on in weary silence as their horses clomped along the stone surface.

With the lack of chatter, Megan's attention returned to oracles and councils and her current conundrum. It was this prophecy nonsense that was keeping her and Jon apart. Yet the whole concept seemed absurd, no matter how much Aylun and Yaomey insisted it was real or how many people believed in it. If she was to stand a chance of proving this prophecy wrong, she needed to understand it and this whole oracle business. Yet all she had now were assumptions, and too many of them didn't seem to fit together.

Even if the prophecy was not about Jon or her, it didn't quite make sense. Becoming a great leader, bringing people into a new age—these were things that only came about through great effort and sacrifice. Why would a stranger care enough to go through that for a people they didn't know? And if this Otherworlder was to learn that they were destined to be that great leader, why would they feel compelled to strive so hard for something they knew to be inevitable? They would see no reason to make the sacrifices it took to become a great leader. The knowledge of their fate would forestall the very blood, sweat, and tears that made it possible.

And that didn't apply to just this prophecy either. Unless there was more to it, the concept seemed unreasonable. If you could predict the future, then couldn't you just avoid anything bad that might happen? If you knew you were destined to go swimming and drown today, you could just stay home and never leave your house—in which case, your vision of the future would have altered events, invalidating the very fate you saw.

It was like the observer effect in physics, where it was impossible to observe a thing without changing it. Prophecies only made sense if the future couldn't be changed, but that seemed absurd. What could force you to go for a swim that you knew was going to kill you?

There were far too many ways in which the whole concept seemed self-contradictory and improbable. There were too many questions to be answered, and they kept pestering Megan as the light of dusk grew dimmer. As night was settling in, Aylun led them to a spot well off the road, where they set up camp a short distance outside the small village of Vadia. He selected a sheltered area in the corner of a field behind a short rock wall. They made camp amid several large gray and brown boulders. They and the wall sheltered them from view but did little to hide their horses. A fire would draw unwanted notice, so they ate an all-too-meager meal in the dark, in exhausted silence.

After agreeing that Yaomey would take the first watch and he the second, Aylun settled on his blanket for the night's sleep. Yaomey sat next to him, perched on one of the taller boulders, which afforded her a clear view in every direction.

Beyond tired, Megan's mind was still filled with troubling questions that would not stop pestering her, so she sat on a smaller rock next to the wall. With her arms lying along its top and her chin resting on her folded hands, she stared at the lights of the village some distance away. Its dirt streets were lined with clay-and-stone buildings, and the dark windows and empty lanes now lay in silence.

Before long, fireflies began to drift up from the fields. They were a wondrous sight, unlike any she had ever seen. As if the different colors were somehow coordinating, they formed swirls of amber, fuchsia, and emerald that enveloped their camp in ever-changing pinwheels of light. After a while, she decided there was only one way to bring clarity to the confusion of thoughts that were keeping her awake.

Megan glanced over at Yaomey. "I don't get it. Why is the council after Jon and me?"

With the moon bathing her face in its soft light, Yaomey sat cross-legged on the boulder, scanning the dark horizon. At the question, she peered over at Megan. "What?"

Megan turned to face her. "The future is the future. So what if they capture us? It won't stop the future."

Yaomey gave a thoughtful nod. "Perhaps, but your basic assertion is wrong."

"In what way?"

"There is no single definitive future."

Megan boggled. "Huh? If there is no definitive future, then what is there to predict?"

Reclining on his blanket with his eyes closed, Aylun responded in a bored monotone. "The future is an ever-branching tr—"

"Aylun ..." Yaomey glared at him.

He looked up at her.

"Do not mindlessly spout Augury adages and expect her to understand. Explain it properly." She returned to her vigil, surveying their surroundings.

Aylun looked over at Megan and gave a weary sigh, but when he spoke, his voice had the patient and careful manner of an experienced instructor doling out well-practiced pearls of wisdom.

"Without oracles, what you say would be true. There would be only one future. And in fact, weak and untrained oracles can only see one course of events. They see a single thread of what is to come. But with proper technique and focus, they can learn through meditation to explore alternate choices, to reveal other branches the future may take. Once revealed, those branches become a permanent part of what they see. It is this knowledge of choices and consequences that allows them to understand and change events."

A bit taken aback by the lucidity of his explanation, Megan eyed him. "That's a bit of a paradox, isn't it? The future only changes because you can see how to change it?"

"Not really. It is a natural consequence, is it not?"

She considered for a while. "Okay, but what good is it anyway, to see a future that might change?"

Aylun shrugged. "It is neither good nor bad. It simply is."

He watched her, seeming to think, while she strolled over to her plush bedroll and lay near him. She set her head down and stared up at the whirling lights of the fireflies before an almost-full moon in a star-filled sky.

AYLUN

Aylun rested his head back on his bedroll and gazed at the heavens with her as he continued his explanation. "Oracles cannot actually see a future that can never be. They can only see futures that are possible. The most powerful describe it as an ever-branching tree. They say each branch represents a change in the course of events that would result from a choice someone could make if given the right impetus."

Megan puzzled. "Huh? Every minute of every day, we make choices. How could you possibly see all those branches?"

Aylun paused for a moment, seeming to contemplate the question. "Most choices are not life changing. For example, suppose I had gotten you the black stallion instead of the spotted mare. I doubt it would have altered the course of your life."

The notion alarmed her. "Hey." Megan propped herself up on her elbows and stared at him. "You can't go changing Yuki like that. She likes her red mane and spots. To her, they are life changing."

His patient-instructor facade melted into an expression of utter confusion. Aylun opened his mouth to respond but then halted. His brow creased, and he gave a quick and bemused shake of his head, then paused as if in thought. He tilted his head. "So the fact that she's female is not life changing?"

Megan grinned and waved off his statement with a flick of her wrist. "Oh, well, that goes without saying."

The conversation went silent for a while before Aylun resumed. "Anyway, decisions that are life changing tend to be made by a person's character. They are free to make other choices but never would."

Megan's brow furrowed. "I don't see how."

"What about you? When you came out of Islong's lair, if you knew what I was going to do, would you have asked for help anyway?"

The mention angered her, and her reaction was sharp and instantaneous. "Are you kidding me? Of course not."

"Really?" He peered at her with a skeptical look. "You would have left Jon alone and frightened in a dragon's lair and not even tried?"

"No, no. That's ... that's not what I meant."

"You were terrified for your friend. The way you looked, I think you would have tried anything at all to save him, even knowing what would happen."

Megan pondered for a while. "I suppose that's true. I mean, what choice did I have?"

"Exactly." He gave an approving nod.

She set her head back down, and they both remained silent for a time as she watched fireflies drifting through the dark and starry sky. While the concept of seeing multiple possible futures did explain how a prophecy might not be self-defeating, the notion still seemed off, as if there were untold problems with the very concept. She rolled the framework he had described around in her head until she found a clear question to which she could give voice. "Okay, but it makes no sense. What you described earlier is sheer chaos."

Aylun opened his eyes and glanced at her. "I never described anything of the kind."

"But you did. All those oracles changing the future all the time. If it's constantly changing, there is no stable future to predict."

"That is purely a figment of your imagination."

She rolled her eyes. Was the man deliberately trying to be unhelpful? What had happened to the patient instructor of moments before? Megan folded her arms and huffed.

Aylun must have heard her reaction because he sighed. "There are rules ... natural laws that govern prophecy and prevent complete chaos. Besides, the whole mission of the Augury is to make sure—"

Yaomey gasped. Her gaze whipped down, and she glared. "Aylun!" she spat out, her voice as scolding as her creased brow.

Megan glanced over at her. What was that about? Had he almost revealed a secret he shouldn't have?

Aylun seemed surprised and defensive. "What? You were the one at Islong's lair talking about the Shou, and prophecy, and Other-worlders, and all kinds of Augury business right in front of her."

"Hey, I was not thinking straight. I was flustered."

Megan watched the exchange with intense interest. Perhaps they would allude to some well-guarded secret that would be the key to debunking this whole Otherworlder nonsense.

Aylun *tsked* her and shook his head. "Talking in the open about a prophecy."

"Hey, I only told her part of it." Yaomey jutted her chin out. "It was you who revealed the whole prophecy, word for word."

"We are on a mission to prove it is not about her. She will have to know at some point."

"There was no mission when you told her."

Aylun propped himself up on his elbows and glared. "Even so, my transgression does not excuse yours. You are Shou. To reveal a prophecy to one you believe to be its subject? That is not a little thing, Yaomey. You know better."

She folded her arms and stared down at him. "Hey. You were going to kill yourself, and she was in a panic for help. What was I supposed to do?"

He grumbled, "It is done now. She already knows more than she should."

"So we just tell her more?"

"Fine. From now on, I will only tell her what she could learn if she asked the right people on the street. If all she wants are a few answers, we owe her that."

"Fine." Yaomey closed her mouth and yanked her gaze away. There was a ferocity in the way she returned to her vigil, scanning the pricks of amber and fuchsia drifting above the sea of still grass. It seemed more like a reaction to Aylun's scolding than a real focus on potential threats.

Aylun lay back down and returned his attention to Megan. "Anyway, there are rules to how prophecy works that preclude complete chaos."

She huffed again. "Oh, so now I'm part of the conversation?"

He shrugged and closed his eyes. "Fine, if you did not want the answer …"

Megan squirmed. She had let their entertaining exchange distract her. "Well, no ... it's just ... I forgot what I was going to say."

Aylun sighed and turned on his side, facing away from her. "It is just as well. Get some rest."

For a moment, she lay there, the elusiveness of her unvoiced question nagging at her. Her stream of thought lingered right there, right on the tip of her tongue. If only ... "Oh, I remember. Are there a lot of oracles or just a few?"

He rolled onto his back again and turned his head, eyeing her with a solemn expression. "We need to rest."

"Now, when the conversation was just getting interesting?"

His calm words were slow and deliberate. "I do not exist for your amusement."

Megan scowled back. "I know. You exist to abduct people, so you can be rude to them."

His solemn expression never faltered or soured. "Expect it. From here on, I intend to be a thorn in your side."

She pointed at him and smiled. "Hey, you admitted it. No taking it back."

Aylun shook his head and again rolled back over to face away from her. "Go to sleep, Megan."

She stared in shock. The name had come from his lips with surprising correctness and clarity. "Oh, you used my actual name. I'm so honored."

His voice remained matter-of-fact, as it often was, but this time there was an uncharacteristic note of concern. "We have a long way to go tomorrow, and we must rise early again. Go to sleep."

Megan considered further pursuing her questions, but he had offered information with a minimum of his usual acerbic attitude. His approach to her seemed to be softening some. Perhaps it would serve her better to nurture the change, regardless of how repulsive the notion might be that he was becoming more friendly toward her. She laid her head back down and stared again at the swirling firefly lights wafting across the grassy expanse beyond scattered boulders. She focused on them, trying to give her mind time to process the new information. Tomorrow would be another day and another chance to find more answers.

Chapter Eight

EYES IN THE MOONLIGHT

Aylun awakened to his name being whispered. He smiled as his eyes crept open to see Yaolin's form crouched over him, nudging his shoulder. Her face was questioning, waiting for some sign that he had awakened. It was so familiar, and yet … A sudden sadness cut through him, and his eyes flew wider; it wasn't Yaolin at all, but Yaomey.

He strived to put on a more impassive demeanor as he rose and dragged himself up to the stony perch she had occupied on a large flat-topped boulder. He steadied himself and gave a muted sniffle. Then he stretched and raised his head to the almost full moon hanging in the sky. It was the darkest part of the night. Yet the pinpricks of starlight and soft glow of the white orb looking down from above were a comforting reminder that the darkness was not complete. No matter how wretched he might feel, at least he was not back in that horrible land of darkness and death. At least he was not in the Dead of Night.

He glanced down at Megan's sleeping form. Not wishing to awaken her, he drew several slow, silent breaths as he peered out across the darkened plains. His eyes stung, and his head was foggy, but he pushed through his sleep-deprived state to remain alert. It was time for his watch, and they were far from out of danger.

The sadness that had saturated his awakening seemed determined not to abate. It brought back memories of his sister, Ayrue, and Megan's innocent question the day before. Ayrue loved to travel. Each mission was an adventure to her. She would read and study maps of each place before embarking on a mission, and she was sharp too. She

183

could remember the name and location of every road, stream, village, and town, no matter how small. Her mood had been jovial to the point of annoying as they entered Talus along the Eastern Trail.

He could recall with the clarity of yesterday his offhand remark that she needed to take the mission "more seriously."

She pouted and grumbled, "You mean be more grumpy, like you?"

"It is called being serious minded," he shot back.

"No, it is called not showing any faith in me."

He scoffed.

She graced him with a smile full of exaggerated sweetness. "What if I prove I am better prepared than you?"

"In what way are *you* better prepared?"

"Name the next three cities along this road."

He had fallen into her trap, but he couldn't admit it. "Um, Krosia—"

An accusatory finger shot out at him. "See, you don't even know the next village is Dulfi."

He rolled his eyes. "How am I supposed to remember the name of every backwater town in Talus?"

She frowned. "There are no backwater towns, Dulfi-for-brains. To the people who live there, every stone and piece of wood is precious."

He huffed, but she never let it drop, teasing him the rest of the trip, calling him "Dulfi dunder head," "dumb as Dulfi," and a variety of other not-all-that-inventive names all the way to the Dead of Night.

He could picture every detail of her smiling face. Then in a sudden burst, as it often did, the picture around that face blackened to sinister darkness. Her smile transformed into an expression of horror as her eyes locked on to him. Dark shapes swirled around her, slashing her body again and again with jagged claws. He threw himself against the mass in a feverish haze, hacking and slashing with everything he had. At the edges of his vision, sprays of light shot through the darkness. Her eyes begged him as she called out, "Elder Brother, please—"

184

AYLUN

A guttural grunt cut short her plea, and her body fell. Dark forms descended upon it, enveloping it in a flurry of claws and teeth. Panic took away all thought and reason. Time seemed interminable as her cries of agony kept coming and coming. Then, all at once, she fell silent. It seemed like an eternity before he had decimated the last of the shadowy things. When he finally reached his sister, what was left of her was so bloody and shredded it was barely recognizable as human.

He retched as he noticed she was still breathing. His mind refused to accept it. Plans and schemes whirled through his head. He had to get her to safety and ... and ... Then the mass below him shuddered and he knew his dear, sweet sister was suffering. She would never survive this. No one could survive this. He let out a wail of anguish as he jabbed his blade through what seemed like the left side of her chest and all movement stopped.

In a flash, he was back in the moonlit campsite. Every muscle in his body suddenly clenched, and he shook as he strove to banish the memory. He looked back down, and Yaomey's questioning gaze had transformed into an ever-deepening look of concern. With well-practiced effort, he pushed back the painful memories and forced his body to relax. He was needed here and now. There were vows to fulfill. He hadn't time to let the ghosts of his past drag him back down into that blood-filled pit of despair.

A peaceful stillness pervaded the night, seeming to soothe his turmoil as below him Yaomey settled herself in for a short rest. A calming sense of purposefulness took root as he sat and scanned the horizon, alert to anything moving in that dark expanse. The constant attentiveness required for his watch left little room to dwell on his discomfort. So he remained vigilant as the moon slid lower in the sky, the night air cooled, and the fireflies dwindled until they'd all but vanished. And for a brief time, all that filled his thoughts were the sights and sounds of the plains below a cloudless sky.

The dawn remained some time off, and he was focused toward the east, where the protector might approach, when a sparkling pinpoint of yellow flashed far off in the grass. It appeared and vanished in an instant, leaving him wondering, Were his eyes playing tricks on him? Was it a mere illusion of shadow and light, or perhaps the moonlight reflected off a drop of dew?

His suspicions strengthened when it didn't reappear, so he resumed his scan of the fields and village while keeping a watchful eye for the return of any phantom lights. The air had cooled, helping stave off his sleepiness as he surveyed the dirt street of Vadia, now as still and dark as the night. He was turning his head away when he caught the pinprick of yellow again out of the corner of his eye. Without moving his head, he shifted his gaze to the east, watching and waiting for its return. Aware that his motionless state might give him away, he released his tension and resumed scanning as he kept an even more wary eye to the east.

As time passed with no return and more chances to consider the possibilities, he had almost written it off as a few straggling fireflies when something new caught his eye. To the east again, but much closer than before, a dark shape ... no, *two* dark shapes were moving through the grass with effortless stealth. He focused on them, and they froze as if aware of his interest. They remained still for a long time, seeming to disappear into the dark grass. Then, in tandem, a pair of roundish shapes rose out of the grass. Two sets of yellow dots flashed out from them. They gave every impression of two sets of eyes reflecting the moon over his shoulder.

As he stared, a dark hopelessness filled him. It was not the kind that had accompanied him since the Dead of Night. No, there was something worse in the feeling, a morbid dread that made him sick in his soul. He shivered and averted his gaze. Perhaps he was merely letting the ghosts of Yaolin's death run away with his imagination. No doubt the yellow dots belonged to a pair of wolves or coyotes or even stray dogs. He returned his gaze to the dark shapes, but they were moving off.

It took a moment before it sank in. The far distant sound of hooves against cobblestone had been growing louder for some time, and he had been too preoccupied to give it his attention. His gaze spun around to a torch-bearing rider racing down the Eastern Trail toward town. There were few reasons why someone might gallop down a remote road in the middle of the night, and almost none of them would spell good news for Megan or her goal.

Without a sound, Aylun slid from the rough boulder and bounded over the rock wall. With a watchful eye for the rider's attention to turn in his direction, he kept low and raced across the open field to the edge of town. Hidden in shadow, he crept up behind a squat home built of heavy brown stones. He peered around the corner at what appeared to be a woman on horseback barreling into Vadia.

The clomping of hooves halted, and the rider launched herself from the back of her brown horse. She turned away from Aylun and raced up to the first home on the street. The pounding of her fist on the heavy wooden door echoed down the deserted streets. After a long delay, a disheveled and droopy-eyed man opened the door a crack. Aylun strained to catch their hurried conversation, but the voices were too low.

The rider turned around, and Aylun yanked himself back around the corner. This was futile. Someone was going door to door, inquiring about something. He paused for a moment. Perhaps it mattered little what their concern was. Any interest at all, any search, any lookout for anything was bound to make remaining unnoticed more difficult. He peeked around the corner again and waited as the rider marched down the street. As soon as she eyed the next door and her gaze was away from him, Aylun stooped low and sprinted back across the field to their camp.

He vaulted the stone wall and landed near Yaomey with a deliberate thud intended to jar her awake. His breathing remained heavy as Yaomey's eyes popped open and Megan stirred from her sleep. He pulled his gaze from the village and glanced back at Megan as she propped herself up on her elbows and squinted at him through the darkness.

Yaomey began to rise. Aylun motioned to them both to keep low, then returned his attention to the village. The streets were still silent and dark, save for the lone torch of the rider and her shoes thumping against the stone walkway as she strode to the next door.

He looked back at the two puzzled women and whispered, "We should leave. There's something going on. I heard a rider come into town. I went to investigate, and she appears to be going house to house."

Megan lurched to her feet but remained crouched below the wall. "Looking for us?"

"I did not ask. It does not—" The pounding stopped, and the faint sound of voices carried across the fields. He peered back over the wall, remaining still as he strained to catch even a word or two. He pulled back below the wall. Eavesdropping was turning out to be a futile waste of precious time. Aylun spun around and began to scoop up his belongings. "It does not really matter. Whatever their business, it is dangerous for us to be seen. We are leaving. Now."

Striving to remain as silent as possible, they packed up and readied their mounts. At every stir of the horses or clank of metal, Aylun turned a watchful eye to the intruder, but whoever it was remained oblivious to their presence. In the cold and dark of predawn, they set off, trying to stay out of the rider's view as much as possible. As they left, Aylun kept one eye on the road ahead while making frequent checks behind them, watching the town and their former campsite.

The stars shone in a swath above the sleepy homes as the rider carried her torch farther down the street. Its light flickered across the fields, lending faint illumination to a pair of dark shapes creeping into their now-abandoned camp.

Even with their noses to the ground, scouring the area, they were taller than the tallest boulders in the camp, making their size extraordinary for even the largest of dogs. They lingered for a while, milling in the darkness, then raised their heads, and their yellow eyes flashed in the moonlight, staring straight at Aylun. They looked away.

The torch and rider moved down the street, and the dark shapes disappeared into shadow.

As they sped farther away, the sounds from the village became muted, falling below the croaking of frogs and droning of insects. Lights appeared in a few windows, then became distant until they vanished in the darkness. Afraid of encountering more riders, Aylun once again led his charges in a lazy zigzag. He kept an eye out behind them for the dark shapes he had spotted earlier but kept his glances brief so as not to alert them to a concern that might be unfounded. The horses thudded across the dark grassy expanse, the moonlight guiding his way while the glowing white orb drifted ever lower in the sky.

Indistinct pinpricks of amber light eventually appeared on the road, and as they grew closer, they became lanterns and torches hanging from carts or held in the hands of half-awake travelers.

It was still dark out when they passed another town stirring from its slumber. Smoke billowed from several large chimneys, and signs of activity appeared in a few of the lighted windows.

After a while, as dawn was upon them, Aylun's glances turned into staring behind him, scanning the broad, flat plains, now lit by the faint orange glow of the skyline.

Apparently, his interest had become too obvious to be mistaken as simple vigilance, because Yaomey pulled up next to him and asked, "What is it?"

He continued to stare as he spoke. "I do not know. Last night there was something in the grass to the east of our camp. All I could see were what looked like two pairs of yellow eyes reflecting the moonlight. They seemed to be watching us from a distance."

Yaomey puzzled for a moment. "Yellow eyes ... Could they be coyotes or wolves? Or perhaps simply a pair of stray dogs?"

"They were larger than a wolf or a coyote, or even the largest of dogs. And their actions did not seem random. After we left, they entered our camp."

"Perhaps checking for any scraps of food we left behind?"

"Perhaps." Aylun nodded, then waited for some kind of comment from Megan, but she seemed unconcerned. In fact, she still seemed half-asleep, so he let it drop. Things stayed quiet for a long while as the light of dawn grew brighter and the sun began to peek up over the horizon.

At the farthest point of one of his zigzags, he turned his head to check behind him and caught a fleeting glimpse of movement. It was not where he looked but far out to the south, away from the road. Details were impossible to see at this distance. All he could make out was some kind of bloodred form leaping over something. Two more followed, almost together, and even though they were just shapes on the horizon, there was an unmistakable familiarity in the effortless stealth of their movement.

Aylun sat taller in the saddle. "There they are again. Only I think there are three now." Then the implication of their position and direction struck home. "I swear they are flanking us. And from the glimpses I just caught, they are huge and dark red, I think."

Yaomey followed his gaze to the south. "They could still be strays, merely looking for whatever scraps we might leave behind."

"Perhaps, but what animal tracks you for this long, over such a great distance, for a few leftover crumbs? And they are stealthy and big. Why stalk three people? Why not hunt small animals?"

Megan chimed in, "Could we do something to throw them off our trail?"

Aylun twisted around in the saddle. "The watchtower. The one outside Egina. That is where we will cross the Eastern Trail to head around the city. When we do, if they change direction and continue to follow, especially across such a well-traveled road, we will know for certain their presence is not a mere coincidence."

He returned to his scanning, this time accompanied by both Megan and Yaomey. The group remained quiet save for the sound of hooves against the grass-covered ground. This time, all three kept a watchful eye on the growing stream of travelers trudging along the Eastern Trail, as well as any movement on the southern horizon. As

AYLUN

Aylun scanned the road, an unsettled feeling grew, a sense that something was off.

It wasn't until the sun had just made its way above the horizon and the sojourners on the road were thinning out that it occurred to him. It had been the peak time for merchants and buyers to head to market, yet there were far fewer than the day before. They were riding toward Egina, the capital city of Talus. That meant they were traveling into areas of ever-increasing population, so there should be more people, not fewer.

He puzzled over this as the travelers thinned out and the sun crawled its way up above the horizon. Several more towns passed, and it was well past midmorning when the edifice came into view, a tall stone tower atop a small hill, nearly shrouded in the hazy distance. Even from this far out, it seemed massive compared to the cobblestone road that threaded around the base of the hill. It and its two companion towers to the north and south were enormous structures of stone and clay. They had been made tall enough for sentries posted at their top to spot anything approaching the city long before it arrived.

Aylun halted and pointed to the tower as he glanced back at Yaomey. "The watchtower. We cross here, circle the outskirts of Egina, and pick up the old road headed toward Katapa." Aylun stopped his lazy zigzag and paralleled the road as he waited for an opening. He kept enough distance to make out the form of each traveler, but not their faces. He pointed to a small group of people straggling down the cobblestones. "We are crossing at the busiest point in the road. We have yet to be spotted. If we want to remain so, we will have to time our crossing with care."

He shoved aside the questions of dark shapes and the dearth of merchants and focused instead on each distant traveler on the Eastern Trail. Soon only one remained, a man on foot headed toward them from Egina. As soon as he passed and his back was receding, Aylun angled toward the road, trying to make their crossing a hasty one.

Now committed to the endeavor, he kept a sharp eye on the departing traveler over his shoulder as he scanned either end of the

191

road. Before they'd even made it halfway, a rider appeared far down the path in front of them, plodding toward them from Egina, and unless they changed their course or speed, they were bound to run smack into one another.

Aylun tensed. They were a brief ride outside the military capital of the highly disciplined Talesh empire. All it would take would be one report of their presence to the wrong person and things would get very complicated. Their jaunt through the realm could devolve into a frantic race as they tried to make it to Katapa while evading a couple dozen well-armed, well-organized, and very well-trained soldiers.

He turned and peered back at Megan. She was staring at their new arrival with a look of grave concern. With a quick glance at Aylun, she spoke in a low voice. "Should we turn around?"

He shook his head. "Too late. Any sudden change in speed or direction would seem suspicious now. We don't want to appear to be avoiding people." He waved her and Yaomey on. "Follow me."

He increased their pace ever so slightly and led them through a slow, casual turn. Soon they were angled back toward the traveler headed away from them, with their faces almost hidden from the new approaching one.

As the road neared, yet another rider arrived, this one moving at a fast trot, headed for the receding traveler and on a collision course with them.

Surprised and alarmed by the pace of this latest arrival, Aylun faltered and clenched Juzhi's smooth leather reins. It was a little too tight and brought him to an unintended halt. For a few moments, the horse pranced in place, stirring restlessly as he swished his tail. Feeling nervous and embarrassed, Aylun glanced back again at his companions.

Yaomey had noticed the rider too, but Megan had her eyes fixed on him. At his unintended stop, a look of concern had spread across her face, and she brought herself up taller in the saddle. Then she noticed Yaomey's gaze, and her eyes followed it, locking on to the rider galloping down the path toward them.

AYLUN

In a soft voice, Aylun spoke over his shoulder. "Do not stare. It is suspicious." He turned his eyes ahead and urged Juzhi forward.

He led them again through another slow, gentle turn, this time in the other direction until they were headed straight toward the Eastern Trail. As the road approached, the horse became visible. It was a familiar shade of gray.

Aylun checked behind them to see if Megan had noticed the gray horse. She was trying hard to be inconspicuous, but her anxiety was apparent. With her eyes fixed on the latest arrival, she brought herself up even taller in the saddle. As she tensed, she clutched Yuki's reins, causing the mare's head to rise and her ears to prick.

Aylun looked down the road to find what had caused such an extreme reaction and the new traveler was now much more visible. It was a woman with rich brown hair in all-too-familiar brown leather armor.

Megan's worried gaze turned to Aylun. "That can't be the protector, right? That can't be Dellia?"

He hesitated as he considered the possibility. Then he shook his head. "Alone? I do not see how, but I suppose it is possible."

"What do we do? Make a break for it?"

"No—if we act strangely, it will only attract attention, and right now, we need to remain as inconspicuous as possible."

A clomping came from the cobblestones underneath as, one by one, each set of hooves crossed the road.

With a less subtle touch, Aylun turned Juzhi at an angle toward Egina, one that would partially put their backs to the brown-haired woman flying down the road toward them. He kept a careful yet subtle watch over his shoulder. As they left the Eastern Trail behind, the woman came to an abrupt halt. She appeared to greet the receding traveler, then a discussion ensued.

While she was still occupied, Aylun turned to Yaomey. "Forget subtlety. We need to get out of here."

He urged his horse forward and broke into a fast trot. Megan and Yaomey followed, and the three thudded swiftly away.

They were almost close enough to see the face of the traveler headed toward them from Egina when the leather-clad woman broke from her conversation. She eyed them for a moment, then surged to a gallop, heading straight at them.

Aylun motioned to Megan and Yaomey to remain steady. "Do not panic and give us away."

No sooner had he said it than a new group of three travelers on horseback appeared, headed down the road from the capital city.

As they came into view, the brown-haired woman brought her steed to a stop. She dallied a few moments, her dapple-gray horse prancing beneath her as she studied the two sets of riders on the road from Egina. Then she threw one last glance at them and galloped off toward the Eastern Trail and the new arrivals.

Aylun relaxed, and behind him, Yaomey breathed a sigh of relief. As they continued forward, she turned her head toward him and her voice was low. "Was that Dellia?"

Aylun puzzled for a moment. "It did look exactly like her."

Yaomey gave a thoughtful nod. "But she knows our horses. If it was her, why break off from us?"

"Agreed. It makes no sense, but we have no idea what might have happened since we last saw her." He considered for a moment longer, then drew a deep breath. "I think we must assume it is her and act with even greater caution. Right now, a direct encounter with anyone could be a disaster. It could alert authorities to our presence when we are a short ride outside Egina, and it is almost certain they are searching for us by now."

He and Yaomey returned to their quiet and intense watch, throwing frequent glances over their shoulders at the receding cobblestones. Aylun maintained their course, and the road soon grew small behind them. The woman had just engaged the second group of travelers on the road when she faded from view.

Almost at once, Aylun altered their direction, angling a little away from the city. He heaved a sigh of relief as the road, and the imminent threat of interception, faded in the distance.

He faced forward again, reminding himself that the threat was not gone, only stayed for the moment. They remained a few minutes' ride from the military capital of Talus, and every soldier had, no doubt, received orders by now to detain them if spotted. He had risen early with little sleep and kept watch half the night. Then they had traveled almost a day's journey before half the day was over. He had long ago passed the point where weariness had taken its toll, yet he could not keep his vow to protect Megan if he let his guard down now. So even as his tensions eased, he persevered, raising his bone-tired head and remaining alert and attentive as he kept a sharp eye on every speck of his surroundings.

He glanced behind him. Yaomey appeared to be in not much better shape. She wore her fatigue on every aspect of her features, while her keen gaze darted here, her attention to detail no less than his own. Megan was another matter. She remained tense and on edge as they worked their way around the city and the sun crept higher in the sky.

A field of yellow and scarlet wildflowers appeared to their left, their brightly colored faces nodding in the gentle breeze. After a while, rolling hills appeared beyond them in the distance, the first break from flat terrain in almost two days. As they drifted closer, houses came into view, dotting the slopes like specks of snow on a vibrant green lawn. It was a comforting sight, a clear landmark that provided certainty he was guiding them along the right path.

After a while, he slowed their pace, and the atmosphere began to relax. The flower-strewn field expanded into their path, and they waded into a sea of green dotted with vibrant yellow and red. The sun was nearing its peak when a depression appeared in the distance off to the left, and at its center sat a small pond as blue and clear as the crystal sky. Its shoreline was below the surrounding land and might block them from view of anyone passing by.

Aylun veered toward it and turned in the saddle. "I don't think that woman is following, and I have not seen the wolves since we crossed. Even so, it has been too long. Our horses need rest. We have to stop and water them."

They pulled up and dismounted at the edge of the reflective pool, with bright sunlight glimmering on its nearly calm surface. Dense sprays of tall grass and cattails formed clumps along one side, while large half-buried boulders were strewn along the other. The horses strolled down to where the shorter grass and bright flowers met the pond's surface. As their steeds began to drink, the three travelers each found a suitable boulder on which to rest.

Wanting nothing more than a brief respite from his endless vigil, Aylun stared at the smooth surface disrupted only by ripples from the horses' drinking. He lay down, and with the cool rock beneath him and the gentle pool beside him, the warm sun began to melt away his anxiety. They would soon need to resume their trek away from Egina, but now, protected from view, he could let his guard down for a little while.

After a time, he heard the rustle of Yaomey rising. He turned his head and opened his tired eyes to spot her as she scooted over to face Megan. "What is your gift called?"

Sprawled out on her back, Megan opened her eyes and squinted up, seeming confused by the question. "Called?"

Yaomey continued to stare down at the reclining woman. "Soon, I must report back to the Augury, and a name would be useful for my report."

Megan lifted her head a bit and froze, seeming taken aback. Then she scowled. "You're thinking of leaving?"

"I have not made any firm decision, but I am not sure going to Lanessa is the right thing for me to do."

"What?" Anger radiated from Megan's face. "The journal in Lanessa was your idea in the first place, and now you're thinking of leaving?"

"You were about to cave in Aylun's skull. The only way I could think of to stop you was to suggest the journal as a way to find the truth and fix the problem of the prophecy separating you and Jon. My being here was never necessary."

196

"Wait a minute. You agreed to help me in whatever way I chose. Now you've decided on your own to leave? What was all that talk about promises and vows? Just empty words?"

Yaomey's discomfort was apparent as she averted her gaze and looked down at the cool clear water of the shoreline. "I will abide by whatever decision you make. I promise. But I ask you to consider my father. He just lost one daughter, and it would kill him to lose another."

"That is not my problem. It was your idea to stick by whatever I decided. You should have thought of your father before you made that promise."

Yaomey bowed in deference. "I understand, but Aylun is all the help you need, and the Augury is powerful. They could stand against the council or even spread the truth. I may be able to do more for you by returning to them."

Megan lay back down and gave an almost inaudible huff. When she glanced his way, Aylun avoided her gaze. It was clear she was upset with the course of the conversation. She crossed her arms and stared up at the bright blue sky, seeming as if she wanted to vent but was holding it in.

What was just as obvious was that nobody at the Augury would care what Megan's gift was called, which meant Yaomey's question had little to do with a name. She was attempting to draw Megan out, to learn as much as she could about her and her gift. While it was annoying that she had not discussed her desire to return to the Augury with Aylun, it was a minor annoyance, and nothing she had said about leaving was incorrect.

Wanting to assist her, he caught Yaomey's eye and gave her a small knowing nod. Then he sat up and peered down at Megan. "It would still be useful to have a name. What shall we call your gift?"

Still lying on the rock with crossed arms, she opened one eye to look at him. "Call it whatever you like." She snapped it shut again.

He smiled, putting on his most affable air. "Come on. It must have a name. Where you come from, what is it called?"

This time her eyes remained closed, and her response was short and sharp. "I never had it before I came here."

"Obviously. But it must have a name for those who have it."

"There are no gifts where I come from."

Aylun leaned away in surprise. "What? No gifts? How is that possible?"

"No. It's this gift of mine that is impossible."

He remained as calm and reasonable as he could. "That makes no sense. It exists, therefore it is possible."

Megan opened her eyes and shot him an angry stare. "No, it is not."

Bemused, he shook his head and let the subject drop.

After a moment, Megan sat upright and shifted around to face him. "Look. Everyone knows that thoughts are just tiny electrical impulses inside your brain. About seventy millivolts, if I remember from my biology class. Even if such a small impulse could somehow escape your skull, how could it affect anything outside of it? It's impossible."

The barrage of unfamiliar words confused, yet he understood the gist of what she was saying. Aylun puzzled over it for a moment. "I ... do not think that is right."

Megan reacted with her typical expression of annoyance. "What do you mean, not right? I've seen brain scans. I've seen how emotions and thoughts light up different parts of the brain."

More confusing words, and this time he was far less certain what they meant, so he tried a different tack. "Then explain your gift."

She scowled, looking exasperated. "That's what I'm saying. I can't. You think I'm wrong"—she crossed her arms—"you explain it."

Aylun paused. He had run across a few theories in his travels, and most seemed incomplete, inconsistent, or preposterous. However, there was one he liked. It had been explained to him by an elderly monk in Kirwan. Tsaoshi had sent him there to thwart some dishonest negotiations. The whole thing had turned into a rather oversized fiasco, complete with side deals, theft, and bribery. There had even been an assassination attempt. But the one enduring moment he brought back was the monk's explanation of how gifts work.

He looked down, trying to recall the exact details. "In Erden, many believe in a universal consciousness. It is said to infuse every living thing, transcending the veil, binding all that is or ever will be. Perha—"

"The veil," Megan scoffed.

He waited for her rude interruption to end, then tried again. "Perhaps all gifts work through that consciousness, allowing a gifted person's thoughts to influence it and, through it, alter what we perceive as the real world."

She shook her head and muttered, "Universal consciousness ... bunch of hocus-pocus nonsense."

"How can you disparage other people's deeply held beliefs with such disdain? Is there no room in your world for universal consciousness or Adi or anything that gives life greater meaning?"

"Adi? I don't know what that is, but if you're asking if I believe in God, no, I don't. No more than I believe in psychic hotlines, pyramid power, or other superstitious nonsense."

"Nonsense?"

She laughed at him. "I believe in what I can see, what I can measure, what I can hold in my hand. The electrical impulses that make up thoughts can be measured. I believe in them, but how can I believe some made-up flight of fancy like universal consciousness?"

Fed up with her dismissive and disrespectful attitude, Aylun shot back, "Then you explain it. There has to be more to it than your trisical impluses."

Megan covered her mouth, not completely suppressing a giggle. "Trisical impluses? You sound like a two-year-old." Her face lit up. "Say it again."

Frustration welled, and several biting retorts came to mind, but he simply scowled and grumbled, "I do not exist for your amusement."

She scoffed again, then let out another mumble designed to be overheard. "Clearly, you do not understand how our relationship works."

Not wishing to continue a pointless exchange, Aylun clammed up.

She remained sitting and watched him.

Still in need of rest, he lay back down on the rough stone surface and closed his eyes. He inhaled a breath laced with the refreshing scent of lake water, trying to unwind in the few precious moments he had remaining. Why did exchanges with her always have to end up being so annoying?

Once again, he focused on the soft breeze and the cool rock against his back as he lounged in the bright sun. A fish made a delicate splashing near the shore while the song of birds and rustling of grasses soothed his jangled nerves.

He cracked one eye and peered up at Megan through his eyelashes.

She was studying him with a thoughtful expression.

He opened his eyes and stared up at her.

At his gaze, she looked away. After a moment, she inhaled a deep breath. "Okay, so neither of us can explain how my gift works. But when you told me to move the rock, you said I needed to imagine it moving and believe it would." She looked down at him. "How did you know that was going to work?"

He sat up in surprise. "You surely cannot believe I expected that to work. I was trying to prove you were delusional."

"Still, you must have made that specific suggestion for a reason."

"Why? Why do I have to have a ..." He shook his head in exasperation. "Look, it just made sense."

"Why? You mentioned other gifts. Is that how they work?"

The earnestness of her thirst for understanding banished most of his annoyance, and he considered for a moment before responding, "No. I suppose not. Not really. Dellia has the Gift of the Heart. It is described as being like another sense to her, like sight or hearing. It is always present. She always senses what you are feeling. She just has to pay attention to it. Her mother, Sirra, has the Gift of Passage. She must picture the location where she wishes to go, but she opens a portal to it by willing it to open."

Megan frowned, seeming surprised. "Huh? Then why did you tell me how to move the stone?"

He brushed it off with a wave of his hand and lay back down. "I told you. It just made sense." He took a deep breath and looked back up at the clear blue sky. "Is that not the way of all things? To accomplish anything in this world, you must first be able to imagine doing it, then believe that you can."

Megan seemed to give his response thoughtful consideration. She remained still for a long moment, then eyed Aylun. "So, what you're saying is you have no idea why you suggested it."

He gave a quick and baffled shake of his head. "I started by saying that." It was his turn to mumble, loud enough for her to hear, "Apparently, it takes three times to get through to her."

That exchange seemed to end the conversation, and he shut his eyes for a few more fleeting moments before hauling himself up off the rock. "Let's go." He held out a hand to help Megan up.

She looked at it with a mixture of disgust and apprehension, then she reached out and took it.

Yaomey rose with her, and Aylun looked over at the two. "We may have been followed, and I am uncomfortable with how close we are to the capital of Talus."

Megan and Yaomey nodded, then followed as he headed for the horses. The three mounted and rode off once again to continue their long trek, this time headed away from Egina.

Megan glanced behind her at the pond growing smaller in the distance, wishing she could have had more rest. With little sleep, little food, and a morning ride that seemed endless, all she wanted was to close her eyes for a few minutes, but Yaomey and Aylun wouldn't let her be. What was with the pestering about the name of her gift? What did it matter what it was called anyway? She sighed and faced forward again, letting Yuki carry her along.

The hills to their left faded behind them, the flowers of the field thinned out to just grass, and a cobblestone road appeared, angling off in the distance before them. Aylun informed them it was the same Eastern Trail as before, only this time leaving Egina for Katapa. They returned to following it again in the now-familiar wavering parallel.

Ahead of her, Aylun and Yaomey seemed far more alert than she felt, scanning their surroundings with an intensity that never seemed to fade. Travelers on this side of Egina appeared to be less numerous, and they thinned even more with each passing hour. The day dragged on, seeming as interminable as the long cobblestone road beside them and the vast plains around them. Three more towns passed, each smaller than the last and each given a wide berth.

The sun was nearing the horizon when they stopped again beside a small gurgling stream. Megan cooled her sore feet in the frigid water as she watched Aylun. He seemed preoccupied with a dense layer of billowy clouds that had appeared in the distance behind them, in the east. They glowed with a warm golden-orange radiance cast by the setting sun. After a short while, he turned his attention to the road ahead and urged them to press on. As Yaomey mounted, she stopped with one foot in the stirrup, her eyes fixed in the direction of the cloudy horizon behind them.

Her gaze remained steady as she finished mounting, and her voice was calm and measured. "They are back: yellow eyes. I count two ... no, three pairs, and I think they may be following us."

Aylun twisted around in the saddle and stared off in the direction Yaomey was facing. "I don't see them."

"They were there only briefly."

"Then we need to keep moving."

The interest of her abductors was somewhat difficult to comprehend. In their conflict with the protector, they seemed accustomed to fighting. Enough so that it seemed odd that three wolves would cause them so much concern. In fact, on Earth the beasts tended to keep to themselves, but, then again, these weren't acting like ordinary wolves. So her ill-ease grew, even if she wasn't quite sure what they expected these wolves to do.

With Aylun leading and Yaomey behind him, they set off again, traveling in silence. The clouds drifted in from the east, rolling across the sky until they obscured the deep blue heavens. As darkness shrouded the world, they returned to the now-vacant road. The cloud cover continued to deepen, and a breeze picked up, beginning to feel and smell like the air before a storm.

When the world around them became too dark to see, Aylun produced a palm-sized glass ball Yaomey called a flamestone. Megan couldn't keep from staring at it, fascinated by its steady, golden light. It spilled around them, lighting the cobblestones as they clomped down their endless length.

With the flamestone came an unexpected change in Aylun's demeanor. He seemed to become visibly anxious. His posture became stiff, and he began to jump at every sound. On occasion, he would even shudder when there was no sound. It was clear something was bothering him. Yaomey noticed it as well, seeming concerned with his agitation. After a while, she called out ahead to him and suggested they stop. His few words dripping with edginess, Aylun refused. So, without another word, she passed him, snatching the flamestone from his hand as she shot by. Then she continued ahead to take the lead, leaving the man to fall back in front of Megan.

She studied him as he jostled in the saddle, expecting him to calm down now that the pressure of leading no longer fell on his shoulders. Rather than his tension easing, he seemed to fixate on the glowing yellow ball now in Yaomey's hand. Over time, his anxiety continued to grow until it became palpable.

It was hard for her not to empathize. Once, her history teacher asked for an essay on the history of the printing press. She got a poor grade because instead of starting with Gutenberg's introduction of the printing press in 1450, she began with Bi Sheng's use of baked clay characters in the Song dynasty around 1040. That evening, when her father saw the low grade, he called her a show-off and a "hopeless idiot," lacking humility for bringing Chinese history into a Western history class.

When she tried to defend herself, he became red-faced and accused her of talking back. He grabbed her by the arm and flung her in the closet, where she banged her head on a heavy wood shelf. He locked the door and stormed away, leaving her scrunched down, in pain, and crying in the dark. Her fear only grew as she imagined savage beasts lurking in the dark, hungering for her. When it became too much and she began to wail, he'd stormed over and kicked and pounded the door. When she pleaded for food or water or just to go to the bathroom, he'd yelled at her to keep quiet and shouted that he wasn't going to let her out until she "settled down." It wasn't until the afternoon of the next day when she'd collapsed from fear and exhaustion that he finally unlocked the door so she could let herself out.

A part of her—the part that was still that little girl locked in the closet—cringed at the stormy darkness around her now. It still made her uneasy, as if there were ghouls and ghosts hiding in the shadows. It was creepy and unsettling, and only Yaomey's steady light helped hold her unease at bay.

As Megan watched Aylun's obvious discomfort, a seed of sympathy sprouted in that long-ago-girl's heart. It tugged at her, growing and growing until she relented and pulled up beside him. His expression was as bad as she had imagined, made even more dramatic by the dark shadows cast by Yaomey's glass ball.

It grated on her nerves to show even a shred of sympathy for the man, but then the words slipped out on their own, soft and concerned. "Are you okay?"

Aylun clutched his reins in white-knuckled hands as he remained focused on the road before him. "I will be fine."

Stuck about how to help him and not sure she even wanted to, Megan remained silent for a while; but eventually, her conscience wouldn't allow her to stay mute. She glared at him and spoke in an accusatory tone. "I asked you a question before, and you refused to answer."

He shot her an annoyed expression. "Can it wait?"

She leaned closer to him. "No. You owe me an answer. Oracles—are there only a few or many?"

Aylun shook his head. "We are being chased by something unknown. Storm clouds have come in, threatening to rain any minute. We are trying to navigate dangerous territory in the pitch-black—and the burning question that cannot wait for an answer is how many oracles there are?"

Megan sent him a smile and a firm nod. "Yes."

He started to object, then appeared to stop himself. "Wait. Are you pestering me to distract me?"

Her smile broadened, and she eyed him sideways. "That depends. Is it working?"

Through what remained of his anxiety, Aylun chuckled and said, "Yes." He forced a weak smile. "Thank you."

She feigned indignation. "Don't change the subject, just answer the question. Are there few or many?"

He gave a respectful nod. "It is rare to be born with the gift, but Elore has many people, so there are quite a few who are born with it. There are always several new recruits training in the Augury."

"Then if each of those oracles can change the future, it has to be complete chaos. I mean, how can anyone predict anything with all of them changing the future all the time?"

"I told you, that is purely a figment of your imagination."

Megan humphed. "And you telling me that does nothing to answer my question."

Aylun sighed. "Look, there is an old saying among oracles: nature abhors a paradox."

Megan scrunched up her face. "What does that mean?"

"It means the way their gift naturally works prevents them from seeing things that cannot be."

"Like, for example?"

He held up three fingers. "There are three natural laws to prophecy that prevent paradox."

"Hmm, a paradox ... like a puzzle. I like it. Okay, hit me with one."

Aylun paused as if about to object, then yielded. "First." He held up a single finger. "An oracle cannot see any event they would be compelled to change. For example, only the most enlightened oracles, the ones who have come to accept their destiny, can see their own death."

She considered his puzzle for a while. "A paradox. Two things that contradict one another ... that cannot be at the same time. Let's see ... If they could see their own death, they would be compelled to avoid it, and that would make it not happen. If their death did not happen, then there would be nothing for them to see. Right?"

"Exactly. Not bad."

Pleased with herself, Megan chirped, "More."

"Okay. Second." He held up two fingers. "An oracle also cannot see a future they are destined to act upon that another, more powerful oracle would be compelled to change."

"Oh. That's harder. Two oracles. Hmm ..." Megan mulled it over for a while, then snapped her fingers. "Oh, got it. It's like you said before. Oracles cannot see that which cannot happen. And if a more powerful oracle is compelled to make sure it doesn't happen, then there would be nothing for the less powerful oracle to see."

He smiled, then held up three fingers. "Third, an oracle cannot clearly see an event that has already been acted upon by a more powerful oracle."

She struggled for a moment, trying to reason it out. "Hmm. Already been acted upon—so, a paradox involving time. ... Oh, I get it. It's the same as the last one. The more powerful oracle would have seen the less powerful one undo it and stopped them, so it is a future that cannot happen." Megan froze for a second, then cocked her head. "Wait, you used the words 'cannot clearly see.' Does that mean they can see it, but it's ... it's ... Okay, what does that mean?"

Aylun gave an appreciative nod as if applauding her astuteness. "It means they may see some of that event or the things around it, but it is as if nature were conspiring against them. As if it were determined to prevent them from seeing enough to act upon."

"Is that only true in the third case or all of them?"

"It is always true. They may be able to see flashes or hints, but enough will remain hidden that they will be unable to make the connections needed to act upon it and create a paradox."

Megan pondered for a moment as a horse whinnied somewhere far off across the plains. "More, please."

Aylun seemed puzzled. "More what?"

"More paradoxes, these are fun."

He scowled, and his words were slow and deliberate. "I do not exist for your amusement."

She shook her head. "You know, you keep saying that, but I'm just not buying—"

Lightning flashed through the distant sky, and Aylun thrust out a palm, cutting off Megan's words. "I think we have to set this discussion aside for now. It appears that rain is coming, and we need to find shelter fast."

Yaomey looked back at him and nodded.

Having been interrupted midsentence, Megan scowled to herself. What was she doing anyway? The man had abducted her, terrorized her, and dismissed her, as if her own opinions about her life didn't matter. He had treated her like she was less than human, and here she was, trying to ease his discomfort. Then again, there had been flashes in the past day, moments when it was as if he were a different person. She shook her head. It wasn't worth even thinking about. He was a means to an end now, nothing more. So she turned her attention to Yuki and the dark world around her.

Something caught her eye, and Megan glanced down at the roadside. A pair of glowing yellow eyes peered up at her from the grass. Aylun's warning echoed in her thoughts, and she bolted upright in her saddle and gasped. He shot a glance at the pair of shining orbs and gave a derisive shake of his head. Then the face in the grass jerked over toward him, and it became clear the beady eyes were merely reflecting the glow of Yaomey's flamestone. The eyes turned away, and a small furry shape with a hairless tail waddled into the darkness. It was only some creepy nocturnal critter trying to scare the daylights out of her.

Apparently satisfied that Megan's alarm was a mere waste of time, Aylun sped up, thudding up next to Yaomey. After a brief discussion, the pace of the group sped up. At the next crossroad, Yaomey took off down the right branch and then the left while Aylun held Megan up and informed her Yaomey was seeking a sheltered spot out of the rain.

The pattern repeated, with them clattering down the road and halting at each intersecting path, walkway, or crossroad to send Yaomey scouting them out. She would hold the light aloft and wander far away, scanning by its bright glow. As the first chill raindrops streaked through the yellow light of the glowing glass ball, Yaomey returned and announced she had found the perfect place to rest.

They hurried through the ever-denser drops to a squat stone hay barn with massive dark timbers supporting a gently sloping roof of clay shingles. They entered and looked around. The walls appeared thick and solid but nonetheless showed signs of decay from lack of upkeep. They led the horses into an area with a dozen or so stalls. Beyond them lay a couple large piles of loose hay, and behind those were two banged-up old doors.

A quick exploration revealed that the doorways led to a pair of empty rooms, each with its own exit out the back. As the rain began in earnest, they fed the horses and settled them in their stalls for the night. Yaomey and Megan each chose one of the rooms and dragged hay into it to make a bed, while Aylun remained on watch in the front.

After Megan finished, she tested her makeshift bed. The hay was prickly and not much softer than a hard floor, but at least she would be dry and protected from the elements.

AYLUN

She returned to the front where Aylun warned, yet again, that food was short and had to be rationed. They partook of a minuscule meal eaten in weary silence born of the long day. It was remarkable how good the same boring meal of dry bread and nondescript jerky tasted when you were ravenous. Megan was beyond sore, and her only desire was to lie down and sleep—but as she went to retire in her hastily tossed-together bed of hay, Aylun stopped her. He motioned to Yaomey to go on ahead, and his partner walked off, disappearing in the back, leaving Megan alone with him.

He pulled her aside and stared at her with a solemn look. In the soft yellow glow of the flamestone, his face seemed much too earnest and sympathetic. Whatever he was after, she wasn't going to like it. She tensed. "What? You're scaring me."

From his pocket, he produced a dark metallic ring with a dashed line of jade around the center. He held it out to Megan. The metal was unusual, not painted or anodized, as was almost always the case when the metal of an object was dark. It was blackish yet polished and shiny, with elaborate etched patterns that crossed the seamless metal and deep green jade.

She eyed it with a touch of wonder and a dollop of suspicion. "What is it?"

Aylun appeared reluctant and pulled it away as if there were some deep and difficult meaning connected to it. Then he seemed to gather his resolve and thrust it out farther. The dark metal and polished jade shimmered in the soft light as he held it where she could grab it. "A ring. Take it. Put it on. As long as you wear it, I will be able to find you, no matter where you are."

Still harboring strong suspicions, Megan hesitated as she picked it up from his palm. As she went to slip it on, she paused, looking at it next to her finger. It was way too large, and she was about to object when it occurred to her a demonstration would be simpler and result in less contention. She slid it over her finger, and, as if the size had been an optical illusion, it now looked and felt like a perfect fit.

She held it up on her finger, examining it in the light. It was beautiful, and the ancient-artifact appearance suited her to perfection. She dropped her hand as her mood soured. "It's really not my style," she said, then turned a wary eye to Aylun. "What's wrong? Why the sudden concern about finding me?"

He looked out at the rain like a little boy reluctant to confess some mishap to an angry parent. "We made good time today. We will reach the ruins of Katapa tomorrow."

"But that's a good thing, right?"

Aylun shook his head and spoke with quiet reverence. "Only someone oblivious to the danger would think so."

Her suspicion deepened, and she took a step back. "No. What are you planning? I don't like it already."

His manner turned calm and soft. "I promised you I would bring you and Jon back together, and I will. I will go to Lanessa, and I will find the journal." Aylun shook his head. "But I cannot take you with me. It would be far too dangerous."

Anger and frustration welled within her. "Of all the …" She looked away, considering the pieces of this puzzle that didn't fit. "But why change your mind? Why now, when we're almost—"

Aylun cowered and winced as that contrite little boy returned. "I was just trying to find—"

Megan's gaze snapped back to him, and she glared as the pieces came together and the picture clarified. "Because this was your plan all along, wasn't it?"

His face turned red. "Well … not exactly."

She stiffened and began to fume. "What is it with you people? You throw around all this big talk about vows and promises, but then you casually discard them when it becomes inconvenient."

Aylun leaned toward her, his expression earnest. "I am not discarding it. I made a vow to Jon to keep you safe, and I made a promise to you to bring you back to Jon. I cannot keep either of them if you die."

210

AYLUN

Her words came out biting and brittle. "I don't buy it. Every step of this trip, you've been on edge, telling me how dangerous it is to be here, that I could be captured, tortured, or even killed if discovered. And now you think it's safer to stay here than go with you?" She crossed her arms. "I don't believe you."

Aylun pointed out into the rain and darkness, where a flash of lightning crackled across the sky. "The place we are going was the capital of Talus, the military center of the most efficient and well-trained empire Meerdon has ever known. It fell in a day. From that moment until now, those who value their lives have shunned the ruins because whatever destroyed the city comes back at night."

"Why should I believe you?"

"Why would I lie?"

Megan huffed. "You already did."

Aylun slumped and sighed. "Be reasonable, this could—"

"Be reasonable? Really? You are the most unreasonable, unscrupulous, unfeeling tyrant I have ever met, and you want me to be reasonable?"

He took another deep breath. "You are obviously upset. Perhaps we should talk about this tomorrow."

"Oh, and did I mention condescending and dismissive? Fine … what's the point? You've already made up your mind."

Too angry for words, Megan whipped around and stormed off. A flurry of feelings whirled inside her: anger, frustration, bitterness, betrayal—but the one that cut the deepest was her disappointment. Not in Aylun, because he had only behaved down to her worst expectations. No, her chagrin was directed at herself for sympathizing with him, for trying to help him, but most of all, for trusting him for even a second.

Halfway across the room, she stopped and spun back to face him. "You know, I almost felt sorry for you earlier. And the thing is, I knew better. I knew it was a waste to have even a shred of sympathy for the likes of you. Do whatever you want. I'll find a way to go to Lanessa without you."

Aylun hung his head as Megan whirled again and marched away. She stomped into her room and threw herself onto her newly made bed of hay.

Overwhelmed by anger, she let out a quiet grumble as she kicked her feet. They had lied to her and led her on. With that in mind, her decision came with remarkable ease. This was over. She had had it. If she could not count on that man, then it was pointless staying with him. As the rain poured down outside, she tossed and turned, trying to get to sleep. And she resolved that, come tomorrow, she would be done with those two and show them she didn't need or want their help.

Chapter Nine

ALL AROUND THE WATCHTOWER

Aylun swatted at the finger poking him in the shoulder. Even through closed eyelids, the warm glow from what seemed like a lantern aggravated his tired and stinging eyes. He slung his arm over them, blocking the light. The soft crunching of hay under feet barely rose above the rumble of rainfall against the clay shingles of the roof. He had taken the first watch, and Yaomey the second while he slept, which meant it was most likely her attempting to rouse him. And from the gentleness of her effort, it was no doubt just morning rather than some urgent matter that needed immediate attention.

He lifted his arm and cracked his eyes, squinting up at her face in the dim light. In a soft voice, he inquired, "It is still raining?"

She granted him a nod.

He shut his eyes again and groaned.

"I know. I know." She patted his shoulder. "I do not see how the protector could be following, but if she is, the rain will not stop her."

Aylun grumbled and braced himself against the chill morning air. With a reluctant nod, he dragged himself up to a sitting position. He brushed away the scratchy bits of hay stuck to his face and hair as he recalled his discussion with Megan of the night before.

Although he was entirely sympathetic to her feelings of betrayal, it could not be helped. He could not take her with him. And if it was a choice between suffering her outrage at being left behind and putting her in peril to placate her, the decision was obvious.

213

He glanced toward the darkness of the dusty room where she had vanished the night before. "We should let her sleep. What do you say we get the horses ready first?"

Yaomey nodded.

He rose and sleepwalked through his chores, feeding and outfitting their mounts by the soft light of the lantern set in the windowsill. As they worked in the damp and clammy stone stable, the roar of the downpour outside tapered to a trickle. The pair gathered their gear, setting aside three meager portions of dried meat and stale bread for their morning meal. The last drops of rain having fallen, they led their packed and outfitted steeds outside. In the dark and turbulent atmosphere, they squished across the rain-soaked ground to tie them to an old hitching post at the side of the squat stone building.

After returning inside, they set about eating. No sooner had they sat on the floor and parceled out the usual paltry meal than Megan trudged from the back. The timing of her arrival could only mean one thing: their rustling had already roused her, but she had chosen to sequester herself in her room, most likely to avoid interacting with him.

Eyes only half-open, she shuffled up to Yaomey and held out a hand, like a child asking for sweets.

Yaomey placed her measly portion in Megan's hands, but before anyone could say a word, she had spun around and marched off toward her room. Aylun called out to her as she left, but her only response was to scoff as she ducked through the doorway, returning to her self-imposed isolation.

With Megan in the back and unseen, Yaomey scooched closer. She threw a quick glance at Megan's room, then turned her back to it and, in a quiet voice, asked, "*Now* what did you do?"

Aylun grumbled and replied in just as quiet a voice, "How should I know?"

His words contained little conviction, and Yaomey shot him a skeptical stare.

He eyed the entrance to the room. Then, as his partner had done, he scooted up next to Yaomey and put his back to the door. In a quiet yet exasperated voice, he replied, "I tried to protect her, okay?"

"I don't see why ..." The dawn of understanding lit up Yaomey's face. "Oh. You mean the 'abduct her to protect her' kind of protection?" She crossed her arms, and her voice dripped with sarcasm. "Of course. Why would she be upset about that?"

Aylun looked out the almost closed stable door, where drops of water from the still-wet roof dribbled into dark puddles on the well-trodden ground. "Exactly."

Yaomey shook her head. "People tend not to like it when you force them to do what you deem best for them. Perhaps you should have considered that the first time you took away her ability to make her own choices." She leaned closer. "Perhaps you should reconsider now."

Aylun lowered his gaze and sighed. "I cannot. I promised her friend I would protect her. Taking her into Katapa is the opposite of protecting her."

Yaomey gave a nod of agreement before her expression turned sour. "Wait a bit here. ... If she is not going with you, then where is she going?"

"I told her"—he peered over at Yaomey and winced—"you would take care of her."

Her reply was more than a little indignant. "I see. I am to be left with the burden of ensuring her safety. Right. And at what point exactly were you planning to inform me?"

"Hey, you never consulted me before deciding to return to the Augury."

"That is different. My plan was about what *I* was going to do."

"Which would leave her with me, regardless of what *I* planned to do."

Yaomey rolled her eyes. "Well, what am I supposed to do with her? We are all the way across Talus. It will take days to get her to safety."

215

ALL AROUND THE WATCHTOWER

Aylun gave her an earnest stare. "You know as well as I do that it is foolish to take her to Lanessa with me."

Yaomey paused, seeming to calm as she considered his assertion, and when she replied, there was a note of exasperated acquiescence in her voice. "I suppose."

"And you know the Augury could use that journal to help figure out what is going on."

"That is true."

"And we need proof that she is not the Otherworlder if we want to protect her and Jon and the prophecy."

Yaomey scowled. "Yes. Okay. Fine. You win. You go alone, and she goes with me."

Aylun offered a deep bow of his head. "Thank you."

They ate in silence for a moment before he addressed her again. "Can you talk to her? Convince her that this is what is best for her?"

For a moment, Yaomey seemed reluctant. Then she huffed. "Fine," she said with a hint of exasperation.

Aylun kept eyeing her, and after a while, she seemed to get his message.

She sighed. "Right now?"

"Please."

She shook her head as she stood and started to leave, then stopped and turned back to him. "You know she does not like me all that much more than she likes you."

She spun around and marched across the room, then ducked out of sight in the back. No sooner had she disappeared than a snapping twig caught Aylun's attention.

He glanced up.

The stable door opened farther, and a silhouette appeared in the opening.

Lit from behind by the faint glow of the western horizon, a woman stood with a commanding air. Dressed in all-too-familiar leather armor, she had one hand wrapped around the hilt of her sword and the other on the pommel of her dagger. She remained motionless for a moment, her blue eyes peering down from beneath her soft brown hair.

Aylun gawked at her. "Dellia?"

Palm resting on the rough brown stones of the arched doorway, Megan peeked through, watching the seated pair. She ducked out of sight as Aylun shot a glance her way, then peeked out again to see him scoot over next to Yaomey and turn his back. Last night, she had made up her mind. She was well past the point of being tired and fed up. She was tired of the abductions and lies and fed up with these two miscreants deciding where she would go and what she would do. What they had both made crystal clear was that they planned to abandon her at the first opportunity.

Late into the night, she had tried to talk herself out of leaving them behind, repeating that she was just upset and reminding herself of all the reasons she needed them. Yet what was the point of assistance that forced her to do things she didn't want to do? In the end, all her indecision had only led to one conclusion: she would be the one to decide her own fate. And if this last day had taught her anything, it was that regaining control of her life meant getting away from Yaomey and especially from that cretin Aylun. So, while they were leading the horses outside, she had prepared her things to leave.

Now all she needed was the right opportunity, so she ate her few bites of food in haste while she strained to catch their hushed conversation. If she was going to free herself of these two, then now, when they were occupied, was the best time. Unable to make out a single word, she let out a muted huff, ducked low, and snatched her pack. The hay gave off a soft crackling as she slunk to the back door. With slow, quiet movements, she opened it, ducked lower, and slipped through.

The crisp, clean air of the morning after a storm hit her as she eased the door closed behind her. The sky had cleared in the east, where the sun was rising, while turbulent dark clouds above were still drifting off to the west. The mud was wet, and it squished underfoot as she traipsed around to the side of the building. She untied Yuki and turned to walk her away, but when she lifted her gaze, the view stopped her in her tracks.

A line of distant mountains shone brightly against the dark and gloomy horizon. Their peaks, lit white by the dawn sun, sparkled against the heavy, turbulent cloud cover. Shrouded behind a curtain of rain on the left, they wound their way across the vast horizon like a silver thread, disappearing into the distant haze on the right. Lightning flashed across their peaks as Megan renewed her slinking.

The squish of Yuki's hoof-falls in the saturated, muddy ground became buried beneath a rumble of far-off thunder as the pair snuck away. Here, far from Egina, few houses, farms, or any sign of civilization appeared on the vast expanse before her, only the decaying stable behind her. For a moment, she wondered about the presence of the lone building out here where no other signs of human life were to be found. Then it occurred to her it might be a shelter for patrols, who maintained it as a place to rest and feed their horses.

Once she was far enough from the squat stone building that the chirping of birds and buzz of insects would mask the thud of hooves, she mounted and galloped off. She guided Yuki onto the road. Lily-like flowers of vibrant orange graced both sides, their dark foliage and bright blooms dripping with rainwater as she galloped down a ribbon that disappeared in the distance. The crisp air was bracing and the view exhilarating, but neither seemed able to cut through her trepidation. Wild horses, once a novel sight, seemed more abundant now. The distant herds trotted, pranced, and reared, appearing restless in the dark and turbulent ambiance.

After a while, she slowed to a trot, but when she glanced behind her, there was Yaomey, galloping toward her. She gasped and spurred Yuki on, clattering down the overgrown cobbles. The chill air whipped through her hair, and a blur of orange blooms fled past, bright against the lush green plains beyond. Ahead, silver peaks shimmered against the storm clouds as she sped toward the dark horizon. Megan shot frequent glances behind, trying to outpace her pursuer, but Yaomey remained a constant distance.

She had hoped neither of the two would check on her until their meal was complete, giving her a good chunk of time to forge ahead. It hadn't seemed as if she had dallied that much or her pace was slow, yet here was Yaomey, catching up to her in far less time than expected.

Then it hit her, and she mumbled to herself, "What am I doing? What am I afraid of?" She slowed to a trot and waited, not looking back as hoofbeats rushed up.

Yaomey pulled up next to her and stared at Megan, looking nervous. "Do not slow down. She could be coming for us."

Confused by the reference, Megan glanced over.

Yaomey was peering down the cobblestones behind them. "That was quick thinking, getting out so fast after that protector arrived."

A flash of fear struck, and Megan boggled. "Dellia? Here?"

Yaomey sent her a peculiar look of confusion and suspicion. "But, if you didn't see—"

"Oh … yeah," she stumbled. "I … I heard someone approaching, you know, from outside. But I didn't actually see who it was."

"Oh. I see." Yaomey nodded as her suspicions seemed to drift away. "Well, I only saw her briefly, just an outline in the doorway, but Aylun called her by name. I think he recognized her."

"What do we do? She'll catch us."

"She was talking to Aylun when I left. He will find a way to delay her, but it is up to us to stay ahead of them."

Megan nodded.

Yaomey spurred her horse on. Megan followed suit, and the two raced off toward the glistening snowcapped peaks. The arrival of the protector and resulting intrusion by Yaomey had made a shambles of her plan to strike out on her own. With no idea what would happen next, all she could do was play it by ear, follow Yaomey's lead, and trust that Aylun would handle the protector.

Still seated on the cold and dirty floor with the last crumbs of his paltry meal in hand, Aylun stared up at the figure in the doorway. Light from the dim western skyline silhouetted her brown-leather-clad frame as she stood in the rough stone entry to the stable. He tensed, unsure what would happen next and uncomfortable that his seated position would place him at a severe disadvantage in any impending conflict.

Her hands still rested on her two weapons in an ominous manner, but when her voice arrived, it had an unexpected young and excited quality. "Dellia? You know Dellia?"

She stepped into the light of the lantern on the windowsill, and it became clear this woman was not Dellia. Her nose was a tad too long, her eyes a bit wider apart, and she appeared a smidgen younger. She also exuded an air of impulsiveness and unease that didn't match Dellia's self-assured manner. Still, the resemblance in every other respect was eerie, right down to her identical outfit, armaments, and hairstyle, not to mention her dapple-gray horse, visible just outside the doorway.

An enthusiastic smile graced her face as she looked down at Aylun. "She's my cousin. She is fearless and beautiful and works tirelessly to serve all of Meerdon. I always wanted to be just like her."

Flustered, Aylun could not help his slight stutter. "I—I can see that. You even have the same clothes and hair."

Her smile broadened, and she swayed back and forth, showing herself off. "You like it?"

Aylun smiled back and nodded. It was still dangerous to be discovered, especially by what was undoubtedly some kind of Talesh soldier or scout. So, for now, his safest course would be to play along. He cocked his head. "And you are ... ?"

"I'm Brita," she said, then asked again with hesitancy, "So, you know Dellia?"

Aylun paused. The connection might earn him some slight grace with the woman, considering they were relatives, and she appeared to be enamored with the protector. He nodded and smiled again. "We met on the road a few days ago."

She brightened. "Really?" Then her disposition took on a sudden somber aspect. "Then you know about the wolves?"

Caught off guard and a little alarmed, Aylun rose to his feet. "Wolves? What wolves?"

"The Blood Wolves." She pointed to the east. "Dellia discovered bodies, two travelers, killed on the plains. Last night, they attacked a man who was staying with Sirra. He killed a pair of them. Not only that, but his only weapons were a pitchfork and a wood axe. Can you believe it?"

He froze. The idea that the yellow eyes flashing in the night might belong to Blood Wolves had never crossed his mind. Even though the size and color were right, it had been decades since one had been spotted. Not to mention, they were suspected to be familiars, so it was unheard of for them to travel alone. Even without that, they never ventured more than a half day's ride from the Alundeer Mountains. To spot them near Egina was unprecedented and more than a little concerning.

Then the rest of her statement sank in, to sobering effect. It was Dellia who had encountered the wolves. She was with Jon, while, at the same time, yellow-eyed wolves had been following him and Megan. That made it a foregone conclusion there were at least two groups of Blood Wolves. The possibility that two sets of such rare beasts would happen to be following the only two people who had come out of Islong's lair was far too remote to be mere coincidence.

Then it hit him, and he stared. "Sirra? You mean Dellia's mother, Sirra?"

She nodded.

Aylun took a step back, stunned. It was another set of circumstances that was too improbable to be pure coincidence. That Dellia's mother would wind up being involved only made sense if Dellia had taken Jon to her home and the wolves had followed. And if that was the case, then the man they attacked might very well be Jon. If the wolves were attacking people, and especially if they attacked Jon, then what threat did they pose to Megan? The idea of the woman he had vowed to protect, the woman he had abducted and taken to this remotest of places, being savaged by Blood Wolves shot a wave of terror through him.

He was practiced at hiding his alarm, yet he still blurted out, "I think I saw some near Egina."

Brita was looking away and nodded, seeming oblivious to his reaction. "Me too. I was on the road, warning people that there are three more loose on the plains."

"Three?"

"That's what Commander Prian said, but I have seen more than three."

"More than three?"

Brita looked back in his eyes and gave an even more enthusiastic nod. "Yesterday, I spotted three, but this morning I saw another pair on the other side of the Eastern Trail."

"You saw them in the dark?"

"I have a sunstone." She pointed to a small net hanging from her belt. "Their eyes reflect its light in the dark."

Aylun strived to appear calm. If Brita saw Megan, it could blow everything. She could tell Dellia of their location or, at the least, report their presence to her superiors. What's more, he needed to get rid of her as soon as possible so he could confer with Megan and Yaomey. The news put a kink in their plans, one that needed to be unraveled right away. He donned his most concerned expression. "I have a companion in the back. I will warn her. But the mission you are on is far too important for me to delay you any further."

"Yes. Stay indoors." Brita backed away out the door as she spoke. "Do not travel unless you must. I saw someone headed west. I have to warn them." She waved goodbye. "Stay safe." She pivoted and swung up onto her dapple-gray horse.

As she turned the beast down the road, Aylun marched across the debris-covered stable floor to the back. He barged through the doorway, expecting to find the two women eavesdropping on his awkward exchange. A sinking feeling burrowed its way into his stomach as he surveyed the empty room.

He flew out the way he had come and around into the second back room only to find it, too, abandoned. He raced out the back door and squished through the mud around to the side of the building. All that remained was Juzhi, standing alone. He spun and stared down the road at Brita, galloping away toward the far-off, white-capped peaks.

If Megan and Yaomey were gone, there was only one possibility: they had taken the opportunity to flee Brita while he was talking to her. It was all wrong. He needed to be with Megan. He had to or he couldn't keep his vow. But he also had to stay with Brita in order to keep her from catching up with them. Unable to do both at the same time, he closed his eyes and let out a deep and frustrated groan. "Perfect, just perfect."

He launched himself onto Juzhi's back and chased after Brita. It took some time, but she eventually slowed, and he caught up.

As he pulled up alongside her, she shot him a puzzled look. "I told you to keep indoors."

"You did." He nodded to the orange-bloom-lined road before them. "But apparently, my companions decided to go on ahead and never told me. I am worried about them."

Her puzzled look deepened. "You only mentioned having one companion."

"That is true." He nodded. He had to cover his misstep, and the best cover was always the one that most closely resembled the truth. "The other is a client, a researcher, who asked us to guide her to the ruins at Katapa."

Brita's expression turned skeptical. "That is terribly dangerous."

"So we repeatedly told her, but she is stubborn and insistent."

The young woman became quieter, and her hand seemed drawn to the pommel of her dagger. Then, after a moment, her tension appeared to ease, and she inquired with a nonchalance that sounded forced, "Are you all three Elorians?"

Aylun gave a hearty laugh. "No, no. My partner is, but our client is not." It was the truth, after all. Megan was not Elorian; she only looked it.

Brita glanced down at his spotted horse. "That was you outside of Egina, wasn't it?"

He put on his most convincing puzzled expression and answered with practiced casualness, "I don't know what you mean."

"I was on the road yesterday, warning people about the Blood Wolves. I saw three travelers crossing the Eastern Trail near Egina. I tried to catch up to them, but they seemed determined to disappear on me."

He shrugged. "Could have been us. We did cross the road east of Egina yesterday."

Brita appeared to turn even more pensive. "Huh."

He squinted and peered up at the dark and cloudy skies, attempting to act casual. Brita was suspicious now, and her questions and reactions all but confirmed that she had orders to look out for three Elorians. On the one hand, Megan was unaware of her dangerous situation. On the other, it was now imperative that Brita never lay eyes on her or learn of her Elorian appearance. This would be tricky. He had to seem to be in a hurry while he did all he could to delay her.

Aylun turned to face her, regarding her with calm dispassion. "We should hurry. I doubt my partner is aware of what has been going on, and it sounds dangerous."

She flashed him a not-very-convincing smile and nodded. "Yes, it is dangerous out here. We need to catch them." She returned her focus to the long road ahead.

AYLUN

Aylun closed his eyes and sighed. This was going to be tricky, indeed.

Still bright against an ominous layer of dark rolling clouds, the sparkling mountain range appeared to have a minute crack in it. Megan squinted and stared at the overgrown stone path winding out before her. Though it vanished into the verdant panorama, it seemed as if it just might be headed for that tiny gap. She patted Yuki as if to calm her, yet the act seemed to do more to dampen her own unease. Yaomey, beside her, seemed nervous herself as she scanned their surroundings with an intensity that seemed more driven than vigilant.

As the world continued to emerge from night, the mountains loomed larger. After a long while, the dark and gloomy cloud cover began to break. Then a tower appeared out of the distance, a mere needle poking at the heavens next to the winding river of vegetation and cobbles. As they approached, it soared into the sky. What at a distance had seemed to be a minuscule crack had become a gaping chasm. It looked as if some titan had broken the mountain range in two and shoved the halves apart. And it was clear now that the road ahead led into that broad canyon framed by towering cliffs on both sides.

Across the landscape, herds of wild horses stirred and milled with an uneasy tension. No longer peaceful, they seemed apprehensive, reacting to every rumble of thunder or howl of a wolf.

A sudden bright light appeared out of nowhere to the far left of the road. It plunged from the distant clouds above the base of the mountains. They both stopped their horses and stared as a massive ball of fire plummeted from the sky, a plume of thick dark smoke trailing behind it. All turned still and silent, as if the entire plains were holding its breath, as the mass of flames hurtled toward the far-off peaks. Soon after it passed in front of them, an almost inaudible roar of fire arrived, mingled with faint sounds of screeching and pained cries. It continued, banishing the eerie silence as the fiery comet fell past the mountains and disappeared from view at the horizon.

The two stared at the place where it had vanished as Megan began a quiet count of the seconds. A moment later, a faint vibration passed beneath her feet, startling her and almost disrupting her count. As she reached twenty-two, a long low rumble echoed across the vast plains. Far-off herds pranced and whinnied, then bolted away from the sound, and as they did, barking and plaintive howls broke out all around.

Megan muttered to herself, "Just over four miles away." Spooked at the unease all around her, she turned her head to stare at Yaomey. "What was that?"

With a puzzled expression, Yaomey shook her head, and her voice reflected a mixture of fear and awe. "I have never seen anything like it in my life." After a moment, her puzzlement deepened, and she pointed to where it had fallen. "That was near the southern watchtower of Katapa." She turned her wide eyes back toward Megan. "It was at the Recluse Tower."

Megan leaned away. "Is that bad?"

"I do not know, but nothing good ever came from that place. All my instincts are telling me to flee, but we cannot go back and risk encountering the protector."

"Then what should we do?"

"I do not know." Yaomey scanned the gray and turbulent horizon. "We should seek shelter." Her eyes came to rest on the cobblestone road ahead, and she pointed to the enormous stone tower off to its side, reaching up for the cloud-scattered sky. "There. It was once the eastern watchtower of Katapa. It was abandoned along with the city when it fell, but it was built to withstand an assault, so the entrance is most likely well fortified. I think we should hole up there for a while and see what happens."

They veered toward it, with Yaomey leading the way. Jittery and uneasy, the woman surveyed their environs as if she expected the sky to fall at any moment. As they neared it, the edifice loomed tall and dark before them. They headed straight for the generous entry, jutting out some distance from the central tower.

AYLUN

As they stopped, Yaomey looked behind them, staring back down the road meandering off beneath the still-bleak cloud cover. "I do not know. I am worried about Aylun. He may need my help, and we need his. What if I leave you inside the tower entrance, and you can hide out there while I go back and get him?"

Megan peered at the dirty and decaying old tower and cringed at the prospect of being left alone inside. "You mean leave me here? Is that necessary?"

Yaomey nodded. "If the protector is with Aylun and we both go back, you could be captured."

"No, I mean, do I really have to hide inside that?" Megan pointed.

Yaomey followed her finger to the tower, then turned her gaze to stare across the plains to where the blazing mass had disappeared. "I fear it was an ominous sign. Balls of fire do not simply fall from the sky for no reason. Seeking shelter, at least for a while, would be the smart thing."

"You're being superstitious."

"I'm trying to keep you safe."

"I agree, balls of fire do not just fall from the sky, but whatever it was seemed to be screaming, which means it's alive. It had plenty of time to reach terminal velocity. Assuming its density was similar to that of a person, it would most likely be going a hundred and twenty miles per hour when it hit the ground."

Yaomey cocked her head. "Den city? ... Miles per hour?"

Megan nodded. "It would be like ... like falling off a very high cliff. No living thing could survive the impact, much less avoid being consumed by flames."

"I don't know."

"And I don't know your world, but I know a little math. Land area increases at pi times the square of the radius. There would be something like fifty square miles of land within four miles of that tower."

Yaomey shook her head. "I don't understand any of what you just said."

227

"You don't have to. Trust me, the odds of them randomly wandering close enough to see us would be like … like one in forty thousand."

Yaomey shook her head. "Okay, if you say so. But you say you can't explain it. Well, what if another one appears right above us?"

"And if wishes were fishes we'd all be as rich as kings."

Yaomey gave her a screwy look. "What is that supposed to mean?"

Megan hesitated as it all returned to her. She was tired of having her fate decided for her, of being hamstrung by the whims of these two. She had decided to set out on her own. For the last several hours, she had even been considering how to separate from Yaomey, and here the woman was, handing her the perfect opportunity to set out on her own.

Megan nodded. "No, you're right. Let's do that. Even if the risk is small, Aylun is still out there. He could be in danger, so I'll hide out in the tower while you make sure he is okay."

Yaomey eyed her with a curious look, seeming put off by the abrupt acquiescence.

Megan peered over at the massive wooden door. Its heavy timbers seemed far too solid, given its purported antiquity. The two grabbed hold of a giant metal door pull, and both heaved until the door grumbled open. They led Megan's mare up to it, and it was easily large enough for her to pass through. The spooked animal seemed reluctant to enter, but with a fair amount of persuasion and several handfuls of grass, they managed to coax her inside.

Megan remained inside as Yaomey slipped out, then she pushed the door partway closed. She turned and stared at Megan through the opening. "When I return, I will give two rapid knocks, then three slow ones." She pounded on the wooden frame in demonstration, each bang echoing through the dark and daunting space.

As the reverberations subsided, she pulled a jangling pouch of coins from her pack. She reached through and dropped it into Megan's hand with a muffled clank. "If I do not return, head north.

Keep out of sight as best you can, and find the small town of Naliq. I will meet you on the bridge in the center of town at sunset on the night of the next full moon."

Megan hesitated as the reality dawned on her: she was setting out on her own. She wouldn't have these two to depend on anymore, no lookout for soldiers, no insight into this world or its ways, no guide to tell her where to go, and no protection from its dangers. She straightened, steeling her resolve.

As Yaomey turned to mount, Megan recalled that she had meant to apologize for her words of the day before. A pang hit at the realization she would not get another chance. She poked her head through the gap in the door and called out, "Yaomey?"

The woman halted and turned back to face Megan, her eyes questioning.

Megan pulled her head in and lowered her gaze. "I shouldn't have said what I said yesterday … you know, at the pond, about your father losing a daughter."

Yaomey's face clouded, and she glanced away. "It is okay."

Megan hesitated for a while, then looked up. "No, it isn't. I know what it means to lose a sister." Her words caught in her throat. "I would never wish that on anyone, and what I said was awful and rude and insensitive."

Yaomey held her gaze and paused, as if reluctant to speak her mind. After several long moments, she stepped forward. "Yaolin was not just my sister … she was Aylun's partner. It was his job to protect her, just as it was hers to protect him. In many ways, she was the only family he had left. She loved him with all her heart, and I think he cared for her too, in his own way. Though he was too stubborn to admit it."

Megan scuffed her feet. From snippets here and there, she had figured out that something had happened to make Aylun so angry and volatile. She had assumed it was his nature, perhaps aggravated by a nasty argument or breakup. What she hadn't expected was for it to be something so profound or so close to home. Her gaze fell. "Oh."

Yaomey continued, "You said you want to understand. That you want answers. Well, here is one: Aylun was *right there* when Yaolin died. He went to the dragon because he wanted to end his life. He wanted to die."

Megan paused as the man's words came back: "Remorse is all I feel." More memories returned of all the things he'd said and done, and as they did, it all began to make sense. At the dragon's lair, she had interrupted a man so racked by grief and remorse he was on the verge of killing himself.

"Oh ..." she repeated as she stared down at ancient bits of stonework sloughed off the tower over its vast existence.

Yaomey sighed. "Well, what is done cannot be undone, but we are both trying to make it up to you in our own way."

Megan looked up as Yaomey drew another deep breath and let it go. "Take care of yourself, Megan. Stay safe." She turned and began to mount again, then stopped and turned back, looking Megan straight in the eye. "And please, do not do anything foolish." Before Megan could find a response, Yaomey finished mounting her horse and bolted off down the road.

Megan looked over at her only remaining companion, Yuki. Then she yanked on the inside door pull, and the door groaned shut, leaving the stone floor and walls in deep shadow. The only light was a beam of pale white from a window high overhead. Above the restless stirring of her spotted mare, the muffled clatter of hooves against cobblestones grew more distant, telling her Yaomey was heading away.

She waited with her ear to the door, straining to catch every hoofbeat as the light from above grew dimmer, then brighter again, with each cloud that passed overhead. As the sound faded to nothing, she untied her bedroll and grabbed it from Yuki's back. She heaved the door open a crack and wedged it into the opening. Beyond the slit, the clouds were already clearing some. She watched as Yaomey, now a tiny speck in the distance, disappeared altogether.

Megan gathered her mare's reins and shouldered the sturdy door wide open. Seeming eager for the light and open spaces, Yuki led the way out. Megan watched for a long moment, scanning the path for any sign of Yaomey. Satisfied that her former companion was gone, she took a deep breath and mounted. She guided the beast away from Yaomey and down the cobblestones toward the mountains. The path before her now meandered off into the gaping canyon, with sheer cliffs on either side. From what she had gathered in conversations with Aylun and Yaomey, it led straight into Katapa, then through it and beyond to the lost city of Lanessa.

As she trotted down the road, the mountains grew larger, soaring into the heavens. Their peaks, white with snow, seemed much more daunting now that she was alone. No fireballs appeared in the sky, yet the atmosphere remained restless as if the clearing storm were a prelude to some even greater cataclysmic event. Plaintive cries of far-off wolves drifted across the verdant plains, and horses in the distance no longer grazed. Instead, they pranced and whinnied then bolted away, most heading with her toward the fallen city.

Seated atop Juzhi, Aylun remained still, transfixed by the sight of a massive ball of flames plummeting past the distant mountains to disappear at their base. A sudden heaviness grabbed ahold of his chest, choking out his breath as a wave of anxiety paralyzed him. Whatever had just happened might be a threat to Megan and Yaomey, and he was too far away to do a single thing about it. Even worse, he had been dragging his feet, delaying Brita and leaving them unprotected.

Without a thought of how the Dellia look-alike might react, he spurred Juzhi forward, breaking into a gallop. He clutched the reins in his tightened fists as the fear of yet more people dying on his watch propelled him headlong down the overgrown cobbles.

Brita pulled up beside him and shouted above the clatter of galloping hooves, "What are you doing? Slow down!"

With his thoughts consumed by anxiety over the fate of Yaomey and Megan, no room remained to contemplate a response.

She tried again, yelling, "Answer me!" When she got no answer, she whipped her dagger out of its sheath, flung it over in front of Aylun's neck, and shouted, "Stop!"

More alarmed at the prospect of the delay than the weapon jostling inches from his throat, he pulled Juzhi to a quick stop. Brita did the same, managing to keep the blade at his throat. With an economy of movement, he bent backward and smashed the flat side of the blade upward. Her hand flew over his head, and as she brought the weapon back down, he whipped his reins around the sharp edges and yanked it from her grasp. It tumbled through the air, but he caught it and held it out of reach.

She grabbed for her sword.

He leaned over and seized her wrist.

Her every move having been countered with such ease, she stopped and stared. "You're no guide. Who are you?"

Aylun let go as he regained some measure of calm. "There is no time for this."

"I have a duty to this realm."

He threw her an annoyed glare, and the careless words slipped out. "At least Dellia had the sense to try to talk first."

"What? What do mean 'try to talk *first*'?"

He ignored her as he squinted and scanned the plains. "Whatever that was, it could be a danger to all of us, and I am not going to lose another partner. So you can either help me, and we can protect each other, or you can keep this up and—" He spotted Yaomey approaching along the road in the distance.

Brita continued to stare at him. "And what?"

"And just see where this blind devotion to duty of yours leads us all." He released her wrist and tossed Brita her dagger as he urged his steed forward again. Juzhi lurched ahead, clattering down the cobbles toward Yaomey. As he reached her, he guided Juzhi up beside her. "What happened? Where is she? Where is Megan?"

"Holing up"—she pointed in the direction she had come—"in the eastern watchtower of Katapa."

"What?" His alarm deepened again. "You left her? Alone?" He glanced over as Brita clomped into the group. "She was threatening to run."

Yaomey straightened in her saddle. "Run?"

"She told me she did not need us, that she would go to Katapa without us."

Yaomey scowled. "And you didn't think that was important to mention earlier?"

Brita appeared even more puzzled and alarmed. "You said she hired you as a guide. Why would she run away from a guide?"

Anxious to find Megan and annoyed at the needless questioning, he scowled at her. "Because she was upset with us. Because she is a bullheaded, irrational, stubborn, inconsiderate, foolish, irresponsible ..." He eyed Yaomey. "I have to go after her. She is my responsibility."

Brita balked. "I'll go with you."

Irked at the suggestion, he glared at her. "She is most likely headed into Katapa."

Her eyes widened, and she leaned forward. "Katapa? Into the actual city?"

"Yes, and I cannot be responsible for taking you or anyone else into that place."

With Brita's focus on Aylun, Yaomey sent him a subtle knowing nod and put a hand on the woman's arm. Brita turned to face her, and Yaomey spoke with an unusual degree of cheerfulness. "Aylun can handle this. You and I should go back and wait for his return." She nodded her head with exaggerated eagerness.

Brita seemed to consider for a moment as she looked at the canyon with fear and trepidation written on her face. Then she glanced back the way they'd come, then at the mountains again. She faced Aylun. "Okay, but I will be forced to detain your friend here"—she nodded to Yaomey—"until you return."

Yaomey acted scared, feigning sweetness and innocence. "Detain? What did I do wrong?"

It only took a moment to catch on to her act. Aylun eyed her and spoke as if to a child. "It is okay, Yaomey. Do not worry. She will not hurt you. Just stay with this brave and pretty lady. She will protect you until I return."

Yaomey gave a slow nod with a hint of a pout. "Okay."

Brita glanced at her, and her eyes narrowed in an are-you-kidding-me look. Then she turned her gaze to Aylun.

With her back turned, Brita could not see Yaomey send him an emphatic shake of her head and silently mouth, "Do not return."

He endeavored to keep his expression calm and earnest. "I took a vow to protect her, and I must fulfill it."

Still seeming suspicious, Brita turned her gaze back again to Yaomey.

For her benefit, Yaomey gave an exaggerated wave goodbye, and her voice was bright and full of feigned innocence. "Bye-bye, Aylun. Come back quickly. I will worry about you."

He granted her a deep bow.

Brita sputtered for a moment, but before she could find the words to object, Aylun spurred Juzhi forward and galloped off the way Yaomey had come. He raced down the road, his focus ahead as he clenched the reins in his hands. With the cloud cover almost gone, the bright sun poured down on the tower that appeared on the horizon.

As he approached, his concentration was broken by an awareness of movement on either side from horses, turning and prancing in uneasy circles. As he reached the tower, he spotted two pairs of yellow eyes. They had returned, flashing out from far beyond the restless horses. They danced across the distant grasses, circling out around the herd, moving among them with stealth and purpose.

He reached the tower door to find it wide open. Nothing but stillness and silence greeted him as he slipped from his horse. With an anxious gaze, he peeked inside only to find it dark and deserted. He made a hasty job of tying Juzhi's reins to a nearby twisted shrub, then raced inside. Through the entry, down the stairs to the second door, and into the base of the tower he flew, pulling out his flamestone as he ran. His footsteps echoed through the foreboding space as he raced across the cracked stone floor, searching for any sign of Megan.

Spinning and scanning, he stared upward, light flashing across a spiral stairway that wound its way around the inside wall. It was crumbled in several places, one of which, a short way up, would have made it impossible to lead a horse higher into the tower. He called out Megan's name, then cocked his head and froze—but all that met him were the echoes of his own voice as it faded away to an ominous silence.

Fatigued and out of breath, he sprinted back outside and stared down the road as he slumped to the ground. In the distance, beyond the nervous horses, movement caught his eye once again: pairs of yellow eyes moving in tandem, drifting through the grasses. A wolf howl floated on the air, then another, farther away, and another. He lifted his gaze, following the road out to where it disappeared in the distance, then beyond to the gaping chasm that marked the ruins of the Katapa. The tightness returned, squeezing his chest again. Megan was out there somewhere, alone and unaware of the danger.

As Yuki carried Megan toward the fallen city, the cloud cover dissipated, leaving the bright sun drifting lower in an azure sky. Ruins appeared at the base of the canyon, indistinct, half-standing homes and shops strewn like rubble between the pair of sheer cliffs. Rising above them stood the partly crumbled remains of gigantic pavilions, temples, amphitheaters, and monuments. With their enormous fluted columns and massive roofs of stone, it was like peering into history. It was as if she were viewing the ancient Acropolis of Athens from a distance.

As she approached, the houses grew larger, and the herds thinned, then disappeared altogether, as if afraid to be infected by the decay of the city. Yuki clattered up to a huge carved boulder at the edge of the road. Megan dismounted and stared down at the lettering in disbelief. Though they were half worn away, she recognized them in an instant from her math and science background. Etched in the stone were letters from the Greek alphabet. With an odd sense of comprehension, she stared as she mumbled to herself, "Kappa, Alpha. Tau. Pi." Then she read the whole word aloud: "Katapa."

She stumbled in disbelief, then lowered herself to sit as her mind boggled at the realization, yet the clues were all there. They had been, almost from the start. The name Dell-yuh was just a different pronunciation of Deal-ee-uh. One much closer, in fact, to the place from which it was derived: the Greek island of Delos. The protector's armor, down to the skirt made of leather strips, was in a style reminiscent of Rome or Greece. The somewhat Greek-sounding names of the cities—Katapa, Egina, Vadia, and Krosia—the letters on the boulder, and even the vast ruins before her—they all pointed in one direction. While different in many subtle ways, they nonetheless had an unmistakable similarity to ancient Greece.

This couldn't be the Earth of the past. The geography and city names weren't consistent with any historical record. Moreover, outside of fiction like *The Iliad* and *The Odyssey*, no written record even hinted at physical laws being broken on the scale she had experienced. Yet here on a world that could not be her own were what appeared to be the remains ... no, not the remains, some kind of living offshoot of a long-dead Earth civilization.

Her mind rebelling against the craziness of it all, she slumped back against the stone marker. As she did, her gaze rose to the stunning ruins that now filled her view. The road branched as it neared the city, with the Eastern Trail becoming the primary thoroughfare. It wound its way into the crumbling remains where countless decaying stone homes lined either side. The nearest buildings now obscured the colossal monuments that had earlier been visible above their jagged walls and collapsed rooftops.

She stayed that way, resting against the stone marker, eyeing the vast sea of decay with trepidation as the many dire warnings about the place rolled around in her head. She fidgeted as she stared down the road, contemplating whether to heed the warnings and turn back now or face them head-on and press forward.

Absorbed in thought, she paid no attention to the far-off whinnying as it grew quiet. Nor did she take note when it was replaced by a barely discernible low rumble. After a while, the shuddering of the ground beneath her became too strong to escape her notice. She sat up straight, her vague anxiety turning to out-and-out alarm.

She rose to her feet and turned. There, in the distance, thundering toward her, was a broad line of horses that almost filled the horizon. Panic struck. She had to get out of here, now.

Her hand reached for Yuki's reins as she took a few steps to the north.

She froze. There, far away and moving effortlessly toward her, was an enormous deep-red wolf almost as large as she was.

She whipped around and headed the other way but halted at an even closer predator with its front end lowered, leering at her with disturbing yellow eyes. It slunk toward her with slow and cautious steps, stalking her as if she were mere prey to be taken down, taken apart, and consumed.

A sick, morbid dread struck at her, and she glanced away. The crumbled houses of the ruins would offer little protection, even if she could reach them in time with massive wolves on either side chasing Yuki down. And if she made it to one of the homes, then what? How could she fit an animal as large as Yuki inside, or make sure the building didn't collapse on top of them with the ground shaking as it was?

Crippled by indecision and fear, she turned once again to face the vast herd pounding toward her. Like a tsunami of streaming manes and rippling muscles, it poured over the green sunlit expanse. It was unstoppable, threatening to obliterate her beneath a torrent of raging bodies and hammering hooves. She was trapped, a cornered animal, and her chance of survival was growing more distant with each passing second.

Chapter Ten

RAGING INTO RUINS

An edgy, nervous tension saturated the air as if the entire plains were waiting for the heavens to fall. Aylun clutched the reins with sweaty hands as he drove Juzhi forward at a steady yet rapid trot. Herds of horses abounded now, and there seemed little doubt they were being herded here by the Blood Wolves. As difficult as it was to fathom, it had to be some kind of trap for Megan.

A contagious apprehension seemed to jump from one skittish clutch of horses to another. Fear showed in their wide eyes and quick, jittery movements, and in their snorting and milling. Yet, he dared not take his focus from the search for his fleeing charge.

Movement flashed at the edge of his vision. His gaze whipped over to catch another pair of yellow eyes and a desperate whinny. A not-too-distant body plummeted to the ground, landing with a thud and a pitiful screech. The surrounding horses broke to a gallop, causing Aylun's chest to tighten even more and his breath to grow short. He had to reach Megan and make sure she didn't suffer the same fate as that poor beast. He spurred Juzhi ahead, and he flew to a gallop.

A rush of nearby horses transformed into an all-out race. Aylun split his attention, trying to stay ahead of the surging crowd while he strained to catch any glimpse of Megan.

As if it were a wave rippling across the plains, panic struck here and there. More and more herds bolted, racing away from the Blood Wolves and toward Katapa. Before he could puzzle out what to do, he was buried deep in the middle of a stampede, trapped in a blind race

239

of terrified beasts, barreling without thought or reason toward the gaping chasm and decaying remains of the once-majestic city.

Then he spied a woman in the distance. Near a marker outside the crumbling outskirts, she rose to her feet. Her ginger hair, bright in the warm rays of the almost setting sun, made her easy to spot across the long green plains ahead.

His chest twisted into knots at the sight. It had to be Megan. He ignored the heaving and jostling of the galloping bodies all around and focused instead on her.

In a frenzied flurry of motion, she grabbed Yuki's reins and darted to the right. She halted as she spotted a giant bloodred wolf, far away and stalking toward her.

At the sight of it, the weight on his chest swelled, the pressure becoming oppressive.

Megan spun and lurched in the other direction. Again she froze at the sight of a second wolf, head down and slinking toward her from the other side.

His breath grew rapid and shallow. Heads bobbed, bodies heaved, and the rumble of countless hooves filled his ears, crowding out every thought. The woman he had vowed would come to no harm was in dire danger, a cornered quarry, moments from being obliterated. And he was trapped and helpless to do a single thing about it. As he watched her, the sea of charging flesh seemed to close in on him, tightening his chest even more and crushing out his breath.

Megan turned to face the onslaught and gawked for a moment. Her face filled with terror as she stared at the tide of bone and hide pouring toward her.

Just out of her line of sight, Aylun released the reins and waved his arms with frantic motions, but she continued to stare off to his side and no sign of recognition passed her face.

With the wave of hooves and flesh nearly upon her, wolves closing in from either side, Megan flew up onto Yuki's back. She whipped her around to face the jagged homes and shops that lined the edge of the city. Above them, in the distance, towered a hill littered with crumbling monuments, statues, and temples, gleaming and white in the late-day sun.

With a heavy kick, she spurred her steed toward it. The spooked animal broke for the broad main street into the city just as the throng surrounded them, carrying them along like driftwood in a flood.

Aylun tightened his grip on the reins and pulled to the left, trying to steer Juzhi toward Megan, but to no effect. His horse was as spooked as all the terrified beasts around him and ignored his attempts to guide him. Like a raft in rapids, they carried him farther to the side, away from her.

The mass of surging bodies bore him along as they poured into an all-too-narrow side street. He glanced over as Megan disappeared into the main thoroughfare on the next road to the left. Then he and Juzhi were carried along into the city. The crumbling homes on either side closed in, amplifying the roar of hooves and breathless snorting. Dust filled his eyes and stung his lungs. Horses jolted and jarred against him, slamming into his legs. Juzhi lurched and heaved, flying over the rubble and debris strewn along the cramped avenue.

All of a sudden, the horse to his left hit the wall and stumbled to its knees with a shrill cry. The sweaty beasts on the other side shoved Juzhi over in its place, and Aylun had to pull his shoulder in to keep it from raking against the jagged stonework. One hard jar and his leg would slam into it. His horse would fall, just as the last one had, and its sheer weight driving him into the sharp stones would tear him apart.

Above the river of heaving bodies, the crumbled remains of a fallen wall appeared straight ahead, blocking his half of the street. Horses thundered into it. They collided and stumbled over each other as they struggled to clamber up the pile of wreckage. Those that swerved to avoid it heaved into others, crowding into what remained of the already narrow avenue.

Aylun jerked his reins in the other direction, to the left. He guided Juzhi through the ragged opening made by the fallen wall and into what remained of a home. All went dark as he charged down a hall. Juzhi heaved beneath him, almost throwing him off as he flew over a jumbled pile of collapsed stonework. The building around him shook and loose chunks of rubble fell, one of them whistling past his ear. The ceiling opened up, and they barreled into the light. Aylun ducked, barely avoiding decapitation as Juzhi leaped through the enlarged opening of a former window and clattered onto the decaying side street beyond.

The turn was too sharp, and his stallion slipped and stumbled along the gravel and debris. Ahead, an impenetrable wall of horsehair and flesh screamed by where the cross street met the broad main thoroughfare. Aylun glanced behind him. A similar torrent of frightened and frenzied bodies streaked past the other end, making an exit at either point impossible.

Before he could pull his gaze away, the heaving flood of bodies shouldered a horse into the side street. Unable to make the turn at racing speeds, the poor beast collided with the wall. Its neck bent at a horrible angle, and it cried out as it toppled to the pavement. Another came right behind, stumbling down on top of the first.

A woman's scream rose above the snorting and rumble of hooves. His gaze whipped back ahead, trying to find its source. With Juzhi struggling for balance, Aylun raised his hand and stared at the dark ring with a solid jade line around the middle. He concentrated, and a silvery thread darted from it, leading to the end of the alley where a tidal wave of horses continued to roar past on the main avenue beyond.

Frantic and determined, he tightened the reins and whipped Juzhi down a tight winding alleyway parallel to the main street. He charged off just as a massive bloodred wolf leaped onto the fallen pair of horses while they were still trying to gain footing and stumble their way upright. Its teeth sank deep into soft flesh of one of their bellies and yanked, rending a chunk of flesh from the frantic animal. Its guts spilled onto the dirt as it disappeared from his view. The decaying stone walls closed in on him even further, making navigation a nightmare in the cramped and crumbling space.

Glimpses of the main avenue flashed by, then a protruding brick fragment slammed into his upper arm, slashing deep into his skin. Blood flowed down the limb as he drove Juzhi harder. They twisted and wound down the claustrophobic alleyway at breakneck speed, watching through each slender crossway for any sign of Megan. Suddenly, the thread pointed straight down an alley as red hair flashed by.

Aylun straightened, and Juzhi leaped over some rubble, sending him lurching into another jagged stone, digging a deep gash across his leg. He winced at the sudden sharp pain. They landed and forged ahead, winding around a turn to a steep incline that angled away from Megan. Juzhi braced himself as he slipped and skidded down the alley to emerge on the banks of a broad stagnant river.

High above, a stream of horses surged from the next street over onto a heavy stone bridge. The massive structure crossed the murky water and ended in a curve that led the road along the opposite bank. The silvery thread pointed near the head of the bridge, where glimpses of Megan appeared as she surged onto the crumbling stonework. As the walls and supports grew lower, he suddenly gained an unobstructed view of the woman. She was clinging with everything she had to Yuki, and what little he could see of her receding face appeared pale and shocked as the mob swept her along with them.

Aylun spurred Juzhi forward and hugged his neck. Rubble and dust flew into the air as he thundered to a flat-out gallop, racing down the riverbank. The roar of hooves echoed along the decaying channel as he glanced back and up at the throng. Near its head, Megan forged onto the curve that would bring her parallel to him on the far bank.

Several lengths behind the petrified woman, a bloodred wolf sprang onto the haunches of a horse, dragging itself up onto the beast's back. The poor animal struggled under the weight of the canine almost half its size. It cried out, bucking and twisting, but the wolf clamped its jaws down on the neck and shook. Its victim spun to the ground as the predator leaped and dove after the next horse.

Aylun's anxiety exploded as he watched a white-faced Megan clinging to the reins. Her entire focus was ahead, unaware of the massive wolf bounding after her. Its powerful jaws and daggerlike canines were only a few horse lengths behind and gaining fast.

He kicked harder, surging down the opposite bank. Movement caught his eye as another wolf flew out of the alley behind him. It never paused as it leaped after him. Aylun leaned even lower and steered Juzhi toward a somewhat intact bridge, with one end fallen onto the shore ahead. The other end emptied high up on an intersection ahead of Megan, one that would carry her away from the river.

The wolf behind made rapid gains, bounding after him with easy, flowing movements, its yellow eyes watching him with singular intensity.

As he passed by a pile of rubble from a collapsed lamppost, Aylun reached out and snatched a heavy rock from the heap. In a single fluid motion, he swung it down and whipped it at the wolf's head.

The beast swerved to the side, but the stone caught it in the haunches, sending it spinning and tumbling across the dirt and gravel. It landed in a slimy puddle but soon staggered up from the muck. Runny sludge splatted the shoreline as it shook off the blow. Then it lowered its head, braced itself, and broke into a run, chasing after him with renewed determination.

Juzhi leaped and clattered onto the low end of the fallen bridge, then headed up the steep incline to the other side. He stumbled and struggled, trying to bear Aylun's weight as he surged upward.

Above, a traumatized Megan galloped at blinding speed toward the other end of the crumbling bridge. Her wide-eyed expression told of her trauma and all her attention remained on the river of surging flesh ahead, making it doubtful she would notice him or the wolf gaining on her from behind.

Aylun leaped off the struggling Juzhi and sprinted up the fallen bridge toward the opposite bank to intercept Megan. He slipped and skidded on dust and debris underfoot as he pushed forward, all the while yelling encouragement to Juzhi. Every hoof-fall dislodged gravel and stones that skipped and clattered down the bridge. Several chunks hopped over its edge to plop into the water below.

He had reached the midpoint when the Blood Wolf leaped onto the base of the bridge. Aylun whipped around to face the bundle of fangs and fur bounding up the incline toward him. From the angle of its ascent, he could tell it would need to get very close before it could pounce on him.

Aylun flipped a large rock onto the top of his foot. Tense and out of breath, his heart pounding in his ears, he waited.

The beast was almost upon him, its yellow eyes now bright and vicious.

He popped the stone into the air in front of his chest, then jabbed his palm out, slamming the rock toward the wolf's head.

It struck the side of the beast's skull with a *thunk* as Aylun whipped around and kicked the heavy thing midleap. It let out a sharp cry as the blow sent Aylun flying backward and the wolf plunging off the edge of the bridge. Before it could splash into the stagnant water below, Aylun was pulling himself back upright. He grabbed Juzhi's reins and pulled her behind him as he sprinted upward.

As they reached the top, Megan was rounding the curve to head away from the river. He flew onto his steed's back and barreled down the street just in time to shoulder his way up beside her and Yuki. The torrent of charging, leaping bodies pummeled his legs. A deafening clatter of hundreds of hooves roared in his ears. It echoed along the avenue as the musty scent of sweaty equine flesh assaulted his nostrils.

He looked over at Megan. Her face was still pale and terrified. Every shred of her focus was bent ahead as she clutched the reins with white-knuckled hands. Her breath rasped out, short and frantic, her hair whipped behind her, and her eyes bulged.

His heart went out to her, even as a small portion of his anxiety eased. Despite having no notion of what to do next, he was back by her side, and that meant he was close enough that he might just have a chance of protecting her.

He leaned toward her and shouted above the deafening roar of hooves and snorting breaths, "Megan!"

Her gaze whipped over, and she stared, but no sign of recognition or relief crossed her face. He had seen the look before when Tsaoshi sent the Shou to help victims of a landslide. Megan had reacted to his voice and even turned her head to look right at him. She could hear, see, and respond to what was going on around her, yet her expression remained vacant. It wasn't that she didn't recognize him. Her mind was just in a profound fog. She was shocked beyond the point of response. This was bad. If they hoped to survive, they needed every advantage they could get, and, right now, Megan's gift could be a crucial one. Only she wasn't in a fit state to use it, and all he could do was wait for her fugue to pass.

Megan's gaze rested on him for only a fleeting moment before a chilling shriek yanked her attention away. A bloodred wolf stood squinting at her with eerie yellow eyes from the back of a horse two lengths behind. It snarled, then sank its teeth into the middle of the poor animal's spine. Using its jaw, the wolf pulled itself up farther along the animal's back, then let go and lunged, clamping down on the terrified beast's head. The skull crackled, blood spewed, and the frantic animal crumpled to the ground, disappearing below the thundering hooves.

Megan gasped as the giant red body reappeared from the storm of dust, leaping and bounding after the horse just behind her.

Aylun's gaze flew across the half-standing homes and shops that raced by at the edges of the avenue. They were trapped in a rush of surging flesh, and unless something happened, Megan was mere seconds from being the huge carnivore's next victim. As they rounded a curve toward the center of Katapa, a massive parklike plaza came into view.

The street emptied into a gigantic open paved area that stretched off to surround an enormous hill. Scattered across its slopes were massive half-crumbled monuments, statues, and temples. Though some of the roofs had collapsed, the remaining fluted columns and heavy stonework shone white and polished in the almost setting sun. Stretched across the top, high overhead, stood a massive rectangular temple, seeming intact. Its heavy stone roof was supported by the same kind of giant pillars, rising several stories tall.

Aylun pointed to the bottom of the hillside. "There!" he shouted above the deafening rumble.

Megan followed his finger to a debris-strewn ring of steps jutting far out from the base. They rose more than two stories high to a smaller version of the temple at the top of the hill. Half in a daze and heaving in the saddle, she looked over and nodded. A cinder of hope ignited in his heart. Her wits were beginning to return.

Like the waters of a flood, horses poured out in all directions as they charged into the open plaza surrounding the hillside. Side by side, Juzhi and Yuki barreled through the middle, heading straight for the nearest set of steps.

Only partway there, another frantic screech came from just in back of them. Aylun and Megan twisted around in their saddles as a wolf clawed its way up onto the back of the horse right behind them. The terrified animal stumbled and struggled under the weight of the enormous wolf crouched on its back.

Then, it hit him that he had a throwing weapon. Aylun yanked a heavy shuriken from a harness on his belt.

Megan stared at the gleaming circle of sharp blades. "A throwing star?"

The wolf pounced onto the head of the horse. Its neck bent down under the weight as the wolf then leaped for Megan.

Aylun flung the hunk of metal at its skull. It sank deep into one of its yellow eyes, and the weight jerked its head to the side. Off-balance, it let out a piercing yelp as it twisted and flailed. It slammed into Yuki's rear as Aylun flung a second shuriken, slashing the beast's neck.

Blood sprayed across white-and-brown-spotted flanks as the deep-red body plummeted to the cobbles below, then disappeared under a deluge of pounding hooves.

As the stream of horses emptied into the large open plaza, the exhausted herd slowed. Aylun pushed harder, urging Juzhi up the nearest set of rubble-strewn steps. Yuki followed, and their hooves clattered against the carved marble as they dodged between massive chunks of fallen stonework.

They cleared the last step and flew off their horses onto the marble floor of a huge column-ringed pavilion. Relieved to no longer be trapped in a panicked mob of raging hooves, Aylun yanked his staff ends from his back. His gaze locked on to one of the wolves, its yellow eyes peering up at them from its bloodred face. With disturbing purpose, it weaved through the mass of prancing hooves, headed for them. Beyond the sea of equine flesh, the ruins of the city spread out like gravel lining the sides of a plethora of winding streets, avenues, and alleys. Here and there, small markets, parks, and plazas broke the seemingly endless crisscross of decaying stone roads.

A pair of bloodred beasts emerged from the milling throng and leaped onto the base of the steps. A third and fourth appeared next to them. From another direction, a fifth, sixth, and seventh bounded onto the side steps. Then four more leaped onto the opposite staircase.

His anxiety returned as he watched each group slink upward together with cautious, stealthy movements. Then all at once, they fanned out, moving in unison to surround them, as if the pack were a single well-trained unit.

Behind the wolves, horses slowed to a stop, snorting and whinnying restlessly across the broad park, churning like turbulence in a stormy sea.

AYLUN

Aylun turned to face the first group of stealthy carnivores. Megan remained pale and unresponsive, but took Juzhi's reins when he handed them to her. With careful steps, he began to back away. He shoved the staff ends together and twisted. With a click, they became one continuous staff, and blades sprang from each end. The noise drew Megan's attention. For a moment, she stared with vacant eyes at one of the glittering knives, then her gaze drifted back to the wolves.

Aylun struggled to track each wolf, his gaze flittering across the marble temple ruins. He shot Megan a fleeting glance. "Are you all right?"

Her face was still white and shocked, and she never responded, her eyes remaining fixed on one of the yellow-eyed beasts.

He raised his voice above the din below. "Are you unharmed?"

She nodded.

He turned away, but her voice caught his attention. Quiet and mouselike, it eked out, barely rising above the clatter and snorting below. "You came for me."

At the sound, relief spread. She was lucid enough to form a coherent sentence. Her wits were returning. He looked back at her, and her face held an expression somewhere between confusion and terror.

He endeavored to sound stronger and more reassuring than he felt. "Of course I did."

Her head turned, and she looked up at him with wide eyes. "I mean, after everything I did, after I yelled at you, and ran away, and everything ... you came for me. Through all of this, you found me. You came for me."

He gave a single resolute nod. "Yes. Now, protect the horses." He pointed to Juzhi.

As they backed away, Megan glanced at him again. "How?"

"You like playing with your gift. Now would be an excellent time."

Seeming relieved to have some sort of plan, she gave a rapid nod. "Yeah, yeah, that's right. I could do that." She glanced at the wreckage spread everywhere, the ground littered with hunks of the crumbled temple, from mere pebbles to massive fragments of fluted column and pieces of the flat roof adorned with ornate etchings and scrollwork.

Her eyes fixed on a chunk the size of her fist. She waved her hand, and with a puff of air, it shot away, skipping and bouncing down the rubble-riddled stairs. It cracked against a step, then took a hop and headed straight for one of the wolves.

The lithe beast leaped away with casual ease. As if the stone were a signal, every single wolf flew away, diving into hiding behind the pieces of fallen stonework that lay strewn down the ring of steps.

Aylun stared in surprise. "What the ..."

Without removing her eyes from the scene, Megan leaned closer. "It's me. It's my gift. They're ... *hiding* from it."

He shot her a skeptical look.

"Can't you see it? It's obvious from the way they reacted, the way they moved."

"You mean, all at the same time?"

She nodded. "Yes, they're coordinating somehow, and from their faces and posture, they're hiding in fear." There was a pause, then she mumbled, "Wait a minute. I would never have noticed that before. How can I see it so clearly now?"

Their survival was more important than her musings, so Aylun kept his focus on his surroundings. At the edges of his vision, a dark red body slipped upward only to disappear behind a massive fallen hunk of a column. His gaze whipped over to catch its movement, and on the other side, another bloodred blur leaped and dove behind a broken segment of the roof.

Megan seemed to notice as her gaze followed his, then she turned to him, her voice filled with apprehension. "They're only moving where we're not looking."

He watched her as she glanced around at the horses milling in nervous circles all across the vast parklike area, then up at the monument-riddled hillside and the massive temple towering above it all.

Her eyes came back down to rest on an enormous doorway far across the pavilion. Only partly visible above the ruins, it led to what appeared to be a large room enclosed by half-standing walls. "There." Megan pointed. "It'll at least provide some protection."

Aylun returned his attention to the wolves. "And how do we get there?"

"Horseback?" she ventured.

"No. I have seen it. These wolves are faster than horses."

She stared at him as if his words didn't make sense, so he elaborated. "Trying to flee would be like surrendering. It would trigger their hunting instinct, and chasing down prey, cutting off escape routes, surrounding and attacking from all sides—that's how wolves hunt. We cannot play that game."

His gaze shot around the pavilion and came to rest on a large corner piece some distance behind them. It lay on its long side, the peak shooting up much taller than a person. "If they want to hide, then we need a higher vantage point." He motioned her to come.

Megan followed, coaxing the nervous horses as she scanned the cluttered steps on all three sides. Her skittish charges pranced and snorted, but she seemed to know just how to urge them along. She backed up to the enormous stone peak, and the horses followed, the entire group protected by another giant piece of the roof on one side and a fallen column on the other.

Aylun crouched down and sprang, then pushed, pulled, leaped, and bounced his way up to the peak. He rose to his feet and looked down at Megan and the horses below. Then he began scanning the cluttered stairs. Movement flashed on every side, but each time his eyes rested somewhere, the scene before him froze. The wolves there remained hidden behind cover while at the edges of his vision they continued their advance. They darted from behind one hunk of stone to another, skirting and ducking to hide again, moving inexorably closer.

He pointed to the steps on one side. "There. Can you spray some rocks there?"

"'Spray'?" Megan cocked her head. "Like, more than one rock?"

He nodded. "If you can."

At his request, her still-terrified expression became tinged with intimidation. Undaunted, she took a deep breath and hoisted a large piece of rubble. Signs of effort showed on her face, and wind spun around her as she flung it high in the air. It landed at the edge of the pavilion with a loud crack and shattered, sending a spray of fragments bouncing down the steps. The wolves remained hidden as stones pelted the stairs, clattering into the chunks of roof and column that hid the beasts.

Megan's eyes whipped over, following something on the steps.

Aylun followed her gaze as, closer now, a wolf landed behind a giant slab and disappeared from view. He looked down at Megan. "It is not working. It needs to come down from above if it is to get behind their hiding places."

She stared up at him with a frightened, are-you-kidding-me expression. "How am I supposed to do that? It's hopeless."

Too busy tracking the ever-shifting pack working their way toward them, he threw out a less-than-thoughtful response. "You are clever. You will think of something."

It appeared to be just the goading she needed, though, because her gaze flew around in a frenetic search. Aylun glanced down as her attention seemed drawn to a intact column standing a couple stories tall at the edge of the stairs. Wind whirled around her as she hoisted another chunk of rubble in the air. Her brow furrowed as she eyed it with unwavering concentration. Then, with a roar of wind and tremendous effort, she flung it upward.

Movement raced at the edges of his vision, much closer now, and still, every time he shifted his focus to catch the wolves, they dove out of sight or hunkered in their hiding places.

The chunk of marble arced through the air to strike the top of the decaying column and shatter with a loud crack that echoed across the vast ruins of the fallen city. The enormous piece of stone wobbled from the blow as fragments showered down on the steps.

AYLUN

A yelp echoed from behind a slab of stone, but it lacked conviction. It seemed more like a whine of annoyance than the wail of anguish from a severe injury.

Aylun looked down at her. "This is not working."

She looked up. "What do we do?"

"I will protect you. We make our stand here."

Seeming unsatisfied with his proclamation, Megan eyed the intact column again. Wind blasted around her as she lifted an even larger fragment. Her face scrunched in intense concentration as she held it high. In a gale of wind, she launched it to arc through the air.

At the burst of wind, Aylun lost his balance, the force nearly toppling him from his perch.

With a jarring *whack*, the boulder struck high up on the side of the column, away from the wolves. The pillar teetered as Aylun used his staff to recover his balance.

A deep-red wolf leaped onto the fallen column next to Megan. It eyed the horses with rabid greed, then turned its creepy yellow stare on her.

With the back of her hand, she swatted like she was shooing away a fly.

In a rush of wind, the wolf shot upward, tumbling through the air like a rag doll to hit the same spot on the teetering column with a thud and shriek of pain. The bloodred body ricocheted off and plummeted head over heels far down onto the steps, landing with a deep guttural grunt.

As if in slow motion, the column began to fall.

Another wolf leaped onto the slab of roof next to Aylun.

He jabbed it with the blade end of his staff, piercing its shoulder. The blow sent it plunging backward off its perch with a loud anguished yelp as blood sprayed his clothes.

The column crashed down on a pair of wolves hiding on the steps. It shattered into large fragments with a loud crack and a short-lived screech of agony that reverberated across the chasm.

A nearby wolf darted away. Midstride, it froze, then raised its head high, and a pitiful howl echoed across the vast ruins.

As if it were a signal, all the remaining wolves scampered away down the steps. They raced around the ring of stairs, forming into lines that weaved in and out of the hunks of marble debris.

Aylun glanced down at Megan, who stood on tiptoe to peer over the column. She was trying to see what was happening. He garnered her attention. "They are retreating."

As the wolves headed away from the temple, the lines merged into a single file, racing off across the open area. They scattered as they hit the remaining horses, disappearing beneath them. Like the wave of a shark running near the surface, horses bucked and spun as the wolves dashed between their legs, only to disappear into the alleys and streets at the edge of the park.

Aylun peered down at Megan as she slumped and bent over. He depressed a pair of buttons on his staff and twisted to separate the two halves. Still holding the buttons down, he pushed both blades against the slab of stone on which he stood. The pressure forced them back up into the staff ends, where he released the buttons, and they clicked into place.

As he returned the pieces to his back, his attention was drawn again to the ruins of the fallen city. Though the wolves had vanished for now, something in the pit of his stomach told him their retreat was strategic. All his instincts were shouting that although he had won this battle, the war was far from over.

Her mind clearing from its adrenaline-fueled haze, Megan tried to relax and unclench her body, but it refused. The wolves' hasty retreat was not at all reassuring because it meant they were still out there and could do who knows what, who knows when. At any moment they could rush back, and she and Aylun would be no better off than they were moments before.

AYLUN

Crouched over, she crept to the end of the enormous hunk of fallen column that had been sheltering them and peered out in the direction Aylun had been facing. She scrutinized the crisscross of roads and alleys, bordered by half-standing homes, amphitheaters, and monuments. There remained no trace of any bloodred wolves. In fact, except for the sea of restless horses, no movement at all showed across the sprawling ancient ruins and even beyond to the rocky ground that stretched out to meet the towering chasm walls.

The stifling pressure to escape this death trap still suffocated her. Megan pointed to the horses milling at the far end of the plaza and eyed Aylun. "We need to get out of here."

Still standing high above her, he seemed to give her apprehensive urging serious consideration. He glanced around for a moment, then motioned across the enormous plaza as if presenting it to her. "It will take a long time to work our way out through all those horses, and if the wolves return, we will get caught up in another stampede."

Megan peered across the city and hillside again, searching for a place of refuge. She stopped as she faced the back of the pavilion, then pointed across the wreckage-strewn floor. There at the back stood a broad opening leading to an enclosed area, with parts of the walls and roof fallen away. "We could hide there."

He peered at it for a moment, seeming to ponder her suggestion. "It is half fallen down. I doubt it is defensible. It could also be a problem for the horses. They're our way out of here. If we lose them, it is over." Aylun glanced all around, then up and down the hillside. He pointed to the much larger temple spread out across its top. "I think it would be safer up there. It seems intact."

Before she could respond, he slid down a short way, then leaped and bounced off hunks of stone to land on the ground before her. No sooner had he hit the ground than he spun and took off the way they had come. He wound around and through the hunks of debris spread across the pavilion floor as Megan struggled to keep up, leading the horses behind her.

Then, for the first time, she looked up at Aylun. Not just glanced at him while in a rush of raging horses or under the threat of approaching wolves, but really *looked* at him. He was limping, literally staggering, ahead of her. She rushed up and reached for his arm, but it had a horrible gash, and his clothes were soaked with blood. The sight of that much gore hit her in the gut, making her reel with nausea. She reached around and tugged on his uninjured arm, pulling him to a stop.

She pointed to his leg, where the worst of his injuries was visible beneath a tear in his garments. "You're wounded."

He seemed surprised, then brushed it off. "I can walk. It will be fine." He tried to wrest his arm free and take off again, but she held firm.

"No. It needs bandaging."

"With what? Besides, there isn't time."

"I can work quickly, just—"

"No!" he shouted.

Megan jumped and let go.

"I told you not to give my welfare a passing thought. Getting you to safety is all that matters."

Taken aback at the fierceness of his rebuke, she stood motionless for a moment, her gut still queasy. It was the exact phrase he had uttered before, but now, with them in dire danger and his life on the line to protect her, the reality of his demand took on a much more disturbing meaning.

"Go!" he shouted again.

She jumped a second time, but before she could object, he yanked his arm free, clamped down on her wrist with a sweaty hand, and began dragging her behind him. Startled by his impudence and still clinging to the reins, Megan pulled the horses behind her. After a few steps, she resigned herself and stopped resisting.

They skirted the partially collapsed walls and half-standing pillars of the main enclosed area around to its back, where a ramp wound its way up the hillside toward the temple at the top. No sooner had they started up the incline than a sudden chorus of plaintive howls broke out, halting her in her tracks. Aylun stopped with her, listening as the cries overlapped at different pitches, beginning and ending, again and again. A multitude of echoes ricocheted across the vast decay of the fallen city, filling the gaping chasm with its bloodcurdling melody.

Megan peered out in the direction of the howling as a feeling came over her that she knew what the sound meant. She turned her attention to Aylun. "Are they calling to their lost pack members?"

"Or worse, calling for reinforcements." Aylun let go of her wrist as he spun and faced the incline. Then he took off, scrambling upward with what appeared to be a renewed sense of urgency.

The horses clattered behind Megan as she tried to keep pace.

The howling came to an abrupt halt, the echo seeming to bounce off the sheer cliffs on either side, repeating and repeating as it faded. A disquieting silence followed. Then, as if in answer, a much more distant sound rang out. This time a horn, blowing loud, deep, and persistent. Like the howl, it echoed across the sprawling ruins of Katapa.

Megan froze and turned to stare. Past the southern edge of the city, a host of swarming shapes poured out of scattered dark holes at the base of the chasm wall. They pooled at the dim edges of the sheer rock cliffs, a mass of gray and reddish shapes, too distant to make out any one of them. She stood, terrified and transfixed by the slithering carpet gathering in the shadows, filling every space with moving bodies.

"Oh no." Aylun's apprehensive voice rose above the deep, resonant moan of the horn. "I think we are about to find out what comes here at night."

The sound ceased with an ominous abruptness, the echo fading in slow rounds, leaving only another chilling quiet.

Aylun turned to face Megan in profound alarm. "Go. Hurry. Those shadows will lengthen. They won't contain whatever that is for long."

The two renewed their climb, racing up the incline. They were not even halfway to the top when the distant horn blared a second time. Megan whipped around to spot the gathering swarm leave behind the shadows to pour out across the broken ground toward the city. They split around hills and flowed over fallen trees, turning and moving in concert as if they were a single coordinated unit.

Aylun pulled his eyes from the scene. "This is no time to stop and stare. Go!" He yanked on her arm, and they began moving again.

Megan continued to throw glances around the horses behind her at the waves of gray and red washing toward them, darting, leaping, and weaving in unison. An impression struck her and through labored breath, she forced out a few words. "It's like a flock of birds. They're all moving and turning at the same time." She peeked back at them again. "As if they're all reacting to the same thing, or they each know what the others will do."

A low roar, the thundering of a thousand feet, reached them. High up the incline, Aylun peered behind him and over her head. Her anxiety grew as his gaze rested there. "No, not birds. They move like hunters." He glanced at Megan. "Like wild dogs hunting prey. Like ..."

"A pack," she finished.

"Yeah, like a massive pack."

As they finally neared the top, she looked up at the tall marble columns of the temple looming above them, over four stories high by her estimate. Below, as the swarm of beasts poured over the horses still milling in the plaza, it became clear that many of them were different and much larger than the Blood Wolves. They slammed the horses with their massive chests, knocking them down and trampling them beneath a different and more destructive kind of stampede.

As she followed, Aylun rounded the corner and headed to the base of the pavilion as the roar grew louder. The lack of yipping, growling, or yelping had an odd and chilling air about it as the sea of creatures reached the bottom of the hill and charged up it.

Megan yelled, "They're coming for us!"

They rounded another corner, this time into the pavilion proper. Their footsteps echoed around them as they passed through the enormous columns that ringed its edge. Before them appeared a broad, dark opening to an enclosed temple building. Megan sprinted across the unpolished marble floor in a flat-out race. The horses, no longer trailing, pulled up beside her; all four abreast, they flew toward an opening wide and tall enough to fit them all.

As the entry neared, the roar of countless paws suddenly jumped in intensity as a wall of creatures crested the hill, racing behind them into the pavilion and through the ring of columns.

Leading the way were massive canine-like creatures, their heads higher than Aylun, who had now begun to lag behind her. Everything about them seemed threatening, from their heavy legs and paws to their broad bodies and thick muzzles brimming with jagged teeth. Their canines looked like they could punch right through her arm. Covered in the coarsest of gray fur, they charged across the marble floor with their backs sloped down to shorter, heavily muscled rear legs. The arrangement thrust their heads up high and made them move like some terrifying ape-dog hybrid.

Megan glanced back as Aylun slipped even farther behind. The sight was disturbing. His face was pale and sweaty, his limp more pronounced, and now fresh blood was oozing down his leg.

She shouted, "Are you okay?"

At her question, he seemed to gather his strength. He scrunched up his face in determination as he put on a burst of speed, staggering faster across the pavilion floor.

The massive gray beasts behind him were gaining at a frightening pace. Among them were dozens of dark scaly things, their only fur a bloodred strip down their backs. Supported by gangly sticklike arms with curved fingers like daggers, their front legs were longer than their back, letting them charge across the ground semi-upright, like the larger creatures. Weaving in and out between them raced dozens of giant deep-red Blood Wolves, and every one of the beasts possessed the same creepy yellow eyes.

As Megan flew through the opening, faint light burst into the massive marble chamber. It sent a golden brightness reflecting off the polished walls and swirling marble floor. Near the end of the hall, the light grew brighter, seeming to radiate from an enormous statue of a woman in flowing robes.

Perched on a massive platform, she stood more than thirty feet tall. Her bearing haughty and regal, she held a golden-tipped bronze spear upright in her right hand. Her left gripped the edge of a giant shield, with the far edge resting on the ground near her feet. Light from the majestic effigy reflected off a pool of crystal water behind her. It glimmered off the still waters in a glittering display that filled the entire back of the temple with a golden glow.

Aylun halted as he entered.

Megan looked back to spot his gaze flying across the vast chamber. "It is a death trap. There are no places to hide."

She barely caught his mutterings above the clatter as she and the horses barged across the marble floor into the enormous open space.

He whipped around and shouted over his shoulder, "Help me!"

She stared in puzzlement. "Help you do what?"

"Hold the entrance."

"How? It's too big. They'll surround us."

Aylun hesitated. "Then hide."

"Where?"

He pulled his staff pieces from his back and stood firm.

Megan stared for a moment at the massive pack of vicious claws and teeth now charging across the pavilion. She looked at the doorway, and a plan occurred. With her gift, she reached out and pulled down on the stone frame in a burst of wind that jarred her backward, almost knocking her off her feet. The force should have been enough to do *something*, even if it didn't collapse the entrance.

She tried again, putting all her concentration into it, pulling down on the doorframe. A gale of wind whipped through her hair, and she began to slide across the floor. A shriek forced its way out; at first borne of her effort, it soon turned to one of frustration, yet the stone doorframe refused to budge even the tiniest bit.

Megan turned away from it, breathing hard as she staggered toward the back of the temple. In reluctant capitulation, she began scanning the chamber for hiding places. Yet the enormous statue somehow drew her attention, an object of intense, glowing fascination. Her gaze wandered up its length to the face, then flew down to the pool of water. The oddity of it all hit her in one blast, striking with staggering force.

The light was impossible. It had come on as they entered, but to create light required energy. Energy that entropy would have long ago dissipated. Baffling too was the absurd pool of water. Without a source of fresh water to renew it, it would have evaporated eons ago. Yet the roof appeared intact, allowing no rain to seep in and fill it. Even without that, the walls and bottom of the pool should have become coated in a thick layer of algae and sludge. Yet the pool was as crystal clear as a mountain stream. The temple was intact too. In fact, the entire city should have been buried in layers of dust and decay, yet too much of it remained looking like new.

The light, the water, the pristine temple, the city itself, even the doorway her gift couldn't collapse—all of it was utterly wrong. Something was protecting it, protecting all of it. Some source of mind-boggling power had preserved it, something perpetual, something immortal, something of … godlike power.

Her head whipped up, and she stared at the piercing eyes of the statue as a sudden crazy, improbable, and ridiculous epiphany struck. In sheer desperation, she dropped to her knees on the smooth marble floor.

She spoke in a soft and reverent tone. "Help us."

The beasts almost upon him, Aylun jammed the two staff ends together with a click. He glanced back at Megan. "Have you lost your ever-loving mind … again?"

Her whisper became even softer. "I implore you, please help us."

He braced himself for the impending assault. "We are about to die, and you think begging a mythical deity for help is—"

A loud crackling of rock against rock resonated through the hall as the chin of the statue dropped, and it glared at Aylun with glowing marble eyes.

The enormous beast at the front leaped in a blur of wiry gray fur. It arced through the air to descend upon him, its long, curved claws, sharp teeth, and wicked canines ready to rend Aylun limb from limb.

The haughty statue crackled some more as it waved its hand to dismiss the beast. It and all its brethren across the enormous pavilion were scattered away like chaff in the wind. Time seemed to slow, then come to a stop, leaving only Megan, Aylun, their horses, and the statue still moving.

Megan stared in stunned silence as the marble sculpture left its spear and shield standing and stepped down from its ornately scrolled podium, becoming smaller as its stone feet clacked against the marble floor.

Aylun's jaw dropped and he stared in awe. "How did—"

"Silence!" the statue demanded, its commanding voice reverberating through the chamber.

Megan startled.

The statue crunched with the sound of breaking stone as it approached her and began transforming into a real-life woman. Her bright white robes flowed around her with an otherworldly quality, and even as marble turned to flesh, she continued to radiate an ethereal golden light.

Now perhaps only eight feet fall, the former statue's sandaled feet stopped just in front of Megan, her silver eyes fixed on her as her voice sounded out strong, yet suffused with compassion. "As admirable as your supplication may be, child, I cannot help you."

Dumbfounded, Megan pointed to the now-empty pavilion. "But you did that ..."

"I brushed away a nuisance, nothing more. One that would profane my temple with your blood. They will soon return, and I will not stop them a second time."

"Return?"

The statue nodded.

"Can't you send them away for good?"

"If only it were that simple, but alas, I will not."

"Why?" Megan pleaded, her panic flaring anew.

"There could be consequences."

"Consequences?" She boggled. "For who? ... You? But you are a god."

The statue seemed to take her words as an affront. "A godd*ess*," she corrected, then her expression softened. "And no, I am not. There was a time when we were believed to be gods. Perhaps we even let ourselves believe it, but I am as human as you."

"But surely someone as powerful as ... as ..."

The woman looked down at Megan. "I have been called many names: Parthenos, Areia, Hellotia, and many more." She smiled. "But you may call me Athene."

Megan stepped back as memories of college textbooks on ancient Greek culture and mythology rolled around in her head. She recalled a large and heavy tome that contained a lot of pictures. One of them was of a statue much like this one. In an instant, she made the connection. "Athene, as in ... goddess of warfare?"

The woman smiled again as if admiring Megan's astuteness. "I prefer goddess of wisdom and courage."

Her suspicion confirmed, Megan's mind raced as she tried to recall all she had once known of the Greek goddess Athena. She stepped forward again. "... and heroes and stuff, right?"

Athene granted her another soft smile, then her expression grew distant as if recalling some fond memory. "I have encouraged those who undertake heroic endeavors, yes."

Eager to gain her favor, Megan blurted out, "We're trying to reach Lanessa, isn't that heroic enou—"

"Heroic?" Athene's voice boomed out as she pointed to the now-empty pavilion. "This is what you consider heroic? You get caught in a lethal trap by a foe you do not yet begin to comprehend? You pray for help when you have no idea what powers you call upon? You toy with terrible forces, child. Did your brush with Islong teach you nothing of the dangers with which you trifle?"

She stared for a moment, then lifted both palms. A sudden lightness came to Megan's pocket as her dragon key appeared on the goddess's right hand and her dark metal ring on the left. "By rights, these are mine."

"Yours?" Megan stepped closer and reached out for her treasures.

Athene's face filled with disapproval, halting her midswipe. As soon as she stopped, the soft and patient manner returned. "They are made of Elysium. That can come only from one place and only through me."

"But I may need them, and I—"

Athene's eyes hardened as her voice became stern and reproachful. "And you think your need entitles you to them?"

Megan shrank away and bowed her head. "No, but ..."

A distant and remorseful tone filled Athene's voice. "I have no use for champions any longer, but this world may soon have terrible need of them." She seemed to consider for a moment as Megan lifted her gaze. "Keep your treasures. Prove you are worthy, and they will be yours."

They disappeared from Athene's palms and returned to their original places.

Megan pointed out past Aylun and the broad doorway to the pavilion beyond. "What about those things out there?"

Athene dismissed her question with a simple wave of her hand. She motioned to the platform where her bronze spear and shield still stood, and they slid forward with a low grinding noise. She pointed to a now revealed stairway leading down into darkness. "You may leave my temple. It would be a tragedy for it to be profaned with your blood."

AYLUN

She lifted her palm again, and a glowing glass ball appeared in it, looking much like Aylun's flamestone except the light had the same golden quality as that radiating from Athene. With gentleness, she placed it in Megan's hand. "It will be dark down there. You will have need of this."

"What is it?"

"Merely a bauble, an aetherstone. Its light will never dim."

Athene shot a glance over to Yuki, drinking from the pool of water. She shook her head in disapproval, and with a wave of her hand, both horses vanished. "Keep your beasts out of my temple."

Megan's jaw dropped. She stepped forward, and her voice became demanding. "Give me back my Yuki."

At her defiant tone, a look of approval and admiration crossed Athene's face. "If you survive, I will return her. For now, she is in a place with abundant food, few dangers, and sun-drenched fields in which to run. She is far better off than with you."

She turned and addressed Aylun with a stern voice. "And you. You choose to be her protector?"

He had been standing still with a stunned expression, but at her question he gave a scant nod.

She pointed out to where the raging beasts once stood. "And you accept the cost?"

He nodded again, seeming reluctant to open his mouth.

Athene's irate voice boomed out. "Then you are a liar, a fool, and a coward."

Aylun stumbled back, seeming even more shocked.

Her manner softened, and her gentle voice and radiant face showed genuine concern. "I feel for you, Aylun. To see every person you love perish before your very eyes, it is a grievous burden. Yet you have lacked the wisdom to find meaning in their sacrifice. And you speak of honor while seeking to place the burden for your suicide on the conscience of another."

Aylun's head dropped.

Her voice took on an even stronger note of grace and empathy. "Be sincere in your efforts to protect her. Do not flinch in the face of death, but do not seek it." She pointed again to the pavilion. "And do not accept it. Only if you live can you continue to protect her."

Athene grew larger again as she turned and stepped back up onto the platform. Her robes flowed around her as she faced them again, looking down on them from more than three stories up. Her voice rang out, sure and strong. "If you are to live through this, it must be by your own efforts. It will be a test of skill and strategy, but there is a way." Her gaze rose as she resumed her original pose and returned to stone.

In an instant, time resumed, as if the world had been a video on pause and Athene had pressed the play button again. The roar of pounding paws returned, growing louder as the beasts mounted the hill and, once again, charged across the pavilion.

Still appearing awed and shocked, Aylun limped over to where Megan stood and ushered her to the top of the stairway. He pointed down into the blackness. "Go. I must stay to ensure your escape."

Megan balked. The idea of leaving him alone to fend for himself tied her stomach in knots. "But it's suicide. Didn't you hear her?"

"I have no intention of dying, but if we both flee, we will both be hunted down and killed."

Tears came to her eyes. "I already left Jon behind. Don't make me leave anyone else. Don't leave me alone. Don't make me do this."

The rumble continued to grow, becoming alarming in its volume. Aylun pointed down into the foreboding darkness. "Find a place to hide, somewhere with a strong door. Wait for me. I can find you."

She began to object, but he stepped toward her. As if drawing on some hidden strength, he became calm, and his voice confident and reassuring. "I will find you."

She hesitated, and he gave her a small shove down the stairs. She took a few reluctant steps, forging through the darkness of the arched stone stairwell. Her light spilled across the dark gray stones from which the structure had been built. The few hesitant steps soon turned into quick, careful ones. Guilt and concern tugged at her, wanting her to slow further.

Then the pounding of countless paws and clacking of claws against marble reached her, echoing down from the chamber above. Terror won out, driving her faster and faster on the rough-hewn steps. Soon she was flying downward, with only the lighted glass ball to show her the next few steps in front of her.

She glanced behind as a massive body of gray leaped to the top of the steps and lunged down the stairwell toward Aylun. A vicious snarl bellowed out as it slashed forward at his head with jagged teeth. She gasped and slowed as Aylun jabbed and thrust, swinging his bladed staff with astonishing speed and precision as he held the enormous beast at bay.

Megan stopped and yelled up at him, "Aylun, come with me, we can do this tog—"

"Go!" he shouted as he fought.

Megan turned and raced downward. She glanced back at Aylun one last time and fought the impulse to choke up. He was surrounded now by a ring of enormous creatures. Silhouetted by the light from the temple behind him, he fended off attack after attack with a flurry of thrusts, dodges, blocks, and parries.

Every fiber of her being told her he was in trouble, that she had to go back, that he was wounded and exhausted and needed her help; but even though his position seemed hopeless, she had to trust him. He was more capable, more knowledgeable, and more experienced than she. So, with aetherstone in hand, casting its golden glow across the stone walls and stairs, Megan did as Aylun had demanded and raced downward into endless darkness.

Chapter Eleven

HIDING OUT

Megan plunged down the dark and damp stairwell, the knot in her stomach growing with each step. She clutched the smooth aetherstone in her hand, its golden light splashing across the gray stone walls and uneven steps as they streaked by. She kept her head down, focused on the slabs that made up the stairway as she struggled not to lose her balance.

The clatter of the fight behind her intensified, growing more frantic even as it faded, eventually becoming a mere rumbling echo, mixing with the clatter of her own footsteps and labored breathing. Down and down she raced until she was gasping for air and her legs wobbled from fatigue. Still she pushed on, slipping and stumbling on the carved stone steps.

The bottom came unexpectedly. Megan's feet crumpled under her, and her shoulder hit the unforgiving rock of the opposite wall where the passage rounded a corner into what appeared to be a straight arched hallway. She winced and rubbed her shoulder as she gathered herself up. The flat rock floor seemed to be a single unbroken surface, which made for better footing, so she picked up the pace. Soon she was racing along a tunnel that appeared to be built from the same dark gray stone as the stairwell.

At the thought of Aylun behind her, tears began to fall. For over a decade, she had strived for independence, never again wanting to be reliant on anyone or anything. She had even taken martial arts classes so she would never be vulnerable, never need anyone for protection. Yet here she was, fleeing in abject terror. Leaving an injured man, a man she despised, a man from whom she had just run away, to fight and quite possibly die so she could survive.

Megan forced her attention back to the immediate danger and the urgent need to escape. She had promised Aylun she would hide, yet the uninterrupted corridor offered no shelter, no door or room, not even an offshoot, grate, or tunnel into which she could disappear. As she ran, the echo of her gasping sobs and the clatter of footsteps almost drowned out the fight behind her, now only echoes of echoes.

A sudden change in the quality of the sound caused her to halt. She silenced her gasping breaths and choked back her tears as she turned and raised an ear to listen down the hall. The low rumble remained but had become quieter now.

Unable to guess what led to the change, she faced forward again, but as she did, a dull flicker of light caught her eye. She waved her aetherstone, hoping the movement would repeat the flickering, and it did. A faint light reflected back to her, a barely visible silvery glint from the lower part of the wall a short distance ahead.

She raced up to the spot and dropped to her knees, squinting through the soft golden light as she felt along the rough stones of the wall. Then she found it—a spot of cold, smooth metal. The flash of reflected light had come from the dull metal surface of a spike or rod embedded in rock. Flush with its face, the piece was centered on one of the larger stones that composed the wall. She checked around it. This was the only sign she'd seen of anything but rock and mortar, and it had to mean something.

She scanned the stonework again and soon found another dull circle of metal a few feet to the left, at the same level, buried in the center of another stone. The existence of two such pieces at the exact same height and both centered in a stone couldn't be a mere coincidence.

More certain than ever that she had stumbled onto something, she glanced down below the dull metal and located a dark crack where the wall wasn't attached to the floor. She ran her finger along its length. It extended a foot or so beyond each metal rod and came to an abrupt end at a point where she found the mortar that joined the wall to the floor. If the section in front of her wasn't attached, then perhaps this was some kind of false wall. It had to be.

She was too anxious and engrossed to take note of another change in the rumble reverberating down the hall. As she worked, it grew in volume until it became too obvious to ignore. She turned her head back in the direction she had come, listening to the sound of countless scraping claws and pounding feet growing louder and louder. The creatures must have gotten past Aylun, and now they were coming for her.

She froze as it occurred to her that if Aylun was no longer protecting the stairwell, the most obvious explanation was that he was no longer able. He had succumbed to the endless tide of creatures. No, that couldn't be. She had to assume he was still alive. He must have abandoned the stairwell as part of some strategy. Any other conclusion was unthinkable.

Megan's breath turned rapid and shallow as she turned her attention once again to the wall, waving the golden light over it as she felt for cracks in the mortar. Then she spotted one—a jagged line that weaved down between the stones until it reached the gap at the floor. She stood and stepped back, eyeing the wall in the golden light as more cracks now jumped out at her. It was just as she had hoped. The cracks formed the shape of a short door.

She pushed against it, and it gave back an encouraging groan but didn't budge. The roar of paws and scratching claws took a sudden jump in volume. Gripped by alarm and terrified to look for fear of what she might find, Megan glanced down the hall. Bounding toward her were countless pairs of yellow eyes, reflecting the golden light of her glass ball.

She turned her back to the door and pushed, but it still refused to give way. With a mass of creatures almost upon her, she was committed now to moving the door or dying in the effort, and a sudden determination came over her. She calmed herself, then clenched every muscle in a last tremendous push.

The door *thunk*ed and ground open a crack. Megan shoved again as the wave of fur and teeth hurtling at her became visible in the light of her aetherstone. She heaved again. The door opened further, and she was able to squeeze through. She swung around to push the door closed and a gigantic paw full of broken and ragged claws swiped through the narrow opening.

She dodged away from it, then took another step back. More claws came through, and she jumped at each set that reached out for her through the opening. Unable to close the door with even one heavy paw jamming it open, she waited until all of them had disappeared, then leaped and flung herself against the door, pushing hard.

Another huge paw swiped through and froze as it became pinched in the closing door.

Megan let go, and the paw pulled back.

She heaved again, and it closed some more.

A thinner, longer set of curved claws jabbed through the door, this time catching her arm.

She thrust her arm down and pulled away as the claws scratched her skin. With all the force she could muster, she flung herself at the door in one final push.

It ground shut, shearing off several of the thin, dagger-like claws. A shriek of pain shot down the hallway, then the wailing that followed grew muffled as the heavy slab of stonework *thunk*ed back into place. The wall once again appeared to be a single, uninterrupted piece of dark gray stonework.

Trembling, she slumped down, facing the jagged rocks of the door. Through the crack beneath the door came a disturbing medley of barking and growls that reverberated down the long passage. With her golden aetherstone clutched in a shaky hand, she turned sideways and began stepping away, following the interior wall.

A bench hit her behind her knees, and she sat down hard, sliding in a layer of grit and grime that coated its surface. She pulled up her feet and clutched her knees to her chest as her tears fell. The odor of dust and decay hung heavy in the air. Her trembling refused to abate, and all at once, she was that little girl again, cowering in the dark and dusty closet. Only this time, it wasn't ghosts and ghouls in the corners and on the shelves. There were actual monsters behind the door.

Wait ... was she sure? How certain was she that no terrors lurked here in this new room? She scanned her surroundings, trying to untie the anxious knot in the pit of her stomach.

The floor resembled the floor of the hall, a continuous flat surface of rock. On either side of her stood walls that seemed constructed of a mixture of light and dark gray stones. She squinted at a second bench standing against the far wall, unable to make any details of the items on it in what little light reached it. The uneven sheet of rock behind it and the jagged ceiling above were of the same material as the floor. Together, they gave the impression of being natural, as if the entire room had been built out of a preexisting cave.

Reassured that she was most likely alone, she turned her attention to the door, which was obscured by the shadows, lines, and curves of the strange mechanism that supported it. For a long while, she stared at the severed claws lying on the floor. She jumped as one of them twitched, no doubt a postmortem spasm, a nerve reflex. It didn't matter that she could explain it. She was still creeped out and shuddered at each loud bang or vicious snarl from quarreling beasts in the hallway.

The image returned of Aylun fighting like mad against a ring of snarling, lunging faces, and she mumbled to herself, "You promised to protect me. You told Jon no harm would come to me by your hand or any other. But where are you now? Idiot ... cretin ... stupid, stupid Aylun." Megan raised her voice. "How could you do this to me? How could you send me off alone and leave you to—"

She stopped and sniffled, then sniffled again. Here she was, trapped and alone in a dark hole of a room, crying because of him. She was crying because she had left him back there because he was trying to be some kind of ridiculous macho hero. Even when he was no longer here, he couldn't just leave her in peace. He had to make her worry about him, worry that he was dead or suffering.

A sudden revulsion hit. *He* was the one who had abducted her. *He* was the tyrant. How dare he make her worry about him? He had been nothing but horrible to her, and now here she was, crying over a despicable despot. Revulsion turned to anger as she realized he hadn't been entirely detestable. He had gone all noble on her, promising to bring her and Jon back together and even risking his life to do it. Even her concern for him was his fault. He had no right to appeal to her that way, to touch her emotions, to make her uneasy about not forgiving him.

She eyed the door, and her heart cried as the image returned of Aylun on the stairs, bloody clothes clinging to his leg and arm as he struggled to hold back a swath of vicious teeth and fur. Megan whispered to the image, "I'll make you a deal. I'll close my eyes and count to ten, and if you come through that door before I finish, I'll forgive you."

"One ... two ... three." A yip and bark made her jump. A vicious-sounding fight broke out in the hall. Bodies thudded against stone, and she clamped her eyes shut tight. Full of growls, snarls, and screeches of agony, the distraction interrupted her over and over, but she persisted. "Nine ... ten."

A desperate wail cut through the clatter, and the hall fell silent, save for the last whimpers of a dying animal. No sign of Aylun occurred, not even the sound of his footsteps or him fighting in the hall outside the door.

Her trembling now even more uncontrollable, Megan lowered her eyes. The mental image returned of him fighting for their survival on the staircase, and her voice became ever so soft. "Okay, I'll give you one more chance."

She began counting again, much slower this time. A rapid digging came from the door, threatening to interrupt her count, but she only slowed. It stopped, and a series of sniffs shot through the crack at the bottom, ending with a louder blast of air. She jumped as the frantic and determined scraping resumed. Over and over, it repeated: the sniffing at the crack, the dust shooting from the floor, and a new and more desperate round of scraping claws. With each, she startled and slowed more, until her count came to a stop.

Anger swept through her veins. Here she was, giving him a chance to be forgiven, and he didn't even care. Through her shivering, the tears began to flow in earnest. "Stupid, stupid Aylun."

The hall went silent for a time. Then the digging at the door resumed and intensified. Megan spent what seemed like an eternity paralyzed by terror. She trembled and jumped at every vicious bark, snarl, or growl and each desperate cry of pain from the hall outside her door. In unending dread, she hunkered against the wall, certain they would break through any minute and it would be over for her. As time dragged on with no sign of Aylun, she succumbed to despair. Then exhaustion overtook her, and she fell into a fitful sleep.

Aylun's attention was everywhere at once. In constant motion, he parried every advance from the wall of snarling faces that ringed the edge of the dark stairwell. They shifted and dove as they crowded around him, ready to exploit any opening he might leave, no matter how slight. Determined to ignore the ache in his leg, he dodged and danced out of reach, his staff darting, anticipating, flying to intercept every lunge, swipe, and snap of teeth in a perpetual standoff.

He glanced up into a pair of yellow eyes, and a sick, morbid feeling crept into his soul—the same dark dread as the last time he had peered into those eerie, yellow eyes. In his rush to tear his gaze away, he slipped on a stair, and several bodies dove at him at once. He whirled his staff before him, putting it between him and each attacker in turn, halting them as he regained his balance.

He changed his focus to the many legs surrounding him as he calmed his mind and slowed his breathing. No Shou trained to follow opponents only with their eyes. To do so would be to leave oneself vulnerable to attack from behind. Like all of his kind, he had to be adept at using every ounce of his faculties. He had been taught to hear, feel, sense, and even smell his opponents, even when they struck from outside his field of vision. And now, he would live or die on how well he had learned those lessons.

He avoided their eyes and expanded his awareness to include all his senses while over his shoulder, Megan's footsteps grew more distant. Eventually, they disappeared below the rumble of movement in the temple and growls and snarls around him. A modest relief washed over him. She had a fair head start. Now, he had only one goal: to hold the tide of creatures at bay as long as he could and give Megan her best chance of escape.

Creatures were jammed together, shoulder to massive shoulder, along either side of the stairwell in a continuous ring of claws, fur-covered faces, and jagged teeth. One dove too close, so he dodged out of its reach. A lightning lunge from a pair of glistening white teeth threatened to capture the blade end of his staff.

He jerked it back. The moment they disabled his weapon, an onslaught would ensue, and it would be over in the blink of an eye.

A sharp clack jangled in his ears as the beast snapped its jaws in the air where the blade had been.

He jabbed forward, piercing its face just below one eye.

The creature let out a deep yelp that resounded down the hallway behind him as the standoff resumed. On instinct alone, he watched the stairway and reacted to every move at the edges of his vision.

He held them off until long after Megan's footsteps had disappeared beneath the shuffle of feet, growls, and yips. One of the massive gray creatures leered down at him with huge yellow eyes as it shoved through the crowd and brought itself low at the edge of the stairs overhead. It was preparing to pounce. If it leaped down on top of him, he would be forced to defend against a falling weight many times his own, leaving him vulnerable to attack from every other side. Far from being defensible, the stairwell had just become a death trap.

AYLUN

Alarmed that his position no longer remained safe, Aylun spun into action. The time for a standoff had ended; it was now time to cripple and kill. He jabbed and slashed everywhere, slicing faces, piercing eyes, and slitting throats as he pushed his way up the stairs.

Creatures began pouring over the edge into the stairwell behind him, forcing him to defend on every side.

He reached the top few steps, wounding and maiming with a flurry of stabs and swipes. Creatures upon creatures retreated, injured, but not out of the fight. For every one that backed away, more followed, ringing him in a shifting barrier of red and gray fur, blood-spattered faces, curved claws, and sharp teeth.

Through his hail of slashes and blows, he took another step up and glanced across the softly lit temple, now visible above the backs of the throng that surrounded him. Night was falling outside, meaning the siege had only just begun, and a vast sea of creatures stretched far out across the pavilion and beyond. It was an army no one person could hold back.

He returned his attention to his advance, throwing glances at the inside of the temple. The smooth marble floor and sheer white walls offered no cubby, wall, hole, ledge, or perch where he could seek refuge. The raised pool was wide open and indefensible, so he stared up at the glowing statue towering above him. Perhaps if he could climb high enough, he might be out of reach of all the creatures; but its smooth surface seemed slippery, and climbing it could be treacherous.

Aylun unleashed a burst of energy, one last push toward the statue. His staff whirled around him, slashing paws and faces.

One of the enormous gray wire-haired beasts leaped into his path. It turned and bared its teeth in a threatening display as it hunched low between him and the statue. His blade plummeted down on its throat, slicing it open in a spray of blood. The beast wobbled for a moment, then dropped to the ground. His staff whistled through the air as he swung it around and jabbed the tip into the dying body to anchor it. He winced in pain as he gave a tremendous push with his injured leg, vaulted over the carcass, and headed for the statue.

One of the beasts reared up on its muscular haunches, and a huge paw full of broken and jagged claws came in from the side. It caught him midair, sharp edges digging into his stomach with a jolting shot of pain. It threw him back in the other direction, and he flew over the dead creature and tumbled into the pool at the back of the temple. Lukewarm water splashed everywhere as he leaped to his feet and sloshed backward through the water.

The droplets spattered fur and scaly skin in a rain that caused a deafening chorus of shrill shrieks and desperate whimpers. The barrage of pained cries echoed through the overcrowded temple chamber. Aylun stepped farther and farther back, his feet splashing through the clear pool until he hit the corner of the room. His wet clothes clung to his body, and the point of his staff, painted red with blood, jerked back and forth in front of him in anticipation as he held it between him and the creatures.

None followed.

Shocked at their cries of discomfort and puzzled at not being chased, he heaved from exertion as he studied the mass of canines and claws and regained his calm. The creatures milled just beyond the border of the pool, a wall of gray and red fur and white teeth shifting and swerving among one another.

A few approached with tentative steps, halting at the water's edge to swipe in his direction. Yet, each reaching paw was pulled back as if the action caused the beast a shock of discomfort. Then it came back to him: a short time ago, the horses had been drinking from the pool with no hint of pain or displeasure. That meant it must be a bane only to these creatures. But would mere pain or discomfort be enough to stop them from entering the water?

He watched and waited for a while as hope began to rekindle. Then movement outside the temple drew his attention. A thin woman was winding her way through the dark throng spread out across the pavilion. Twice as tall as he, she appeared atop one of the massive gray canine-like creatures. Confident and in command, she swayed with a dignified ease as the beast's heavy shoulders rolled beneath her and its massive paws thudded across the pavilion floor. Those shoulders were much higher than her mount's haunches, not only lending it its creepy, apelike appearance, but also thrusting her up high above the throng. Her clothes were loose and tattered, barely covering her deep-red skin. A human-looking face poked high above it, perched on a longer-than-normal neck.

Her mount halted at the edge of the broad temple entrance, and she stared in with a look of disdain, as if loath to enter. Creatures between her and the pool backed away, giving her an unobstructed view of Aylun and he of her and her mount. She craned her long neck as she surveyed the interior, and her huge yellow eyes came to rest on Aylun. A profound despair and morbid dread gripped him as she let out a low, rumbling growl as authentic as any dog's or wolf's.

Wet clothes, as cold as her eyes, hugged Aylun's body, and water dripped from his hair to roll down his face as he held her gaze. For a moment, she scowled at him, then slipped from the muscular shoulders of the enormous beast. She broke her gaze and the despair faded as quickly as it had come on.

As if it were as natural as walking on two legs, she lowered herself down onto all fours. She stood on her fingers and toes as her heels turned into hocks and her long fingernails into jagged claws jutting from thick paws. As her head bent to the ground, her human features distorted, the nose and mouth extending into the pointed muzzle of a wolf.

Then she sniffed the floor, lingering for a moment to take in the scent of one particular spot. If his memory served him, it was the exact spot where Megan had entered the chamber. A smile spread across her face as she returned to her human form, and she rose back up onto two legs. The smile persisted as she cocked her head, staring at Aylun as if he were a bug she could squash or mere prey for her to toy with.

With the commanding air of a general ordering her troops, she glanced at two of the enormous coarse-furred beasts. As if they understood some unspoken command, they strolled over to the pool, and each grabbed a wolf carcass in their powerful jaws. With feet braced and violent jerking movements, they dragged the bodies away. A pair of carcasses at a time, they cleared a long swath of slick white marble smeared and spattered with blood.

Having created an open path leading to the pool's edge, one of them strolled to its far end. It brought its head low, leering at Aylun with its giant yellow eyes. It hovered for a moment as a different dread entered Aylun's heart, this time fear over what he knew was coming. He glanced all around the temple again, searching for a place of refuge, but his gaze was drawn back to the statue.

In a scraping of claws against swirling marble, the gray monstrosity broke into a sprint, bounding across the floor in tremendous leaps, headed straight for Aylun.

Water splashed all around as he sprang to his feet and yanked his staff out in front of him.

The massive beast landed with one last thud and leaped over the edge of the pool, its powerful haunches uncoiling in a tremendous push. It sailed through the air in an arc that would send a weight many times his own crashing down on top of him.

Aylun dove forward and raised his staff, ducking under the beast. His blade whipped up and sliced the length of its chest open as the monstrosity fell. The tip of the staff came down at the edge of the pool, and he leaped, using it to pole-vault through the air.

He landed on the upper edge of the statue's shield. With beasts leaping after him, he bounced off it toward the marble body as his staff clattered to the ground. He used the folds of fabric, the belt, and the spear to spring, pull, and bound upward, propelling himself higher until he reached the spear arm. In one last giant leap upward, he grabbed hold, hanging on to a limb many times larger than his own. He dangled for a moment, high above the beasts swirling below.

They leaped at his legs as his hand began to slip. He pulled himself up to get a better grip, but the smooth marble surface resisted any attempts to gain a solid purchase. Again and again, his hands slid as he reached higher and higher, trying to get a firm grip. Then, all at once, he yanked himself up and flung his chest over the statue's arm, then pulled himself up to sit on it.

The angle at which she held her spear made the limb a perfect resting spot, so he leaned back, his wet clothes even colder against the cool, hard marble. For a while, he sat there, panting, as he surveyed the chaos below.

Creatures jumped and scrambled, trying to clamber up the statue, but he remained well out of their reach. The beast in the pool still clung to life, moaning and whimpering as it dragged itself toward the edge. The woman outside the chamber scowled and let out a pitiful howl. All the creatures stopped in their tracks, raised their heads, and joined in, creating a wail so loud it compelled him to cover his ears.

As the clamor ceased and its echo reverberated through the marble chamber, the woman waved her clawed hand as she marched toward her mount. At her signal, a stream of creatures turned and headed for the stairway where Megan had disappeared. As the woman rode away into the darkness, Aylun watched, helpless, as beast upon beast poured down the stairwell after Megan, with nothing and no one to stop them.

The wounded creature in the pool dragged itself over the wall. In an instant, it was set upon by its brethren. They clamped down on its various parts. Furious screeches of agony rang through the chamber as they tugged and pulled until they tore off limbs and rent the flesh. The pitiful wailing whimpered to an awful silence as they strolled away or hunkered down to consume their prizes. The spectacle stood as a vivid preview of what awaited him if he allowed himself even one slipup. He slumped against the white marble of the arm, eyeing the throng below as he waited.

The creatures beneath him had soon consumed their wounded member and licked the floor clean of its blood and entrails. As if waiting for him to fall, they began to pace below him. Then, a few at a time, they gave up and lay down until, eventually, there were dozens of them sprawled out across the smooth polished floor. A brief compulsion hit him to do as Megan had done and pray to the goddess for help, but then he recalled all that Athene had said. She had been quite forceful in telling them she would not help and if they were to get out of this it would have to be by their own efforts. Not wishing to further suffer her anger, he refrained from entreating her.

Aylun peered down, eyeing his staff. It lay on the ground surrounded by a sea of gray and bloodred bodies. With only one small throwing star left, he was virtually weaponless, and he would die of thirst if he remained trapped on this perch. The creatures were not known to roam the city during daylight. They only ventured into it at sunset, so, his only hope now was that some or all of them would leave before the morning light.

He leaned back on the unyielding marble and closed his eyes against the statue's constant golden glow. He quieted his mind and ignored the impatient grumbles and snarls from below, determined to get a few moments' rest before sunrise. Morning would come soon, and perhaps the situation would have changed enough to give him a fighting chance to reach Megan.

Her sleep was fitful, every yip and scrape from the hallway bringing Megan half-awake. A morbid dread haunted her deeper slumber, yellow eyes chasing her through her dreams and into a cramped, dark closet. The closet would expand into a vast hall. The eyes would reappear and chase her down again. Terror would drive her through corridors and rooms, yellow-eyed monsters nipping at her heels until they found another dark closet to chase her into. Then the vicious cycle would begin again, repeating over and over, never giving her a moment's rest.

AYLUN

At a loud bang, she jumped and snapped wide awake, her breath short and her hands shaking as she stared into the dim light of the room. All was quiet now, but the noise had sounded like it came from inside. Then again, her half-dreaming state made it impossible to be sure.

Megan rubbed her throat and gulped a dry swallow. The sound was not her only worry. These past days, their meals had been meager and her hunger growing until it was now a constant gnawing. Even worse, it had been morning when she'd last taken a drink, and all her food and water had gone wherever Yuki had gone. With not even a sip in almost a day, her mouth had already become parched, and a nagging thirst hounded her. If food and water were to be found, she would not find them by cowering in a corner.

She scanned the dingy space by the golden light from her aetherstone, looking for the source of the bang. While the hallway beyond the door was silent now, she had no illusions; it was bound to be filled with now-hungry carnivores. The light jittered in her shaky hands and was too dim to penetrate the chamber's darker recesses, so she braced herself. Nothing could be learned from the confines of her small corner of the bench, so she resolved to venture out into the room to check it over firsthand.

Still uncomfortable in the dark, she rose, alert to even the slightest sound. Her shoe clacking against the bare stone of the floor broke the near silence, and a deep, resonant bark erupted from beyond the door. First one voice, then another, and another, higher, then deeper, spreading farther and farther until it became a continuous roar. Trembling, she hunched over, as if by making herself smaller she might be protected from the source of the barking. With her aetherstone clutched to her stomach, she ignored the deafening chorus and crept across the room. With each step, shadows from the giant wheel and metal rods of the door's strange mechanism stretched farther across the gray walls.

She stopped in front of it and stared for a while, her mind foggy and unable to function with all the noise. From this side, it was clear the metal spikes she had seen in the hall were not spikes at all. They were the flat ends of a bent rod, extending out from the rocks of the door far enough to hold a carved stone wheel on which its entire weight rested. High above, a heavy metal counterbalance protruded well past the center of the wheel, helping negate the stone door's substantial weight, so that not all of it rested on the ground.

Two curved metal levers provided a mechanism for closing and opening. Both were attached to the ceiling and rested on the counterbalance above, and, when pulled, they would lift the door and push it at the same time. One on the outside pushed it closed, while another on the inside pushed it open.

As she finished examining the door, the barking thinned. Then a sudden deep and sonorous howl rose from right outside the door. At the very edge of holding it together, she staggered away toward the rough rock wall opposite the bench. Like the barking, the yowling spread until it almost drowned out the barking or turned it to yips that were half bark, half baying. She slumped as she reached the table before the wall, leaning on it to steady herself.

An image flashed through her mind of Aylun out in the hall with that noise. It was followed by more imaginings of him fighting through its endless length filled with those things. She covered her ears, trying to shut out the unholy cacophony, but it was no use. At the limits of her tolerance, she fell apart and shrank down, crouching in a ball as memories of her father's dark closet rushed back.

Scenes hit her of the many times he had picked her up and tossed her in there for yelling at him to stop shouting at Mother. As vivid as yesterday came scenes of their hallway and the times he had dragged her kicking and screaming into that cramped space for trying to flee his angry, yelling face. The threatening noises beyond the stone wall blended with these horrid memories, roaring in her ears, and she began to wail.

It might have lasted only a minute but seemed like forever as she hunkered there, crippled by worry and terror and that horrible, ceaseless howling. After a time, she managed to pull herself together.

Her breath shuddered as she gathered her courage and struggled upright. She had to resume her search.

When she reached the near end of the wide table, she stared down at the collection of items heaped on it. Every one of them was covered in a layer of gray sand and dust. Megan reached with shaking hands to wipe the layer of debris off a row of slender metal objects. They bore a vague resemblance to the tools a dentist might use to scrape your teeth. Behind them lay what appeared to be heavy metal pry bars. The howling diminished as, with shaky steps, she moved farther down to the middle of the table.

From there to the far end lay stacks of clothes, from drab linen rags to colorful finery and an assortment of wigs in many styles and shades. In a chest on the floor at the end lay a jumble of cloth and leather bags, purses, and other containers, looking as if they had been casually tossed in a heap.

The howling drew to an end, stopping as quickly as it had started. The only sound that remained was the restless movement of the creatures in the hall. Her brain still mired in shock and fear, Megan stood back and studied the whole table. Through her haze, a vague sense gathered in her consciousness. Something about them spoke to her, telling her these were tools of the trade for pickpockets or thieves. She looked over the collection again, struggling through her jumbled thoughts to reason out what had led her to that impression.

The clothes varied in style and condition too much to be a simple wardrobe. After all, who would collect worn and dirty woolen rags alongside new silken robes? No, it was clear: The vast differences meant they were costumes. They were used to dress for various roles. The small slender metal objects didn't exactly resemble dental tools. In fact, they were even more reminiscent of old-fashioned lock picks. They, along with the pry bars, were tools for opening that which others did not want you to open.

Even the pile of pouches fit. They appeared to be leftover remains of stolen purses and satchels. After all, who would need or want so many? And the fact they were on the floor in a heap whereas the other items had been somewhat neatly arranged said they were unwanted and discarded. She nodded to herself as the hall remained silent and her mind continued to clear. She was right. The mixture of items painted a picture, a distinct impression. This place had once been a hideout for pickpockets and thieves.

Feeling better now that the hall had fallen silent, Megan tiptoed to the next point of interest—a second door, this one of heavy metal embedded in a substantial wall of stone. Situated across from the door she had entered, its surface was replete with intricate scroll-work, and on the right side, it had a simple handle and keyhole. She set her shoulder against it and shoved, but it refused to budge, making it seem likely that it was locked. It looked like the door to some kind of safe, so she continued on, until she ended her survey back at the gray marble bench.

With her search having yielded no source for any noise inside the room, or any water, she lay back down. The barking and howling left her more unnerved than ever. With nothing to distract her wandering mind, she shivered at the stirrings and clicking of claws from the pacing monstrosities in the hall. As time wore on, any germ of hope she still nurtured died a suffocating death. By now, Aylun had to be dead, and even if he wasn't, the hope that he might reach her seemed a forlorn one. Spent and harried, Megan lay there for an eternity, jumping at every scrape and scuffle until exhaustion drove her back down into a fitful sleep.

The ache of his weary and bruised body kept Aylun's sleep light, as did the sounds of licking, yawning, and quiet stirring from the throng below. They interrupted his slumber again and again, only allowing him to drift off for a time near dawn. Sometime later—it was impossible to tell when—morning light roused him for good. It glowed through openings in the wall near the ceiling, filling the entire chamber.

He stretched and rubbed his sore neck. Then he shifted his position, trying to gain some comfort against the chill of the unyielding marble. From his perch, high on the spear arm of the statue, he had a clear view of the entire chamber. Patches of coarse gray fur were interspersed among the bloodred creatures lounging across the shiny marble floor. Sheer walls surrounded them, stretching more than three stories high, leaving no accessible place that was not open to attack.

Only the cool, clear pool below offered any protection, and as last night's foray had demonstrated, it provided no permanent shelter from the beasts. Out past the entrance, the pavilion lay bare. The army that had last night laid siege to the temple had abandoned it. The creatures remaining inside were a force of daunting numbers, spread across the floor, down the dark stairway, and who knew how far beyond. But at least it would not be an endless fight that would pound him into exhaustion. No matter how remote his chance of survival was now, it was preferable to a fight with no hope at all.

The animals below seemed asleep, or at least not on high alert. He had only one throwing star left, and his staff lay on the ground out of reach. The element of surprise might still be his, but how to use it when he was weaponless and too far up for a direct assault? He surveyed the reclining bodies at the feet of the statue as a strategy began to organize itself in his mind. It was an old one: make a noise in the east and attack from the west.

He took a slow, deep breath, then slipped around the statue's arm and dropped to her robe. On the balls of his feet, he bounded from the belt to the folds of fabric to land without a sound on the upper edge of the shield. For a moment, he perched there, waving his arms to regain his balance as he stared down to make sure the throng below had not heard his movements.

From his sheath, he slid out the last shuriken, raised it to his mouth, and clenched it between his teeth. Balanced on the rim of the enormous shield, he lifted first one leg, then the other, and slipped off each shoe. Back again on both feet, he flung the shoes far out across the pool. The shoes arced over the water and slapped into the marble wall with a pair of loud claps.

As they did, he dropped quickly and quietly down behind the shield, hidden between the legs of the statue and the enormous round shield of stone.

Heads whipped up and swung around with ears pricked and aimed in the direction of the sound.

As the claps reverberated through the temple hall, a barefoot and silent Aylun dashed out from behind the shield and headed for the pool, snatching his staff from the ground on the way.

As he slipped through the throng of bodies, faces turned toward him.

He flung the shuriken, embedding it in a giant yellow eye on the right as he dodged a set of flashing ivory teeth on the left.

A massive gray blur lunged out in front of him.

He tossed the staff over the beast as he dove under it. Jaws snapped in the air behind him as he rolled and leaped over the edge and into the pool. He twisted around as the staff came down, and he caught it with one hand. His back hit the surface of the pool and he kicked and flailed, splashing water as far as he could. Beasts skittered away as he sprang to his feet with his bladed staff in hand. He flew after them, attacking the retreating throng, slashing necks and stabbing through eyes. Five beasts fell before he retreated and dove back into the pool.

The assault had proved one thing beyond doubt. The Blood Wolves may have blinding speed, but the larger creatures were slower, and he could use that. Still, he had only so much energy—one bite, one mistake, and it would be over. Now was not the time to cripple and maim. Every blow had to kill.

As the beasts stepped closer to the edge of the pool, Aylun removed his shirt, submerged it in the water, and tied the dripping fabric around the end of his staff. Then he whipped it around his head, spraying water everywhere and sending all the creatures scurrying. While they were off guard, he launched another attack, felling several more before he sprinted back to the relative safety of the pool.

This time, the creatures did not return to the lip of the pool. Instead, they scrutinized him from a fair distance back. Perhaps they were afraid, or maybe they were trying to lure him out. Yes, that had to be it; their movements seemed more deliberate than simple caution, more like a tactic. They were faster than him, so if they were to get him away from the pool, they could slip by and surround him.

Aylun considered for a moment as he redrenched his shirt. Then he dove out of the pool and headed straight at the group, leaving only enough room on the left that any beasts trying to get past him would have to stick to the wall.

Creatures on either side began to encircle him.

He waited for the perfect moment, then swung the soaking shirt in a circle again, raining pool water on all sides as he lurched to the left, heading straight at the group against the nearest wall.

As expected, they split, leaving part of the group stranded.

He made straight for them, trapping them between him, the pool, and the wall.

The few now-isolated creatures turned and tried to flee to the safety of the pack, but he stabbed and slashed, cutting down three more. Then he raced back to the pool.

Not sure they could be fooled a third time, he used his staff to create a wave in the pool that splashed water well out across the smooth floor. Its marble surface now wet and slick, he dove out and rushed the beasts. Struggling to avoid a fatal slip or fall, he stabbed at them as he jeered.

They dodged away from his blade.

He taunted for a brief moment, then turned and ran.

As wolves do, the group gave chase.

When he reached the slippery floor before the pool, he skated across it as if it were ice.

When the beasts hit the slick, wet stone, they lost their footing, crashing to the floor and sliding across it in disarray.

Aylun leaped and somersaulted over the wall of the pool as beasts slammed into it. Water splashed as he landed facing them. He lashed out with a flurry of quick slashes as they stumbled for footing. Soon he had felled all the beasts that had chased him. Their bodies lay at the pool's edge, their blood flowing onto the marble and mixing with the splashed water.

With only a brief rest between runs, bit by bit, a handful of creatures at a time, Aylun cleared the hall. Near the end, their reluctance to enter the relative brightness of the pavilion became apparent. He used that to his advantage, trapping stragglers at the entrance, where he put an end to their threat.

The temple now littered only with dead carcasses, he turned his attention to the stairway where Megan had escaped and the host of creatures hiding in its dark depths. His shoes were still floating in the pool, so he retrieved them and put them on. He filled his waterskin, donned his soaked shirt, and placed his flamestone in a holder on his belt.

Since a fight in the cramped space of the dark stairwell would prove awkward, he twisted his staff and pulled the two halves apart. Rather than retract the blades, he gripped each half in one hand, flourishing them to give himself a feel for their weight.

So far, his attacks had been brief forays across the temple floor, then a return to the cooling waters of the pool to recover and prepare for the next bout. The stairwell would be a different matter. It would offer no rest and no cooling water. He would either fight his way to Megan or succumb to exhaustion and die.

It would also be a different kind of fight. The temple was open, with lots of space to maneuver, while the stairwell was cramped and dark, with no room for error or escape. It did, however, offer one advantage: his attackers would all come from in front of him, allowing him to focus his efforts on a single front.

He readied himself, quelling his doubts, calming his mind, and steeling his resolve. It was not a matter of *if* he could reach her. He had no choice. He *must* reach her. With a bladed staff piece in each hand, Aylun ventured down the stairs with quick, quiet steps. The unforgiving stone walls closed in on him.

The yellow eyes of a gray behemoth dove out of the dark, its massive canines ready to tear him apart.

He spun and slashed through its throat as two more pairs of Blood Wolf eyes darted into the light. He stabbed through the eye of one and leaped over it, launching himself off the head to come down and slice the throat of the other.

Darkness enveloped him as another set of enormous eyes appeared, racing toward him. He sprang over the dead body. The yellow light of his flamestone splashed across the gray stone as he banked off the wall and came down with the beast's neck between his legs. After two lightning slashes, one on each side of the throat, the body slumped to the floor.

He spun around, facing down the stairwell again, his breath already labored. There would be no stopping now, no room for retreat. He either reached Megan or fought to the death.

More eyes raced at him.

He darted to the side and leaped downward toward them.

Megan sat hunched over on the long bench with the ball of golden light clutched in her hands, staring into the room. Hunger and thirst gnawed at her, and she was too well rested to sleep further. So, with nothing to do but wait and worry, she watched the shadow and light shudder across the gray stones of the wall with each trembling of her hands. Every scratch or snarl caused her to jump and shake as her thoughts drifted from Aylun to Jon.

The fate of each was now tied up in that of the other. It seemed impossible that Aylun could still be alive. He had said it himself: The temple was a death trap. It contained no hiding spot in which to seek shelter. With no place of respite and an endless supply of creatures to assail him, Aylun's survival seemed impossible. Countless hours had passed, and nobody could fight for that long without making a mistake or succumbing to exhaustion. The admission that he might be dead or dying upset her more than she could have ever dreamed possible, given his treatment of her.

Perhaps what upset her more was that if Aylun was dead, her own prospects for survival became far more dismal. Without his help, she would never fight her way down the hallway. Gift or no gift, she was trapped in this dirty, smelly, noisy room, and she would soon die of hunger and thirst. Her inevitable demise would leave Jon to cope with this horrible world and find a way home on his own. In that case, it would only be a matter of time before the protector arrested him, and his life would be over.

Tired of her dreadful imaginings and how they always led to the same conclusion, she rose. The hall seemed quiet now, its inhabitants either asleep or waiting. Seeking distraction from her defeatist thoughts, she crept back to the table and dusted off, sorted, refolded, and restacked all the clothes, from rags to silken robes. Then she cleaned each pick and pry bar with painstaking care. The most ragged of the clothes she used to wipe the grit and grime from the gray marble bench and rock floor around it, in the hopes it might not creep her out so much to stay here. Once done, she settled down again on the bench to reconsider her situation.

Then from the hall came a sudden flurry of pounding feet and scratching claws. Growls, snarls, and thuds dragged on and on and even seemed to grow in volume, filling her ears with a symphony of horror. She pulled her feet off the floor again and hugged her knees to her chest, her breath short and ragged.

She clenched the lighted ball in her hands, shaking with anxiety, waiting for the horrible noise to stop, but it only grew more intense. Then came a rapid tapping of what sounded like metal against stone.

Megan froze for a moment, unsure what she had heard, as the scratching and thuds from beyond the heavy stone door grew even more frantic.

Then the tapping came again, too precise and rhythmic to be mere chance or a beast. It had to be human.

Shocked and not quite believing she could be right, Megan leaped up from the bench. Light from her aetherstone washed across the wall as she flew to the door. She grabbed the lever above that opened the door and pulled down with all her strength. It pushed the counterbalance down and away from the wall, lifting it and prying it inward. As the door scraped open a short way, she let go.

Golden light from her glass ball poured through the crack as she held it to the opening, trying to make sense of the flurry of gray-and-red movement from beyond.

Then, in a flash, she spotted it: Aylun's face, lit by the flame-stone held on his belt. Drenched in sweat and blood, claw marks on his arms, his clothes ripped and torn, and heaving from exertion, he was still alive and fighting like a possessed madman. Creatures leaped around him, crowding him from both sides. With a bladed staff end whirling in each hand, he thrust, jabbed, vaulted, and bashed. His desperation and exhaustion were palpable, yet he persisted, beyond all logic and reason. And his speed and grace were more astonishing than anything she had seen since the portal in Jon's lab.

With her bare hands, Megan pried the crack open further. She leaned through it and yelled, "In here!"

His glance caught her, and in a flash, he dove for the opening. He rolled inside as a jaw snapped through the crack behind him. It opened to lunge at him again. From the floor, he thrust the blade up through the gaping maw, piercing the soft pallet.

The creature dropped to the ground, and Aylun kicked its muzzle until he'd shoved the head back out through the crack.

Another bounded over it as Megan grabbed the second handle and pulled down with all her weight. The lever pushed on the counterbalance, lifting the door and forcing it closed.

The beast's face hit the closing door and fell. Paws shot through the crack above it, swiping at her until they became caught in the narrowing opening.

Aylun leaped up and hacked at them, breaking limbs, severing them, and kicking them out until the door finally ground shut.

Megan backed away, staring at him, soaking wet and blood-spattered. Beneath his rent clothes, blood oozed from long gashes on his side, and nasty scratches and puncture wounds riddled both arms.

She gawked for a second. "Are you okay?"

His breath heaving in huge gulps, Aylun stumbled toward her. He stood motionless, staring at her for a moment, giving no sign of recognition. Then he flung his arms around her neck and slumped his head onto her shoulder, leaning on her as he hugged her.

His weight caused her to stumble and almost lose her balance, but she braced herself against the wheel of the door, then froze there for a moment, standing upright with her arms at her sides, too stunned and puzzled to react.

His body began to tremble.

Her eyes flittered here and there in confusion. "What's the ma—"

His breaths began to come in gasping waves.

She stiffened again, but after a few moments, she relaxed. Her arm came up, and she began to give Aylun ever-so-gentle pats on the back. "Are you ... crying?"

He didn't answer, but his heaving slowly calmed as the ruckus in the hall tapered to a stop.

With his head still resting on her shoulder, Aylun rubbed his sleeve across his face. Then his voice came out, pitiful and shaky. "I thought it was happening again." He hung there for a moment, then let go and stumbled toward the bench.

Megan pulled up beside him and hooked her arm under his, lifting his weight. She stared over at his shocked face, watching beads of sweat roll down it, masking any tears. As they reached the long stone bench, she set him on it. Then she guided him onto his back, his breath still labored.

She knelt down and held her light above him as she peered through the frayed edges of his torn clothes, examining his injuries.

"This gash in your side is pretty nasty, and these wounds on your arms are no joke either. But otherwise, you seem … unharmed. How are there so many rip—"

"But my leg." Aylun glanced down. "Before, in the alley, I cut it when I … hit …" He stared at the unscathed leg beneath his lacerated clothes. An expression of profound puzzlement filled his face. "Huh."

Megan puzzled over it for a moment, recalling his distinct limp but unable to find any injury that would account for it. With no way to solve the mystery, she set her aetherstone on the rock floor and strolled over to the far wall. She gathered some simple white linen clothes from the stack on the bench. Remnants of debris still clung to them, so she shook them off and dusted them again. Then she tore them into strips and squares, using her teeth to start each rip.

She hurried back and lifted him enough to pull his shirt up. Then she knelt on the floor, examining his wounds again. "Do you have any water?"

He offered her his small waterskin. "I filled it in the pool up there, but do not use much. I would rather suffer with my wounds than have both of us die of thirst."

Megan paused for a second, then looked up from his sweat-and-blood-soaked clothes and nodded. With a square of cloth, she sopped up beads of perspiration from his brow. Taking care to be gentle, she used the cloth to wipe away the blood and grime around one of the slices on his side. Then she dribbled a few drops of water onto another of the cloth squares and gently dabbed the slash itself.

He winced as she touched the raw flesh of his open wound but remained silent.

She concentrated on her work as she spoke. "How did you find me?"

He stared into space for a moment as if the words didn't register. Then he raised his hand and stared at his dark metal ring with a solid jade line around it. His remark came out emotionless, only this time it seemed more from shock and exhaustion than disinterest. "The ring. It led me to you."

"Oh." She paused for a moment. "But how did you get here with all those things out there?"

He closed his eyes and gave his head a tiny shake. "It is a long story."

Megan shrugged as she continued to work. "Are you in a hurry? Is there someplace you need to be?"

He shifted his position, seeming to get more comfortable, then sighed. "I climbed the statue and waited till dawn when the things outside the temple had gone. They won't enter the pool of water, so I hid in it. From there, I eliminated the ones remaining inside the temple, a few at a time, and fought my way down the stairs to the hall."

"And then?"

He shrugged. "The ring led me to your door. I tapped on it and you found me."

She remained quiet for a moment as she cleared more sweat and blood from the wounded area. "See, not that long a story after all."

Aylun smiled. "It sounded longer in my head." He flinched as she blotted the raw flesh of another open wound.

Megan stopped and peered up into his face. "Are you sure you're okay?"

He gave a slow nod.

She picked up another square of cloth and resumed cleaning around the third of the deep scratches in his side. "When you came in before, why did you say that? What did you think was 'happening again'?"

He didn't respond right away, but when he did, his voice possessed a quality of deep regret. "This is not the first time I have gone into a place like this to retrieve a journal such as this one. Two times already, I have witnessed the people I care about die."

Shocked, Megan looked up from her work. Yaomey had told her part of his story, but hearing the anguish in the voice of the one who had lived the experience was different. After a moment, she returned her focus to cleaning his bloody wounds. "Was one of them your partner, Yaolin?"

Even in his exhausted state, he showed surprise at hearing the name. He paused for a moment before nodding. "Yeah. The other was four years ago. My sister was my partner back then. We were sent along with two of my closest friends."

Megan reeled back in surprise. "Your *sister*? Your actual sister? Into a place like this?"

He nodded. "We got into some trouble. I thought something had taken her, and I sort of went out of my mind. The thought of something happening to her made me abandon all reason. In my panic, I chased after the wrong person and left her alone. In the end, everyone died because I didn't manage my fears."

She continued her work for a while before replying. "It sounds like you think you were to blame because you were afraid for your sister."

"How could I not think that way? I cared about her, so I panicked, and bad things happened."

"And that makes sense to you? How can you not care about your sister?"

"But this was a mission. I should have reined in my emotions and kept my wits."

Megan shook her head as she tended his wounds, not altogether sure she bought his assertion. When she finished cleaning the last of the bloody scratches, she slipped her arm under his back, sat him up, and turned him so his feet rested on the floor. She lifted his arms over his head, and he held them there as she began wrapping a large swath of cloth around his waist, binding his wounds. "Okay, fine. You went twice before to find something like this journal we're looking for. I still don't get it. This isn't the same. You don't care about me."

Aylun stared down at her with a difficult-to-read expression and tilted his head. "Do you have any idea what it is like to be the only one to survive?"

She halted at his soft and remorseful words. Her gaze rose to his face as old memories resurfaced, reopening wounds she had struggled to heal. After a while, she gave a nod and an "uh-huh," then returned her focus to her work. "I watched my family die. Not in an instant, like yours, but slowly, painfully, over many years."

He seemed surprised at first, then inhaled a deep breath. "Your mother and sister?"

She nodded. "Even now, it hurts when I think about them. I feel like I failed them. Like I should have been able to save them."

Aylun nodded with her. "I understand. You blame your-self. ..." He glanced down at her face as a puzzled look came over him. "But you also blame your father?"

She remained focused on her work as she spoke. "I blame him because he is to blame."

Rather than object, he simply nodded once again.

"He was cold and demanding and unforgiving. No grade at school, no job at home, no meal, no amount of effort was ever good enough. He pushed and pushed. I watched my sister and mother sacrifice everything in an effort to please him. But he never cared. He never spoke a single word of encouragement or showed them the slightest bit of empathy or love."

Aylun remained quiet for a long time as she wrapped his stomach. He seemed ill at ease, and his discomfort appeared to grow until, eventually, he spoke his mind. "Disapproving fathers have always been with us, but it usually does not end in death. What happened?"

She shrugged. "It's a long story."

He mimicked her earlier manner and tone of voice. "Why? Are you in a hurry? Is there someplace you need to go?"

She grew uneasy and looked away. "Seriously? Is my life story what's important right now?"

Aylun paused for a moment. "Yes. It is helping keep my mind off your ruthless tending of my wounds."

Megan flashed him a fake smile, trying to make light of his less-than-humorous humor. She continued her work for a while longer, pulling the bandage tight and tying it off with a firm knot that would not unravel on him later, even with a fair amount of movement. Then she leaned him back down so he was lying on the bench again, and she sat down on the floor where she had a better angle from which to work on his arm.

It wasn't until she rolled up his sleeve and was holding the light over one of his dark puncture wounds that she gave in to the urge to talk. "I think it started when my sister did poorly on a geography test. My mother was recovering from cancer at the time. …" She hesitated, unsure if he would be familiar with the term. "An illness."

His voice remained soft and unemotional. "I know what cancer is."

She nodded. "My sister had to take my mom to her checkup, but she was so nervous and distracted about the test that she ran a red light and got into an accident. My mother ended up in the hospital." Megan stopped her work and glanced up at his face, but his eyes were closed and his expression relaxed.

She finished cleaning around the second puncture, dribbled some more water on the cloth, and dabbed the wound. "My sister already felt guilty enough about it, but my father would not let her be. One night, after hours of scolding and punishment, my sister went to our room and couldn't stop crying. Then while I was asleep, she got ahold of my mother's heavy-duty painkillers and took a whole bottle."

She lifted his arm and began wrapping it, bandaging his wounds. "After her death, my mom just seemed to give up. She stopped talking to us and went downhill from there. The cancer came back and spread, and she died not long after."

Aylun glanced at her. "Leaving just you and your father?"

She leaned away, shocked at the suggestion. "Oh no. I got out of there as fast as I could. I packed up my stuff, took some money, and left. I was only sixteen, too young to live on my own, so I answered an advertisement for someone looking for a roommate. I moved in with her, got a job, and never looked back." She glanced over again at

Aylun. "That's actually how I met Jon. The woman I was renting the room with was in the same group of friends. They would meet up sometimes, so I tagged along."

He regarded her with an expression of admiration. "Being on your own at such a young age, that must have been difficult."

Megan stopped and squatted before him, peering into his face. "No, not really. Watching my family self-destruct, that was tough. Watching my sister and mother try to change to please someone else, that was hard. I mean, it wasn't all on my father. That took me a long time to realize. My mom and sis, they both loved him, so they kept sacrificing more and more to please him, but the harder they tried, the more unhappy they became and the angrier he got. If they'd just stopped trying to please someone who could never be pleased, it would have all ended so differently. I left because I decided that was never going to be me. I was going to be the only one to decide who I am and what I want. Nothing and nobody was ever going to decide that for me."

Aylun sat up and looked down at her. "Not even a stupid prophecy?"

She widened her eyes. "*Especially* not some stupid prophecy."

He lay back down in the other direction.

Megan reseated herself on the floor, rolled up his other sleeve, and began to examine that arm.

After a time, in a soft and tentative voice, Aylun ventured, "Perhaps your father was just trying to teach his family to be strong, to survive. And when it was not working, he became profoundly unhappy and didn't know how to get out of it."

Megan stopped and glared. "Unhappy? He drove my sister to suicide and made his sick, grieving wife give up on life. I told you not to ever stand up for him." Tears gathered in her eyes. "Why are you even saying this?"

Aylun turned away. "Because I think ... perhaps ... Yaolin might have said the same thing about me."

She froze and stared in shock.

He turned his head to look at her, heartrending grief written on his features. "That I was unforgiving and cold, that I never showed her the love and sympathy she needed."

Megan peered into his eyes, stunned. "But, Yaomey said she loved you with all her heart."

He nodded and held her gaze. "And I did not have it in me to accept it. I pushed her away because I thought I needed to. I thought that was the lesson of my sister's death, not to get too close. That way, I would never again panic when someone needed me the most." He gave his head a meek shake. "I was wrong. It only made her miserable and distracted her at the worst possible moment."

Aylun laid his head back down and stared up at the ceiling, becoming still and his voice soft. "I may not have killed her myself, but I might as well have thrown Yaolin to the creatures that tore her to shreds." A dark cloud settled over his mood, and he withdrew into sullen silence.

Megan held up his arm, but it was like a dead weight, as if he were in a catatonic state. The uneasy noises of prowling beasts in the hall carried on while Aylun stared at the ceiling, seeming to fight off sleep.

She finished, then turned her back and sat on the floor in front of him. Worry about the severity of his wounds hounded her as she pulled her knees up to her arms and stared into space. Soon, the sound of slumber came from the man behind her. She leaned back, expecting to feel the hard coolness of marble. Instead, she was met by the reassuring warmth of his shoulder against her back.

Sympathy tugged at her as she finally understood his story and how, in so many ways, it resembled her own. She tried to fight back her empathy and rekindle her justifiable anger. Sure he had suffered, but he had taken out his anguish on her. It was wrong, and no amount of sympathy for his plight would justify using her life and her fears as his emotional punching bag.

Yet, even as she repeated the words to herself, they were insufficient to reignite the grudge she had harbored this whole time.

He was frail and human after all, more vulnerable and pathetic than she could have ever believed. The more she came to grips with that reality, the more disturbing her circumstances became.

They were trapped in a former den of thieves with monsters behind the door waiting to get in and rip them both to pieces. Right now, the only person she could rely on for her survival was wounded and weak. It did not help her sense of security to believe he was also pathetic and vulnerable.

For what seemed like forever, Megan sat and listened to the pacing and movement in the hall. Soon, groans and mumbling came from Aylun behind her, no doubt from some wretched horror that stalked his sleep. Sympathy tugged at her, and she could not bring herself to disturb what might be the only rest he would get. As the torturous minutes wore on, she began to shake and jump again at every loud noise or snarl and snap of teeth. Hunger and thirst still gnawed at her as she sat and waited for her only hope of escape, for her vulnerable and traumatized companion to awaken from his nightmares and most likely die trying to get them out of this mess.

Chapter Twelve

DARKEST HOURS

The urgency to escape this trap of blood and death tugged at Aylun. Over and over, it dragged him out of his slumber and up into half-consciousness. After many bouts, he fought all the way to wakefulness, staring at the rough stone ceiling.

The warmth of her back against his shoulder and brush of her hair draped over his arm caused Aylun to glance over, and there was Megan. Dirty and disheveled, she sat on the floor, leaning back against him while she clutched her knees to her chest and trembled. Her aetherstone rested on the ground next to her, casting its warm light into the cave-like room and bathing her jittery face in its golden glow.

To see her so small and frightened filled him with sympathy. It was a stark contrast to the Megan who had fought by his side against the wolves. According to every sign he could read, her shock and fear then was greater than now, yet she'd faced that threat with unflinching determination. That fact alone made her almost as brave as most Shou. Perhaps even more so because so many of them were without fear. It was one thing to stand against an enemy you knew you could defeat and an altogether different one to remain unyielding against a foe who struck terror into your heart.

He reached out and gave her shoulder a gentle tap. "It is time."

She flinched at his touch, then scooted around toward him, peering into his face with a look of relief. Almost at once, her expression turned to one of questioning concern. "Time for what? You just fell asleep ... well, not *just* fell asleep, but you've only slept for a couple of hours. You need more rest."

For a fleeting moment, Aylun was struck by the word "hour" coming from the mouth of one who appeared Elorian. It was a unit of measure used in Talus where they divided the day into twenty-four intervals. Most Elorians would have used "shi," for a twelfth of a day. Yet the incongruity mattered little. Other issues were more pressing, so he began to pull himself upright, but the soreness of his body and ache of his wounds argued him back down. He winced as he stared upward at the golden light casting jagged shadows in the recesses of the rough ceiling. "I have to go back into the hall and clear it so we can get out of here."

"What? No." Her eyes widened. "You need to rest and recover."

He closed his eyes as the image came back. On the temple pavilion, the strange red-skinned woman had slid from the back of the massive gray beast. She had transformed into some kind of wolf thing and bent down to sniff the ground. He turned his gaze back to Megan. "They can smell us. I am sure of it. When night falls, they will come back and track us to this room." He pointed to the gray stonework door. "When they do, they will flood the tunnel again. And I will have to fight through all of that, all over again. I have to get you out now, before nightfall."

He pulled himself up a short distance, but Megan placed her small hand on the ripped clothes covering his chest and shoved him back down to the hard marble bench. "No, you need to rest."

He pushed against the warm palm holding him down.

"Look at you. You're so weak you can't even fight against me, and I'm only using one hand."

He shot her an earnest expression. "I made a vow to—"

"Oh, just shut up about your stupid vow." She flung her whole arm over his chest and pushed down, using her entire weight to smash his back onto the smooth surface of the bench. "If you stay and rest, maybe we have a chance. If you go out in the hall and die, I'm toast."

Her arm, still shuddering and warm against him, softened his resolve. Puzzled and concerned, he peered at her grime-streaked face. " 'Toast'? I do not understand … 'toast.' "

She didn't budge. "If you die, I die. So rest and live."

"Look, we have no food. It was all on the horses. We have little water. We will have to get out of here in a few hours, not days."

Her expression softened. "Then at least rest for half a day and regain your strength while we try to find another way out of here."

His resolve gave way. After everything he had done to her, she was more worried about him than herself. Here she was, literally throwing herself on top of him out of concern, even after he had, on two occasions, told her, "Do not to give my welfare even a passing thought."

Aylun gazed into her eyes. "Megan, this is life and death—your life, your death."

Through her obvious anxiety, she donned a warm smile. "Then I should have a say in it."

He considered her assertion for a moment, then sighed as he relaxed. "Then I would like to go on the record as advising against it."

Her expression remained soft yet resolute. "Noted. Now rest." She kept her arm slung over him as he drifted off again, this time into a deep sleep.

Aylun awakened a second time to a warm weight on his chest and the softness of her hair draped around it. He pried his weary eyes open and lifted his head to peer down at Megan's peaceful sleeping face. The streaks of dirt across her cheek and disheveled ginger hair were lit by the steady golden glow of her aetherstone. Her arm remained heavy on his upper body, but her head had slipped from it and now rested next to his chest. She looked peaceful, a state that would dissipate the moment she awoke. It was almost certain that their chance to escape before nightfall had passed. So he set his head back down, listening to movement in the hallway as he drifted in and out of sleep for what seemed like an eternity.

After many rounds of fitful slumber, he came all the way awake and could no longer get back to sleep, so he lay still for a long time, unwilling to disturb Megan. She had already been subjected to a harrowing experience beyond what anyone should be forced to endure. The image of her curled up and trembling at every sound made it impossible to wake her for fear it would turn her peaceful rest back into a terrifying nightmare.

So he turned his attention to their current predicament. The sense of urgency had not eased while he slept. Rather, the desire to escape had only grown. They were trapped in a room with no food or water and beasts outside that would sooner or later find their way in. Over and over, he reviewed his options. Yet there were too many unknowns about where they were and their potential avenues for escape to reach any conclusions.

With time, the stiffness became too much, and he lifted Megan's head and arm with gentle care. She stirred, and her eyes opened, but she merely mumbled a few indistinct words. He slipped out from under and set her back down on the now-warm bench, where she soon lapsed back into sleep.

Careful not to disturb the creatures in the hall, he crept over to where Megan had retrieved the cloth she'd used for bandaging. He sifted through several stacks of clothes of many disparate types and selected two velvet robes. With silent steps, he returned to her. He folded one of them into a pillow and slipped it under her arm and head. The other he covered her with.

He scooped up her lighted aetherstone and held it out as he ran his fingers over his bandages and pressed on each wound, attempting to gauge the severity of the damage. To his surprise, not only were the dressings well done, but his condition was much better than expected, given the amount of fighting he'd done. In fact, there were wounds, like the gash on his leg, that he remembered getting but were absent now.

AYLUN

At a loss to explain it, Aylun turned to a mystery of a different sort. He looked down at Megan. It was impossible to tell whether it was sheer insanity, or reckless whimsy, or perhaps just incredible insight, but she had saved them back in that temple. She had gained help from an impossible source when all he'd had to offer were doomed strategies. Somehow, she had pulled a miracle out of a hopeless situation, and he found he no longer wished to return her to Jon merely to fulfill a vow. Now, as he gazed upon her face, a new desire had taken root. He wanted to return her to Jon for the simple reason that it was where she wanted to be.

With that change had come another. It was said that all of life is a dream walking and all of death a going home. A couple of days ago, all he had yearned for was that sweet going home, but his destiny had taken him along a different course. That path had given him something he wanted to accomplish, someone he had to protect. If that path led to his death, he would not flinch—but Athene was right. He couldn't protect her if he was dead.

The goddess had been right about another thing, too. He had found no meaning in the death of his sister, his friends, or Yaolin. He had never even considered the notion. Now, in the wake of her words, the idea that their deaths may have served a greater purpose was like a life raft to a drowning soul. If there was a meaning to be found in their sacrifice, he had to find it.

He stayed there for a long while, watching Megan sleep, before he left, carrying the glowing glass ball with him as he toured the room. His first stop was the door to the hall. There, he undertook a thorough examination of the ingenious mechanisms, with its carved stone wheel, metal counterbalance, and two levers.

When he finished, he moved on to the heavy stone table set against the solid rock wall. He picked up and scrutinized each metal lockpick and pry bar and each item of clothing. With care, he rummaged through every bag and purse in the basket at the end of the table.

Next, he moved on around the room to the second man-made wall, opposite the first. The remaining walls, floor, and ceiling were natural rock formations that appeared to be those of a cave. Someone had used the construction of the tunnel to create this hidden room. Rooms that were hidden tended to be so for a reason.

When he reached a second door of pure metal, he ran his fingers over the coolness of its etched surface. It seemed sturdier than the massive stone wall in which it was set, though that could be an illusion. Since that wall stood across from the stone door he had used when entering the room, perhaps its presence meant there were two ways in and out of this space. He put his ear to it as he gave it several soft raps with the side of his fist. The deep, long echo from beyond told of an enormous chamber rather than the confined space of a room or vault.

That echo only confirmed his suspicion that it was likely a second door out of this place. The way the room had been hidden with such care, along with its contents, lent every impression of being a den for thieves. And what self-respecting thief would risk being trapped in a hideout with only one exit?

While it was encouraging to imagine the door might be another way out of this place, he was reluctant to let that enthusiasm carry him too far. The door would be solid metal, and given the room's purpose, breaking through the wall that held it was probably not an option. Any architect would have also designed the masonry to be downright impregnable. So he turned his attention to the lock, brushing his fingers over its cool surface, looking it over and peering through the keyhole to the blackness beyond.

No matter how he positioned the light of the aetherstone, the mechanism was too shrouded in darkness to make out the cylinder or tiny pins. Without seeing them, it would be impossible to determine what he needed to do to manipulate them. The more he examined it, and the more he considered the matter, the more his hopefulness faded. Given its appearance and location, it was a fair bet that it would not be an easy lock to pick. Perhaps the whole door was some kind of formidable artifact that would never open without the correct key.

After he finished, he returned to sit on the bench next to Megan. The pressure to find their best option for escape weighed on him. For what seemed like more than half a day, he wracked his brain, but it was futile. Every avenue went back to the hallway and the direct approach of fighting through whatever lay along its unknown length.

After a long time, Megan stirred and brought her head up, blinking with soft and sleepy eyes as she peered over at Aylun. "You're up?"

He nodded and stared at her. "Are you okay?"

She nodded back. "A little stiff, not to mention famished and thirsty, but that's all. You?"

"Sore and banged up, but I will be fine."

Megan looked at his stomach. "I need to check your wounds, see if they're clean and uninfected."

He grabbed his waterskin and offered it to her. She tried to take it, but he held it firm for a moment as he eyed her. "We have to ration this well. A small swallow every couple of hours."

She took a sip, then handed it back to him. As she turned her attention to his wounds, he took his own sip. Then he snatched a small piece of cloth from the stack of bandaging Megan had made. He dribbled a little water onto it, and as she squatted to examine his wounds, he raised it to her face.

She pulled back. "What do you think you're doing?"

"Just be still." Aylun put his hand around the back of her head and pulled her face toward his. With care and concentration, he used the wetted cloth to blot the streaks of grime from her face.

She held very still, and there was a slight widening of her eyes in a reaction he couldn't quite read. When he had finished, Megan scowled and glanced away. "Was that really necessary right now? I thought water was precious."

"You're welcome."

With an exasperated sigh, she turned her attention back to his bandaging. She unbound his wounds and seemed surprised when she looked at them. "They're healing fast. You must have a strong constitution." She tore up more bandages and rewrapped his wounds. When she finished, she sat on the bench next to him.

He gazed at her. "Thank you. You seem to know something about medicine. Was that your vocation?"

"No. I suppose I just picked most of it up. You know, I've watched quite a few medical shows. I can spout TV medical jargon with the best of them."

Aylun puzzled for a moment, then decided "TV" must refer to some strange form of theater and let it go. He rose and scanned the room. "Have you looked around?"

She nodded. "I didn't find much of use."

He pointed to the slab of metal in the wall. "I think that door leads out of this place, but it did not budge. I gave the lock a quick look, but it does not appear to be an easy one to pick."

"Oh, are you an expert on picking locks now?"

Aylun cocked his head as he considered her question, then gave a firm nod. "I do okay."

Megan seemed surprised. "Oh."

He glanced at the door he had entered through. "That leaves the hallway."

"But it's full of those things, and we don't know how long it is or even where it goes."

He took a deep breath. "Well, I have an idea." He paused for another long moment. "If I draw them deeper into the tunnel, perhaps you can slip by and get out through the temple."

She stared in apparent surprise. "Okay, but then how will you get out?"

Aylun's gaze fell, and he hesitated.

"No. No. Don't tell me. ... You don't think you'll make it." She gave an adamant shake of her head. "Absolutely not."

310

"Be reasonable. It may be your only chance to get out of here alive."

Megan's tone became calm and measured. "I am perfectly sane and reasonable, and please understand that I am not saying this just to contradict you ..." She stomped her foot. "But are you out of your ever-loving mind? Being torn to shreds by those abominations is not reasonable."

"Fine, then what is *your* brilliant idea?"

She looked around the stone walls, seeming to give every aspect careful thought. Her eyes rested on the silvery metal door on the far side of the room. "Wait ... you said you did okay with locks, yet you're giving up without even trying. There are some pointy things on the bench. How about—"

"Pointy things? They are—"

"Yes, pointy things. How about you use them to pick the lock on that door?" She pointed to the huge slab of metal.

Aylun sighed. "They are lockpicks, and even if I could, we are not certain where it leads."

"Humor me. If you have actual lockpicks, isn't that even better?"

"No, it is not. They, and the costumes and empty purses, make it likely this is a thieves' hideout. What are the chances you can pick the lock of a door to a den of thieves?"

Megan pouted. "Just try ... for me, okay?"

He sighed again and lowered his head. It was almost certain to be a waste of precious time they didn't have. Then again, there was no way to tell if it was still night out, and if it was, the entire massive pack of those things could be right outside the temple, making any escape impossible. Perhaps trusting Megan would be best. She had proven she had better instincts than him, and for better or worse, this was *their* venture now, and not just his. If she was determined that he make the attempt, then he couldn't ignore her and do what he deemed best.

His flamestone had gone dark while he slept, having not been recharged by setting it near some form of fire. So he grabbed Megan's inexhaustible aetherstone and went to the bench. With care, he reexamined each lockpick, gathering the ones that seemed most suited to the task, and headed to the door.

Megan sat on the bench, watching as he knelt down before the metal door and began to finesse the lock. As he'd suspected, it was almost impossible to manipulate. The mechanism never made a sound, nor could he sense any clicking when he moved the pins, so it remained sheer guesswork. Restless creatures in the hall never ceased their movement, serving as an unrelenting reminder that there wasn't time to waste on lost causes.

The day passed with painful slowness. He found himself groaning and grumbling a lot but kept pushing himself, working long stretches with infrequent rests. Each time he stopped, he found he had grown more weary and tried to convince Megan of the uselessness of continuing. However, she was foolishly determined to save him from himself and kept insisting he try over and over.

After half a dozen long sessions, he had his ear to the door when a touch of dizziness struck. It had been there all along, but he had been so focused on his task he'd tuned it out. He pulled away, hoping Megan wouldn't notice, but the rapid movement made it worse. He fell sideways and had to put out his hand to steady himself.

Megan sprang from the marble bench and raced over. "Are you okay?" She looked down into his face.

He remained still, endeavoring to appear normal as he fought his light-headedness. He had overexerted himself in the hallway and had had little to drink since. The slight fever wasn't a surprise, but they needed to conserve water, and Megan wouldn't let that happen if she knew of his overexertion and dehydration, so he kept his concern to himself. With all of Megan's focus on him, he became aware of how flush he felt.

He was contemplating how best to distract from any sign of his condition when she put her hand to his forehead, then yanked it away. "You're burning up."

"I am fine," he lied, not wanting to get bogged down by useless worry over the state of his health.

"No, you need to lie down and rest."

Aylun hesitated.

She shoved her face close to his. "Don't make me pin you down again."

Despite being worn out and wobbly, he laughed.

She encouraged him up and guided him along as they returned to the bench. After laying him down, Megan sat on the floor next to him again. The muted scraping of claws and growls from the hallway outside never ceased. After a while, a fight broke out. Megan turned and grabbed hold of his upper arm and leaned into him. She remained there, clinging to his arm, as occasional squabbles continued to resound from the hallway. until, at last, he fell asleep from fever and exhaustion.

Aylun awakened the third time to find Megan sitting in silence next to him. Her face held an expression somewhere between fright and concern as she stared into the room. How long he had slept he had no way of knowing in this dark space, but it must have been a fair span of time because her lips had become dry and cracked. It was troubling because time was not their friend. Each passing moment they were deprived of food and water narrowed his chance of survival and Megan's chance of escape. It was reckless to squander precious time on unproductive rest.

He sat up a bit but slowed as his body informed him he was more sore and stiff than he realized.

Megan looked over at him, and relief filled her face. "Are you feeling better?"

"Yes."

"You still don't look good. Do you need more rest?"

Aylun peered into her face. "Perhaps, but we do not have time."

"Then make time."

"You do not understand. Feel my forehead." He took her hand and set her palm on his head.

She pulled it away. "You still have a fever."

"Yet I am not sweating, and my mouth is dry. I fear I am in the early stages of dehydration. Because of my fever and all the exertion and sweating from my fight in the temple and hallway, it is happening faster to me than it is to you. In a day, or possibly a little more, I will become dizzy and overheat easily. After that, I will begin to faint and eventually lose consciousness entirely." He leaned closer to emphasize the point. "Time is something we do not have now."

He began to rise but found he was unsteady on his feet. Apparently, this was not lost on Megan because she glanced down at his legs. "You're not thinking about going out in that hall again, are you?"

He nodded.

"That's crazy. You can't even stand straight on your feet, much less fight."

He took a careful step past her toward the door.

She leaped after him. From behind, she wrapped her arms around his waist and held firm, stopping him from moving forward.

Shocked and surprised, he stood motionless for a moment. Then he relaxed. "And what if I prove I can fight?"

Megan hesitated.

When she didn't answer, he steeled himself, hardening his heart for what he needed to do. He grabbed her little finger and yanked it back, forcing her to unwrap her arms. He reached around, took hold of her wrist, and twisted it, wrenching her arm behind her back. The pressure on her shoulder forced her down onto her knees on the uneven rock floor.

More clever than he expected, she took a deliberate tumble forward, releasing the force on her arm. As she rolled away, she wrapped her leg around his grasping arm.

Rather than be pulled to the ground, he let go and yanked his arm free.

314

She rose to her feet. "All you proved is you can surprise me."

Aylun nodded. "Not bad. I am impressed."

Megan smiled. "Thanks, I try."

He could see her concern for him in the lines of her face, but he had no choice. Time and the imminent threat outside in the hall allowed him no room for sympathy. He needed to eliminate her concern and show her he was more capable than she thought. To do that, he needed to be cold and hard, so she would be cold and hard. And he needed to show her how brutal he could be. He let his arms drop to his sides and relaxed, trying to appear at complete ease. As he did, he shoved all concern for her from his mind. She was a mere opponent now.

He shot her a look as cold and unfeeling as he could manage. "You have three tries to hit me. If you can land even one blow, you win, and I stay. If you cannot, I win and prove I can still fight." Of course, the test proved nothing about surviving the hallway, and Megan would sense that, but that didn't matter. She would take the bait to stop him, and all that mattered now was using the opportunity to harden her heart so she could let him go.

Megan didn't seem surprised by his change of demeanor, or if she did, she didn't let it show. She gave a slow, contemplative nod. Before her head rose the last time, she jabbed out for his throat with her fingers stiff and straight.

He slapped her hand away, then slammed his fist into her shoulder, causing her to twist badly and stumble sideways. "Ouch! Do you have to—"

"Again," he demanded as he motioned her to come. Then he went loose again.

She put her fists in front of her and took a wide fighting stance.

Aylun remained at ease. "That is good. You are not completely without skill, but what—"

Megan feinted a punch to his stomach. When he moved to block, she pulled back and swung her elbow at his head.

He simply bent away from her blow. As her elbow flew over his head, he pivoted and lurched backward, grimacing as he jabbed his elbow into her stomach.

She cried out and stumbled backward, holding her side and wincing from the pain. "What are you doing?"

He strived to keep his expression cold and emotionless. "That was a mere tap. If I wanted to, I could have broken several of your ribs."

"Well, stop it. A demonstration of skill will do. I don't need a demonstration of pain."

Aylun nodded and grunted agreement. This wasn't working, and it bothered him too much to hurt someone who had done nothing to deserve it, even if it was for her own good. He had to try a new tactic, something to remind her of just how much she hated him. He took a casual stance again, letting his arms fall loose at his sides.

Megan took up her fighting stance.

He waited until she started to step forward, preparing to punch.

With all the speed he could muster, Aylun jabbed out. He struck her in the sternum with the palm of his hand before she could unleash her blow.

She straightened in surprise at his speed.

He grabbed her partially outstretched arm, spun away from her, and thrust out his leg, pulling her hand forward and throwing her over his shoulder.

She hit his shoulder and flew into the air over it, then plummeted down in front of him, headed for the cold hard rock floor.

He lunged forward and caught her in his arms, right before she hit the ground.

She stiffened.

He lifted her up and brought her uncomfortably close, so close her hot breath brushed his dry lips.

She froze for a moment or two, looking into his eyes. Then, with a loud squeal, she pounded his chest with her fist as she tried to wriggle free. Her squirming continued as he set her down on her feet with slow and gentle care.

316

She backed away and glared. "What do you think you're doing?"

Aylun granted her a broad smile. "A demonstration of skill?"

Megan huffed. "A demonstration of creepiness, you mean."

He hardened his manner again. "I win. We go with my plan."

She darted between him and the door and thrust out her arms to either side, blocking him. "No, I won't do it. Not until we have no other choice."

Coldness hadn't worked. Causing pain hadn't worked. Even acting like a creep hadn't worked. She remained admirably determined, and it did soften his resolve. "And if I am too far gone by then to put up a decent fight, or to buy enough time for you to escape?"

She relaxed. "So what? What if we do as you say, and I get to the temple? You think they won't follow me after you're down? You think I can survive this city long enough to get out? And then what? The council hunts Jon and me down?"

She was right, but it didn't matter. "It is the only plan I have."

"It's a crappy plan that gets you out of protecting me and leaves me to fend for myself." Tears gathered in her eyes. "You're just like Athene said. You want to put your death on my conscience while you wriggle out of your vow by dying. Well, fine"—she pointed to the door—"just go and die, if that's what you want so bad." Megan slumped to the ground and looked down at the rock floor as she stifled any further tears.

Aylun stood for a moment, peering down at her as his resolve crumbled until all that remained was the desire to see her live. "Look, I do not want to die, truly."

She glanced up as he crouched before her.

"I want to stay with you and protect you, I do."

"Then do it."

Time was still running out, and the urgency of that reality still nagged at him. Yet he found himself pausing for a long while, unable to summon the will to push the issue. Eventually, he nodded. "Okay, how about we agree? For another half a day, I will give it everything I have to get that metal door to open. But if I start to feel like I am running out of time, we try my plan as a last resort. Agreed?"

Megan sniffled and nodded.

The only way to end this would be to put to rest the idea of picking the lock. Aylun returned to the table and gathered all the pry bars and remaining lockpicks and set them on the floor near the metal door with its ornate engravings. For what seemed like an interminable time, he pried, pushed, and jerked, straining each pry bar to the limit until they bent, and he destroyed them all. He worked on the lock, trying to finesse it and manhandle it. He pulled every trick he could imagine and broke one lockpick after another until he was exhausted.

As he worked, Megan watched, seeming to hold her tongue, unwilling to distract him. As time wore on, the hopeful expression on her face faded, and she appeared more and more despondent.

Weary, unable to make any headway, and with all his tools broken, he returned to the bench. Despite his fatigue, hunger, and wooziness, he hadn't allowed himself to rush or be sloppy; he'd given it his best effort. Aylun looked down at her. "I am sorry."

Megan took him by the wrist and set him down next to her on the smooth cool bench. "Rest first."

His first reaction was to object, but he held his tongue. She was right. He needed rest, even if just a little to restore some strength, so he nodded. He scooted over and lay down near her. She slipped a folded velvet robe under his head, and he closed his eyes.

Chances were good he'd frittered away the last of his strength in his attempt to pick the lock, and he would not last long in that hallway. He could hold off the few creatures he'd seen before he dove into the room, but not much more. The bouts of dizziness were coming with greater frequency now, and in a fight of any real length, it was almost certain he would pass out or grow weak and slow. Aylun let out a deep breath. There was nothing either of them could do about that now, so he closed his eyes and drifted off.

AYLUN

Images swirled in a chaotic dance, an endless fight in the hall-way, gray and deep-red fur darting around and around in dizzying circles. Creatures merged and spun one into the other as Aylun grew smaller and smaller. The hallway began to tilt. His stomach lurched as he began to slide down it, struggling to keep the beasts from bury-ing him as they grew and multiplied. Out of nowhere, Megan blinked into existence, and he needed to protect her, but she kept drifting out of reach. He slipped and stumbled for footing as the attack grew into a swirling storm of claws and teeth. All of a sudden, the floor grew too steep, and he was falling down an endless shaft, yellow eyes leering, jagged jaws of white teeth slashing as they whipped around him. Megan screamed ... or was it him?

Aylun's eyes flew open, and his heart pounded fast and hard in his ears. He lay there for a while, his lips cracked and his mouth dry, as the fog of sleep lifted from his mind. The dream was nowhere near the worst he'd suffered in the last several years. What made it distressing was the air of feverish delirium that suffused it. They were symptoms. The surreal disorienta-tion of his fever-induced dream, his parched mouth, and the thumping in his ears—they were all signs his dehydration was getting worse.

He pulled himself up into a sitting position.

Megan glanced over at him. She watched for a while as he stretched his sore and aching arms. Then she scooted up next to him on the bench.

Still stiff from the long stretch of inaction, he took a few slow and deep breaths and twisted and bent his neck both ways to limber up the muscles. Megan seemed to understand what he was preparing to do. Without a word, she rose and offered him a hand. He took it and let her help him up. Then they both crossed to the door with slow, reluctant steps.

Megan turned to him, seeming about to speak. She stared for a moment, then lowered her head.

Mild dizziness hit him. He struggled against it, not wanting to show any sign. With slow, deliberate moves, he pulled his staff ends from his back and pressed a button on each. A blade sprang from each tip with a clank. He took another step toward the door, and Megan grabbed his arm. It steadied him, for which he was grateful, but it also puzzled him. He looked down at her hand, then back into her eyes.

She peered into his face. "Don't die. Please?"

He paused, uncertain of what to say. Awareness of one's body was a practiced discipline for all Shou. That awareness told him he was not in good enough shape to withstand a prolonged battle. The fight would be disorienting, arduous, and painful, but he had to endure it for her, so she would have the best chance of escape.

It was a foregone conclusion he was not going to make it. Even so, he couldn't give in to thoughts of defeat, so he nodded. "I will try with everything I have."

Megan reached up and grabbed the lever to open the door. She pulled down, dangling all her weight, and it ground open a short distance. Her grip slipped, and she fell onto the wheel of the door with a loud clank of metal on stone.

At the sharp sound, the heads of beasts strewn along the hallway turned and stared through the crack.

The world began to slide sideways from dizziness, and the clanking confused him. It was like the sound his blade had made as he tapped it against the door to get in. Puzzled and uncertain about whether the sound had been real or a hallucination, he glanced down at the metal blades of his weapons.

They were nowhere near any stone. "What was that clanking?"

Megan looked down at her legs. "Oh, it was my pocket. It was just a ... key."

Out in the hall, the beasts began to rise as Megan's gaze shot up, her eyes widening as she stared into his. She reeled back and inhaled a slight gasp.

AYLUN

Aylun returned his attention to the door. He stepped up to the crack as the hall began to crawl with movement. Every beast rose, and a few lowered their front ends, slinking toward him with cautious movements.

Megan dove upward, grabbed the closing lever, and yanked down, pushing the door closed.

As barking and low growls broke out beyond the door, Aylun turned to her, distraught that she might be trying to stop him yet again. In his current condition, it was now or never. He bowed his head. "I know you—"

"Wait." Megan fished in her pocket and produced the dark metallic key. The bow had a serpent or wingless dragon winding around its outer edge, and in the center sat three jewels sparkling in the golden light from her aetherstone.

Aylun eyed it with surprise. "What is it?"

"A long shot. A really, really, *really* long shot." She raced to the metal door.

As the turmoil in the hall seemed to settle some, he followed as best he could, struggling against his disorientation. He watched as she held the key near the lock. Its size and shape appeared to be all wrong.

Megan looked over at him. "It came from the dragon. She seemed upset with me for taking it."

Shock struck him dumb. The idiotic woman had stolen a key from Islong. She had spit in the eye of a god.

Megan took a deep breath and jammed the key into the key-hole. He stared in shock. It was a perfect fit. Like his Rings of Pairing, it was as if it had been a perfect fit all along, and what he'd seen a moment ago was an illusion.

She turned it, and with a low clunk, the door moved open a hair's breadth.

A wave of relief washed over him that was every bit as intense as Megan's expression of wonder and satisfaction. It seemed to carry his dizziness away with it, and he rushed over, grabbed the handle, and eased the door open a crack.

Golden light from the aetherstone flittered out through the opening and across the brownish stone floor of a large dark cavern. It reflected off the glittering pool of water at its center, sending beams of light across the whole area. It was a thing of beauty, but then again, anything would be that wasn't that dirty, smelly hole they'd been trapped in.

Megan rushed to go through, but Aylun flung out an arm and stopped her. "The air could be poisonous." Through the cracked door, he waved odors from the cavern to his face and sniffed. "It is damp but appears to be fresh."

He snatched Megan's aetherstone from her hand and jammed it through the opening. The golden light scattered across the large cavern, revealing a tall, jagged ceiling and a wide stone floor that skirted a large body of clear water. Curtains of stalactites and stalag-mites ran through the area, creating passages and pockets all around the crystal pool.

A drop of water fell from the tip of one of the longer stalactites and plopped into the pool, sending circular ripples across the still surface. Aylun glanced over at Megan. "This is good. It is by no means a certainty, but the water dripping into the pool from above makes it likely it is drinkable."

Not seeming all that impressed with his revelation, she ducked under his outstretched arm, through the cracked door, and into the cavern.

He followed, and the air hit him, damp and sweet. The change was almost surreal after being trapped for days, sick and sweaty, in that small space.

They both raced to the water's edge.

He swept out an arm again to hold her back. "Let me try first." He scooped water to his mouth and sniffed it. It gave off no unusual odor, so he lapped up a small amount. The liquid stung as it hit his cracked lips and seemed strange in his parched mouth. Despite the pain, he wanted to plunge his head into the pool and drink until his stomach burst. He settled for taking several hurried sips before turning back to Megan. "It seems fine, not sweet or bitter, fresh like a stream."

They both scooped water to their faces, but after a moment, Aylun halted and grabbed Megan's wrist. "We have to take it easy. Too much too fast, and we could get cramps, or vomit it all back up, or even lose consciousness."

They switched off, each taking a short drink and resting for a while as they watched the other. As time passed and his wooziness faded, Aylun began to scrutinize the area, taking it upon himself to find a way out. Passages wound by the still water, leading to pockets shrouded in shadow. Reflected on the pool's surface were numerous scattered ridges, collections of stalagmites that reached upward toward the stalactites that riddled the ceiling.

There appeared to be several passages out of the cavern, but their best hope lay with the one just to the left since it led in the same direction the hallway had been going. After another half-dozen rounds of careful drinks, Aylun thrust his finger into the water and stuck it into the air. There seemed to be no detectable airflow.

Dissatisfied, he rose and headed to the narrow corridor to their left. It appeared to go off for some distance beyond the room, which added to the impression it might be a passage out. He stuck his finger in his mouth to wet it and positioned it in the opening.

He turned to Megan. "It is hard to tell, but I think I feel air movement. If we follow it, we may find the way out."

Megan's aspect brightened. "Really?"

"It is possible but by no means certain. But first, you have to pick. Right now, is it day or night?"

She pondered for a moment. "What time was it when you found me?"

"Afternoon, probably."

"Then I think it might be night."

"Air often flows into caves at night, and since the air is flowing out of this passage, it means outside is most likely this way."

He returned to Megan and sat by the pool, and they continued to alternate small drinks with long breaks. After a while, his thirst dwindled, leaving only powerful gnawing hunger.

Aylun refilled his waterskin, then turned to her. "Feeling more optimistic?" He smiled.

She smiled back. "You have no idea."

"Then let's try getting out of here." He offered her his hand and helped her up.

They returned to the opening and squeezed through. Aylun led the way down a maze of rock, winding along jagged corridors, across shallow ledges, down narrow shafts, and through open chambers. Eventually, they crawled on their stomachs down a low passage and through a shallow pool of water. Then they squeezed through a crevice and out into a large sheltered pocket with a broad entrance to an open rocky field.

A light breeze brushed across his face, igniting an intense sense of liberation that spread throughout his whole being. He raised his head, reveling in the vastness of the night sky and the swath of brilliant stars spattered across that dark canvas. It was as if a miracle had occurred. They had spent so long trapped in that dirty room, soaked in sweat and blood, that the gentle rustle of grasses and croaking of frogs seemed surreal.

Megan dove past him, headed for the wide-open spaces.

Aylun jumped in front of her. "It would be best to wait until morning. We do not know what might roam this place at night."

She scrunched up her face. "But, I'm famished."

He puzzled. "And what were you going to eat?"

She pouted.

Aylun set her down on the rocky ground. No sooner had he come to rest beside her than a faint white mist appeared, materializing out of thin air. It gathered and grew, becoming more and more dense until it coalesced into a woman in white robes. One and a half times as tall as Megan, she seemed aglow with a golden light.

AYLUN

Athene looked down at them with silver eyes and smiled. She raised her hand, and Juzhi and Yuki appeared behind her complete with saddle, bags, bit, and bridle. "As promised, your beasts of burden."

Megan and Aylun both stood and bowed before her.

Megan stepped forward. "Can I ask a favor?"

A hint of displeasure disrupted her serene face. "I have explained, I cannot help you."

Megan waved both hands and shook her head. "No, no. I remember. Not help. It's just … Jon has no idea if I'm okay. He must be out of his mind with worry. Can you tell him I'm fine?"

Athene shot a disapproving stare. "You want me to serve as a common messenger?"

Megan lowered her head. "I guess not."

Athene stood motionless for a moment, then nodded. "And if I do, will you grant me a boon in the future?"

Not sure if she would understand the word, Aylun stepped up next to her, leaned closer, and whispered, "A favor."

Megan jabbed him with her elbow. "I know what a boon is, doofus."

Athene scowled at them.

Megan bowed again. "Agreed, a boon."

"You agree, though you have no idea what I might ask?"

"I will count on your kindness and benevolence."

Athene smiled. "You really are a naive one, child." She faded away into the darkness.

Driven by a relentless hunger, Aylun rushed to the horses and grabbed a couple meager portions of bread and dried meat. They had only a day or two of rations left and who knew how many days ahead of them in dangerous territory where hunting would be risky. Now more than ever, they needed to conserve. He handed one portion to Megan. "Take it slow, do not wolf your food, and chew well."

The pair sat in the mouth of the cavern, staring out at the star-filled sky as they ate.

After a while, Aylun glanced over at Megan. "It feels good, does it not?"

Megan smiled back and nodded. "It's good."

They consumed their inadequate meal in comfortable silence, buoyed by a renewed sense of optimism. After they had eaten, they spent a long while staring at the sky in relative silence, broken only by the occasional round of discussion. Megan seemed surprisingly at ease as they each recounted their worst moments, greatest fears, and other impressions of the last few days' events. And as they sat, and ate, and shared their thoughts, the dark sky brightened, and a light breeze began to caress the grassy field before them.

Chapter Thirteen

BOX OF TOYS

It was hard for Megan to take her eyes off them as she heaved gently in the saddle. In many ways, they were like the Grand Canyon, jagged walls on either side, towering far into the mid-morning sky. And then again, they weren't like anything she had ever seen. Compared to that famous canyon, the cliffs seemed much steeper, far taller, and the whole thing many times broader. The floor was different, too. Rather than being a riverbed, it contained a patchwork of rocky fields and woods, with the occasional pond or stream.

The Seteepta Valley, Aylun had called it. It was nothing more than a broad canyon cut far into the mountains. As he described it, Katapa—the seat of power, with all of its armies—lay at its entrance. Far down the chasm, at the other end, stood Lanessa, the main center of production and commerce. The Talesh Empire had chosen the spot for its two most crucial cities because the Alundeer Mountains around them were nearly impassable. By putting their capital and center of commerce behind the soaring peaks, they made them almost impervious to outside attack. It appeared they never expected an assault from within the mountains themselves.

Megan stared up at the sky, and another oddity struck her, a strange combination. The woods and fields had a distinct lack of ground life—no sign of rabbits, squirrels, foxes, chipmunks, raccoons, deer, or anything like them. Yet there existed a startling abundance and variety of birds, big ones with wide wingspans, the kind that liked to make lazy circles in the sky, far up toward the rocky cliffs. As best she could recall, large birds like that were most often birds of prey or scavengers. Yet if ground life was sparse, then what would birds of prey and scavengers eat? Or perhaps they had already eaten it all and were themselves in the process of starving.

Then the most chilling conclusion came to her. The beasts from the temple must roam here. She had heard the ferocity with which they could attack one another, and the birds of prey must feast on the remains of the fallen.

Her gaze returned to the overgrown path before her, a carpet of cobbles and vegetation that stretched far off across the broad patch of rocks and grass only to disappear into a swath of trees and shrubs. Yuki's hooves thudded against the path, and she jostled beneath Megan, adding to her soreness. Weary and stiff, she stretched her aching neck and shoulders as she glanced at Aylun in front of her. "Can we stop and rest?"

Ever alert and scanning their surroundings, he never glanced back. "No, not yet." Gone was the edgy anger that had so often typified their past exchanges, replaced by a calm and patient tone. In that den of thieves, somewhere between the fever, wounds, hunger, and dehydration, something in Aylun had snapped. He had changed. No longer did he play the same obnoxious tyrant. Oh, he could still be annoying and irritable, and he still liked to quarrel and contradict every word she said. But there was an absence of the usual animosity behind it, replaced by an unruffled, laid-back quality.

Megan sped up, trying to get closer. "We were cooped up in a cave for four … two … who knows how many days. We've been riding for hours. I'm sore. I'm tired, and I was never that used to being on horseback in the first place. Can we please just stop now?"

"No."

The world around them turned darker as they passed from the field to the shade of a woodland that wound its way around the rocky walls of a craggy hill.

AYLUN

She heaved a weary sigh. "Not even for a few minutes?"

"We have one day to make it to Lanessa and search a big portion of the city. Every minute we are not moving is another minute we might have to spend dealing with those things from Katapa."

"You really think they're still out there?"

Aylun turned in the saddle and stared at her. "Count on it. No one has ever come back from this far in."

"But to do all that in a day ... it isn't realistic."

"We should at least try."

She scowled, then decided to give up for now. It wouldn't kill her to go a bit farther before she resumed her pestering.

Aylun faced forward again, and the screech of a bird caught Megan's notice. It circled above them as if waiting for their demise. Its massive wingspan made it visible even through the cracks in the gently swaying greenery. Light from the midmorning sun had not yet risen above the eastern cliffs, leaving the woodlands and fields on this side of the chasm in shade, while a warm light splashed the hills, woods, and rocky cliffs beyond.

She turned her attention to a closer stand of trees, puzzling at the moss-covered trunks at the edge of the path. Moss was supposed to grow on the south side, where there was perpetual shade, but from the angle of the shadows across the distant rock and grass, these patches all appeared to be growing on the eastern side, facing the morning sun.

"Are you sure you know where you're going?" She stretched out a hand to touch one of the clumps. "How can anyone make out where they're going in this ... stuff?" Then it occurred to her. Moss grew on the south side of trees because they never saw the sun. She looked up at the cliffs bordering the right side of the path. They blocked the morning sun, leaving the eastern side of the trees in perpetual shadow. Maybe it wasn't all that odd after all.

Aylun's response contained a familiar note of impatience. "The path can only go one place: Lanessa. We have been over this." He shook his head.

329

Well, he wasn't completely different, after all. Megan scrunched up her nose and silently mouthed, "We've been over this" to his backside, then stuck out her tongue. She put on a sarcastic bubbliness. "And we just have to make it there and search the whole city before sundown! Sure, piece of cake, no problem."

Aylun sighed. "Not the whole city. I told you." He turned in the saddle and eyed her with an exasperated expression. "Has anyone ever told you you're kind of a negative person?"

With her reins clutched in her hands, she set her fists on her hips. "Oh, that's rich coming from mister sunshine."

He fell silent for a time. The path took a sharp corner that hugged the rock wall. Their hoof-falls echoed through the dense trees and assorted greenery as the silence dragged on, and the path straightened.

After a while, he glanced back at her again. "There's something I have been meaning to ask."

She nodded. "Okay, sure."

"You once said you loved Jon as much as any wife loves a husband."

Megan closed her eyes and shook her head. It was a thing she had said in anger and not a topic she was yet comfortable discussing with him. "Um ... well, I may have exagger—"

"No. No, I believe it. After everything I have seen you do to get back to him, I believe it. It's just, I cannot figure out why you are not together. Was it Jon? Did he never tell you he liked you?"

She almost laughed. "Oh, trust me, he did. The day we were sent here, he asked me out."

"Then why did you not say you were courting when I asked if you were married?"

Megan giggled. " 'Courting' ... really? What is this, the Dark Ages?" She stopped herself from saying more. Courting wasn't really as old as the Dark Ages, and an age such as this one had never appeared in any history book.

330

AYLUN

Aylun fell silent.

She spent a while searching for a response. When she finally did speak, she was surprised at how much regret her own words contained. "Jon has always been interested in me. Honestly, it was me who kept putting him off."

He dropped back next to her and scrutinized as they rode side by side. "But why?"

She struggled with the question for a while, then began slowly. "Well … I guess … at first it was because I wanted to establish myself in my career, you know, become independent before I got serious about anyone."

He seemed quite puzzled. "Why?"

Megan shot him a look of disapproval. "Would you like the idea of being dependent on someone? Of being supported by someone? Of being unable to take care of yourself if that other person were ever gone?"

Aylun seemed surprised by the question. "I do not think the possibility of becoming dependent on someone would ever enter my mind." He cocked his head. "Still, I don't see the connection."

"What connection?"

He appeared baffled. "Were you not already independent before you established yourself in your profession?"

"I already told you. I was on my own from a young age."

He shook his head in apparent confusion. "But you just now said that you needed to establish yourself in your profession in order to be independent."

"That's not what I …" She straightened and glared. "Hey, are you just doing this to make me confused?"

"It is you who are confusing *me*."

His puzzlement seemed genuine enough, and she found herself wanting to make him understand. "Okay. Fine. Maybe 'independent' was the wrong word. I wanted to become the adult me. You know, the person I would ultimately become."

Aylun appeared thoughtful for a while as the hoofbeats against vegetation-covered stones drifted on the warm air. He peered at her sideways with a quizzical look. "There is no such thing."

"What does that mean?"

"It means there is no ultimate you. People are not like bread, where you bake it and then it is done. Every hardship, every tragedy, every happiness, every person who becomes part of our lives changes us. Therefore, we are always in a state of becoming. We learn, we adapt, and hopefully, we improve. In that way, our experiences shape us, so we are always turning into someone new."

Stunned at his thoughtful response, Megan stared. "I guess. But even so, I wanted to be *more* of the person I saw myself as. So he would know who he was accepting as his partner."

Aylun nodded. Perhaps he finally understood. Then, after a moment, his puzzled look returned. "I ... I am confused. Do you want to marry someday? Is that not a part of who you ultimately want to become?"

"Of course. At the right time. When I'm ready. I was afraid that if I got involved with him too soon, it might never allow me to become who I wanted to be. I wouldn't be me anymore."

He looked into her eyes and nodded. "If being your own person is what you want, if that is more important than being with Jon, then perhaps you were right to not accept him."

She was startled by his comment and uncomfortable with the characterization. "Well, I wouldn't say it was *more* important than him. ..."

Aylun continued, ignoring her response. "Love, marriage, becoming someone's mate, always being by their side, throughout every adversity—it changes you. How could it not? If it does not, then it is not a real marriage. It is just two people who live together."

Annoyed and disappointed that he insisted on misunderstanding her, Megan pouted. "So you just think everything about me and Jon is wrong and dumb."

His response gave every impression of being heartfelt and genuine. "No. Not at all. I never said that. I am merely concerned, that is all."

"What is that supposed to mean?"

"I fear you are setting yourself up for disappointment and heartache."

"Me? How so?"

"You plan to share your life, but only after you have grown separate lives that preclude your other half. You want to become one with another person, yet never have it change you. You seek connection and family, but do not want to depend on anyone. It sounds unrealistic to me. It sounds like a fantasy."

Megan huffed. "Or perhaps you just lack imagination."

He paused and gave a thoughtful nod. "Perhaps."

"And what about you? Aren't you just being a hypocrite? Were you willing to become someone different to be with Yaolin?"

It was obvious her statement had struck a nerve, and he appeared to give her words serious consideration as they plodded out onto another patch of rocky field. Aylun jogged in the saddle as he shot her a fleeting glance. "It is not the same. She yearned for something that was not within me to give. Even so, you are right. I never once made the slightest effort to be who she needed."

Megan winced to herself. It was obvious she had just poured salt on a wound that still remained open. She lowered her head. "I didn't mean that. I'm sorry."

He eyed her with a look of hurt and anguish. "But your words were not wrong. I pushed her away because I wanted us to be stronger. But it only divided us and made us weaker. It was not what she wanted or needed."

"Can we please just drop it?"

"Perhaps I simply have to face the truth: that I was meant to be alone, that I am a liability as a partner."

Megan lifted her gaze. As much as she had resisted it, he was beginning to feel like a friend, and his self-deprecation upset her far more than she would have expected. She scowled at him. "Oh, for ... and that makes sense to you? That you're a liability? That you should be alone?"

He grumbled under his breath, "I thought we were dropping the subject."

He hadn't let it drop when she wanted. It was time to give him a taste of his own medicine. Megan glared. "And this whole thing about your sister, about her dying because you lost your head, because you cared too much ... it's just dumb."

"What?"

"I mean, really, come on. Did your sister panic?"

Aylun shook his head. "No, she actually seemed kind of calm at the end."

"Then, did she not care about you?"

"No, that's not it at all."

"If you think the problem is caring about your sister, if you think that's what caused you to panic, then explain why she stayed calm when you did not?" When he didn't answer, she insisted, "Well, why did your sister not panic?"

Despite his attempt to maintain a calm facade, it was clear the question had not only thrown him, but also stung a great deal. A somber mood descended on him, and his words were quiet.

"Perhaps you were right. I should have dropped the subject." Aylun spurred Juzhi ahead, leading the way as he scanned the rough landscape for danger.

With the abrupt end to their discussion, Megan returned her attention to the towering cliffs. Her inclination was to regret what she had said, to soften it, or take it back, yet they were words he needed to hear. She hadn't been present when those tragedies had unfolded, but even knowing as little as she did, it was clear that his blame was misplaced. Not that she doubted he'd panicked and made things worse, but if that was the case, it was not out of caring too much. Something inside told her this. Call it instinct, call it intuition, but she was certain. He was wrong to blame that part of himself. Caring gave you something to fight for; it made you stronger.

They passed in and out of patches of woods and rocky fields with occasional pools of water. The temperature steadily rose along with the humidity, making the air oppressive. Each new stream or pond called to her, beckoning her to rest and partake of its refreshing coolness. The sun passed overhead, then disappeared over the cliffs on the other side. Towering rock walls passed by, sometimes closer on the left and sometimes on the right, as the path wound its way down the canyon toward Lanessa.

Through it all, Aylun's cloak of glum rumination never faded, making conversation difficult. She managed to goad him into stopping a couple of times for a brief rest and a drink of water. Or perhaps he relented because the horses needed the breather more than she did. Yet, even as they rested, he remained withdrawn, answering questions with a smile and a polite word or two, then returning to his quiet reflection. As late afternoon came, he began to express concern that they hadn't yet reached the city and would soon need to seek shelter.

Against his urging, they stopped again at a lake that touched the sheer rock of the chasm wall. Megan insisted on wading in, using the excuse that she needed to wash the sweat out of her clothes and clean the grime from her face and hair. While it was true that she did feel dirty and unkempt, what she needed more was relief from the stifling heat and humidity. The water was shallow enough to stand in, so she bent over and immersed her body and head in the refreshing coolness.

Meanwhile, Aylun seemed fixated on the cliff that bordered the pool, its folds and cracks making it look like a flowing rock curtain. He rose and approached it.

Megan ducked below the surface for a second time and watched several fish dart away toward the gray, sandy shoreline. As her head splashed out of the water, he glanced down at her. "There is a gap in the wall here. It is hidden from view. It might …"

She watched as he dove in and disappeared below the water. When he didn't reappear right away, she waded over to where he'd vanished. From her new vantage point, it became clear that the solidness of the wall had only been an illusion. In the place where Aylun had headed stood a wide gap that curved behind the wall but couldn't be seen from the side. He splashed up through the surface in front of her a short time later, causing her to jump and let out a small squeak of surprise.

Aylun turned to face her. "There is a cave beyond this. I think it may be possible to hide there for the night."

Megan finished her washing ritual, and they mounted. She retrieved her aetherstone and used it to light their way as they waded into the water and through the craggy walls of the gap. The horses splashed around several folds of the rock curtain and eventually emptied into a large open grotto, with a pool along one wall and a wide beach.

They splashed up onto the shore and settled in the cavern, making camp and tending the horses. It was far cooler than outside but not chilly, and Megan's clothes and hair dried quickly. Sore and tired from a long day that had started in the depths of a den of thieves, they both were eager to recover and relax. So, when they finished, they sat on the beach, watching the golden light from the glass ball reflect off the still waters and scatter across the craggy cavern walls.

Aylun sharpened a stick and left. A few moments later, he returned, having pierced several large fish. By the light of her aetherstone, he skinned and deboned them with a hunting knife, then handed her the hunks of raw flesh. Her hunger more profound that any she had ever experienced, and the bounty he had gathered far more than their recent meals, Megan ate the uncooked fish with feverish haste, telling herself it was no different than sushi.

After a while, a gentle rain began to fall outside, the quiet patter seeming as gloomy as Aylun's mood. Megan closed her eyes. This wouldn't do. She had soured his mood by randomly bringing up his sister, and although he might have deserved it for being such a dunderhead, it was beginning to make her feel guilty.

She glanced at him. "Hey?"

He looked over at her.

"How long are we going to sulk like this?" She flashed an exaggerated pout.

Aylun rolled his eyes. "Sorry, I was just thinking."

"Well, it's boring. Stop it."

He let out a small laugh. "I do not exist for your—"

She pointed her finger at him. "Don't say it."

He presented her with a grave expression and a bow of his head. "Yes, ma'am."

She folded her hands in her lap, sitting prim and proper as she nodded approval. "That's better."

"Then how shall I entertain you?"

Megan smiled. "Um ... tell me what's with this whole Augury deal."

"Augury deal?" He shook his head. "You know you should probably avoid using words you do not understand."

"Really? How do you suggest I ask about it without using the word?" She scoffed and muttered, "Grumpy, illogical sourpuss."

Aylun chuckled again. "Well, as long as you asked nicely ..." He flashed a disingenuous smile.

"All right, I know it has to do with oracles and prophecy, and I know you worked for them, but what's the point?"

"The point?"

"Yeah, why does your world need an Augury?"

He seemed to ponder for a long moment, staring at the soft light reflecting off the water and playing off the cavern wall. The sound of rain outside rose, then dwindled before he answered. "To preserve free will, I suppose."

Megan boggled and responded with indignation. "Oh, no. Absolutely not." She waved her finger at him. "You do not get to say those words."

"What?" His puzzlement appeared to be genuine.

"Really? The person who abducted me can't see why I might object to him talking about his purpose as 'preserving free will'?"

"Oh." He lowered his head.

She let out a soft grumble. "It doesn't even make sense."

Aylun scooted around to face her and sat cross-legged, seeming somewhat enthused about the topic. "I know it seems that way, but how do you know I was not preserving your free will?"

She crossed her arms. "Because I was there?"

"No, I mean, sure, we took it away for a couple of days, but after it was clear you understood, we gave it back."

"You mean after you realized you couldn't force me to go along with your whims any longer?"

"If I had not abducted you, you very well may have been imprisoned and spent the rest of your life with no ability whatsoever to express your free will. Taken in the balance, I may have preserved far more than I took." He seemed quite self-satisfied as he finished his proclamation.

Megan rolled her eyes. He was so clueless. "You realize that doesn't make any sense, right? My choices are mine. Who are you to make them for me? Who are you to decide how and when to preserve my free will? The whole concept is cuckoo."

"But you were not in your right mind, and—"

"Oh, and you *were* in your right mind?"

"Regardless, you were in denial. Nothing I could have said or done would have convinced you of the gravity of your situation. Because of that, you were not capable of making the decision. I have already said that I am terribly sorry for what I did. But even so, I would do it again. I had to do something to impress upon you the danger you were in."

She stared at him for a long silent moment, then gave a crisp bow of her head. "Apology accepted."

Aylun seemed thrown for a second, then laughed. "You are most gracious."

A portion of her anger returned. "Don't get me wrong. It's not that I want to forgive you. I just figure it's better if we go into that city tomorrow on the same side, rather than being at odds with one another."

His expression turned a bit serious. "Now, I appreciate your kindness, I truly do, but it is already getting dark, and I fear those things will return and track us to this pool." He nodded to the cool dark water before them. "If they are right outside, any noise we make could confirm their suspicions that we are in here."

Megan nodded. "See, isn't that better? You explain the danger, I agree, and we work together."

He seemed to consider for a moment. "Then we have a new agreement. Anymore, my only reason for being here is to help you. So I will guide and counsel you, and as long as you agree to take my advice with the sincerity with which it is offered, I will leave the decisions to you."

She nodded. "Now, be quiet. I don't want you attracting any unwanted attention."

Aylun chuckled, but it was cut short by a piercing howl from just beyond the rock wall. Megan fell quiet as impressions of their recent time trapped in the hideout came back. More voices followed, farther away. The chorus of howls echoed into the distance, some plaintive and some piercing, some round tones and some yips. After a while, snarls and growls began to fill the evening air. Megan shrank down and stared at the entrance.

Seeing her discomfort, Aylun scooted over next to her. He leaned in as close as he could get to her ear and whispered, "If they don't come in here after a short while, they probably will not come in at all. They either cannot figure it out or are unwilling to cross the water. Either way, I will keep watch if you want to sleep."

A fight broke out, and she hunkered down next to him, wrapping her hands around his muscular upper arm. No sounds of splashing could be heard, nor did any ripples show on the surface of the water. After a while, Megan gathered her courage and relaxed.

Once she was comfortable that no unexpected intruders would appear, she crept to her bedroll and pulled it over next to Aylun. Then she lay down and soon fell into a jumpy sleep.

They reached the top of the ridge, and with a fair degree of excitement, Megan peered down at the place they'd fought and bled and struggled so hard to reach. The ruins of Lanessa before her were every bit as impressive as those at Katapa. Yet at the same time, it was an altogether different sight. Loose clumps of buildings, separated by large open spaces, sprawled out in every direction. She scanned the crumbling low homes and shops that formed a ring, winding around the base of a gently rolling hill.

Aylun pointed to the center, where temples and monuments dotted the crest, with large open spaces and generous walkways between. "Lanessa was once the center of Talus commerce. By all accounts, nobody has seen this place for hundreds of years."

Far out, beyond the western edge of the city on top of a small hill, stood an enormous and puzzling monument. It consisted of a massive round platform, large enough to hold a small army, ringed by three arching monoliths that tapered as they curved up over it, high into the sky. Aylun's gaze drifted over to survey the gleaming white monoliths and he mumbled, "If only we had a spire stone."

Megan glanced at him. "Why? What's a spire stone? What is that thing?"

"That's a spire. There are almost a dozen of them spread across the three realms. Each one has a spire stone of a different color that takes you to that spire. If we had one of those stones, we could use that"— he pointed to the monument on the distant hill—"to travel to one of those other spires. It wouldn't even matter which one we went to. What matters is that in the blink of an eye, we would be out of here."

Megan nodded as she continued to survey the ruins. Beyond them, chasm walls circled the entire area, surrounding it on three sides with sheer rock cliffs.

AYLUN

Aylun pointed to a few of the many dark cavernous holes at their base. "Come dusk, we will need to find shelter again in one of those caves." He turned his attention to Megan. "Wistra's journal described living in the back of a blacksmith's shop. We have to find it before nightfall."

Megan nodded and resumed scanning, but the buildings were too far away, too decrepit, and too numerous to make out much of anything, much less the use to which each building might have been put. She turned her attention to Aylun. "How exactly am I supposed to recognize a blacksmith's shop?"

He paused for a moment. "Huh. Good point. They probably looked different back then."

She rolled her eyes and spoke with slow emphasis. "Since I've *never* seen one, they'll all look different to me."

He eyed her with surprise. "You've never seen a blacksmith?"

Megan shook her head.

He thought for a moment. "Well, a blacksmith would need a place to burn a lot of wood or coal and a bellows to heat it to a temperature where it could melt metal. Also, some flat stone or metal surface to hammer the softened metal on, and a place nearby for water to cool it. They would also need tools: hammers, tongs, and other implements. Of course, half of that would have decayed into an unrecognizable state by now."

She sighed. "Well, that's sufficiently unhelpful."

It had not been a long trip from last night's camp to the city, so the air still had a tinge of morning chill. The sun disappeared as their horses wandered down the hill, blotted out by a dense layer of clouds. They rolled across the sky, casting a deep shadow that drifted past them and into the city, then across it to the cliffs beyond. The cobblestone road headed straight toward the edge of town, where it branched out. Like the tributaries of a river, it flowed through jagged, half-collapsed remains of dozens of stone buildings.

As they wandered into the sea of crisscrossing roads lined with ancient structures, Aylun proposed a search pattern. The general path would be clockwise around the center. Every two blocks, they would part and wander in opposite directions, Megan toward the center of the city and Aylun away, scanning the buildings for signs of a blacksmith's shop. As they each reached the edges, they would turn clockwise, go one more block, and head back toward each other.

Megan set off, enthused at the prospect of such a rigorous search. Yet, while it all sounded logical and straightforward in theory, it turned out that the city had not been laid out in such a neat grid. As a result, their methodical approach soon fell apart in practice. Instead, she found herself clomping down alleys and cross streets, plodding through the same square over and over or weaving through chaotic nests of buildings. Not only were the haphazard detours tedious, but they also left her uneasy about whether she had examined every structure.

The monotony soon began to wear on her, and she struggled to stay focused as they slogged through what seemed like an endless parade of crumbling stone homes and shops, mixed with the occasional columned temple, sculpted monument, or open market. They'd risked their lives to get here, so it was crucial she stay alert and not let all that terror and anguish add up to nothing. With that mindset, she struggled to remain alert. Yet despite her best efforts, her passion faded as time dragged on and on. Then everything began to blend together, becoming a hazy blur of decrepit stonework, crazy-quilt alleys, and decaying cobbles.

The search did yield a couple of prospects that stood out as possible blacksmith's shops, with stone hearths, places for bellows, and flat surfaces to hammer metal. Yet, when she and Aylun did a further search of each, it yielded nothing in the way of a journal or any sign of oracles or prophecies.

With countless hours spent and only about two-thirds of the city searched, Aylun began to appear nervous. After some time, he announced that because of the cloud cover, he couldn't be sure of how late it had become. He advised that it would be best to quit for the day, seek shelter, and return in the morning. True to his word, he had not taken charge and demanded, but simply explained the dangers, offered council, then accepted her decision.

Though disheartened at the prospect of quitting when they were so close to their goal, Megan nonetheless decided to heed his advice. So the pair clip-clopped along on their weary horses, heading back toward the entrance.

After only a few minutes, Aylun stopped and stared with intensity at an almost intact building to his right. He pointed. "There." He squinted at it. "I think I have seen that before. It is like the pattern on the cover of Wistra's journal."

She looked, and two houses down, beyond a crumbled opening, etched crosswise on the far wall, stood a giant outline of a dragonfly. Below it, visible above the pile of rubble, sat a chest, shrouded in the shadows of a small room.

The position and sprawling size made the dragonfly wall visible from quite a distance, lending the impression of a sign set out for all to see. Aylun spun toward it and spurred his horse on, and with renewed hope, the pair clattered over into the small yard before the building. They slid off and rushed up to the jagged opening in the decaying wall.

Aylun pointed to a nearby ample stone fireplace. "A place for coal."

A smooth, flat stone table stood near it, and Megan pointed, too. "And a place to hammer metal?"

He nodded. "This could have been a blacksmith's shop."

They stepped across the pile of rubble and through the opening. Megan slipped on a loose piece of gravel, and Aylun caught her as they crept into a small stone room that appeared intact. Across the floor, below the dragonfly, stood the small metal chest. Against the adjacent wall sat a dilapidated bed and a little dresser with the top two drawer pulls broken off.

With intense anticipation, Megan hurried over and squatted before the chest. A heavy layer of dust covered some kind of impression on the lid, so she brushed away the dirt and debris.

Beneath it, diagonally on the surface, lay a beautiful and detailed figure of a dragonfly inlaid in jade, ebony, and obsidian. She tugged on the lid of the chest, but it refused to move. Even when she pulled harder, it didn't budge the slightest amount. She looked down at the dirty and corroded keyhole on its front. "It's locked."

"Chances are it is rusted shut."

They both stared for a moment.

"Can you lift the whole thing up and drop it, maybe break it open?" Aylun motioned, indicating it rising from the floor, then falling.

"And risk the contents? What if ..." She stepped back and gasped as she remembered her dragon key. "You don't suppose?" Megan thrust her hand in her pocket, retrieved it, and held it up, the three gems seeming to sparkle even in the dimness of the unlit room.

He nodded. "It is worth a try."

Despite appearing to be the wrong shape and size, it was a perfect fit when she jammed it into the lock. With a quick turn, the ornate lid clicked open a crack. She grabbed the edges and heaved. It grumbled as it gave way, then opened.

She rummaged inside to discover a collection of intricately carved jade dragon figurines, a couple of what looked like puzzles, a string, and a large top of the type you spin. Her eyes rested on a small bag off to the side. Megan grabbed it, untied the drawstring, and couldn't help but smile as she peered down at its contents. "Ooh, marbles. It's a box of toys."

Aylun peered over her shoulder into the bag. It contained quite a few small stone spheres, polished and shiny, in a range of bright colors. Most were a single shade in hues of crimson, burnt orange, chartreuse, lilac, white, gray, midnight blue, jet black, and more. Others were translucent, some clear and others like colored glass, with silver, gold, or copper swirled throughout.

Aylun staggered backward and almost fell over a piece of fallen stonework.

AYLUN

The clatter attracted Megan's gaze, and she puzzled over what could have affected him so.

He stared at the bag in awe. "Those are not marbles." His gaze drifted to hers. "They are spire stones. They are worth a fortune beyond your wildest imaginings. Keep them. Hide them well."

She began to retie the drawstring as Aylun glanced through the missing portion of the wall and out across the tops of the homes. Centered in the opening stood the spire on the hill. Well beyond the edge of the city, its three curved stone teeth were only partly visible above the decrepit rooftops.

His gaze snapped back to her. "Wait … first, hand me the amber one. It is our way out of here."

Puzzled, Megan reopened the bag and grabbed the orangish-yellow marble. She held it up and scrutinized its polished surface, then handed it to Aylun. "So, this will work with that spire thingy to get us out of here?"

"No time for details, but yes. All we need to do is use this stone on that." He pointed to the monument in the distance, rising above the remains of the city. The three stone monoliths arched toward each other as they rose up above the rooftops, shining ivory-white against the steel-gray sky. They didn't resemble a spire in any way. Megan closed and retied the bag and jammed it in her pocket.

Aylun returned his gaze to the contents of the chest. "Is that all there is? No journal?"

His question alarmed her, so she returned her attention to the contents of the chest, rummaging a bit more before she noticed the bottom sat too high off the ground. She knocked on it and was rewarded with a hollow sound. She jammed her finger into a small slot on the right and lifted it. A dry and brittle sheet of wood crackled as she pulled it up, threatening to break in two. All the baubles resting in it slid to one side, revealing a collection of ornate apparel and accoutrements beneath.

On the left lay several colorful silk robes with opulent embroidery in gold. Next to them, tucked into cubbies that were a perfect fit, sat a few gem-laden pieces of jewelry: a ruby circlet, a necklace of emerald and sapphire, and several hairpins that evoked the feeling of birds and flowers. There was even a golden one in the shape of a stick with a crystal dragonfly perched on its end.

Aylun straightened. "What? Wistra was a woman of simple means. She neither cared for, nor would she collect, such expensive and elaborate clothes and jewelry."

Megan considered for a moment. "Chests are for things you want to keep and protect. Perhaps she wasn't interested in their value. Maybe she had some kind of emotional attachment to them."

He shook his head. "I do not know. It does not fit." He glanced around. "She would consider her journal to be very valuable and not something she would want stolen. A chest like this would be where I would expect to find it."

"Is that where you found the other journal?"

"No. It was in a drawer."

Megan glanced over at the ancient chest of drawers. She rose and flew over to it while Aylun took her place, rummaging through the trunk and pocketing a few of the items. She grabbed the top drawer by its edges and pulled, but with no handle and no way to get a good grip, it wouldn't budge. The same held true for the second drawer, but when she tried the bottom one, it slid open with ease and clattered to the floor.

Her heart leaped as there, along the side, rested a small leather-bound book with the same kind of dragonfly symbol scrawled on its surface. It could be the key to freeing her and Jon from this whole prophecy. She stared at it for a second, finding it hard to believe they might have actually found it.

Then she realized the oddity of this situation. Aylun seemed to think the dragonfly was somehow associated with Wistra, but who would keep their journal in the bottom drawer? It should be in a top drawer where it would be accessible.

Megan picked it up with care. It seemed old and brittle as she turned it over in her hands, looking for some sign of its contents.

AYLUN

Aylun had come up behind her and reached over her shoulder to snatch it from her hands.

She glared up at him behind her. "Hey."

"I must see if it contains what we need." He stopped on the first page. "The writing uses her brushstrokes, and she speaks of images that came to her in meditation." He scanned a few moments more. "She even mentions the branches of the tree." He looked up from his reading. "This is it."

He paged through for a while, then stopped. "She refers to a dream here and mentions the Otherworlder." The mention of the prophecy rekindled her hope, and Megan watched with impatience as he flipped through, scanning the pages. "And here too."

He turned a couple more pages and began to read aloud. " 'I had the dark dream again. The one I should never have had. The one I sought to protect against. I gave the Shou a warning against this very thing. That warning was to be kept in the Augury. I even created the Vault of Time to ensure its safety. Even so, I fear the dream may be a portent, that somehow someone has tampered with the timeline. Yet nobody can see what I have done, so I do not know how that is possible.' "

He turned the page. " 'If the dream is real, then I fear my warning will go unheeded. Megan will become—' "

She let out an unconscious gasp at the mention of her name, and her anxiety exploded.

Aylun looked up for a moment, then continued. " 'If the dream is real, then I fear my warning will go unheeded. Megan will become separated from Jon, and she will not be there to stop him from going down a path that he must not follow.' "

Megan lost her balance and stumbled as she heard the words. They were reputed to have been written hundreds of years ago and warned against precisely what had just been allowed to happen.

Aylun paused and glanced up again before returning to his reading. " 'It is a path that would lead to the undoing of all that I have sought to accomplish. I wish I could believe that the dream is nothing more than my fears manifesting. That I see disaster because I have sought to deny it. But if that is not the case, then the fate of humankind may be at risk, and there is nothing I can do about it.' "

Aylun rose and stared at Megan.

Her face flushed as anger ripped away all reason. Her mind flashed back to images of her abduction, her utter terror and breakdown, the flight through Katapa, the horror of being trapped and alone in the den of thieves, the thirst, the horrible hunger, and with each image, her fury grew. It was all a mistake—all of it.

She looked into Aylun's eyes, and her rage found its focus. It was his fault. She flung herself at him and hammered her fists against his chest. "I told you, I begged you. I pleaded with you. How many times did I ask you to send me back to Jon? I can't even count that high." She shoved her face in his. "But no. You were so sure this prophecy crap was real. You were so sure that I had to be kept away from him."

Dizzy with the monumental uselessness of every second of sheer horror she'd lived through, Megan staggered away a short distance and leaned against the decaying wall to steady herself. "I can't believe this. Every crappy thing you put me through, all that ... and ... and for what?" She glared at him.

Aylun stood dumbfounded for a moment. "But ... but ... there is nothing in the Augury about this prophecy. Not in the Vault of Time, not anywhere. It was all from Leanna—"

She stamped her foot. "Is that what's really important right now?"

"Yes. Do you not see? This changes everything. But it also changes nothing."

Megan fumed. "Perfect. Just what I need, more obscure nonsense."

Aylun rushed over and grabbed her by the shoulder, staring into her face with a look of pure sincerity. "No. No. I vowed to bring you and Jon back together. That hasn't changed. Only now it is much

348

more urgent that I do so as quickly as possible, regardless of the council or protectors or anything. You and Jon must be together."

She stared into his eyes. His forceful proclamation was an outright admission that he'd been wrong; he was agreeing with her. And his vow, delivered once again with such conviction and clarity, snuffed out the largest portion of her outrage. She nodded. "Well, at least we agree on that. But still, look what we went through. …"

He shook his head. "For good reason. I know it is not the answer you were hoping for, but we now know that something is *very* wrong. What the council thinks they know might be completely incorrect or invalid. As soon as I return you to Jon, I must find answers."

What he was proposing was not only well reasoned and logical, but exactly what she wanted to hear, and she calmed even more. "I suppose now is not the time to argue."

Aylun looked up at the dense clouds overhead. "Without the sun, it is hard to say what time it is, but it feels late. We have what we came for, and now with the spire"—he pointed to the monument in the distance—"we can be out of here as soon as we reach it. We should go now."

Megan nodded.

He handed her the journal as they headed out of the building. "It is yours now."

"Mine?"

Aylun nodded. "This was always your mission."

Megan looked down at the worn pages and was shocked to find she understood the strange scribblings. What was written wasn't exactly what Aylun had just read, but close enough. For a moment, she puzzled over how she could understand its ancient script when Aylun had gotten parts wrong. Perhaps its age meant it wasn't familiar to him. She shrugged. It was just another in a growing set of pieces to the language puzzle she hadn't yet solved. She closed it with care, slid it in her pocket, and turned her attention to their departure.

The notion that they might soon be out of this den of insanity struck with an intense sense of relief. It was almost over. They reached the horses and mounted, then headed for the monument in the distance. Megan followed, her anticipation growing as Aylun zigzagged through wide alleys and down narrow side streets to arrive at a paved circular plaza. Ringed by what seemed like crumbed shops, at its center stood a statue of a tall graceful beauty. Dressed in a flowing robe, her head and half an arm had broken off, and their cracked and shattered remains lay at her feet.

The gray marble form sat at the junction of seven roads, and the view down the westernmost one was uninterrupted. It exited the city over a small bridge and led far off across the grassy countryside to the hill, then up it to the spire. They quickened their pace, clattering along its length as the clouds deepened and the area grew darker.

With the dusky environs, her anticipation gradually turned to dread. It was almost certain that the things that had followed them, that could track them by smell, that would kill them given half a chance, were incapable of telling time. When it grew dark enough, they would be back, regardless of the exact hour.

The bridge at the edge of the city led over a small stream that emptied into a modest pond. Aylun halted and turned to Megan. "Though time is short, we must stop long enough to water the horses."

Her sense of foreboding having become quite intense, she balked. "Why, if we are almost out of this place? Wouldn't it be better to wait until after we are somewhere safe?"

"Where we are headed is arid. No water."

She looked at the darkening gray sky, then back at Aylun, and nodded.

As Aylun topped off his waterskin, the horses drank their fill. After leading them back onto the road, their heads swung around. Far off in the distance, rising above the buzz of insects, a familiar and chilling horn sounded long and low. They both looked toward it, back in the direction from which they'd approached Lanessa. Far off in the distance, the darkened crest of the hill overlooking the city crawled with a blanket of gray fur, dotted with bloodred. The beasts were back and racing toward them at an alarming pace.

Panic rose within her.

Then, as if in answer, a piercing screech came from the opposite direction. Megan's gaze whipped around, and there, off in the distance, pouring out of the dark holes at the base of the cliffs, were countless enormous spiders. They crowded together, scurrying across the rocky ground, as just above them, whirling far into the sky, gathered a cloud of what appeared to be some kind of flying creatures.

Megan looked back at the wave of fur racing across the ground toward them, then over at the spire in the distance. Her breath grew short, and her words tumbled out. "We're … we're never going to make it."

She looked over at Aylun standing next to her, and he was frozen, staring at her with an expression of sheer terror.

Chapter Fourteen

BEGINNINGS

A horn sounded far to the north, the direction from which the creatures from Katapa would approach the city. Loud and low, it sent a chill through Aylun's body and a shiver down his spine. His gaze shot toward the persistent bellowing. There, beneath rolling gray skies, a distant wave of creatures poured over the crest of the hill, rippling and flowing as one, rumbling toward them at a terrifying pace.

His gaze whipped over to Megan. Her breath was already coming fast and deep, and she stood motionless. As if in a stunned trance, her eyes were fixated on the mass of fur, claws, and teeth bounding over the rocky ground.

Then came a chilling response, a grating screech echoing, out from the opposite direction, sounding as much like a call to arms as the horn. Megan's head spun around to face the sound, and he followed her gaze. There, at the distant base of the sheer rock cliffs, spiderlike creatures of all sizes flooded out of dark cavernous holes. They gathered in the shadows and scrambled across the landscape toward them. Above, a massive cloud of flying creatures swirled up into the dark and stormy sky, so dense they obscured the curtain of rock behind them.

Megan glanced between the two waves of creatures, one on each side of them, and began to shake.

Aylun froze as a surge of anxiety shot through him. One of the armies alone was impossible, but two … A wild panic welled within at the prospect of having to protect her from an overwhelming assault on two opposing fronts. Even if he could manage to avoid a savage death, it would be impossible to reach the spire. There was no conceivable way they could survive this.

Images spun through his mind of his sister's face, pleading to him through a whirling flurry of black, his oldest friend crying out as dark shapes swarmed and devoured him, and Yaolin's desperate cries as razor claws dragged her up along the rock wall. The terror of that moment sped back, shoving out all reason and threatening to cripple him.

He glanced over at Megan, and she stood trembling, half out of her mind with fear. At the sight, the tightness in his chest roared back, choking out his breath, and his mind began to slide away, whirling into a panicked daze. Then Megan's simple question came back, rippling through his thoughts: Why had his sister not panicked? Her expression had been resolute and her manner calm as she cried out, "Elder brother, please." Suddenly he saw the moment that had so often haunted his dreams in a new light, and he knew beyond all doubt what she was going to say next. She was going to tell him, "Save yourself."

As if it were the morning sun rising up to banish the darkness, a realization came to him: His dread now was centered on Megan. The source of his fear was not a threat to his sister or his fellow Shou or even his family and friends with whom he had lived and trained since childhood, but to Megan, a woman he had known a matter of days.

And with that epiphany, the answer came to him. It was an answer he had always known, an answer so simple and obvious it was stunning he had not seen it before. It had nothing to do with caring about someone; it had everything to do with trust. Ayrue had trusted him. His sister had not panicked because she had faith in him. She knew, even in the moment of her death, that he had done everything in his power to protect her, and it was her turn to protect him.

He had trusted Ayrue too, but not in that moment. Not when it counted. He had failed to have faith in her ability to handle the assault, and it had driven him into a panic.

Now he studied Megan, seeming so small and frail. She possessed a gift of enormous power, and yet here she stood trembling and afraid. If they were to survive this, it would not be by his skill and training. He had to have faith in *her*, faith in her gift, faith in her instincts, faith in the courage she had shown to him back in that temple. But before that, she had to have faith in herself. And he had to give her that faith.

A sudden surge of strength suffused him as everything became clear, and all the events of his life clicked into place. Yaolin's death, his friend's, even his sister's demise—they gained a sudden sharp and clarifying meaning as he stared at the terrified woman before him. It was her, the companion of the Otherworlder, the one Jon needed, the woman of Wistra's prophecy. She was the reason for all of it. All his friends' sacrifice, his own survival and anguish, every horrible thing that had left him a hollowed-out shell of a man—they had all led him to this moment, so that he would be here for her, so she would trust herself.

Megan began muttering to herself, the chatter growing louder as her panic seemed to spread. "No, no, no, no, no. We'll never make it." She stared at the beasts hurtling toward them. "We're going to die. I don't want to die. Not in this ridiculous, absurd … All I wanted wa—"

"You are not going to die." His proclamation was filled with all the calm certainty of his newfound purpose.

"Are you crazy? Are you delusional?" She glanced all around as her panic seemed to rage out of control. "No, wait … it's me. I'm the delusional one. This can't be hap—"

"Stop." He grabbed her by the shoulders and gave her a small shake.

For a moment, she stared at him with saucer eyes, then her gaze flitted across the two armies on either side, careening toward them, out of control and unstoppable.

Aylun hesitated. They hadn't the time for this. Every second mattered. Yet if he didn't take the time, if he dragged her with him in her current state, he would wind up fighting her fear and the two raging armies at the same time. They would never make it like that. So even as his anxiety spread, he accepted that he must take the time. He had to get through to her, because she was their only hope.

"Okay, then don't stop. I mean, who am I trying to fool? I lost four people in circumstances just like this, people I grew up with, people who were everything to me."

His calm seemed to mystify her, and she stared with wild eyes. "And you're not afraid?"

"Afraid? I am petrified. I am scared down to my bones. Scared that I will fail you, just like I have failed all the others. And every speck of my being is certain there is no way we are ever going make it to that." He pointed down the cobblestone path to the spire rising from the distant hill.

Megan began to shake. "What are you saying?"

"I am saying that all we have is just us two against all of them." He motioned to the two masses, racing toward them from either side. "Even if we could fight them off, they would overrun us and bury us under a mountain of claws and teeth. How could we possibly make it through all of that to reach the spire?"

She cowered away. "If this is a pep talk, it's a really scary one."

Aylun smiled, and he let his voice carry all the calm certainty he could manage. "But that is just our heads telling us what to believe. That is important. Because we have to be careful and smart." He brought his face closer to hers. "But it is not with your head that you believe, so stop listening to your head." He sent her a smile of admiration. "Stop listening to this." He pointed to her skull. "And believe with this." He pointed to her heart.

Megan stared down at the finger. "With my breast?"

Aylun couldn't suppress a nervous chuckle. "No, you dummy, with your heart."

She nodded as the idea seemed to calm her.

With a gentle hand, Aylun lifted her chin, so she held her head up high. "These past few days, you have shown me your heart. It is fearless and determined and heroic and beautiful. It soars above all this, where nothing can touch it. It hopes and dreams, and it *never* gives up. And I know what it is telling you right now."

"You do?"

"It is telling you that you have to make it. That you *will* make it to that spire, even through all of this."

She nodded. "So we can live?"

He granted her another calming smile. "No." He gave a small shake of his head. "Because Jon needs you. He cares about you, and you cannot let him worry about you. You cannot let him mourn you. You cannot let him down."

Megan nodded again. "That's true." She forced a weak smile. "I am beautiful."

Aylun gave another nervous chuckle. "Do not listen to the voices in your head telling you all the things you cannot do. I need you to believe with your heart. I need you to fight with everything you have. I need you to never give up, even to your last breath, and know that you *will* make it, for Jon."

"Okay." She nodded as her wits seemed to return. "But we need a plan."

He grabbed her by the arm and hustled her toward Yuki. "We stay between the two groups. Keep away from either side as long as we can." He heaved her up into the saddle. "You lead the way. Use your gift to clear everything from the path ahead. Make sure nothing stops us. The horses need to run as fast as they can. Keep moving, don't give those things a chance to converge on us, and I will protect our rear and sides." He mounted and turned Juzhi forward. "Got it?"

Megan nodded again.

"Then go."

A determined look came over her as she spurred Yuki forward. That familiar uneasy feeling began to creep back in as Aylun urged Juzhi up close behind. Megan was just one person, and the two of them against ... His confidence began to slip away, but he forced it back. He had to place all his faith in her now, and in himself. There was no more room for regret or doubt. She would fight with all she had, so he must do his part. He had to get her out of this, no matter what it took.

The pair sped toward the spire, faster and faster. At an all-out gallop, they fled down the cobbles, hot breath snorting from their steeds as swarms on either side barreled across the stony fields, surging ever closer. The roar of countless feet pounded the ground, and the shrill chittering of the spiders grated in his ears, growing both louder and more disconcerting with each passing moment.

Aylun glanced to either side, judging distance, then yelled over the clatter of hooves, "This is good! Stay right between the two of them."

Megan stuck out her thumb, pointing up, which her resolute expression told him must be some form of affirmation. Then she returned to her survey of the two groups, her gaze flitting back and forth between them. As they raced toward the curving white teeth of the spire, it grew larger and larger, and the masses on either side continued their relentless charge. Megan and Aylun shot down the ever-narrowing path between them, hooves pounding against the cobbles as the two waves threatened to crash over them.

From the left, flying creatures began shooting into them, stinging where they pelted their bodies. The air turned dark, visibility dropped, and it became difficult to make out the two armies through the swirling airborne mass. Now much closer, their shapes became clear. They were some kind of lizard with tiny sharp teeth and jaws too small to harm anyone.

As the wolves neared the road, Megan reached out with her gift and, in a blast of wind, swatted back several of the leading gray blurs on the right.

Blobs of coarse dark fur flew backward, the massive creatures tumbling through the air to crash into a storm of charging bodies. Spiders leaped over the path in front of them, diving onto a group of Blood Wolves, sending them shooting backward.

The two vast armies collided in a line that threaded far ahead, well past the spire, and behind them, all the way to the ruins. Aylun focused on those right around him, slashing and jabbing, letting his instincts take over, repelling creatures in every direction.

Above the roars and screeching, he yelled ahead to Megan, "They are fighting each *other*. This might work!"

Megan gave a distracted nod as she scooped up a group of spiders from the path in front, and this time flung them forward instead of back, clearing the way. They collided with a wave of Blood Wolves on the other side, sending them all tumbling to the ground. In an instant, the wolves whirled around and turned on the spiders, savaging them, multiple jaws yanking and tugging in every direction, tearing them to pieces.

A pair of the apelike wolf monstrosities charged toward them from behind, gaining with each powerful leap and bound.

Aylun followed Megan's lead, piercing a spider that flew at him from the side and flinging it behind them. The dark body hurtled into the gray behemoths. They yelped as they tumbled to the ground, clearing the road behind them. The pair sprang to their feet and fell upon the spider rather than continuing their chase.

Megan tossed a swath of red wolves and monstrous gray beasts into the air, whipping them forward across the path and into the charging spiders. In an instant, they disappeared, buried in a swarming mound of spindly legs and bulbous bodies. Yelps resounded, bones cracked, and beasts whimpered as they were twisted and crumpled into a ball.

Slashing and jabbing left, right, and behind, Aylun acted on reflexes alone, downing one creature after another as they gave chase.

A Blood Wolf sprang at him from the side.

He pierced it with his staff and hurled it overhead, arcing above the horses and into the spiders leaping from the other side.

He glanced ahead. Through the hail of flying lizards, a ball of swarming spiders and red fur half as wide as the road rolled into the path in front of them.

Juzhi lurched beneath him as their two steeds swerved around behind it. On the verge of being thrown from his horse himself,

Aylun reached out and grabbed Megan's arm to steady her. Snarls, screeches, and the crackling of broken bones emanated from right beside them as they brushed by. Then they veered the other way back onto the path and charged forward down the paving stones.

The area around them became a flurry of wolves crushing and rending spiders, gray behemoths being swarmed and torn limb from limb, and snarls, howls, and screeches from every direction. A carpet of legs and claws, fangs and teeth, blood and pain stretched out beyond them, coating the landscape on every side.

Megan seemed to get the knack of it and widened her focus, flinging creatures not only from the path in front but from either side and even overhead as the horses weaved and leaped through and around the chaos. Aylun and Megan lurched and heaved with them, the wind whipping around the pair as they slashed and stabbed, pushed, flung, and hurled creatures into one another.

They hit the base of the hill and headed up toward the spire, now massive above them. The brunt of the conflict came to bear as they navigated an ever-denser path, and Aylun squinted and strained to see through the storm of flying lizards.

One of them caught in Megan's hair and started to crawl up her head, snapping its needlelike teeth as it crept. She never noticed as she slapped, heaved, and tossed spiders and wolves out of the path in front, struggling to clear the last bit before the massive empty platform.

Aylun sliced the winged lizard in two, and its remains scattered into the raging chaos around them.

Along one side of the spire, flying creatures pelted its invisible barrier. The constant barrage sent a layer of sparkling blue flashes shooting across the curved surface, coating the entire side, reaching high into the dark and stormy sky. Beneath the shimmers of blue, the curved ivory teeth loomed massive and tall.

Megan flicked her wrist and scattered creatures back. They tumbled through the air to hit the unseen barrier that rose from the edges of the empty platform. Larger flashes of blue shimmered across the surface from the impact as the bodies tumbled to the ground. Megan swept them to the side in a roar of wind as they neared the edge.

Aylun kicked hard and surged past her, shouting above the constant roar of the bloody battle, "The barrier will not stop us—keep going!"

Juzhi heaved again beneath him as he and Yuki leaped in unison through the barrier and onto the huge open platform. As he and Yuki clattered down, a crackling came from above, barely rising above the clamor of yips, roars, and pained cries.

Creatures clashed and bled, fought and died all around as a glimmering water-like curtain appeared above at the peak of the spire. Its surface shimmered like the reflection of a star-filled sky in a pool of water. It stood out, a shocking contrast to the stormy gray cloud cover surrounding it.

Creatures began to pour onto the platform from every direction.

Aylun yelled back to Megan, "Keep the base clear! The stone you gave me just took away the barrier."

Megan responded, swatting massive creatures, spiders, and wolves one by one or in bunches as they scurried and leaped onto the round stone surface. As Juzhi reached the center, they both flew off their horses. Megan started to race in a circle around the group. She stretched out her arm, and a vortex swirled around the center as creatures scrambled for the edge of the platform. As her palm passed over them, her invisible hand flung them back so that they collided with one another and cleared the edge.

Aylun fished in his pocket for the spire stone.

The wind became a roar as she sprinted in circles around them and flung creatures on top of one another, clearing farther and farther back from the edge.

She began to wobble from dizziness as Aylun found the round amber stone and yanked it from his pocket. He lowered himself and faced one of the massive polished teeth. As Megan raced past, he dashed for the spire, wind blasting him, almost blowing him off his feet. Wailing, screeches, and snarls washed over them, resounding from every direction as he leaped and sailed through the air. He landed and smashed the stone against a magenta symbol on the spire.

Surrounded by dark heavy clouds, the shimmering watery curtain of stars in a dark sky began to fall toward them. The world roared and cried in pain as creatures raced at them, and Megan flung them back, continuing to spin, stumbling and staggering.

The shimmering curtain passed over them.

The clattering, screeches, and snarls fell silent.

Megan tumbled to the intricately carved rock floor as the portal dropped to the ground and disappeared.

Aylun bent over, heaving from exertion, his and Megan's deep breaths the only sounds breaking the peaceful stillness of a star-filled night. The almost full moon hung over the dark horizon, its warm light glinting off the smooth ivory teeth above and bathing the flat arid plains beyond in a soft and serene glow. The still air was hot and dry.

Aylun looked down at Megan. She lay trembling, her shocked and pale face beginning to streak with quiet tears of relief. An intense sense of gratitude filled him as he beheld her sprawled out on the rune-covered stone of the platform, quivering but unharmed. What she had done was nothing short of a miracle. Not only had she brought them through it, but she had done so while managing to keep them and their horses unscathed.

She looked up at him and smiled through her tears, and her trauma seemed to ease. He took his time recovering, and as she rose to her feet, her soft countenance filled with gratitude.

He stepped back and granted her a deep, long, and respectful bow. "Thank you."

Without the slightest warning, she leaped on him, grabbing him, and pulled him close in a firm hug. "I was sure we were dead."

Aylun stiffened, startled at her embrace. His discomfort grew with his awareness of her warm body pressed against his. It was the sort of embrace a wife might give to a husband, but not an altogether appropriate one for an unmarried Elorian woman to give to any man. She clung to him for a while before letting go, then smiled as she pulled back.

Her eyes peered into his. "That was beyond horrible ... and beyond amazing ... whatever it was."

Still transfixed by her face, he stared as she paused for a second. Then she raised her eyes to the dark shadow of the spires above, with a swath of pinprick lights spattered across the peaceful sky beyond. Her face seemed to glow in the pale light as she looked out at the dry scrubby brush and barren moonlit ground that surrounded them as far as the eye could see.

Her gaze returned to Aylun. "What just happened? Where are we?"

He handed her the amber stone. "As I mentioned back in Lanessa, this is a spire stone."

She peered down at it, small and vibrant in her hand.

He looked up at the enormous teeth arching high above them. "And this is a spire." He pointed to an amber rune on the nearby tooth, its color a match for that of the stone's. It was a simple triangle, with a circle in the center and five equally spaced lines radiating out from it. "There are different-colored spire stones. Each one is keyed to a spire in a different place."

"Then, where are we?" She found her pouch of stones and dropped the amber one into it.

"Erden. Another of the three realms. The amber stone is for this spire outside of Mundus."

"Why here?"

Aylun looked around. "The authorities think we are in Talus, so I wanted a different realm. One where they aren't looking for us. And to be honest, I would rather not be anywhere near the Augury in Kanlu. So that left Erden, and the amber stone is the only color I know in this realm."

He scanned the desolate landscape, but a quiet shuffling of hooves against the dry ground drew his attention to a brown horse. It stood well beyond the edge of the platform, and next to it sat a dark-haired Elorian woman, cross-legged and closed-eyed, in apparent meditation. Her thin dark hair was parted in the middle and pulled tight to her head, and in her lap lay a hideous piece of jewelry that looked like a disembodied indigo eye staring up at her.

Aylun gawked. What in the blazes was she doing here? He called out, "Ruahn?"

Megan glanced at him, then followed his gaze to her.

The Elorian woman's eyes cracked open, and she drew a slow, deep breath, then let it out.

He grabbed the reins and strolled toward her. As he reached the edge of the platform, he called out, "How is it you are here?"

Ruahn rose to her feet with slow catlike movements. In her gray robe, she would have blended into the night if not for the swaths of violet trim at the edges.

She dusted herself off. "I was sent to meet you and Megan. I have been waiting for quite some time."

As they ambled across the still-warm ground toward her, Megan leaned over and whispered into Aylun's ear, "How did she know tha—"

Ruahn shouted to Megan, "The Great Oracle. He told me when and where to find you."

"Then do you also know th—"

"Yes. I have already inquired about Jon, though it was hardly necessary. What took place here is known to everyone."

Megan leaned over again and eyed Aylun. "She likes to interrupt, doesn't she?"

He whispered back, "She was never the most ... affable student." Aylun stopped in front of Ruahn, who peered at Megan with a steady gaze.

"Jon was here, in Mundus, a couple of days ago. He made quite a spectacle in front of half the town. It is all the people have been talking about since."

Megan gawked. "Um ... we're talking about *Jon*, right?"

Ruahn gave an earnest nod. "He is gone now, but a group of Verod will soon leave here to march on Shirdon. Their aim is to confront the council, but after two days on the road, they will encounter Jon."

Megan looked at Aylun. "The Verod?"

He returned her gaze. "A secretive resistance movement. They oppose the council."

"Then we need to find them."

He smiled. "Agreed." He looked to Ruahn.

She bowed her head in respect. "The Verod are quite cautious. I have been unable to obtain the name of a contact. That task will fall to you." She turned her attention to Aylun as she withdrew a pouch from beneath her robe. It jangled with the sound of many coins as she placed it in his hands. "Here. You must be running low on funds. This will keep you for a long while."

Aylun tried to hand it back. "I took my life savings with me when I left. Years of wages while the Augury fed me, clothed me, and gave me a roof over my head. I don't need this."

Ruahn stepped back and put out her palm in front of the pouch to stop him. "Keep it. It is the Great Oracle's order." She looked at Megan, then back to Aylun. "Now, if you will follow me, I have secured a place for you to stay in an area where you will draw little attention."

A fleeting curiosity struck him as to why Tsaoshi would send Ruahn, who had no practical experience. For that matter, why provide her with detailed instructions on what the Verod planned to do but no directions on meeting a contact? He shrugged it off. Who could fathom why Great Oracles did half of what they did?

They all mounted and headed across the arid landscape, aimed in the direction of Mundus. It was no surprise that Ruahn, acting on her own, had been incapable of cultivating any contacts in the Verod. It was a task for which she had no background, experience, or training. Again, he wondered, why send her, of all people? Why not send full-fledged Shou such as Taibok or Zhoujing?

Still, her arrival meant that at least they had a plan now. There remained much to be done, but if all went well, in a matter of days, he would have kept all his vows. He would have made sure no harm came to Megan and returned her to Jon's side, where she belonged. It was a satisfying notion, but first, he had to worm his way into the Verod and convince them to take a pair of strangers with them. No easy feat, but it was just the kind of thing he'd trained for. Until he had accomplished it, he could not allow himself to feel at ease.

Aylun took one last look at the spire growing smaller in the distance behind them and wondered at what they had witnessed to get here. It was a complete mystery what terrible and awesome conflict they had struggled through to get to the spire. Yet, one thing was certain. He had chosen to place his trust in Megan, and she had proved him right. Perhaps Ruahn's presence here at the spire meant he was destined to do that all along, but such weighty philosophical matters were for oracles to ponder, not mere Shou. All that mattered in this moment was that he had chosen faith over fear, and it had paid off. Megan had kept her head, and she had managed the impossible. She had saved them both.

An edgy anxiety still clung to Megan as she rocked in the saddle. Everything from the starlit sky to the barren terrain had a tight, sharp clarity to it as if all her senses were still balanced on the edge of a knife. It gave the peaceful landscape a surreal definition and brightness as they headed off toward some unseen destination beyond the horizon.

That odd woman they had met—Ruahn, Aylun had called her—took the lead, allowing Megan to relax as they thudded along the dry, cracked ground. The woman's presence at the portal had been as much a shock as her unexpected words. It meant that someone had foreseen their arrival, and for a brief moment, it felt as if all their efforts had been pointless. Their arrival was predestined. Then she thought back on all Aylun had told her of oracles and prophecy and realized the truth of it. If they had known they were predicted to make it to the spire, they might not have fought as hard as they needed to make it. They might have died.

With that thought, it all suddenly crystalized for her. Destiny was not written in stone. It was forged from the myriad choices, large and small, she and Aylun had made from the very start. No oracle had been there to make those decisions for them. If they were destined to survive, it was because they were destined to fear for their lives. Because of that, they were destined to fight like mad, and only because of that were they destined to survive. So, in the end, whether their arrival at the spire was foreseen or not didn't matter. They had made their own destiny, and the oracle was just an observer, knowing only that the choices made, of their own free will, would lead them to this moment.

Aylun leaned closer and whispered in her ear, interrupting her rumination. "Later, I will answer all your questions about our escape and this place. For now, just rest. You need it and deserve it." With that, he fell back behind her, following in relaxed silence. This version of Aylun was a little disconcerting. Praise and concern had never been a big part of his repertoire, but relief and the aftershock of it all left her mind blank, with little room to contemplate the difference.

As time went by, the edginess that had come from their harrowing escape dulled, and her heightened state dissipated. Tremendous fatigue settled in as if she hadn't rested in weeks, and her sharp hunger ate at her. In a weary daze, she trudged along for what seemed like an eternity.

Eventually, a sea of broad homes rose up out of the barren moonlit landscape, their silhouetted dark shapes growing larger as they approached. Ruahn led the way to the right, counterclockwise, around the fringes of the city. Soon, in the moonlight, they could see the homes more clearly. Enormous estates with many rooms, elaborate terraces, rooftop gardens, and yards adorned with shrines and all manner of statuary drifted by as the weary horses plodded past them.

These homes reminded her of a movie. Megan's dazed mind wandered back to a time with Jon and a theater near school. In the two weeks before he was to leave for his new job at Delas Labs, all their friends were either busy with final exams or making plans to leave for new jobs. Jon seemed frantic to spend time with her and had asked her to see a movie several times. She kept putting him off. Not just because she had finals herself, but also because the smiling face she needed to keep up had become unbearable. She told him she was too busy studying, and she was. But after her study sessions, she always seemed to find herself at a bar.

She would dance, and drink, and flirt, and laugh, and for a while, she could put it all out of her mind. But she always wound up back at her dorm, and in the few minutes before sleep, the guilt and sorrow would come crashing back as she was faced again with the reality. Soon, he would leave, and she would be alone.

The day before his flight out, they went to one of those multiplex theaters with eighteen screens. One of them was always playing some well-known Hindi movie. Jon had a fondness for them, though she found them a bit sappy. The show he picked this time was wonderful, and the day stood out as one of her fondest memories with him. Its title translated to *When We Met*, and the homes here reminded her of the ones in the film. They were little mansions with large open patios, broad passages, and rows of arched doorways and windows, and everything was adorned with flowers and greenery.

The movie was long, and for those few hours, everything was perfect, and she could imagine they were those two people, living in that world. It was the last time Jon ever tried to put his arm around her or hold her hand. In fact, it was the last time he ever did or said anything romantic until his sweet words the day before the accident in the lab. She could still hear his voice as he told her what he really enjoyed was spending time with her. Now she had the journal they needed, and if she could just make it back to Jon, she could tell him how much she regretted her past cruelty. Then they could make plans to counter the council's lies while she made amends for all the rejections she had dished out over so many years.

After a while, they stopped at a gate to the backyard of a much more modest but secluded home on the outskirts. Ruahn slipped off, and the creaking of the gate cut the quiet of the neighboring yards as she eased it open. They passed through to a backyard consumed by a quaint garden. The meticulous landscape surrounded a low home constructed of giant clay bricks.

Off to one side, a narrow gravel path led to a small stable, and a modest tree stood on the other side. Tucked in the corner, its limbs were well laden with huge, trumpet-shaped flowers. Even from many feet away, their scent wafted on the air, syrupy sweet and heavy. The three led their horses down a path that ducked beneath a generous pergola crawling with delicate vines and scattered with small frilly blooms in colors that were difficult to make out in the dark.

Once they reached the other side, Ruahn instructed them to leave their horses in the yard so she could feed, water, and put them away later. Then she led them across a covered patio surrounded by dense shrubs with thick, turgid leaves. They passed through an arched doorway and into an almost unfurnished home.

The kitchen contained only a modest wooden table and chairs, and the generous living room held just a single low coffee table. The few items stood in contrast to the open spaces around them, making the rooms seem even larger. As they strolled through, Ruahn explained in a bland, disinterested drone that the lack of furniture was because the home was not in use at the moment, and she had arranged for them to have it for a while.

Their footsteps echoed through the nearly empty space as she ushered them across a worn wooden floor and down a short hallway. They arrived at a pair of rooms, each with a row of arched windows opposite a small bed and dresser. A lit candle on each dresser meant someone, most likely Ruahn, must have been here earlier to prepare the place. Their escort proclaimed that her assignment was done, and she was taking her leave to return to the Augury. As her footsteps receded, Megan chose the room facing the street, and Aylun retired to the other at the back of the house.

As soon as she entered, a savory smell struck her. With a haste born of near starvation, she located the source: a small stack of fresh round breads Ruahn must have left on the dresser. They smelled heavenly and their vibrant color was inviting. The flat pancake-shaped delicacies seemed to be made from rice and dried peas of various colors. The taste was peppery, and in no time, she devoured them all. When she finished, for the first time in days her stomach was full, and she turned to thoughts of sleep.

The mattress had the appearance of a futon but possessed a feathery softness. Laid out on top were silken sheets splashed with a large pattern of desert flowers in a yellow as pale as butter. Megan plopped down on it, sinking into its plushness, relishing the feel of lying on something softer than the solid rock or smooth hard marble of the nights before. Beyond the point of exhaustion, she plunged into a dreamless sleep.

A gentle breeze wafted across her face, waking Megan and carrying with it the pungent aroma of spices that seemed like turmeric, ginger, and coriander as well as the refreshing scent of lime. From beyond the comforting walls came the distant lilting of laughter, neighborhood conversations, and children playing. She opened her eyes to a house that was still and quiet, with golden sunlight streaking through the arched windows opposite her small bed. From the color and angle of the warm rays, it seemed like midmorning.

Famished, she stumbled down the hall to the kitchen with its small wooden table and two chairs. Spread out and waiting for her lay a thick creamy-yellow porridge of some kind and, next to it, a small bowl of slices of a rose-colored citrus-looking fruit. There weren't enough segments to make a whole sphere, which she took to mean that Aylun had already eaten, so she decided not to wait for him.

AYLUN

The concoction was smooth and chunky, creamy and chewy, all at the same time. It had a slight sweetness and was filled with crunchy bits of nuts and hunks of dried fruit, most of which she didn't recognize. She ate in the quiet of the warm sunlit kitchen, savoring the meal and the peaceful feeling of finally being well rested.

Assuming Aylun had gone to find a contact in the Verod, Megan returned to her room and settled in for a while with the journal from Lanessa. She spent a long time scanning it, but many of its pages were faded or stained to the point of being unreadable. Much of what could be read was mundane: comments on the places Wistra had been and the people she'd helped, her thoughts about how to heighten her gift through meditation, and philosophical musing on the nature of her prophetic gift. She described many visions, but all were framed as happening in the near future—which meant the actual events had already happened in the ancient past. In fact, it was frustrating and a bit odd that only passages that contained anything useful about the Otherworlder prophecy were the ones Aylun had flipped to and read first.

She slipped the journal back in her pocket and sighed. Then, for a long while, she sat in the quiet of the empty house, watching through an arched window as across the front garden, residents in bright attire passed on the stone street. The lane buzzed with their hushed conversations and the arguments, screeches, and giggles of children playing. As she soaked up the scene, her mind wandered back to that theater long ago, watching that Hindi movie with Jon. There was a similarity to the rustic appearance of the streets, the design of the houses, and the garb of their occupants. Not identical, to be certain, but an echo of that distant memory.

As often seemed the case, her ample rest had left her more sleepy rather than more alert, and she drifted in and out of slumber for a while before coming all the way awake.

Around what appeared to be midday, she spotted a smiling Aylun sauntering down the street, his arms laden with packages and bundles that looked like some kind of food. He smiled and greeted her as he entered, then went about spreading his haul out on the table. He set out a stack of soft, fluffy flatbreads, a bowl of chunky red paste to eat along with them, a saucer of savory potato dumplings, and a white drink that had the color and taste of yogurt. All were tasty, and he seemed like a different person, laughing and joking as they ate at their leisure.

He explained the spires, how several stories attempted to explain how and why they were built. The most popular ones said that the artificer Varish had made them, but nobody knew which, if any, of those tales were true. She found the mechanics intriguing too. The blue flashes they'd seen were a barrier, preventing entry to those trying to cross it without possession of a spire stone. It was possible that she and Aylun might have been repelled too if someone had already entered the Mundus spire with a stone tuned to the one at Lanessa. Both were part of a mechanism to prevent one party from transporting into the space another already occupied.

What most caught her attention was when he divulged that only ten spires were known to exist, and when they checked the color of her stones, it turned out she had one for each of them. In fact, she had more than ten different colored stones, which meant there had to be spires of which nobody was aware. She puzzled over the fact that some of hers were solid and a few translucent. That their maker would color the two sets of stone in such a different manner seemed like an attempt to identify those that were somehow distinct from the rest. Almost all spire stones had been lost over the centuries, and as a result, there were several spires for which no stones were known to still exist, until now. The rarity of them made her stones priceless, and if what she possessed was indeed a complete collection, it could very well make her one of the wealthiest people in the known world.

When she'd offered to sell a few to help bribe their way into the Verod camp, Aylun had paled visibly. He became adamant that her discovery of them might be intentional, that she had found them for a reason. Then he pointed out that they might prove invaluable in the future. They would allow her to travel faster to more places than anyone in this world. When she didn't act adequately impressed, he had forced a promise out of her to never sell them or tell anyone she had them, not even Jon. As if she were some kind of dullard who couldn't grasp that priceless baubles made her a target for thieves.

When it came to the subject of their escape, he had no idea what craziness they had fought through to get to the spire, but it appeared to be a conflict between two groups whose size and nature were unknown. They were now in the holy city of Mundus, home to the palace of the Rhanae, a husband and wife who co-ruled the realm of Erden.

The most distressing revelation was that Jon had not only drawn extensive attention to himself but had been chased from town by soldiers from Shirdon under orders to capture him.

Aylun kept stressing that she must stay hidden and out of sight. As if she weren't smart enough to figure out on her own that if discovered, she might suffer the same fate as Jon. She wanted to give him a verbal throttling for underestimating her intelligence, but the concern in his earnest eyes made that impossible. She even found herself reassuring him that she would stay hidden in the hope her promise might ease his apprehension.

Having made no progress in contacting the Verod, Aylun departed a short time after the meal. It seemed like a tall order, trying to locate someone who could get a pair of Elorian strangers into a secret Verod operation in Erden. Yet he seemed determined and confident ... unless that confidence was just a facade donned for her benefit.

After he left, Megan spent a while in the kitchen, bathing in the ambiance. Spending time in a house together, having him bring her food, tending to her needs, and worrying about her made her feel secure and cared for in a way she had not felt since childhood. It gave her a much deeper appreciation of that simple life Jon was always blathering on about.

She imagined *him* bringing her food and talking to her over a meal, as Aylun had. It only strengthened her resolve to return to him, where she belonged. And the moment they were reunited, she would tell him everything: how she'd always wanted to be with him but was afraid, how everything she'd said in the lab was an lie, and how she still wanted to be with him now. She would clear the air, dispel all the misunderstandings, and then they would start again. It would be their new beginning.

Tired of being cooped up inside on a bright sunny day, she eventually risked the yard, sitting sheltered from view of the plains and outskirts as she lounged in the cool shade of the house. The scent of the flowering tree seemed lighter now in the daylight. In the brightness of the midday sun, its deep-throated flowers shone out a golden-yellow, hanging facedown in large pendulous clumps. Off to the side came the soft pawing of Yuki and Juzhi, resting in the quaint low stable.

A squeaking came from the gate, and Megan glanced down through the long flower-laden pergola as a woman passed through and stood across the yard, scanning the area.

Megan slipped over to hide behind the length of the vine-covered structure. She stood motionless for a while, hoping the stranger would vanish. From the glimpse she'd caught, the intruder appeared to be in her thirties. Her hair was jet-black, her manner demure, and her clothes a simple kurta in a soft cream color with a semitransparent veil covering all but her eyes. She stood for a moment before strolling down the path toward the house as if she owned the place.

Megan stopped breathing. What if she *did* own the place? Even if she didn't, the path led right past where Megan stood. If the woman kept going, she would walk right in front of her. She would be in full view. To remain undetected, she had to move, yet the delicate flower-covered vines scaling the pergola were nowhere near solid enough to hide her movement. No matter what she did, there would be no escaping notice.

Deciding it best not to look more suspicious by scurrying away, she slipped into view and approached the stranger, attempting to appear far less concerned than she was.

AYLUN

The woman seemed unfazed by Megan's sudden appearance and stopped before her. With smiling eyes, she gave a deep bow. "Hello."

The casual chirpy "hello" was a bit odd when paired with a formal bow. Even more odd was the accent. Even though she couldn't place it from a single word, its presence brought back a prior puzzle. Not only did everybody else she'd met speak English, or was it Mandarin, or both … well, whatever it was, she could detect no discernible accent. A little flustered by the woman's appearance and manner, Megan fumbled, unsure what to say or do. "Hi?" she forced out with a note of uncertainty.

The woman seemed thoughtful for a moment. "I'm not sure why I came. I think I just wanted to see you … and maybe make sure you're all right."

"Me?"

The woman bowed again. "I am Prisha."

With the name she could suddenly place the accent. It was Hindi, down to the hard *t* and *d* sounds. Megan hesitated. "I'd ask if you know me, but since nobody here knows me—"

"I know you, Megan."

She startled. Aylun had insisted she stay hidden and unseen, yet this woman not only knew she was here but had sought her out. Aylun would not be pleased. She gave a quick bow of her head as seemed to be the custom. "You *know* me?"

Prisha remained cordial. "And I know you are not from this world."

Megan stood motionless in a state of shock. "How could you know that?"

The woman motioned for her to sit on the back step. Megan fumbled in indecision. Flustered and not sure what else to do, she strolled over and sat.

With quiet elegance, the woman came to rest on the stair below her. "There are many eyes in Erden, and after Jon, I made a point—"

"Jon, you saw Jon?" With a sudden jolt, all the strange awkwardness of the exchange was swept away.

"Many did." Prisha gave a slow nod. "Those that didn't have heard of him. In the Temple of Knowledge, there was a Rakshasa killing and eating soldiers, and another, a huge four-armed Bahkaana. Jon and Garris chased them out in front of a rather sizable crowd."

"Jon? We're talking about *Jon*, right?"

Prisha gave a firm nod. "And Garris, and another. It was quite a sight."

Puzzled, Megan parroted the unfamiliar name. "Garris?"

It seemed as if a smile bloomed beneath the veil. "Big fellow. Warrior"—she pointed to her face—"skin like mine, loves his crossbow."

Megan recalled the large golden-skinned man next to Jon the last time she had seen him. He had been carrying a wicked-looking crossbow. "Oh. Yeah. I think I saw him in the Illis Woods."

"He's an old friend. I owe him my life several times over. He helped me when I was new to this world."

Megan froze again. "What did you just say?"

Prisha stared with big dark eyes. "I am from Earth too." She paused. "You are from Earth, right?"

Megan gawked for a moment. "Earth?"

"Yes, some here call it Prith. I think it's a shortening of Prithvi, the name for Mother Earth."

Megan boggled. "You're from *Earth*?"

Prisha gave another firm nod.

With her revelation came a realization. Prisha was from Earth, and she had a distinct accent. People from this world had no accent. She knew, with ironclad certainty, that it was not a coincidence. There was a reason, even if she couldn't yet see it.

With no way to find the answer, her mind turned to more important questions. "So … you never found a way back?"

Prisha sat taller, exuding a sense of certainty. "No. I gave up my way back."

"Why?"

"That is another story, one that would take longer than I have time for."

Megan pondered for a while, still a bit stunned. "Then, how many of us are there?"

Prisha looked thoughtful. "From Earth? Just three, as far as I know. You, me, and Jon."

Megan looked away, shocked by the sheer synchronicity of it all. "Only three ... and you and I are here at the same time ... and Jon was just here. That's ridiculous. The only three people in this entire world, and they just happened to be in the same city at almost the same time? That's way too big of a coincidence."

Prisha raised her eyes, staring up at the clear blue sky above. "Coincidence?" She gave a small slow shake. "I believe there is a hand that guides all of this, that things happen for a reason. What Jon did, it saved many lives and led me to you. It was not random. It was not a coincidence."

Megan leaned away. "I believe I guide my own life, nobody else."

The soft smile came once again to the eyes above the veil. "Why do you believe those two things are incompatible? Can you not guide your own life whether all that happens around you is random or has a purpose?"

Megan paused for a moment. "You think there's some hand guiding you, but you don't even know why you're here?"

"Often, it is impossible to see the pattern until the whole mosaic has revealed itself." She looked at Megan with earnest eyes. "Perhaps my only reason for coming here is to tell you that you are not alone, that you have a friend, that I have been where you are now, and I know what it is like."

Megan straightened in surprise, shocked at the notion. "A friend?"

Prisha nodded.

"Can you help me find Jon or tell me how to get home?"

"I cannot."

"Then, I appreciate your kindness, but what's the point in making a friend when I'm leaving soon?"

Her uninvited guest remained unruffled and her manner cordial. "You never know when you might need help."

"I need help *now*."

Prisha appeared thoughtful for a moment, then set a hand on Megan's arm and seemed to smile again beneath her veil. "I will find out what I can about Jon."

Megan looked away, unsure why she had asked about finding him when she already had a plan to meet him. All of a sudden, it clicked: here was the opportunity she and Aylun had been waiting for, and she was about to squander it. Her gaze snapped back to Prisha. "Wait. What about the Verod? Can you help me find them?"

Prisha leaned away. "The resistance movement? My existence here is something that must be kept secret."

There was an unexpected tension behind her words, and Megan hesitated. "Okay."

"Powerful forces: the council, the Parishad, the Hordes, Syvis—they must not learn where I am. I do not wish to risk revealing myself by becoming involved in the affairs of the Verod."

"Even if it means helping a friend?"

Prisha considered for a long moment, then the crease in her brow melted away. "What is it you seek?"

"A Verod expedition will leave here in a few days. Aylun and I wish to leave with them."

Prisha seemed startled and eyed her sideways. "You seem to have an unusual grasp of their plans."

Megan smiled back. "I have my own sources."

"As a friend, I must advise you that revolutionaries are not the safest people to travel with."

"Please?"

Prisha seemed to weigh her request for a time. "Perhaps I can find a way. I do have contacts that might help."

Megan bowed her head. "Thank you."

"Now, it is dangerous for me to remain here for long and risk being seen with you. I must go." Prisha rose.

"How will I find you?"

"You will not. I will send someone to you with what I have learned. For now, please avoid telling your companion of my visit." Prisha bowed. "And, I beg of you, whatever happens, do not mention my name to anyone, not to Jon and not even to your companion."

"Okay."

Prisha seemed suspicious of her quick response and enunciated each word with care. "My *life* depends on this."

Megan nodded. "I promise. I promise. I won't tell a soul your name." She puzzled for a moment. Why would a woman whose life hung on remaining hidden reveal herself with no hesitation to a total stranger?

As if to answer her unvoiced question, Prisha bowed again, and her voice was soft. "I was certain I would never see anyone from Earth again, and here I've met two in one week. Take care, Megan."

She turned, but Megan called out, "At least tell me how you got here from Earth."

The woman looked back and smiled. "Sorry, I tried that with Garris, and it didn't go well." She paused for a second. "Even if you believed me, the answer would be of no help to you." With that, she faced forward and resumed her stroll, passing under the pergola laden with soft pink blooms, their throats painted with a pale-yellow glow.

Megan's sense of satisfaction grew as her visitor passed through the gate and out onto the plains beyond. These past hours, she had felt useless, trapped inside, waiting for Aylun to find a way into the Verod. Even though it had come to her by no effort of her own, it was still gratifying to know she had made her own contribution to the quest to get back to Jon.

It was the afternoon of the second day since their arrival in Mundus, and Aylun's apprehension had been growing. It had started last night when Megan seemed off. When he had arrived home, she displayed an abnormal lack of curiosity about his day and whether he'd made progress in finding a way into the Verod. When he made a subtle comment about it, there was a slight avoidance of his gaze, and after that she showed an interest that felt forced. When he asked about her day, she turned rather cagey, avoiding looking into his face as she changed the topic. If his instincts were right, she was hiding something, and she wasn't very good at it.

On top of that, he had made no progress in the day and a half that he'd been scouring the city for contacts in the Verod. In that time, he had exhausted the seedier parts of town, where the unsavory and disgruntled abounded. Often, a few well-placed coins in the soiled hands on those dirty streets would buy you anything you wanted to know, but everyone here seemed remarkably tight-lipped.

The closest he had come was a pair of children stealing fruit from a stand. When he had caught them, they had divulged their names with relative ease, though it was doubtful they used their actual names; but when he mentioned the Verod, all that greeted him were averted gazes, curt answers, and denials that were way too nervous. No matter how he pressed or how much he agreed to pay, they would not speak of what they knew.

Now, in desperation, he had resigned himself to perusing the market areas in hopes of snagging a passing pickpocket or thief. It was a long shot since the shops and stalls were tempting targets for thieves and, as a consequence, were well policed. He had seen firsthand how adept the local authorities were at spotting vagrants and pilferers.

The aroma of kathi rolls stopped him in his tracks. He had been bringing Megan food for every meal. It had even become a little game for him, finding new dishes for her to try and seeing her face light up as she took a bite of something tasty. What was equally entertaining was her curiosity when confronted with a dish, meat or vegetable, that she couldn't recognize. She would make fun of them, laugh over them, and pull the most adorable faces when she found she enjoyed them. The hunt for each new culinary concoction to amuse her had become a welcome distraction from his often-frustrating search for the Verod. The meals themselves were an even more welcome break. She had a tremendous sense of humor, and he found he quite enjoyed their conversations.

He shoved his way up to the cart and peered down at the flaky, crispy rolls filled with grilled meat and vegetables. They seemed like just the type of thing she would enjoy, but now was not the time. They had to be eaten warm to be at their best, and he had more to do today before he gave up the search. So he made a mental note of the location before continuing his search.

He scurried down the stone road, rushing by stands and market stalls. Clusters of browsing customers meandered by as he scanned the area for anyone or anything suspicious. He glanced behind as he passed a shop lined with clothes in a montage of styles and vibrant colors. Suddenly, it flitted by again: a figure in the deep blue cloak. No sooner had he spotted the dark stranger than they seemed to drift back into the shadows at the edge of a tavern. This was the third time the same person had drawn his notice, which made it a certainty now that he was being followed, and not by just anyone but by someone with the Gift of Shadows.

It was one of the more annoying gifts of Erden. Those that possessed it could blend into shadows if they wished. It was a trick of the mind, of course. Nothing changed at all. Your eyes just refused to detect them unless you knew where they were and focused hard. It gave the possessor a frustrating advantage for thieving, assassination, spy craft, and all manner of nastiness.

Aylun ducked around a corner and sprinted past a fruit vendor with his cart of fresh mangoes, moonfruit, lyberries, and persimmons. Without looking back, he whipped around the corner and dove into the first alley. A comforting cloak of dirt and shade enveloped him. With practiced ease, he leaped up the walls, silently pushing off the corners and edges of the huge clay bricks, bounding between the walls on either side as he propelled himself upward.

He reached up and grabbed the edge of the roof, yanked himself over, and rolled to a crouch amid the greenery of a rooftop garden. He quieted his breathing as he turned and peered down between a pair of potted plants, surveying the dusty darkness below.

Moments later, the figure in the dark blue cloak rounded the corner at the other end of the alley. With more than a fleeting chance for him to observe, it became apparent to Aylun that the shape was that of a man. The face was obscured in the shadows of a hood, but his attire and the two curved daggers almost invisible beneath the cloak gave the impression of one proficient in sneak attacks.

The man halted right below him and stood frozen, staring down the alley and out into the busy street. A group of laughing children passed out on the lane as he remained poised and motionless. With the slow, cautious movements of one practiced in stealth, he raised his head and peered upward.

Aylun pulled back from the edge, but even as he did, he caught a glimpse of the face beneath the hood. The man's dark skin was scarred, and his short black hair was wild and unkempt; but most telling was his calm, relaxed expression. Every aspect of his appearance and manner gave the impression of a haggard mercenary, though it was foolish to jump to too many conclusions based on appearance alone.

The man's quiet muttering barely reached him as Aylun hid from view beyond the edge of the roof. "Well, this is no fun."

Aylun sighed. The man knew he was here and even where he was. There was no point in hiding any longer.

Then, it struck him. It was said that opportunity knocks but once, and here, staring him in the face, was the opportunity he had been scouring the city for.

Remaining as silent as he could, he skirted the plants and leaped over the edge of the roof. He dropped to the dirt without a sound, landing in the shadows, an arm's length from the man.

The stranger never startled but his hand slid toward his dagger with subtlety and calm certainty.

Aylun reached out, grabbed the man's wrist, and held firm. Then he yanked out a coin pouch containing the meager portion of his funds he always kept aside for bribes. He made sure it jangled as he thrust it forward where the man could see. "Are you interested in earning some coin?"

The man relaxed.

Aylun let go of his wrist.

In a flash, the man's arm flew out, swiping for the pouch.

Aylun snatched it just out of reach, then smiled.

The man eyed the pouch with a hungry expression. "You ambush me in a dark alley and pull out a bag of coins? Why wouldn't I just slit your throat and take it?"

"Did you not just try to take it?"

"Did I?" His rough lips twisted into a grin. "Or was I merely testing your reflexes?"

Aylun looked him over. "Your eyes are not those of a man who kills without thought or care."

The man gave a low chuckle. "True. But I must refuse your offer. I am entirely too busy with a task of a highly lucrative nature and cannot let myself become sidetracked by the request of a suspicious stranger."

Aylun remained calm and congenial. "Are you sure you want to turn down an offer of easy money? Can you really ever have enough coin?"

The man squinted as he tilted his head.

Aylun smiled. "It might coincide with your current task quite nicely. You'll never know unless you listen."

The man stared at the pouch for a long moment with avarice in his eyes as he seemed to consider the request. Then a smile spread across his leathery lips. "Well ... it never hurts to listen."

Aylun stepped a little closer and lowered his voice. "I am a recent recruit into the Verod in Elore. News has reached me that an Erdish contingent will leave here tomorrow. I must leave with them."

The man's smile broadened. "Done." He thrust out his hand as if expecting payment.

Aylun froze. Did the man not understand him, or was he just that eager? Even if he was, what happened to the "lucrative task" he was on? Was it all just a ruse? He eyed the man with suspicion. "Done? But don't you—"

"A woman named Zala will come to your house tomorrow at dawn. She will lead you to the rendezvous point, introduce you to the Verod, and vouch for you."

Aylun stared for a moment. It was beyond belief that this man could appear and hand him the very thing for which he had been scouring the streets. As he struggled to come to terms with the proof standing in front of him, another truth came to him. He closed his eyes and sighed. "You were tailing me so you could tell me that, weren't you?"

The man smiled again. "You were right. Your task did coincide nicely with my current job." He stuck his hand out further, eager for his payment.

Aylun pulled the pouch just out of reach. "I have just been had, have I not?"

The man shook his head. "No, no. You ambushed me fair and square." He thrust his hand out for the third time.

Aylun sighed again as he set the coin pouch in it.

"It was a pleasure, friend." The man turned to go.

Aylun called after him, "And if something goes wrong, how will I find you?"

The man halted and stared back over his shoulder. "Ask around for Cain. You won't find me, but I will hear of it and contact you."

Aylun bowed.

Cain resumed his exit, then halted again. "Oh … there was also a message. Tell Megan about the arrangements and let her know it is help from a friend."

The comment gave him pause. Megan didn't have any friends here. His mind rattled through possible explanations, but there were only a few that made sense. The most obvious was that she had encountered someone, confided in them, and not told him. That theory would also fit with her evasiveness of the night before. It rubbed him the wrong way to be kept in the dark on such an important matter, and it wasn't at all reassuring to receive help from an anonymous source whose motives he couldn't begin to fathom. Even so, it was the only help he'd found in a day and a half, so he had no choice but to go along and hope it was offered in good faith.

Aylun turned and headed out of the shadows and into the busy market. A sense of satisfaction came over him as he realized he had accomplished what he had set out to do, and now all that remained was to wait. But first, he would head back to the kathi roll vendor. And not only them but many others. He would assemble a feast of the best food and drink he could find. Then he and Megan would have a proper celebration. Tonight, they would eat and drink to their heart's content; then tomorrow, they would rest and play. Because the day after that, they would be on the road again, this time on the last leg to return Megan to Jon.

Chapter Fifteen

LAST TRAIN HOME

Megan had spent the afternoon in her room, the bright sun warming her skin as she stared out the window, anxiously awaiting his return. It had been almost two days, and in that time, her hopeful optimism had turned to nervous foreboding. So it was a great relief when she spotted Aylun strolling down the street bearing a cheerful demeanor and more bundles of food than he could comfortably hold. She raced down the hall to meet him, and he burst through the arched doorway in exceedingly good spirits.

Right away, he announced that a man named Cain had relayed a message from a friend, and they would be leaving with the Verod the morning after next. Relief washed over her. It was really happening. She was going to reunite with Jon. Giddy with anticipation, she squealed and jumped up and down, much to Aylun's amusement. It wasn't a stretch to conclude that the friend he'd mentioned was Prisha. Although Megan could no longer hide that she had meet someone who offered help, she felt obliged to keep her word. So she resisted Aylun's gentle probing into where this man came from or any details of her mysterious benefactor.

As Aylun set about his work, enticing odors wafted through every room, lending their barren quarters a homey feel. On the kitchen table, he laid out a banquet of colorful, savory food and drink. It was enough for a dozen people; and he insisted his news called for a celebration. Excited and relieved, Megan embraced the idea with eagerness.

In their borrowed home, they ate and drank, talked and laughed, until long after Mundus had fallen asleep, its houses dark and still in the cool evening air. Late in the celebration, they ascended the stairway to the rooftop patio. In one corner stood a few potted plants, the largest resembling a palm tree with long, serrated fronds that swayed in the gentle evening breeze. A smooth stone railing surrounded the entire area, with more brightly colored pots and plants arranged along its length.

They spent a long time sitting on a gliding bench, rocking gently as they cooled themselves in the night air and stared out over the city. One of the temples in the distance must have been holding some kind of service. Lights from countless torches and candles cast a serene glow along the horizon, as residents, mere splashes of brilliant color in the distance, drifted down the ornate pillars of a huge pavilion.

Satiated and happy, she and Aylun eventually wandered off to their respective rooms, where Megan slid into her plush bed. She smoothed out the intricate pattern of yellow and white desert flowers, relishing the feel of the silken sheets against her skin. Warm and content, she soon dropped into a sound sleep.

The next day, Aylun had left before she awoke. She stumbled into the kitchen to find a note. The morning sun shone bright and warm on the paper's rough white surface as, sleepy-eyed, she squinted down, absorbing its contents. It let her know that he had headed to the market to gather supplies and a tent for their trip. She looked up from the note to find he had also set out her morning meal. It consisted of leftovers from the feast of the night before, which she enjoyed almost as much as when they were fresh.

He returned midmorning with more food and tended the horses, then spent the rest of the day inside amusing her with several games. He tried to teach her a board game that had a somewhat familiar appearance. Perhaps her father had once played something like it in her presence. One player used a set of white stones and the other black. You tried to surround the other player's stones, and when you did, you swapped them and they became your pieces.

AYLUN

It was a strategy game and so not particularly fun. To make matters worse, she was unfamiliar with its rules, while he seemed to know every trick. She blundered and misunderstood, again and again, and eventually knocked over the board when she'd grown tired of the frustration and humiliation.

After that, they turned to kids' games. There was one that was pretty much the game of jacks, only played with small stones. Another that he called "cat and mouse" was nothing more than the game of tag by a different name. Megan decided it was one game she could win. Eventually, carried away by competitiveness, they found themselves running around the house with the carefree abandon of unsupervised children at an amusement park. They laughed as they chased each other through rooms, up and down stairs, and around the island in the kitchen.

After the giggling subsided, Aylun taught her several other games. But between the smiles and laughter, it was difficult to tell if he was good at them or just pulling her leg by making up the rules as he went along.

Late in the afternoon, he taught her some exercises that seemed a lot like tai chi, with slow, graceful movements. He claimed she had a knack for them, but she wasn't all that comfortable with the stretching of muscles and the long, drawn-out motions. At the end, he told her that when sped up, they were the basis of some of the best fighting techniques and had her try this out. The quicker movements did remind her of her self-defense classes, and she began to feel as if she might have a knack for it after all.

In the evening, after it grew dark, Aylun risked taking her out to show her the sights of Mundus. They strolled the paved avenues, illuminated here and there by lanterns and floating candles. Couples and families in colorful clothes wandered the streets with them as they partook of the wonders.

The palace, where the Rhanae lived, was stunning, with its sweeping spires, high-arched roofs, and tasteful gardens. They visited a number of well-known temples, theaters, and museums, a few still busy with late-day activity. All around the city were houses, from small hovels to massive estates. Even the simplest were adorned with desert gardens and ornate statuary, and many were lit by the soft radiance of flickering flames. The sights were captivating, and with the peaceful, warm glow around the city, the starry night, and the warm air, it felt a little like she was touring an exotic land—which she kind of was.

At dawn the next day, a woman who introduced herself as Zala came as promised. She was younger and shorter than Megan expected, perhaps just nineteen or so. Demure and soft-spoken, she had decked herself out with a conspicuous number of bangles and anklets. The quiet young lady escorted them both well outside the city, where a group of dozens of rough-looking Verod had gathered.

Zala introduced them to the Verod leader, Libena, a modest-looking but blunt woman in a dark red kameez. Seeming quite wary, she let them know in a dour tone that she would only tolerate their presence on the condition that she'd keep an eye on them, and they would travel and camp at the rear of the main group. Aylun was quick to agree, later confiding that he was more than happy to avoid the others if it minimized extra attention.

The first day's ride was uneventful—the flat, desiccated terrain seeming almost endless as they followed the hodgepodge group of rebels north and west. There were no roads or paths, and the group spread out behind the leader, a ragtag assemblage with no formation or structure. Other clusters met and merged with them along the way, the caravan growing ever larger as they plodded along the hot sun-burnt terrain. Throughout it all, Megan's saddle chafed, her legs grew sore, and the hot sun became uncomfortable, but none of it mattered because she was going to see Jon.

The first night, they made camp a short distance behind the main group and spent most of the evening lying in their tent. Megan wanted nothing more than to rest as she soaked in the ambiance. Aylun seemed willing to indulge her, and their talk remained sparse, with frequent long periods of listening to the chorus of laughter and discussion spread across the sprawling camp.

She found herself becoming a bit sentimental, knowing that in less than a day, their trip together would come to an end. For Aylun, the prospect seemed to have the opposite effect, as if the idea of delivering her to Jon had caused his mood to soar. It made him the perfect antidote to her moments of melancholy. Every time it dulled her disposition, he seemed to sense it. He would gently prod her to imagine seeing Jon again, telling him of her ordeals, and traveling with him, and the images Aylun painted made her giddy with excitement.

On the second day, they left behind the arid terrain for plush, grassy hills. Fresh clumps of travelers continued to wander in, folding into the larger group. With each new arrival, the sense of determination grew, and a mood of anticipation filled the air. She developed a headache that lingered all day, making the trip seem unending, and the gruff company made her nervous. But it didn't seem to matter because she was going to meet Jon.

That night, the entire force camped in the valley between the waves of rolling hills. Aylun picked a spot at the back of the main group, but Megan couldn't contain her excitement. Anxious to meet Jon right away, she insisted they find a spot to wait that would allow them to observe the whole area. So they hurried as they set up their tent and tied up Yuki and Juzhi out back. Aylun grabbed a few savory treats he had brought along from Mundus to snack on as they waited. Then they strolled past the clusters of ragged travelers, busy tending their horses, pitching tents, and constructing campfires.

She picked a spot on the side of a grass-covered hill where she could watch every square inch of the camp. Their conversation was sparse again, just a lighthearted word here and there while Megan focused on the ever-changing scene below. At first, people sat around the scattered fires eating, drinking, and laughing as they talked. The atmosphere in the camp seemed both tense and jovial, as if those below were anxious about the conflict they knew was coming and trying to embrace a last bit of camaraderie before facing possible death.

As time dragged on, the activity in the camp slowed, and the mood darkened, as people left behind the talk and laughter and headed to their tents for one final night of sleep. Eventually, all that remained were a few stragglers, staring into dying fires spread along the verdant valley. Having watched it all from her perch, and waiting with dwindling patience, Megan eventually grew anxious.

She looked over at Aylun, seated next to her. "Could Ruahn be wrong? Could he not be coming?"

He remained calm and collected. "Anything is possible, but the night isn't over yet. Be patient."

She mumbled, "Easy for you to say." Even so, his words were somehow reassuring, despite containing nothing new or profound.

She let more time pass, watching the activity of the camp drag to a virtual standstill as the fires became piles of ash. An odd feeling began to grow within her—a realization that soon Aylun would leave and a need for reassurance that he would be okay. Her mind went back to that terrifying first meeting, and that arrogant, unfeeling tyrant who had traumatized her, robbing her of her dignity and sovereign will.

She knew in her mind that the man next to her this night was the very same one as back then, yet her heart refused to connect the two. The Aylun next to her on this grassy hillside was the complete opposite. Then again, perhaps it didn't matter. Her concern for him now was real, and the man beside her on this star-filled night, worthy of it. He had redeemed himself.

She glanced over at him. "So, what's next for you? Will you go back to your Augury thing?"

Aylun looked down at the cool grass between his legs as he shook his head. "No. It is no longer my Augury. It is not my home."

"Then what will you do?"

"I may have to visit there, to search for the warning Wistra spoke of in her journal, but it is no longer a place where I am welcome."

Megan remained quiet for some time. "That's kind of sad."

Aylun shrugged.

She peered over at him again. "You know, you told me the Augury exists to preserve free will, but you never actually told me how or why."

"And you never caught on that it was a secret I was not comfortable revealing."

Megan grinned. "Oh, *that*. Well, truthfully, I just didn't care. I figured I could just annoy it out of you sooner or later."

Aylun grumbled, "If being annoying was all it took, I would have given in a long time ago."

She smiled anew at the remark. "Okay, how about if I take a vow to never reveal—"

"Oh, a *vow*, well that is an entirely different matter. In that case ... no."

She flashed him her big dark eyes. "Please?"

He sent her a flat stare. "Does that actually work on some people?"

Megan batted her eyelashes and pouted, endeavoring to appear even more coquettish. "Pretty please?"

"Oh for ..." He groaned. "Fine, since you are leaving soon ... but you must make a promise to tell no one."

She gave an eager nod. "I promise."

Aylun sat staring at the few remaining somber men around the piles of ash and embers, seeming to consider the question. "I only know what I have been told. I think you have to be a Great Oracle to see it for yourself, but for centuries they have all spoken of it in the same way."

"What?"

"Imagine a world as you described, with many oracles all changing the future. Some would seek personal gain; they would use their gift for power or fame. Others would want money, and many would use their insight to help those close to them. As you suggested, it would be complete chaos. Wistra foresaw that some force was needed to organize prophetic power, to prevent a world of oracles run amok. They say that even one such oracle could wreak great havoc."

Megan nodded. It was similar to thoughts she had expressed to him before. Thoughts that at the time Aylun had said were her imagination. She ignored the inconsistency. "Acting on their own? ... We call that freedom. What you're implying isn't preserving free will. It's taking it away from those whose only sin was to be born with the Gift of Prophecy."

He nodded, seeming to agree. "Perhaps, but it was a significant part of my job to give them a choice. The Shou approach all those with the Gift of Prophecy and offer them that choice, a chance to be taught and trained. Very few refuse an opportunity to become more powerful. Especially when the Shou have the benefit of a Great Oracle telling them how best to appeal to each candidate."

She considered for a moment. "And if they refuse?"

"Then they are told they will be watched; that any attempt to use their gift, even to help those nearest them, would be met with resistance by the full force of the Augury."

"Wow, that's ... rough."

"And if they are exceedingly powerful and cannot be convinced, they can be sent to serve the dragon."

Megan gawked. "What?"

"Islong, the dragon, they are sent to serve her."

She stared at him, shocked at the casual way he treated the possibility. "But isn't that a death sentence?"

He shrugged. "No one knows. I have never seen it happen, but the Augury is said to have an ancient agreement with the dragon, to accept those who will not join and who are a threat. In any event, it would be the end of the life they knew."

She considered this for a while as a cool breeze blew through her hair, adding to the peaceful ambiance of the star-filled night. He had told her that all oracles belong to the Augury and about the means the Shou use to ensure that they join, but so far, he hadn't addressed her original query.

Megan looked up at the waning moon. "Are you avoiding my question?"

"Which one?"

"So, every person with the Gift of Prophecy belongs to the Augury, so what? How does that preserve free will?"

Aylun drew a deep breath and looked out across the camp. "Because joining the Augury means abiding by its rules, one of which is that you can only reveal what the Great Oracle permits. Most are only allowed to act in small personal matters that cannot influence larger events. Even the Great Oracle is subject to rules that allow them to act only when events demand that they do so." He turned back to Megan, peering into her eyes. "You see, the Gift of Prophecy is the greatest threat to self-determination that could ever exist. So the Augury prevents oracles from acting except when the threat is so great they have no choice."

She met his gaze. "I don't get it. How are oracles such a big threat?"

"Because they make people believe that if they simply do the right thing, at the right time, as an oracle has directed, they will lead safe, happy and prosperous lives, without the need for effort and sacrifice."

Megan boggled a bit. "But why put in the effort and sacrifice if prophecy can help avoid it."

Aylun drew himself up taller. "Because that is a fantasy. Prosperity and security come from effort and sacrifice, no other way. Farmers will work and strive from sunup to sundown to feed their neighbors and family, ensuring plentiful food. But not if they believe there is no need, because all-powerful oracles will prevent famine and starvation. Soldiers will train and perfect their skills, so they can protect those they love. But not if they believe they cannot lose because the Augury will guide their hand. Artists will study and perfect their craft to produce great works. But not if they believe they are already destined to do great things without effort."

"I don't know …"

"Take you and Jon. If an oracle told you he was your one true love, would you work as hard to make your relationship work?"

She smiled as she imagined an earnest-looking oracle spouting the solemn words. "Well, first I'd laugh, but if I did believe in that stuff, it would probably make me more confident. Why would that be bad?"

He leaned closer. "Because your confidence would not be grounded in commitment. Marriage is never easy. It requires work and compromise. Believing you are destined to work things out undermines the very commitment needed for that effort. It could stop you from making the sacrifices that would have ultimately made it work."

Megan paused, resisting the reflex to disagree for the simple reason that Aylun had said it. "I guess. I have had similar thoughts, but ..."

"A reliance on oracles would be like a poison in the lifeblood of humankind, sapping them of the will to accomplish things on their own and thereby leaving them impoverished."

She leaned back with her palms against the cool grass and studied Aylun. "But still, how does that make sense? You have this great power that could benefit all humankind, but you squander it and leave people to fend for themselves. Why not use that gift to improve lives? Why not use prophecy to guide people, to rule them?"

He shook his head as if he'd already explained everything, and she just wasn't getting it. "It is like that old saying, 'If you give a man a fish, you feed him for a day. If you teach him to fish, you feed him for a lifetime.' Oracles do not teach people self-reliance. They only breed dependence and despair. A people ruled by oracles would be a destitute people with no belief they can improve their own lot in life. A people for whom hopes and dreams are a waste of time and energy. Who are told what will happen, rather than free to create what they want in their lives by their own will. Such a people would be little more than slaves, working to fulfill the grand schemes of the Augury, rather than striving to realize their own vision of the life they want for themselves and their families."

"But you said it yourself, the problem is a belief in oracles. That belief comes from their very existence. So long as they exist and use their gift, people will believe in them, and if they act, people will rely on them."

He seemed relieved and lowered his voice. "Not if they work in secret. Not if they do only as little as they must, and only in the shadows, so people will not see how they are being protected. The Shou are regarded as myth, so people will not come to rely on them."

Megan mulled over all he had said. It seemed logical and consistent, even if she didn't see how helping someone led to dependence. It certainly never had for her.

At last, she gave a bow of her head, as seemed to be Aylun's custom. "I don't know if I totally agree, but I understand better now. Thank you for that."

She fell silent for a time as the uneasy feeling returned. She still had very little idea what would become of Aylun. So she tried again. "If you don't go back to the Augury, what will you do?"

"I will continue to look into the prophecy. I will stay out here as your eyes and ears, working to protect you and Jon." He had spoken with the nonchalant certainty of someone who assumed it was the only logical thing to do.

Megan gawked for a moment. "What?"

He looked over at her, as if his steady gaze would somehow cause the comment to make more sense. "I will help and protect you in any way I can, until you no longer need my help. This is my oath, my—"

"Don't say it."

"My vow and my promise."

Stunned and more than a little burdened by the idea, she balked. "But you have your own life to live."

Aylun remained still for a while, then eked out a response with a small shake of his head. "No. I do not."

397

"You've already done so much for me. You were hurt so bad in that temple. You could have died of thirst or starvation. Don't ..." Megan trailed off when she saw her words were having no effect, his expression remaining determined and resolute.

He took a deep breath. "This is something I need to do for my own sake. Okay?"

She gave in, not feeling any less burdened but not able to find a reasonable objection.

They both remained quiet for some time, watching the dwindling fires spread across the valley. With the silence, her sense of anticipation grew. After a while, her mind wandered back to a distant time when she had been just as eager and excited. It was the day she flew to Delas Labs for her new job with Jon.

The year leading up to that day had been a long and lonely one. Everyone she'd known had graduated and moved away. Alone, with her own school days coming to an end, the appeal of going out to party and socialize dwindled, and her time was spent in class or in her dorm studying. As the year dragged on, calls and texts from Jon became less frequent, and as graduation approached, the hope of reuniting with him faded to a flickering flame.

Then, one day, she got a text from Jon telling her to go to a particular room on campus at a specific time. No matter how she pressed, he would not tell her why or divulge any details, but he did manage to pry a promise out of her—that she would go. When she arrived at the designated room at the appointed time, all she found was a woman in a sharp business suit and thick black glasses. She introduced herself as Robin, here to recruit new graduates to work at Delas Labs. Her heart soared as she realized it would be a job in the same city, in the same *building* as Jon.

Then she found out it was a decent-paying job as a lab assistant. For someone like her, with only a bachelor's degree in physics, job prospects weren't stellar, so she was elated. Then came the most stunning news of all. Not only would she be working directly with Jon, but he had gone out of his way to request and arrange the interview. On the flight to her new job, she was giddy. She may have been on her way to a foreign city, to do a job she had never done, in a company she didn't know, but she was returning to Jon. She was going home.

A yell from the camp caught her attention. It drew Megan's gaze to the sea of fires, tents, horses, and men below, and she scanned the area, searching for the shouting man. Heads turned toward the head of the camp, and a murmur broke out as, one by one, the travelers spotted the source. She followed the sea of eyes and spied it too.

There, where the valley began, stood a glistening circular curtain a little taller than a person. As if made of water, its surface was dotted with pinpricks of light that shimmered in the gentle evening breeze. The longer she stared, the more they became discernible as distant torches lining roads that crossed a river, as seen through a glimmering curtain of water.

A dark outline blocked out a few of the pinpoints of light. Megan held her breath as a woman appeared through its rippling surface. She stepped forward and stood tall, surveying the camp.

Aylun rose and stared. "That is Sirra, Dellia's mother."

Megan bounced to her feet and began to fidget.

The woman peered back at the circular curtain and motioned, urging someone to come. Soon, a second figure passed through: a hulking, golden-skinned man with a wicked-looking crossbow.

Megan pointed. "That's Garris. That's him, isn't it?"

The warrior stepped up to Sirra's side.

Then Jon appeared through the curtain.

Megan stepped forward, popping up and down on her tiptoes, barely able to contain herself. "It's *Jon*. He's right there." She swung around and beamed Aylun a huge smile as she motioned for him to follow, to go with her to meet the man she had suffered so long to reach. "Come on."

Aylun remained motionless as he smiled back, seeming to share in her excitement, yet unmoving. He stayed that way for a long moment, as if taking it all in. "I am happy for you. Truly, I am." A look of affection filled his face.

When he still didn't stir, a wave of sadness and bewilderment struck, and Megan gawked. "What are you doing?"

He smiled and stared into her eyes, as if studying her, memorizing every feature of a face he would never behold again. "Goodbye, Megan."

Her smile faded, and she gave a small disbelieving shake of her head. "You have to at least meet him." She smiled and once again motioned for him to come with her.

Aylun placed his hand on her shoulder and beamed an even broader smile. "Always be like this." He patted her shoulder, then stepped away. Only, he headed the other direction, toward their tent at the back of the camp. After several steps, he stopped and turned back to face her. For a second, they stared at each other across the hillside, Megan inviting him to be part of the moment he had fought so hard to bring about, and Aylun sharing her joy but unwilling to take one more step with her.

"Take care of yourself." He turned and strolled away.

As she stood and watched, a strange sensation came over her—a feeling of being at odds with herself, of being torn, as if she were on a railway platform watching the last train for home leave without her. A flurry of emotions continued to nudge and pull at her until Aylun reached the camp and disappeared in the sea of tents and horses.

Then her attention was drawn back to Jon. Excitement and affection filled her, crowding out every other thought as she watched him across the hill. Of course she would miss Aylun. He had risked his life to bring her here, and he had been a fierce ally and a more than tolerable companion these last few days.

She began walking toward Jon. So much had happened, and she had risked so much to arrive at this very moment. *He* was her home. With him is where she belonged. She had never been more certain of anything in her life.

AYLUN

She began to rehearse in her mind all that she would tell him: of Katapa, and Lanessa, and all the harrowing things she had been through to get back to him. Then she would tell him, straight and unabashedly, that she loved him; that she had always wanted to be with him but was foolish and afraid. She would make sure he understood that all those horrible things she had said in the lab were a lie, and that she never wanted him to leave her again.

Far away, up at the start of the valley, Jon placed something in the grass, then bent over for a while. As he stood up, a massive formless image appeared in the night, almost as tall as the hills around it. It slowly came together, like a picture coming into focus, eventually becoming an enormous, heavily branched tree. Its autumn leaves of yellow and red shimmered in the night sky, and light from them danced across the grassy hillsides like the laser lights at a stadium rock show.

Megan halted in her tracks, staring up at its glimmering branches. Then a voice boomed out across the glowing embers of the dying campfires scattered across the valley. "The future is an infinite branching tree of possibilities, each determined by free will."

She stood motionless as she watched the image transform into a middle-aged Elorian woman.

PART TWO

THE HIDDEN CITY

Chapter Sixteen

TOGETHER

The last Blood Wolf tumbled into the massive yellow vortex rumbling in front of Jon. In an instant, it was swept up in the roaring wind, disintegrating in a shower of glittering sparks.

Another wave of agony hit, staggering him to his knees. The swirling vortex began to weaken as he concentrated through the scorching convulsion—part burning pain, part seizure, and part overwhelming weight bearing down on his entire body. It was a side effect of his gift. A gift that had allowed him to take the ability of a powerful artifact: the Stone of Syvis. ... No, not the artifact, the power of Syvis itself.

Along with that power, he had gained vast insight. He simply knew a great many things, as if they were obvious, as if he should have seen them all along. He understood how his experiment had played a part in him and Megan being swept into this bizarre and impossible world. In his mind's eye, he could see how this strange shard of humanity had split off from civilizations of ancient Earth; how their people had passed through stable portals to settle on this distant world. He could see with perfect clarity the nature of the existential threat its inhabitants now faced. And he knew why that threat was now unavoidable.

It was through that same knowledge that he understood that his flashes of agony were inevitable, a side effect of a power too vast to be contained by his mere human body. Even as he knew all of that, he also knew the power was fading, because the convulsions were coming farther apart and the pain was growing less crippling. Eventually, when the waves of agony faded to nothing, it would all disappear: the power, the expanded consciousness, and every scrap of knowledge it had imparted. All he might retain would be the few crumbs he struggled to hang on to, or so his new mind seemed to sense.

But right now, holding on to fragments of accidental knowledge was not his focus. What mattered was using the power in one last drive to end the Blood Wolf attack on Mundus. It was the third such attack since he and Megan had arrived—each larger than the last—and it didn't seem random, though he couldn't guess its purpose. Through an agonizing convulsion, he pictured the swirling black portal, far off in the Malthayan Mountains, where he sensed the wolves had entered this part of the world.

With it implanted firmly in his mind, he raised his fist and drew a deep breath, tainted with the metallic stench of blood. He brought it down, pounding the dry, cracked ground, and a brilliant yellow flash sparked through the deep blue sky of dawn, striking that far-off portal and destroying it.

The last of the vortex drifted away in the light breeze.

He glanced around at his companions: Dellia, Garris, and Sirra. They were surveying the desolate expanse littered with hundreds of Blood Wolf corpses. The pitiful creatures had come through that portal only to meet their end here, on this vast patch of desiccated ground. Now, the portal was gone. No more would come.

Jon writhed, and every muscle in his body contracted in an aftershock, the price for using that awful power yet again. As the searing pain eased, he slumped to his knees, a spent heap in the still-cool dust and dirt, wanting nothing more than to lie there, unmoving and unthinking.

The crack of thunder followed by a low rumble echoed across the arid expanse. It was the sound of the flash that had destroyed the portal just now reaching them.

Dellia ran up and grabbed ahold of him, steadying him. Her brown leather armor was blood spattered, betraying the prolonged battle she had endured, yet the arms steading him were firm and strong. He stared up at her adoring face. Framed by her thick brown hair, her blue eyes peered into his, seeking reassurance that he was all right. Even here, huddled amid all the pain and carnage, the sight of her made his heart ache with longing. A longing so deep it had compelled him to give up going home. He had given up his world for her.

It was still impossible to believe she loved him too. She was strong and determined, and in that way, she was everything he was not. Yet, at the same time, she understood him with a compassionate heart of which he would never be worthy. Looking at her, so competent and self-assured, reminded him once again that giving up his world would be worth it if he could be with her.

He forced out the words through a spasm of pain, "The gate is destroyed. It is over."

With great gentleness, she helped him back up, then slid her arm around him, lending him her support. His trembling eased as she caressed his back with gentle strokes.

After a while, he let go and stepped back. A shard of pain rippled through his body again, and the last of his resolve crumbled. He peered at her. "Can we go home now?"

She returned her gaze to the deep golden sun, now a mere sliver, peeking above the mountains. All was quiet and clear. Sunrise was coming once again to the plains of Erden. She turned to Jon and gave a single crisp nod.

Having watched the exchange, Sirra raised her palm, and a colored mist formed in the air in front of it. It grew deeper, coming together, the colors taking form as they coalesced into an image on the surface of a shimmering liquid portal. It was the now-familiar pavilion outside the gates of Shir Keep.

Carved into the bowels of Mount Karana itself, it was the seat of power, where he had confronted the Ruling Council of Meerdon. At the back of the broad cobblestone street, a pair of guards stood, watching from their station at either side of the enormous doors mounted in a wall of solid rock.

407

Jon waited as Sirra headed through the portal, and as he surveyed the scene, his anxiety grew. Beyond that glimmering curtain, beyond the doors, inside the keep, lay a path that was more terrifying to him than all the Blood Wolves they had just faced.

Somewhere along the arduous journey to assemble the medallion, he had fallen for Dellia. But between the council's persecution and this ridiculous prophecy, the prospects for them being together seemed hopeless. They had worked through the night, even moving an entire Verod army out of the valley in which they were encamped to place them out of reach of the council's armies. Now, one long day later, what seemed impossible was within his grasp. He had pulled off a miracle and found a way to stay with Dellia, but at what cost?

To stay with his love, a confrontation with the council was inevitable, and many schemes had bubbled up in his mind before he approached them. At the very least, he had to make them give up all thoughts of pursuing him or Megan, but what had happened in that marble room as he faced those nine council members was not anything he had planned. He had forced them to agree to a reformation of the council. They were to hand power and control back to the three realms so they could each govern themselves. But that was not what petrified him.

Not many days ago, he had been in an outright panic over the prospect of being promoted to a mere project manager. Back then, the thought of being responsible for the careers and accomplishments of a handful of researchers petrified him. Yet, in a moment of desperation, as he faced the council, he had agreed to take on a mantle that would have people calling him leader for an entire human world.

He had done it because it was the perfect plan, so neat and clean it defied belief. It allowed Dellia to remain a protector, a role she had striven for throughout her life. It allowed her to stay and work with him, and it brought Garris back from exile to the work he had initially chosen for himself.

The cost, though, was terrifying. He had been cornered into agreeing to be council leader, and the only thing that had convinced him it was even halfway sane was that Kayleen would represent him. Although he had only met her briefly, she appeared to be quick-witted and competent, with a deep understanding of the political landscape. It was her insight that convinced him that without his taking leadership, his plan to reform the council was doomed to failure. Unable to accept the weight of being in charge, he had capitulated only when she agreed to represent him, to act on his behalf. As the old council leader, she was the perfect person to argue, debate, and decide for him. He wouldn't have to make any actual decisions.

Yes, it was the perfect plan, so neat and clean it was hard to believe. Then again, perhaps it was not all that hard to believe. Since the moment he had arrived, he had been manipulated. From the rumbling dragon, deep in her lair, to the horrors of the Recluse Tower, to the demons in the darkness of the Mundus Catacombs, he had been pushed and prodded. He had been shoved along a path devised seven hundred years ago by Wistra, who some believed to be the greatest oracle who had ever lived.

The most shattering step of all had come in that oracle room in Elore, where he had come face-to-face with the terrifying reality of Wistra's prophecy. In that place, he had seen a bloody invasion, with men, women, and children being trampled beneath the hooves of a raging horde. With it came the delusional oracle's proclamation. She actually believed he was the Otherworlder, a mythical hero who was destined to lead everyone he cared about to their death to stop an invasion. The most chilling part was the invasion itself: he was given a vision of each of the people he loved, their bodies broken and bloody, as they met their gruesome end.

It was pure nonsense, of course. He was not remotely capable of leading anyone in anything, much less to their death, but her prediction was useful. It lent him an imposing aura, so he had let them believe he was something he was not, and never could be.

A blast of pain ripped through him again as Dellia ushered him forward, and he realized it was his turn now. They passed through the shimmering portal to a distinctly darker sky and cooler climate outside the doors to Shir Keep. Beyond those doors lay a world that was foreign and frightening to him, a place where the council met to debate and make laws. It was the horrifying world that his desperate gambit had thrust him into. It was where the price would be exacted for his oh-so-perfect plan.

At his appearance, one of the pair of soldiers vanished into the keep.

Dellia took up her place at his side as the portal turned back into a colored mist that wafted away in the soft morning breeze.

A short while later, Kayleen scurried through the massive keep doors, her should-length blond hair bouncing with each stride. She didn't look the part of a council leader. Her garb was simple and her manner unassuming. Yet in the few moments he had spoken with her it was clear she was a force to be reckoned with. Her expression was expectant as she stepped up to Dellia. "Is Mundus safe? Is it over?"

She nodded. "Yes. The threat is gone."

"I wish I could give you more time, but there are agreements to sign." Kayleen motioned to the keep doors.

Dellia balked. "Now? Already? I can't ask Jon to—"

"It's fine." Jon looked her in the face and nodded. His reforming of the council needed to be set in stone as soon as possible. Most likely, Kayleen's sense of urgency was rooted in more practical concerns. Once there was an agreement signed by all parties, it would be much more difficult for any one of them to back out. His reasons were more personal. He wanted it done quickly because only then would he have secured a way to stay with Dellia. Only then would he allow himself to breathe.

He winced in pain several times as Kayleen led them through swirling-white and pale-purple hallways. Fluttering torches lined the walkways, casting shadows that drifted across the floor and walls as they hurried along. In some places, windows with soaring views to the valley below graced one of the rock walls, allowing warm morning sunlight to fill the walkway.

Soon, they arrived in a small room with a large marble table in the center. On its dark, swirling surface lay several stacks of papers, looking identical.

Kayleen motioned to them. "Each of you read and sign."

Jon picked up one of the piles of thick paper covered in carefully drawn lettering. To his surprise, he understood the unfamiliar script. No doubt it was a new aspect of the gift the dragon Isla had given him and Megan. The Gift of Understanding, she had named it. It had allowed him to understand the dragon's speech, and it must be why he could converse with every person he'd met, even though it seemed doubtful they spoke the same language. He began to read as each of the others did the same. His anxiety returned as he absorbed the words. It was all here, just as he'd dictated, and yet it filled him with trepidation.

Each of the three realms—Talus, Erden, and Elore—already had their own form of government and their own laws. They also had a desire to free themselves from the tyranny of the old ruling council. This new, reformed council would give them the means to do that. Each realm would appoint two representatives to vote for them. Over time, all old laws would be eliminated and the new council could replace them or not as it saw fit.

He relaxed some as he saw it all in writing. What he was counting on was that the three realms would choose to limit laws imposed on them and retain power for themselves. If his plan worked, and the three realms ruled themselves, he could avoid making those terrible decisions that came with power. The ruling council would rule in name only.

Then he reached the part that spelled out the position of council leader, and his tension lifted even more. It was all there, just as he had insisted. Kayleen would become "first advocate" and would debate, vote, and act for him. In fact, she was fully empowered to act on his behalf in all matters, including as liaison to ambassadors, the protectors, and the military. He would be council leader in name only as well.

When he was facing the nine council members and his plan was falling apart, all eyes had been on him, expecting him to be the leader. In a moment of sheer desperation, he had capitulated only because of this clause, because he wouldn't really have to lead. As the prior council leader, Kayleen could not be more perfect to act on his behalf, allowing him to avoid the otherwise inevitable: that his decision would hurt or kill innocent children, women, and men. She would represent him and make those dreaded decisions for him, leaving him free to use council resources to find and protect Megan.

Farther down, he came to a clause revoking Garris's exile, reinstating him as a protector, and another making him and Dellia "high protectors," a position that reported only to Jon as council leader. A third clause dictated that orders from Dellia, Garris, and Kayleen were to be taken as having come from him, which was good. The more people there were who could order others around and make decisions for him, the better able he would be to handle things.

When he got to the bottom, he was shocked by the signatures. In the short time he'd been gone, Kayleen hadn't just drafted the entire handwritten document—four copies in fact. She had also gone on to obtain the signatures of all eight of the remaining old council members, several military leaders, and the ambassadors from Erden and Elore.

Jon signed each copy, as did Dellia. Garris was the last to sign. It was a bit comical to see the big, leather-clad warrior with his golden skin and unevenly cropped black hair, squinting and studying the piece of paper as if it were alien. His rough and sarcastic manner made him the type that was definitely more comfortable with the sword than the pen.

Kayleen stood off to the side, scrutinizing Garris's every move, seeming apprehensive as she toyed with the long sapphire crystal of her pendant. When they finished, she whirled into a dervish of activity, dispatching couriers with copies to various people and places.

Amid it all, she suggested the three of them go outside and wait for a short time until she could see them off.

By the time they worked their way back outdoors, the sun had risen and removed the chill in the morning air. They stood for a while on the barely warm cobblestones, watching as people scurried here and there. It was hard not to imagine that Kayleen was behind much of the frenetic activity.

As he watched the officials hurrying along the streets and walk-ways, it came to him that there had been a third reason for his sense of urgency. Now that the die was cast, he couldn't back out either. It was done. He was committed. His own deep trepidation could no longer drive him away from Dellia.

As the waves of pain dropped to a more tolerable level, his mind wandered back to the myriad ways in which physical laws of Earth were broken on this world with stunning frequency. From Dellia's empathic gift, to Sirra's portals, to Megan's ability to move things with her mind, it was as if basic principles of physics didn't even exist here. In his time in Meerdon, the only theory he'd been able to conjure was that this was some kind of alternate reality, a place apart from the universe of Earth, and that here a different set of physical laws applied. Now, though, in the aftermath of having taken the power of Syvis, that theory seemed simplistic and lazy.

The law of conservation of energy was one of the most basic tenets of the physical sciences. It dictated that energy cannot be created or destroyed. Yet only a short time ago he had summoned a bolt of lightning to destroy the portal through which the wolves had come. There had been no thunderstorm, no clouds, no rain to cause a buildup of electrostatic charge. By his will alone, he had simply created a massive bolt of electrical energy out of a clear blue sky. If such simple laws as the conservation of energy didn't apply here, then what laws did apply? How was he to understand this world and how it worked?

With his pain nearly gone, he realized the normally calm Dellia hadn't been acting like herself. She had become more and more

413

fidgety the longer she stood next to him. He was about to ask if she was all right, when she turned to Garris and Sirra and excused herself. Before anyone could react, she grabbed Jon's hand and took off, leading him along behind her.

She crossed the paved courtyard, through a massive stone arch, into the beautiful circular Shir Courtyard, out of sight of Garris and Sirra. Still a bit stunned at her abruptness, Jon followed in silence as she pulled him along a stone path, past a patch of tall waving grass, and then ducked behind a wall of deep pink blooms, whose sudden sweetness saturated the air. They traveled by stands of orange and yellow lily-like flowers that led to the border of a small pool. Large colorful fish drifted and darted through its crystal waters while butter-yellow water lily blooms dotted its surface.

There, with the cool, clear water beside them and bright blossoms all around, Dellia stopped, grabbed him by the shoulders, and studied his face. His alarm rose at the solemn look in her eyes. "What is it? Is something wrong?"

"Marry me, Jon."

The sound of lively discussion and the patter of scurrying feet outside the courtyard barely reached them as Jon stood, eyes blinking, in stunned silence.

Then he shook the cobwebs away. "What?"

Dellia's voice remained steady and firm. "Marry me."

"But we just ... I mean ... we've only ... how can you—"

"You know"—Dellia smiled—"you're kind of cute when you're flustered."

He couldn't keep the alarm from his voice. "This is serious. We're talking about forever."

Dellia remained calm, but appeared a bit puzzled. "Is that a bad thing?"

Eager to dispel the notion, he blurted out, "No. No. It's what I want, with all my heart, but you hardly know me. What if you wake up someday and realize I'm not this great leader you think I am?"

414

Her expression soured, and she seemed a bit wounded. "Is that what you think, that I love you because of some prophecy or because it says you're destined to be some kind of great leader?"

"Isn't it?"

She shook her head "No. No. I couldn't care less about any of that. I love you because of who you are."

"But that's just it. I'm afraid you don't know who I am. And if we get married, you'll eventually figure it out, and you'll want a divorce."

Dellia cocked her head in puzzlement. "There's that word again. You've used it before, but I don't know what it means."

"What word?"

"Dee-force."

"A divorce, a separation—you'd want to dissolve our marriage."

A look of deep hurt and bewilderment filled her face. "I don't understand."

"What's not to understand?"

"I don't understand how dissolving a marriage would work. If we marry, Garris will know it, my mom will know it. The council and all of Shirdon will know it. The Ephori, my people, for Adi's sake, half of Meerdon will know we have made an unbreakable promise, that we belong to each other. How exactly does that get dissolved?"

This time, it was Jon's bewilderment that was profound. "Surely couples must break up. What happens if a wife wants to leave her husband?"

With the cool water lapping against the rocks behind her, Dellia began to choke up, her eyes becoming glassy with tears and her voice faltering. "I don't understand you, Jon. I'm talking about marriage, and you're talking about leaving me?"

Eager to make up for his botched explanation, Jon gave a firm shake of his head. "I would never leave you, but I'm trying to be practical."

"Since when is love practical? A marriage isn't where you dither around while you figure out who the other person is. It isn't something where you sit by and wait to see if it will or won't work. I'm saying I want to commit to you. I'm saying I will vow to make it work. A vow I will never break, whatever may come. But if that's not what you want, if that's not how you think ..." Dellia turned to leave.

"No, no. Don't go."

She spun back to face Jon.

He sputtered, trying to summon the words to make her stay. "I just ... I didn't ..."

"Look, if there's one thing I know for certain, it's that marriage isn't halfway. You marry because you can't imagine being without the other person. I know it's only been a few days, but Jon, I can't imagine a life without you." Dellia lowered her head. "But I guess it's not the same for you, so I just have to ..." She turned again and began to shuffle away across the plush grass, still wet with morning dew.

Desperation filled him. Dellia was the only reason he had stayed. Without her, none of it meant anything; none of it was worth it. Here she had just offered him more than he could have ever dreamed of—not just now, but forever—and he was bungling it badly.

Jon rushed up to her, and she wheeled around at his approach. He reached out and grabbed her arms. "No. No. That's not true. I was just surprised, you know. I'm a stranger here. I don't know how things work. I just didn't understand, but I get it now. I ... I get it."

"The last thing I want is for you to marry me because I pressured you into it. So let's just—"

With his chance slipping away, Jon's voice couldn't hide his panic. "No, wait ... wait a minute."

"I am being sincere, Jon. You feel pressured. Even if I couldn't hear it in your voice, I can feel it here." She set her palm on his chest. "I don't want you to marry me because you feel pressured."

Dellia turned and began to walk away again.

Jon stood still for a moment, watching the yellow and orange flowers around him nodding in the light breeze, as if urging him forward, telling him to chase after her and fix this most colossal of all screwups. He raced up behind her and threw both arms around

416

her shoulders in a hug that stopped her in her tracks. "Don't go. Please, don't go."

She didn't pull away, so he hung on for a moment longer as Dellia stood there in what seemed to be shock. When he let go, she turned to face him. Her eyes peered into his and rested there for a long moment as Jon calmed.

All of a sudden, it hit him, and he knew what he had to do. He stepped back and dropped to one knee.

Dellia jumped back a step and stared in surprise and confusion.

Jon took a deep breath and pulled together all the calm he could manage. "Tell me, do I seem pressured now?"

Still appearing stunned, she gave her head a small slow shake.

"Then don't just listen to my words, listen with your gift and know, as only you can, that my words and my feelings are true."

Dellia nodded.

"I love you, Dellia. I think I started to fall for you that very first night, when we were sitting by the fire." He smiled. "I thought you were some kind of ridiculous, delusional romantic when you told me what 'one true love' meant. Do you remember what you said?"

Dellia nodded again.

"It turns out I was the fool, because that's how I feel now. I've fallen madly in love with you. I can't wait to wake up next to you each day and see your face. I want to get to know you. I want to know every part of you, every fear and flaw, every wound and weakness. And I promise I will love every one of them, because they are what make you human. And I will love you more, because they make you ... you."

Jon reached out and took her hands in his. "I can't imagine life without you. I don't even want to try. More than anything, I want to commit to you and only you. Marry me, Dellia."

She smiled and her demeanor took on an uncharacteristic shyness. "I don't know. This is all so sudden."

He remained solemn as he stood up and hugged her, pulling her close. "Please, Dellia, marry me."

She spoke in his ear, her soft voice mingling with the rustling of leaves and quiet gurgling of water. "Yes. Of course. I just wish you could know that it is the same for me." She let go, and Jon took her by the hand.

The broadest of smiles spread across her face as he led her back around the water-lily-dotted pond. They skirted the wall of pink blooms, walked around the tall grass, and headed onto the stone path, back to the entrance of the keep and a waiting Sirra and Garris.

Jon glanced back at her. "Do we tell everyone?"

Dellia hurried up to his side. "Can we tell Mom in private? I want her to be the first to know."

"Okay."

As they walked, Jon turned his head away, avoiding her gaze, and in a quiet voice asked, "I'm still staying at your mother's guesthouse, aren't I?"

"Are we married yet?"

"No."

"Then there's your answer."

Jon hung his head. "Okay. Just checking."

After a few more steps, Dellia stopped and glanced over at him. "And one more thing: what was that creepy kneeling down thing?"

"Hey, it was supposed to be romantic."

Her face adopted a screwy look of confusion. "I could force you into that position before you knew what hit you. How is that romantic?"

He tried to hide his surprise. "Because it was voluntary."

As they resumed their walk back to their waiting friends, Dellia mumbled under her breath, "As if I couldn't make you."

Jon paid no attention. He was too pleased with himself. He would be married to Dellia. It was impossible to believe. And not only that, but *she* had proposed to him. He felt positively giddy, recalling her passion when she said she wanted to take a vow to make it work with him, a vow she would never break. He felt the same, and he realized, now more than ever, he was committed to making it work with her.

A small knot returned to his stomach as he realized that it all rested on making his crazy, improbable plan work. He had drawn a fine line that he must now walk. He had to act the part of the leader the council expected, without letting himself be maneuvered into making a bunch of weighty decisions. Because the minute people started dying as a result of his misbegotten choices, they would see him for the fraud he was, and it would all end. He would be deposed. To the council he would become a criminal and to the protectors, an enemy. And with that, he would lose any chance of a life with Dellia.

Garris lowered his gaze against the early morning sun as he stepped along the paving stones. It was the dawn of the day after his exile had ended, and he was headed home. Only, it wouldn't be a pleasant reunion. There were things he needed to say that would make this an awkward encounter for all involved. So he distracted himself by focusing on the promise he had broken the night before.

It was just a little more than a day ago that he had encountered Megan in the Verod camp. During their brief exchange, she had not only insisted that she not meet Jon, but had also extracted his promise not to reveal her presence. Yet, yesterday evening, when Jon was ready to ignore all that was going on around him to run off looking for her, he had broken that promise. He had told Jon he'd seen her.

As if that wasn't bad enough, he had taken it even further. He had talked Jon into a plan to wait a week to see if she would come to Shirdon on her own, and if she didn't, he and Dellia would go find her. Not only had he broken his promise, but he had made plans to track Megan down after he vowed to not mention having seen her. It sat wrong with him to have gone back on his word in such a spectacular way, but what could he do? He had to stop Jon from sabotaging his own plan to become council leader.

Garris strolled up to the open door in the tall wooden fence and stopped there, peering through at the long, morning shadows stretching across the grass of the quiet backyard. Next to him, the early light warmed the back of a modest home of wood and stone, his mother Eejha's home—his home.

It had been fifteen years since he had seen it. Fifteen years in exile. Fifteen years he had missed his mother. The sight hit him with a mixture of nostalgia and dread. So much of his youth had been whiled away in this place, the best years of his life. Not his teenage years spent training to be a protector or his early adult years on the road and serving under Kayleen, but those carefree days, engaged in idle mischief, here in this place. If only he had made different choices ...

Back then, he knew Kayleen had feelings for him—it was obvious every time she looked at him with that expression of youthful adoration. He had destroyed that look and taken away her happiness. The hurt in her voice and anger in her eyes as he told her he was joining the protectors still haunted him. He had shattered her heart and abandoned her. All because he harbored the ridiculous delusion that he was destined to be a great hero. What a joke. That fantasy had come crashing down around him during a mission to Erden where Kayleen's sister, Leanna, was sent to help. Things had started going south. The council grew more and more angry and suspicious until it all came to a crescendo with the death of Leanna and the utter failure of his mission.

The image was burned in his mind: Kayleen meeting him on the road to Shirdon, screaming at him, blaming him for killing her sister, telling him she and the council had voted to banish him and that he should never come back again. It wasn't until two days ago, when he met Kayleen again for the first time since that day, that he learned she had never blamed him. It was all an act. She was playing the noble idiot, cutting ties with him so he could leave the three realms and not look back.

After Kayleen's harsh send-off, he had left the three realms and lived off the land. Banishment meant that killing him was no longer a crime of any kind, so they came, anyone he had arrested, slighted, or opposed. Some were poor saps in search of notoriety—the bragging rights that came with killing a former protector. A good number of them were good people, misled by the notion that he was some kind of enemy of the state. Even more carried forged orders from Kayleen to kill him on sight, no doubt in some kind of organized plot to eliminate him. It was a trail of human carnage, countless faces he would never forget. People with friends and loved ones who had been maimed, crippled, or killed by his hands. For fifteen bloody years it went on and cost untold human lives.

How could he face his mother, knowing what he really was? To hide such a monumental part of his history would be to create a lie, yet what could he possibly tell her of his past? He couldn't. He simply couldn't.

Garris looked away from his childhood home, across the quiet yard to the larger house of similar construction. It was the home of protector Edan, Kayleen's uncle. Edan had built the smaller home bordering his yard as a part of an agreement, a pact between families.

When Garris was still an infant, he'd lost his father in the same tragedy that had taken Kayleen and Leanna's father. Their mother died a short time later while giving birth to Kayleen. Protector Edan, their uncle, had taken the two girls in, but his long trips away from home had forced him to find a caretaker for his charges.

Having been friends with Kayleen and Leanna's parents, Eejha had been the obvious answer. For a small allowance, food, clothes, and the small house for her and Garris, she had agreed to look after the two girls when Edan could not.

So they had grown up in that way: Leanna and Kayleen in the big home across the yard, under the care of their uncle Edan, when he was around, while Garris and his mother Eejha stayed in the smaller house.

Those were carefree days, with Garris, Kayleen, and Leanna as a gang of neighborhood friends, running around, playing in the yard or along the streets of Shirdon, often getting themselves in a great deal of trouble.

His mother had more or less raised the girls, caring for them with a patience and kindness no less than a real mother. Edan had been the closest thing he had to a father, although he doted on Leanna and Kayleen far more than he ever did on Garris. He expected Garris to be like himself, principled and self-sufficient, with an unwavering moral compass. Remembering those long-forgotten days only worsened his turmoil. He was no longer that innocent boy. Because of him, Kayleen had lost her sister, Leanna. Not only had his mother lost a woman she regarded as a daughter, but his banishment had left her without a son to help and support her. He had destroyed his family.

Garris peered farther around the corner at the warm morning sunlight splashing across the circular stone table on the cozy terrace outside the small home. His guilt intensified at the sight of Kayleen, seated at the table, eating her morning meal. He knew Eejha must be there with her, but he hesitated, reluctant to look in farther. Even now, the twisting of his stomach at the thought of facing his mother was dwarfed only by the yearning for even a glimpse of her soft face.

He leaned in even more, and there across from Kayleen sat his mother, Eejha, wrapped in a beautiful blue-green sari edged in deep brown. The sight of her seemed to crush his soul. Everything about her was the same. The same golden skin, the same manner of parting her hair in the middle and tying it back, then covering it in a wrap matched to her clothes. But she seemed so much older now. Her hair, once black and shiny, had turned almost entirely gray, and her kind face, which had been smooth and beautiful, had become creased with worry and age. He had been a horrible son, bringing shame and heartache to a mother who loved him like no other.

Consumed by the vivid reminders of his failed past, he had been ignoring their quiet conversation. Now Garris leaned closer to watch and listen.

Eejha straightened, seeming shocked. "So, all that happened yesterday?"

Kayleen nodded. "Yes, but I haven't told you everything."

Eejha relaxed and smiled. "You can tell me next time. I don't want to make you late for the first meeting of the new council. It's too important."

Kayleen didn't move. "If I have to be late, it will be okay. I need to tell you ... the Otherworlder I told you about?"

Eejha seemed intrigued. "Jon? The new council leader? The one Wistra said would save us?"

"Yes. The one with the strange name. He brought someone with him. Someone who has been helping him. Someone important to him. ... Someone we both love." Kayleen let the statement lie for a time, in that practiced way she had of drawing attention to her words.

Eejha stared with a puzzled expression, then her hand flew to her mouth, and tears came to her eyes. "Where?"

Her reaction hit Garris like a war hammer. His mother missed him. He had abandoned his family to become a protector in the arrogant delusion that he could be some great hero. He had made his mother suffer for fifteen years, with no blood relatand no one to support her. He had taken away someone she had raised and loved as a daughter, and despite all of that, she still missed him.

Unable to see her cry over someone as unworthy as himself, Garris rounded the corner into the yard. He halted as she spotted him.

With stunned slowness, Eejha stood as tears begin to roll down her cheeks. "My precious son."

He froze for a moment, paralyzed by mortification. Then he rushed over and reached down to touch his mother's feet.

She grabbed his shoulders, lifted him up, and threw her arms around him. "You were banished. I thought I'd never ... I was afraid ..."

Eejha sniffled and let go. She was as soft and warm as he remembered. With a quick brush of her hand, she wiped away the tears, then set her hands on his shoulders and pushed him out in front of her, where she could scrutinize his face. She stayed that way for a while, studying him with a smile of gentle affection gracing her face.

Garris remained frozen by remorse, his eyes unable to meet hers. "I'm not banished anymore."

Her tears began to flow again. "What have they done to my beautiful boy?" She turned his chin so she could gaze into his eyes. "You can't even smile anymore?"

His head drooped. How could he tell her all that he had done? How could he break her heart like that? Even if he could, he hadn't even allowed himself to think about it for fifteen years. How then could he explain it?

He stared at the ground. "So much has happened. Kayleen knows all about it. She'll tell you."

It was a lie. Kayleen knew nothing, but she could explain what there was to explain, and if she did that for him, he could escape.

Eejha straightened. "Kayleen? Why would my son not tell me?"

Garris took a step back and turned his head just enough to avoid his mother's gaze. "I've done things, things you shouldn't forgive. Things nobody should forgive."

Eejha moved to his side. "What mother would not forgive her son?"

"When I was banished, killing me was no longer a crime. People came after me. I've killed so many people, Mom." He presented his palms for her to see. "How can you eat at the same table with my blood-soaked hands."

His mother seemed shaken for a few moments. Then she looked into his face. "You did what you needed to survive."

He looked away again, unable to think about, much less express, his utter shame and guilt.

"Whatever happened, it's all right. You're back now to stay, and we can be a family again."

Kayleen rushed to his other side and held on to his arm with both her tiny hands. "This is your home. When you're not out on missions, you can stay here, where you are needed. We've kept your room in the house. It's exactly as you left it. You can stay, and we can eat meals together like we always used to."

Garris looked away from Kayleen, but in doing so, his eyes met Eejha's, and his gaze dropped anew.

Kayleen held tight to his arm. "And when you are ready, you can tell us everything."

He stayed quiet for a while, trying to keep the one image he couldn't shake behind the wall he had built in his memories. When he finally did speak, it was with halting reluctance. "I … can't."

Kayleen tried to look into his downturned face. "You're leaving, aren't you?"

"He's not leaving. Why would he leave?" His mother searched his face with a look of deep concern. "Say something. Why aren't you saying something?"

He closed his eyes. "What would you have me say?"

His mother stepped in front of him. "Tell me it's not true. Tell me you're staying."

Garris finally returned his mother's gaze. "I told Jon I would find his friend, Megan. After that, I plan to leave."

Kayleen gawked. "Why?"

Eejha's expression fell. "If you're going to turn around and leave, then why did you come home at all?"

Garris stepped back, gently pulling his arm free. "To show you I'm fine and—"

"But you're not fine." Kayleen shook her head.

He tried again. "To let you know I am unharmed and to tell you that you will always be in my thoughts, but I can't stay."

Eejha seemed hurt and baffled. "Of course you can stay. Why would you leave?"

The look on her face only amplified his feeling of guilt. He stepped back again, staring at his mother's soft brown eyes. Images forced their way through the cracks: the agony on Leanna's face, her tiny hands clapped down on the dark, gaping wound, frantic to hold back her lifeblood as it gushed through her fingers, the pleading look in her eyes, and the sickening odor of her blood spilling onto the dirt. On the verge of being crippled by his own memories, Garris forced the horrors back behind the wall, then steeled himself.

"Leanna is gone." He pointed to the sturdy squat stone house across the yard. "Every morning, she'd come through that door, with that silly smile on her face. She'd skip across this yard and plop down at this table. Every day we'd gather for our morning meal, right here, and we'd sit and talk and eat, just you and me and Kayleen and Leanna." He sensed he was choking up and paused to compose himself. "She'll never do that again because I put her in harm's way."

He turned to face her. "Your sister, Kayleen. Your *sister*." He shook his head. "She was right there with me, and I ... I couldn't protect her." He shuddered as the memories tried to force their way back. "She's dead because of me. How can I stay when everything reminds me that I ..." Garris turned away, then spoke over his shoulder. "Goodbye, Ma. I'll visit from time to time, but I can't stay."

He strode across the yard as if afraid of his mother's gaze, as if she could see right into his wretched soul. With a sharp turn, he rounded the corner and stepped into the lane, and it was done. The moment he had both longed for and dreaded was over. He had hurt his mother again, but it was a pain nowhere near as crushing as it would be if he'd stayed and she had learned the truth.

He would have left that instant if not for his promise. Jon had reversed his banishment and made it possible for him to roam the streets in peace again. For the first time in fifteen years, he didn't have to jump at every shadow. That was Jon's doing, and he owed him for that. So, his departure would need to wait a week to see if Megan would return on her own, once news spread that Jon had become council leader. Now he simply needed to maintain his resolve for those seven long days, and this would be over.

Kayleen watched Garris turn the corner out of the gate and disappear into the quiet lane. An awful foreboding grabbed ahold of her, telling her this was so much worse than she'd thought. When she had first met Garris after all these years, he had seemed angry, which was understandable, given the despicable things she'd said when she sent him into exile.

She had always been good with words, and she used all that talent to make sure he left behind any hope of returning. Then there were the even more despicable things he *thought* she had done. How could he think she'd send one assassin after another to kill him? To say he was angry was perhaps an understatement; he was ready to kill her. Yet that same anger had been absent with Eejha.

He loved his mother in that all-consuming way Erdish sons do. He had her firmly placed on the highest of pedestals. Anger at Eejha was as inconceivable as the sun rising in the west. No, this was not Garris stomping off in anger. He was running away, but from what?

Every mood of his was a book to her, the pages of which she had read and memorized since before she could even talk. Not one line, not one syllable, had been unknown to her, yet this new Garris was a puzzle. He was not one to run from anything, anytime, any place. So, if he was running, and it seemed likely he was, it must be from something he couldn't fight, something terrible, haunting, and traumatic. Anything that could scar him so terribly would never let him rest unless she made him face it.

She glanced at Eejha. She was standing there, staring at the spot where her son had disappeared out of the yard. Then the stunned mother looked over at Kayleen. "He's hurting so much."

Kayleen nodded. "More than I realized. I'll go after him, talk to him."

Eejha lowered her head. "He's made up his mind. You know how stubborn he can be."

Kayleen set her hands on Eejha's shoulders and smiled. "I talk for a living, and nobody knows him better than me. I will get him to stay. I have to."

Eejha shook her head. "You have that meeting with the new council. It's more important. You can find Garris after, for all the good it will do."

The thought of a delay in talking to Garris frightened her more than the idea of what might happen if she missed the meeting. Political problems she could solve, but if Garris vanished again, her chances of ever persuading him to stay might very well evaporate with him.

He had been lost to her twice. Once when he became a protector and again when she forced him into exile. The thought of a third time shook her to her core. She could not bear to lose him again.

Kayleen took Eejha's hand and set hers upon it. "No. He's here now, and I can't take the chance he will disappear out of our lives again. I will stop him."

Propelled by a profound sense of resolve, Kayleen took off across the backyard, whipped out of the gate, and turned around the corner. She strutted along the tall wooden fence and down the sunny cobblestone lane. Bordered by a few enormous old trees, it was a dead end that ran by only a few houses. With no horses, carriages, or soldiers to interrupt their shenanigans, it had been a favorite spot for childhood games.

She spotted Garris. He had not yet gone far, only halfway down the street. Gravel crunched underfoot as she raced up behind him. Suddenly aware that she'd been tinkering with her long blue crystal pendant, so she let go and calmed herself before grabbing his arm. "Stop."

Garris halted but resisted her tug, not turning around. He simply stared ahead with an air of intense determination and a crispness in his voice. "I've said my piece. There's nothing more to say."

Kayleen kept her voice soft and calm. "Your mother doesn't blame you, and neither do I. Maybe I did at first, but then I realized you did your best. You *always* do your—"

"You can be so frustratingly naive sometimes." Garris shook his head.

He yanked his arm free and began to walk away again down the sunlit lane, but Kayleen chased behind him, her pleading becoming more insistent. "Okay, maybe you don't care that your mother needs you or that I need you, but Jon needs you. How can you be so determined to abandon us that you'd leave him behind right when he needs you the most?"

Garris shrugged off her concern, throwing comments to her over his shoulder. "He has Dellia. Besides, I've known him a couple weeks. I knew Leanna her whole life. How can you even make that comparison?"

"I know Leanna is dead. I know you feel responsible, but Eejha and Jon and I are still alive, and you leaving the people who need you won't bring her back."

This time, Garris stopped, and the rubble ground under his foot as he spun around. "How can you be so cold? Why can't you see it from my point of view?" He motioned to the homes and buildings across the broad plateau. "Every single thing here is a reminder." He presented his palms to Kayleen. "A reminder that blood is on these hands. Not just the blood of the dozens I've killed, but her blood, your sister's blood. This place is a reminder of a stain that will never be washed away."

Kayleen stepped back. Eejha was right. This wasn't going to work. He was on the verge of leaving. Her years in council debate had taught her to remain calm in the face of calamity, but this put a scare in her that was as bad as any political problem she had ever faced. She needed a new tactic, something to shake him as much as she was shaken by him.

She nodded. "Okay, I concede; I can't know what you've been through or how you feel. But no matter how much you think you're at fault, you shouldn't have to pay with your life."

Garris seemed suitably perturbed by her words and stared for a moment in stunned silence. "Paying with my life? What in the blazes are you talking about?"

Kayleen stepped up close in front of him. "Someone has been trying to kill you for fifteen years. We have no idea who it is or why they are so determined to see you dead. Do you really think they'll just stop?"

Garris grunted, then calmed a little. "How do you think I killed so many? They never stop. I thought maybe with my banishment reversed and all, and it being no longer legal to attack me without consequences …" He stopped himself as if coming to his senses, as if realizing he had no reason to explain. "But how exactly does this concern you?"

She crossed her arms, putting on a defensive front. "How does it concern me? I can't believe you said that. Someone is trying to kill my best friend, the man I grew up with, and you think that doesn't concern me?"

His expression suddenly took on a note of concern. "It's wrong, you know, for you to care about me, after what I did to your sister." She puzzled over what Garris meant by the remark as he spun back forward again, ready to storm away. "I'll figure this out on my own." He marched off.

Kayleen stared as her alarm deepened. This still wasn't working, so it was time to up the stakes. She raced up, grabbed his arm, and this time forced him to spin back toward her. "Then what about me? Someone went through a lot of trouble to make you think I was trying to kill you. They poisoned your mind to me. Don't you see? That wasn't by chance. It was a plot to kill me, and they wanted you to be the weapon. Have you really become so unfeeling and bullheaded that you don't even care who is trying to kill me?"

Garris shuddered, and his eyes widened.

This was good. It might actually work.

He shook his head. "No, of course not. If something were to happen to you …"

"I understand that you're not going to stay. Fine. But please, stick around long enough to uncover who's trying to kill you and make you want to kill me."

Garris looked down for a moment, studying the pattern of shadow and light through the branches above as it danced along the gravel-strewn roadway. "I don't see how you can help?"

Kayleen stood taller and made a point of barking out her questions like a council leader addressing her protector. "How many attempts have there been?"

Like a dutiful protector responding out of habit, Garris answered, "I've lost count. Several each year."

"What made you think I was behind them?"

"They carried orders written in your hand. They said the most vile and despicable things about me."

A pang of hurt ripped a hole in her attempts to maintain a confident facade. "I don't understand how you could think I could be that hateful?"

Garris spoke in a quiet voice as he scuffed his huge feet against the dust and gravel. "After Leanna, I despised myself. I still do. How could you not feel the same?"

Kayleen shook the hurt off. She had caught him in her net. Now all she needed to do was pull him in. She regained her commanding air. "So there was forgery involved. Was there anything else they had in common?"

Garris responded again with automatic efficiency. "Yes, many of them carried these gold coins with a strange chimera symbol on them. I began to think they were being paid or bribed with them, or someone had given them for expenses."

His sturdy coin purse jangled as he pulled it out, opened it, and retrieved a burnished golden coin. He flipped it over and there on its head was the image of a beast. It was a chimera, all right—a creature made up of parts from three different animals. In this case, the body of a snarling tiger, crouched with its claws out, the wings of a dragon unfurled around it, and the tail of a scorpion with its stinger poised to strike.

Kayleen peered at it, not at all able to recognize the coin or the creature. "And they all had them?"

He nodded. "Those that had the orders from you all carried them."

Kayleen puzzled over the shiny bit of metal. "If all the coins are as unique as this one, it can't be coincidence."

"Agreed."

Kayleen thought for a moment. Her acquaintance Ahmet might recognize it. He was a fancier of coins and might know where it came from and its history. She looked up at Garris, and when she spoke, it again had the sound of a commander dispensing orders. "Okay, I'll focus on finding the origin of the coins. You find the forger."

Garris stepped back, seeming incensed. "Since when did this turn into *our* investigation?"

Now she had him. Kayleen put on a thoughtful expression. She tapped her index finger on her lips a few times for effect, then gave a quick nod. "You're right. I'll simply have to investigate all of this on my own."

With an air of efficiency, she dodged past him and began to walk away.

Garris turned around and yelled after her in an annoyed voice. "You haven't changed one little bit. You're always scheming and trying to talk me into things. I know you want me to stay, but we're not kids anymore, and what you're suggesting isn't as simple as breaking into Shir Keep for laughs."

Kayleen spun around. "I admit it—this is a scheme to make you stay, but I am *not* wrong. The threat is real, and it's out there even if you choose to ignore it."

"Fine. So how exactly am I supposed to find this forger?"

Kayleen straightened in surprise. "Oh, stop whining. You're one of the best protectors ever born. For crying out loud, act like one."

Garris mumbled, "Well, maybe not one of the bes—"

"And a stop pretending to be humble. It doesn't suit you. So, are we agreed?"

"Okay, but only until we catch whoever's been doing this."

Kayleen lowered her head, acting deferential and meek. "Of course, Garris," she chimed in a soft yet serious tone.

"Oh, don't start that again."

"Whatever you say, Garris."

AYLUN

"You con me into this and then pull that 'obedient little girl' act. Are you trying to tick me off?"

Kayleen looked up, staring with innocent, wide eyes as she shook her head. "I would never, Garris."

"Knock it off." He shook his head and marched past her into the shade of a huge tree.

She turned and trudged behind, looking down and acting repentant. "Yes, Garris."

For Aylun, the three-day trip from the Verod camp to the hills of Erden was a bittersweet one. He had parted with Megan as she was headed for Jon. He had brought her back to the man she loved, and from that very second until now, he had missed her. Yet, from the moment they met, it had been understood that he and Megan would part. She would return to Jon and he to whatever fate awaited him. So his being alone again was no surprise.

It was that same acceptance now that allowed him to set aside his loneliness and focus instead on the sense of rightness in knowing he had returned her to where she belonged. She was in the place where the Greatest of Oracles had ordained she should be. But more important than that, she was in the place that made her happy, and he found that despite his Shou upbringing and desire to protect prophecy, that was what mattered most.

Yet, even amid her absence, in some ways it was still as if they were together. She often visited his dreams, and his waking moments were filled with recollections of her. Their days in Mundus hiding out, working and playing, the trip to meet Jon, and her smile and infectious joy at his arrival—they were all happy moments that sustained him. In that way, they would always be together.

He was grateful too, because through her, he had found a new purpose in life, and it filled him with satisfaction, knowing he would be protecting her. How often had he heard the phrase: if you want happiness for a lifetime, help someone else? To him, the saying had always seemed superficial and trite. Now he understood. He would help Megan and Jon and, in so doing, protect the prophecy in his own way. If, by taking this path, he could contribute to their happiness, then nothing would bring him greater fulfillment.

It was that sense of purpose that had driven him back to Kanlu, despite his trepidation at returning to the place from which he had been so vehemently dismissed. And it was that sense of purpose that had driven him and Juzhi to arrive in a little over three days.

He trod a path into the city under a cloud-streaked dusk, stopping to stable his horse at a discreet place just beyond the outskirts of the town. Careful to not be seen, he entered the city on the edge of night. He skirted through shadows and dove in and out of dusty alleys and darkened backstreets to avoid notice.

He needed to visit the Vault of Time, but it sat beneath Yaochen's quarters in the Augury, making it quite a challenging place to breach. Not to mention being beneath the room of the one man he least wanted to encounter, the man from whom he had taken Yaolin, his daughter. Other than its difficult-to-reach location, it was not well guarded. It was, however, protected by a lock he would never pick, especially not silently, with Yaochen sleeping nearby.

Surrounded by high walls, the Augury itself was a tricky place to break into. Aylun had to swing his way up into a large tree that stood a short distance from one of those walls. From there, he danced out on one of its winding branches, which he used as a springboard to leap to the top of the Augury wall. He bounced off of it toward the other side like an acrobat on a trampoline, and as he fell, he grabbed the sturdy branch of another tree, well inside the wall. The rough bark grated against his hands and raked across the still sore scratches on his arms as he swung and dropped from one limb to another, then fell soundlessly to the ground.

He skirted in and out of shadows, avoiding sentry routes and staying well behind the patrol. At the edge of the first building, he slipped into the shadows behind a row of dense bushes that lined the path, where he could wait unobserved. It was time to

434

"borrow" a key to the vault, and he knew just how to get it. He dug his fingers through the tough grass, feeling for a rock or stick. Instead, he found an old walnut, most likely left by a forgetful squirrel. It was perfect—not too old, since it had not sprouted and had not yet rotted from burial in the ground—so he rubbed away the dirt and debris from its surface.

It was Taibok's turn to be on guard, so Aylun waited until he spotted his friend's tired face approaching along the expected route. His familiar goatee and rounded features were recognizable in the soft light of the lamps that ran the length of the buildings. He waited until his former comrade was about to pass. Then he positioned his hand in front of him with the nut resting on his upturned fingers and flicked his wrist.

The nut arced up over him and onto the roof.

He reached out between the branches of the shrubs.

The nut dropped onto the roof with a distinct clack and bounced along its slope.

When Taibok's head jerked up, Aylun wrapped his hand around the key ring to dampen the sound and gently lifted it from Taibok's belt.

As he moved silently away, he pictured Taibok looking down at the nut, strolling over, picking it up, and examining it. Then his friend would look up at the tree branches, swaying in the night breeze as they hung over the building. Before he finished his mental walk-through of Taibok's movements, Aylun was long gone, having slipped around to the back of the building and into the shadows of the trees looming over the garden. Taibok would check out the area. He was thorough but not very imaginative, which made his routine predictable. When he found nothing out of the ordinary, he would follow protocol and resume his rounds.

Aylun snuck around Yaochen's quarters and up to the porch, taking care not to rouse him. The last thing he wanted was to come face-to-face with the man from whom he had taken a daughter. With excruciating slowness, he crept inside. Stepping across the floorboards without making any noise proved as difficult as he knew it would be, given their age and creakiness.

The keyhole also proved challenging. It was easy enough to get the key through the hole without touching the sides, but it was inevitable that as soon as he turned it, the mechanism would make a noise, regardless of how much care he took. He did his best to muffle the clank, but it caused Yaochen to moan and stir, though he remained asleep.

Careful not to make a sound, he eased the door shut, stopping it just short of latching behind him. Blocked from anyone's view, he withdrew his flamestone and cupped it, so most of its steady amber light was cast down the stairs. After another bout of slow creeping he was, at last, in the dank confines of the Vault of Time. In spite of its fancy title, it was nothing more than a dirty, clammy basement filled with sturdy, well-crafted shelves, most of them empty. Only one held the dozen or so neatly arranged chests he needed to check.

He stepped lightly over to them, the warm light of his glass ball gleaming off of the lock and metal plaque displayed on the front of each. Engraved on the plaques were the signs that would indicate the time for their opening. Augury rules required that each plaque have at least three signs. A single sign might be misinterpreted, and two might appear by coincidence, but all three would be difficult to misinterpret or misconstrue. And each sign was given scrupulous consideration by the Great Oracle of that prophecy.

He held up the flamestone as he scanned the row, reading the first sign on each chest. Mounted on the oldest and most worn was a plaque that spoke of a time when the first "high protectors" would be absent from the seat of power. He contemplated it with care, as he had been taught. He had never heard of such a thing as high protectors, which meant that the sign could not yet have come to pass.

He moved to the next one, and it spoke of the discovery of the fifth realm. Again he considered with care, but no one inside or outside of the Shou had ever heard of a fourth realm, much less a fifth, so he went to the next chest.

AYLUN

The first line spoke of the rise of an Otherworlder and the second of a time when their mate would search for them. It was a sign he had read hundreds of times since his youth. Now he couldn't help thinking of Megan as the mate searching for her husband, Jon. The notion of them marrying brought a pang to his heart and a smile to his face.

The bittersweet memory returned of the fiery anger and passion with which she had proclaimed that she loved him as much as any wife loved a husband. It warmed him to think of how happy it would make her to marry Jon, how right it would be.

His smile remained as Aylun moved on to the next chest. So it went, down the row, and in every case, there was at least one sign that had not yet come to pass. After studying each plaque and finding nothing, he steeled himself for what he must do next.

He climbed the stairs, striving to be as silent as he could, closed and locked the door, then slipped out into the night. Retracing his steps, he weaved his way back through shadows and behind bushes and buildings to the place in the path where Taibok had frozen upon hearing the nut. He placed the key ring on the ground, in a spot where it was partly visible from the patrol route; it would seem plausible that it had been dropped by accident and overlooked on subsequent rounds.

Then he slipped through Tsaoshi's window and knelt beside his sleeping figure. The man liked to sleep with the shutters near his bed open, so the air was cool and brisk as Aylun peered down at the darkened form.

He had grown up revering the Great Oracle, as any son might a father. Yet as he stared at him now, nestled in his bed, he seemed different somehow—more human, more vulnerable. Or perhaps Aylun himself was the changed one, now that he was no longer a part of this place.

He took the flamestone from his small pack and cupped it in his hand so the soft yellow light illuminated Tsaoshi's familiar and serene face but was shielded from the open window. He kept it covered as he set it on the floor near the wall, then gently placed his other palm over the Great Oracle's mouth.

The man awoke and tried to sit up, but Aylun held his head down with a firm hand as he signaled him to be silent.

Tsaoshi nodded.

Aylun uncovered Tsaoshi's mouth and whispered in his quietest voice, "I am sorry, Chenyu, but I must speak with you."

Seeming a bit sleepy but otherwise unfazed, Tsaoshi gave a single slow nod.

"I have been to Lanessa and recovered one of Wistra's journals."

Tsaoshi did not startle or seem surprised. Instead, he whispered back, "Yaomey has already told me of Megan and of your intent to recover the journal. She has been quite thorough in reporting what happened up to the point where you were poised to enter Katapa."

Aylun paused. He had forgotten his concern for Yaomey. He leaned closer. "Is she back? Did she arrive safely?"

Tsaoshi nodded. "I assume the contents of the journal have something to do with this visit?"

Aylun continued in a whisper, "Wistra wrote of a warning she placed in the Vault of Time, but no such warning appears to exist, nor are there any signs that would allow for the revealing of any new warning."

Tsaoshi's hand crawled up from beneath his covers, and he held it out. "Where is this journal? I must read this warning for myself."

"You cannot. It is with Megan."

Tsaoshi seemed a little surprised. "The one who arrived with Jon?"

"Yes. It was Megan who retrieved the journal from Lanessa. I merely assisted."

Tsaoshi rolled his eyes and grumbled at that. He probably saw the turn of phrase as a simple semantic difference. "Why would you leave such an important relic in her hands? It belongs in the Augury."

Aylun's voice rose a bit as he failed to entirely hide his irritation. "By rights, it is Megan's. It was her insistence that led me there.

Why then would I take it from her? Why would I bring it here? I am no longer Shou. I am no longer the hand of the Augury. If you wish to have it, send Shou to fetch it. Send Yaomey. She knows Megan quite well."

Tsaoshi lowered his voice even further, as if it were an antidote to Aylun's relative outburst. "No need to be defensive. I am merely concerned that something that could reveal so much about this place is outside these walls."

"It is safe with Megan."

Tsaoshi paused for a while, in apparent thought, then whispered. "And you are certain it is a real journal from Wistra? You interpreted her writing correctly?"

Aylun considered for a moment, recalling the precise wording. "The writing was older and some of the characters not as we make them today, so there was some interpretation, but yes, I am quite sure."

"And you have considered all the signs in the Vault of Time, and none fit?"

Aylun nodded.

"And what is the nature of this warning? Perhaps it has already been revealed."

Aylun shook his head. "It spoke of Jon the Otherworlder and the need for Megan to remain by his side."

Outright concern clouded Tsaoshi's usually serene features. "When Jon came here, she was not with him."

"I have returned her to Jon, but they were separated for some time, and I must know what Wistra was afraid would happen."

Tsaoshi sat up. "You returned Megan to Jon?"

Aylun nodded.

Tsaoshi remained silent for a while, then drew a long breath. "If Wistra wrote it, we must assume it is true; we must assume she placed a warning in the Vault of Time. So, if it is not there now, then it must have been lost or taken."

"How? Its absence would have been noticed."

Tsaoshi nodded. "And it would have been recorded in the archives of the Augury."

"Unless the records were also taken."

They both went quiet again, mulling over the incongruity.

Tsaoshi perked up as if struck by an epiphany. "Perhaps it was not lost here. Perhaps it was left behind when the vault was moved."

Aylun paused out of confusion. "Moved?"

"Oh yes. The Vault of Time has not always been in the Augury. For the first five hundred years, it was southwest of Daobai, along the northeast bank of Kinshai Lake."

Aylun considered for a moment. "I do not see how it could have been left behind. Still, it makes little sense to check here and not go search for it there. So I guess I must find the old Vault of Time."

"As you have so ... *fervently* reminded me, you are no longer Shou. I can no longer tell you what to do, but I believe what you propose is the wisest course of action."

Aylun rose to leave.

Tsaoshi tugged on his pant leg. When Aylun looked down, he motioned him to come closer. Aylun leaned over, and Tsaoshi whispered, "Return here. Tell me of what you have learned."

It sounded more like an order than a request, and Aylun sent him a flat stare.

"Please."

Aylun gave a crisp nod and a sharp, "Hmm."

"Perhaps I should tell the Shou to allow you entry."

Aylun gazed in puzzlement. "What in the world for?"

Tsaoshi waved him off. "Yes. What was I thinking?"

Aylun smiled as he slipped out of the room, less soundlessly now that Tsaoshi was aware of his presence. He moved quickly through the shadows of the overhang and the large, heavily branched tree of the courtyard. The posts that supported the awning were sturdy, so he scurried up one and pulled himself up onto the shingles of the roof.

One of the roof's peaks was near the Augury wall, so he scrambled up, leaped to the top, dropped to the street outside the Augury, and slipped into the shadows. He would return to Juzhi and the stables and catch a couple hours of sleep before heading to the old site of the Vault of Time. If he moved quickly, he would be there by midday tomorrow.

Still, the question nagged at him: if he found nothing there, then what was his next step? How could he find the missing vault contents when he had no idea when or even where they had gone missing?

Chapter Seventeen

HONEYMOON

Dellia stared up at the blooms of the tree. The morning sun shone through their pink petals and the thin green leaves around them, lending the whole architecture a soft glow. It contrasted with the dark twisting branches, imparting the impression of a living, growing work of stained glass that bowed and swayed in the gentle breeze.

It was her favorite part of the day and one of her favorite spots. Reachable only through a winding dirt path off the main stone walk, and surrounded by huge plants and dense shrubs, it was sheltered from view on all sides. That made it the perfect place for a private moment with Jon.

It had only been five days since he confronted the council and proposed marriage to her, three since they were married. Her people were not inclined to an overabundance of pomp and formality, so the ceremony had been a simple one, having only the essential elements. It had been held here, in the beautiful Shir Courtyard gardens in front of a handful of witnesses that they exchanged promises to stay together forever, whatever may come. Its simplicity served to highlight all that mattered in a marriage ceremony. A vow made in front of friends and family that bound them for all time.

In the days since, the depth of her affection for Jon had only grown. As her contentment spread, her gift strengthened with it. The Gift of the Heart was like that. Like having another sense, it let her feel what others were feeling. That ability weakened when she was in turmoil and her own emotions crowded it out, but it blossomed at times like this, when she was at peace and content. So it was with

443

profound clarity that she could feel the burning of his love and desire for her growing with each passing hour.

She slipped her arm around Jon's shoulder and pulled him close. He glanced over and smiled. The adoration in his eyes matched the flood of affection pouring from his heart. An affection that only intensified as his gaze rested on her for a long moment. The feelings mingled with her own until it became almost overpowering.

The last few days had been intoxicating in that way. Every time she looked at him, the impulse called to her to reach out with her gift and revel in his feelings for her. The wonder and harmony of them fed her gift like nothing else could, expanding it and clarifying what she sensed, until it saturated her being.

Yet even now, even as she relished her time with Jon, a familiar feeling had begun to tug at her. It was an itch she couldn't scratch, at least not as long as she remained here, in Shirdon. It was that tiny grain of guilt, that sense that her idleness was wrong, that she was somehow betraying her kind, that she was forsaking her duty and her destiny. That itch wasn't going to go away. It hadn't since she was a young girl. It was what had led her to become a protector in the first place.

She wanted to share her thoughts with Jon, but he seemed perfectly content to ignore their future. Then again, maybe he wasn't simply ignoring it. Perhaps it was more than that. Perhaps his evasiveness, whenever she brought it up, was not as casual as he made it appear. Maybe something deeper was behind it. After all, even in the most peaceful moments, there burned in his heart an anxious fear, buried deep down where nothing she did could touch it.

She had assumed it was merely a reaction to the responsibility he had taken on. Something that would ease with time and experience. Still, his silence mystified her. Why keep his troubles bottled inside? Why avoid discussing a future he feared? Wouldn't it ease his burden to share it, to get it out in the open, to talk about it?

Whatever the reason, his avoidance had made it impossible to get him to contemplate their future. Yet, there were things they needed to discuss. Things that could not be put off much longer. So, perhaps now would be the time to nudge him into face their future head-on.

She sighed as the gentle breeze made the leaves above flutter in their familiar dance. They whispered their quiet song as she smiled at Jon. "Happy?"

He smiled back and nodded.

She leaned her head over and rested it on his shoulder. "One part of me wants to stay here like this forever, with you. But you know this 'honeymoon,' as you called it, it is not the way of my people. Hiding out like this—"

"Hiding out?"

She could feel his sudden hurt at her words, so she lifted her head and looked into his eyes. Yet all she found there was affection.

Jon granted her a smile full of warmth and tenderness. "It's not hiding. We are getting to know each other, acclimating to married life."

"But that's just it. This is not 'life' we're acclimating to. It's not. I get what you're saying, but life isn't isolating yourself. It's complicated and hard and messy. The way of my people is to face that life together. To get to know each other as we confront each day and each challenge, as a family."

He went silent for a while. "It's only been three days, Dellia. If it were up to me, this would be our life: simple and easy, enjoying each other's company as we work and live."

She nodded. "I understand, but staying away from everything is not your life. You are council leader now. You serve the people, and I want nothing more than to be out there serving the people just as you are."

Jon froze, staring ahead at the base of the tree, where a cluster of tall white flowers hugged the heavy trunk. His gaze intensified as that familiar anxiety of his returned.

She turned her head to look at his face. "What?"

He delayed, clearly hesitant to speak his mind, and perhaps afraid, too, of how she would respond. After a moment, he glanced at her. "When we met, you were on a mission. In fact, most of the time I've known you, you were out on the road. Do protectors spend a lot of time away from home?"

Dellia looked up into the intricate artwork of light and shade, flower and branch, as she came to understand what had disquieted him so much. She paused, considering her words, as a pair of tiny brown birds hopped and bobbed along a branch. They were identical, except one of them had a rose tinge to its head. She kept her gaze on them as she spoke. "That's the job, Jon. Some people say protectors aren't allowed romantic relationships for this very reason. They are gone all the time."

His disquiet turned to mild panic. "You mean you might be gone? I might have to face all of this without you?"

At his reaction, her impulse grew to assuage his fear, to remind him that he had ultimate control over where she went and when. Perhaps that would be best. After all, she had just betrayed him out of a false sense of duty to a corrupt council. Here she was, mere days later, letting that same sense of duty tug at her again, and after she had just told Jon that her duty lay with him now.

She hesitated. No. This was different. This was not a duty to some unscrupulous council. She had made a vow, and even if the part of it that bound her to that council was no longer valid, she still had made a solemn promise to serve the people. She still felt a compulsion and a yearning to fulfill that vow.

She looked over at him, trying to figure out what to say. Should she mention what Garris had told her—that Jon himself had decided that in a week, she, as a protector, would be sent with the big guy to locate Megan? Should she make sure he fully understood what being a protector meant? Should she tell him she could be sent on a mission at a moment's notice? Should she point out that he might return home one day to find her gone, without even the slightest warning or goodbye?

No. Her heart rebelled against the idea. She had already stressed her point enough by explaining why protectors didn't have romantic relationships. There was no need to send him even further into a panic. But had she perhaps been too strong? Should she try to soften the blow?

No. This time it was her mind that rebelled against the idea. She had said what she must. Trying to minimize it would only create a false expectation and end up hurting him. She had been blunt, but that was what she needed to be. Now she needed to stand firm. He had to accept this.

Her attention remained with the pair of birds as one of them flew away, leaving behind the one with the rose tinge to its head. It saddened her in a strange way. Or perhaps it was her decision that saddened her.

She drew a slow, deep breath as she looked away toward Shir Keep. "I have watched Kayleen for years. The role of council leader is no small thing. It is a huge job, and I think you will find it keeps you so busy you will hardly notice I'm gone."

The notion shocked Jon as expected. What she hadn't expected was that his fear would explode. She focused on her gift, sensing an intensity in him akin to that of a trapped animal.

His gaze whipped over to her. "That's what I'm afraid of. You know what happened to me. I took charge of an entire class and got them all killed, even my stepsister. That's what being in charge means to me. It means my decisions get people killed. It terrifies me. How am I supposed to cope with that without you?"

"But Kayleen will represent you. All you have to do is give advice."

"And what if that advice hurts or kills people? What if it sends Kayleen's uncle Edan to his death? Or angers the Verod, and I have to send soldiers to fight the very people who helped me? Or what if my advice causes two realms to go to war?"

Dellia softened her tone. "I think you're letting your fears run away with you."

At her gentle words, his panic took on an intense edginess. "Am I? Look at the little lie the council told. They changed a few words in a prophecy, and you know firsthand the kind of devastation and pain it caused. It could have killed everyone in the three realms. That is not a power I, of all people, am supposed to have."

She took his hands into hers, her touch calming him. "No. Don't worry. I heard you. What was it you said? You don't know this land or its customs or its people. I figured that was why you need Kayleen. She could represent you so you didn't have to bear all that responsibility." She pulled him close and hugged him. "I know this isn't the simple life you wanted. So don't make yourself miserable. Lean on Kayleen and Garris. Use them. When I'm not here, they can support and guide you."

Jon startled and pulled back, his reaction almost making her jump. "You realize you just suggested I look to Garris for support?"

She laughed. "I know. What was I thinking?"

His tone turned serious again. "Besides, Garris is leaving."

"Leaving? Why?"

Jon shrugged. "He explained, but I'm not sure I really get it."

He fell silent for a long while, and his emotions churned as he seemed to consider what she'd said. She tilted her head and rested it on his shoulder again, trying to lend him comfort and reassurance, trying to let him know that she was still his, even if she wouldn't always be here to hold him. For a time, she was content to stay that way, as the shadow of a couple strolling the main path drifted along the dense greenery.

After a while, Jon spoke. "You realize I don't really know Kayleen at all, right?"

Dellia lifted her head, looked at him, and nodded.

"That said, I will try. Because even as scared as I am, I want to be with you more. If that means I only get to be with you part of the time, then I'll just have to adjust." He gave a sly smile. "But you have to promise me that when we are together, you'll make up for all the time we were apart. You'll owe me that."

She returned his sly smile and gave him a playful punch in the shoulder.

His smile faded. "I'm serious."

She grabbed him and hugged him again. "I would have, even if you hadn't asked. Because I feel the same way."

Jon returned his attention to the gardens around them. "Now, we only have a short time left. Can we at least pretend to be newly-weds instead of council leader and protector talking about realms and councils and duty?"

Dellia squeezed him tighter as she felt his tumult of emotions ease. "Deal."

She let go, and they both leaned back, staring at the flowering tree in front of them. A cloud had blocked the sun, extinguishing the glow of the leaves and petals, and the faces of the flowers were now pale and drab in the shade of the tree. Gone, too, was that harmony of two people feeling as one. All her talk had soured the mood. Getting it out in the open and discussing the future hadn't made Jon feel one bit better, and with that realization, a tinge of self-doubt clouded her certainty.

She had just told her new husband that she wouldn't be around much. It reminded her of all the times she had told him how much she believed in love and family. In a sense, she had just betrayed all the values she had extolled with such conviction. And in a small way, in so doing, she had betrayed him, again.

That shard of guilt didn't change anything, though. She still felt that tug, that feeling that her idleness was wrong. Nor did it change the fact that she had made a vow to serve the people.

The sound of soldiers marching outside the courtyard told her that the noon hour had arrived, and she breathed a deep sigh. She had made a choice. She would find a way. She would make it work. After all, he was still right beside her. And yet, as close as he was, he seemed more distant now than he had been in days. She had brought him to a beautiful spot, to one of her favorite places, and she had only hurt him and ruined their perfect day together. This wouldn't do.

She rose and offered her hand. "Let's go."

She could sense Jon's puzzlement and surprise. "Where?"

Dellia shoved her hand out further. "Back home."

He cocked his head. "We just came from there."

"I think we should go down to Shirdon later and eat." Jon slipped his hand into hers, and she smiled. "But first, I had a sudden urge to take a nap."

"An urge? … To take a nap?"

"Yes, and I want my new husband, who I adore, to take it with me."

Jon smiled as he suddenly seemed to sense her drift. "Will this nap involve more than sleeping?"

Dellia sent him a coy smile, and her cheeks flushed. "It might. We'll have to see."

He rose and followed. And as they traveled out to the main path and down the rough stone walk toward home, his tumult of emotions faded, leaving one singular desire—a desire for her.

Kayleen rounded the corner out of the still coolness of the mountain keep and into the heat of the bright afternoon sun. A light breeze blew through her hair, and the cobbles clacked underfoot as she scurried down the street toward Ahmet's home. Things had not gone well, and now she needed an ally to help set them right.

Ahmet was an old acquaintance. One who loved to talk and who considered himself important. Not that he wasn't an important man; he was. It was just that those who were influential and liked others to know it were among the most useful when it came to council politics. She had spent many a noontime meal with him, bending his ear. Drop a subtle hint or two that there were questions about his influence, then ask for a favor, one that might make use of said influence, and invariably he would be much more inclined to grant that favor and, by helping, prove his importance.

On one particular summer evening, she had made dinner for him. It was not something she liked to do often for single men, since it could send the wrong signal. The last thing she needed was for some man to get the wrong notion into his head and have a collaboration with a political ally turn awkward. In this case, though, it was an important matter. The council had become aware of counterfeit coins flooding the market, and they seemed to originate in Erden, Ahmet's home.

So she'd slipped into the conversation that his name had come up in a council debate about some fake coins. That seemed to puff up his ego nicely. When he was feeling his most self-congratulatory, she mentioned that Braye had argued against Ahmet's help, doubting he would hold sway with the right people. Ahmet became as defensive as a little boy whose father's honor had just been impugned.

It was during that exchange that she had found out he once worked as a designer, crafting coin stamps for the Erdish Mint. He claimed to have worked in close collaboration with the Rhanae and a litany of other high officials. She had never known him to be prone to exaggeration, and she did know many of the names he mentioned, so his claim seemed genuine enough.

After that, she didn't even need to ask for his help. He interjected himself into the whole affair, insisting that he get protector Shal into the right places and in contact with the proper people. In the end, Ahmet's importance was reaffirmed, and he proved instrumental in helping locate the counterfeiters.

She hoped he might be equally useful this day. In her desperation to convince Garris to stay, she had made herself late for the first meeting of the new council. Not only had she given the impression it wasn't important enough to be on time, but her absence had also allowed the council to wander into topics she would have rather they avoided. It was supposed to be an organizational meeting, to lay out the agenda for subsequent meetings. But without her there to keep things on track, the discussion had taken an undesirable turn. They had made it their first order of business to discuss the dismantling of all of Shirdon's military resources.

Well, technically, according to the agreement she had just drafted and convinced everyone to sign, in three months *all* powers of the old council would expire. In those three months, it would be up to the new council to decide which powers to retain and which to send back to the three realms. The new council was made up of direct representatives of each of the three realms, and unless they decided otherwise, the power to form and keep a standing army would soon disappear. So the matter the new council had blundered into was whether there would be any reason for Shirdon to continue to have military power.

The desire to eliminate it was understandable. Centuries of feeling oppressed by the council and its overbearing laws had led the new council, guided by the three realms, to seek a permanent end to that possibility. What better way than to remove any force Shirdon might possess that could be used as an instrument of oppression.

A consensus appeared to have rapidly formed around the idea that each realm would maintain their own militia, with Shirdon able to take control, but only in the most dire of emergencies. It seemed clumsy and untenable, leading to too many unanswerable questions. What defined a dire emergency? What if disagreements arose over the severity of the threat? Who would arbitrate? Who would decide?

It seemed an especially egregious plan, given the prophetic vision of a massive invasion Jon had received. How was a leader with no military resources supposed to defeat such a dire threat? Had she been present when the topic came up, she could have perhaps pointed out all of that or steered the discussion elsewhere. As it stood now, she needed Jon's input to decide how best to handle the situation. All she could do in the meantime was gather influence, which was where this visit to Ahmet came in. He did have influence, particularly with the two Erdish members of the council, as well as with many of their contacts and supporters. At the very least, she could try to enlist his aid in casting doubt on the idea of dismantling Shirdon's forces.

However, there was a secondary motive for this visit. One that was closer to her heart. Kayleen pulled out the coin Garris had given her, the one he had found on the body of one of those sent to kill him. She flipped it over, so the head faced up, and examined the unusual image on its glittering gold surface. Crouched there, with its claws out, was a snarling tiger with the wings of a dragon and stinger of a scorpion. As far as she could recall, it was not a symbol associated with any realm, organization, or mythology.

Gold was more valuable than silver, and the tendency was to put significant or beautiful images on gold coins. For anyone to put such an off-putting and intimidating image on such a valuable coin seemed odd. Her hope was that as a former designer of coins, Ahmet would know its origins. That, at least, would give her a place to start her investigation.

As the street curved around in its circular path, she sped past Dellia's quaint house of wood and stone. Perched at the edge of the plateau, it was one of the smaller homes in the row, a little cramped for two people. She had offered Jon a larger one, but he wanted Dellia to stay in the home she had known. And he seemed particularly fond of the idea of living his life in the simple way that she had. Kayleen smiled. In some ways, his views were similar to her own, such as finding it repugnant to flaunt his status.

Kayleen glanced ahead as Ahmet's home came into view. It was larger than Dellia's, and, like the homes of many of the more influential, it sat on the edge of the plateau with a spectacular view of the mountain, woods, and hills below. The moment she spotted it, the wrongness of the scene struck her, and it took her only a moment to realize what it was.

The windows were still shuttered, and the sturdy wooden door was ajar. Only it wasn't just ajar—it stood almost half-open. To leave the windows shuttered during the day was a bad sign on its own. It usually meant the person wasn't home or was too sick to get up and open them to let in some light and air.

She had never known Ahmet to leave Shirdon. It was hard not to suspect their association might be two-way, that perhaps he was using her and others to keep abreast of council politics and report back to the leaders in Erden. If so, his constant presence in Shirdon was not happenstance. It had a purpose. Either way, for him to be missing was a bit unusual. Even if he had left the city, who would take a trip and leave their front door half-open? The breeze remained too light to have blown it that way, and with no sign of anyone in or around the house, the situation had a peculiar feel to it.

Her thoughts went to a host of worst-case scenarios. Perhaps he was ill, or someone had broken in, or both. Perhaps a theft had gone wrong, or he had been injured and was dead or dying.

She mounted the steps and peered through the doorway into the rooms beyond. It wasn't entirely dark—not all of the windows were shuttered. That, too, seemed odd.

She called his name several times, her voice resounding within the modest stonework walls. When she got no answer, she announced her intention to enter, shoved the door the rest of the way open, and stepped inside.

Light streamed through the window at the back of the house, drenching the kitchen in its warm yellow light and spilling into most of the other rooms. The window side of the house sat at the edge of the plateau, and through the large opening, she could see the shadow of the mountain, stretching far out across the rolling hills of Erden.

Kayleen called out, froze, and raised an ear, listening, but the house remained still and quiet. She called out and listened again, but all that met her ears was the sound of birds chirping, echoing up from the mountainside far below. It took only moments to check every room in the house, but there were no signs of anyone home and no signs of theft. Every room seemed neat and clean and in order.

Her mind went back to the oddity of the one open window, when all the others remained shuttered. She strolled up to it, glancing around for any sign of where Ahmet might be or what might have become of him. On a desk near the window, she spotted a note, set out as if left behind for a roommate to read. But Ahmet lived alone.

She bent over to examine it. The writing looked just like his familiar chicken scratchings. How someone with such abysmal handwriting could have once designed beautiful images stamped into coins remained a mystery. She stared down at it, feeling a little like she was intruding into his private life, but was urged on by the unsettling nature of the whole situation.

She leaned over and read the page's three simple lines:

I grow sicker each day.
The pain is unbearable and getting worse.
I want to end it now while I still can.

It was signed AHMET OF DULE, his native home.

It took quite a while—or so it seemed in the dim light of the main room—for the meaning of the note to sink in, the meaning of the phrase TO END IT. Or perhaps the words had sunken in the instant she read them, and her mind simply refused to accept the obvious conclusion. It was a suicide note.

Even the very concept wouldn't sink in. The man she knew, the one who imagined himself important, wouldn't give up like this. He would snarl or laugh in the face of such a cruel fate.

Kayleen scanned her memory, trying to summon recent images of him. Two days ago, while in the market buying food for Eejha to prepare for dinner, she had spotted him in the distance as he ascended the long stairway carved of stone that led from Shirdon to the plateau. He had bounded up the steps with no limp, hunch, wince of pain, or other sign of infirmity. In fact, if he was sick, she had no recent memory of him that betrayed it.

Then her gaze rose from the chicken scratching to the window. In an instant, it took on a whole new and menacing meaning. She approached it with terrible trepidation. Placing one hand on the wall, she slid her head through and peered down. There, at the base of the cliff, lay a body, bloody and twisted. Ravens pecked at his face as the wind blew through the ragged shreds of his red-stained clothes. Even as mangled as it was, it resembled Ahmet's stout form.

455

For a moment, Kayleen stared in shock and disbelief, her mind still refusing to accept what met her eyes. Then she yanked her head back inside and froze.

She did not scream or cry or even become nauseous. She was not the kind to panic at the sight of bloody and broken bodies, and she had seen enough sickness and death in her life to avoid the queasiness. Yet, below, at the base of the cliff, lay the lifeless remains of a man she knew. One she had broken bread with.

He was not someone she was overly fond of or who she even called a friend, but he was a life. He had friends and family. There were people who would mourn him.

Then her heart sank even further. He was a man of some importance, and she was the one who had discovered his body. Of course, as "first advocate," the representative of the council leader, the task would fall to her to inform his friends and family. But he had no family in Shirdon. In fact, he had never talked about them at all. Who would she even contact, and where would she find them? She wanted to walk away and ignore it, to indulge her shock, but she was here to act for the new council leader. It was her job to handle things.

She pulled herself together. The Erdish members of the council might know whom to contact. They could help her. But the barracks would have to be her first stop. She would need to get the guards working on retrieving the body, and it wouldn't hurt to have them take a closer look at the house.

As Kayleen headed across the room, something much more troubling gathered its dark and disturbing shape in her heart. In one blow, she had lost her best asset in helping prevent the dissolution of the Shirdon military and her best chance to find information on Garris's mystery coins.

A part of her, the part that often proved invaluable in council politics, wanted her to be suspicious. This could be a blow to Jon and his fledgling council. Rumors would spread of Ahmet's death occurring so soon after Jon took over. At a minimum, it would be considered a bad omen or a sign of a leader unable to protect the people of Shirdon. If this was a politically motivated killing aimed at harming the new leader, it was striking in its elegant simplicity; it killed several birds with a single stone.

As she stepped out of the house and back into the bright afternoon sun, she shook off her unease. She was letting her imagination run wild. After all, if the goal was to harm Jon or Garris, there were far more direct ways of doing so than killing Ahmet, a man who wasn't a part of the government here or anywhere.

Kayleen turned her attention back to immediate concerns. Yes, she would stop first at the barracks and put her newly promoted captain Alkis to work retrieving the body. Once she had finished there, she would need to visit Fraysha and Haarash, the Erdish members of the new council. It would be her duty to inform each of Ahmet's death so they could determine what they wanted to do with the body.

When she finished all that, she planned to settle in her room and have a drink in memory of an old acquaintance. She would rather share that drink with her oldest and dearest friend, but Garris was indisposed, at least to her, and likely to remain that way for some time. Tomorrow would be a new day, and she would definitely get to the bottom of more than one mystery, not the least of which was whether there was any proof of this illness Ahmet had supposedly come down with so abruptly.

Dry needles crunched underfoot, grating on Garris's nerves as he tried to move quietly down a mostly dirt path that weaved its way through towering pines. Not that he needed to move quietly. It was merely a long-standing habit, a side effect of years of constantly being on guard. He was headed for the home of a fellow named Ruepo. His cabin was situated a short distance outside of Shirdon and far enough from the base of the plateau for the pines to give the goings-on at his residence year-round privacy.

This whole search for the forger had turned out to be a bit of a fiasco. On the surface, it had seemed straightforward enough. Kayleen wanted to find whoever was out to kill him. She was council leader, and he a protector, following orders. It wasn't like this was new to him. Once upon a time, he had worked for Kayleen when he had been the protector assigned to her as a council member. During that long-ago time, he may have kept things a little casual in his interactions with Kayleen, but he had always been strictly business when it came to anything related to carrying out an assignment.

Yet, while he was once again a protector and she a council leader, this felt completely different. Well, to be precise, he was a "high protector," but he'd never call himself by such a hoity-toity title. And well, actually, Kayleen wasn't a council leader either. She was "first advocate," she represented Jon, and Jon was … well, Jon. It wasn't like he needed to impress the man, or follow his orders, or even keep a straight face when he gave those orders, but that was beside the point.

Perhaps what really made this seem different was that this hadn't been an order. In that respect, it had seemed more like one of Kayleen's misadventures. Like the time she had talked him into breaking into the Shir Keep kitchens after dark to whip up a midnight snack. He had envisioned pastries and pies, but all they found were slimy fish eggs and whipped duck liver—yuck. To top it all off, they'd been discovered, yelled at and dragged in front of Eejha for more humiliation and scolding.

Then again, it didn't feel like one of Kayleen's debacles either, perhaps because this was about him and who was out to kill him. Somewhere in the back of his mind, he sensed he ought to be more concerned that someone was out to "off him." Yet, he wasn't. Perhaps because he had merely become used to the idea of assassins out to get him, but it seemed like more than that. It seemed like it didn't really matter. If he was dead or alive, banished or home, hated or loved, none of that could erase his past or change the things he'd done.

The large cabin built of rough-hewn logs jumped out at him as he rounded a corner. Forests crowded it on three sides, as if to hide its presence. The shutters were closed tight too—a sign that no one was home—and several large bells stood in the yard hanging from expensive-looking decorative mounts. The ornate bells and custom-made mounts didn't quite match the wilderness setting or the crude look of a cabin, as if someone of generous means was trying to appear mundane.

Garris stepped lightly up the walk, stopped in front of the sturdy wooden door, and gave it a solid rap. No answer. So he waited.

It had been a twisted path to get here. At first, he had no idea how to find the forger. He had grown up in Shirdon and at one time had known almost everyone, if not by name, then by reputation, and he'd learned of many dark secrets, treacherous lies, and covert deals. But he had been absent for fifteen years now. A stretch of time easily long enough for all the familiar players to have been rearranged. Those who hadn't grown old or died had moved away or become different people. He could no longer tell who was who.

A whole new crop of younger troublemakers had grown up, and he had lost his implicit feel for the place. He couldn't discern the shady characters from the trustworthy. With no contacts and no place to start his search, his first thought was to go around asking to borrow money. Forgers, counterfeiters, and money lenders were not all that far apart. Even if he couldn't locate a forger, he might meet a money lender with insight or connections that could lead to a forger. At the very least, he might find someone who was like he used to be, someone with their finger on the pulse of the goings-on in the city.

A wooden creak came from inside the cabin. He paused and listened. It might just be the house settling or a dog, so he knocked again and waited. No answer.

Trying to find a money lender seemed the best option available to him. It was true, he was a protector, and by now, he was well known, but a part of that knowing was that he had been exiled. Which meant he had some credibility as a less-than-upstanding fellow. He had hoped that very reputation might work in his favor, that it might predispose the less desirable elements of the city to hold their tongues a little less.

He was wrong. In practice, it had worked against him at every turn. The upstanding among the residents of Shirdon remained cautious of him, not wanting to be seen in the company of one they deemed to be of dubious integrity. The less-than-upstanding wanted nothing to do with the law, or councils, or any of the trappings that came with a protector.

So, as he worked on the problem, he had found the task much more complicated than he had first envisioned. He toured all the drinking establishments in town, pretending to be drunk and staggering up to nearly every young stranger, bellowing that he needed more drink and asking if he could borrow money. It got him nowhere except a reputation as a stupendous drunkard who could drink in half a dozen establishments in a single night.

Another sound came from inside the cabin, a scratching, like something moving across a wooden floor. Claws maybe, or a chair sliding, or a foot dragging. He knocked a third time and waited.

Asking for money had gotten him nowhere, at least until he became strapped for cash and used one of the chimera coins he had appropriated from an assassin to pay for his drink. The bartender picked it up and stared at it as if it were tainted with disease. Garris had set about reassuring him it was real gold, when the man gave him a flat stare and said something unexpected. He responded that he knew it was real; he'd seen one before.

When pressed by Garris, in his best slurred voice, the bartender couldn't recall who had given it to him. He even scoffed at the idea of remembering who paid for each drink and with what. So it seemed to be another dead end, but as he staggered up from his chair and feigned stumbling over the leg, the man froze for a second, then said. "Ruepo."

Unsure what a Ruepo was, Garris wobbled back around to face him.

The man snapped his fingers. "That's who gave me the coin, Ruepo. I remember now because he was new in town, and I wondered where he came from to have such an odd coin."

460

AYLUN

Not wanting to draw attention to his curiosity, Garris nodded, then pretended the movement had thrown him off-balance. He slurred out an almost unintelligible "thanks" and then went on his way. There would always be a chance to come back and ask more questions, but he deemed it best not to appear to be interrogating the man.

He spent the remainder of the day making discreet inquiries about Ruepo in various corners of Shirdon, but there seemed a curious absence of information. Most people were known. Things they'd said, places they frequented, their interests, were all fragments of information the observant in town would note. Those fragments got repeated, merged, and spread, and over time they painted a public picture of who that person was. Ask about anyone, and you'd eventually get enough comments to form an image of at least who they pretended to be, the side of them they let people know.

With Ruepo, he found nothing. He was rarely seen, spoke little, and avoided inquiries into his background. Of course, that alone told you he was a bit reclusive and secretive. It also made people suspicious, and so there were more than a few comments about Ruepo being involved in black market dealings, or the Verod, or simply up to no good. With no other leads on anyone or anything, rumors of black market dealings were more than enough to warrant a visit to the man.

Yet he had knocked on the door in front of him three times now and received no answer, so here he stood facing another dead end. He turned and started to walk away, when another wooden creak came from inside. This time, the quality of the creak made it certain—something or someone was inside the house. Garris returned to the door. With the recent death of Ahmet, he could justify entering by claiming a heightened concern that something similar might be happening to Ruepo. After all, he was a protector, and it wasn't outside his domain to investigate something suspicious, like noises inside a supposedly empty house. He pulled the door open and crept inside.

In an instant, movement drew his attention to a man sitting behind a desk. He was Elorian, with long black hair and sideburns. His solid look and neat grooming lent him an imposing air, made more so by his long angular face, thick mustache, and short beard. He looked up, and something flashed across his face, subtle surprise perhaps. "You ..." His expression turned to one of annoyance. "You barge into my home unbidden?"

Garris held still for a moment. Who used the word "unbidden" these days? He granted the man a brief bow of his head. "Apologies. I heard noises from inside, and after what happened to Ahmet, I was concerned that ..."

The annoyed look deepened, but when Ruepo spoke, his voice seemed more derisive than irritated. "That I was going to kill myself? Is that it? Did it ever occur to you that I merely didn't want you to disturb me? Isn't that more likely?"

There had also been a commanding quality to his questions. It bore a striking resemblance to the tone many council members used when you questioned an order they didn't care to explain. For a moment, he had the impression he was speaking to one who was used to being in authority.

Garris granted him another brief bow of his head. "Well, it's clear I am unwelcome here, so I apologize for the intrusion." He brought himself up taller and started to turn away, then paused. "It's just ... well ... never mind." Garris bowed for what he suspected would be a final time. This wasn't going well.

Ruepo rolled his eyes, obviously seeing his ploy for what it was: a transparent attempt to slip a question into his departure. The man sighed. "You came for a reason." He stated it in a flat voice, then paused as if waiting for a response, but his intonation had not been in the form of a question.

Uncertain whether to leave or respond, Garris paused and acted as if he was thinking.

Ruepo became impatient. "Well, what is it? Why were you knocking on my door?"

Garris took a cautious step forward. Not that he needed to be careful, he just needed to buy time to consider how to broach a tricky topic. Asking Ruepo if he knew of any forgers would almost certainly be met with indignation and denial, regardless of whether he knew any or not. Still, in this brief discussion, the man had been very direct, and he struck Garris as one who appreciated others who were equally direct.

He took another step forward. "I think someone has been trying to kill me."

Ruepo showed no sign of surprise or shock, remaining unusually unaffected for someone who just heard about an attempted murder. "And you think that someone is me?"

"No, no. Not at all. It's just that … well, you can understand that I might be highly motivated to find out who that someone is."

"And what would make you think I'd know anything about it?"

"I don't. In fact, I know very little about you. Only a word or two mentioned by strangers."

Ruepo sighed, seeming annoyed again. "Look, I could ask you why you came here if you don't know anything about me. We could go around and around while you stand there and beat around the bush. But I don't really care why you're here, and I have no desire to play guessing games." He leaned forward with his elbows on the desk and pressed his fingertips together. "So, in the interest of getting rid of you as quickly and permanently as possible, let's skip all that and get right to the point. Why do you think people are trying to kill you, Protector Garris?"

Garris stood for a moment absorbing all the man had conveyed in that short statement. Ruepo, if that was his real name, recognized him and knew he was a protector. He hadn't flinched at the idea someone was trying to kill him, and his assertion that he didn't care why Garris was here seemed completely believable. Yet his question made it appear as if he had just made an outright offer to help—an odd approach to someone he could just summarily dismiss as an unwanted intruder.

Maybe it was exactly as the man said: he wanted to get rid of him, and proving he would be of little help was the quickest and most permanent way to do it. Garris stared right at him, trying to judge the best way to elicit his aid. This man was even more direct than he had seemed at first and remarkably calm for one who might construe a protector's interest as an accusation of involvement in shady activities.

Garris didn't mind being direct either, so he nodded approval. "In my exile, there were several attempts to kill me every year. Some were understandable. Retribution, you might call them. However, quite a number were by people who I know were hired under false pretenses."

"And you know they were hired under false pretenses how?" The man suddenly seemed quite interested, as if intrigued by the puzzle of it. Normal people tended to be put off by the idea of assassination. For a moment, he had the impression that to this man, the last fifteen years of Garris's life was a murder mystery, and he the detective who loved to unravel such puzzles.

Garris withdrew one of his glittering gold coins and placed it heads up on the desk with a clank. "They all had the same unusual coins on them. Unusual enough that it seemed likely they'd been paid by the same person. And each one had written instructions that I know were forgeries. Quite good forgeries, in fact."

"And these forgeries, they were all signed by the same person, I assume?"

Garris nodded.

Ruepo stared into space, then looked back at Garris. "Isn't the simpler explanation that the letters are real rather than forgeries?"

Garris gave it serious consideration. The letters had been from Kayleen, but she acted as if she had no clue about them, and he liked to think he knew her well enough to spot a lie. Yet, he had been in exile. How much did he really know about her after fifteen years? Still, he rejected the idea. Kayleen had no apparent reason to want him dead. She had helped vacate his exile and regain his title as protector, and she'd gone to great lengths to convince him to stay. None of those acts spoke of someone with secret plans of revenge.

Perhaps even more importantly, he didn't *want* to believe it. He had just reclaimed his faith in her and didn't want to go back to believing she loathed him. Somehow, believing she still cared about him was preferable, even if it might be a dangerous delusion.

He shook his head. "No. The letters aren't real. They're forgeries. I'm certain."

Ruepo spent several moments in apparent contemplation. Then, he leaned back in his chair. "I do happen to know of a few forgers ... by reputation only, you understand. But I don't see how that could help you. The chances that any of them is your forger is remote, at best."

"Even one might be useful. They are likely to know of others."

Ruepo nodded. "Were the letters sealed?"

"Yes."

"And the seal, did it look authentic?"

"Perfect, actually."

Ruepo fell silent again for a while. "And when did you find the first assassin? Or rather, when did they find you?"

"The year I was banished."

"So, fifteen years ago. And the last?"

Now it was Garris's turn to pause. It hadn't really occurred to him, but he had found the last note almost two years back. Long enough to make the gap unusual. "Just shy of two years ago."

"Hmm." Ruepo leaned forward. "Could be Ujaan. He was fairly well known in the right circles. Fifteen years ago, he had just started making a name for himself, and he dropped out of sight around two years ago."

Garris nodded. "I don't suppose he lived in Shirdon at the time of his disappearance."

"No, in a house just outside of Ghokal, northeast of Indare."

Garris sighed. It was a long shot, the sort of wild goose chase he didn't care for. He was likely to travel all the way to Ghokal and find an abandoned house with no sign of Ujaan and no clue where he had gone. Or worse, find a new resident who'd obliterated every trace of the man.

Still, it was all he had, and it would get him out of Shirdon for a few days. "Thank you. If I need more informa—"

"Oh no. I want you gone permanently. I thought I made that clear from the start." Ruepo leaned back in his chair. "Now, I've given you all you'll get from me. Don't come back."

"Good day, then." Garris spun around and marched out the door. Pine needles crunched underfoot as he traversed the same mostly dirt path back toward Shirdon.

He could be packed up and ready to go before nightfall. He'd stop by and bid his mother a brief farewell. She would accept his leaving if she knew where he was going and when he expected to return. Then he would be away from this unfamiliar hometown and its uncomfortable, yet familiar, faces. And at least for a few days, he could go back to pretending that he was okay, that he had no past.

Aylun looked down from the bluffs to the bright sun, glittering on the waters of Kinshai Lake. The light shimmered off the ripples rolling toward a white beach. Once in a while, when he was young, he and a few of his fellow Shou would go missing for a day, to the extent that anyone could go missing when they lived with someone who could see their future. For that brief time, they would head north along the shores of Kinshai Lake and spend an evening laughing and playing, singing, and dancing on a beach much like the one below.

It had been a day of playing hooky, a brief respite from responsibility and everything else the Augury stood for. Ayrue always relished those days, running along the beach, teasing her friends, climbing the bluffs, and generally acting out in wild antics. Megan would love it too. She seemed to be the same kind of free spirit, one who knew how to revel in cutting loose.

AYLUN

Aylun turned his attention to the treacherous path ahead. Somewhat worn with use, it jerked and twisted upward, over ragged rocks, around jutting boulders, and through gravel-strewn ruts. The location Tsaoshi had described was in this vicinity, but Kinshai Lake was vast, and the territory he needed to cover, enormous and inhospitable. The only description he had to go on was that it lay southwest of the village of Daobai, near the edge of the lake.

He had already spent hours wandering back and forth, first toward the village, then back to the lake's edge. Juzhi needed a rest, so he took a break around midday near the bluffs, with the cool air blowing off the water.

As he sat, he surveyed the vast expanse. Fishing junks were still spread out across its breadth, pulling in the day's catch from beneath the shimmering waves. Slope-roofed houses dotted the shoreline here and there, collecting into scant villages, and along the lake's edge ran a jagged road that nearly dipped into the water in places.

His gaze rose up along the bluffs to the ridge that ran along the border of the lake. A short way back from that ridge, far across the rock face, he spotted it: a twisted old plum tree. It appeared ancient, to be sure, and it didn't much resemble the tree outside the oracles' chambers at the Augury. It was broad, and even from this distance, he could see it was dense and heavily branched. But it was much larger, far more twisted and gnarled, and thoroughly unkempt and wild. It beckoned to him, as if to say, "You know what I am, I have always been the symbol of the Augury." There was little doubt that somewhere near it, he would find the old Vault of Time.

Feeling better now that he could see what was surely his destination, he finished his brief meal of sweet, dried apricots and smoked fish, and then struck out for the tree. It was late afternoon by the time he arrived. On closer inspection, he became more certain than ever. The tree was older and less vigorous, but it was the same variety as the one in the Augury. It had been planted in a dirt-filled rut in the otherwise solid rock of the ground. A short distance away lay a small, square building of heavy stone, overgrown with vines. Beyond an encroaching tree and a generous overhang was a dark hole where a door had undoubtedly once stood.

Aylun dug out his flamestone, slung it in a net, tied it to his belt, and ventured through the dark opening. The amber rays revealed a set of carved stone stairs leading downward. At the bottom lay a broad, dark room. The walls, carved from the native stone, were riddled with cracks and large holes near the floor. They were generous enough to fit his hand into them with his fingers out-stretched, as if they could have been made by some type of enormous, dog-sized rat.

In the corner to the right of the stairs stood a set of empty shelves. If any doubt had remained that this place was the one he sought, the shelves dispelled it. Their type and notched construction were an exact match for the ones in the Augury.

With great care, he scanned the shelves, but they contained no chests or items of any kind. As expected, whatever they once held had been moved when the vault was relocated. He kicked through the debris and dirt covering the rest of the floor, but the room was barren, except for the empty shelves and the remains of a giant rodent skeleton crumbled in one corner. He kicked it apart, but all he found were bits of hair and bones, fragments of wood, and dry twigs.

In the entire room, there were no papers, plaques, boxes, jewelry, or any other trappings of human civilization. But, as he turned to leave, he noticed the dirt on one of the walls had an almost impercep-tible rectangular indent somewhat taller and wider than he was. It had the shape of a door.

He strolled over and held up his flamestone as he swiped a finger across the surface. Beneath a thick layer of crud and dust was a hard, cold metal surface, covered in ridges. He used his sleeve to wipe away the coating. At first, what lay beneath reminded him of the door they had found in Lanessa, in the den of thieves. It was gleaming metal with intricate engravings and had a similar handle and keyhole.

When he finished clearing away the dirt, he stepped back and held the flamestone high to view his handiwork. The results were stunning. The light glinted off a dark metal door with an arching branch inlayed in obsidian that ran from one corner to the other. The branch was lush, sprouting leaves of jade and smothered in delicate blossoms of mother-of-pearl.

He peered through the keyhole, but all that met his eye was darkness—no sign of what kind of room lay beyond or what it might contain. Still, it was suspicious. Who would invest in such an intricate and beautiful door if not to protect something of great importance? If it still remained here, that thing of importance could easily be a warning from the Greatest of Oracles. It even made sense: if the old Vault of Time did indeed contain a warning of such dire consequences, then why not keep it securely locked away until the right moment? Yet, there were no signs or writing of any kind near the door to reveal when that right moment might be.

He spent quite a while examining every detail of the door and frame, then moved on to each shelf, corner, and rafter, searching for even the slightest clue, yet found nothing more. He sighed. His only option now was to return to the Augury and find out if the Tsaoshi, the man who had known of this site, perhaps knew what lay behind the door or how to open it.

Morning was approaching by the time Aylun made it back to the Augury. Too much in a hurry for his normal route, he found an inside corner in the wall, one near Tsaoshi's quarters. He scaled it by bouncing off the edges of stones on either side to propel himself up and over the wall. He remembered the usual routes for patrols, so he skirted them on his way to Tsaoshi's chambers, then dove through his side window and rolled to a crouch next to the bed. Tsaoshi was sleeping, as expected, so he held his flamestone over the Great Oracle's face.

He stirred, and Aylun signaled him to be quiet. "I found the old site of the Vault of Time."

The Great Oracle's eyes lit up. "And?"

"There was nothing left behind, at least not that I could find. However, there was a locked door, and I have no idea what might lie behind it."

Tsaoshi considered for a while. "Hmm. I cannot recall ever hearing of such a door. It is not mentioned in our archives."

"That seems odd."

The Great Oracle nodded. "A locked room implies something valuable. What you seek may very well be behind it."

"Agreed. But if you were unaware of the door, then I suppose you do not know of any key that might unlock it."

Tsaoshi paused, then shook his head.

"Hmm. I gave it a great deal of thought on the way back here, and I have an idea how I might open it."

"A way to open it? Care to elaborate?"

He paused. Megan's key, the one she had taken from the dragon, had to be an artifact of great importance, given the way it seemed to open things it shouldn't. That made it a secret he shouldn't reveal, even to the Great Oracle. "I can't say more. Just trust me. I will return and let you know once I have succeeded." Aylun turned to go, then remembered his prior oversight.

He stepped back to the bedside and knelt next to Tsaoshi. "Oh, I am sorry for my negligence during my last visit. I failed to offer my thanks for sending Ruahn to help us in Mundus. Without your help, it would have taken much longer to find Jon and return Megan to him."

A stunned look came over Tsaoshi. "What?"

"Thank you for sending Ruahn to guide us to Jon."

He shook his head. "I never sent Ruahn. She simply disappeared one day."

Aylun froze. "But she knew where Jon would be. She knew the exact time and place of his arrival days in advance. If you didn't send her, then ..." He stared down at Tsaoshi, the warm yellow light of his flamestone sketching dark shadows on the features of his former master's face. He remained crouched there for a time, frozen as the implication drew ever darker shapes in his heart.

If the Great Oracle had not sent Ruahn, then why had she lied about it? What was her purpose in helping them? Then a disturbing truth struck him. He had fled before he witnessed Megan walk up to and meet Jon. If Ruahn foresaw where Jon would be, then did she also foresee that Aylun would leave Megan alone and unprotected before he saw their actual reunion? Could she be working with someone else? The camp was filled with so many strangers that anyone could have hidden there unnoticed. Had he just sent Megan into some kind of terrible trap?

He stood up. "I think I need to find Megan as quickly as possible."

Tsaoshi nodded again and motioned for him to make haste.

Chapter Eighteen

MEETINGS

Exhausted, Jon covered his eyes and leaned his head back. With an exasperated sigh, he tried to untangle the confusion of topics scrambled up in his head. This was worse than any cram session he'd endured in school, particularly because it wasn't merely that he was being force-fed information. He was being asked to make decisions—decisions that affected lives.

Trapped in this small room, he had spent what seemed like forever staring out its one window at the sweeping view of the hills below, while Kayleen hashed over one controversy after another. She droned on until her voice no longer registered, and the topics all blurred together in a slurry of muck that he was certain would splash back on him the moment he uttered an opinion.

Illegal goods, black markets, smuggling, trade negotiations, bribery, kickbacks, graft, protests, taxes, extortion, defamation, arms, religion, policing, and you name it—they were all areas about which Kayleen had come to him for opinions. And, in each case, there were all kinds of gray areas—situations where he was expected to take a stand. But he didn't want to take a stand. He didn't want to have an opinion. Opinions led to debate. Debate to laws. Laws led to activities being illegal, policing of crimes, and some-one getting hurt.

Each detail, each implication, each crumb of minutia was a trap that would snare him and bring him down like a hunted deer. All he had wanted was to let the three realms rule themselves, but Kayleen was determined to make that impossible.

473

He had entered this first meeting with high hopes that she and the three realms would do most of the deciding for him. Instead, he was being worn down by an endless stream of controversies that seemed to be just the kinds of things the rulers of Talus, Erden, and Elore wanted them to stay out of. This wasn't working out at all as he had envisioned.

He uncovered his eyes to catch Kayleen scrutinizing him with strained patience, or at least it seemed strained. Surely, she must find this all as trying as he did. At several points, he had even gotten the sense she was as frustrated as he was and just very practiced at hiding it.

Her solid wooden chair didn't creak as she leaned forward. "This is the"—She began silently counting off on her fingers but gave up partway through. "It's at least the thirteenth topic, and I am more confused than ever." She interlaced her fingers and set her hands on the swirling-black surface of the polished marble table between them. Then she leaned forward as if to emphasize her point. "I simply cannot represent you if I do not know what you want or what you think. You have to give me something to go on here."

Jon considered for a moment. He thought he had done well. It seemed like he'd deftly steered away from every decision, implying Kayleen or the rest of the council should figure it out without him. Yet, her patient facade seemed to be eroding, and with each passing hour, her responses betrayed a growing dissatisfaction.

He was puzzled. What could be behind her discontent? What was so wrong about leaving the three realms to rule themselves with almost no council interference? Why was that so unacceptable to her?

She straightened and pointed at him. "See? Right there. There's something going through your head. I can see it on your face, but you're not talking; you're not saying what you think."

He hesitated. She was right. He had been dancing around what he really thought this entire time—hinting at it by his refusal to take a stand on any topic, but never outright saying it.

She leaned back and seemed to relax. "Don't be embarrassed or worry about what I'll think. Just speak your mind. I promise, I will not pass judgment. ... Okay, I *will* pass judgment, but I promise, I will understand."

Jon nodded. She was perceptive, that's for sure. She knew he was holding his tongue. Then it occurred to him: why exactly *was* he keeping quiet? He'd spoken his mind just fine with Dellia. But this was different. Every opinion he conveyed to Kayleen might translate into action. Action that his history assured him would lead to disaster on every level.

He pulled his eyes from the shiny surface of the black table and looked her in the face. "You want the truth?"

Kayleen nodded, her eyes begging. "Please. For Adi's sake, yes, please."

"The whole idea behind handing power back to the three realms was so I could avoid making decisions. I worry ... no, I am *certain* that whatever I decide will turn around and hurt or kill people."

This time, she remained quiet for a long while, then nodded. "You're right. It will."

The admission sent a jolt through him. She was confirming his worst nightmares. He stared at her. "See, that's what—"

Kayleen held her palm up to stop him, but her expression remained calmer and more patient than it had been in hours. "I'm glad you realize that. It's something Braye and Aapri and Shaon and most of the old council have long forgotten. All decisions have consequences. When people make their own decisions, they only have themselves to blame when things go wrong. When you, as a leader, take their power by unnecessarily making decisions for them, any ill consequences they suffer are your fault." She smiled. "It encourages me that you can see that, when so many leaders feel entitled to control the lives of their subjects. But that doesn't mean you can avoid making all decisions."

"What's wrong with letting the three realms rule themselves? Let *them* make all those decisions."

"I agree, in part, but there are things that no single realm can do by itself."

"Like what?"

"A few basics, such as laws against killing each other. That shouldn't be up to the realms to decide. Beyond that, they need protection, and not just from threats, but from each other. And someone has to ensure they treat each other fairly."

Jon sighed and turned his head from the cramped room to stare out the window at the beautiful blue sky and soaring view. Where could he even begin? None of what she had mentioned required the new council to interfere. It could be done by agreement between the realms. They could sign treaties and form pacts to cover them. He returned his gaze to her face.

A map lay on the table, and before he could respond, Kayleen pointed to Erden. "Look, what if someone from Erden murders someone from Talus, then flees back to their home realm?" She walked two fingers across the map to Talus, motioned stabbing the map, then finger-walked back to Erden. "Does the murderer go unpunished because they didn't kill in their own realm?"

"No, of course not. But can't the realms just have some kind of agreement to, I don't know ... extradite murderers or something?"

"Sure, but what if Erden doesn't want to spend any resources to track down the murderer? Why waste their time hunting down someone who killed a person from another realm? After all, their resources are better spent protecting their own people, the ones who depend on them, the ones who support them with their taxes."

He considered for a moment. Perhaps she had a point, yet there had to be a way that didn't involve imposing his will on them. "I don't know ..."

"What about the reverse? What if a dignitary from Talus murders someone while visiting Erden and gets caught? Can an Erdish tribunal put a Talesh dignitary on trial? Could they imprison or kill them, or does the dignitary get away with killing a citizen of Talus?

Wouldn't it cause a rift between the two realms if such matters were not decided in advance?"

The idea of causing a disagreement between realms sent his tension skyrocketing, but before he could speak, she tried again. "Okay, let's go back to our very first discussion, the one about the military."

Jon closed his eyes and groaned. "The one we spent the first two hours on?"

Kayleen gave a firm nod. "Yes. Suppose Shirdon has no standing army, and a huge invasion occurs in Talus, something bigger than they can handle on their own, something that threatens all three realms?"

"Then why couldn't Talus have the power to call on the Erdish and Elorian military?"

"You mean, call on another realm to send a force of unknown power along with its military leaders to invade your homeland?"

"Invade?"

"Yes, that's exactly how it would be seen." She shook her head. "Why would you invite a foreign power to take up arms on your own soil? And even if they were so inclined, how would that work? Send an envoy to beg for assistance? That would take days and place them at the mercy of the other two realms. And if those other two realms did provided assistance, it would take even more days to get the troops into position to help. Those days could mean the difference between standing against the invasion or falling."

She pointed to Erden again on the map. "And what if Erden has a minor problem of their own and doesn't want to spare the troops? What if they simply preferred to have Erdish soldiers die protecting Erdish people and lands?"

Jon sat up straighter in the stiff wooden chair and shuddered at the image of soldiers he commanded dying, even as Kayleen barged ahead. "You need a central military not beholden to any single realm. One that can move to provide assistance at a moment's notice. Not realms negotiating with each other for help that may or may not come until days later."

He pondered for a moment. "Why not use the protectors? They could be given the authority to command the other realms' military forces as the council sees fit."

Kayleen leaned forward and paused in that theatrical way she had that seemed engineered to emphasize her point. Then she spoke in a clear, slow voice. "What protectors?"

The statement hung in the air as he struggled to understand what she was getting at. "What do you mean? A ... a protector like Dellia."

Kayleen shook her head. "You don't get it. They view the protectors in the same light as they do an army. They don't want protectors mucking around in their realm any more than foreign armies. When they are talking about doing away with the military, that includes the protectors."

His stomach lurched as if he were on a plunging roller coaster. Jon stared for a moment in stupefaction. "Oh, man." He slumped back into his chair as the implications of all this theoretical policy stuff suddenly hit home in a very personal way. "We're talking about Dellia's job here. We're talking about her *life*."

Kayleen seemed more than a little put off by his off-the-cuff statement. "Jon, it's not just her. My uncle Edan feels as strongly as Dellia does about his calling. All protectors do. And career military as well. How can this only matter to you when it involves Dellia?"

The words barely registered. It was already happening. His decisions were destroying lives. It was he who had dissolved the old council. It was he who had created the new one. It was his idea to take away all the old council's power and give it to the three realms. He had done this. He had done all of this. The protectors faced extinction, and it was all his fault. How could he stand in front of Dellia and tell her he had destroyed her lifelong dream? It would shatter her world.

Then a tinge of panic hit as he recalled the multiple occasions when she had him pinned to a wall with a knife to his throat. They were fond memories, to be sure, but also a bit frightening. He peered out the window at a distant flock of birds soaring down to light on the boughs of the pines far below. "I don't even know how I would explain it to her."

Even as the words left his mouth, it hit him: the agreement, the one everyone signed. It named Dellia and Garris high protectors reporting only to him. That couldn't be undone, not without breaking the entire agreement. So at least Garris and Dellia would always be protectors.

He heaved a mental sigh of relief as he returned his attention to Kayleen. She seemed more satisfied than she had in hours. "Then we are at least agreed on one thing. We agree to keep the protectors."

Jon froze. He had already made one horrible mistake. The idea of compounding it with another sent his imagination reeling. He recalled the demons in the catacombs in Mundus, the swarm of dead in Kanlu—and how close both had come to being unmitigated disasters. His mind spun through the countless ways they could have gone wrong.

Protectors do dangerous things, things that involve life and death. If he advocated for keeping them, then whatever happened to them, or to Dellia, or Garris, or to the people they tried to protect, would be his fault. If he sent a protector into a situation that was far worse than he thought, then he would be to blame. If they died or other people got killed, it would be seen as his decision that killed them.

As soon as the people saw who he really was, he would be disgraced and ousted, and his chance to be with Dellia destroyed, just as his actions may have already destroyed the protectors. He couldn't let that happen either. He couldn't make things worse than he already had.

He put both hands out as if to stop her. "Wait. Then in some way, anything the protectors do that goes wrong becomes my fault because I wanted to keep them."

Kayleen seemed astounded. "Are you saying you don't want to keep the protectors? Are you serious?"

He shook his head. "No, no, that's not what I'm saying. What I'm saying is: Why does it have to be my decision? Why can't we just let the three realms decide whether to keep them or not and in what form?"

"You mean abstain?"

Jon gave an eager nod.

Kayleen appeared to drop her patient facade and let her manner betray her exasperation. "Look, leaders make decisions. For better or worse, you are a leader. You will have to make decisions."

"Why? Why can't I just let people make their own decisions, then if it goes bad, it's not my fault?"

She closed her eyes and leaned back in her chair. After a moment, she sighed and looked him straight in the eye. "I don't think you've thought this through." Her gaze remained locked on his, unrelenting and unflinching. "Fine, you want to abstain. Sometimes that's best. Most of the time, the ideal outcome is achieved when people are given control of their own destiny. That's perfectly understandable. But if you abstain from every single decision, you will be seen as a weak leader, and nobody will follow you."

She placed her hands down on the smooth black tabletop and leaned forward again, stressing her point. "If people even heard a few seconds of you talking like this, they would lose faith and stop following you. Trust me on this."

Kayleen halted for a moment as if to let her words sink in. "If this new council of yours is going to work, you will need to have an opinion on all of this." She motioned to the stacks of notes she had brought with her. "If you abstain, it will have to be backed by something more than 'I don't want to be responsible.' You will need a compelling reason for every decision you make or decide not to make. People will look to you for that. Because you are a leader, and that's what leaders do."

Jon sat in silence. She was right. This was the flaw in his plan. Still, he couldn't do it. If he made decisions, they would go bad, and then people would stop following him anyway. Dellia's duty would never allow her to be with a disgraced and deposed ex–council leader. He had to find a way to make this all work.

He pointed at Kayleen. "But you're a leader. Dellia says you have been doing this for years. Why can't you just make the decisions for me?"

She gave another exasperated sigh. "Because it won't work. Sooner or later, someone will ask me what Jon thinks, and I refuse to lie or make things up to cover for your lack of … spine or maturity or whatever is behind this crazy aversion to making decisions." She paused for a second as her expression softened. "Sorry, but it's the truth, and you need to hear it."

The accusation left him stumped. He looked away. "I need time to think."

She gave a crisp nod. "Fine. That's the first intelligent thing you've said this afternoon. Here are my notes." She piled the stacks of paper, one onto the other, and slid the resulting single large stack over to his side of the table. "I have outlined all the major issues in detail. I will stall the new council. I'll tell them how complicated it all is and how you are studying the issues. Which will be true. Because you *will* be studying my notes." She paused, as if to make sure her insistence would be heard and recognized for the ultimatum it was.

Jon gave a reluctant nod.

Kayleen continued. "I think I can buy you a few days, a week at the outside. Think long and hard about whether you want this to work, and if you do, then come back here with an opinion on every single one of these issues." She began to rise but stopped halfway up. "And if you want to abstain, I will support you with everything I have, but you absolutely must have a persuasive reason as to why it is best for the realms to decide. One that is rooted in the best interests of everyone, not one that is about *you* or what *you* want." She finished standing and turned to go.

Jon blurted out, "Can you not tell Dellia about the whole 'end of the protectors' thing?" He stared at Kayleen's back as she froze in her tracks. It was the wrong thing to do, and he knew it, yet he needed time to figure out what to do and how to tell her.

She stared back at him over her shoulder, with a hint of disdain in her eyes.

He hesitated. His heart told him he should reconsider, he shouldn't hide the information from Dellia, but instead, he gave in to his fear and let it speak for him. "Nothing is decided, and I don't want to worry her unnecessarily."

Kayleen raised both eyebrows. "Fine. Whatever you want. But if she asks directly, I won't lie." She faced forward again and stormed out of the room, shaking her head as she went.

It wasn't much of a town, more like a large village, really, which was good. Everyone in Ghokal had been there forever and knew everyone else. Small towns were like that—tight-knit and gossipy—making information easy to come by.

Garris trudged down the narrow dirt-lined street past a newer hodgepodge of a shack, slapped together from whatever seemed to be available at the time. It was a barely standing fusion of old lattice-work, discarded farmhouse wood, and even unused fencing. Across the street stood an older flat-roofed home of brick and clay, splashed with a fading emerald-green wash.

The contrast was emblematic of Ghokal, a blending of the large and small, the new with the old, the run-down alongside the pristine. He visited many homes and shops and stopped every person he met. Almost all of them had an opinion on Ujaan. Most were so similar that it became obvious they were not unique observations but the parroted views of neighbors, friends, and family.

The man was tall, and he had a reputation as reclusive and secretive. He often entertained strangers who liked to hide their faces, and not one native soul had ever visited his place. All agreed that he had disappeared a couple years ago, and no one had any idea where he had gone.

His house lay to the southeast of town, a short ride across the grassy hills. It was a sturdy but run-down building of heavy blocks of clay. It couldn't have included more than four small rooms. Off to the side and set away from the main house stood a small barn with chickens outside, pecking for food in the sunbaked yard.

Garris circled around the property as he closed in, wary that it might be a trap. Ruepo had been a bit too forthcoming for one who seemed so opposed to a protector visiting him. He had been much too difficult to read, and he was either trying to get rid of Garris as quickly and thoroughly as possible, setting him up, or perhaps just sending him on a colossal waste of time.

All signs of life were absent as he neared the front door. He burst inside, banging the door against the wall. His footsteps clapped against the wooden floor as he barged through its three rooms, checking to be sure he was alone. Once finished, he paused for a moment, listening, but all was silent.

Then he performed a more thorough examination of the rooms. Everything appeared long abandoned, being covered in a thick layer of dust. Only a few scant pieces of dilapidated furniture lay scattered around the house, and there were cobwebs draped in the corners of all the rooms. He found not a single thread of clothing or crumb of food in any closet or cupboard.

Based on the amount of dust, it seemed plausible that the house had been empty for about two years. In the main room, a desk and chair remained, appearing prominent amid the empty space around it. The top drawer squealed as he opened it to find a collection of stoppered ink jars, all of them dried out, and many brushes and feathers resting beside them. Brushes were more common for writing in Elore; quills from large birds more so in Talus and Erden. Because of this, most individuals used only one type of writing instrument, and the presence of both lent credence to the idea that whoever lived here had been a forger.

The drawer below held a sizable collection of different types of bark and paper for writing. The bottom drawer was almost empty, except for a cracked seal that contained the mark of Parishad in Indare and a couple stubs of colored candles in brown and purple.

Given that the house seemed to have little to do with Indare, it acted as further evidence that forgery had been done here.

The ready availability of evidence prominently placed in the front room seemed like reason for suspicion. A good forger wouldn't keep his tools where anyone might find them. They would be in a hidden room, or under the porch, or stashed below floorboards, or placed in a secure safe, or even locked in a desk drawer. Still, it wasn't proof of anything, just reason for caution.

Despite the time and energy spent rummaging through the home, he found no maps, writings, or other clues to where Ujaan might have gone. When done, he ventured outside. While not promising, a check of the barn was mandatory. It would be idiotic to invest so much time to get here, only to skimp on his search of the place. The barn door wasn't fully shut, and it groaned as he pulled it the rest of the way open.

The inside was barren and silent. Sunlight shone through cracks in the walls, drawing beams through the dust that drifted aimlessly in the air. The place seemed long abandoned, with nests and debris lying in an unkempt jumble in every cubby and corner.

He poked his head farther inside and checked left and right and around each corner. A small chest at the far end of the barn drew his attention. It seemed newer and less dusty than the rest of the contents, so he took a cautious step toward it, and then a few more.

The soft sound of movement came from the rafters behind him.

He moved to dodge, but a pair of boots swung down and slammed into his back, sending him sprawling.

Garris drew his sword as he twisted and rolled to his feet.

A red-haired figure hit the ground and charged toward him. The man was at least as large as he was and moving with alarming speed. Decked out in leather armor coated with shiny metal studs, and his expression grim, he brandished a gleaming two-handed sword with one hand.

The weapon flew down at Garris. He barely had time to intercept, and the blow sent him farther backward. It was the first of a barrage of hits, striking in rapid succession. The blows never relented long enough for Garris to regain his balance, and they drove him back until he tripped over the chest against the far wall.

Garris pushed off a wooden stud and dove into the man's stomach, wrapping his arms around his waist and lifting him up. He drove his assailant backward across the dirt floor.

The butt of a sword jabbed into Garris's back, and with a shot of pain, he stumbled down onto his face. This man was stronger and faster than he was.

Garris rolled out of the way, catching a glimmer of the sword plummeting down at him. His own weapons lay next to him, so he reached over, grabbed the hilt, and yanked it over his throat to protect it, dragging the tip through the dirt. With his arm braced against the ground, he caught the blow. Then he reached for the man's feet, hoping to pull them out from under him, but his attacker suddenly stiffened, then fell forward, landing on his face in the dirt and dust.

This had an odd familiarity, similar to a not-too-distant day in an alley in Mundus. He looked behind the red-haired man and spotted the stealthy and enigmatic Cain. He recalled the annoying man from that same alley. He'd been of grudging help during that whole nasty business with the demon in the temple. The last he'd seen of the man was when they were being chased down a path through the Malthayan Mountains by a half dozen angry Blood Wolves. Cain had stopped to face the wolves so Garris could escape, and he hadn't seen hide nor hair of him since. The scruffy fellow smiled at Garris. His leathery dark skin was scarred and his short black hair still as wild as his unpredictable personality.

Garris flew onto the attacker and bound his hands behind his back with a piece of rope he'd snatched from the wall.

Cain rolled his eyes. "No need to rush. He won't wake up for a while."

Garris finished and stared. "Weren't you supposed to be dead?"

The man scoffed. "Your faith in me is inspiring."

"Last I saw, you were facing a half dozen of those Blood Wolves."

Cain shrugged. "Three of them went right by me and took off after you. Thanks for that, by the way. I killed one right off. I don't think they're shadow creatures, but it didn't make any difference. They use their noses more than their eyes. I just climbed up high, kept quiet, and waited. Then took care of the other two before they could sniff me out."

Garris stood and offered him his hand. "Well, this is downright annoying. You've helped me three times now."

Cain grasped it and gave it a firm shake. "Helped you? I saved your life."

Garris grunted. "Now whose faith is lacking?"

Cain mumbled, "And it's cute, you thinking it's only been three."

"What?"

He motioned to the man on the ground. "How did you miss this big fella here in this tiny barn?"

"Just sloppy, I guess."

"And the house? I don't even know what you're looking for, and I smelled a trap."

"I just don't like jumping to conclusions."

Cain gave a derisive shake of his head. "Or taking basic precautions, apparently. You see a great big distraction sitting there"—he pointed to the chest—"and you just go for it?"

Garris glared. "And what about you? How did you find me?"

"I got sources."

"And an obsession with me, apparently."

"I could swear back in Mundus I mentioned—I get paid very well. Plus, you did ask every blasted person in Ghokal about Ujaan. It wasn't exactly hard to figure out where you were headed."

Garris gave up. Cain was right. He hadn't tried to hide his trail at all. Why would he? He wasn't banished anymore and unprotected by law. But as much as he hated to admit it, being a protector again had made him careless. He motioned to the man, still lying facedown. "I suppose we have to wait for him to wake up."

Cain reached in a satchel he carried under his cloak. "I can wake him. Let's put him up against that wall there first." He motioned with his head.

They both rose and hauled the man over to the wall, then sat him down, leaning him back against one of the rough timbers with his hands still tied behind his back.

Cain grabbed the man's hair and used it to wrench his head back. He poured a drop of liquid from a vial into the man's mouth, then reached in and rubbed it over his gums with his finger.

In a short while, the man jerked awake and struggled against his bindings.

Garris and Cain sat in front of him and watched.

A mild panic showed on the man's face as he realized he was bound and not able to wriggle free.

Garris sighed and spoke in a low monotone. "What's your name?"

The man froze at the calm in Garris's voice, but his bright brown eyes darted back and forth, panic still reflected there. "Um, Lagesh."

Cain pointed to Garris and grinned. "You know, you attacked a protector here."

Lagesh turned his wide eyes to Cain, staring as if the scruffy man were demented. "I was told he was going to assassinate Ujaan, and I needed to stop him."

Cain's manner remained calm and matter of fact. "No. He's Protector Garris." He reached out and plucked a large and rusty nail from a rotted portion of the wall timbers. His eyes got a curious look of longing as he caressed the roughness of its corroded surface with his fingertip. "Now, if you don't want him to start sticking things in you, I suggest—"

"I'm not sticking things in anyone." Garris glared at Cain.

The color ran out of Lagesh's face.

"Oh, I'm sorry. I misspoke." Using his other hand, Cain pulled out one of his gracefully curved daggers with the azure pommel and brandished it near the man's eyes. "What I meant to say was, if you don't want him to be indisposed while I stick things in you, I suggest you answer all his questions."

Lagesh turned his gaze to Garris, staring with ever-widening eyes. "You're not Garris. He was banished."

Cain grinned. "He doesn't keep up with current events, does he?"

Lagesh shook his head. "No way did I get the drop on a protector, especially not Garris."

Cain eyed Garris again. "See, sloppy."

Garris produced a small wooden tube, removed the paper within, unrolled it, and held it up for Lagesh. "See that there, it says High Protector Garris. And this here"—he pointed to an ink stamp—"that's the seal of the Ruling Council of Meerdon."

Lagesh squinted at the paper. "High protector? There's no such thing."

Cain's grin widened. "It means he's untouchable. He can do anything he wants to you, and nobody will lift a finger to stop him."

Garris shot Cain another disapproving glare. "That's not what it means." Then he grumbled. "I told them not to call me that."

Still seeming panicked, Lagesh stared at the stamp on the official paper. "It could be forged."

Garris ignored him and rifled through Lagesh's belongings. He found a half dozen of the chimera coins and tossed them on the dry, packed dirt near the man's leg. "You were paid with these, weren't you?"

Lagesh looked down at them.

Garris pulled a dozen of the same coins out of his own purse and sprinkled them next to the ones already on the dirt. "Where do you think I got these from?"

Lagesh turned an even lighter shade of pale.

Garris nodded. "That's right. From the last two dozen sent to kill me."

The huge man stiffened. "I wasn't going to kill you. That's the truth."

Garris nodded. "I see. So that sword you brought down on my neck wasn't to kill me. It was cosmetic—to remove my unsightly head? Is that it?"

Lagesh gave a rapid and vehement shake of his head. "It was the heat of the moment, that's all. I swear."

Garris scooped up all the coins, including Lagesh's, and dropped them back in his own purse. "Well, attempted murder of a protector ... that ought to get you locked up for ..." He started counting off on his fingers. "Add the two ... carry the five ... let's see. Ah"—he glared—"pretty much forever."

At that, Lagesh's alarm seemed to reach a breaking point. "Wait."

Garris put his face very close to the man's and lowered his voice. "Look. I've got no argument with you. You're just a big pile of muscles-for-brains that got dragged into something that's not your affair."

Lagesh nodded vigorously.

Garris leaned back. "I want to be reasonable here. So just tell me everything you know about the one who hired you, and I'll forget about the whole attempted murder thing."

Lagesh relaxed some, then eyed Garris. "There's not much to tell. I was approached by this man, Ujaan. He claimed you were a banished mercenary hired to kill him. He said—"

"A mercenary?" Cain scoffed. "It's an old tactic, deflect suspicion by accusing the other guy of the exact same thing you're doing."

Garris motioned to Ujaan. "Go on."

"He said you were going to come to his house, and I should ambush you here to send a message to leave him alone."

Garris grumbled. "And there was no mention of killing?"

489

"Well, he did suggest you'd be mighty determined and not likely to stop going after him. He said you might fight back, and since you exist outside the law, I shouldn't hold back either—that I should do whatever was necessary to stop you, for ... um, for good."

Garris looked back toward the main house. "Describe this Ujaan."

"His face was covered. I couldn't see much."

"Short or tall?"

"Tall. A bit shorter than me."

"Did *he* approach *you*?"

"Yeah."

"Where? In public?"

"Yeah, on the street."

"And his voice?"

"Low, I suppose."

"Did he have any kind of accent?"

Lagesh seemed surprised by the question. "No, but ..."

"Go on."

"He didn't sound exactly like a genuine native either. I could swear he was faking it, covering up an accent."

Garris rose to head outside.

When Cain stood to follow, Lagesh's alarm seemed to rise with him. "Hey, you aren't going to leave me here, are you?"

Garris glared at him as he walked out the door. "Be still."

Cain followed until they were out of earshot.

Garris turned to face him. "The man he's talking about is not Ujaan. Ujaan is secretive. He wouldn't contact someone on a public street. Especially not someone who could implicate him in a murder plot. Plus, I asked a lot of people about him, and not a single one mentioned an accent, which means, to them, he sounded like a genuine native."

Cain nodded. "The house seemed staged. Everything was laid out nice and pretty for you to find."

"Ujaan hasn't been seen for two years. The dust in the rooms would seem to confirm that, but that desk, it didn't have two years' worth."

Cain nodded. "Not to mention, someone who has been missing for two years just *happened* to know you were coming and set up an ambush?"

Garris considered for a moment.

Cain moved closer and lowered his voice. "Someone tried to paint a pretty picture for you. One that looks all sparkly on the outside, but if you dig a little deeper, it's rotten."

"No, you're missing an even bigger picture." Garris locked eyes with him. "I came here to find the one who hired Ujaan. I never suspected him of anything more than a bit of forgery. He's a mere two-bit player and not worth killing over. Ujaan would have known that. He would have known he's more use to me alive than dead. So the whole idea of him trying to ambush and kill me turns him from a forger to a murderer. It's just plain stupid, and you don't get to be a well-known forger by being stupid."

Cain nodded again. "Agreed. Someone *is* trying to kill you, but it isn't Ujaan."

Garris looked back at the barn. "I'm not so sure if trying to kill me was even whole point either. I mean, sure, no one would've shed tears if it had worked, but maybe it was all just a big distraction."

"How do you figure?"

"Only one person knew I was coming to see Ujaan. That means all of this must somehow go back to that one person. It has to. He also had to figure there was a good chance I'd survive and figure it out. And that means his real purpose wasn't necessarily to kill me. It was to send me away, so I wouldn't be around to stop him. What I don't know is what he was planning. What didn't he want me around to stop?"

Cain nodded once again.

"I need to return to Shirdon right away." Garris eyed him.

He stepped back. "What? I'm not going with you."

491

"You said you were well paid?"

Cain nodded.

"Well enough paid to clean up this mess for me and send Lagesh back to wherever he came from?"

Cain grumbled under his breath, "Sure, go. It's not exactly like I'm unaccustomed to cleaning up your messes."

Garris took off. He wondered what Cain had meant by his last remark, but he needed to get back to Ruepo's house as quickly as possible. He returned to Kyri, leaped on her back, and took off. Kyri's hooves thundered along the dirt road, and in no time, the farm had faded behind him.

A short while later, the town, too, had become a memory, lost behind the grassy hills of Erden. He knew he should resist the temptation to jump to conclusions, but his gut was telling him Ruepo was somehow in the middle of all of this. The coins were the key. Their appearance now, in this encounter, one that only Ruepo could have orchestrated, made him more certain than ever that he was linked to the repeated attempts, stretching back fifteen years, to kill him.

Kayleen paused outside the heavy wooden door to Braye's chambers, remembering the last time she had been here. It had been a less than pleasant experience. But this time, she held the upper hand. She was still council leader, or at least she stood in for one. Braye no longer possessed that power, a power he coveted. She had influence she could dangle in front of him like a carrot in front of a horse, and he would prance and bow at her command, because that carrot was sweeter than any he would have for some time.

No, there was no doubt she would get what she wanted, and she wouldn't need to lord her status over him. He would do it willingly because they now shared a common concern. The loss of the protectors would diminish Shirdon's power. Braye still held on to a small portion of that power, and he would never be one to sit by and let his status or control be diminished under any circumstances.

So she'd come here not to condemn him but to recruit an ally. He was a dangerous ally, though. He still maintained connections and leverage of his own in his estimable sphere of influence. Moreover, he had opposed Jon more directly and fully than anyone else on the council, and it remained unclear to what extent he had undermined Jon behind the scenes. Or, for that matter, what part he might yet play. So, first, she had a matter to clarify.

Not bothering to knock, she shouldered open his heavy wooden door and strolled inside Braye's garish chambers. He had decorated it with a heavy hand and an emphasis on priceless artifacts and rare weapons. They had always seemed designed to rub his station and influence in every visitor's face. Now, with his much lower standing, and no direct ability to make law, they seemed to mock his overblown self-importance.

Braye glanced over as she strolled across the huge bearskin rug near the entrance. He stood there, short, bald, and pudgy, stroking his salt-and-pepper stubble as he returned his attention to the giant map of Meerdon that consumed most of his wall. It seemed like another sign of his self-indulgent lifestyle—as if by painting it on his wall, all of Meerdon was his to tinker with, his to control. Well, no more.

As she approached, he looked over at her again with eyes that were deceptively bright and cordial. She recalled the day, not long ago, when they had been far from bright or cordial. For that brief time, he had shown her how cruel and unfeeling he could be as he told her all the reasons he had voted to kick her off the council. He turned to face her, seeming unfazed by her unannounced and uninvited entry.

Braye bowed his head in deference. "First advocate." His eyes met hers. "To what do I owe the pleasure?"

Kayleen halted close enough to make him uncomfortable, then glared. "I have business with you, Braye of Wenford, business that I should have attended to days ago."

It was all she could do not to let his manner throw her off-balance. He had always played the part of a competing council member with opposing views. This deferential manner was a new wrinkle in their twenty-year relationship. Perhaps it was designed to unsettle her. Perhaps it was having the intended effect. But it was she that needed to throw him off-balance, though that was unlikely to happen. Braye was extremely shrewd.

She kept her gaze hard. "Assault. Kidnapping. Torture. And not just any torture, you used a form that's been outlawed for centuries."

Braye seemed flustered, but his aptitude for subterfuge made it impossible to tell if it was genuine. "What? I have no idea what you're talking about."

"Are you denying you kidnapped Jon, tortured him, staged a rescue, and then led him into an ambush so Shirdon soldiers could come to his rescue, making you the hero?"

He stepped back. "Wait a minute. Why would I risk losing a man I already had by leading him into an ambush?"

"Because your torture wasn't working. You needed a new tactic. One that would predispose him to trust you."

"That's absurd. Okay, I admit I tried to fool him with that ambush in Kanlu, and I did arrange for soldiers to get him out of it. I wanted to gain his trust, but the rest you have all wrong."

Kayleen evaluated his face. It was a foolish exercise. He was too practiced at telling bald-faced lies with genuine sincerity. She leaned even closer, hoping to increase his discomfort. "Then tell me why I shouldn't call soldiers in right now to arrest you. Convince me this is all merely circumstantial."

She paused, waiting for a response. It was a threat devoid of substance. She lacked any evidence, save for the word of three soldiers of somewhat dubious repute. Soldiers who wouldn't want to implicate themselves since they were at the heart of Braye's plan. Still, she needed to hear his answer. At least then she would have a starting point to untangle the truth of what really happened.

Braye smiled. "Look, I heard about his abduction from an informant."

"Who?"

494

"Ahmet. He said word had come to him through his contacts in Mundus."

Kayleen paused. It was both entirely plausible and, at the same time, entirely too coincidental. The one person who could corroborate his story was dead. She stared at Mundus on the map covering the wall. "It doesn't fit. You claim you had nothing to do with his abduction and torture, but then who was it that rescued him?"

"How should I know? Look, Ahmet offered to send a mercenary who had the Gift of Maya. He said she'd make herself look like Rillen, then rescue Jon and lead him to Kanlu. He gave me a time and place to set up the ambush and rescue, that's all."

Kayleen considered. It sounded fishy. How could a rescuer give a time and place to meet when the rescue hadn't happened yet? Too many variables might affect the time line. Still, he might be abbreviating the story for her benefit.

It didn't matter anyway. His story was plausible enough, and with no evidence or witnesses to disprove it, there was nothing she could do. Right now, she needed an ally. Jon had once said, "Keep your friends close and your enemies closer." At the time, she had considered it an extraordinarily reckless idea, yet here she was doing exactly that.

She sighed. "You conspired with the three soldiers Grekor, Nikosh, and Pedrus in all this, correct?"

"Conspired? I asked them to keep an eye on you."

"No, you asked them to spy on me."

He shrugged. "Semantics."

"And you asked them to get Jon out of an ambush *you* arranged."

Braye took a deep breath. "I've already admitted as much."

"So, how much do you trust them?"

He seemed thrown by the question.

Kayleen suppressed a smile. Now was the time to draw him into her plan. "Ahmet's death concerns me. He died as I was approaching him to advocate for preserving the protectors."

He nodded. "Ah. And that leads you to believe that Ahmet's death might be suspicious. You want to know if you can trust those three to help you investigate whether it really was a suicide."

"Discretion is utmost."

Braye smiled. "I wouldn't have sent them if I didn't trust them. Not only to get the job done but to stay tight-lipped about it."

"Good. Then write me a letter of introduction."

He gave her a quizzical look and snapped a scornful response, "They are soldiers. You order them about. You don't introduce yourself."

His scolding struck her as uncharacteristic. It let his now obvious grudge leak into his words. She leaned closer and used a more direct and commanding manner: "This needs to be investigated in complete secrecy. Not a single word must get out. In this matter, we are on the same side, and I want you to leverage that goodwill of yours to bind their hearts and tongues to me."

Braye heaved a huge sigh tinged with exasperation. He was hesitating.

She strolled to his ornate, oversized desk and pulled open a drawer.

He rushed over to stop her from rummaging through his belongings but stopped short of interfering with her.

She grabbed a crisp sheet of paper and slapped it down on the smooth surface, then snatched up a quill and thrust it into his hand.

He hesitated again. The reason was obvious. Those three soldiers were resources—*his* resources—and he didn't want to give them over to her. Which is why she had to give him no choice. If she was to keep her enemy close, she needed to take away his allies and make them her own.

She slammed the desk drawer shut with a bang that made Braye jump. Then she glared at him and demanded, "Write. And be as persuasive as I know you can."

He stalled a little longer, then dipped the quill in ink and set it to paper.

AYLUN

Kayleen leaned over his shoulder and watched him write every word. She would make sure this letter made all three of those miscreants *her* miscreants for good.

Chapter Nineteen

THE EYE IN THE BOOK

Out the window, Jon watched a hawk circling above a patch of rocky slope far below. A sudden empathy for its prey came over him. He was like that poor animal, waiting for disaster to plummet from the heavens and tear him apart.

With a weary sigh, he lifted his gaze to the pines that stretched out from the base of Mount Karana, and then past them to the green fields and the line of carts and travelers on the road leaving Shirdon. It threaded its way almost to the horizon, then forked. A few days back, Dellia had pointed to it out her window and explained where they were going. One half wound its way southeast through the rolling hills of Erden, then across the plains to Mundus. The other headed northeast toward Kinshai Lake and Kanlu.

He let his gaze fall and drew a slow, deep breath. As breathtaking as the view might be, it was not why he'd come here. He was avoiding his work, and he had too much he needed to accomplish to be indulging his desire to escape it all. The smooth windowsill was now cool in the afternoon shade as he pushed off from it and returned to the dark marble table.

Kayleen's notes, now dirty and smudged from overuse, lay scattered in piles across the surface before him. They were all words he had read a dozen times or more, until he almost knew them by heart. Yet understanding the issues and knowing what to do about them were two different things. He pulled the notes on keeping state secrets up in front of him and returned to his studying. It was a tangled mess of details, and he fretted over each one as he tried to arrive at an opinion, as he'd promised he would.

This was the same room where he had met with Kayleen, with the same mauve-swirled marble floor and walls. Like the entire keep, its makers had carved it out of the solid rock of the mountain. Yet it was as level and square as any room he had ever seen. In a remote corner of the keep, off the beaten path and away from any distractions, it was a perfect place to read and concentrate in quiet, for all the good it did.

He had spent two arduous days, countless hours, trying to study and think. If there was anything he was good at, it was studying and thinking. So it wasn't that he didn't understand; in fact, he understood all too well. It was that the problem was insoluble. So each time he stared at the pages, his anxiety grew, and he became more disheartened.

Hamstrung by dread and plagued by the thousands of ways each issue could backfire, his imaginings blurred his focus. Bickering between realms breaking into open conflict. People who had harmed no one rotting in jails. Corruption and graft running rampant. Citizens starving to pay their taxes. Soldiers dying in bloody fields because he hadn't collected enough taxes to train and equip them. It went round and round, never-ending, always culminating in red-faced crowds with torches and pitchforks storming his door like that scene in *Frankenstein*, shouting at him, pointing out the obviousness of his blunders and demanding he pay with his head.

The only thing that kept him coming back to this small room, the only thing that allowed him to persevere, was Dellia. After that first arduous day with Kayleen, and each day since, he could return home to her beautiful face, her kindness, and her warmth. Those moments with her were an oasis of happiness in a desert of misery. It had all seemed so simple in the abstract as he imposed his plans on the council, but the reality had become torturous.

This day's session had started at dawn after an almost sleepless night. He had slipped out of his sleeping wife's embrace and come here in the dark to watch the sun peek above the horizon. Since then, he had focused on his studies, consuming countless hours, with the knot in his stomach twisting and coiling around his insides like a burning snake. Every minute became more unbearable as his mind swam through rivers of anxiety-saturated sludge.

He had found an argument in favor of leaving almost every issue in the hands of the three realms. Yet Kayleen's demand still rang fresh and ominous: if he abstained on every issue, he would be seen as a weak leader and expelled. On the other hand, if he didn't, his decisions would go wrong, people would blame him, and he would be expelled. How could he face Kayleen again and ask to abstain on all these complicated issues, knowing she would refuse and he'd be no better off than he was days ago?

A sudden storm of footsteps echoed down the long hallway, drawing his attention away from his task. They clattered toward him with an ominous fury. With his focus worn by hours of study and trepidation, his head came up in a blank stare as Dellia rounded the corner and burst into the marble chamber. Confronted by her taut, angry expression and intense, irate steps, his apprehension exploded, turning his mind the rest of the way into a pile of mush. She marched across the polished floor and stomped to a stop before him, disheveled, with sweat still clinging to her brow.

Afternoons were her time to practice and teach new recruits at the training grounds. She attacked those sessions with a fervor that bordered on mania, and her devotion to her craft and that of her charges was almost obsessive. The room suddenly seemed tiny as she stood above him, her manner as stiff and hard as her gaze. "Would you like to explain to me why I had to learn from one of my students that the protectors might be disbanded?"

Jon gawked at her. With his head still buried in a half dozen political issues, her words swam through molasses as he tried to process them and bring them together into a coherent thought. "What?"

His gaze was drawn to her hand, twisting around the pommel of her dagger. "The protectors. Your new council is considering doing away with them."

His mind finally cleared enough to grasp why she was here and what had prompted her anger. Flustered, he spat out the stupidest comment imaginable. "Oh, that."

The unintended dismissiveness of his comment seemed to infuriate her. She leaned on his desk, her eyes scorching holes in his head. "You didn't think to mention this to your protector wife?"

"Look, I ... I didn't want to worry you. Nothing has been decided yet."

She bolted up straight. "Oh. So that was your plan? To keep me in the dark until it had already been decided, and it was too late for me to do anything about it?"

Jon stared in bewilderment, trying to figure out what she meant. "Do anything about it?"

Dellia seemed taken aback, becoming even more fierce in her accusation. She leaned over his desk again, her fingernails scraping its unyielding surface. "Yeah, like remind you that you should be making sure your wife doesn't lose the most important thing in her life."

The words struck with tremendous force, stabbing through his stew of anxiety and jarring him most of the way out of his daze. He stood slack-jawed, not even knowing how to respond to the dagger embedded in his still-beating heart. His new wife, the woman he loved enough to give up his world for, had, in the most forceful way possible, just told him he was not the most important thing in her life.

He knew it to be true, but to have it shouted at him with such cold and angry force left him stammering. "The most ... important thing?"

Dellia remained emphatic. "Yeah. The thing I dedicated half my life to becoming."

Jon shook his head in a vain attempt to clear away his disorientation. "I ... I left it in the hands of the three realms to decide." He reached out to take her hand, wanting to ease her consternation, but she yanked her arm away as if he were a leper. He let his hands drop to his side, his voice remaining soft and conciliatory. "It doesn't matter what happens in the council. You will always be a protector. I will see to that."

Her fury only seemed to grow. "You don't get it, do you?" She pointed out toward the plateau. "I trained with these people. I fought with them. Edan, Rillen, Shal—these are my friends. How am I supposed to face them when my husband ..."

Jon held her gaze. "It's not that I don't get it. It's just, we have to let the process play out."

"No. You have to make sure this doesn't happen."

"How can I interfere when—"

"Inter*fere*?" Dellia took a step backward, seeming shocked. "No. You can lie to yourself, but don't you ever lie to me."

"I'm not lying."

"Yes, you are. You're afraid—afraid to lead." The accusation hung in the air for a moment before she pointed to the papers strewn on the black marble desk. "You've spent two days locked up in here, trying to run away from making any real decisions. You don't think I see what's happening?"

The truth of her words stung, but he was desperate to make her understand. "Because I never wanted this. I wanted a simple life with few responsibilities, remember?"

Dellia folded her arms. "So, you're just going to do nothing?"

He closed his eyes and lowered his head, but before he could respond, she cut him off. "If you're so determined to be useless, then why are you even here?"

Jon froze again as the dagger in his heart twisted and dug even deeper. The woman he loved with his whole being had just asked what good he was. As if his only value to her was what he could do for her. She didn't even care how hard he was trying or what difficulty he was going through to stay with her. He looked into her eyes. "It was the only way I could be with you."

New footsteps brought their exchange to an abrupt halt. They beat through the doorway at a frantic pace, then stopped. Jon's gaze snapped over, and he glared in frustration. "What?"

A tall, muscular Elorian man stood in front of them, dust from the road still clinging to his face and clothes. His breathing labored, his apprehension hung thick in the air as his gaze darted between Jon and Dellia. "I am sorry to intrude. I cannot seem to find Megan. No one seems to know where she is, but she must be here."

The sudden change of subject jarred Jon out of the prior discussion, and he shook his head. "What do you mean? Megan is with …?" A glimmer of recognition lit up his slow and weary mind. This was the man who had been with Megan in the Illis Woods. He stepped toward him. "Wait. You're the one who took her."

"Yes. My name is Aylun."

Jon's confusion roared higher. "But she's with you."

A contagious panic suffused the man's voice and manner. "No, she has to be with you … it is imperative that she be with you."

"What are you talking about?"

"This is so bad. She was supposed to meet you. I left her in the Verod camp. We saw you arrive. She started toward you, so I left. She has to have met you."

Fear gripped Jon as the picture clarified, and anger swept through his veins at the colossal negligence of it all. "What? You left her? That was over a week ago. You lost her? You lost Megan?"

Aylun seemed even more distraught than he was. "I am sorry. I don't understand how this happened."

Jon's rage took over, and he pointed out the window at the road snaking through the rolling hills of Erden. He raised his voice. "She's been out there alone … for a week? If anything happens to her …" He took another step forward and jabbed his finger at Aylun's chest. " 'No harm will come to her.' Those were *your* words. I trusted you. You made a vow."

Aylun bowed to Jon and kept his head down as he spoke. "I am so deeply sorry."

504

Jon's face became even more hot and flushed, and he shot out the words: "Don't bow to me. Don't say you're sorry. Fix this. Find Megan. Do as you promised, and bring her to me."

Aylun bowed even more deeply.

"Now!" Jon shouted, his voice bellowing through the small chamber and echoing down the hallway outside.

Aylun jumped at the sharpness of the rebuke and flew out of the room.

Dellia stared at Jon for a second, her expression one of utter disbelief. "If only you spent a fraction of that passion protecting what matters to your *wife*." Before the meaning of her words could even register, she stormed around him and out of the room.

Jon returned to the table and sank into his solid wooden chair. She was right. He had mishandled this terribly. Even as he sat paralyzed by indecision, he knew he was wrong. He rarely got angry, yet he had acted like an angry child when Megan's safety demanded he keep a cool head, and he had failed to show equal concern when his wife needed him.

It all just served as further proof that he shouldn't even be here, but it was too late now to fix any of it. He had no desire to slow down Aylun, and it would only compound the problem to run after Dellia and risk further quarreling with her in her present state, not to mention in full view in a public hallway. It wouldn't do to have half the council see her pin him to the wall with a dagger to his throat. Although it had been many days since she'd done that.

Then a chilling thought occurred to him. This was even worse than he'd imagined. Dellia had been his oasis in the desert, but he feared tonight, when he returned to their simple home of stone and wood, that what he'd find would be an unrelenting sandstorm of fury and accusation. Sure, he would still be greeted by her beautiful face, but it seemed certain that the kindness and love in her eyes would be replaced by anger and coldness. Even if that were not the case, her face would only serve to remind him that he had utterly failed to make her happy.

The honeymoon was over now—well and thoroughly over.

He buried his head in his arms, wishing he could disappear into the darkness of the marble table.

Dellia barged down the swirling-marble hallway, propelled by frustration and a bitterness as deep and acrid as any she had ever experienced. The fluttering torches on the walls flew by, their reflections dancing along the polished floor as she tried to calm her distraught heart. The man she loved wasn't even willing to lift a finger to protect what she cared about. He was letting his wife's lifelong ambition be dashed into a million pieces without so much as a word of defense. It was infuriating to be so helpless when one so close had the power to save something so dear to her heart.

She resisted the temptation to whirl around, to go back and pin him to the wall with a dagger to his throat and threaten him into doing something, anything to stop this. As satisfying as that might be, it wouldn't accomplish anything. No, there would be no talking to him. He wouldn't want to do anything. He was determined to be useless.

She caught sight of Aylun, and it served as an instant reminder of the disturbing ferocity of Jon's reaction to Megan's being lost. He felt more strongly about her than his wife's dream. And to send one man to find a woman of such importance, especially of such importance to Jon, was foolhardy. You needed many eyes to do a thorough search.

Any rational, courageous council leader would have carefully considered the best approach, then organized a thorough search for Megan. This was anything but. Instead of a well-devised plan, what Jon was doing seemed more like the hysterical knee-jerk reaction of an overprotective, lovestruck idiot. Not to mention, this was the kind of job the protectors had been created for. She or Garris should be the ones going. But then again, Jon didn't seem to see the value in having protectors at all, much less sending them with Aylun.

Then it came back to her: until minutes ago, that had been the plan. Garris had told her that if Megan didn't appear in a week, the two of them would be sent to find her. It had already been over a week. That meant two protectors were supposed to have been sent to find her a day or two ago—so what was Jon thinking.

Obviously, he wasn't thinking. He had forgotten, or he wouldn't have allowed Garris to go gallivanting off. Obviously, his passion was clouding what little judgment he possessed, because here he had sent a lone man of unknown capability and honor in place of two protectors. Then it hit her. If Garris wasn't here, and the plan had been to send her two days ago, then the obvious course of action was …

Her steps clattered down the hallway as Dellia raced up behind Aylun. She grabbed his arm and swung him around to face her. "I'm going with you."

He stared for a second before responding. "I can find her. I do not need help."

Even with her gift nearly crippled because of her agitated state, she sensed his certainty. It was well beyond simple confidence. He knew he could find her, but how?

It didn't matter. This was important. Dellia stood firm. "Garris and I were to be sent to find Megan. The plan was for us to leave a day or two ago, but it got delayed. I still need to go, so sending you separately makes little sense."

Aylun shook his head. "I cannot wait, and I will not be slowed down."

She brought herself up taller. "*Me*, slow *you* down?"

He gave a polite nod. "No disrespect intended, Protector, but you would need time to prepare provisions and belongings for the trip. I was already on the road."

She held her ground. "I am a protector. I am always prepared for the road. Is your horse at the plateau stables?"

Aylun nodded. "But I really don't need—"

"This isn't a debate or a request. I will meet you there momentarily." She took off at a jog down the marble hallway.

Side passages and doorways to barren rooms flew past as her ill ease grew. Something bothered her about both exchanges with Aylun. She had sensed it first when he realized Megan was missing. His exact words still rang in her ears. "This is so bad," he had said, but it was not the words themselves, it was the feeling behind them that had stuck in her memory. It was one so powerful as to punch through her barely functioning gift. It had not been the panic of a person who had just lost a loved one. His reaction didn't even feel as if it was directed at a single person. His dread was more profound than that. It was a feeling she was accustomed to when serving under with Kayleen. He was in fear for many lives.

She had sensed it again just now. He was hiding something, just like he had during their encounter in the Illis Woods when he said there were things he had taken a vow not to reveal. On every level that mattered, she sensed the man to be rational and trustworthy, which meant that even if she didn't know the cause of his concern, she had to take it seriously. The conclusion was clear: Aylun believed the absence of Megan would have profound implications and that any delay in finding her could be catastrophic.

Dellia sped up. She couldn't afford to get bogged down in haggling or debating with Jon, nor could she waste time soothing his anxiety or bruised ego. Going back to talk to him now was not an option. She couldn't risk losing her chance to leave with Aylun. She would go home and scrawl out a brief letter. It would only cost a few minutes, and Aylun would not be pleased, but the delay was unavoidable.

She had just begun contemplating the contents of her note when Braye rounded a corner and headed past her. She dodged in front of him with both arms out, bringing him to a halt. "Councilman, I need a favor."

Aylun continued past her, and for a moment, she watched him recede down the hallway. Then she returned her attention to Braye.

He gave her a bright and cordial smile as their eyes met. "Of course."

AYLUN

Dellia kept her words quick and sharp. "I think eliminating the protectors is a grave mistake."

He gave an approving nod. "My agreement could not be stronger."

"Jon seems hesitant to support them. Could I ask you to see if you can talk some sense into him?"

He hesitated, and she sensed a vague apprehension. "... I'll see what I can do."

"I have an urgent matter and must leave Shirdon right away. Can you relay a message to Jon for me?"

Braye seemed a bit surprised but continued to study her, waiting for her to speak.

"Tell him I won't be home for a couple of weeks, at least. I am going with Aylun to retrieve Megan. Deliver that message, and perhaps you can use the occasion to slip in a word or two about keeping the protectors."

Braye stroked his salt-and-pepper stubble as he nodded, seeming to approve of the idea. His smile broadened. "Of course. I appreciate the opportunity. Is he still studying in the back room?"

She nodded.

"Don't worry. I have a matter that I must attend to first, but as soon as I finish, I will go to Jon and relay your message. And I will do all I can to convince him to support the protectors."

Dellia hesitated. The delay bothered her. But if Jon did as he had done for the past couple of days, he would be in that room until well after sunset, so it shouldn't pose a problem. With a deep bow, she hurried around him. Now there would be no need to go home. She and Braye seldom interacted, but in this matter, they shared a common goal, and he seemed to appreciate being given a pretext to talk to Jon. It seemed certain her message would reach him.

She maintained a set of supplies and equipment at the stables for just such a rapid departure. As she neared the rough-hewn building, she spotted Aylun waiting outside, with his spotted horse ready to ride. Annoyance and frustration swarmed around him like a cloud

509

of angry bees. He continued to wait, deftly managing his impatience, as she tossed a blanket and saddle over her dapple-gray Ulka and readied him for the trip.

Then, without a word, the two trod past the keep entrance and down the long ramp to Shirdon below. The wind swayed the peaks of the pines as Aylun and Dellia grew closer, then the breeze vanished as they continued down beneath to the base of the woods. The comforting shelter of the trees did little to assuage her anger as they continued for a time, then turned eastward through Shirdon to the road out of town. Pleasant faces glanced up from the busy city streets as they trotted by, their smiles unable to soften her mood. She granted an efficient nod to the sentries posted at the city gates and received surprised looks and a polite acknowledgment.

Time wore on, and her temper cooled as the dirt road rolled by beneath her, and the plateau grew smaller over her shoulder. She stared back at the long stairway that led from Shirdon to the plateau above and used it as a point of reference to locate her home at the cliff's edge. Jon would soon arrive there. At the realization, a horrible consternation clawed at her, but she struggled to set it aside. She needed to focus. The amber orb of the sun was already headed toward the forested edge of Mount Karana, and they wouldn't make it far before they had to stop for the night.

Yet as time passed, apprehension and guilt shoved out her frustration. She had just left Jon without a word after arguing with him and calling him awful names. No action she had taken was wrong, she reminded herself. She was accustomed to making snap judgments under stress and never let her anger or hurt lead her to make a strategic mistake. From any point of view, this was the prudent course of action. Why then did she feel so wretched? Why did she want to run back and tell him it was okay?

She pulled herself up taller in the saddle. This was her duty. She was doing what was right. This was the correct course of action for Jon, for Shirdon, and for the three realms. Megan was connected to the Otherworlder Prophecy, and that connected her to all that was important in this world. She was a crucial figure in everything that had transpired and needed to be found with all due haste.

So Dellia turned forward, focusing on the long road before her. She needed to put all her personal concerns out of her mind. When she returned, she would mend fences with Jon, or at least she hoped she would. Until then, her duty was all that mattered.

The rattle of a rickety ladder registered somewhere in the depths of Megan's despondent fugue. After a sluggish moment, her gaze wandered up from her book to the odd man. What was his name … Pretaj or something? The scene went by, barely penetrating her haze, as, with shaking legs, the man inched his way upward. She stared ahead, trying to recall how she had come to be in this place, as he examined the bookshelf before him, scanning each row with a crooked finger.

Her mind finally managed to summon the memory. She was here because Zala had brought her and introduced her to the strange little man with his thinning white hair, bald spot, and crook in his nose. In fact, it was Zala, the demure young woman with all her bangles, who had been her support at a time when nothing mattered anymore.

Megan returned to her absent-minded flipping of pages. Names and pictures of hideous creatures and things of beauty drifted by on its faded, yellow pages. Paintings and drawings of multiple arms and heads, exotic chimeras and shape-shifters, a collection of the alluring, delicate, bizarre, and repellent, all went unnoticed as she paged through in a grief-stricken haze. Her fingers continued to turn the pages automatically as her mind was drawn again and again to those final minutes that seemed to have broken her soul beyond repair.

It had been nighttime, and she was watching Aylun walk away. It had all been so perfect. Jon was right there, just across the grass-covered hill, at the head of the camp. All she had to do was hurry over and reunite with him. She was giddy with anticipation, only a few steps from a moment she had envisioned a hundred times in the past few days.

As she hurried toward Jon, he set something shiny and metallic in the grass. He bent over it, and in a few seconds, a ghostly image appeared ... that horrible, beautiful image. It came together, like a picture coming into focus, slowly gathering itself into a glittering likeness of a heavily branched tree. It towered above the Verod camp, almost as tall as the hilltops. Lights of red and yellow from its bright fall-colored leaves danced across the tents and horses and flittered along the dark and grassy slopes.

Then came that voice, serene yet terrible as it boomed out through the dwindling fires. "The future is an infinite branching tree of possibilities, each determined by free will."

Above her, the image transformed into that of a middle-aged Elorian woman. The swath of stars and moon that graced the night sky twinkled and distorted as they showed through her translucent likeness. Then the voice said more about being the oracle of the prophecy and something about deception, but Megan's gaze was drawn back to Jon, watching as he stood close to that woman, very close.

A sick feeling wormed its way into her stomach as she watched them together. There was no single movement or gesture that she could cite, no glance or expression that gave her pause, but dread began to fill her, nonetheless. Then the booming-yet-serene voice said something that caught her attention, and her gaze rose up.

A scene was playing in the air above her, bloody and horrible. A seemingly endless army of twisted creatures raged through a small village. They beheaded proud fighters, smashed skulls, trampled men and women, and obliterated small girls and boys under the hooves of their massive steeds. They raved on, cutting down everyone in their path as if they were mere wheat before a scythe, until nothing remained that could be recognized as human.

Above it all, that woman's voice boomed. "You see, I have known for most of my life that humankind will soon face extinction."

In an instant, all of Aylun's concerns, all the Augury's interest in the prophecy and in the journal, it all made sense. Memories of him saying the Augury was reluctant to act unless the need was dire replayed in her head. Oracles didn't tinker with a few lives here and there. Aylun had said as much. They only changed the natural order of events when the threat was dire. That meant this was never about such paltry lives as hers or Jon's or even the ruling council. No matter how central they might be to coming events, they were only ever a means to an end. This prophecy wasn't about them, it was about those future events. This was about the end of everything, the end of every life here. It was about the fight against extermination.

She looked down at Jon at the head of the camp, and her apprehension deepened. There was something different about him, too. He seemed more determined, more certain of himself. He'd never looked like that. Then, he leaned over and whispered into the ear of that woman next to him ... into Dellia's ear. It was not the act of a captive speaking to a captor. It was not a word shared between pursued and pursuer. No, this was the act of a confidant, of a friend whispering to a friend, of a ... lover whispering to his beloved.

Megan's heart stopped. Then, Jon slipped his hand into Dellia's, their fingers intertwining. The protector didn't pull away. She accepted his hand. She seemed as eager for it as Jon did for hers. Dread turned to crushing horror as she stared at the proof of her worst fears. They were together.

Jon looked over at Dellia in a way that he had always looked at Megan. Those were the eyes that had been for her and that was the expression that only she could elicit. Except now, as she watched, the face that had been her face and the eyes that had been her eyes weren't searching for her affection—they were looking for that woman's. They belonged to Dellia.

The booming voice spoke a name that snapped her attention back to the scene of the serene middle-aged woman looming above her. "... Jon. You were destined to be one of our greatest leaders. The one sent to save us all."

Megan's attention flew back to Jon as everything crashed in on her. Jon? The one sent to save them? It didn't make any sense. She stared at him, at her Jon, her sweet, kind, perfect Jon, standing up there with his hand intertwined with that protector's.

Her mind went blank, unable to function, as the woman's words rolled over her. "So, I wrote only the truth, that you would bring about a new age, knowing it would let the council spin their comforting web of lies."

Dellia moved closer to Jon, leaning into him, and he wrapped his arm around her waist and pulled her even closer.

Megan stared as the sight tore away any last shred of hope. She wanted to break down and weep. She wanted it all to go away. She wanted to dissolve and disappear, and still, the words would not cease. "It was a path to prepare you through trials and cut years of pain and suffering from your rise. Yet, only you can lead us safely through the perilous events ahead to a time of peace and prosperity."

Finally, the words cut through her daze. He was a part of all this. A part of something big and important. Something that could save every life here. Something that could forestall extinction. Megan reeled as the truth hit her. She was insignificant, a forgotten friend, an old flame that never took. There was no place for her here, no room for her in this world ... no special spot for her in his heart.

Her feet moved, almost without her directing them, and Megan dove into the sea of campfires, headed for Yuki. She flew around tents, tethered horses, and murmuring soldiers gathered around piles of ash and embers. The only thought that could pierce her haze was the compulsion to get out of this place without being seen, without discovery. She had to make it to Yuki. That was it. Yuki was still her friend. Yuki would take her away.

As she swerved through the campground, a sudden voice bellowed out from behind her. "Megan!"

She kept going, not so much ignoring her name as crippled and incapable of response.

Footsteps raced up behind her, and the man's voice called out again. "It's you, isn't it?"

She froze, feeling dead and hollow inside. Only one desire filled her mind, the compulsion to run and hide. But, able or not, she could no longer avoid responding to the one pursuing her. She forced out a smile as best as she could and turned.

It was the huge, golden-skinned man, the one she had seen before with Jon, the one called Garris. He was another of Jon's new friends, another of the group of which she was not a part. "You were the one with Jon, right?"

He seemed surprised to see her. "What are you doing here?"

She neither wanted, nor was capable of, mounting an explanation that would cover even a fraction of how she had gotten here. Without thinking, she pointed toward Yuki and spat out the first excuse that came to mind. The one that would get her out of here as soon as possible. "Sorry, I was in a hurry. I was headed to meet Aylun … you know, the guy who was with me. We were looking into something super important."

Garris motioned her to follow. "You have to come with me. Jon has been worried about you."

Her heart shattered into a million little pieces as she recalled the image of Jon pulling Dellia near to him. To see it up close … no, she couldn't. Then the rest of his assertion hit her. Worried about her? Jon had been worried about her? Her gaze drifted up the hillside where Jon still had his arm wrapped around Dellia. Megan slowly shook her head. "It doesn't look like that to me."

A puzzled expression came over Garris. "Is something wrong?"

Panic struck her. She couldn't stay. She just couldn't. Unless she got out of here right now, she might even break down in front of this man. She gave a crisp shake of her head. "No. I guess I'm just surprised to see them together like that." Unable to gather a plausible reason to excuse herself, she blurted out the truth. "Whatever is going on here, it sounds important. I don't want to interfere with it."

Garris gawked. "Interfere?"

She had let it slip, and now he was expecting her to explain, so her hampered brain slung together the best lie she could manage. Not a bald-faced lie that wouldn't make sense, or crumble under scrutiny, or seem odd upon later reflection. It had to have enough truth to it to make him understand. She gazed into his eyes, trying to seem genuine and certain. "We went to Lanessa. We fou—"

"You?" He seemed to startle. "You went to Lanessa? Are you kidding me?"

She plowed ahead. "We found something there. It's incredibly important that we follow up on it, and we don't have much time. I ... I can't stay." She spun around and hurried away.

After a few steps, Garris called out. "So, what exactly am I supposed to tell Jon?"

Terror struck again. Jon couldn't know that she was here. If he knew, he would try to find her, and he couldn't be allowed to find her. She would be mortified. The idea of having to face him and that woman together gutted her. She wouldn't be able to survive it.

Trying to drag it out as long as she could, she turned and walked back to Garris. Her mind waded through its haze to find some plausible extension of her half-truth that would convince him to hide her presence here completely.

She stepped up to him and forced a smile. "What we found in Lanessa"—She pointed off toward Jon—"it said that this, what's happening here, it's important." Her heart broke again as she stared at him with that protector at his side. She brought her attention back to Garris. Her only hope was to tell him enough of the truth so he would understand. "This is where Jon belongs. Here, with you and that woman. I have answers of my own I have to find. They might amount to nothing, or they could change everything. The thing is, if I let Jon get dragged into that, it could put an end to all he is trying to do here. He doesn't need that."

Then it slipped out. "He doesn't need me."

The truth of the words struck her to the heart of her being. She forced herself up taller. "I won't become the reason he fails. Don't tell him you saw me. Please."

Garris seemed shocked. "Are you serious?"

"Yes, completely serious. Promise you won't tell him."

"You're asking me—"

"Please, it's important to both of us." She shook her head. "Don't tell him."

The huge man stared at her, obviously dumbstruck.

She felt her heart racing as she waited to see if the part of her words that were true and heartfelt were compelling enough to balance out the rest of the crap she had just spouted.

After a while, his expression returned to normal, and Garris shrugged. "Okay. If it's that important."

Relief spread through the part of her that wasn't already numb with grief. As she assumed was the custom from watching Aylun, she clamped her arms to her side and bowed from the waist. Then she raised her head and peered into the burly warrior's eyes. "You give your *word?*"

He nodded.

"Thank you."

Megan gave a second solemn bow, then whipped around and scurried off. She held it together until she reached the tent; then tears began to fall as she gathered her things. The tent flap lifted, and she stared up at the unexpected intruder. The young and demure Zala, the woman who had gotten them into the Verod camp, stood peering down, watching her pack her things. "Are you leaving?"

Megan nodded through her tears.

"I think I should go with you. Are you returning to Mundus?"

She managed to nod again. It didn't matter where she went, as long as it was away from here. What she appreciated more, what she needed but hadn't expected, was that she might not have to be alone.

Zala nodded back. "You go. I'll catch up and guide you."

Megan nodded a third time, then turned away to finish collecting her meager belongings. Nothing further interrupted her as she hauled everything outside into the cool night air and readied Yuki. Then she mounted and spurred her on.

As she trotted away, hoof-falls approached, and Zala pulled up alongside her. Megan glanced over. Decked out in all her bangles and anklets, she suddenly seemed more mature than she had at first impression. The young woman smiled, then forged ahead to take the lead. They mounted the crest of the hill and headed down the far side, into the moonlit valley below. The camp behind them disappeared into a dull glow above the hilltops, but Megan never paid attention, never paused, never looked back.

A loud clatter jarred Megan's attention back to the unkempt library surrounding her. She looked up from her tome and then over at a pile of books lying on the floor. Not one of the semiorganized stacks scattered here and there on every surface and even on the floor of the library, but a jumble, heaped in disarray in front of one of the shelves that packed each of the six walls. She looked up and there was Pretaj with his arm still outstretched and his crooked finger pointing to the empty spot from which the heap must have tumbled.

The odd man turned his head and stared at Megan with an accusatory expression. "Did you do that?"

Her imagination still stuck in the past, she shook her head.

"Oh, well, yes. I suppose. It happens even when you're not here." Pretaj clambered down, leaving the books lying in a pile on the floor. He strolled around the tree in the middle of the room to stand across the circular table from her. "Books fall, and you just watch? Didn't I hire you?"

Mired in confusion and her mind sluggish, Megan shook her head. "No …"

"Oh, but you are here to help?"

She shook her head again. "No. I'm here to read and learn."

"Oh, right. I'm the one who is supposed to be helping *you*." He looked down at the massive tome before Megan, her fingers poised to turn the next page. "And was that book helpful?"

She paused for a moment as she struggled to find the memory of how she had come to this library. Zala had escorted her from the Verod camp back to Mundus just as promised, then insisted she stay with her. Zala's home was one of the palatial places that housed a large extended family, and Megan was able to find a corner room in the back where she had hoped to hide away from the world. It didn't work since Zala seemed determined to check in on her often, each time seeming more concerned about her than the last. After a day or two of catatonic moping, Megan picked up a book to distract her addled mind. Zala saw and seized upon it as some form of medicine, insisting she come to this library where she would find an endless supply of distraction.

The first day felt awkward, with the odd man in the wrinkled linen clothes buzzing around her, but she found he tended to keep to himself, except for his habit of mumbling a lot. The outing and new surroundings had done a lot to keep her mind occupied, and so she'd kept coming. However, she had trouble concentrating, making absorbing words problematic. So she was drawn more to the books with lots of pictures, like the one before her.

Megan stared down at it as her sluggish brain tried to process Pretaj's question and decide if the barely noticed book had been helpful. "Oh, I guess, I kind of drifted off."

His interest seemed piqued. The chair groaned as he seated himself across the table. "Oh, really! Is that your gift? Where did you drift off to? Kanlu? Shirdon? Egina?" He lowered his voice, speaking to himself, "I could swear she was here the whole time."

Megan raised her voice as if he were hard of hearing. "No, I mean I wasn't paying attention."

He rubbed his chin. "Oh, yes, I see." He leaned closer as if sharing a secret. "Do all people from Prith read books without paying attention? It seems inefficient."

She hesitated at the reference. "Um, no." Then it came to her that Prisha had told her Prith was the name sometimes given to her home world, Earth. "I mean ... I don't think."

Pretaj scratched his chin. "You don't think? Doesn't that make it hard to read?"

"No, my mind was just kind of a blank."

The chair creaked as Pretaj leaned back in it. "Oh, yes, I see, you were meditating."

Megan stared at him. "Meditating?"

"Yes, you know, focusing on one thing, clearing your mind. That sort of thing."

"No, I know what it means. I wasn't meditating."

"Are you sure? You look Elorian. Elorians meditate."

When she didn't answer, he leaned forward again and eyed her book. "Is that why you were looking at the Eye of Syvis?"

"Huh?" Confused, Megan looked down at the ancient-looking drawing on the faded page. It was a dark, sickly-green orb with an iris-like circle of indigo in the center and three red scratches radiating out like the vessels of a bloodshot eye. There was a familiarity about it. She had seen it before, she was certain, and yet her hampered mind couldn't summon any specifics. "Ew. What does that have to do with meditation?"

Pretaj cocked his head. "Nothing, I suppose ... and everything."

She contorted her face. "Who would meditate on that anyway? It's gross."

"Someone who wants great power."

"Oh, really? What does it do?"

"Well, that's the question, isn't it?"

She shook her head. "If you don't know what it does, then how do you know it has great power?"

"Artifacts from Syvis are always powerful. Why make them otherwise?"

Megan stared down at it again, trying to recall where she'd seen it.

Pretaj's wooden chair grumbled as he rose from the table. "If you want to know what it does, why don't you ask the Mirhal."

Megan cocked her head. "The who?"

"The Mirhal. Centuries ago, the Eye of Syvis disappeared into their hands, or so the myth goes."

She shook her head. "Sure, I'll just ask people who lived centuries ago?"

Pretaj leaned over the table. "Oh, that would be interesting. Can I come along?"

She stared into his eyes. "It was sarcasm. You do get the idea of sarcasm, right?" She looked back down at the picture and mumbled, "How would I even ask people who lived centuries ago?"

Pretaj shrugged. "There are ways."

She brought her gaze back to his and stared, not certain if he was being serious.

Before she could ask, he smiled and said, "If you really want to know what it does, then why don't you try meditating on it. Maybe the answer will come to you." He let out a quiet cackle as he turned and walked away. "Meditate on it ..." He continued to chuckle to himself on his way back toward his heap of books.

Megan shook her head and mumbled, "It wasn't that funny."

She glanced again at the faded page on the table in front of her, trying for a third time to recall where she'd seen the repulsive artifact. After a fruitless moment, she shook her head and turned the page as Pretaj bent down to pick up books from the pile on the floor.

Chapter Twenty

MISSING HOURS

Jon sighed and opened his eyes. His ability to concentrate crippled by his argument with Dellia, he gazed vacantly down at the handwritten stacks of notes strewn across the table. Even with the contrast of white paper against black marble, the pages seemed smudged and worn by overuse. He once again pulled the stack on the keeping of state secrets in front of him and tried to concentrate. Words drifted by as his mind refused to focus, and after several pages had drifted by he realized he hadn't absorbed a single word.

He got up and paced a few times across the polished marble floor, trying to set aside his worry and guilt, so he could sort out what to do. After a while, he stopped and stared out the window at the jagged shadow of the mountain peaks zigzagging across the woods and grassy fields. Feeling an intense sense of shame for letting Dellia down so terribly, he lowered his head, studying the scenic mountain-side below. The pines at its base seemed to mock his anxiety with their gentle swaying in the light afternoon breeze.

After a brief time, he tore himself from the window and paced across the floor a few more times before giving in to the futility of it all. He needed to find Dellia, even if he didn't know if it was a good idea, much less what he would say. With haste, he scooped up, stacked, and straightened the piles of notes, then shoved them into the soft leather satchel Kayleen had provided. He slung the strap over his shoulder and strode from the room.

An awful sense of dread and urgency tugged at him, drawing his steps faster and faster. He flew through the torchlit hallways, out of the keep, and across the sun-drenched plateau to the training grounds. It was a complex of sorts, with a half dozen large fields for group classes and a dozen rings and enclosed combat areas. Everywhere you went, there were weapons: spears, pikes, bows, crossbows, shields, daggers, axes, maces, clubs, flails, morning stars, and an impressive array of swords of all kinds and sizes.

He stopped a few of the well-muscled, leather-clad fighters as he sped down passages and across open spaces. Each person he asked bowed to him with respect and informed him they hadn't seen Dellia. A few politely added that the last they'd seen of her was when she excused herself to go see him. It didn't bolster his confidence when a handful even said she'd "gone to see the council leader," not knowing they were *speaking* to the council leader.

Having made a thorough enough search to be sure she wasn't at the grounds, Jon returned home. It was the place he imagined she was most likely to be, but he found it deserted. In the hope she was perhaps trying to calm herself in the gardens, he searched the huge circular courtyard, poking his head into all her favorite places. Eventually, with the sun low in the sky, he returned to their home to sit on the floor near the front door and wait.

Out of desperation to find any clue to her whereabouts, he decided to use his gift. It was not a thing he liked to tamper with because, as Garris had once pointed out, it was dangerous. He could take someone's ability with his gift, but not their wisdom and experience in using it. Moreover, it represented power—power to control, power that could hurt or maim or destroy—and he didn't want that kind of power. So he used it only when circumstances compelled him, but Dellia's absence was more than compelling enough.

He picked a tiny pebble from the floor, no doubt a piece of debris that had been dragged in on the bottom of a shoe. He had toyed a few times with the size of objects, trying to understand how his gift was possible under any set of physical laws. He concentrated on the fragment he held in his fingers and the sounds from outside slowed, then stopped, telling him he had triggered his gift. The real world grew dim, and a shimmering likeness of the room sprang up, overlaid on top of it.

As he had done in the past, he turned events backward, watching the play of light across the room betray the rewinding of time. The detail of the image was stunning, which only deepened the puzzle. He had used his gift before, looking back hundreds of years, but the amount of data needed to store that much detailed, three-dimensional imagery was staggering. It was more than the number of atoms in this tiny grain of rock between his fingers. If this was a reality apart from that of Earth and if its physical laws different, then what were those laws? What could account for what he was seeing? If this fragment of stone was too small to contain the images he was viewing, then where did they come from?

He spun the scene back to his entrance to the room, then reviewed events backward from that point. There was no sign that Dellia had ever entered the house. When he finally found her, it was earlier in the morning, when they had left together. Dellia hadn't been back all day.

He rewound a little more, until he could see her walking toward the door, and then he froze that moment. For a while, he gazed upon her gorgeous face. If he wanted, he could concentrate on her and take on her fighting ability, as he had when he faced Aylun and his companion in the Illis Woods. Or he could even take her gift, though that idea was troubling. A part of him feared knowing what people felt about him. All he wanted now was to see her, to know where she was and what was happening. Yet all he had managed to learn was that she had never come home, so he let go and the image dissipated, the world brightened, and time resumed.

With nothing to do but worry, he sat in the quiet of their home as his imagination ran wild. He feared she had gone because she never wanted to speak to him again, that she had lost faith in him, and that he had forever damaged their relationship. It remained inexplicable that she had chosen him in the first place. How could he expect her to return when he never understood what she saw in someone like him? Now that she'd encountered the real Jon, she wouldn't come back.

Time passed with excruciating slowness as the house grew dark. With it, a sense of loneliness, regret, and dread closed in on him. It grew and grew, taking over more and more of his thoughts, until worn and overwrought, he shut down, staring into the dark corners of the room as his despairing soul bled out. Sounds drifted in from the street: the guard changing, the soft cooing of a couple strolling by on the street, the outside world going on and on without him.

Eventually, drained by regret and his fearful imaginings, he pulled himself together and sought out Kayleen. She seemed somewhat worried but had no idea where Dellia might be. She sensed his concern and advised him not to worry too much—that Dellia was a big girl and could take care of herself, and that she would be back when she was good and ready. None of her reassurances was entirely comforting, since each one could cut either way. Maybe taking care of herself meant admitting she was wrong about marrying him. Maybe she would be good and ready when she was done with him.

As he was leaving, drained and disheartened, she threw him a lifeline, suggesting the soldiers posted around the area might have seen her. Then she amended her suggestion, advising that a visit to the barracks might be a more efficient way to find out where she had last been spotted.

After a hurried march through the dark streets of the plateau to the fires outside the barracks, he caught the clamor of loud talk and laughter coming from the dining hall. He barged through the door to a large room with rough-looking soldiers gathered around ale-soaked tables, laughing and drinking. The odor of alcohol, leather, and sweat assaulted his nostrils, and the din of discussion saturated the air with a festive ambiance. It drew a sharp contrast to his utter despondency.

At his entrance, one by one, all ceased their babble and turned their eyes to him.

AYLUN

Jon's gaze drifted across the room as his mind froze, unable to summon the right words now that he had suddenly become the center of attention.

One of the assembled, with hair as long as his face, called out, "It's our fearless leader."

A few chuckles followed, then a lean, sinewy man with a broad smile yelled out from the back of the room. "Did you stumble into the wrong building?"

The heavyset man next to that one almost stepped on his line. "Need directions?"

A big, bearded fellow with a paunch stood and pointed as he belted out a jovial remark. "Shir Keep is in that big mountain there. You can't miss it."

A round of hearty laughs broke out, blending into raucous discussion. Seconds later, a sturdy man with square shoulders and the air of a leader spoke, his voice deep and commanding. "Can I help you?"

The room quieted, and all eyes turned back to Jon.

He nodded. "I was hoping someone might have seen Dellia."

A complete quiet came over the assemblage. Then the bearded man with the paunch spoke again, his tone as jovial as before. "You don't know where your *wife* is?"

There were a few snickers.

The sturdy fellow with the square shoulders bellowed, "Have some respect!"

A brief silence ensued, then a shorter man with a sour expression spoke out from the front. "I saw her leaving earlier today with some Elorian guy. They were headed out of the stables."

Farther back, a somber man with his arms crossed added, "I saw them ride out of town to the east, toward Erden."

Jon froze. She'd left him. She'd actually left town without telling him. This was worse than he'd imagined. Why was she with Aylun? In the Illis Woods, Megan had chosen to leave and go with that man, and now Dellia had made the same choice? He remained paralyzed by shock as a round of soft

527

"oohs" came from almost everyone in the room, then faded into a few stifled laughs.

Then the bearded man with the paunch shook his head as he called out, "You've been married less than a week, and your wife ran away with another man."

The room exploded with laughter.

Humiliation stabbed Jon with agonizing sharpness. He wished he could melt into a puddle, then disappear through the cracks between the floorboards. He'd always known he wasn't worthy of Dellia, and apparently, everyone else in this entire world did too. Despite his certainty that she would never run off with another man, a knot of vicious jealousy tore at his insides as the entire room continued to roar with laughter.

Then another voice added, "You must not be keeping her very happy. If you know what I mean."

The laughter intensified. This had been a bad idea ... a really, really bad idea. Flush with embarrassment, his voice eked out, barely loud enough for him to hear himself over the laughter, "Thank you."

He spun around and endeavored to appear nonchalant as he strode from the room, stumbling over the threshold at the door. Trying to outrun his mortification, he rushed past the fire pits outside the barracks, around the first corner, and down the dark lane.

Heavy footsteps followed behind him, and a giant of a man raced up to his side.

Jon glanced over at the rough-looking fellow dressed in red leather armor with a crude likeness of a flaming horse embossed in the front.

The man eyed Jon. "You need help finding them?"

He stopped and turned to face the brute. The man was familiar. He was one of those who had helped him out of an ambush in Kanlu. Jon stepped closer. "Could you?"

As soon as the words left his mouth, he regretted them. Blundering around in the dark, chasing after a woman who had fled in anger, seemed like another stupendously bad idea. Besides, what would he say when he caught up to her?

The man seemed like a crude sort of fellow, but his aspect brightened at the request. "Sure. I'm no tracker, but I asked around quick, and I found out they were on the road to Erden. I know when they left, and I have a suspicion what path they took, and even where they might stop for the night."

Jon hesitated, trying to come up with a way to back out but not altogether sure he wanted to. Eventually he had to do something, so he thrust out his hand. "I don't think I know your name."

The man smiled as he clasped Jon's forearm and gave it a firm shake. "I'm Grekor."

"By the way, thanks for helping me out in Mundus."

The hulking man seemed surprised and positively beamed. "Aw, it was nothing."

Jon motioned for him to take the lead.

Grekor marched around another turn and headed down the street toward the stables.

After a moment, he dropped back next to Jon and eyed him. "Want me to bust him up when we find them?"

Jon turned his head and stared as they walked, not quite sure he'd heard what he thought he'd heard.

Grekor gave him a knowing nod. "I think you should. I mean, Dellia's no big looker, but plenty of men'll find her serviceable enough. You gotta set a precedent. If you know what I mean."

Jon gaped. "Hey, that's my wife you're talking about." Was the man blind?

"Sorry, no offense." Grekor seemed sheepish at the rebuke.

Feeling defensive, Jon quietly added, "She's more beautiful than anyone else I've seen in this world."

At that, Grekor smiled. "Ahh, love. It affects the eyesight."

A moment of silence followed. Then the urge to clarify came over Jon. "If she decides she doesn't want to be with me, then how can I force her to stay?"

Grekor's response was instantaneous. "Ooh. You mean just let her go? Bad idea." He glanced at Jon. "I mean, Dellia may not be the prettiest in Shirdon, but she's a bit out of your league, if you know what I mean. You might want to rethink that."

Jon gaped again. "Hey, that's *me* you're talking about."

Grekor grumbled, "Well, you think about it. It'll take a while to catch up with them." He pulled ahead again and rounded the corner into the stable.

Jon strolled over to outfit Enna, but Grekor grabbed his arm with an iron grip and pulled him to a stop. He pointed to a sleek black horse with three white socks. "Take him. He's fast, and he can keep to a gallop. If we push our horses, I think we can catch them in less than an hour."

Jon nodded and readied the designated steed. Outside the stable, Grekor mounted a lamp on a long pole and shoved one end into a holder in his saddle, so the light was held high. Then the two mounted, and Grekor led the way past the keep entrance and down the ramp to Shirdon, then east out of town. He pushed the pace to frantic limits, his lamp swaying and jostling, its light dancing across the cobbles as they flew by beneath.

Jon paid little attention. His muscular horse heaved beneath him as his concentration was torn between staying in the saddle and what he would say to Dellia.

True to his word, in about an hour, Grekor slowed and swerved off the road, heading for the flickering light of a blazing campfire. Seated before the flaming pile of logs, Dellia and Aylun rose and stared at Jon as Grekor led the way up to their camp. The giant warrior stayed on his mount as Jon climbed down off of his.

Jon gaze stayed on the lamplit dirt as he struggled to decide what to do or how to explain why he was following Dellia. He wanted to let her know he was sorry, to assuage her anger, and to tell her that he hadn't thought it through—that he should have told her right away about the protectors. His only desire was to beg her to return. He yearned to tell her how much he needed her, how much he relied on her.

Unsteady on his feet and his legs still wobbly from the ride, he stepped forward. His gaze came up and drifted from Dellia to Aylun, standing there gawking at him. At the sight of the pair shoulder to shoulder, almost touching one another, the laughter and mocking of the soldiers came back, stabbing him with a fresh wound of painful jealousy. Then Grekor's reminder that she was out of his league came to mind, heaping on the humiliation.

He struggled to remain calm as he took another step toward Dellia, stopping a few feet away.

The sudden familiarity of the scene swept away all his resolve with breathtaking force. She really was leaving him with the exact same man and in the same way that Megan had. Every one of his carefully chosen lines flew from his head, and the words slipped out, biting and accusatory. "Do you want to explain to me why I had to learn from the soldiers at the barracks that you had left me?"

A look of surprise came over Dellia, and her tone seemed more defensive than apologetic. "Braye was supposed to tell you."

"Do you have any idea how humiliating it was to be told that my new wife has just run off with another man?"

She seemed thrown by the rhetorical question, but soon regained her indignation. "Really? The protectors are being dismantled by *your* council. *Your* Megan is lost. Who knows what is happening to her right now, and the most important thing here is your ego?"

Caught off guard by the unfairness of her accusation, Jon stared. "My ego?" He shook his head.

Dellia stepped closer. "Yes, and you're so insecure you had to run off and track me down?"

The comment reminded him again of the soldiers deriding him over his runaway wife. Flustered, he let his passions get the best of him again. "And what about you? You wouldn't even let me stay in your house before we were married, but here you are alone in the dark with a man you don't even know."

Dellia took another step closer. "And you think you're not insecure? What are you afraid of?" She pointed to Aylun. "Do you think he can force himself on me? Or do you just have so little faith in me?"

Jon scoffed. "What were you afraid of when you refused to let me stay with you before we were married? Did you think I could force myself on you, or did you just have so little faith in me?"

Dellia's face became bright red with anger. "You have no right to vent your petty jealousy on me when you still have feelings for Megan."

Hurt and rendered mute by the crazy accusation, he stared.

She seemed to sense his surprise and barked out, "You freaked out and demanded immediate action when you found out she was missing, but you won't lift a finger to help me."

Bewildered by the ferocity of her assertions, Jon just stood there for a moment, agape. She had often seemed a bit volatile, but she was never one to make outrageous and nasty claims like this. His gaze drifted from Aylun to Dellia, then to Grekor over his shoulder.

When it fell on the huge fellow, Grekor shrugged and mumbled, "Don't look at me."

Jon whipped around and stormed back to his steed. If his presence here was such an affront to Dellia and every word out of her mouth was only going to hurt more and more, then coming here, chasing after her, had been a colossal mistake. No good would come from staying a second longer.

Grekor brought his mount around as Jon swung up onto his, then the pair galloped off. Jon never looked back. He could only imagine an unconcerned Dellia strolling back to her fire and chatting with that man as he rode out of sight.

After a moment, Grekor pulled past him and took the lead, the two clattering down the lamplit cobbles at breakneck speed. This time the frantic pace was not born of an anxious desire to catch Dellia, but of a need to flee her, as if his haste might somehow help him outrun the sting of her words or the awfulness of this feeling.

AYLUN

Time passed, and the miles flew by, but the hurt and terrible jealousy never faded.

As the chill wind whistled around him and the lamplit roadway raced by beneath, Jon's dread grew with each pounding of hooves. He had mishandled this all so badly. Rather than mend fences, he had only fueled the inferno of her ire. He had given Dellia even more reasons to never return.

As Shirdon sped closer, the reality loomed large and heavy in his mind. All that awaited him back there was an empty home, anxiety over the collapse of his marriage, and endless anguish over insoluble political issues. With each passing minute, his apprehension mounted and with it his desire to be anywhere but the place he was racing toward.

Shadows of the tall pines arced across the dark needle-strewn ground as Kayleen, with lantern in hand, stepped lightly along the dirt path. A cacophony of yips, barks, and howls arose from a distant pack of coyotes, lending the night a spooky air, made even more so by the halo around the half-moon sometimes visible through the branches above. More than a little nervous about this venture, her edginess heightened her senses, and her gaze darted toward every hoot of an owl or scurry of another nocturnal critter. This outing was not without risk.

She had waited until the night had settled in before setting out. Then, just as she was leaving, she'd received a visit from a frantic Jon searching for his missing wife. He had shown poor judgment in hiding the demise of the protectors from his protector wife. Doing so had made his quarrel with Dellia inevitable and her fiery outrage fully justified. Yet as much as he had brought this on himself, his concern had been touching and endearing to watch. And knowing Dellia, the bulk of her anger was almost certainly temporary. So Kayleen had sent him over to the barracks to seek word of her whereabouts.

After that, she'd set out for Ruepo's, staying out of sight as much as possible and only lighting her lantern once she entered the woods. What she was doing might not have been illegal, but it was not the kind of thing that she wanted to make public either.

It was that weaselly-looking Nikosh who had set this all in motion. The man had turned out to be a complete surprise. He was far more tenacious and resourceful than he had first appeared. As fate would have it, he had also proved to be quite talented at rooting out information on the chimera coin. He had shown it around and found a barkeep that recognized it as coming from a man named Ruepo. The enterprising soldier had then scouted out the man's house, only to find it continually quiet and shuttered.

Unable to catch sight of him in a day and a half, Nikosh had sought out Kayleen, having the sense to find her in a private spot where they could speak unobserved. It was there that he suggested that a little late-night tour of Ruepo's residence might turn up some helpful information. However, he had the wits to realize he didn't know why he was searching for the coin, so he needed more information about what to look for before breaking into the place.

Wanting to encourage the man yet keep him at arm's length, she had told him the truth—that it was about finding someone who had hired a mercenary to commit a murder—but avoided divulging any further details. Instead, she suggested that since she had a detailed knowledge of the incidents, it would make more sense for her to scout out Ruepo's house, and she would let Nikosh know what she found. It wasn't quite the truth, because scouting was not what she intended to do. No, breaking and entering would be a better description, and if the man was at home, he might take offense at having it entered without permission.

She rounded a bend to see the outline of a lamplit log cabin, looking dark and deserted against the silhouette of pine trunks. From the arrangement of bells in the yard, it fit the description of Ruepo's house. The crackle of pine needles came from some distance behind her, and this time, it didn't have the quality of an animal. It sounded like she was being followed.

Kayleen's alarm deepened, but rather than glance behind her and give herself away, she sped up, listening and stepping along the dirt path with more care, avoiding twigs and needles that might make a sound. No further noise came as she tiptoed up the steps to the porch and lowered herself onto her knees before the door. She listened with great attention to the absolute silence as she pulled out her tools and slipped a gleaming pick into the rusty lock.

A whisper came from behind her. "What do you think you're doing?"

She jumped, then breathed a sigh of relief as it dawned on her that she knew the voice. "Don't scare me like that." With no small degree of annoyance, she glanced up over her shoulder. Garris was peering down at her, his face lit by the lamp beside her. "I'm breaking into a man's house, obviously." She scowled. "Have you been following me?"

He smiled. "No, I was keeping an eye on the place, looking for Ruepo, when you blundered along."

"Blundered?" She scoffed. "I'd ask why you were here, but I suspect it's for the same reason."

He nudged her aside, grabbed the door handle, and shouldered the heavy wooden structure. The crack of splintering wood echoed through the dark trees as the door jerked open.

Kayleen pulled herself up from her knees and mumbled, "Any fool can break down a door. I was trying to be at least a little stealthy."

As Garris walked past her into the house, he looked over and shrugged. "Why?"

She picked up her lamp and followed him inside.

He turned and eyed her. "I doubt we're here for the same reason. Unless Ruepo tried to ambush you too."

Kayleen froze and stared as Garris lifted the lantern from her hand. His statement was more than a little alarming, and she remained still as he set the glowing box on the desk and turned up the flame.

She nodded to herself as the light flittered across the book-shelves and walls of the room. "So you must have tracked the coins to Ruepo, just like I did, and he sent you on a wild goose chase?"

"More of a wild goose *trap*." Then he mumbled, "I could swear I mentioned him trying to ambush me."

Kayleen pondered for a moment. "But that means he had to know there was a chance you'd come back." She paused to consider the matter a while longer. "Which also means the house probably isn't just empty. It's abandoned."

"And if he's clever, which he appears to be, he destroyed any real evidence."

She began to scour the room. "Let's see if there's anything he overlooked."

He followed her lead, talking as he scrutinized every feature and facet. "Don't you have people to do this kind of thing for you, Madam First Advocate?"

"People? Yeah, I have you, but you're determined to run away from me."

Garris merely grunted at the remark. He sauntered to the old walnut bookshelf and began combing through the aged and worn books, examining each, opening it, and scanning a few of the faded pages before returning it.

Likewise, Kayleen opened every drawer of the mahogany desk, took out each unremarkable item, and scrutinized it. She wasn't sure what she was looking for, so each piece of paper, pen, writing brush, and stamp needed to be considered with care. Time passed, and it was looking like the search would be fruitless, when Garris stepped back and froze.

She glanced at him, then stopped and stared. "What is it?"

"Come here."

She hurried over, scanning everything before him as she walked. He pointed to the floor. "Look at that scratch."

536

The floor had many scratches, but where he pointed was one that didn't stop before the bookcase. It kept going right up to its edge, as if the base were partially covering it.

Kayleen shrugged. "So they put the bookcase over a scratch, so what?"

"Nah, it was made more recently than that."

Kayleen examined it more closely, and it seemed he was right. The scratch wasn't dark like the others—it appeared to be a newer one. She looked up at the shelf itself. "These books aren't right either."

He shot her a puzzled look. "I examined each one, what's not right?"

She pointed to the bookshelf on the left. "See here? We have a group of books on economics and below it, some on artifacts and art." She pointed at the bookshelf to her right. "This shelf contains books on philosophy, and down here are ones on warfare and history." Then she pointed to the shelf between. "Look here. You have fiction interspersed with folklore and herbs and medicine."

She nodded to Garris. "The books on either side are well organized, but the ones on this middle shelf aren't organized at all. They were thrown together hastily, with no thought to their content or order."

He nodded back, then began tossing books from the shelf. Kayleen stepped back as he moved faster, sweeping armfuls of books and scattering them across the worn and scratched flooring, until he had emptied the entire thing.

Then he yanked and pulled on the bookshelf itself, but it failed to yield. It was nailed down. He seized the top and heaved it forward with a tremendous yank. The base squealed, groaned, and cracked as the leverage of the shelf splintered wood and pried nails out of the floor. When he forced the bookshelf down onto its face, it revealed a door hidden behind it.

The remnants cracked and snapped as he kicked and yanked the shelving, breaking it into pieces and shoving the books and debris out of the way. He reached for the door handle, but it had been removed. Kayleen returned to the desk and scooped up the lantern, holding it up as Garris regarded the door. Nails showed around the edge where it had been secured to the frame.

He ran his fingers over the heads of a few nails. "He hides the door, removes the handle, and nails it shut. Well, that's just plain redundant."

She nodded to herself. "He certainly went to a lot of trouble to make his secret hidden door really stand out."

He eyed her. "It's just plain dumb. It's not like it's going to stop anyone from getting in."

She smiled. "Well, if he's inviting us in, it would be rude of us to turn down the invitation."

Kayleen trailed Garris as he strode outside, hefted a large, jagged rock, and toted it back in. With both arms, he raised it before the door and brought it down against the sturdy wood. The door and wall rang with the blow, but barely moved. He raised it again and again, hammering repeatedly. With each impact, the door shuddered more, until the boulder punched a hole through it.

He continued to bang at the ragged edges, chipping away until the hole became large enough to step through. Then he resorted to his hands, his muscles tight and arms bulging as he heaved the splintered remains, prying and pulling them apart until he had torn away most of the door.

Kayleen smiled. "You're efficient."

With a bit of a flourish, he motioned her to go through. "Councilwoman."

She ducked through to a curved wooden stairway leading downward. Debris covered the steps, so she kicked and shoved it aside as she descended. The stairway creaked, and pieces of wood clacked against one another with each step.

When Kayleen neared the bottom, light from the lamp in her hand flickered across a large cave-like room. Near one side stood an ancient-looking desk, and against the opposite wall stood a cabinet with a giant faded map of Meerdon mounted above it. Kayleen

538

stopped and stared, surveying the area. Placed on every surface and mounted on every wall were ancient weapons and artifacts of astounding artistry. Those she recognized were of impressive value. Each surpassed anything adorning Braye's chambers, making his look paltry by comparison.

Garris halted on the stairs behind her. She looked back as a wide smile spread across his face. He pointed to the gleaming bronze blade of a long, curved scimitar mounted behind the desk. "I want that." He pointed to a pair of jeweled daggers on the desk itself, their gems sparkling in the warm yellow lamplight. "And that, and that." Then he pointed to a massive crossbow mounted on the far wall as his smile broadened. "Ooh, and *that*."

She shook her head as she strolled over to the map. "You and your fascination with weapons."

"Said the woman with the dragon-claw obsidian dagger."

Kayleen smiled as she set her hand on the hilt of the weapon sheathed at her side. "Point taken." She returned her attention to the map hung on the wall. Large and ornately adorned, it was a work of art in its own right.

Garris came up beside her and studied its markings. Then his brow furrowed as he pointed to a small brown X in the northwestern part of Erden. "That's Ghokal. I was just there." His eyes drifted across the map. "Oh … I don't like that."

Kayleen glanced at him. "Don't like what?"

He pointed to a series of X's marking spots on the map. "I was ambushed there, and there, and there, and attacked outright there." He pointed to more faded X's near the Neri Mountains, where he had told her he'd hidden out most of his exile. "These are all spots where attempts were made on my life." He looked down into Kayleen's face.

She pointed to one of the X's. "Isn't this where that Setlander incident occurred?"

Garris glanced at her. "Yeah, I was there."

"You were there?" She pointed to another X. "This is where a scouting party was mysteriously ambushed. It caused quite an incident. I spent a lot of time smoothing that over." She pointed to a third X. "This is where Ambassador Rotus was betrayed by some on the council."

His eyes widened. "I was at all of those incidents. Not all of them were ambushes, but things went bad, and I almost got myself killed."

"So all of these were places you almost lost your life."

He nodded. "Yeah, and I'm the only one who knows where they occurred. Which means—"

"Ruepo must be somehow connected to most, if not all, of the attempts to kill you."

Garris nodded as he scanned the map a moment longer. "Some of these go back fifteen years."

Unsettled by what they'd uncovered, but feeling the pressure to learn more, Kayleen left Garris and strolled over to the wide desk. Intricate carvings adorned its sides, mingling with faded yet still gorgeous paintings of flower-laden plum boughs. She ran her fingers over the carvings as she stepped around to the front.

At its side lay a lacquered black chest with a branch full of delicate white blooms and buds winding across its shiny surface. Inlaid with mother-of-pearl, it seemed as extravagant as the rest of the furnishings. Kayleen set the lantern on the desk, so it still illuminated the map and cabinet below it. Then she reached down to lift the lid. It creaked open to reveal it was stuffed with golden chimera coins with the exact same image as the one Garris had given her. She stared in surprise. So much gold had to be worth a fortune. To leave it behind seemed unfathomable.

She looked up at Garris. "There's a chest here full of those coins of yours."

He turned his head. "Full?"

She nodded. "I'd say there's enough to live quite comfortably for many lifetimes."

The mention of the coins ended his review of the map, and his boots clunked against the rock floor as he strode over to stand beside her. His eyes fixed on the glittering coins in the chest, he stood agape. "Well, that's something."

"It's looking more and more like Ruepo is in the middle of many of the attempts on your life, but why? What did he have against you?"

He shrugged. "I have no clue. I just met the man a few days ago. I'd never seen him before that."

She turned her attention to the set of drawers on the right and Garris to the ones on the left. She opened each one and took out and contemplated each item, searching for some clue as to how this all might be connected. She found paper, bottles of ink, brushes for writing, stamps, and other items commonly found in a desk. All of them were of much higher quality than those inside the desk upstairs. She stopped as she found a note written in a familiar script. Then it hit her; it was *her handwriting*.

The note was a letter commissioning a mercenary to serve Shirdon by eliminating Garris. In her own hand it claimed that he had betrayed the three realms out of a blind thirst for fame and glory. That he had been so eager to get credit for information, that he tortured the suspected Otherworlder Prisha after the council had given a strict order to bring her in for questioning. Her torture had dragged on for days as she begged him to stop, and when he had so crippled and disfigured her that she pleaded for death, he left her to bleed out alone. It went on to explain that he had kidnapped a council member's sister, Leanna, and made her watch the entire ordeal, then killed her to silence her.

In her own distinctive script, the letter asserted that Garris was utterly without conscience or honor, that his word shouldn't be trusted, and that interacting with him in any way was exceedingly dangerous. It finished by insisting he should be hunted down like the animal he was and killed on sight for his "heinous crimes." Her eyes flew to the bottom where she found her own signature. Even she would have believed she'd written it, if not for the fact that she knew she hadn't.

Not wanting to touch such a vile pack of lies for one more instant, Kayleen dropped it on the surface of the desk and eyed Garris. "This is awful. I didn't write this. ... I would *never* write this."

He was studying the worn pages of some tome he had retrieved from one of the drawers. At her indignant tone, he pulled his head out of the book. His eyes drifted down to the letter, and he scanned the contents for a moment. "Oh, that. It's like the ones the mercenaries who came after me carried."

Kayleen scowled at him. "Oh no, you don't get off that easy." He looked over at her, and she captured his gaze. "How could you think I wrote this? Have you ever heard me use the words 'heinous'? And you think I believed you tortured someone?"

Garris shrugged. "I believed you were upset over the loss of Leanna, that you blamed me, and that you were angry enough to dissemble."

She glared. " 'Dissemble'? You mean, you thought I was mad enough to spin outrageous lies in order to kill you."

"Fine. My judgment is terrible. I have dishonored you. I am so sorry. My contrition is only dwarfed by the magnitude of the lie your council spun about the Otherworlder ending civilization."

Their eyes locked, Kayleen keeping her stare unfazed and steady. "Apology accepted. Now, can we get back to figuring out what's going on here."

He tossed the old tome he had been reading on top of the letter, open to one of its pages. "These are accounting records. They include payment, times, dates, and places. My memory isn't perfect, but a bunch of these times and places seem to line up with the attempts on my life."

"So, more proof Ruepo was involved."

He pointed to the last line on what appeared to be the last page with any writing. "What's interesting is this entry here. The amount is much bigger. The place is in Talus, west of Egina in the mountains south of Nydri, and the time is three days from now."

Kayleen stared down at the entry.

He pointed. "There's a red X on that map marking a spot in that vicinity, and it seems more recent than the others, just like the one at Ghokal."

She nodded in acknowledgment. Then they both returned to their search of the desk, looking for any further clue that might betray Ruepo's possible intentions or current whereabouts. Then they switched sides, Kayleen taking the right drawers while Garris reexamined everything on the left. Once they had exhausted the desk, they expanded the search, looking over the cabinet below the map, and every sword, flail, crossbow, vase, and delicate jade sculpture in the room. It was like viewing the contents of a museum display.

Having done all they could, they headed back outside, but Kayleen's thoughts kept returning to the incongruities of the situation. She pondered them as Garris led the way in silence down the dirt path, across to the base of the ramp, and began his ascent to the plateau.

Eventually, as they walked side by side, she tried to articulate her thoughts. "So Ruepo sent you to Ghokal knowing you might return. Because of that, he abandoned his house, yet left behind its rare and ridiculously expensive contents, as well as a chest full of gold that implicates him and clues to where he might strike next. Does that about sum it up?"

Garris gave a thoughtful nod. "Well, either he is brimming with confidence or everything we found here we were intended to find. Given the way he made his secret hidden door so obvious, I tend to favor the second explanation."

"So there's a high probability it's another trap?"

He nodded again. "And only a fool would expect me to fall for a trap the second time."

"And since Ruepo doesn't seem like a fool, it means this trap is a well-hidden and well-planned one, and therefore dangerous."

Garris sighed. "I'll leave at first light."

An enormous clatter arose from behind them, and the sound of hooves echoed through the forest. Kayleen stopped and turned to face it. A lantern was approaching, jerking and leaping above a sleek black horse. Behind it, a second dark steed remained partly hidden from view. The pair galloped up the ramp toward them, and as the first flew into the light of her handheld lamp, she spied Grekor hunched low on its back. He eyed her and gave a polite nod as he flashed by.

The second horse flew into the light, this one with Jon on its back, his haggard face staring vacantly ahead. Apparently, his search for Dellia had led him out of town, and whatever had happened had left him quite upset. He glanced down as he passed, then yanked his steed to a stop and brought it around to face her.

The beast pranced as it turned, and hot breath shot from its nostrils as Jon guided it over to address Kayleen. "I found her."

She stared up at him. "Dellia?"

Jon nodded. "She decided to go get Megan without consulting me or even telling me. I just came home to an empty house and no clue she was gone."

To Kayleen, it sounded more like a whining complaint than an attempt to inform her, but his genuine agitation and despondence made it impossible not to sympathize.

Garris stepped over to Kayleen's side and looked up at Jon. "I'm sorry. I promised you that Dellia and I would find Megan together. Now I'm afraid I can't join her. I need to go out of town for a few days for an investigation, and I have to leave right away."

Jon shook his head, seeming tired, worn, and defeated, then looked at Garris. "It's all become a big mess. That Aylun guy is with Dellia, so don't worry about it. It doesn't seem much like they need you or me or anyone else. If there's something you've got to go do, just do it."

Kayleen looked down. He said he'd found Dellia, and by his tone of voice, it sounded like an argument had occurred. Working with Jon had already proved difficult, and adding agitation to the mix wouldn't make things easier. She peered up at him as he began a slow turn of his horse up the ramp. It gave the impression he was reluctant to return home.

Then he halted and addressed Garris a second time. "Just … let me know when you get back, okay?"

He began to direct his mount up the ramp again, then made a second sudden stop and eyed Garris with intensity. "Wait. Instead, take me with you."

Kayleen stiffened. The entire notion caught her off guard. She had given Jon an ultimatum to develop an opinion on all the issues she had outlined, and instead, he was proposing that he run away from them?

She stepped toward him, trying to draw his attention. "You can't just leave now."

He looked at Garris. "How long will it take?"

"A week maybe, but—"

Jon set a hand on the satchel he had been carrying with him. "I have to study these notes anyway." Then he returned his gaze to Kayleen. "Heck, I've spent two days studying them already. I know most of it by heart, but I can take them with me."

She gave a firm shake of her head. "No. Absolutely not."

"Why?"

"What if I need your input on something?"

He rushed his words out. "You said you'd hold off the council for a week."

"A week at the *outside*."

"Before I finish studying the issues, I won't have any real input."

Kayleen hesitated. "This is not a good idea."

"Come on. It's a lot of time on horseback to think and decide, and I could really use the time away to help calm down and focus."

"These are the crucial first days of a new government. It's not the time for our new leader to go running off."

"You've been council leader for years. I'm not necessary. You can handle things."

She stood there, certain this was a terrible idea but not sure what to say.

Jon clasped his hands together and stared down at her with pitiful eyes. "Please."

"What am I supposed to tell everyone?"

"They already think I'm considering the issues. Tell them I'll continue to do so as I help Garris investigate."

Garris stepped forward. "There's no time. I need to leave right away—tonight."

Kayleen eyed him and whispered, "You said at first light tomorr—"

"I changed my mind, okay?" he whispered back.

Jon leaned forward. "I'll be ready in an hour."

Garris looked to Kayleen as if expecting her to object. She hesitated as she recalled Jon confronting the dead in Kanlu. He had destroyed a veritable army while being pursued. When he faced the council in Shir Keep he had turned the Eye of Syvis to dust as if it were nothing. In both cases, he had done things no known gift could do. Things that demonstrated he was clever and wielded immense power. Garris was heading into a trap, and having that kind of power at his side might make the difference between living and dying.

Torn between needing Jon in Shirdon and needing Garris safe, she finally threw up her hands. "Fine. Go help Garris. It will make me feel better anyway. I'll … I'll make some kind of excuse."

Jon folded his hands together again and bowed from his saddle. "Thank you." He eyed Garris. "I'll meet you at the stables within the hour." This time, Jon brought his shiny black horse all the way around and galloped up the ramp.

Kayleen watched him disappear into the dark. The whole idea of his leaving while his new government was forming, and possibly unstable, filled her with foreboding. But her concern for Garris was more immediate and powerful. As adviser to the council leader, she had just made an irresponsible choice. But as one who feared for Garris's safety, it was the only choice. She would just have to find a way to make it work.

AYLUN

Their steps echoed through the dark forest as, once again, the two of them headed up the ramp. Garris shook his head at her. "I was trying to help you out there, give you another reason to make Jon stay."

"I know. But honestly, with the miracles I've seen him pull off, I'd feel better if he accompanied you."

"I don't mind the company, and Jon has proven he can be a big help, but what are you going to tell everyone?"

Kayleen closed her eyes and sighed. "I don't know. Something along the lines of what Jon said, I suppose." She looked into his face. "I'll figure out a way to keep the new council occupied. Just be safe, okay?"

Garris smiled.

A smile seemed an odd reaction to her heartfelt expression of concern, and Kayleen cocked her head. "What?"

"You used to tell me 'just be safe' each time I left on a mission, remember? It's been a long time. It feels good."

She mumbled loud enough for him to hear. "I'm glad my discomfort brings back fond memories for you."

He set a steady hand on her shoulder. "Your concern makes me feel good."

She couldn't help the broad smile that filled her face. Then she recovered and scoffed as she motioned up the ramp. "Just go. And bring him back in a week … in one piece."

"Yes, ma'am."

"I mean it."

Garris never responded. He just continued to smile as they climbed the ramp side by side. It did feel good. She was sending him off on a mission again. It was familiar and comfortable. But more than that, since Jon was going with him, it meant Garris would have to return. She had maneuvered him into coming back, and he'd never even given it a second thought. And since Jon was going along, they would bond just a little more, and it would make it just a tiny bit harder for Garris to leave for good. This was one of the reasons she loved him. He was so thickheaded and predictable, she could push him a little closer to staying, and he would never even notice.

Chapter Twenty-One

LANTERN IN THE NIGHT

The dried logs and branches in the fire crackled and popped, burning with a ferocity no less than her anger, frustration, and disappointment. Dellia lay on her bedroll, watching them as time dragged on, and Aylun, who lay nearby, fell asleep. Her agitation seethed well into the night. But as the crackling thinned out, leaving only the soft flutter of the flame accented by an occasional pop, her fury settled with it. It was impossible to sustain such rabid intensity for any length of time, and after a while, it burned itself out.

As the flames turned to embers, her thoughts turned to the damage she had done and the words she had spoken—words she would not be able to take back, or even soften, for many days. She had accused Jon of running away from his duty, of hiding away out of fear, of being determined to be useless, of being insecure, and of letting his ego run away with him. They were harsh words, and the utter conviction with which she had delivered them preyed on her conscience, erasing her anger and replacing it with apprehension and doubt.

As time dragged on and sleep refused to come, the words stuck with her, repeating in her memory, over and over, sparking a deep regret and shame. They were said in anger, in the heat of the moment, and even if there was truth in some of it, or even in all of it, there had not been a single grain of sympathy or understanding. For one who knew firsthand how important, how delicate, and how fragile feelings could be, she had gone out of her way to wound the heart of the one who loved her enough to give up his world. This was not who she wanted to be.

With the fire cooling, the dawn came, followed by a red sun lighting up the long, flat clouds that drifted along the horizon. That scarlet orb set the sky afire as worry and regret turned to a red-hot flame burning in her soul.

Her mind stuck in the events of the day before, Dellia rose, tended her dapple-gray Ulka, broke camp, and set out with Aylun, headed down the dirt road away from Shirdon and away from Jon. As the two horses thudded southeast along the dark road that wound through the rolling hills of Erden, she fidgeted and worried about the man she had left behind and the way she had left things.

Her angst grew with the rising of the sun, becoming as bright and blinding as that yellow orb peeking through the clouds scattered across the azure sky. Pastoral hills drifted by without a single word being spoken, as she and Aylun clomped down the long road that took her farther and farther away from Jon.

It was as if their relationship was being stretched and strained with each passing town, until it was torn and tattered by the distance between them. After a while, the chasm became too great, and Dellia could no longer stand it. She pulled in front of Aylun and stopped, blocking his path.

He looked up at her in surprise.

Dellia leaned forward in the saddle and stared for a moment, striving to bring peace to her heart and clarity to her gift. "Tell me again that you don't need my help." She couldn't resist the note of desperation in her voice.

Aylun stared in puzzlement. "What?"

"You said you don't need my help. Say it again, just like you did in Shirdon."

"What is this about?"

She hesitated. "I know it is my duty. That I have to help find Megan. That I *should* find her. That I *must* find her. But Jon ..."

He gave a knowing nod. "Ah. You are regretting the disagreement you had last night."

Dellia looked down.

Aylun's tone turned sympathetic and earnest. "I understand. Are you all right?"

"I'm trying to be."

"Then focus on my certainty."

She nodded and looked up at him.

He left a pause before speaking, and when he did, his voice was as strong and sure as his heart. "I have told you before, I can find Megan without you. I don't need any help whatsoever."

Dellia hesitated, pondering the iron strength of his conviction. "For you to be that certain, you must have a way of locating her."

He nodded. "I do. Megan ran away from me once before, and I found her at the outskirts of Katapa. A second time, I told her to flee and hide while I protected her escape. I found her again in an abandoned thieves' den, hidden beneath the city."

Dellia stared in astonishment. She sensed no subterfuge in his assertion. He had absolutely done what he said, but to do what he claimed was incredible. People didn't simply waltz into Katapa and return.

Aylun held her attention with a steady gaze. "I can find her no matter where she goes or what she does." His eyes flashed down for a fleeting moment, then rose and gazed to the southeast. He pointed just to the right of the road. "She is that way."

"You're sure?"

"I could not be more sure. Based on the direction, I suspect Megan has returned to Mundus."

Dellia nodded. "Then find her, and bring her to Shirdon, to Kayleen. I think I have to go save my marriage."

He smiled. "Go, and rest easy. Do not worry about your duty. I guided Megan through Katapa to Lanessa and brought her back safely. By comparison, getting her to Shirdon is a simple task. Trust me. I've got this."

He seemed solidly built, calm, and capable, and there was an absolute certainty behind every word he spoke. Moreover, he was far more worried about Megan and far more desperate to find her than she was. That combination of urgency, concern, and confidence was entirely convincing. More than that, it meant she was adding little to the search.

For a moment, she wondered who he was, where he had come from, and what he was really doing here. He had an aura about him that convinced her he was no normal man, nor did his sense of responsibility and honor fit that of a mercenary. But then her urgency took over, and Dellia spun Ulka around and spurred him on.

As her confidence strengthened that Aylun was capable and motivated to an extent far beyond her own, it was as if a tremendous weight was being lifted from her shoulders. She was here out of duty. To him, this was personal. With the removal of that weight came a sense of relief that grew as Aylun disappeared behind her. She pulled herself tight to Ulka's neck as he surged down the path that would return them both to Shirdon and to Jon.

Yet as the towns flew by and the sun dropped lower in the cloud-filled sky, her relief waned with it, turning again to apprehension. Her confidence that she could work this out with Jon faded the more she pondered what she would say. She could understand why he was doing everything. She even had tremendous sympathy for him, but the fact remained, she was right. He had been running away from his duty. He had been hiding away out of fear, and he remained steadfast in not wanting to help her. His coming after her had been in part born of his insecurity, and it was clear he had let the jokes of a few soldiers bruise his ego.

She wanted to take back what she had said, but to do so would be a lie. So what could she say? What could she do to set this right? Those worries followed her all the way back to Shirdon as the afternoon wore on.

Dellia dragged out the task of putting away and feeding Ulka, hoping that with time she would find the perfect words to heal their wounded union. When nothing came to her, she set aside her concern and sought Jon in the keep, but he was not in any of his usual places.

Puzzled and worried, she checked all the other spots he knew of: her home, the courtyard, and the shops in Shirdon proper.

She even scouted out the dining hall at the barracks, taking care not to draw attention to the woman they all knew had run away from her husband. As she surveyed the boisterous soldiers from an inconspicuous corner, it came to her that she had slipped in the back door and spied from the shadows out of a desire to avoid humiliation over "running away with another man." From his description, Jon must have come in the front door in order to confront this raucous crew directly. She had called him insecure, but in so many ways, he had been braver than she was being.

The same "insecurity" kept her from Kayleen. Unwilling to subject her ego to the battering it would suffer from admitting she couldn't find her husband, Dellia headed home and waited. There she sat, in her small home on the plateau, and fretted.

As the sun sank down past the horizon, worry began to burn in her heart as bright and fiery as that brilliant orange skyline. Had he left her? Had he moved out of her house, or even worse, headed back to his own world? She didn't even want to contemplate how much sense the latter made, how it seemed like just the kind of thing he might do. The intensity of his discomfort at being council leader was as clear as the relief on his face at coming home to her each day. And if she was not there, then what awaited him in this world but everything he dreaded? Without her, why would he stay?

As dusk settled on the plateau and Jon failed to appear, hope faded, and her despair became as dark as the descending night. She had always loved her little home on the plateau, but now it seemed lonely, empty, and bereft of life.

As the sounds of the night guards changing carried across the plateau, a dark cloud of despondency set in. All her earlier fretting over what she would say to him seemed so insignificant now, when all she wanted to tell him was: "I love you, I miss you, please come home." After a while, her heart grew heavy with the weight of it. Why was she always hurting Jon? And as she imagined him out there, thinking she didn't care about him, she began to weep.

What would she do if he never came back? Then the most horrifying possibility of all came to her. Could she have just driven the Otherworlder from the world he was supposed to save? Had she just doomed everyone? Her fears grew until they consumed her every thought. She lost all track of time as the evening wore on and it became more and more apparent that he was never going to come home. Yet this was the only home he knew. If he was not here, where could he be?

Eventually, out of her mind with worry, she broke down and visited Kayleen in her chambers. Her earlier reticence seemed so utterly frivolous now. If admitting she didn't know where he was would help find him, then the price was worth it.

Dellia gave a soft rap on the door, and after a brief shuffling from inside, Kayleen appeared and greeted her with drowsy eyes and a puzzled look. She had been asleep. Kayleen's puzzlement soon turned to concern, and Dellia realized her own distress must be showing on her face.

Kayleen motioned to her. "Come inside."

As Dellia passed into the room, she sensed Kayleen's concern growing.

The first advocate peered into Dellia's face. "What happened? What's wrong?"

Dellia shuffled to the chair against the wall and crumpled down onto it. "I've made such a mess of things." She looked up at Kayleen as tears welled again in her eyes. "I must have chosen to become a protector because of my gift. I knew that because of it, I could never make a marriage work."

Kayleen's puzzlement deepened as she lowered herself to sit on the floor in front of Dellia. "What happened?"

"My gift has been so strong lately because of Jon. But when he found out Megan was missing, he got so angry. I didn't even know he could get that angry." She lowered her head. "But he did, and it wasn't over me. It was over her. I felt every scrap of it with him, how worried he was, how much he cared about her, and how protective of her he felt. I couldn't handle it. I yelled at him. Then I left to help find Megan without even talking to him first."

Kayleen nodded. "Oh, a quarrel. Is that why he was so desperate to find you?"

Dellia froze. At the image of Jon out of his mind, not knowing where she had gone, she couldn't stop her tears. "He was desperate to find me?" She sniffled and covered her eyes, trying not to break down completely. "Oh Adi, he must have been so worried, and I yelled at him when he caught up to me. I've driven him away, and now I can't seem to find him."

Kayleen set her hand on Dellia's. "He went with Garris. He begged me to let him go along to investigate a threat to the big guy."

At the news that he truly was gone, her heart fell. "So I really have driven him away." Yet there was also a tinge of relief that at least she hadn't driven him back to his world.

Kayleen patted her hand. "Then go after him."

Her tears halted as she peered into Kayleen's face. "And say what?"

"Oh, come on. Where's that dedication to family the Talesh are so famous for? He is your family now. What would you say if you and your mother had an argument?"

"It's not the same."

"It's obvious to everyone that he loves you as much as you love him. There's nothing you can't solve if you cling to that."

Her words were heartening, and Dellia found herself nodding.

Kayleen smiled. "Go after him. They're headed to a spot in the mountains south of Nydri. I'm sure they wouldn't turn down your help, and it would make me feel better if you were with them. I'm worried Garris is walking into a trap."

A smidgen of Dellia's optimism returned at the idea of going after Jon and helping him and Garris. "But they have a day's head start. I'll never catch them."

"If I remember correctly, you still have that red spire stone you used to go investigate Jon's coming to this world."

Dellia nodded. "Yeah, I do."

"Then use it. You can get there a day ahead of them and track them down."

Dellia sniffled and nodded again. "Then is that an order?"

Kayleen smiled. "Of course. Go protect our council leader, Protector Dellia. If he is headed into a trap, the only place you need to be is by his side."

The decision having been made for her, it was as if a burden had lifted once again from her shoulders. Things with Jon still seemed bleak and broken, but she knew where he was and that he hadn't entirely left her or this world. She could fix this.

As she rushed by the fluttering torches lining the marble hallway of the keep and on the way down the lane to her home, a tremendous fatigue set in, both mental and physical. She had slept not a wink the night before, which made it more than a day and a half that she'd gone without sleep. The ride back to Shirdon had been physically taxing, and her anger and worry had drained her emotionally.

As she climbed into her small bed alone, she reminded herself that she could only afford a short bit of shut-eye. She needed to rise early and get ahead of Jon and Garris. Her best hope would be to come up on the path in front of them and run across them on their way. If that didn't work, she had tracked Jon before, and because of the ordeal, Enna's distinctive hoofprints remained seared into her memory. If she could intercept his trail, she could track Jon down. One way or another, she would find him and somehow set this right.

Aylun wiped the sweat from his forehead as Juzhi rocked lazily beneath him. The outskirts of Mundus lay dead ahead—a line of houses, yards, and gardens spread across the hot, sunlit plains. He glanced down to the Ring of Pairing on his finger. As he had done so many times in the last few days, he concentrated on the dark ring with the solid jade line. A winding silvery thread spun out from it, floating over the desiccated brush and sunbaked ground. It was headed straight to the heart of the city, and the other Ring of Pairing, the one with the dashed jade line.

Yet again, he fought back the ugly notion that the ephemeral thread might not be leading him to Megan; that the ring may no longer adorn her finger. He preferred to cling to hope. Because if it was no longer hers, the potential explanations were all grim and his chances of finding her remote.

Still, Mundus made sense. The Verod would have returned to their homes here after their mission had fallen apart. That Megan would follow them back seemed only natural. So he headed around the city, destined for the vacant home they had once shared. It was the only place Megan knew. When they'd parted, she carried with her enough provisions for an extended trip, and the bag of coins Yaomey had given her. As long as she still possessed both and the house remained deserted, she could hide out there indefinitely.

A quarter of the way around the city, with the houses and gardens looming larger, he passed another major road, one that curved as it headed into the edge of town. He looked down and used the ring again. It was a trick he had employed before to pinpoint a partner's location. When one of the dark rings was used at two widely spaced locations, it would provide two threads pointing in two different directions. The place where those threads crossed would be where the other ring would be found.

He looked up, expecting to see the twisting silver line skirting the edge of the city, aimed at the location of the abandoned home. To his surprise, it darted off between a pair of homes at the outskirts and headed toward the shops and markets at the heart of the city.

His anxiety grew. The other ring was not at the abandoned home. Still, the lines intersected somewhere in Mundus, so if it was Megan, if she still wore the dark band, she was located somewhere in there. If it was not her, whoever possessed the ring would know where they had acquired it. So whatever may have happened, he would find out within the hour.

He pictured a map of the area and imagined where the two threads might meet. Then he turned Juzhi and plodded down the main road, past weary travelers headed out of the city. The late-day sunlight rained down on the cobbles as he clomped down the busy street, past clay-brick homes, desert gardens, and intricate ornamentation. Once he neared the area where he expected the lines to meet, he dismounted and led Juzhi on foot.

He strolled along the paving stones as he scanned groups of smiling golden faces. Lively discussion filled the air as pedestrians draped in cheery clothing meandered past. With a quick glance down, he checked the ring once again and adjusted his course, weaving through a few side streets until the thread aimed straight up one of them.

He continued to scrutinize each passerby as they approached until, at last, he finally caught sight of her. It was Megan, but the scene made his heart drop. Her head was up and her eyes forward, aimed in his direction, but they had a glazed-over appearance, and her face bore a mournful look. He rushed up to ask her what was wrong, but she sidestepped him and Juzhi as if they were mere obstacles, never appearing to notice his presence or anything else for that matter.

His mind went back to that time when the Shou were sent to help victims of a landslide. He had seen that same look in the eyes of a man who had watched his beloved wife and newborn child perish in the collapse of a building. For days afterward he could be seen wandering the streets in a trance, as if his mind were still trapped in that tragic moment. Megan's vacant stare and obliviousness were a heartrending reminder of that man's tragic fate.

Aylun froze and turned to watch her back as she walked away. Something very disturbing must have happened. The spotted Juzhi continued his restless movements beside him as he stood frozen by hesitation, reluctant to approach again until he had a clearer idea of how Megan had come to be in this state.

AYLUN

He led his horse around in a half circle and followed Megan as she trudged down the narrow lane, never responding to a single sound or action around her. After a short while, Megan rounded a corner, walking through a gate and into the yard of a huge and ornate home. He gazed at her, his heart frozen by the sight, as she shuffled down the walk, up a step, and into the simple house.

Aylun remained motionless for a while, staring at the door as he contemplated her unresponsiveness. It was clear something terrible had happened that had affected her deeply and made her despondent. That it involved Jon seemed obvious. He had been her sole focus the entire time Aylun had known her. She had fought and struggled through tremendous heartbreak to get back to him.

That night in the Verod camp, she had been so excited to see him. She had even been headed to meet him before stopping to say goodbye. Yet from Jon's reaction upon hearing she was missing, it was obvious that she had never made it to him. In the moments after his departure, something had changed completely. She had gone from seeking him to fleeing him, and given Jon and Dellia's marriage, the most plausible explanation was that she had seen them together.

Aylun brought himself up taller. He didn't truly know what was going on in that head of hers to make her like this, but it mattered little. She needed him, and he would be there for her as long as necessary. But first, he had to make sure he understood her situation.

He returned to the same modest home he once shared with Megan and moved back in. The barely furnished abode was not the same without her there, the emptiness and quiet seeming unnatural. He rose at dawn the next day and seated himself across the street from the house she had entered the evening before.

The road remained shaded, with the sun not yet above the rooftops, as he watched and considered what to do. Few pedestrians strolled the street as his vigil dragged on. Then, a young woman with a conspicuous number of bangles passed by a window. It was Zala, the one who had introduced them to the Verod. Another piece of the puzzle fell into place. Megan was here rather than at the abandoned house because Zala had brought her back with her and given her a place to stay.

It was a bit puzzling, though. The young lady had been introduced as a mere contact, and yet she had made the effort to ensure Megan was cared for. Which meant she was most likely more than just a contact. Whoever Megan's mystery benefactor was, she hadn't only arranged for Zala to get them into the Verod camp, she had made sure that the young woman would look after Megan's welfare.

He was still enumerating the implications when a woman in reddish-brown armor covered by a deep green robe plopped down beside him. He glanced over and startled. Though he had never met the woman, the air about her, her outfit, and the abalone clip that held back her golden hair made her instantly recognizable. It was Protector Rillen. He sat staring at her, confused and flustered because she was not only here but had arrived in Mundus and located Megan before he did.

Aylun remained seated and eyed her as he spoke softly. "Did ... Jon send you?"

Rillen mused for a moment, then slowly cocked her head. "... Yes."

The contemplative pause and hesitant answer were puzzling. It wasn't a complicated question. Aylun turned his attention back to the house for a while as he mulled over her pensiveness.

Then he eyed Rillen. "How did—"

"You took your sweet time getting here."

Aylun paused. "Excu ... excuse me?"

Rillen returned his gaze. "Why the confusion? Did you expect your presence here would go unnoticed? You and Megan lived here in Mundus for five days." Her tone turned accusatory. "And you left her before making sure she was safe?" Rillen shook her head as she tsk-tsked. "You didn't even wait to see her meet Jon."

He stared in bemusement. "How did you—"

The door opened, and Megan shuffled out onto the front porch. Her head was up, but her expression remained sad and glazed over.

560

She stepped mechanically down the stone walkway, her vacant eyes aimed straight at the street in front of them, yet she never showed the slightest hint of recognition.

The gate creaked as she swung it open and turned out onto the paved street. She passed only a few feet in front of Aylun and marched away as if in a stupor.

Rillen stood and looked down at him. "I've been watching for several days now. I promised I would tell Megan where Jon was and help her in any way she chose, but she has been like this since I arrived." Rillen motioned him to come.

As the pair followed some distance behind Megan, Rillen glanced over at Aylun. "She is safe, and I couldn't bring myself to disrupt her. Whatever happened, I think she needs time. So I have watched and waited."

Aylun studied Rillen, trying to puzzle out why she talked as if she'd been here for many days and what set of events had transpired to bring her to this place. He was on the verge of asking when she halted. "The promise I made to tell her about Jon and help her in any way she chose—I would share that obligation with you now. Do you accept?"

It took a moment to process the concept of sharing a vow. In a strange way, as odd as the notion was, in this context, it made sense. Not to mention, helping Megan had been his plan from the start.

Aylun gave a slow nod. "Yes. I understand, and I accept."

"Good. Then Megan is your problem for the time being. I'm going to go rest. I'll find you later." With that, Rillen spun around and marched away.

Not wanting to lose Megan, Aylun sped up, soon walking mere steps behind her. She wandered into a small six-sided library, and he backed off, waiting nearby where he could remain unobtrusive as he kept watch on the door. It wouldn't do to make residents or authorities suspicious of a strange man stalking a young woman.

He spent the next day and a half following her at a distance while he mulled over Rillen's assertion that Megan needed time. He also needed to learn all he could about the situation and consider what to do. It was a disturbing experience, watching the Megan who had once been so animated wander to and from her home in a profound daze, her face always lost in an expression of immense sadness. She was so consumed with grief that she never once noticed him.

Her routine was simple. She would leave Zala's clay-brick home in the morning, trudging down the same warm, sunlit streets to the same library, then disappear inside. Around midday, she would reappear for a brief time. With her head down, she would meander into the street to consume a meager snack at a nearby street vendor. Often, she would consume only a few bites before discarding the rest and returning inside. In the evening, she would appear again and plod back along the same path to Zala's home, where she would disappear, presumably for the rest of the night.

By the afternoon of the second day, he decided he had learned all he was going to learn, and it was time to put an end to this. So, he left his vigil at the library and spent a long while scouring all the busy market areas until he found an importer of Elorian sky lanterns.

Made of thin bamboo strips and white rice paper, the lightweight lanterns were spherical, with a hole at the bottom where a small, thin candle sat. The flame heated the air inside, making it lighter than that surrounding the lantern. The warmed air rose into the body of the lantern and carried it into the sky. In ancient days, generals used them for signaling between Elorian troops in times of war. In recent times, they had become associated with special occasions and ceremonies, and their popularity had spread to Erden.

Having purchased the item, he spent the next stretch of time selecting Megan's favorite comestibles from lively vendors spread across half the city. He brought his collection of tasty treasures to their vacant house that he had once again "borrowed." With care, he laid out a plentiful table, tastefully arranging the colors and appearance of each dish. When done, he covered it with a cloth to keep it warm, then stacked some logs in the fireplace. He set a flint and a few long dry twigs next to it. The sky lantern, he placed on the mantle.

AYLUN

Done with his preparations, he camped out on the stone street in front of the gate to Zala's mansion of brick and clay. There he sat and waited for Megan to return from the library.

Again, she approached without the slightest hint of recognition as he rose to his feet. She almost passed right by him, but he stepped in front of her. After nearly colliding with him, Megan looked up, and recognition appeared in her eyes. "Aylun?" He waited for a moment for her to say or do more, but all that came out was a soft and sad, "How are you here?"

He peered into her face. "Are you all right?"

She lowered her head to stare down at the worn stones of the street. "I'm good," she said in an even quieter and more sorrowful voice.

Aylun nodded. "Good. Good." He pointed to the house. "And this is where you live?"

She glanced at it and gave a halfhearted nod. "Uh-huh."

He nodded along with her, then stopped and stared. "Is that all you have to say?"

She shrugged.

Frustration bubbled up within him. "You intend to stand here and act like everything is just fine? Is that it?"

At his stern words, she tried to hurry around him. "Out of my way."

Aylun stepped in front of her again. "Pack your things. You're coming with me."

Megan shook her head as the sadness returned to her voice. "No, Aylun."

"We are leaving."

"No." She tried to sidestep him again.

He jumped in front of her. "Stop this and come with me."

She peered at him with eyes bereft of joy and warmth. "This is my home now."

In the face of her quiet insistence, Aylun's frustration grew. "Do not make me laugh."

563

"Move."

"No, you are coming with me," he insisted.

She glared at him. "No, and you can't make me."

He crossed his arms and stood taller. "Of course I can, or have you forgotten?"

Megan stormed around him, but he grabbed her wrist and spun her back to face him.

"Stop being so stubborn." Aylun took off, hauling her down the street by her slender arm.

She tugged and squirmed, trying to free her wrist. "So, what? You're just going to abduct me ... again?"

"If I have to."

She went loose in his hand, halting all resistance, stumbling along after him as her voice became pleading. "I can't accept any more help from you. No more, please. You've done too much for me already."

He stopped and let go, staring at her in disbelief. "Me? I have done too much for you? Are you joking?" He shook his head. "I would be dead now if not for you. Do you not get it?" Aylun stared for a moment, letting it sink in. "The only reason I am standing here now is because you gave me a new life, a reason to live, a purpose." He set a hand on her shoulder, and the appreciation in his voice matched the gratitude in his heart. "The nightmares are gone. For the first time in four hellish years, I get up in the morning and look forward to each day." He peered into her eyes. "And that is all because of you ... only you."

She hesitated, seeming struck by his heartfelt words.

He stepped back and crossed his arms. "Do you get it? Or do I have to put up with more nonsense about this being your life now and not wanting to owe me?"

Megan stared for a moment, and a hint of a smile came to her face. "Okay, I'll come." She turned, strolled through the gate and down the walk, and disappeared inside.

He waited, not sure if she was being sincere or if her acquiescence was a mere ploy and her smile prompted by her cleverness in getting rid of him. It proved to be the former when she returned a short time later with her pack. Dusk had arrived and the streets were empty as they strolled in silence back to the vacant house.

Megan smiled at the feast he had prepared, then her expression fell, and she appeared distraught again.

Sensing that she might feel burdened, Aylun made haste to cover. "Oh, that stuff." He motioned to the abundant food and shrugged. "I did not know if you would be hungry."

She lowered her head.

"Look, there are no strings attached, honestly. I had to eat anyway, so you do not owe me at all, okay?"

Megan nodded, then seated herself, and they ate their extravagant meal in silence, with her mood not much improved.

As the feast ended, and she sat picking at the leftovers on her plate, Megan looked away from him. "How did it get like this?" She sniffled. "I'm so stuck. I can't go home to a world without him, and I can't face him." She raised her head and stared into Aylun's eyes. "He has this whole big important thing he's a part of now, and there's no place in it for me." She shook her head. "If I appear in front of him now, I will only make him feel obligated. I will only ruin it all for him."

She paused for a moment and lowered her head. "There's no more place for me in his heart." She sniffled again. "He said he knew a way home, but I can't even go to him and ask without messing up his life." She looked up at Aylun. "Every day, I try to figure out what I should do, but there's nothing."

Anger and frustration welled in him at seeing her so heartbroken and helpless. He realized it wasn't Jon's fault, but he couldn't stand seeing her like this. He leaned forward, trying his hardest to hide his frustration and be firm but understanding. "It is over, Megan. You have to let him go. He has his own life and his own world now."

Her attention whipped back to him. "You've seen him?"

He hesitated, then closed his eyes and nodded. "He is married, Megan."

She blinked a few times and stared in shock, then her head fell, and her voice came out weak and feeble. "No." Her tears fell anew. "What do I do?"

Aylun clenched his fists in frustration. All he had wanted was for her to be happy, but here she was paralyzed by grief and despair. He stood. "Do you have something of his? A memento?"

Megan looked up at him. "Huh?"

"A ring, a bracelet, a letter, something from him."

"Why?"

"You are going to let him go."

She nodded. "I have a picture of us together."

Confused, he stared at her. You could draw a picture, or picture someone in your mind, but the way she spoke was as if a picture were an object, a tangible thing. It had to be slang for a drawing or painting, so he smiled. "Perfect."

Megan found her pack and rummaged through it until she located a small reddish-brown purse. She opened it, unfolded its layers, and slid out a shiny piece of paper. With haste, she jammed everything else back in her pack, turned, and handed the square of paper to Aylun.

He froze when he looked down at it in his hands. Then he ran his fingers over its glossy surface, feeling the smoothness. He turned it over, scrutinizing the white back, then stared at the front again. "This is amazing. It is not a painting, but it looks real."

He pulled his attention back to the matter at hand and returned the picture to Megan. She stood watching as he strolled to the fireplace and lit the logs with a flint he always carried. Then he retrieved the spherical sky lantern and set it on the table next to her.

She smiled at it and looked up at him.

He pointed to the picture in her hand. "Smear some of that sticky curry paste on the back, and glue it to the side of the lantern."

She hesitated as she looked at the image of her and Jon's sunlit faces with strange metallic structures of some kind in the background. After a few moments, she drew a deep breath and dragged her finger through the red paste remaining in the bowl. With rapt concentration, she smeared it all over the white back of the paper, turning it a translucent red. Then she stuck the strange picture to the side of the lantern, smoothing it out with her remaining clean fingers.

Aylun smiled and nodded approval. "Now, use your finger to write 'Goodbye, Jon, I set you free' on the other side."

Megan smirked like a child breaking some unwritten rule as she dipped her finger in her bright green drink. Then, with intensity and care, she wrote the message down the other sides of the lantern. She rose and stepped back, admiring her handiwork, seeming to approve.

He strolled to the fire and used it to light the tip of one of the long dry twigs. He handed the burning stick to Megan. Then he grabbed the lantern and led the way up the stairs to the rooftop patio.

Megan followed, cupping her hand to protect the flame as they ascended the steps.

He set the lantern on the railing of the downwind side of the rooftop patio and turned to face her. "Light it."

She nodded, becoming more enthusiastic by the second.

The flame at the end of the stick danced in the light breeze as Megan brought it over and touched it to the wick of the small, flat candle of beeswax at the base. It lit, causing the lantern to glow and spread a warm, steady light across the patio around it.

Aylun held out his hands at a good width for holding the lantern. "Put your palms out like this."

She blew out the burning twig and set it on the stone railing, then positioned her hands as he'd instructed.

With gentle care, he lifted the round lantern and set it on her palms, with the picture facing Megan. "When you feel it pulling upward, let it go."

He could see her excitement growing as she held it, her attention flittering between the lantern and Aylun as her smile broadened. After a while, she let go, and it lifted off. She clapped her hands like a child with a new toy as it rose above the patio. Then she wandered below it with her neck craned up as it drifted to the railing and beyond, out toward the center of Mundus.

Megan leaned over the railing, beaming and rocking to and fro as the glowing orb floated higher into the night sky. It soared over the sprawling estates, gardens, and terraces, becoming smaller and smaller against the swath of stars in the night sky. The spires of the distant temple glimmered with its reflected light as it rose above them. After a while, it left the city behind, becoming a mere dot of light meandering above the barren plains.

Megan turned to Aylun and he to her. Smiling, she held his gaze for a long moment in earnest gratitude and admiration.

He nodded and smiled back, sharing the moment of gentle release. "Better?"

She stepped forward, then flung her arms around him and squeezed. "Thank you."

Megan lingered for a while, and he let her, feeling the comfort of her warm embrace. Then he regained his senses. He was here to help her let go of Jon. Aylun let his arms fall to his sides. Megan stepped back, and he averted his gaze as a sudden awkwardness came over him.

"We are friends." Aylun gave a quick nod. "It was just a hug. Friends can hug, right?"

Her smile broadened, and she gazed with fondness, seeming to take amusement in his discomfort. She nodded agreement, and they both turned their attention back to the tiny dot of light, watching as it passed below the moon and out of sight.

Chapter Twenty-Two

BREAKFAST ON HIGH

Dellia set out from the Shirdon stables in the cold and dark of an overcast morning with a steady drizzle. The dismal weather made a perfect match for her downbeat mood, which remained as bleak as it had been the night before. She trod to the spire outside Shirdon, where drops of rain pelted the intricate carvings of the round stone base. As she guided Ulka onto it, a liquid portal appeared above her, where the teeth were closest. Painted on its surface was a different gray sky, the one at her destination.

She pressed her red spire stone to the white symbol on one of the three toothlike spires arching up high above her. The shimmering curtain passed over her, and she arrived in the large, flower-strewn clearing outside the western edge of the Illis Woods. Here, the sky remained just as bleak and the ground was still wet, but the rain had ceased a short while earlier. It gave her heart a small pang to recall that day only a few weeks back, when she had arrived at this same spire in the same clearing, to a warm, sunlit day as she headed to meet Jon for the first time.

The trek west, out of the rain-soaked woods, was a miserable one, and she left the trees and shrubs behind, cold and soaking wet from brushing against the still-dripping foliage. Beneath gloomy gray skies, she headed due west across the flat, grassy expanse of the Talus Plains, keeping the distant mountain range on her left to guide her. Constant worry and regret followed her over how broken she had rendered their marriage in a matter of hours. Why was she always hurting Jon?

While the weather might have been miserable, the dark and wet were perfect for a horse like Ulka. Both allowed him to exert himself for long periods without overheating. So she kept a brisk pace, trying to cover as much ground as possible before the heavens made good on their threat to once again pour cold, hard rain down upon her. It was late afternoon, and she had just passed Egina when it finally came, this time decidedly heavier than a mere drizzle. The downpour reduced visibility to near zero, and if it kept up, it would make all her hard riding pointless. Even if she could reach the path Jon and Garris were most likely to take, a pounding rain would muddle any prints to the point of being useless.

After dark, she continued by the light of her sunstone until Ulka had almost reached his limit. Unable to carry on, Dellia headed for the nearest town and stayed at a local inn for the night. She arrived late enough that she had to wake the surly innkeeper to obtain a room, and left at dawn before the town had roused from its slumber.

The next day remained as dreary as the first, though the rain had let up. A morning fog obscured everything, including the mountains she relied upon to guide her. She had to use instinct to find her way along the nearly featureless landscape. Near midmorning, the fog had abated, and soaring, snowcapped peaks were once again visible on her left, set above the vast carpet of green. She made good time, heading cross-country to arrive at the road north of Nydri around midafternoon.

The darkness of sunset came early due to the overcast sky, and she passed through Liaka, the town north of Nydri, without spotting any sign of Jon or Garris. She kept heading north until it seemed certain that if they had come this way and made reasonable time, they would have already passed south. So she turned Ulka around and headed back, making a second pass south over the same still-muddy roads, searching for any tracks she might have missed. None showed, and she made it all the way to the far side of Nydri before stopping to consider whether to give up her search for the day.

AYLUN

She was staring at the ground, contemplating where to stay, when she spotted the two sets of hoofprints barely visible in the light of her sunstone. One displayed the distinctive jagged line of Jon's Enna, and the other seemed like it might be from Garris's horse, Kyri.

In an instant, the sight lifted her mood. After two days, she had finally found their trail. Feeling more encouraged, she traveled along the path south, holding her sunstone high and squinting down to catch sight of each track. Then it occurred to her that the only place to stay south of Nydri was a small stable and adjacent barracks that served as a way station for patrols. With the sky again threatening to let loose, it seemed the most likely spot Garris might choose for the night's rest.

Paying little attention to the hoofprints, Dellia headed straight for it, arriving in no time. Not wanting to rouse anyone, she strived to remain quiet as she led Ulka into the crude stable. As she entered, she saw all of her efforts rewarded by the familiar faces of Enna and Kyri. Ulka seemed to appreciate being settled in for the night in the stall next to Enna. She could only hope her presence might give Jon as much comfort.

Once she finished, she made her way to the nearby barracks. It was really nothing more than a rough log building with a single hall down the middle, flanked on either side by a half dozen cramped rooms. She snuck through the sturdy timbers of the doorway and was a short distance down the hall when she spotted Garris in one room and Jon in another on the opposite side. It seemed doubtful that Garris wouldn't have noticed her arrival, but if he did, he never gave it away.

Dellia tiptoed through the low entry to Jon's small quarters and over to his cot. Staring down at him, lying on his side and so peaceful in his slumber, gave her a tremendous sense of relief. She was near him, and that meant she was one step closer to setting things right.

The bed was barely large enough for one person, but her heart told her she needed to be with him, and that being here and spending the night next to him was important. The tiny cot gave a soft creak as she slid into it behind Jon and pulled herself close to his back, barely fitting between him and the edge of the bed. She slipped an arm around him and hugged him close.

At her touch, he stirred, and his sleepy eyes glanced at her over his shoulder. "Dellia?"

She kissed the back of his head. "Shh ... sleep."

He intertwined his arm with hers and hung on to it as if afraid that this was some half-asleep imagining that he might awaken from any moment. She set her sunstone on top of her pack so she could watch him by the light reflected off the rough-hewn ceiling. After a while, he slid to one side, lay on his back, and pulled her head over to rest on his shoulder.

She curled up next to him, content to lie where she could hear his heartbeat.

Jon stroked her hair with a soft, mesmerizing touch. "Listen, there's something I need to say."

She looked up at his face. "Then say it."

"I love you, Dellia."

The knot in her heart unwound at his softly spoken words. "I know."

"I mean, I really love you, and Megan doesn't even have any feelings for me."

Dellia paused. It seemed an odd thing to say. She had sensed the woman's true feelings when the two parted in the Illis Woods. There had been a moment when Megan told him, "You have no idea how much I want to grab you now and go away with you, away from all this." The longing and affection behind those words remained every bit as vivid in her memory as the words themselves. Megan had feelings for Jon. That much had been obvious.

Not long after, on the way to her mother's house, she had even attempted to convince Jon of that fact. Yet he had been insistent that Megan wasn't interested, that she had told him it was "never going to happen" between them. That the woman wasn't interested in him was a complete lie, of course, but it was not for her to contradict him and reveal Megan's heart. Particularly when the woman had gone so far out of her way to create that impression. For whatever reason, Megan must have wanted to cut off any chance of a relationship with Jon. To oppose that effort would be to abuse her gift, so all she could do was to push the subject with a few gentle questions, hoping Jon would rethink it. Yet, he remained adamant, so she let it drop.

Nothing had changed since. It was still not for her to divulge Megan's secrets. Besides, another woman's emotions were hardly the point. Dellia looked up into Jon's eyes. "I know how Megan feels."

His soft stroking of her head stopped, and he peered down as a hint of surprise appeared on his face. "What does that mean?"

"Megan's feelings are private and not something I can talk to you about."

"Are you saying there's something to talk about?"

Dellia paused again. This was not going well. She wanted to make amends, and talking about Megan was not a road that would ever lead to that destination. "Look, what I'm trying to say is that it's not Megan I married. It's you. It's how you feel that matters."

Jon lay still for a long while. When he spoke, there was a note of tenderness and understanding in his voice. "It would be a lie to say I have no feelings whatsoever for Megan. How could I not care about her? How could I not worry about her? We've known each other for ten years. She was my best friend."

She felt obliged to correct his characterization. "You were in love with her."

"It's not the same." His reply was instantaneous, and even though she knew his words to be true, the swiftness of his response somehow made them more reassuring.

Jon laid his head back down and looked up at the crude timbers of the ceiling. "I think what attracted me wasn't really her. It was the idea of the life we could have had together."

"A life you can never have with me."

He looked back at her face, her head still resting on his shoulder. "A life I gave up because you were more important."

He reached out with a gentle hand and brushed her hair back out of her face. "It's you I want to touch. It's you I want to hold. It's you I want near me. You are the one I want to see each day when I wake up." He lifted his head and looked into her eyes. "How can you not see the difference? I sent Aylun to get Megan. If you were the one missing, heaven and earth would not have stopped me from going myself."

His softly spoken words took her breath away. They were everything she had wanted to hear for the last two days. He continued to search her eyes as she considered how to reply. She knew his heart, and she knew the truth of every sweet word of reassurance he had uttered. Even so, she couldn't help how she felt. As petty as it might be, he was hers, and it bothered her that he had any feelings at all for Megan. Still, she knew there existed no shred of doubt or conflict in his heart. He was right: what he felt for Megan paled in comparison to how he felt about her. Perhaps that was all she could hope for.

She lifted her head enough to give a slight nod. "Okay."

Jon continued to search her eyes. "Okay?"

"Yeah, you're asking me to trust your heart." Dellia nodded. "Okay, I believe you. I trust your heart." She put her head back down and lay still for a while, listening to his slow breathing.

He began his soft caressing again, this time of her back.

Then it occurred to her that Jon had gone out of his way to set her heart at ease. Her motive in finding him had not been to gain his reassurances, but to make amends. Which meant that it was her turn to do the same for him. She needed to set *his* heart at ease.

She lifted her head again and looked at his face. "I'm sorry if I let my insecurity over Megan get the best of me. I know better than anyone how you feel."

Jon smiled. "You're entitled." He stayed quiet for a while, his fingertips wandering slowly up and down her spine. Then he added, "I didn't really go after you to give you a hard time, you know. I think I just let Grekor get inside my head."

"Grekor?"

"Yeah, the guy who tracked you down. He made some off-hand comment about you and Aylun being alone together. He said plenty of other men would ... um ... find you attractive. Then he reminded me I'm ..." Jon let the half statement hang.

Dellia gazed up at him. "You're what?"

His gentle caresses stopped again as he seemed to summon the courage to finish saying what he had started. "Oh, let's face it. You could do better than me."

"What?"

"So when I saw you and Aylun together and him being so tall and muscular and all, I just kind of snapped. I let my jealousy get the best of me."

"Oh Adi, Jon, what's wrong with you? How can you even think that way? I choose who I'm with, and I've given myself to you. I'm yours, nobody else's."

He smiled at that. "I know. It's stupid."

Dellia smiled back and kissed his chest. "... In a sweet, flattering kind of way." She set her head back down, feeling the warmth of his heartfelt words as the room drifted into silence. For a while, she lay still, thinking about the last few days and what had weighed most on her mind. She had so much she wanted to say. But now—in a cramped cot, in the middle of the night—was neither the time nor the place for a lengthy discussion.

Eventually, she summoned the courage to speak of what burdened her heart the most. "You know I left Aylun and went back to Shirdon."

"You did?" Jon seemed to mull it over for a moment, then added, "Oh, I suppose you had to, or else how would you have known where to find me."

She nodded. "Do you know what the worst part was?"

He stared at her, his eyes asking her to answer her own question.

"It was finding an empty house. It was sitting at home with no idea where you had gone or what you were doing."

575

"Oh, I'm sorry. I thought—"

"No, that's not what I'm saying. You had every reason to leave. You thought I wouldn't be around to miss you. And to be honest, I had set the precedent. It was me who left you without letting you know."

Jon searched her face again, clearly wondering what her point was. "Okay?"

"I'm saying, I don't ever want to feel that way again—not knowing where you are or what might have happened to you. Imagining the worst."

"The worst?"

"That you were gone. That you'd left me."

He considered for a moment, then let out a soft breath of exclamation. "Oh."

She gazed into his eyes. "What I'm saying is: I'm sorry. I didn't put myself in your shoes. I didn't think about how you'd feel. So, can we make a new deal?"

"What kind of deal?"

"Unless it's life or death, or literally impossible, neither of us leaves the other again without talking about it first, without saying goodbye."

Surprise filled his face. "You would do that? You'd make that promise?"

"Yes." There was no hesitancy in her response.

Jon seemed eager to take her up on her proposal. "Then, of course, I agree. I will never leave without telling you first, and if that's impossible, I'll make certain that you find out where I went and why."

"And I vow to do the same."

Content that they had reached a new understanding, Dellia snuggled closer and lay her head back down on his shoulder. He pulled her head closer to him, then his fingertips wandered down along her arm in light, hypnotic strokes.

From the next room, a voice boomed out: "Now, if you two are quite finished, I'd like to get some rest tonight. ... And put away that light."

She scooped up her sunstone, dropped it into her pack, and closed it tight. Then she peered at the doorway through which the voice had come. "Sorry. See you in the morning, Garris."

A grunt came from the other room, and with that, all discussion ended.

As the heartache and conflict of the last few days drained away, Dellia's gift came back, nearly as strong as ever. With it came a new and worrisome perception. Jon was more at peace now, but somewhere, deep inside, there was a distance between them that hadn't been there before. She mulled it over, trying to quantify it, to understand it.

They had talked it out. Jon was even lying next to her, caressing her arm with gentle strokes. If they had reached an understanding, if they'd cleared the air, then what accounted for this veil that still existed between them. Then it dawned on her. It was a kind of apprehension. She had broken the bond of intimacy they had shared a few days ago. Still, in the past, she had quarreled with Jon, but something was different now.

A sadness came over her as she realized where the difference lay. After their marriage, Jon had trusted her with all his heart. He had never once shown the slightest reluctance to open himself up to her. He had been willing to be vulnerable. Her harsh words and her disappearance had pushed him away. They had broken his trust, and now he was hesitant to be as open with her again.

She breathed a small sigh and buried her head into his shoulder. *She* had done this. No matter how confident he may seem on the outside, he was like most men: loath to admit weakness, especially where feelings were concerned. Her gift allowed her to sense those feelings even without him expressing them. Still, what had made Jon special was his willingness to trust her, to be open and honest, to admit his innermost feelings without reservation. Her harshness had destroyed that willingness. She had not taken care of his fragile heart, and there was no telling how long it might be before she could rebuild his faith in her so he would trust her with it again.

A soft breeze wafted across Megan's face, waking her. From beyond the row of open windows opposite her small bed came the distant lilting of laughter, neighbors chatting, and children playing. A quiet rustling came from that direction, and Megan opened her eyes. Aylun was sitting there watching her, his head backlit by the sunlight streaming through the window behind him.

Those warm rays lifted her spirits as they brought back memories of the happy days of anticipation she'd spent in this room. Yet, like the irresistible pull of a black hole, the memory of that terrible night in the Verod camp began to tug on her, threatening to crush her under the oppressive weight of her own insufferable dilemma. Then Aylun sent her a smile of gentle sympathy and encouragement. The familiarity of the scene and warmth of his concern held back the heaviness of her heart.

As if sensing the two opposing forces tugging at her, he stood, strolled to her bedside, and thrust out his hand. "You're awake. I have somewhere I want to take you."

She blinked through sleepy eyes as she stared up at him, wondering how long he had kept vigil over her. His comforting presence and her curiosity over where he intended to take her banished that oppressive weight. She decided to indulge him and try to face the day with greater optimism.

With a mischievous smile, she shot him a sideways glance. "You lie in wait in a lady's bedroom, and as soon as she wakes up, you demand she go with you? Does that approach work with a lot of women?"

Aylun rubbed the nonexistent whiskers of his chin. "Honestly, I do not know." His smile broadened. "Tell you what, I will go try it out on a lot of women and let you know."

He turned to go.

A strange and familiar feeling hit her: he was walking away again. Megan called out. "Wait ... it's just, a lady has to be careful."

He halted and turned to face her, his smile still as reassuring as ever.

Megan put on her best demure act. "I've heard crazy stories about men who up and abduct women without so much as a please or thank you?"

Clearly playing along, Aylun gave a knowing nod. "Yes, I have heard of scoundrels like that." He strolled back to the bed and peered down at her. "I assure you, my motives are as pure as the driven snow. My only wish is to treat you to a morning picnic with a fantastic view."

She nodded in acquiescence. "Okay."

Anticipation of this mystery picnic buoyed her spirits as she rose and hurried through her morning rituals. They set off in the brilliant morning sun, winding through one avenue after another. Along the way, the sights of the city and liveliness of the brightly clad residents strolling along the roadways kept her sadness at bay.

Eventually, they arrived at a vibrant market with savory smells floating on the still air. Aylun hustled her past the stands selling fresh meats, vegetables, and grains of all kinds. They stopped at a number of vendors roasting, boiling, and baking delicacies to eat fresh off the stand. He explained each dish, its flavor and texture, history, and reputation. He even reminded her of her previous remarks on each, as well as which she seemed to have favored before.

The atmosphere was lively, and the diversion exactly what she needed. She let herself become caught up in the moment, enjoying Aylun's discourse and the enchanting sights, sounds, and smells. Altogether, he kept her too busy to focus on her own sorry state of affairs.

They gathered a plentiful selection, then he ushered her off to a small, squat brick building with a broad tower shooting up two stories above the rooftops. It had the appearance of a guard post—a well-fortified perch where vigilant lookouts could keep an eye on the homes and streets below.

To her surprise, he opened the door, and they passed through to a spiral staircase that wound its way to the peak. As they stepped up through a hatch to a flat platform at the top, they were greeted by a panoramic view of the city that was every bit as fantastic as promised. They settled in the open, airy space, with heavy columns at each corner supporting a generous wooden roof. Aylun spread out their fragrant meal in the shade of its overhang, and they ate at their leisure, enjoying the tastes and smells as they surveyed the bustling market and sun-filled streets.

He kept the conversation light, never asking where she had been or what she had done since they parted. With deftness and tact, he steered the conversation away from every topic that began to cloud her mood. The warmth of his company, tenderness of his care, and breathtaking view left no room for thoughts of the past to take root in her heart.

Near the end of their picnic, Aylun smiled at her, and it seemed as if tiny gears were whirring in that little brain of his as his gaze turned to the shoppers below. "You know what I think would help?"

"Help what?"

"Help you."

She gave his question due consideration. "Getting rid of the annoying man who won't let me wallow in my own self-pity?"

He shook his head. "No, that … that would not help at all."

"Are you sure?"

"Yes. What you really need is to let it all out."

"Oh, I don't like the sound of that. What does that mean?" Megan shrank away from him and crossed her arms over her breasts. "Let all what out?"

He chuckled. "Not that." He peered again at the crowd below. "I want you to yell."

She stared at him, not sure if he was being serious.

He motioned out toward the spires and rooftops. "Go ahead and shout."

AYLUN

She looked at the people milling in the market below, then stared at Aylun. "Right here? Right now?"

"Yes. Let it all out."

"I can't."

"All your pent-up anger, sorrow, and frustration. Every awful thing you have suffered through—bring it to mind, then pour it out in a big, loud yell."

"No."

He shot her a glance full of ancient pain and loss, then let loose with a resonant howl. It was a sort of plaintive cry that hurt her heart. Like the bellowing of a warrior mortally wounded in battle, it flowed out of him loud and long, echoing down the streets of the city.

People in the market turned their heads upward, watching the pair of lunatics at the top of the tower.

He looked at her sideways. "Now, you do it."

At his display, she'd felt the walls of propriety weakening and her desire to join him in his escapade growing. But she still resisted. "Aylun!"

"Come on. Do it."

"I can't."

He stood and let fly again with an even more plaintive yell. It resounded through the busy market, and in it, she felt the loss of his sister, the agony of surviving when his friends perished, and all the years of pain, sorrow, and regret that followed. It battered her own heart, moving her, making her want to cry out, not just for herself, but for him. "I ... I ..."

Almost without meaning to, Megan let out a scream of her own. It poured from the depths of her soul, carrying with it all her pent-up despair and frustration. Swept up in the moment, she let her gift take hold, and wind began to whip around her. Crumbs, a half-eaten piece of fruit, and the basket he had brought the food in rose from the ground as her cry echoed through the busy square. Then it ended and they all dropped to the ground.

Aylun stood for a moment staring around at the fallen items. Then he seemed to snap out of it and motioned to the crowd below, most peering up at them. "Now yell at Jon. Not by name. But tell him how he made you feel."

She hesitated.

"Make him feel your suffering all the way back in Shirdon."

She nodded and rose to her feet, then bellowed to the crowd below, "How could you do this to me?"

He nodded encouragement and motioned for her to continue.

"We were friends! I thought you cared about me! I thought you loved me." The women below began nodding approval and talking among themselves in soft and sympathetic tones. It encouraged her.

Aylun motioned to them and nodded. "Come on. More."

She shouted out with everything she had. "I left for a few days! I risked my life to protect you, and while I was going through hell, you ran off and married another woman? Do you know how rotten that was? Do you have any idea how that made me feel!"

The men looked away or fidgeted while more approvals and a few claps came from the women below. Megan stood on tiptoe and screamed at the top of her lungs, "How could you do this to me!" Then, out of words, she crumpled down into a sitting position, feeling spent, while the brilliant, sunny day, full belly, and clapping from below caused her spirit to soar.

Aylun beamed at her as he came to rest at her side. "Feel better?"

She smiled back. "Yeah." With her gaze held steady, she paused for a brief time, then added, "Thank you."

They sat in silence, basking in the moment, as the clapping from below tapered to a stop. Despite the warmth and sun when she awoke, it had been a struggle to keep the day from seeming gloomy, but now she felt refreshed, and at least for a while, her troubles seemed more distant.

The rough sound of a throat being cleared disrupted her reverie. It had come from the stairway behind them. She twisted around to spot the head of a black-haired, golden-skinned woman rising up through the hatch. It was soon followed by a short body in official-looking attire. The woman's piercing gaze fell first on Megan, then Aylun. Then she spoke in a harsh and accusatory tone. "How did you get in here?"

Before Megan could answer, Aylun stifled a laugh.

She shot him a disapproving glance. From his casual manner, she had assumed this was all aboveboard. What maniac cheers someone up by doing something illegal? This was just like him. She slapped his arm and let out a loud whisper, "What have you gotten me into?"

He ignored her, eyeing the intruder with a sincere expression. "I could swear that door was open, ma'am."

The woman seemed taken aback and leveled a skeptical glare. "You could swear?" A smirk broke through her stern expression, but she quickly suppressed it and folded her arms. "No, it wasn't."

He shrugged. "Huh. Really? Are you sure?"

"I should arrest you, just like the guard who locked the door insisted I do."

Megan stiffened. "Arrest us?"

Aylun set a hand on her shoulder and sent her a reassuring glance. Then he looked up at the woman. "She had nothing to do with this. Surely you could just overlook—"

"Fortunately, Antar Gatia only wanted you escorted out of here by armed guards."

Aylun shot Megan a grin and winked, then bowed his head. "Yes, ma'am." He began to gather their things.

The woman put a stop to it as she blurted out, "Even more fortunately, Asina heard your outburst." She peered at Megan. "She is entirely sympathetic. She had me intercept the guards and take over in this matter."

Aylun stopped and looked up at the official-looking woman. "Asina? One of the rulers of the realm? The Rhanae?"

"Yes, and her orders are much more lenient. She has no desire to disrupt your outing. Finish what you are doing, take your time, and clear out when you're done." Her stare became much sterner. "But no more theatrics, understand? Or there *will* be arrests."

Aylun smiled. "Of course. No more yelling."

With crisp efficiency, the woman turned to go. She yanked the hatch open, then straightened and paused. Her expression softened as she eyed Megan and mumbled, "I'm sorry about that man who married someone else. Forget him. You deserve better." With that, her brisk manner returned, and she marched down the stairway out of sight.

Once the hatch was shut, Megan glared at Aylun and shook her head. "What is wrong with you?"

He chuckled.

She huffed. "You're incorrigible."

He beamed a huge smile. "It is one of my better qualities."

Despite her peevish state, she couldn't help but laugh. She began to pick up the remains of their meal, feeling a sudden need to leave no speck to betray they had been here.

Aylun reached out and put his hand on hers, stopping her.

She raised her head, and her questioning eyes met his.

He looked at her with a profound expression of sincerity. "I need you."

Megan froze as her heart stopped. "What?"

Aylun held her gaze for a moment. "Do you remember how Wistra's journal said she had left a warning in the Vault of Time?"

She shrugged. "I ... I guess."

"Do you remember me saying there was never any such warning?"

She nodded.

"I found the site of an older Vault of Time. It is the place where the warning would have originally been kept. It is empty, except for a door with a lock I cannot open." He let that sink in a moment. "I need your dragon key."

She shrank away from the idea. Going on this picnic had required no small amount of talking herself into staying positive. The idea of going out in the world—it was too much. She had just begun to feel human again. Her knee-jerk reaction was to go back to hiding away. To shelter herself and protect her heart.

She balked. "I could just lend you the key."

Aylun shook his head. "No. I want you to come with me."

"But you could just—"

He rushed out an explanation. "It is in Elore, but with your spire stones, we could be there this afternoon and at the old site by evening. We could poke around tomorrow and be back here by the day after."

She hesitated for a moment. It was just as she feared when he showed up wanting her to come with him. This was why she didn't want him helping her. She lowered her head. "You like me a lot, don't you?"

Aylun seemed surprised. He delayed for a while, then looked down and spoke with quiet reluctance. "How did you know?"

She stifled a giggle. "You are so clueless. How could I not know?"

He raised his head and stared, shocked and perplexed.

Megan averted her gaze as she began to pick up crumbs around her. "It's in every line of your face, in every action you take." She looked up into his eyes. "You get angry when I won't let you help me. You look wounded when I hurt. You get happy when I crack the smallest smile." She looked away for a moment, then returned her gaze to his. "It's all I've thought about since last night. You aren't here to take me to Jon. You're here because you're worried about me, as more than just a friend."

He smiled a warm smile and nodded. "Yes, I like you."

"Oh, Aylun ..."

"I like you a lot, but that is *my* problem. How I feel ..." He placed his palm on his chest. "My heart is my responsibility." He stared into her eyes. "I promise, I will never make it yours."

She hesitated.

He smiled again. "I am not asking anything from you. I am not expecting anything, okay?"

"But I don't want to lead you on. I don't want to give you the wrong idea. If we travel together again, it will only hurt more when I have to leave. This isn't right."

Aylun nodded. "It is Jon who is in your heart. He has always been in your heart. That is good. That is what is right. I made my peace with that from the very beginning."

"You'll get hurt. That's not okay."

"It is *my* heart. I know it better than you do. So, it is okay if I say it is okay. Just let me help you. That is all I ask. It is all I need to make me happy. Okay?"

Her resistance crumbled as she ran out of objections. She paused for a while, torn, then nodded and smiled. "A trip does sound kind of fun."

Aylun beamed. "A mission."

"An adventure."

They finished up and descended the tower. As they reentered the market, fleeting glances met them along with hushed discussions, but the looks were more sympathetic than annoyed. The sun had crawled some distance up the pure blue sky, and the morning crowd and vendors of the market were thinning. They pushed through and soon hit the open spaces of the lane home.

Not long after they cleared the dwindling shoppers, a golden-haired woman hurried up beside Megan. She had the sureness of foot and confident bearing of a fighter. That impression was only enhanced by her leather armor, the color of burnt umber, and the deep green robe that covered it.

She shot Megan a cheerful smile as she pulled up beside her and chirped, "Are we going somewhere?"

Taken aback, Megan glanced over at her. "Ex ... Excuse me? 'We'?"

AYLUN

Aylun sighed and pointed. "Megan, this is Protector Rillen. Rillen, this is Megan."

All his dire warnings about protectors came screaming back, and Megan jumped away as if Rillen were radioactive. "Protector!" She banged into Aylun, tripping them both up and almost knocking them to the cobbles in a painful heap.

He caught himself and righted Megan, but then shrank away a bit. "Oh, I may have neglected to tell you. Jon became council leader. Protectors work for the council." He pointed again at Rillen. "She works for Jon."

Megan's jaw dropped. "Jon? We're talking about *my* Jon, right?"

Rillen reached across and punched Aylun in his arm. "You didn't tell her?"

"Ouch!" He rubbed the spot.

Megan laughed. Then she grinned and nodded as she bugged her eyes. "Hit him again."

Rillen raised her fist.

Aylun put out his hands to block her. "Do not hit him again!"

Rillen hesitated, then shrugged. "Sorry, I'm supposed to help her in whatever way she chooses."

Aylun ducked behind Megan.

The protector danced around to get a clear shot.

He skittered back and forth, thrusting Megan between them as if she were a shield. "That's it, she is not coming with us."

Megan stifled a giggle as she ducked, giving Rillen a clear shot, which connected nicely with an impressive thud.

Aylun grabbed his arm and winced as he moved away. "Hey! That's going to leave a bruise."

Her giggle turned to a full-throated laugh. "Oh, she's totally coming with us." Suddenly liking this woman, Megan threw her arm around Rillen's shoulders.

The protector smiled, seeming to take the stranger's embrace as totally normal.

One arm still around her new friend, Megan walked away,

leaving Aylun standing there rubbing his shoulder and staring after them.

She glanced at Rillen. "Any way I choose?"

The protector nodded. "I'm paraphrasing, but yes, I vowed to help you."

Aylun scrambled to catch up to the pair.

Megan smiled. "Oh, a vow." She couldn't suppress another snicker.

Chapter Twenty-Three

THE SOUTHERN LIGHTHOUSES

Jon stared at himself, standing on the stage of the Laminus Theater outside Egina. At his feet lay the medallion the dragon had given him, with its three leaves: one of black metal, one of gold, and one of silver. Above it loomed the translucent image of a serene middle-aged Elorian woman. It was Wistra, the oracle of his prophecy. Over her shoulder, the red crescent of the moon shone out from between drifts of clouds that billowed across the evening sky.

Light from the oracle's glimmering likeness flittered through the trees swaying in the gentle breeze. In the seats beneath their rustling boughs sat the five Ephori, the ruling body of Talus. They stared upward to the stage, transfixed as her voice boomed out, calming yet sure, carrying with it the seven-hundred-year-old prophecy from the Greatest of Oracles.

"… A vision. Not to prepare you, but to ease my conscience. A warning. So that if you accept this burden, you know the ultimate cost."

The image faded away, leaving Jon standing alone on the stage. For a moment, the scene lingered, then melted into a new one, of him watching himself as he sat around a table in Antar Gatia's bright and sprawling home. The shiny medallion rested on the table between Jon, Gatia, and the rulers of Erden, the Rhanae. Above it floated a massive image of Wistra, almost reaching the ceiling. They all watched as the same image repeated, precisely as before.

589

"... A warning. So that if you accept this burden, you know the ultimate cost."

The image faded again, leaving the four sitting around the table. Then it shifted into a third scene in the emperor's palace in Kanlu and a fourth in the grassy vale of the Verod camp. Each time, Jon watched himself as the image replayed, every word and gesture repeating in exact detail.

The image of Wistra faded for the fourth time, and in a sudden burst, he was back standing in the dark confines of the oracle room, where Wistra had first revealed her prophecy. This time, he was not a spectator watching himself but back in the scene, reliving it as it had played out that day. Surrounded by a dozen Shirdon soldiers with their swords drawn and their bows aimed at him, Jon watched the round platform where the image of Wistra repeated a fifth time.

"... A warning. So that if you accept this burden, you know the ultimate cost."

The message finished, and Wistra faded, as usual. Only this time, a new image of her appeared, standing right on the platform. On the floor before her sat the medallion with a second image of her own likeness hovering above it. She bent over and touched each of the three leaves: first black, then gold, then silver. The figure above the medallion dissipated, leaving only one image of Wistra, hunched over and pulling her finger away from the silver leaf.

With quiet grace, she stood and turned to face Jon. Everything seemed to slow to a crawl as she looked right at him, her gaze lingering on him, as if she could see him. ... No, not as if she could see him. Her eyes were staring directly into his. He felt those eyes watching him. She smiled a tender smile as she continued to hold his gaze.

Then, as if in slow motion, she reached down and plucked a round stone from the center of a symbol on the stone platform. It was a ruby circle inside a triangle, with five golden lines radiating out from it.

AYLUN

The small round stone magnified, becoming larger in his mind's eye. It was translucent, with swirls of gold and glittering ruby red. No sooner had she lifted it from the ground than everything dissolved into darkness.

Jon's eyes cracked open, staring at the rough-hewn beams of the ceiling and listening to the soft rummaging of Garris in the room across the hall. He drew a deep breath of brisk morning air, taking comfort in the warmth of Dellia snuggled next to him on the cramped cot. He lay for a while, listening to her slow breaths as he waited for the dream to fade, but it refused, lingering longer and more vividly than any dream he could recall.

Then it occurred to him: they were all memories, scenes he had lived through, but with the exception of the oracle room, the dream was different. ... No, not different, really. They were identical in every minute detail. What had changed was his viewpoint. He was watching himself. Each scene had unfolded exactly as it had that night, and until the oracle room, each had replayed at an angle from which he could not have seen it. People recall memories from the same point of view every time, the one they experienced it through. This was new. This was different. It was a memory he could not have had.

And there was another difference, too. The sequence had highlighted an aspect that had escaped his notice. ... Well, it hadn't entirely escaped his notice. He had puzzled over it the first time he replayed the message, in private, while rehearsing before his appearance on the Laminus Theater stage. Afterward, he had forgotten the oddity of it in the confusion of that night's rush of events. And it seemed as if the dream were his mind's way of focusing on the difference.

In the dream, as in real life, each of the four scenes had ended with the image of Wistra fading away. The first time he'd seen it, in the oracle room, it had not ended there. It had transitioned into another image. One that never appeared in any subsequent replay.

One where Wistra was looking directly at him. One where she caught his gaze and their eyes met.

In the dream, it had seemed so real. As if Wistra were watching him from the seven-hundred-year-old oracle room. It was the same impression he had been given during that first viewing. She was seeing her prophecy play out in real time. She was visiting him in her future.

While the dream might be his mind's exaggeration of a minor detail, the difference itself was real. He had locked eyes with Wistra *herself*, across the centuries, in that oracle room. He tried to put the whole thing out of his mind. It was just a stupid dream, random synapses firing in his brain. Or was it? It didn't have the quality of a dream. His mind refused to let go of the memory, and every instinct told him it was important, it was crucial, that his mind had hung on to those moments for a reason.

He tried to distract himself with warm thoughts of Dellia near him and remembrances of their conversation of the night before. It was a feeling he still hadn't gotten used to. She had missed him. She had come here to be with him. She had *chosen* him.

As if sensing his thoughts in her direction, her sleepy voice came from beside him. "I don't like where you're going."

A little surprised to find she was awake, Jon twisted onto his side to face her. She didn't move—her beautiful countenance near his, her soft eyes peering into his, and her warm breath caressing his face.

He gazed in puzzlement. "What?"

She sent him an affectionate smile. "As your protector, I must advise you that I don't like you going so close to the mountains."

"As my protector?" He mused for a moment, then brushed her hair away from her eyes. "And what about as my wife?"

She smiled, seeming more awake. "Oh, well, as your wife, I'd strictly forbid it." By her tone of voice, he could tell she was serious about the danger, but at the same time, she was toying with him.

He played along. "Really?"

Dellia nodded.

"Why?"

She sat up and turned her back to him, her voice taking on a sudden serious note. "Nothing but death comes to those who linger too near the Alundeer Mountains. This outpost is as close as patrols go because it's not safe to go closer." She stared over her shoulder at him. "Most who disappear are never seen again, and what's left of those who are is gruesome."

Her warning nudged something deep inside him, perhaps some forgotten bit of acquired knowledge. It reached down into his soul, stirring dark and dreadful memories he couldn't quite bring to the surface. Images flashed through his mind of vast armies deep below ground, of facing row upon row of dark and twisted creatures, horrors of every imaginable shape and size, stretching back as far as the eye could see, and the words "we have to stop it," spoken by his own mouth. But why he had uttered those words? He couldn't quite recall.

Then again, perhaps he was overthinking it. Perhaps it was just Dellia's assertion itself. The people of Talus were skilled fighters, trained from youth. For such well-disciplined and well-organized warriors to retreat from anything was an unsettling prospect. Or perhaps this feeling was just another remnant of his odd dream.

Unable to comprehend the root of his unease, Jon turned his focus to his wife. "Then can I ask a serious question?"

She scooted around to face him. "Always."

"Do you think you can stop Garris from going?"

Her response was a flat and unhesitating, "No."

"Do you think we should make him go alone?"

"No." She rose and began to prepare herself for the day. "You know, it's not very much like a council leader to debate these things with your protector. You order, they go."

His response was instantaneous. "And how does it go over with a wife, to order her to go?"

She granted him a playful smirk. "That would be very bad."

Jon nodded. "I see."

He rose as well, snuck up behind Dellia, and slid his arms around her slender waist. "Look, I'm not just going to avoid Shirdon or politics. I'm going because it's important to Garris. To him, it could be a matter of life and death. How could I not want to help him?"

She wrapped her arms around his and hugged them. "Okay. And I would go in a heartbeat to help Garris. It's just I don't like *you* going."

He smiled. "Oh. It's like that, is it?"

Dellia hugged his arms tighter. "Uh-huh."

After that, he busied himself with preparations for the day's journey. They set off early, supposedly headed straight for the mountains. A light fog coated the featureless expanse, making it impossible to tell where they were or where Garris was leading them. In fact, mile upon mile passed with nothing to greet them but light-gray vapor and green grass that faded into mist in every direction, leaving no visible means by which to guide their path.

It didn't seem to bother Garris, who plodded along with a purposeful air that made it seem as if he knew precisely where he was going. After a while, the puzzle of it became too much, and Jon called ahead. "How can you tell where you're going?"

Dellia and Garris both responded in unison, "The road."

Jon scanned the area around him, yet all that met his gaze was flat grassy terrain disappearing into gray fog beyond. "Huh?"

Dellia leaned closer. "The Saranik Road. It's partly buried here, but if you pay attention, you can feel a difference in hoof-falls between the cobbles just below the surface and ordinary dirt."

It was an answer that raised far more questions than it cleared up. Roads connected places, but Garris had said Nydri was the southernmost city before the mountains, and Dellia had asserted that the outpost where they had spent the night was as far as travelers went. So then, where would this Saranik Road go?

Moreover, a cobblestone road out here would have required extensive, backbreaking labor to construct and no small amount of

594

upkeep. Even more if seldom used. To be worth all that effort, the road had to go somewhere important and well traveled. Yet there appeared to be nowhere south of here to go. Assuming time would provide the answers, Jon let the topic lie and returned his attention to their mist-shrouded surroundings.

In the past, it had been the convention for Garris to take the lead while Dellia followed behind, the pair protecting him as if he were as fragile as a cracked egg. This time, Garris took the lead, as usual, but Dellia had chosen to ride at Jon's side. When asked, she commented she was more worried about what was ahead than behind, and she was better prepared to protect him from all sides by being close. He would have liked to imagine that she just wanted to be near him, but her matter-of-fact delivery made it hard to maintain that fantasy.

For most of the following hours, he tried to focus on political issues, knowing Kayleen would expect answers upon his return. But his mind flittered among all the questions that crowded his thoughts.

It wasn't just the road to nowhere that puzzled. Garris seemed to think that he was being lured here, that this was all a trap. But why lay a trap days away from Shirdon? The entire area around the city was a wooded wilderness. If your only goal was to ambush someone, why not do it an hour away instead of days away, at the far edges of the human world? So, the notion that it was a simple trap seemed far-fetched. There had to be another agenda, another reason the ambush needed to be laid way out here. But what could that be?

From time to time, he couldn't keep his thoughts from drifting back to Dellia's discontent with him. Guilt ate away at him over her accusation that he was determined to be useless, particularly because it was true. That was precisely what he was doing. Yet, the whole effort to hand power back to the three realms was both earnest and deliberate. They wanted control, and he didn't want to get involved in decisions like ending the protectors. It seemed like just the kind of thing where his input would invite disaster for him and his plan to remain as council leader.

It was clear he was letting Dellia down in an epic way by not acting, yet what could he actually do? His was but one voice on a council of nine. If they decided to do away with the protectors, there was little he could do to stop it. So he kept trying to bring his thoughts back to Kayleen's list of issues, but distractions undermined his efforts.

When the fog finally cleared, the mountain range filled the view before them. Now only a short distance ahead, it loomed massive and imposing. Jon had seen some part of the same mountains before, from far away at Sirra's house on the Talus Plains and up close at the Recluse Tower, but it looked very different here. To the right, peaks soared higher than those behind that tower. They rose to wispy clouds that shrouded their white-capped tops. On the left, the range remained somewhat lower and more jagged, like a torn sheet of paper.

In between, the two halves rolled inward to a broad gorge with sheer cliffs. Directly in the center lay a massive tower, rising stark white and glittering above the vast grassy expanse. It wasn't like the Recluse Tower at all. Its base seemed heavier and more squat, and it was perhaps only a hundred and fifty feet tall, whereas the Recluse Tower seemed to be over two hundred and fifty feet. At the top, held aloft by the pair of massive pillars nearest them, stood an enormous metallic disk, hiding whatever else lay there.

Jon pointed. "What is that?"

From the saddle in front of him, Garris yelled back. "They call them the Southern Lighthouses."

Jon puzzled over the assertion. There was only one in view, yet Garris had said "them." Moreover, the "lighthouse" reference made no sense.

He eyed Dellia next to him. "But there's no water here, and if there was, it would partly submerge that thing."

Garris shot him a glance over his shoulder and shrugged. "Things change?"

Dellia peered over at him and added her own shrug.

596

Neither of his companions' responses was helpful in any way. Lighthouses aided in navigation, particularly of treacherous waters. To make them more visible from a greater distance, they were almost always placed at high points in the landscape, such as upon cliffs overlooking the sea. To put a lighthouse here, at the lowest point in the terrain, with no water anywhere in sight seemed ludicrous.

Then there was the disk at the top. It did resemble an oversized parabolic reflector of the kind a lighthouse might have, but it was aimed toward the mountains, where there could be no ship to see it.

Unable to make sense of it and reasonably sure any answers he got would be no more helpful than the last ones, Jon shouted ahead to Garris. "Is that where you're headed?"

He glanced backward. "Nope. We're headed there." He pointed to the gorge beyond the tower.

Jon watched it for a while as the wide chasm and towering rock walls grew larger with every heaving of Enna beneath him. Then he turned his attention back to the tower as they began to pass it. It had an open doorway through which its massive walls were visible. The stones had an appearance similar to that of white granite, glittering in the late-morning sun. The structure seemed taller than simple stone and mortar could support. It was of a size that would require steel-reinforced concrete to prevent it from collapsing under its own weight.

Time and the elements had worn the stones of the outside wall smooth, but the mortar that held them together seemed unaffected. It was white and sparkling like the stone itself and gave the impression of being much sturdier than the rocks it cemented. Perhaps the sparkles were flecks of quartz or even diamond. Perhaps the sturdier material might even account for its soundness and immense size.

Beyond the door, at the back of the tower, a spiral stairway hid in the shadows. Under it lay many metal chests, their newness and lack of dust seeming out of place in their ancient-looking surroundings. The contrast meant one thing for certain: despite Dellia's warning, someone had been here, near the mountains, in recent times.

As they plodded past, what was hidden behind the giant reflector at the top became visible. In front of it, over the center of the tower, lay a tarpaulin covering some kind of massive sphere that filled well over half the space there. A tarp of simple cloth would have decayed within decades, if not years, meaning it couldn't possibly match the age of the tower.

His neck sore from craning and unable to fathom the tower's purpose or presence, Jon returned his attention forward. With the morning haze now gone, and the sun high in the sky, the gaping crack in the mountains was lit up, bright and clear. Sheer cliffs rose on either side as the horses clomped into the enormous gap.

The grass disappeared as the rock walls closed in behind them, and farther ahead, covered in spots under patches of rubble, the cobblestones peeked through. Able to see it for himself now, it became undeniable: the Saranik Road Dellia had spoken of was real, and it did go somewhere. It went through this chasm, but to where?

The group plodded around a bend, and suddenly their surroundings felt claustrophobic. The space they were in was wide enough. It was, perhaps, several hundred feet from wall to wall, but the soaring height of the sheer cliffs made it seem closed in and confining. Jon glanced behind as the open plains disappeared from view, leaving only solid stone walls on every side. Suddenly it came to him that he hadn't been nearly inquisitive enough about where Garris was taking them.

Jon glanced at the man. "It occurs to me I might have a few dozen questions."

Garris grumped back, "Not now."

Dellia leaned closer and whispered. "We may be riding into some kind of trap. Now is not the time to chat."

Jon went quiet. It wasn't exactly idle chitchat he was after. If they were headed into a trap, it might be useful to know a thing or two about this road, these "lighthouses," and where they were going. He returned his attention to their unsettling surroundings, the clatter of hooves seeming to multiply as it echoed between the sheer rock walls, making it sound like a dozen horses.

Time crawled as they wound their way along the gorge for a couple hours or more, and the sun passed above from one side of the cliffs to the other. Then it appeared around a bend: a second "lighthouse," just like the first, standing smack in the center between the two walls, with the cobblestones leading right by it. It even had the same enormous reflector at the top, this time aimed down a long, straight channel of rock that stretched out behind it, a half mile or more in length.

Garris turned his head and pointed to the glittering structure. "This is it."

Questions and concerns still raced through Jon's mind, but Garris returned to looking around with an intensity of focus that said he was on high alert. Alarmed that he remained too much in the dark about too many things, Jon decided to ask anyway. Enna rocked gently beneath him as he leaned forward in the saddle.

Dellia must have sensed that he was about to speak because she set her hand on his arm, and when he looked over, she sent him a subtle shake of her head, as if to say, "Not now." Then her expression turned to one of intense alertness as she scrutinized the tower and the area around it.

His two companions' silent survey continued as his alarm grew, and they came to a stop at an open door. Garris slipped from the saddle and stepped to the ground. He peered inside the tower base, looking left, right, up, and down. With a quick motion, he signaled Jon to stay put. Then he sent Dellia some kind of hand gesture and returned to creeping around the base.

She must have understood because she followed suit, checking the inside and outside wall, then stepping around in the other direction as she surveyed every inch of her surroundings with an edgy intensity.

Jon followed, but Dellia made another hand motion that was almost certainly an order for him to stay put.

The two soon vanished around either side, leaving Jon standing alone, feeling useless and vulnerable. Then more new-looking chests caught his eye again. They were like the ones at the other tower, dust-free and lurking in the dark recesses under the stairs. They called to him, inviting him to satiate his curiosity.

He crept over and surveyed the dozen chests stacked in neat piles beneath the steps. The lid of one let out a squeak as he lifted it, and he was shocked to find it jammed full of ancient-looking glass balls, most the size of the palm of his hand. He picked up one, wondering at its familiar size and shape. Lost in concentration, trying to trigger the right brain cells to recall where he'd seen it, he paid little attention to the light source approaching from behind him. It traced his outline against the wall, growing brighter until it streamed down into the chest from over his shoulder.

Jon startled at a presence near his face. He glanced over, and Dellia's head was right next to his. She was holding her sunstone high as she peered over his shoulder. All at once, it hit him: the glass balls resembled her sunstone. That was where he'd seen them before. He peered down again as the entire contents of the chest began to glow with a faint light.

Garris appeared, glancing over his other shoulder, as Jon whispered, "They're sunstones." He scanned the stacks of chests. "Hundreds of them."

Then a bizarre and improbable notion occurred to him, and he glanced up, expecting to spot some kind of light or mirror at the center of the top, but darkness was all that met his eyes. It didn't matter. It didn't change his hunch, and he murmured to himself, "This really is a lighthouse."

Now convinced he was right, but more confused than ever about a lighthouse in the middle of a canyon, he eyed Garris, then Dellia and whispered, "But why build a light—"

Dellia raised a finger to his lips. Then she interjected, her own voice almost too quiet to hear, "Questions later. We need to check out the rest of the tower."

AYLUN

Garris led the way up the staircase that hugged the wall of the tower. Yet, its inside edge was not square, unlike the walls that supported it. It curved to make a perfectly round spiral at the center of the square tower.

Their silent climb was a not-at-all-subtle reminder of their experience at the Recluse Tower a few weeks earlier. Memories came back of the bloodcurdling screeches and roars, scurrying walls of flames, and Dellia falling, and his alarm returned, as did his appreciation for her insistence on quiet and concentration. With no barrier or railing of any kind, one slip or stumble would lead to a quick death.

The climb up the stairway seemed interminable—fifteen flights of silent ascent and intense alertness. It was plenty of time to notice that a spike, sticking into the center of the tower, came out of the inside edge of each carved stone step. Each one bore a loop of metal at the end that was perpendicular to the climb of the stairway. And each struck him as the perfect size and shape to cup a sunstone.

As they neared the top, light from Dellia's own sunstone glinted off the dark, curved surface of a massive glass sphere. It rested in a hole that filled the entire center of the ceiling. The hole in which it sat was large enough to allow it to arc below the ceiling, hinting at its enormous size.

Jon's vision of the lighthouse shifted in his head as he realized what it was: a massive sunstone, perhaps as much as fifteen feet in diameter, based on its curvature. He staggered to a stop, staring at it as they reached the ceiling. Caught in a stupor, he stood there as designs for the lighthouse rolled through his mind.

Garris heaved open a hatch in the ceiling, and Dellia gave Jon a gentle nudge. All three passed through and stepped out onto the open top, which only had an ankle-high lip around the edge. It was all that stood between them and a hundred-and-fifty-foot fall. Heavy-looking chains crisscrossed the area, wrapped around four sturdy white pillars that marked each of the corners. Most were slung over the tarp covering the massive ball at the center, arranged as if to secure it in place.

601

Jon crept to the edge and peered down. The lip might as well have been nonexistent, and the sight of the horses and road so far below was vertigo inducing. He stepped back as Garris and Dellia seemed to relax.

She looked over at the warrior standing next to her. "If this is a trap, I don't get it."

Garris nodded. "This is the time and place, but I don't understand either."

Jon turned his attention to the tarp. From the ground he had seen a covering of an identical shape, size, and color at the top of the first tower. That made it a near certainty that whatever was under this tarp was the same as what lay under that tarp. He lifted the edge and peeked beneath. It was, as he suspected, an enormous, smooth glass ball. "It's a sunstone, isn't it?"

Dellia sent him a curious glance, then bent over to peer underneath the tarp. She stepped up next to his side and shoved her own sunstone beneath it, lighting the enormous, curved surface. She shook her head. "The color is wrong. It's tinged yellow, not clear."

Garris spoke up from behind them, seeming annoyed. "Fascinating. So it's a flamestone. Can we get back to the reason we're here?"

Jon kept quiet. He wanted to make some snappy retort, but a vague anxiety filled him as he examined the chains and tarp. The chains were older, ancient perhaps, but the tarp seemed new. Someone had put it here not long ago, just like the sunstones in the chest.

Sunstones were about light and the sun. Which meant the giant flamestone at the top and sunstones in the chests must somehow power the lighthouse from the light of the sun. The tarp covering the massive flamestone at the top of each of the two towers meant someone had disabled both of them in recent days.

Constructing such enormous towers, here in the middle of nowhere, was no simple task. It meant rigging huge scaffolding, hauling massive amounts of rare white stone and mortar, and lifting them many stories high. There were no trucks and cranes, no dynamite or motorized winches, no heavy machinery of any kind. So all of that required astounding amounts of raw man power. No one would build such a massive structure here, in an uninhabited area, unless they had a very good reason. And whatever that reason might be, someone had disabled it.

His mind spun, trying to figure out how this could be the trap. He was so absorbed in thought, he paid little attention to Garris's voice behind him. "This would be a fine spot to shove someone off."

Dellia's voice came in reply. "If you mean attack someone and throw them from the top, it seems risky. You could easily die yourself."

Garris grumbled as something far out along the gorge below drew Jon's attention. He rose to his full height and froze as a deep dread came over him.

He remained that way, staring into the distance as Garris continued. "Maybe they saw three of us and called off—"

Jon gasped as his gaze flew from the massive flamestone to the giant reflector, then followed its focus to the dark thing in the gorge below. Suddenly it all clicked. "Guys, where does the Saranik Road go?"

Dellia chirped back, "Saranik, obviously." Then her voice softened as she answered Garris. "But there was no one around when we got here. Maybe they haven't arri—"

"Is it dark there?" Jon's voice failed to hide his alarm.

Garris shot back, "Yes. … No. … Kind of. … Saranik was lost to the Dead of Night."

"What? What is this Dead of Night?"

"It's a darkness that blankets the entire region."

"Did it look like that?" Jon pointed to a black cloud slowly rolling toward them down the shadow side of the gorge. Only *rolling* wasn't the right word, nor was *cloud*. It possessed the appearance of fog, only black, darker than black, so dark it became difficult to see if it even had a shape. It was as if it were absorbing the sunlight, and with so little light reflected back to reveal its shape, it appeared almost featureless, almost formless—a moving, shifting absence of anything.

Dellia and Garris turned and stared at it. They all stood frozen as Jon's dread grew, filling him with an awful foreboding. It reminded him of the feeling of looking into the Blood Wolves' eyes. The sight touched some forgotten memory within him, just as Dellia's warning about going near the mountains had, and he knew with unerring certainty that they wanted to be as far as possible from whatever hid in that darkness.

A sudden clank, followed by a banging, came from below the hatch.

Their gazes whipped down.

Garris flew to the hatch and yanked, but it refused to budge.

Jon motioned as if presenting the dark void to his companions. "Well, I think we just figured out your trap." He glared at Garris, still crouched and tugging furiously on the handle. "Perhaps if someone might have allowed me to ask a question or two, I might have figured this out sooner."

Garris froze again, and his head swung up. His eyes focused on Jon with alarming intensity. He continued to stare as he rose to his feet. "Figured out what?"

"Someone has disabled this lighthouse. The sunstones mean it's powered by the sun. This tarp here"—Jon pointed to it—"is new. It was put here recently. It blocks the sun." He motioned to the base of the tower. "The chests below contain sunstones. They've been removed from inside the lighthouse. They somehow work with this thing to create a bright light, or heat, or something." He traced the beam's path from the stairs below to the flamestone and to the parabolic mirror. "The reflector sends that light down the canyon to ... that." He pointed once again to the darkness flowing toward them like a slow-motion flood washing down a canyon. "My guess is these lighthouses were constructed to stop that, or at least keep it from passing them."

You could almost see the gears whirring in Garris's head as he stared.

604

Dellia gawked at the dark cloud. "Oh Adi, no." Her eyes turned to meet Jon's as an uncharacteristic look of panic filled them. "You can't be right. You just can't be."

Garris's face turned a shade lighter. "Who would do that?"

Their reaction was far more alarming than he'd expected, and Jon's gaze shot between them. "What?"

Dellia stared at him with eyes wide. "The Dead of Night destroyed Saranik. It was unstoppable. The entire southern quarter of Talus was completely obliterated in a matter of days. It turned it into an uninhabitable terror land. If it reaches the rest of Talus …"

Garris nodded. "Being trapped up here will be the least of our concerns."

Stunned silence reigned, broken by the distant whinnying of spooked horses far below.

Before the implication dawned on Jon, Garris had unslung his crossbow and flown to the edge of the lighthouse.

Dellia joined him, and by the time Jon reached the edge to peer over, Garris had loaded an arrow and taken aim. With a twang, the dart rocketed from the bow. It whistled through the air to graze the hand of a sturdy, bald-headed man below as he reached for Ulka's reigns.

The man didn't raise his head or even glance up. He just broke into a run, zigzagging down the gorge, leaving the horses behind.

Garris grumbled as he loaded another arrow. "Of course, if he was going to trap us here, he'd kill or steal the horses too." He took aim. "Just for good measure, you understand."

The arrow flew from his crossbow and whooshed downward to graze the heel of the fleeing man. Garris nocked another as his target continued darting back and forth down the gorge, then dodged behind a bend and disappeared from view.

Garris stopped and glanced up at Jon. "Okay, Mr. 'Figure It Out.' How about you figure out a way to get us down from here."

Jon stared, dumbfounded. Since when had anyone paid attention to anything he said on this trip? He pointed to the floor. "The hatch?"

Garris grumbled and shook his head. "I already tried, and it's probably a waste of time trying to bust through it. If the fellow who locked us up here is smart, he'll have wedged something beneath the hatch that blocks the hole."

A screech followed by a distant scraping echoed up from the haze of nothingness billowing down the canyon toward them. Jon glanced over as a chill ran through him. The sound gave every impression that something was hiding in that darkness, and he was sure it was not a thing he ever wanted to see up close.

Dellia's hopeful gaze flew to Garris. "We have dragon boy." She turned to Jon. "What good is a dragon if you can't call them when you need them?"

"How?" Jon boggled. The only thing that had allowed him to ask for help last time was that he was already face-to-face with the dragon in her lair. He had no secret bat-phone with which to contact Isla. He still recalled the nightmare-inducing moment he had asked for her help. Her face inches from his and her hot breath blasting his face, he had been frozen in terror by the utter disdain in her eyes and the growl in her voice at the very suggestion. He shook his head. "Besides, Isla isn't *my* dragon. She barely tolerates me. She took a pretty dim view of helping me last time."

Garris grumbled, "Useless dragon."

Jon glared at him. "Yeah, I'm sure her biggest concern in life is how she can be of use to me."

Dellia thrust her hand in front of his face and pointed to the ring her mother had given her. "My mother's gift. Take it and use it to open a portal to the ground."

Garris snorted. "You told her about your gift?"

Jon eyed him sideways. "She's my wife. You think I trust you more than I do her?"

Garris tilted his head and nodded. "Fair point."

Jon returned his gaze to Dellia. "I don't think I can."

"What do you mean?"

606

"I've never been able to use my gift to take the same ability more than twice from the same person."

Her eyes pleaded. "Do you think it's possible?"

He faltered. "Maybe … I mean, it feels like it."

"Then try."

Jon glanced at the dark stain pushing relentlessly down the chasm toward them. Like a wave, it rose from its billowing front edge, making it much higher and far more massive than when it first appeared.

He interlaced his fingers with hers, her touch soothing his jangled nerves. He closed his eyes and concentrated, summoning as much of his will as he could. With the warm metal against his skin, he pictured Sirra opening the portal on the Talus Plains. The image was strong and clear in his mind, but nothing happened.

He took a slow, deep breath as Dellia had taught him.

"That's good." The appreciation in her voice told him she sensed him calming himself. The recognition strengthened his resolve, encouraging him to redouble his efforts.

He concentrated again, harder this time, and the memory roared back. For a moment, he sensed the power of that image reaching out to touch his gift. It lingered there before him, a forgotten word, lost on the tip of his tongue, beckoning him, taunting him with its familiarity. Then it slipped away again.

He gave it a third go, and it became even stronger. The image seemed almost real, and time even appeared to slow, as if his gift had taken hold. Then, the world sped up again, and it all drifted away. He opened his eyes. "It's no good. It's not working."

He shot another glance at the darkness, then eyed Garris. "Can you climb down?"

The warrior looked out at the black patch now engulfing the far quarter of the gorge, towering high along the cliff walls. He moved to the edge of the tower and leaned over to run his fingers across one of the smooth white stones of the wall.

He stopped and regarded the wall's surface stretching far down to the ground below. "I want to say yes, that there's nothing I can't climb. But to be truthful, these stones are as slick as polished marble. I think I would be inviting a fall. I doubt anyone could make it."

Jon considered for a second. "Do you have a rope?"

"With me? No." Garris pointed to the horses tied up below. "In my pack, yes." He paused and mumbled, "Why didn't I think of that?"

Jon's gaze flittered here and there across the broad top of the tower as he backed up. Then he bumped into one of the chains. Faster than he could form the thought, his mouth blurted out, "The chains." He scanned them crisscrossing the area. "How long are they?"

The top where they stood was at least thirty feet, side to side. Some sections of the chains passed from one corner to the opposite corner, running over the tarp at the center. That was a distance of over forty-two feet by his calculation, and there were at least four such lengths. He nodded and answered his own question. "They've got to be at least a hundred and sixty feet. They'll reach the bottom."

He scanned the chain link by link, looking for the method by which it had been secured, but Garris spotted it first and grumbled. Jon glanced at him and followed his gaze to an oversized, ancient-looking lock. Corroded and pockmarked, it had been looped through one of the shiny links near either end of the chain. Jon pointed. "Can you open it?"

Garris strolled over, ducked under some of the chains, and came up next to it. He pulled and tugged, dislodging some of the dirt and rust that coated the outside. "It's pretty sturdy."

"What about picking it?"

"Not a skill I ever had."

Jon looked to Dellia.

She shrugged. "Me neither."

He stooped under the chains to come up next to Garris. "Then we'll have to force it."

Dellia sent a puzzled look. "How?"

"Ever see a tourniquet?" Jon pointed to the pair of chains next to one another.

Garris stared as he let out an "Oh."

Jon looked at the weapon at Dellia's side. "I need a sword."

Garris balked. "You'd destroy it."

"It's either her sword or the Dead of Night, you pick."

"I have more than one. Use mine." Garris unsheathed his blade and thrust the hilt out for Jon to take.

It reminded Jon of the first time Garris had handed him a sword, during his initial lesson in how to use one. Back then, he had taken the weapon gingerly, as if it would attack him all on its own. In the daily lessons since, he had become far more comfortable. So, this time, Jon took it right away and threaded the gleaming blade through one of the links, almost to the hilt.

He stopped as he realized he didn't have any idea what kind of metal the chain had been forged from. It was lighter than iron or steel. It shone like silver, and though it was old and dirty, it remained free of rust or other corrosion, like titanium or aluminum. He glanced again at the cloud of nothingness flooding down the gorge and began torquing, using the weapon as a handle to twist the two adjacent lengths of chain around one another.

As he turned, the chains tightened, the lock groaned, and a crackling came from the stone columns they were wrapped around. He twisted again. The chains pulled tighter, scraping along the hard surfaces of the columns and flinging chips of white rock as they went. He turned again, and again they sprayed chips and grated as they tightened.

Garris lent his muscle, applying force with care to the blade of the sword. The pitted and scratched lock deformed, then broke open with a loud clank, and the silvery chains rattled to the floor. Jon slipped the blade out of the link and handed it back to Garris.

Meanwhile, Dellia began to unwind one of the chains from the posts. With a metallic clatter, she pulled the loose end from around one pillar and heaped it in a pile next to her. Then, she moved to a new corner and started again, pulling the length from around the next pillar to unwind the old heap and make a new one at her side.

Garris joined her, feeding lengths of chain from the old pile over the tarp and out around one side of the post, while Dellia pulled them back in around the other.

Jon stood back, unsure what to do or whether he would be more of a hindrance than a help. Upon finishing the second-to-last post, Dellia left the chain around the last pillar and pulled both ends up to her.

She glanced over at Garris. "Grab the end. We'll lower you down." She thrust out the last few links of the longer piece for him to take.

He snatched them from her. "It'll be faster if I climb down."

He rushed to the corner adjacent to the post with the chain wrapped around it and started feeding lengths over the edge, hand over hand.

Dellia grabbed the other end and scooted over to the corner opposite Garris. She wound the end around her arm to secure it, then spun in place to wrap it behind her back. Then, she leaned back against the pull and braced herself. She motioned with her head for Jon to come over. "Don't just stand there. Help me hold this steady."

He rushed over to a spot right in front of her and took hold with both hands. Then, he followed her lead and leaned back against the increasing weight. The friction of the chain around the post would help keep it from slipping, but if it did slip, it would pull both him and Dellia toward the edge or maybe even over it. He put the possibility out of his mind. There were two of them, and Garris couldn't be that heavy.

In hopes of following his progress, he craned his neck, trying to watch Garris at the opposite corner, but the massive tarp-covered sphere between them made it impossible. So he tried to crank his head around to see how Dellia was doing but couldn't quite hang on and twist around far enough to see her right behind him.

Then a sudden nerve-jangling jerk of the chain sent his feet skidding on the smooth white floor. His panic mounted as he slipped and slid across the slick surface. Then a yank from Dellia behind him brought him to a stop. It served as a jolting reminder that they were now holding the full weight of a pretty large man. Perhaps he had underestimated the mass of the warrior decked out in all his weapons and armor, not to mention the entire length of metal that held him.

Jon avoided focusing on the chain tugging him toward a fatal fall by keeping an eye on the dark mass growing ever more imposing as it rolled down the gorge. His frequent glances made him keenly aware they had little time to get off the tower and away from here. To make matters worse, his feet slipped several times, and his muscles burned from exertion, threatening to give out as he held the chain with sweaty palms. Yet, with Garris's life literally in his hands, tiring out and giving in were not options. So he held out until, at last, the weight vanished, and he almost fell backward into Dellia.

She fell on her rear with a grunt of pain.

He spun around. "Are you okay?"

She nodded. "Shouldn't we remove this tarp and try to get this thing working?"

Jon reached down and helped her up. "I don't think it will." He pointed down toward the center of the tower. "There are holders the right size to fit sunstones all along the inside of the stairs. I think this flamestone thing at the top lets the light of the sun pass through to those sunstones." He made a motion to show sunlight funneling down through the glass sphere. "They must store it to power the lighthouse. But someone removed all the sunstones from inside. They took them and put them in the chests at the bottom of the stairs."

"Then we put them back."

He glanced at the cloud of nothingness. Now consuming half the gorge, it rose in billows, filling a space between the sheer rock walls as tall as the tower. It wasn't moving fast—only a little faster than a brisk walk. He did a quick calculation of speed and distance. Then he did another estimating the number of steps on the stairway and the time it would take to put all the sunstones back in their holders and repair the tower. He returned his attention to Dellia. "There's no time."

"Then Garris and I will hold off whatever that is, or whatever hides in it, until we get them put back."

Jon shook his head. "What if the horses die? Then how do we get out of here? What if it covers the top of the lighthouse and blocks out the sun? Without the sun, it will never work, and we'll have wasted all that time for nothing." He paused as he did another quick computation, comparing the relative speed of the cloud to that of a running horse and the distance covered, to determine the time they'd gain if they retreated. It was all guess work, but it seemed as if it would be more than enough time. He pointed back the way they'd come. "It would be better to fix the one back at the start of the canyon."

"But that will leave only one lighthouse to stop it."

"And if we die here, nothing stops it. It's smarter to fall back and fix the other lighthouse, where we have plenty of time."

Dellia gave a crisp nod, as if complying with an order, and they returned to waiting. There were about fifteen flights of stairs, and even someone as fit as Garris couldn't take that many stairs at a run. If he could do each flight in ten seconds, it would still take him two and a half minutes to get to the top.

Dellia fidgeted, a thing she never did. In fact, he had never seen her in a panic before, and it was more than a little disconcerting. She stopped and stared at him, her face pale and drawn. "It was critical information, Jon. My entire homeland is in danger. You should have spoken sooner."

He froze. This was why he didn't want to be in charge. Already, he was being blamed, and his only blunder had been to be a little slow on the uptake. "Sooner? ... I tried to ask a question, and you stopped me."

"I know, but you're the leader here. It was your responsibility to weigh Garris's concern against the threat and speak up if you thought it was important."

Jon boggled. How was he supposed to know it was a threat to an entire realm? Not once during this trip had either Dellia or Garris acted like he was in charge. In fact, she was the one who had shushed him as if he was a mere underling whose thoughts were of no consequence. Now she was telling him he was in charge and shouldn't have listened to her?

He shook his head. "This was Garris's mission. I didn't know what was happening any more than you or he did. I just had questions. Besides, I would rather we work as a team."

"Why? So you won't have to be responsible? If you don't want to stand up for me, that's one thing, but to be a menace to every life in the three realms, I—"

Dellia's head swung down to the sound of banging from below the hatch.

Jon stared at her. The unfairness of her accusation stung, and he wanted to defend himself, to explain he didn't speak up because he'd had nothing concrete yet. But he'd already said that, and it went in one ear and out the other. Besides, Dellia was afraid. Fear didn't seem to be in her vocabulary until today, and arguing her out of it was a fool's errand. It was not the right way to help her.

He reached out and rested his hand on her shoulder. "Don't worry too much. We will get to the other lighthouse and get it working. We will stop this thing, whatever it is."

She turned her gaze from the persistent noise below and locked eyes with him. Her expression softened. The fear was still there, but her irritation was replaced by a hopeful glimmer in her eyes. She gave a small and grateful nod as the hatch burst open, and Garris's head appeared.

His breath was heaving from exertion, and he gave an energetic motion for them to come. "Let's get out of here."

Garris disappeared, and Dellia ducked through the opening.

Jon took a quick look out at the darkness drifting down the gorge toward them. Echoing up from it came a disturbing medley of screech-like cries, scraping, and the flutter of giant wings. Clouds didn't screech and flutter like that, and it reenforced the impression that something lived within that darkness. Almost two-thirds of the chasm had disappeared now, blotted out by a vast void that terrified even Dellia. There was time to reach the bottom and outgallop it, but the disquieting nature of what hid in that impenetrable darkness urged him to all haste.

He flew through the hatch and plunged down the steps, struggling to catch up to Dellia.

Garris was well ahead of her, dropping two and three steps at a time, a disconcerting feat, given the absence of any railing to protect him from a dozen-story fall.

Dellia's feet were a blur—she was almost keeping pace with Garris—but Jon lagged, his breath growing heavier and his heart hammering harder with each flight.

By the time he reached the bottom, Garris had pulled the dapple-gray Enna around, ready for Jon to mount. The massive warrior's muscles bulged as he reached down into the doorway, grabbed Jon by the hand, and yanked him up by his arm, flinging him onto Enna's back.

As his steed came around, Jon took one last look back at the enormous wall of nothingness, now filling his entire view of the gorge behind them. Like a wave washing down the chasm, it towered dark and massive above them, rising well above the height of the tower. In no time, it would eat the lighthouse whole.

His gaze lingered for only a split second before he urged Enna forward, and all three of them surged to a gallop. The clatter of the horses' hooves alternated between a dull thud when they pounded the dirt and a loud clack when they struck raw cobbles, the rumble echoing down the sheer cliff walls as they raced back the way they had come.

Jon glanced behind them to watch the darkness disappear around a bend in the path. Though he could no longer see it, his sense of urgency didn't ease. Instead, it only grew. This was a gamble. He was guessing as to the purpose of these lighthouses, how they

worked, how to fix them, and how long it would take. In fact, everything he had said with such confidence was based on nothing more
than a loosely strung-together series of assumptions. If he was wrong,
the consequences would be unthinkable. Still, he had set them on
this path. There was no turning back now.

As they rounded another corner, the sturdy, bald-headed man
from before appeared. Though he was still attempting to escape
down the gorge, his pace had become nothing more than a slow jog.

Garris surged forward, aiming to fly right by him.

As he passed, the man glanced back, revealing a scraggly blond
beard and wide brown eyes that held an expression of terror.

Garris reached down and plucked the man from the ground by
his shirt. He clocked him on the back of his shiny skull and slung his
limp body over the saddle in front of him.

They continued down the gorge for what seemed like forever.
Just when Enna was growing weary, the vast green expanse of
the plains came into view along with the first lighthouse, soaring
into the sky.

Jon yelled ahead. "The chests below the stairs. I think they
contain sunstones. There are holders along—"

"Orders? What orders?" Garris peered at him as his body heaved
up and down in the saddle.

Jon shook his head and raised his voice even louder, trying to
make himself heard over the thunder of hooves. "No. Not orders,
holders. Holders for the sunstones. They are on every step of the stairs.
We have to return the sunstones to the *holders*." Garris nodded, and
Jon continued. "Then, at the top, we have to remove the chains and
the tarp and pray it works."

Garris nodded again and bellowed out, "I'll haul the chests.
You and Dellia get the sunstones from them and put them back in
the holders."

Jon nodded back. "Good. Good. That's good. We have a plan."

The moment they arrived at the lighthouse entrance, Garris
tossed the saboteur's limp body to the grass and launched himself

from Kyri's back. There were a dozen chests under the stairs. He yanked two of them out, hoisted one onto each shoulder, and raced up half the first flight of steps.

Jon followed with Dellia on his heels.

Garris set the first chest down in the middle of the first flight and carried the second one farther up along the second.

No sooner had the first chest hit the steps than Dellia threw the lid open, snatched several sunstones, and raced down to the bottom.

Jon followed suit, carrying several sunstones farther up.

Each holder was a simple metal rod, with a looped band of shiny metal at the end, formed to be open on either side but still cup the sunstone. They had been angled to follow the rise of the stairs, such that the open sides of each faced the holders on the steps above and below.

Jon peered through the loop, and sure enough, the next couple of holders were aligned to form a spiral. He pushed one of his sunstones into the band of metal, and it popped into place with a soft click. He continued up and filled the next two as Garris clomped down past him.

By the time they emptied the first chest, Garris had already placed the next chest three-quarters of the way up the second flight, the perfect spot to fill the holders quickly. It was a shock to find that Garris, of all people, could divide the number of flights of stairs by twelve chests in his head to figure out where to place them.

Jon continued alongside Dellia, the pair working in silent haste to place sunstones along all fifteen flights of stairs, as Garris clattered along the steps behind them, carrying full chests up and empty ones down. Even the sturdy warrior needed to rest near the end, after having hauled pairs of containers up and down a dozen flights of stairs. Afraid there might not be enough sunstones, Jon breathed a sigh of relief as he popped the last one into the final holder.

Dellia flew to the hatch and held it open.

Garris burst through to the top, located the lock, and flew to it before Jon even had a chance to look around. It appeared heavier and newer than the previous one. The hulking warrior did as they had last time and jammed his sword through a link in the chain to twist a pair of adjacent chains around one another.

Jon joined in, heaving with him as the links creaked and scraped along the corner pillars in showers of chips. They pushed one more time. A low crack came from under the tarp, and the chain slacked ever so slightly.

He grabbed Garris's arm. "Stop. We're going to crush the flamestone." Jon hesitated, then pointed to the tarp. "Leave the chains. We'll have to pull the tarp out from under them."

In a flash, Dellia rushed over and began to tug on the edge of the heavy fabric.

Garris flew to her side and joined her.

Jon unwound the twisted chains, slid the gleaming sword out, and dropped it to the white stone floor with a clatter. Then he shook the chains lying on top of the tarp, hoping to disturb their weight and make it possible to slide the tarp out from under. But with multiple lengths of heavy links slung on top of one another, they were too heavy.

Still yanking on the tarp, Dellia looked over at him with pleading eyes. "It's no use."

Jon stopped, pondered for a second, and snatched the sword from the stone floor. He thrust it into a fold in the fabric near the chain. With a ripping noise, it tore through. Then he yanked on it, and with a louder tearing, he cut a slit down the fabric.

Their attention drawn by the sound, Dellia and Garris stopped their tugging and joined him, each retrieving a knife with which to slice away sections of the sturdy tarp.

As they peeled away the first pieces, the light of the sun hit the stone, and after a while, it began to glow. Jon stopped to peer into the dim light inside the orb, and it was as he suspected and feared: the stone had a gigantic crack in it where the chain had pushed down too hard. They had damaged the lighthouse.

All he could do now was hope it still worked. So he returned to helping Garris and Dellia, working feverishly to cut away swaths of fabric and pull the remnants out from under the chains. The more they carved away, the more of the stone they exposed to the sun, and the brighter it glowed, until all three had to squint to see what they were doing.

As soon as they finished, Garris bellowed out, "This is blinding. We need to get out of here, now!"

Jon covered his eyes as Dellia yanked open the hatch. He peered down into the tower through the cracks in his fingers. The inside was flooded with an intense white light. The sunstones along the stairs were ablaze, much brighter than any he had ever seen. A beam of brilliant light wound its way from blinding sunstone to blinding sunstone, spiraling up the entire length of the stairs.

It struck the enormous flamestone on the side exactly opposite the reflector. The angle was just right to send the beam through the flamestone to hit the mirror and send it down to blanket the entire entrance to the gorge. Light from the sunstones and the beam had turned the walls and stairs inside the tower a blistering white, making it hard to see anything.

Jon faced Dellia. "It's extremely bright in there. It can damage your eyes. You need to cover them." Then he paused. "Just a minute." He picked up a piece of the rough cloth and pricked two tiny holes in it about as far apart as his eyes, then peered through. The frayed edges of the fabric obscured his view, but it did shield his eyes enough to see ... sort of. He held it over his face. "Use the fabric we just cut off. Make two very small holes to see through, then use it to cover your eyes."

He handed the cloth to Dellia and bent down and grabbed a second piece. As he came up, his shoulder brushed against the flamestone, and it was quite hot. Somehow the sunstones were concentrating the sunlight coming through the top and sending it back up to the flamestone to heat it. Even more alarming, it had become much hotter in just the short time since they'd finished

618

removing the cloth. Who knew how hot it would get? Perhaps as hot as a laser. If they stayed much longer, they might even bake.

He called out to Garris and Dellia, "It's getting hot. Avoid that beam of light going through the sunstones. It might burn right through you."

He moved to go through the hatch, but Dellia caught him. She snatched the piece of fabric covering his eyes, repositioned it, and tied it behind his head, so his hands would be free.

Garris finished tying a piece of cloth around his own face and barged past and through the hatch.

Dellia finished hers right after, and Jon went ahead of her, following Garris down the stairs. The light was so bright that even through the frayed edges of the hole, it washed out most of the details of the stairs and walls, making it difficult to make out anything.

Garris plunged down the stairs ahead of him, again taking two and three steps at a time, and soon disappeared below.

Less sure of his footing, Jon kept one hand on the wall as he hurried downward. Dellia's footsteps came from right behind him. It was apparent she could go faster, but she was watching out for him. He stumbled in his haste and lurched for the edge, but Dellia caught him and shoved him forward, guiding him with one hand on his shoulder.

The air became hotter as they descended, and after what seemed like an interminable time, they stepped through a doorway, leaving behind the stifling heat and light. The cool breeze of the plains hit them as they dodged around to the side of the lighthouse.

Jon removed his eye covering, but a ghost of the blinding light lingered in his vision, obscuring his sight. He waited for it to clear, then looked up. The light from the top of the lighthouse was extraordinarily bright, even in the daylight. Yet it didn't seem as blinding from down here as it had above. He glanced out across the grassy expanse, and the reflector was sending a beam down to blanket the entire base of the gorge in bright yellow light.

Dellia looked to Jon with apprehension in her eyes. "Do you think it will stop it?"

He paused, trying to calm himself and not betray his anxiety. "I don't know. I think it was designed to, but we damaged it. Still, that seems pretty bright to me."

A groan of disgust came from Garris and Jon glanced over. The warrior was shaking his head and staring at the ground where he had dumped the unconscious body of the saboteur, but the burly bald-headed fellow was gone. He must have awakened and fled while they were fixing the lighthouse, and with him had gone their best lead on who was behind this.

With nothing to do but wait, they sat in silence for a long time, all eyes on the chasm. Dellia seemed to grow more anxious with the setting of the sun and the coming of dusk. After a while, she faced her two companions. "If this doesn't work, we'll have to get out of here as fast as possible. We'll need to spread the word so people can evacuate."

The word "evacuate" struck Jon with a brutal impact. It meant not just failure, but people fleeing for their lives. Intense guilt racked him at the realization: he wouldn't just have failed on a few trivial political issues. He would have caused an apocalypse. It was an echo of that long-ago classroom with the distant sounds of rifle fire ringing down the hallways. All at once, the memories came rushing back.

The teacher's eyes had been wide with alarm as she left him to monitor the class while she went outside to investigate. The panic in his stepsister's voice still haunted him as she and her classmates pleaded with him to flee down a nearby stairwell, but he didn't listen. He was so smug and sure that he knew better, so he told them to stay put and shelter in place. Yet, the gunshots grew louder until they were right outside the door.

He fled the classroom, hoping to lead the shooters away, but fell down the stairs to the sounds of their laughter and taunting. When he came to and ran back to the classroom, they were all dead. His stepsister, his classmates, all lying lifeless in a bloody scene of carnage because he'd been in charge. His stepmother and stepbrothers never let him forget that their flesh and blood had perished because he was foolish enough to think he could make decisions for others.

This time, no one had called upon him to stop whatever this darkness was, nor had he signed up for it, but even so, he felt the weight of all of those untold men, women, and children of Talus, as if they were his own personal responsibility. It terrified him. He drew a deep breath and reminded himself the crisis was ongoing, and Dellia's idea might save lives. He had to acknowledge that, so he nodded. "Good idea. That's good. If this doesn't work, we flee and alert others."

Garris glanced at Dellia and motioned with his head to the east. "I'll head toward Egina while you and Jon head to Nydri. We can spread the word faster that way and get the residents of each town we pass to spread word of—"

A roar echoed across the plains, and all eyes turned to the gorge entrance. The darkness had arrived, but upon hitting the light, it was as if it was being burned away, exposing whatever hid within. Flickers of fire and showers of light flashed in flurries here and there across the vast expanse of nothingness, each accompanied by a distant screech or deep cry of anguish. No detail could be seen from this distance, yet somehow, he sensed that the flashes and cries were living beings. Now, exposed to the brightness, whatever monstrosities hid within were being burned alive.

For a while, the three watched in stunned speechlessness. The fireworks of light and flame against the black cloud mingled with the medley of pained cries, the sight becoming deeply unsettling, but Jon couldn't tear his eyes away. It connected once again with those forgotten bits of knowledge left over from taking the power of Syvis. They touched something deep within him, filling him with an intense foreboding. Whatever this dark wound on the landscape was, it was intent on infecting all of Talus, but it was being cauterized by the blazing brilliance of the lighthouse.

He sidled closer to Dellia and leaned into her, hoping the comfort of her nearness would calm his anxiety. Perhaps sensing his ill ease, she slipped her arm around him and pulled him closer. For a while, they remained like that, watching the flames and swirls of sparks flash across the cloud of darkness. Then, it seemed to withdraw, retreating to the cover of the gorge.

Jon closed his eyes and breathed a sigh of relief. "Thank goodness. It seems to be working."

Dellia pulled him closer. "Thank Adi."

They waited for quite a while longer as the sky grew dark and night settled on the plains. As they watched, the darkness tested the light again and again, but each advance ended in retreat, and it seemed as if it might burn away altogether if it kept pushing forward.

Jon closed his eyes, and as he relaxed, a shudder ran through his body. For now, at least, they seemed safe. Still, he couldn't shake the overwhelming gravity of their situation. He had wounded the last lighthouse, and who knew how much longer it might keep the Dead of Night at bay. Death had arrived at the doorstep of Talus, and all that stood between it and the obliteration of its entire human population was a tiny bit of ancient machinery that he had damaged in his recklessness.

Chapter Twenty-Four

FLORA MAJORA

The shimmering curtain passed over Aylun, and, in a sudden flash, the hot, barren plains of Erden were replaced by the cool air and hilly forests of his homeland, Elore. He pointed to the symbol on the spire, the one Megan had touched with the azure spire stone. It was a triangle with a circle in the middle and five lines radiating out from it. "Did you see? When the portal passed over us, the shape and position of the rune remained unchanged. Only the color changed from amber to clear blue."

He kept the volume of his voice a little raised and pointed to the southwest. "We are now north and east of Kanlu, the city of the Emperor of Elore, and of the Augury." He leaned a little closer to Megan and spoke softly into her ear. "Rillen cannot come with us. The warning we seek must not be revealed to a stranger."

Megan glanced at the woman a short distance away. She was watching them intently from atop her reddish-brown mare, Laal. Megan replied in a quiet whisper, "Oh, yeah. I forgot. It's secret Augury business. What do we—"

Rillen guided Laal up next to Aylun. "I understand your desire for secrecy, and I make a solemn promise never to reveal anything that happens here."

He stared at the protector, unsure how she knew what they were talking about or how to respond.

She must have sensed his confusion because she glanced at Megan then Aylun. "I can read lips, dumbo."

Megan giggled.

Then, Rillen seized Aylun's arm and yanked him closer, whispering into his ear in a voice so quiet only he could hear. "If I wanted your silly secrets, I'd have taken them when I snuck past you in the Augury. You're not all that great at keeping watch, now, are you?"

He pulled away and studied Rillen's face, trying to discern if she was bluffing. That she might have learned he was a part of the Augury seemed improbable. The Shou were a secret guarded with no small amount of care. That she would make up such a far-fetched bluff seemed equally unlikely. It lent credence to her claim that she'd seen him there.

Then her assertion sparked a memory of Tsaoshi and his words to him before his mission to the Dead of Night. "A few weeks ago, a protector breached our walls. ... She handed me three letters. Each appeared to be ancient and bore the seal of the Augury." Those words were followed, a short time later, by the most telling revelation of all. "It feels as if we are being guided by the hand of one more enlightened than I."

There were only four female protectors, and everything he had seen of Dellia said she couldn't have been the one to break in. The other two had supposedly been far from Kanlu for many weeks. So given what Rillen had just said, it seemed almost certain that she was, in fact, the protector who had found Tsaoshi. Still, despite how improbable, he couldn't rule out it being a clever deception born of something Rillen had seen or overheard. He had to be absolutely sure.

He recalled their first conversation. There were parts of her story that didn't ring true, so Aylun nodded. "Okay, but why should I believe you? When we met, you said that Jon had sent you? Then why, when I met him days earlier, was he so surprised to find Megan was missing? Why did he insist on sending me to find her if he had already sent you?"

Rillen shrugged. "How should I know? Was I there?"

Unimpressed, he continued to stare, waiting for a real explanation.

624

Eventually, she gave in. "Because Jon had found a way home, and I was supposed to help Megan follow."

"Help her follow? Now *you're* not making any sense."

She let out a sigh of exasperation. "Before Jon confronted the council, I sought him out. I went to find him, to help him."

"Before he was council leader? When you worked for the old council?"

"Yeah. Exactly. I caught up with him near Kanlu and he had me guide him to the dragon's lair. He'd found a way home. He was going home."

Concerned she would take the news poorly, Aylun glanced at Megan. She had a look of dismay on her face as tears welled in her eyes. "He was going to leave me behind?"

Aylun's heart fell at the sight of her, so dejected. He had been there when Megan herself had urged Jon to go home without her. At the time, it struck him as a noble gesture. Yet, it didn't mean she actually expected him to do it. To find out now that he really had intended to leave her behind could be a tremendous blow.

He reached for her. "He must have had good reasons for—"

"Because he was scared." Rillen rushed out her explanation. "I don't think I've ever seen anyone quite so scared. I have no idea what happened to him or what made him think so, but he kept going on about how he was going to bring death to everyone he cared about. That would include you, right?" She looked at Megan. "But even as scared as he was, he made me promise—it must have been fifty thousand times—to find you, to protect you, to help you follow him home. I can't ... no, I won't go back on that promise."

Aylun crossed his arms. "You claim he was going home. Then why is he still here in this world, in Meerdon?"

"That's between him and the dragon. I left him there, took his horse, Enna, and had it sent back to Shirdon. Next thing I hear, he's become council leader and married Dellia. That's all I know. Trust me, I'm as confused as you are about how I left him at the dragon's lair and next thing I know he's council leader."

Her story was detailed enough, and it did explain a lot, but there were still suspicious holes. "You expect me to believe the council sent you to help Jon? When? Before or after they lied about him ending civilization?"

She glanced away, her blond hair blowing in the soft breeze as she stared into the feathery greenery beyond the spire. For a long moment, she stayed that way, seeming to compose herself. Then she nodded and peered at Aylun. "I wasn't sent by the council."

He stared, stunned. "Then who?"

"I can't answer that, but I was willing to throw away being a protector because it was something I believed in with all my being."

A little voice in his head told him she had just confirmed what he suspected, yet he needed more. "But you said Jon asked you to help Megan follow him home. This is not helping Megan go home. So, why are you still here? Why are you not helping Jon or at least doing as he asked?"

"Because Jon didn't go home. Because helping Megan *is* helping Jon." Rillen paused. "Look, I did as I was supposed to. I helped Jon. I escorted him to the dragon's lair, and it was over. He didn't need my protection anymore. I never knew why I was supposed to help him, only that it was important. While I was with him, his insistence I help Megan was pretty extreme. So strong, in fact, it made me think it might be a big part of the reason I was sent to help him in the first place. As long as there's even a tiny chance that's the case, I cannot let Megan out of my sight."

Aylun studied her face for a while, unable to shake his suspicious nature. "You are a part of this, right? Jon, Megan, the Otherworlder Prophecy, you are a part of all of it?"

This time, there was no rushed response, and Rillen lowered her head and spoke in quiet voice. "You of all people should know that's not a question you should ask, nor is it one I should answer."

For a moment, he was back, reliving one of the many times Tsaoshi had uttered the exact same rebuke. Which made this the second time Rillen had as much as confirmed she knew him and the

Augury. She had to be the one who broke in and met Tsaoshi, and the Great Oracle believed in her. He had done as she asked. That meant it would be foolish for lowly Aylun, an ex-Shou, to mistrust her.

Still, he had vowed to help, not to make decisions, so he pointed to Megan. "It is her mission. I am here only to help her. It is her call whether to come with us or not."

Megan leaned away. "What? First, you're all take-chargy, and now it's my decision?"

He nodded. "Yes, I am funny that way. About protecting secrets that could hurt you or Jon."

She rolled her eyes and stared. "Fine, then do you believe her?"

He hesitated, then realized they all knew enough already that it would be foolish to get cagey now. "Yes. Her story holds up."

"If you have no objection, then why would I object?"

He turned his gaze back to Rillen. "I don't like it, but I am willing to go along on one condition."

The protector seemed relieved. "Then say it."

"Everything that happens, everything you see and hear from this point on, stays between the three of us." He pointed to each of them in turn. "Agreed?"

Rillen nodded. "Agreed. I will not speak of it to anyone you have not already revealed it to."

Megan smirked. "Then should we teach her the secret handshake?"

Rillen looked sideways at her. "There's a secret handshake?"

Aylun grumbled, "There is no secret handshake."

Megan dismissed his statement with a wave of her hand. "Don't pay any attention to him. He doesn't know it. It's a secret."

Deciding it best to ignore the silliness, Aylun headed out in front, guiding the way and putting an end to the discussion of secret handshakes.

He led them down a long-abandoned wooded road. Only two spire stones were known to exist for this spire, three if you counted Megan's. The owners tended to charge exorbitant sums for their use. So merchants and travelers seldom used this particular spire, and only to transport valuable cargo when the owner couldn't afford the delay of transport by horse or wagon. As a result of disuse, the road was in a general state of disrepair.

After a brief ride, they met a much broader and more well-traveled route that ran along the valley between two rocky hills. It wandered beneath sweeping maples and twisted pines that clung to the hillsides, eventually arriving at the sandy shores of Kinshai Lake.

However, the old Augury site stood elsewhere, on the cliffs overlooking the water. So as the warmth of the afternoon sun worked its way through the loose canopy above, Aylun veered off the road. Using a set of narrower dirt paths, he weaved his way up the hills toward a ridge that ran above the road for quite a ways before turning southeastward.

He had traveled these paths as a youth, on those occasions where he and his friends would "go missing" for a day. Now, everything seemed smaller, and the forest had evolved in ways that made it barely resemble those long-ago times. Perhaps it was also a matter of the memory being worn and faded so that navigation was, in many ways, a matter of guesswork. They plodded up and down the rocky hills, each upward climb a little longer than the prior downward one, until, at last, they reached the tall cliffs overlooking the lake.

Almost at once, Megan seemed taken with the view. As soon as they reached the ruins, she dismounted and strolled to a precipice overlooking the lake. The late afternoon sun glimmered off the water, as single-sailed junks skated along its surface, headed back to quaint villages. The little hamlets were scattered all along the length of the shoreline. Most were nothing more than a small cluster of slope-roofed buildings, some lining the beach, while others surrounded cozy courtyards.

From their vantage point, high over the lake, they could see the road from which they had veered off emptying onto the lakeshore. There, it met a larger road of cobbles that weaved along the shore. It ducked away from the lake, around white beaches, and through villages until it disappeared into the distance in either direction.

She peered down at the bleached sands. "It's more than expected."

Aylun stared at her, pondering her comment.

After a while, she expounded. "It has a vague resemblance to pictures my grandparents had of the lake near their village." She turned her gaze to Aylun. "I don't think it's a coincidence you and I look the same. Or that Jon looks like the people of Talus. I don't know how, but your world and mine are linked. This is sort of like the land my grandparents came from. Somehow, here in this world, there's a culture similar to that of my ancestors. Not exactly the same, you know, but enough that the architecture and aesthetic are recognizable if you just look at them the right way." She cocked her head as she peered down at a two-wheeled, hand-drawn cart rattling along the shoreline road.

It took a moment for the implication of her words to sink in. "Are you saying my people and yours are related?"

She appeared to give his question a good deal of consideration before answering. "I'm used to dealing in facts and hypotheses. I can't jump to any conclusions, but the resemblance is deeper than a few minor parallels. The similarities are too many and too varied to be a simple coincidence. That's a fact. That your people and mine share some common ancestry is a reasonable hypothesis. It fits the facts, but I can see no way to confirm it."

Aylun smiled. "You know, you could just say it is possible, but you cannot be certain."

"Yeah, but that would lack a certain 'I'm a college-educated know-it-all' quality." She took in the scene below awhile longer as Rillen tended the horses and began to make camp.

Eventually, the protector shouted over to them. "Megan, are we sharing a tent?"

She looked thoughtful, then yelled back in an animated voice, "Sure, we can have a sleepover, but why don't we explore the ruins first?"

Rillen appeared puzzled at the reference but went back to her work.

Aylun decided to offer his advice, trying to honor his long-ago pledge to only give options. "Other than the door, there is not much to see. The light will be gone soon, and it might be better to start first thing tomorrow when we are fresh and have plenty of time to examine the room beyond."

They both returned to their spotted horses and busied themselves, preparing for the night's stay. Afterward, they sat around the crackling fire that Rillen had built, listening to her regale them with stories of her encounters with Jon.

She giggled and smiled as she told of her first impression of the "blond-haired man who could make Dellia crazy" upon meeting him at Sirra's home in Talus. Her demeanor became more serious as she described how distraught he had been when she caught up with him. Then she amended her earlier story, looking Megan in the eye she revealed that "Jon wasn't really going home when I met him, he was going to look for you."

Her exasperation was palpable as she related how it took every bit of persuasiveness she could muster to talk him out of it; to convince him that it would only imperil them both to go poking his head into city after city while the council was actively pursuing them. Even at Islong's lair he refused to leave until he had extracted a vow from Rillen to "move heaven and earth to find Megan and help her get home." Rillen knew the breeder of Dellia's horse and that Jon's Enna had come from the same farm. So, after they parted, she returned Enna to her breeder and paid her a hefty sum to deliver her to Dellia in Shirdon.

Throughout the evening's discussion, Aylun amused himself by prodding and probing the holes in Rillen's story. There was the matter of how she had known where and when to find Jon so she could escort him to Islong's lair. And afterward, how had she found out where Megan was hiding. After all, he had taken great care to shield her presence from any potential scrutiny that might lead a dangerous ruling council to locate her. Rillen dismissed his gentle inquiries with a passing remark about being a protector and how they find people.

AYLUN

The evasive nature of her responses kept bringing him back to Tsaoshi's proclamation that Rillen was a part of this—that she was guided by a hand more enlightened than his. If that was true, if Rillen was a part of another Great Oracle's plan, then it stood to reason that she could have been given unnatural insight into where and when to find Jon and Megan. But it seemed equally unlikely that she'd tell him anything more than necessary.

Here they were, at the sight of the old Augury, searching for answers about this prophecy, and he couldn't shake the feeling that Rillen knew more about it than she was letting on. And for the first time, he gained an appreciation of how puzzling it could be to deal with the Shou and their determination not to reveal any part of what they knew.

Afterward, he lay in his small tent, listening to the chirping of insects. As he tried to beckon sleep, his thoughts turned to a conundrum of a different kind. There had been a powerful sense of rightness in his search for a contact in Mundus and afterward with the Verod as he escorted Megan to meet Jon. With Jon was where Megan wished to be, and by his side was where Wistra's journal proclaimed she must be.

That sense of rightness traveled with him now, as he strived to uncover the missing warning. In finding it, he could determine how dire he had made things by taking Megan away from Jon and how to fix that. Even as he searched for the missing Megan and then tried to cheer her up, he felt as if it was the perfect path for him. Yet here, at the threshold of finding the answers he had sought with such earnest determination, that sense of rightness had abandoned him. Megan was correct. There was no place for her any more with Jon. So their trip was simply delaying the inevitable: that she must return to him, where she would be miserable.

In that Verod camp, when Jon had arrived, Aylun had fled. He had left her behind because he didn't want to see them together. Even then, he'd had feelings for Megan. Sure, he wanted her to be happy, but he had no desire to see her hug Jon, kiss him, hold him, or take

631

pleasure in his company. It was a moment for the two of them to share and not one he could stand to be a part of. Yet, here he was, on the verge of returning her to a situation very much like the one he had been unable to face.

And then there was the missing warning in the Vault of Time. It was the eve before he might find the answers he sought, but were they answers he still wanted to find? It was hard to imagine any scenario where the secrets they uncovered would not encourage Megan to return to Jon, where she would be forced to endure seeing him married to another woman.

The part of him that wanted to protect her needed to know the answer. It needed to know she would be safe. Yet, the part that wished Megan every happiness was filled with foreboding over the prospect that the answers they sought would put an end to what little contentment she had reclaimed.

The words rattled around in Megan's head. A saying so buried in her past, she had no remembrance of when she had first heard it. She stared beyond the cliffs at the fiery red horizon of sunrise and mouthed the words, "Red sky at night, sailor's delight. Red sky in morning, sailors take warning." She returned her gaze to the lake below. The clouds above, painted a blazing pink by the scarlet morning sun, were sending bright shimmers of reflected rose across the peaceful waters.

Having awakened early and unable to get back to sleep, she had come to the cliffside to watch the sunrise. Yet, what drew her interest instead were the fishermen, mere ants crawling along white beaches below as they prepared their ships for the day's work. Aylun's arrival had allowed her to forget her troubles and find some moments of happiness in each day. But in quiet moments like this, the insufferable nature of her circumstances gained crystal clarity.

She had set out to protect Jon from a dire prophecy, but that threat had turned into a position of power for him. He no longer needed her protection. So, what was she doing here? Oh, it was clear why she had come on this expedition of Aylun's. Her affection for the man had grown by leaps and bounds these last few days, and it was out of a desire to help him in his goal that she had agreed to come. But if she stayed longer, she would only become a hindrance to him.

It hurt her heart to think of him frittering away his precious existence by allowing his every action to revolve around her. It was obvious he was meant for greater things. She recalled his earnest proclamation in that Verod camp that he would protect her and Jon. That vow had led him here and it had urged him to bring her with him. It was also proof that she was a burden to him, someone who contributed nothing, but whom he felt obligated to help and protect.

As fascinating and distracting as this trip might be, it wouldn't change that. It wouldn't change anything. No matter what they found, the fact would remain that there was no place for her in this world, no purpose she served by being here. She was a hindrance to Aylun finding meaning in his life and a mere distraction to Jon.

As she watched the ships drifting out from the shore, the conclusion that came to her over and over was simple. She would not return to Jon, and without him, her time in this world was pointless. Aylun had drawn her out of the depths of her despair enough to come to grips with one unalterable truth: it was time to go home, with or without Jon.

When Aylun had found her, she felt stuck because she couldn't go to Jon and couldn't leave without him. But he'd helped her regain her strength, and she understood now. Jon was married. He was happy here. He was never going to go home. So that left her only one choice, to return without him.

Sure, she had grown fond of Aylun, perhaps too fond, but she also missed her cozy apartment and her car. She missed being able to talk to anyone whenever she wanted and being able to drive to a store in minutes. How she longed for the simple pleasures of watching shows on her big-screen television, getting takeout at local restaurants, microwave ovens, and the thousands of conveniences of modern life.

More than all of that, though, it was her home. Back on her world she had a life and a job for which she had spent years getting an education. All she could be here was a burden to all around her. So she would help Aylun in this one last task, to set his mind at ease. Then she would ask Rillen to do as she had promised, to help her in any way she chose. And she chose to go home.

As her thoughts churned, Megan had been oblivious to the quiet activity behind her. But it became impossible to ignore when Rillen strolled up next to her and sat cross-legged at her side. The protector remained silent as she stared with her at the lakeshore below.

After a while, Megan peered over at her. "You say you're here to help me in any way I choose?"

Rillen nodded.

"I think the time has come for me to go home, but I may need your help."

Rillen continued to stare down at the peaceful blue waters, splashed with reflections of the blazing sky. "Whatever you need. Just ask."

Megan lowered her gaze to the rocky ground between her legs. "I want to go home, but I don't know how. You say Jon was going home?"

"Yes, he said he found a way."

"When we finish here today, could you find him for me and ask him how I can get home?"

Rillen seemed puzzled. "Are you sure? You don't want to ask him yourself? You don't want to at least say goodbye?"

"What would be the point? He's happy here, and he's serving some big important purpose. Why disrupt that?"

The blond-haired protector seemed to want to say more, but she just bowed her head. "Of course. I will do whatever you ask."

Megan stopped and peered at her with a steady gaze. "You were a good friend to Jon when he needed one. I want you to know how very much that means to me."

Rillen smiled. "Your gratitude is appreciated but unnecessary. I did it because I must. Because it was the right thing to do." She put her arm around Megan's shoulder and pulled her close. "I will do the same for you. Not because you ask, but because it is what is right."

Megan just nodded, then motioned with her head to the ruins behind the camp. "Let's go find this warning of Aylun's."

She took one last look at the horizon, spreading out its fingertips of rose. Then she stood and headed back to the camp as she whispered to herself, "Red sky in morning, sailors take warning."

Side by side, they strolled back toward the camp. And as Megan contemplated her plan to leave, a sense of completion filled her. She really was going to leave Jon behind. It was the end of an entire chapter of her life, but also the start of a new one. In that spirit, she resolved to make the most of her time in this place. Aylun had brought her here to unravel a mystery, to uncover a secret. She liked unraveling mysteries. She liked uncovering secrets.

As they approached, they found Aylun had been sitting in silence, watching them. He rose and went to his pack to retrieve some flatbreads that appeared to be stuffed with some concoction. He thrust one out for Megan to take. The other he tore in half and shared with Rillen.

Megan smiled as the flavors burst into her mouth from her first bite. Apparently, he had prepared for the outing by purchasing them in the Mundus market well before he'd mentioned the trip. He was a confident one. She rather liked the audacity of buying supplies before he had even talked her into the outing. It turned out the breads were stuffed with a generous portion of dried cherries and some deep red apricot-like fruit mixed with spices and nuts, and the whole thing made a sweet and hearty breakfast.

After they had downed the last crumb, Aylun led them to a small stone room with an open door next to a rather large tree trunk. He brought out a glass ball she had seen him place in the fire the night before. As he entered the doorway, it lit up in the darkness.

Megan followed and stood looking down a set of stone steps at the dark, dingy mess below.

To the right of the stairs, a set of dilapidated shelves stood on debris-covered slabs of stone, and the crumbling walls were riddled with holes that looked like the burrows of giant rodents. It was disgusting. She followed Aylun down and around to a beautiful dark metal door set in the cracked and pitted wall. An exquisite etching of a branch jammed with flowers inlaid with jade crossed the door's dark, shiny surface. He presented it to her with a flourish.

She admired its gentle beauty for a moment, then retrieved her dragon key. Unlike prior occasions, when she brought it near the keyhole, it appeared to be a perfect fit. It slid into the slot and turned with little effort and a muffled clank. The door groaned as it opened toward them, all on its own. They stepped back, as all at once, a flood of air blasted them, accompanied by a brilliant light.

Megan stared in shock. She had expected a room, but on the other side of the door lay a sunlit field, brimming with bright flowers in vibrant shades of magenta, indigo, and fuchsia. The blooms and lush green foliage nearest the door flailed back and forth, battered by the wind rushing through the doorway. Her mind unable to make sense of the scene, she gawked at the decrepit wall, then back through the door it held to the colorful sunny field beyond.

Rillen's hair streamed behind her, blown back by the air whistling through the doorway. "Well, there's something you don't see every day."

Aylun reached his hand through. "It is like a portal, but without any curtain. It is like someplace else is right there, on the other side of this door, where you can reach out and touch it."

Megan stood regarding the spectacle as a vibrant yellow butterfly shot through the doorway and whipped past her face. Whatever was battering the flowers near the door, it was not a simple wind, or flowers all across the field would be blown about by it. Which meant it was probably the result of a difference in air pressure on either side of the door. Perhaps the land on the other side sat at a lower elevation with more air pressure, or a high-pressure weather system was perched over the area. Whatever the reason, there was a steady and forceful stream of air rushing through the doorway.

Megan put her hand out, letting the wind pass through her fingers. "This could be a whole different part of the world, or even a whole different world … it might even be *my world*." A twinge of curiosity hit her. "I want to go through, but will we be able to get back?"

Aylun shook his head. "Who knows?"

She studied the flowers, the field, and the wind roaring through the doorway for a while. Something about it told her they'd be able to get back, even though she couldn't yet explain why. "Well, my instincts are telling me it's safe enough."

"Safe?" He took another step backward.

She considered for a moment. "Yeah. The door explains why the warning couldn't be moved. It wasn't in the vault itself. It was out there." She pointed through to the lush field spattered with bright fuchsia and indigo. "And if Wistra put it there, she meant for it to be read and the reader to return with the warning. Otherwise, why bother?"

Aylun turned to face her. "I do not like it. I cannot see why she would have done this."

She considered his question. It did appear to be a rather elaborate way to hide a warning that didn't seem like it needed to be hidden. Still, something told her it must be safe. "Perhaps Wistra didn't trust the Augury with it. Perhaps she foresaw that a warning kept in the actual vault would be at risk of being undermined."

He cocked his head. "Then how was it supposed to be found. Surely you cannot be suggesting Wistra intended *us* to find it like this, that hundreds of years ago she foresaw us standing here doing this."

"No, that doesn't hold up. She left the warning so I wouldn't separate from Jon, which means she intended it to be found before I got to this world. To plan for us to find it through information we obtained because I was separated from Jon would make the warning pointless."

He stood taller, as if planting himself on the spot. "Then how was it supposed to be found?"

"What does it matter? The reality is, things got mixed up. She must have left instructions with someone. Maybe it was like you said; maybe it was sabotaged. Maybe they got lost or misplaced. Maybe Wistra isn't infallible. I don't know, but whether the warning is in a small room or in an entire universe behind a strange door doesn't really matter. It isn't relevant. It doesn't change anything."

He crossed his arms. "So, you think we should just barge through, even though we have no idea where to find what we are after, and no idea if the door will even be there in that field when we get to the other side?"

She shrugged. "Sure. Why not? My gut is telling me it's safe enough."

Aylun heaved an exasperated sigh. "That is a completely reckless plan that could strand us in a place of unknown and possibly lethal dangers with no hope of ever getting back."

Megan shot him a smile dripping with feigned sweetness. "Yeah, but would that be so bad?" She motioned between her and Rillen. "I mean, you'd be stranded with us."

Rillen glanced at her. Then, as if catching on, she moved her head next to Megan's, smiled an oversized smile, and repeated the gesture. "Yeah, you'd be stranded with us."

Aylun just shook his head.

Rillen set her sights on the still-open doorway. Her expression turned resolute, and with a sudden flourish, she marched through, staggering at the threshold from the force of the wind. Blond hair whipping around her, she whirled around amid the flailing flower stalks.

Aylun and Megan stood frozen by surprise.

Rillen shouted back from the other side. "You guys really do like to overthink things. It's a door. You go through. You go back." She strutted back through, and the wall of air shoved her forward to stumble up in front of them.

Megan stared at Rillen with her hair still billowing around her face. At the sight, it became apparent why she wasn't worried about getting back. If the wind could blow through, then of course a person could also walk through.

Rillen pointed back over her shoulder. "Besides, there's a spire."

Aylun stood straighter. "A spire? How could a spire be here? Are you saying there's a hidden spire no one knows about?"

She nodded. "I think so. Well, it's also in the middle of a bunch of ruins. Did I forget to mention the ruins?"

Megan smiled. "Ooh, a hidden warning, behind a hidden door, in a hidden city, with a hidden spire."

Aylun glared at Rillen. "Fine. You have swayed me through your utter recklessness and cavalier disregard for your own safety." He sighed and turned his gaze to Megan. "But we should at least bring the horses. It will make finding this warning and getting out quicker." He marched up the dark and dreary stairs toward the doorway to the warm sunlit outdoors and their camp.

As she followed him, it occurred to her that the existence of a spire and ruins on the other side of the door made it impossible that the door led to her world. No such historical find existed that she had ever heard of, which ruled out Earth, or at least the Earth of her time.

Getting Aylun's Juzhi and Rillen's Laal down the stairs was pretty straightforward. They were both well trained and could be coaxed through the dark narrow doorway and down the stone steps despite their obvious unease. Yuki required quite a lot more coddling and a bit of food. Before long, all three stood in the generous confines of the basement, and each rider led their respective mounts through the river of wind whipping through the doorway.

As Megan passed out into the vast field beyond, a sudden sense of wonder struck her. Surrounded by an ocean of brilliant purple and rose, she watched as shimmering butterflies of sapphire blue and sunny yellow flittered all around her. She lifted her gaze to the azure sky. The wisps of red that had clouded the heavens at the lake were gone here, replaced by a bright yellow afternoon sun dangling in a cloudless sky.

This wasn't just anywhere. It was somewhere very far away. Far enough that it was a sunny afternoon here and a cloud-streaked morning back at the lake. If this was the same world, it was one-fifth to a quarter of the day later. Which made it one-fifth to a quarter of the world farther east of the spot where they had started. Chances were they had just walked through a door to an altogether different part of the world.

Megan peered off in the distance. There, across the blanket of brilliance, stood a line of ancient stone remains. Crumbled walls adorned by a scant few columns were spread across the broad horizon. They were the remnants of some long-gone civilization—who knew what she would find there.

In the distance, straight ahead, a dark metallic needle thrust high into the bright blue sky. Scribbled along its entire length were jade-colored markings that appeared to be runes or symbols of some kind. Megan held up her hand, comparing it to the ring Aylun had given her, and the colors were a near-perfect match. That, and their age, argued that they must be some kind of jade inlay. They made the tall dark edifice stand in utter contrast to the warm yellow stone surrounding it. It was like a marker shouting out to them, "Over here, come and get me!"

Just beyond the ruins lay a large flat lake—like a mirror reflecting the rugged mountainous terrain that rolled back as far as the eye could see. The excitement of exploring an unknown and ancient city, a hidden city, buoyed her optimism. Megan squinted beneath the warm sun and smiled as she pointed to it. "What do you think?"

Aylun smiled back, seeming as eager as she was to explore the new and unfamiliar. He nodded to the dark spire rising above the horizon. "I think those are the colors of the Augury."

They mounted and headed for the dark needle with its jade markings. As they neared the sparse ruins, it became clear they stood at the opposite bank of a narrow gorge, with a massive stone bridge. They clattered across and down the modest street, surrounded by architecture whose origin were unclear. It didn't have the sturdy Greek look of Katapa's fluted marble pillars and ornate scrollwork. Nor did it have the intricate carvings and statuary that were all over Mundus. What remained of the buildings hinted at long, low structures, but without the geometric symmetry and ringed courtyards that abounded in Elore.

Instead, the walls were simple and straight, and the few columns that remained were smooth and unadorned. The streets were different as well. Instead of small cobbles, they were pieced together from large flat slabs of rock, with fine gravel ground into the cracks. The implication was difficult to escape. Whatever culture had built these ruins did not appear to have the same roots as those of the three realms. At least not the parts she had seen. These were, perhaps, the remnants of a fourth realm.

Rillen stopped as they passed the single intact wall of an otherwise crumbled-away structure of yellowish brick. She stood, staring at a symbol that consumed most of the area to the right of an open doorway. Carved into its old and cracked surface was a chimera: a crouching tiger with its claws out, the wings of a dragon, and the stinger of a scorpion.

She peered at it with intense concentration. "I swear I've seen that symbol before." Her gaze wandered to the other side of a door, and her face clouded as she spied a large ring of rusty metal hanging from the wall right above head height. She gave a visible shiver, then turned and walked away.

Megan's gaze followed her. "What?"

She shook her head. "It looks like a place to tie people up in public, to humiliate or punish."

Aylun grumped. "Or worse."

Megan shuddered as she stared for a moment, trying not to imagine what they meant. Then she hurried after. "My, aren't you a cheery pair."

They continued on through the sparse, crumbling remains of an ancient city, passing the remnants of walls and foundations, to arrive at the dark spire with its jade markings. It stood tall and sharp, seeming to serve no purpose beyond that of a marker to draw attention to itself. It sat atop the roof of a small dark metal dome, at the middle of an eight-way intersection, with narrow roads fanning out like the spokes of a wagon wheel.

They headed down a ramp and tied up their horses on some brush near the door. Then they strolled through a short entryway to the interior. On a platform, at the opposite end, stood a single chest, highlighted by the light from an opening above. Aylun pointed to it. "It's like the chests in the Vault of Time."

Megan eyed it with curiosity. Was it normal to leave such an important warning with no indication it was here or instructions on when it should be read? Then again, this was an oracle they were talking about. They seemed to thrive on secrecy. So perhaps it lay hidden in an unmarked location on purpose, or the journal in Lanessa contained some yet-undeciphered clue to its location and use.

Her thoughts were interrupted by Aylun leading the way over to it and heaving the lid open. Inside, resting on a faded blue velvet cloth, sat a tome, looking much like the one they had found in Lanessa, only thinner. Its pages were yellow and brittle from extreme age, and it bore the outline of a dragonfly scribbled across its leather-bound exterior.

Megan mentally added it to the list of curiosities. Was it normal for an important warning to be left just lying around in an unlocked chest where anyone could take it? Then again, this place might not have seen a single soul in decades or even centuries.

Aylun picked it up and turned it over in his hands, then he handed it to Megan.

She peered up at his face, uncertain why he had given it to her.

He smiled. "It concerns your fate and that of Jon. What it contains is for you to discover."

She opened it with care and found that only the first page contained writing, which she read aloud: " 'Fifteen years after the arrival of the first one from another world, two others will come, Jon and Megan. The Shou must ensure they are not separated under any circumstances.' "

Megan looked over at Aylun, afraid he might take the message as poorly as he had when he'd heard it in Lanessa. When he appeared unfazed, she continued. " 'If they are, Jon will become infatuated with the protector, Dellia. He will eliminate the Ruling Council of Meerdon to be with her, but his passion for her will be short lived. Jon needs Megan to guide him, and he needs her to help him rise above his conflict with the council. And he needs the council, just as they need him. For only the council can hold together the three realms, so they can be united against what is coming.' "

Megan halted, taken aback. It was everything she wanted to hear, yet it didn't seem right. She couldn't say why, but she had a strong sense that it didn't jibe with what she already knew about Jon, about herself, about Dellia, and about the prophecy. It was a puzzle with two sets of pieces that could never fit together.

Then again, maybe the problem was just how repugnant the whole idea was. With all the talk of free will, where was Jon's in all of this. He seemed to have become a mere puppet for an ancient oracle to carry out her crazy schemes. This wasn't prophecy at all, it was one woman's machinations masquerading as prophecy. Or perhaps the feeling of puzzle pieces that didn't fit had a more mundane explanation. Perhaps it was her own mind rebelling against the idea of her and Jon together. She had just now come to the point of acceptance and wasn't sure she wanted to go back. Jon had married another woman. It felt like they didn't fit together anymore.

Aylun seemed to sense her puzzlement. "What?"

Still distracted by the strangeness of it all, Megan glanced up at the source of the question.

He stood studying her with a concerned expression.

She hesitated, trying to put her misgivings into words. Unable to understand them herself, she gave up and returned to her reading. " 'If Jon defeats the council, my plan for him will have failed and the consequences will be swift and far worse than if he and Megan had never come. If that happens, the only way to save any part of humanity will be for Megan to go back to the beginning and undo it all. For her to stop them both from coming to this world.' "

Megan froze for a moment, unable to understand how she could go back, how she could undo anything. Then she lost her balance and put out a hand to steady herself as she grasped the meaning of the words. Of course she could undo it, but the cost. How could she?

Aylun studied her face. "What? You know a way? You might be able to undo this? To put events back with you and Jon in your world, like you never came?"

Megan nodded. "I think so. Not now, but there will come a time. I don't know when or how, but there will be a way to make sure Jon and I never traveled to this world in the first place."

"Then it is perfect."

Megan looked at him in horror. "How can you say that?"

"You will have been returned to Jon. My mistake will have been corrected, and you and Jon will be together, back in your world, just as you wanted."

"But at what cost to you? Do you remember when we first met—the nightmares, the guilt?"

Aylun shook his head and gazed at her with earnest eyes. "I would suffer them all to make you happy."

Caught off guard by the sheer strength and power of his simple proclamation, tears came to her eyes. "Aylun, this isn't right."

He set a hand on her shoulder. "It is not just your happiness. Countless lives could be saved. You have to do this. If not for yourself then for them."

She shook her head. "But I don't know how. All I know is I visited myself from the future, a future that hasn't happened yet. That means a time will come when I can visit myself in the past. All I have to do is use that time to warn myself, to warn Jon about the accident in the lab, and this will never have happened."

He smiled. "Then we will find out how."

"I wouldn't even know where to begin."

"Then start with Jon. He seems to know how to get you both home."

Rillen nodded. "That's true. He may—" She stifled herself.

"What?"

"It is not my place to counsel you. I am merely here to assist."

"Then assist by telling me how Jon could help."

Rillen considered for a while before speaking. "I will only state the obvious, that if Jon knows how to get you home, he may also know a great deal more. At the very least, he commands the protectors. If asked to investigate this, they may find the answer to how you could visit yourself in the past."

Megan balked. "I don't know—"

Aylun stepped in, not allowing her a chance to object. "No. Do you not see? This is what you want. And it is what is right. You have to do this."

She finally nodded. It still felt off, wrong somehow, and she hated bringing this kind of news to Jon, but it concerned that prophecy of his, so he should at least hear it. Not to mention, in many ways, she did want to see him again, and if they kept their visit brief, it might not be too uncomfortable seeing him with Dellia.

Rillen motioned to the door and lowered her voice. "Let's get out of here. We don't know what dangers this place might—"

A distant snarl froze her like a statue. It drew her attention to another noise, one that had been steadily growing but had so far escaped their notice—the whisper of myriad flapping wings. i Rillen listened for a moment, then held them back as she crept to the door and peered out. She snuck back and whispered, "This is bad. We have visitors, and our horses are out there with them." She urged them forward.

As the outdoors came into view through the doorway, a lump formed in Megan's throat. It was like a scene from the movie *The Wizard of Oz*: a cloud of flying creatures descending on the ruins to the north. Except instead of flying monkeys, they were those winged tiger-scorpion things. They didn't move like Hollywood flying monkeys either. They swooped and dove like birds of prey coming down to perch.

Megan mumbled to herself, "Well, Toto, I guess we're not in Kansas anymore."

As the cloud of beasts came to rest on the walls, pillars, roads, and grounds of the vast crumbling ruins, Rillen turned to her two companions and whispered, "It's those things. That etching on the wall, a tiger with wings and a scorpion stinger."

Megan eyed Aylun. "What if they get Yuki?"

He ignored her and remained calm, addressing Rillen in a businesslike manner. "How many do you suppose there are, and where?"

She moved closer to him. "I only got a moment's look, but it seemed like dozens, maybe as many as a hundred, north of here, between this building and the spire."

Megan whispered, "We could break for the spire, like in Lanessa."

Aylun shook his head. "Into the densest part of them? Plus, they can fly. We only got out of Lanessa in one piece because they were on the ground and fighting each other." He looked at the ruins outside the door and mumbled to himself, "Make a sound in the east, then strike in the west."

Rillen spoke almost to herself. "A distraction. The sixth stratagem."

Aylun stared at her in what seemed to be surprise.

Megan gawked. It would appear they both took a page from the same book on strategy.

Rillen granted him a knowing nod. "But how? And even if we could, it might draw attention to us and trap us rather than let us get away." She stood still for a thoughtful moment. "What about the eleventh stratagem? What if we sacrifice a plum tree to save a peach tree?"

"What?" Aylun sent her a disapproving stare. "You mean sacrifice one of us so the others can get away? No, absolutely not."

Rillen shook her head. "Not a real sacrifice—no one dies ... more like the twentieth stratagem?"

"Disturb the waters to catch a fish?" He considered for a moment. "Hmm. Catch them unaware and get them to act before they can prepare. I like it. What did you have in mind?"

Rillen moved a hair closer as if sharing a secret. "I fly out of here screaming like a banshee and acting crazy. I head straight for them and just start killing anything that doesn't run. If it doesn't scare them, it'll at least confuse the daylights out of them. I keep moving like that and use the terrain to keep them from swarming me. The moment I have their attention, you two ride across the bridge and straight through that door. I'll follow."

Aylun drew a deep breath. "You must realize those stingers are probably poisonous. One sting, and you could be dead. I know you are a protector, but that seems a little crazy, even for one of your kind."

She beamed a smile. "I specialize in crazy. I majored in it during training, and it's always been my weapon of choice."

He paused for a moment, then turned to Megan. "Did you follow all that?"

She nodded. "The part that matters. Rillen wants to go all kamikaze and draw them away while we escape."

He seemed a bit confused by the reference, but, after a moment, appeared to puzzle out the approximate meaning. "I think it's risky to confront them head-on like that, but she seems confident. What do you say? It's your call."

Megan nodded. "I appreciate that, but your whole stratagem-secret-code thingy convinces me you two know better than I do what will work. So my decision is to rely on your judgment."

Aylun eyed Rillen. "Okay. Are you certain you can pull it off?"

She gave a crisp nod.

He glanced out the door. "All right, we do as you say. You draw them away. I will protect Megan as we head for the door in the field." He looked to Megan. "Your job is to use your gift to send anything I miss straight into the ground, hard as you can, okay?"

She nodded.

With that, a mischievous glint appeared in Rillen's eyes. Then a broad smile spread across her face and she bolted for the door. With a single leap, she bounded onto the back of Laal and headed for the biggest, nastiest-looking creature in view.

When the striped beast spotted her, it crouched low in a threatening pose and snarled, its long, curved canines showing, and its stinger raised high above its head. It unfurled its wings, making it seem much larger and more imposing.

Rillen responded by urging her steed faster, racing at the creature as if determined to cause a head-on collision. Megan began to wonder if her craziness was an act or real. The protector kicked harder, rose in the stirrups, and let out a bloodcurdling whoop.

A dozen tiger heads shot up, faces pivoting toward Rillen as she charged down on the orange-striped beast.

Its display of fangs, claws, and stinger having been ignored, the creature crouched lower and froze, then with lightning quickness, it tried to dart away.

Rillen moved quicker, swerving along the wall as she swung her sword fast and hard.

The beast's head sheared off and disappeared behind the crumbling stonework as the body crashed to the ground in a spray of blood and dust.

Megan snuck farther out the door to get a better look. She glanced at Aylun. "Now? Should we make a break for it?"

He pointed to a few creatures behind Rillen. "Not yet. We are still in their line of sight."

As if on cue, the protector turned her red steed and took off, heading parallel to them. She bore down on the largest group—three of the striped monstrosities perched atop a jagged wall. One of the three fled, but the other two took off toward her, bounding down the ridge of narrow, ragged remains with lithe movements.

Rillen roared like a lion as she leaned forward and raised her sword.

The pair sprang, unfurling their wings, as first one then the other sailed through the air toward her.

She screeched and lurched away, avoiding the stinger of the first. She lopped off its wing as it passed, then spun and pierced the chest of the second.

A fourth leaped into the air with a powerful flap of its wings and arced down on her from behind.

She whipped her sword above her, end over end. It hit hard, piercing the belly of the creature above her head. She snatched the sword out of its tumbling body as it fell past her to the pavement with a thud.

She was almost out of view when Aylun clamped down on Megan's wrist and tugged. "Now."

They took off, sprinting toward Yuki and Juzhi.

He suddenly grabbed her by the waist and threw her onto her steed. In a flash, he dove up onto his, and the two barreled off toward the bridge at the edge of town.

Megan glanced behind her, ready to play her part in this strategy. Two of the creatures leaped to the top of a wall, their yellow eyes leering as they watched their quarry head away. Then, as a pair, they shot after, spreading their wings to sail down from the wall, then leaping and bounding across the broad slabs of the road.

Megan kicked harder, and Yuki responded, galloping down the road like her life depended on it.

Aylun struggled to keep pace while, little by little, the creatures gained on them.

She glanced back again and spotted Rillen atop her fiery red horse, far back and racing down a parallel street. A cloud of creatures swirled around her, claws swiping and stingers jabbing. She downed them in rapid succession, blood splattering everywhere as she dodged and darted, twisted and swerved, avoiding every attack.

Megan faced forward as they clattered onto the bridge, headed for the flower-laden field. With her gift, she lifted a stone as they passed, and in a burst of air, she hurled it back behind her.

The agile beasts swerved out of its path with ease.

So, she picked up an entire fallen segment of the stone railing and, in a roar of wind, tossed it behind her. Half fallen apart, it disintegrated as she threw.

Both beasts unfurled their wings and, with a forceful flap, rose to soar over the fragments, but they caught the leading one full in the chest with a crunch of bones. Rocks tore through its wings, and it crashed backward onto the ground. The other creature bounded off of a flying piece of stone and began to glide down.

As they plowed into the carpet of flowers, Megan did as Aylun had suggested. She reached out with her gift, grabbed the creature in midair, and smashed it to the ground with a grinding of flesh against stone. When she was done, it lay there unmoving.

A wave of exhilaration shot through her as, now free and clear, they charged through the green field, heavy with scarlet, fuchsia, and indigo. They approached the doorway, and it seemed strange and dark amid a sunlit flurry of color.

Megan glanced back at Rillen. The remains of the city were like an obstacle course to her as she did as planned and employed the terrain to keep the beasts off her. Using the wall as a shield, she and Laal shot through their midst, hacking them down as she went. With effortless grace, she vaulted over another wall, ducked under an open doorway, and weaved into a narrow alley, losing almost all of them. As she shot out the other side, she swerved around a single standing column, scraping off stragglers. The bridge lay to her left, so she angled for it and galloped across before most of them could catch up. With her sword whirling around her, she downed creatures as soon as they caught up to her, sending them to the ground like hail in a storm.

AYLUN

Megan reached the dark door with its dismal confines beyond. She flew down off her horse and hurried Yuki through, into the generous basement. Aylun followed, leading Juzhi. They moved their horses out of the way, spun, and put their shoulders to the door, ready to slam it shut the moment Rillen came through.

Megan turned and stared agape as the protector flew across the field, with a pack of creatures giving chase, and Rillen taking them down as soon as they reached her. As the door neared, she never slowed. With her sword whipping around her in lightning slashes, she bounced up onto her feet on the back of Laal and crouched. The door almost upon her, she leaped to the ground and rolled through behind her shiny, reddish steed.

Megan and Aylun heaved the door shut as creatures slammed into it with a rapid series of bangs. Megan jumped at a last loud thump, then all fell silent.

Rillen whooped. Her blond hair streaked with dark blood, she turned to them and beamed a smile. The entire left side of her face was spattered red. "What did I tell you: piece of cake."

Megan giggled. "You are a crazy one."

"I told you." She slapped Megan on the back. "Now, let's go find Jon."

It wasn't even noon yet when they led their horses back up the stairway into the clean, brisk air above Kinshai Lake and broke camp. And on their way down from the cliffs, headed to Shirdon to meet Jon, a strange feeling began to grow in Megan, almost below her awareness. As she watched Aylun rocking in the saddle in front of her, it came to her in a rush. It was a feeling she had experienced once before in the Verod camp, the sensation of standing on a railway platform watching the last train leave for home without her.

Chapter Twenty-Five

RUMORS

Perched atop of Enna, Jon glanced behind him at the lighthouse, a glowing beacon in the darkness. It bathed the chasm and base of the mountains with its warm yellow light as the dark void tested it with screeches and roars that resounded across the vast plains. It was as if the Dead of Night were a living thing—a child touching a cookie from the oven and finding it too hot to pick up. Long pauses came between each attempt, making every new refrain an unnerving surprise.

Riding next to him, Dellia remained somber, her concern evident in the drawn expression on her face. After a while, she turned her head and leered at him. "I can't believe you went to do something this dangerous without me."

Jon boggled. "What? It's not like I knew it was going to be this dangerous." He pondered the topic for a few seconds. "Wait a minute, isn't that what you expected *me* to do—to sit home while you go out and do dangerous things."

Her gaze snapped forward. "It's not the same." Her response was quick, then after a few seconds, she added, "Besides, I trained to do dangerous things."

"Really? So, tell me, if you and Garris had gone alone, could you have died?" No answer came, only the rhythmic thudding of hooves against the dimly lit grass. Her silence was confirmation enough. "Be honest. The reason it's not the same is that it would have been you sitting at home waiting for a husband that might never return. But you expected me to sit home waiting for you while you did life-endangering things?"

Dellia didn't respond right away, and he began to regret his quarrelsome words. She was visibly upset, and now, while she still feared for her homeland, was not the time to get drawn into such a contentious discussion.

She gave him a solemn look. "You could die."

"We're all going to die, Dellia—you, me, Garris, Megan, and a lot of others. I told you the vision I had."

Her discomfort seemed to grow, and he realized he had done it again. He had spoken without thought to how it would make her feel. This was why he had always tried to consider what he said with care. It was easy to give a snappy comeback out of the impulse to win an argument. It was much harder to undo the damage a careless word would cause. She needed reassurance, not a reminder of how fragile their existence was.

"I'm sorry, Dellia, I didn't mean that. Scratch that." He eyed her, trying to summon the voice of his better angels. "You may have just saved Talus from a horrible fate. That's what you trained for. That's what your life is about. Remember that. Hold it in your heart. Take comfort in it. We did good here today."

She smiled at him, but it seemed a little forced. A few words, no matter how heartfelt, were not going to erase the whole unnerving incident.

He faced forward, watching Garris jogging in the saddle, carrying a flickering torch as he lit the way. Its warm, fluttering light spread out across the grasses that never seemed to end in this part of this world.

Dellia fell silent, and her mood remained dark. His own concern echoed hers. This had been way too dangerous, and now, all that stood between Talus and devastation was a beam of light from a half-broken lighthouse.

As the edifice grew smaller behind them, a row of lights appeared in front, a couple dozen or more pinpricks bobbing in the darkness. After a while, it became apparent they were torches. With time, the flickering flames grew larger and eventually stopped in front of them, lighting the solemn faces of over thirty sturdy riders.

They appeared to be soldiers, and at their lead, he spotted Commander Prian. While her armaments and her commanding manner matched those of the Talesh soldiers around her, her pitch-black hair and brown skin betrayed her Erdish descent. He recalled from Dellia's description that she had an intuitive grasp of battle strategy that was uncanny and an understanding of her soldiers that made her an ideal leader.

Mounted next to her was another familiar face, the sturdy and regal-looking Saneya. Her dark hair, olive skin, and pronounced features were striking, enhancing her sharp and imposing air. It was suitable for one of the Ephori, the elected leaders of Talus. He had encountered them both when he was in Egina trying to enlist the support of the Talesh leaders in confronting the council. In fact, it had been Saneya who had convinced the other Ephori that he was being truthful when he professed his respect and admiration for their people.

However, it was not Saneya who drew his attention, but one of the less conspicuous among their number. There, in the midst of the imposing riders, sat a woman who looked just like Dellia, at least in this dim light. She was of a similar size and shape and had coiffed and outfitted herself in a way that made her seem like a near-perfect replica, right down to her hair, armor, and weapons.

Next to him, Dellia seemed flustered. She leaned closer and whispered, her voice barely rising above the restless movements of horses and the flutter of a dozen torches. "Stop staring at my cousin. It's rude. And Saneya is one of the leaders of my people." Her first words were sounds of annoyance, but when he continued to stare, they turned to a sharp rebuke. "Do not show disrespect by ignoring her."

He complied by tearing his eyes from the Dellia look-alike and turned his attention to their leader, Saneya. She seemed upset in that tight, controlled way he had seen when facing her at the Laminus Theater.

He bowed his head. "Apologies, Saneya. It was just—"

"That you were ogling Brita while your wife sits at your side."

A hot flush burned his cheeks. "No, no, it's the resemblance, it's ... uncanny."

Saneya drew herself up taller in the saddle. "It is of no importance." She glared at Jon, her face appearing more stern than usual in the sharp light and shadow of flickering torches. "What are you doing here?" There was a sharp edge to her voice that matched the penetrating look in her eyes. It went beyond simple accusation. It seemed to say she didn't appreciate him being here and wasn't going to like anything he had to say.

Not sure how to explain the winding path that had led the three of them to this moment in time, Jon hesitated.

In the silent interval, Garris jumped in. "They're helping me. We came—"

"Does a disgraced ex-protector now speak for the leader of the ruling council?" Saneya's annoyance grew.

"Well, that's a bit harsh," Garris grumbled.

It was Dellia's turn to speak up. "We came to investig—"

"Does he have no tongue of his own? Does he have to hide behind his Talesh wife, or will he speak to me with his own voice?" She glared at Dellia, then turned her icy gaze to Jon. "We were warned you would be here, and here you are. I want to know why?"

Jon gave his head a slight shake. "Warned?"

"Yes, a rumor has reached us—"

"A rumor? We just got here, how could a rumor—"

"Yes, a rumor that the wolves you killed in Mundus were a long-standing enemy of the Dead of Night. That they had pinned it down, and without them present, only the Southern Lighthouses were holding it back. That you were here, and your bungling had damaged the lighthouses, and if not stopped, you would eventually let the darkness loose on all of Talus."

The accusation struck with brutal force. Countless lives were at risk, and she was saying he was to blame. As the implication hit home, an ancient but familiar feeling took hold. It was as if he were back in that classroom with the moans of the wounded echoing down the halls. His stomach twisted as he recalled the warm morning sun streaming down on the bloody bodies of his classmates, friends, and family who had died because he promised he would keep them safe. Saneya was claiming an entire realm full of people might die because he killed the wolves and tried to fix the lighthouse.

She leaned forward, the torchlight dancing in her eyes as her words became even more forceful. "So, I ask you, for the third time, what are you doing here?"

He faltered, his mind still muddled by the idea that he might have put Talus at risk. "We … we came to investigate. Garris found a map with a mark at one of the lighthouses. We thought it might be a trap for him. So—"

"A trap? For your protector? Is that how this new council of yours works? The council leader investigates threats to their protectors?"

Jon cringed. He felt like a cowering schoolboy trying to placate a disgruntled teacher. Even so, it wouldn't do to play the part. Doing so would only worsen the situation. So he pulled himself together and tried to act leader-like. "And is it customary for one of the Ephori to investigate idle rumors?"

She gave a disapproving scoff. Yet it was hard to escape the feeling that his insolence had earned him a tiny grain of respect and not only with Saneya, but with her soldiers as well.

He dismissed his own statement with a wave of his hand. "Anyway, it seemed important, so I came, and I was right. We discovered that someone had sabotaged the lighthouses. They even tried to trap us at the top of one."

Saneya paused, and, for a moment, she seemed somewhat concerned, but maintained her commanding posture. "So, you deny the rumor? The wolves had nothing to do with the darkness moving, and you didn't damage the lighthouses?"

"You asked why we were here. I answered."

Her response was short and immediate. "I come here to investigate a rumor about you, and you don't feel the need to respond to it. Fine, then I will ask directly, is the rumor true?"

"The rumor has two parts, so you are asking two questions, and I will respond to them in order." He held his gaze fixed on her and leaned forward toward Saneya. Two could play this game. "The Dead of Night is moving. That much I can tell you for sure. We saw it coming down the chasm with our own eyes."

Muttered comments broke out among Saneya's soldiers.

He raised his voice to speak over them. "The truth is, I have no way of knowing whether it has anything to do with the killing of the Blood Wolves ... *halfway across Meerdon.*" He let that fact sink in before continuing. "I mentioned that someone sabotaged the lighthouses. After examining them, I agree they were built to hold back the Dead of Night."

Disapproving moans followed by a hushed murmur ran through the group in front of them.

He raised his voice once again as he pointed back the way they had come, where a faint light still glowed along the dark horizon. "We figured out how they worked and repaired the sabotage to the nearest lighthouse." Jon leaned forward again and peered straight into Saneya's eyes. "And we did damage it in the process, but it is working. It is holding back the darkness."

Prian motioned to a pair of mounted soldiers at either end of the row. They took off, thundering away toward the lighthouse, their hoof-falls carrying across the plains long after the night had swallowed them.

Saneya turned her attention back to Jon, concentrating with an intensity that seemed familiar. It reminded him that Dellia had told him Saneya possessed the Gift of the Heart. She could sense emotions like Dellia, only to a lesser degree. The look on her face now said she was using it to determine if he was being truthful. When she spoke, it was with a more even-tempered tone than before, as if she had put on her former ire for the benefit of her soldiers or perhaps simply to throw him off-balance. "So, as far as you know, the entire rumor could be true?"

He considered for a moment before speaking. "I cannot deny it, because I have no evidence one way or the other to prove the wolves had anything to do with the Dead of Night." He paused. "However, I would point out that neither do you. You are asking me to defend against a baseless accusation." He jabbed his finger at Saneya. "Is that your idea of justice? Is that how it works in Talus? A wild rumor gets thrown around, and you assume I'm guilty until proven otherwise?" He paused again, letting his rhetorical question gain weight. "As for the damage to the lighthouse, it occurred earlier this evening."

He raised his voice again, just the way Saneya had. "So now it is your turn to explain to me. A rumor reached you of an accident that had not yet occurred. How does that fact not cast doubt on the veracity of your whole accusation?"

She remained unshaken and seemed to consider his assertion for a while. "I cannot explain the timing of the rumor. But let me—"

"No, not good enough. I did not ask you to explain the timing. So, I will ask a second time. Since the rumor reached you before the lighthouse was damaged, does that not prove it is a false one?"

"All right. Granted. But let me ask you this. Was it not you who stood on the stage of the Laminus Theater and begged us to let you represent the Ephori in loosening the council's grip on this realm?"

Well, "begged" was a bit hyperbolic, and the change of topic an all-too-typical tactic for one who had just lost an argument, but it gained him little to quibble, so Jon nodded. "Yes."

"And did you also not then bargain with the council to hand control of Talus back to our people?"

He sensed where this was going but could summon no counter-argument. "Yes."

"According to the bargain that *you* made, you have no authority to do what you have already done here?"

Jon was stunned. They had saved the lives of countless Talesh people, and she was chastising him for it. "We saw a threat and

659

stopped it. Should we have done nothing and let it run rampant through Talus while we awaited your kind permission?"

Saneya bowed her head. "And we are grateful for your good intentions, even if it resulted in damage to the lighthouse. However, I must insist that you and your protectors cease your meddling in this matter and let us handle it."

Despite Saneya's condescending manner, letting her handle it was precisely what he wanted. He had no desire to be responsible for the safety of untold Talesh lives. Jon bowed his head in agreement. "By all means. I leave the matter in your hands now."

With that, she motioned to Prian, and the commander belted out order after order: to make camp here, to set up patrols, to monitor the darkness, and to police the immediate area.

Jon dismounted and relaxed as he watched the activity of the camp. After a few minutes, the commander came over and glanced first at him and then at Dellia. "I have instructed that a tent be pitched for you and Jon, and I will make sure Garris gets one of his own." With that, she marched off.

Jon glanced at Dellia, and her face held the same fiery look as when she'd learned the protectors might be dismantled. He had no idea what he had done wrong this time. Before he could ask, she spat out a few quiet words. "I won't be waited upon. I will go help with the tent." Then she spun around and strode off in the direction Prian had pointed.

Not sure talking to Dellia now was a good idea, Jon wandered over toward Saneya. If she was in charge, there were things she needed to know. As he approached, she seemed lost in thought, staring at the distant lighthouse, a mere speck of bright yellow light in the vast sea of darkness. She seemed surprised when he stepped up to her side.

He decided to drop his former act and be himself. "I'm sorry, Saneya. We were as surprised by all of this as you are. We came here thinking someone was after Garris and found this whole mess."

She shot him a hard look, but her words were more efficient than irate. "I have bigger concerns right now than an apology that fixes nothing." For a while, her attention remained on that glowing dot on the dark landscape, then she turned her full attention to Jon. "What would have been helpful is if you three had found a patrol and notified them of your presence and intent, not for our sake but for yours. It would have given weight to your story. As it is, you are now just another problem for me to deal with."

"This rumor concerns me far more than you know. That I may have caused this, even a small part of it, horrifies me."

She seemed annoyed. "I couldn't care less how you *feel* about it. What does it matter who is to blame?"

"I … I don't understand. Then why all the questions about the rumor?"

Saneya shook her head. "You say someone sabotaged the lighthouses, and the darkness is on our doorstep. Countless Talesh lives could be at risk. Blame can be assigned later. What concerns me now is the danger to my people."

He stared, unable to fathom why she had focused so much on the rumor if the danger to her people was her real concern.

She seemed to sense his confusion and sighed. "How can you be so slow-witted? We are in imminent danger. I could use an ally now, especially one with two protectors. But you haven't just made that impossible, you've made yourself into a problem I have to manage." She seemed to calm some and become more sympathetic. "Look, I believe your intentions were good, but the rumor arriving before word of your presence will cast doubt on your motives, making it impossible for me to enlist your aid and requiring me to monitor and report on your activities."

Jon ignored the part about monitoring him and instead focused on the line about enlisting his aid. "Come on, there must be something we can do."

Saneya sighed again. "You can stop distracting me with useless apologies, excuses, and insecurities. I have work to do."

He nodded. "Then, at least let me tell you how I think the lighthouses work and how they were sabotaged."

Her stern expression softened.

He eyed her. "At the top of the tower is this giant flamestone. The stairway leading to it is lined with holders for smaller sunstones. Sunlight comes through the flamestone at the top and hits the sunstones. I don't know how, but it generates a beam of scorching light. That beam hits the flamestone and heats it up, creating a light that bounces off a giant reflector which sends it down to the chasm."

He paused, and Saneya seemed lost in thought for a moment, then looked back to Jon.

He continued, "Someone brought chests all the way out here. They took all the sunstones from the holders on the stairs and stuffed them in the chests. Then they stuck the chests under the stairway. That alone was enough to disable the lighthouse, but they did more. They threw a tarp over the flamestone at the top and secured it with chains to keep the sun out."

"Sounds like overkill."

"It's more than that. If they wanted to disable the lighthouses, they could have destroyed them, smashed the stones. Heck, we cracked one without even meaning to. Or they could've hauled away all the sunstones and sold them. I assume they would draw a fair price."

Saneya nodded, now appearing intrigued. "They're rare. Of course they're expensive."

"So why keep them around unless you want the possibility of restoring them? Whoever did this didn't want to destroy the lighthouses. They wanted to disable them, and they wanted to be able to put them back in working order quickly."

She regarded him with a contemplative look. "That is all solid information, but none of it is very actionable."

He nodded and jumped in before she could say more. "Then let me suggest you get some flamestones out here, as many as you can lay your hands on, and do it as fast as possible."

She seemed about to chastise him, presumably for ordering her around, but he put out his palm and signaled her to hear him out. "There's a flamestone at the top of the lighthouses but not inside. There must be a reason. Perhaps the light of sunstones doesn't hurt the Dead of Night, or at least not as much. What I do know is the light of the flamestone at the top destroys whatever creatures hide in that thing. It keeps the whole thing at bay. We have seen it."

Saneya nodded approval. "So flamestones may provide some defense against it. That's very useful."

"You could spread them around camp."

"We could ring the camp with fires and keep flamestone in them, so they are always ready. The longer we keep them in a fire, the longer they will put out light. If we get overrun and have to retreat, we can use them as a temporary defense."

"That's good." He paused for a moment. "And one more thing. We caught the man who trapped us at the top of the tower, a big bald guy with a blond beard, but we couldn't watch him and fix the lighthouse at the same time, so he got away. He's involved in this. So, there's a good chance he knows how and why the lighthouses were sabotaged. If you can find him—"

"Consider it done. I will have Prian send someone to you, Dellia, and Garris to compile a description, then, in the morning, we'll dispatch trackers to find him."

They continued to talk and speculate and discuss strategy for a while longer, as tents rose and campfires sprang up behind them. After a short time, Saneya thanked Jon in that perfunctory way she had of making it seem like a formality rather than genuine gratitude. Then, she dismissed him.

Feeling better that he wasn't in charge but had divulged what he knew to the one who was, Jon headed back toward the area Prian had pointed out as the spot for Dellia and his tent. He strolled by leather-clad warriors, some even outfitted in chain shirts or skirts. Fires were beginning to crackle and roar as smoke and sparks whirled into the night sky. Prian's troops were each engaged in their own tasks: building fires, fixing food, tending horses, or securing shelter. It lent the entire camp a purposeful air.

He passed a tent with Garris inside using a device that looked like a small portal of the type Sirra made. Through it, he was speaking with Kayleen. Jon stopped for a moment, not really paying attention to their conversation—something about chains. What interested him more was the nature of the device. It was a metal bar with a mist rising off it that thickened into a water-like curtain. On its surface sat Kayleen in her simple quarters, conversing with Garris in his newly pitched tent. It was obvious he was reporting what had happened today to Kayleen.

In many ways, it was a mundane sight, like someone chatting with a friend on their laptop. Only it wasn't mundane. Without the Wi-Fi, cell phone towers, internet backbone, and other network infrastructure to facilitate the long-distance exchange of data, it was impossible.

The scene reminded him of the incomplete nature of his theory that this reality operated on a different set of physical laws. Then as he gazed into the tent, his focus fell on the metal bar, the chair, and then Garris himself. They were all made of molecules and atoms that looked and felt identical to their counterparts on Earth. In fact, in every way he could imagine their behavior was the same. And as he imagined the periodic table that described the construction of the atoms that made up that matter, it came to him that the rules of this world couldn't be all that different.

Wood was wood. Iron was iron, and water was water. If the atoms that made up that matter weren't attracted to each other in the same way, if they didn't seek to fill up electron shells in the same way, matter, as it appeared and acted on Earth, couldn't exist. Flesh, blood, bones, the tens of thousands of different proteins and enzymes the body used and made every second of every day had to be the same. They had to combine and react with one another in the same unfathomably complex manner as on Earth, or life would cease to function.

He and Megan were proof that the fundamental nature of matter hadn't changed. They had come from Earth. They were able to eat the same food and drink the same water as the people here. If that food and water were different on an atomic or molecular level their bodies wouldn't be able to process it. Their very sameness to the people here implied that matter hadn't changed. Yet somehow things were different on this world. Some unknown new set of rules made it possible for dragons to fly and oracles to predict the future ... or for Garris to see Kayleen on that device that now sat before him.

Perhaps it had to do with the veil so many had mentioned. He had a distinct impression they were referring to some kind of barrier between realities. As outlandish as the concept was, it would explain a lot. Perhaps Garris's device was allowing him to peer into a reality where space and time were somehow warped or folded. It might be like the tesseract in *A Wrinkle in Time*, allowing two disparate points in space to be brought together. If that was true, then maybe nothing was being transmitted at all. Perhaps Kayleen's room was literally just on the other side of that curtain.

Jon's musings came to a stop when he spotted Dellia, a short distance away. Her back was to him as she stared off across the encampment. He wandered over, slipped his arms around her, and rested his head on her shoulder. He lingered there for a moment or two, then whispered into her ear, "You seemed upset earlier."

She stiffened.

Then it hit him. His arms didn't fit quite right around her waist. Her shape seemed odd, and her scent unfamiliar. Jon looked up, hoping to find out what had caused such an abrupt reaction, and his eyes met Dellia's, standing a few feet in front of him, watching his every move.

A voice came from the woman he had his arms around. "If you don't get off of me, I will break both those arms of yours, cousin-in-law."

He let go and jumped back as a hot flush came to his cheeks. "I thought. I mean ..."

Brita raced up to Dellia. "I'm sorry. It wasn't my fault. He just grabbed me out of the blue."

Dellia's voice had a flatness to it. "I saw it all. Please go away. I'd like a word with my husband."

"Of course." Brita turned and glared at Jon with scorching intensity. "First, you eye me like a fish at market, then manhandle me. And to think, I was looking forward to meeting you." She raced away.

Dellia grabbed his arm and hauled him into a tent. When she turned to face him, he was met by an angry fire in her eyes. "What is wrong with you? It was bad enough that you wouldn't face the council and stand up for the protectors, but then you give in without a fight when Saneya sidelines Garris and me." She stepped closer. "We are protectors, Jon. This is the kind of thing we train our whole lives for. It's what we live for. It's fine if you want to act like a child pretending to be council leader, but don't render me and Garris useless in the process."

Jon stood there, hurt and stunned. "That was never my intention."

She didn't even seem to hear the comment. "And what about you? If this goes wrong, are you really going to watch others die while you stand by and do nothing?"

He shook his head in dismay. "Did I stand by and do nothing when the darkness was coming down the chasm? No. We fixed it. We contained the threat. We saved lives. Why does it feel like that counts for nothing with you?" A sharp pain hit as the last words left his mouth, and he regretted them for the third time in as many hours. He had always strived to be thoughtful in how he responded to people, because he so often won arguments he shouldn't and later came to regret it.

This was a perfect example. That he had figured out the lighthouses and how to fix them was a fluke of stupendous proportions, driven by fear and necessity, not a desire to help Talus. It was not a thing of which he should be proud or an act for which he wanted or deserved credit. Yet, in his frustration, he had accused one of the most empathetic people he had ever met of being unsympathetic, of not giving him credit. Even more, he had no desire to quarrel with Dellia, yet here he was, fanning the flames of her ire. Why did it always seem to work out this way?

To his surprise, she seemed shocked, and a bit hurt herself. The reaction only deepened his sense of shame for words uttered in frustration.

When she spoke again, there was more sadness than venom in her voice. "I just don't like doing nothing while others are in danger."

Jon stepped closer. "I spoke with Saneya. She wants your help as much as you want to give it, but she has to be careful when there are rumors that we are the ones responsible for setting the darkness loose."

Dellia softened even more. "You spoke to Saneya?"

He wanted to come over and hug her, to reassure her he would try his best, but his nerves were still jangled from her rebuke, and he feared her reaction. "I had to. There were things she needed to know." He considered for a moment, as Dellia remained silent. "Look, she told us not to meddle. That doesn't mean you can't observe or investigate. Of all the things Saneya needs, information is pretty high on the list."

"But what if something happens while I'm investigating? How do I let something terrible happen while I do nothing?"

He drew a deep breath. So many times in recent days, he had let her down, but in this, he had authority. He could be her shield. "You work for the council, not for Talus or the Ephori or Saneya. Forget what I told her. If you see something and think you need to help, then don't hesitate, just do it, and let me worry about the consequences."

"But you're asking me to break your word. You're asking me to make you a liar and put you in a difficult position."

"I trust you, Dellia. I trust your judgment and your heart. I would never blame you for doing the right thing, regardless of the position it puts me in. And, I have no fear of arguing to Saneya that your actions were justified." He stepped up in front of her and softened his voice. "It would be unreasonable for anyone to ask you to do nothing and let others get hurt. I don't think Saneya meant for us to do that. She just doesn't want us acting on our own without her knowledge or consent."

"I know Saneya. She wouldn't ask us to stand down and not have Prian keep an eye on us. If Garris or I go poking around, she'll know."

Jon considered for a while. "Figure out what you want to look into, and I'll see if I can speak to her in the morning. Maybe she'll let you do it if Brita accompanies you."

Dellia shot him a sideways look. "Brita? You heard the name once, and now hers is the first one that comes to mind?"

"Oh, for crying out loud, am I the only one who thinks it's strange she looks just like you?"

"Just like me?" She seemed hurt by the comparison. Then she lowered her head. "Am I not allowed even a little petty jealousy?"

"You're allowed as much jealousy, and to be as petty, as you like."

He moved to hug her, but Dellia shied away. "Do not hug me with arms that have hugged her."

Jon smiled. He deserved that. After all, he had just told her she could be as petty as she liked. They settled in their cozy tent and lay down to sleep on a plush blanket Prian had provided. The murmur of a dozen discussions, crackling of many fires, and rustling of horses both near and far carried on the cool night air.

Eventually, he slid over near Dellia, though he feared she might refuse his touch a second time. To his surprise, she slid closer and laid her head on his chest.

He looked down at her dark hair draped across him. "Are they comforting sounds?"

She tilted her head back to glance up at his face. "What sounds?"

"The camp. Being out here with your people."

She fell silent for a time. "Did you ever wonder why I became a protector when my mother is one of the Ephori, one of the leaders of our people?"

He puzzled. It did seem odd. "No, but now that you mention it, why didn't you become a Talesh soldier or officer?"

"Because of my father."

He recalled another time when they were on the flat grassy plains of Talus. They had been headed to Sirra's home when he mentioned Dellia's father. She had flinched in discomfort and her face had clouded over He recalled her exact words. He repeated them softly, almost to himself. "He died when you were very young. You never knew him."

Dellia pulled back and stared at his face. "You remember?"

He gave a small smile. "When it comes to you, I remember everything important."

She laid her head back down on his chest. "He died at Githeo, saving my mother and me." There was a long pause that told him this was a difficult topic for her. After a while, she continued.

"He was sent to lead a small group of soldiers in protecting a village. Because of an unfortunate accident, my mother and I ended up in the same village during an assault. My father was their best fighter, but instead of staying to protect his men, he ran away. They say he fled to hide me and my mother on the second story of a nearby home. He abandoned his post as his own soldiers and the villagers he was sworn to protect were dying in the streets. By the time he fought his way back, most of his contingent were already dead. Few men survived, but my father wasn't one of them. They needed him, and they might have suffered fewer losses if he had been there to fight alongside them. Instead, he and many others died because he chose to save us instead of protecting them."

That she had been a part of such a bloody tragedy was a little too close to his own story, and a wave of sympathy racked Jon.

Dellia moved closer and scooted up, so her head lay next to his. "Thank you for understanding." She kissed his cheek. "Blame for the defeat was laid at my father's feet. Many of my friends had parents that died at Githeo. Afterward, I became an outcast. My friends tried to hide their resentment, but I could still feel it, even if they never said a word. I knew they thought I should have died instead of their fathers and mothers."

Jon pulled her closer, unsure what to do to ease the pain he could hear in her voice.

"So, I suppose I fled my people. I became a protector to redeem my father's sin. I wanted to prove I wasn't him, that I would always choose duty."

Without another word, Jon finished the sentence in his mind: she would always choose duty over family.

Suddenly the picture became crystal clear, and he understood why her duty was so important to her and why the council's betrayal was such a blow. And he understood, with deep sadness, why he would never be as important to her as her duty. She resented her father for saving her at the expense of the people he was sent to protect. Without realizing it, she was indirectly telling him that if she found herself in similar circumstances, she would not do the same. She was telling him she would let him die if it meant fulfilling her duty.

She paused for a while, seeming unaware of his disturbing train of thought as she nestled closer. Perhaps the turmoil she'd stirred up by delving into her painful past had dulled her gift and distracted her. She glanced again at his face. "Those feelings of resentment are long gone, but I'm still not comfortable being back here among my people."

He tried to shake it off. He was overreacting. "I'm your people now. You and me, that's all we need. Okay?"

She never answered, and they both lay there as the sounds of the encampment became few and far between, until all that was left was the soft rustling of patrols walking the perimeter. Jon kept trying not to go over the words Dellia had said, the meaning he kept reading between the lines. Yet, he knew that on some level, he had heard correctly. He wasn't wrong. She was his world. He loved her with all his heart, and yet he would never be the most important thing in her life. After a time, weariness overcame him, and he dropped into a restless sleep.

Aylun sat staring down the broad road that curved off through the woods. He followed it with his eyes until it disappeared behind the trees and around the rocky slope to which they clung. His nerves were jangled and his mind a mess. He needed to find a focus, so he aimed all his attention on the rhythmic wash of distant waves rolling onto the sandy beaches of Kinshai Lake.

He drained every thought from his mind, trying to forestall the anxiety and oppressive guilt that were clawing at him again. The demons were back, pounding on the door of his conscience, and they were more furious than ever. It was all at the prospect of returning to the life he had before Megan.

He had remained back from the shoreline as he sent his two companions to bathe in the lake. Rillen didn't seem to mind her appearance, but riding around with a blood-soaked and spattered woman was bound to raise a few eyebrows in such a serene part of the world. The protector also teased him about coming along to bathe with them, or at least it seemed like teasing, but doing so wouldn't have been appropriate. More than that, he needed time to himself. He had talked Megan into trying to undo her coming to this world. He had told her it was worth it if it made her happy, but he was far from okay.

The idea of going back to his former self gutted him. The recurrent nightmares, the constant anxiety and dread—he would do almost anything to keep from returning to that existence. *Almost* anything, because despite what it would mean for him, he had to do this. Not because the greatest oracle who ever lived said so, but because setting things back would return Megan to Jon. It would put her back where and when she belonged. She would be where she had wanted to be from the very beginning, and he would do anything to ensure her happiness.

Yet, the compulsion to flee, to escape this fate, was almost overpowering. All he could do now was hold on and remind himself that in every way that mattered, this was the right thing to do. This was what had to happen. He must come to terms with it. For a while longer, he sat and focused, trying to summon the calm of the waves lapping against the shore. Then he caught hoof-falls returning along the cobblestone road.

A short time later, he made out Rillen's chirpy voice. "What makes you think a puffin would make a good pet? Do they lick your face or rub up against your legs? No, because there's no affection there."

He could imagine the indignation on Megan's face as she responded, "You just don't get it. They're cute."

"Then get a puffin statue or a painting. The real thing would poop all over your house and spend half of its time in the water."

"Oh, a statue sounds nice."

Aylun stood as they brought their horses to a stop in front of him, their hair and clothes still wet with lake water. He gathered his resolve, ignoring his dread and sadness as he smiled up at them. "I see you have solved the world's problems. War, poverty, famine, disease, and whether a puffin would make a good pet."

Megan looked at Rillen and gave her head a small shake. "He'll never get it. He's just a stick-in-the-mud."

Aylun pulled himself up tall and sang out in a cheerful voice. "We need to find Jon. Last time I saw him, he was in Shir Keep. Everyone I ran into said to look for him with Kayleen or Dellia."

Megan had been all smiles from the moment she came back from the lake, but at the mention of Jon, a dismal and pensive cloud fell over her. "How can I face him? What am I supposed to say to him?"

He gave her a warm smile. "Nothing you do not feel like saying. I will do all the talking. You need only say what your heart bids you to say."

At that, she became more agitated. "That's great, except my only goal since this started was to protect Jon. How is it protecting him for me to tell him he has to give up the woman he just married?"

"But this is what you wanted. If you undo Jon's coming, he won't even remember having met her. It won't hurt him because he'll never know."

"But I'll know."

"No. You won't remember any of this either. See, it's perfect."

Megan glared at Aylun. "I don't like it."

He paused as he summoned his softer and more understanding side. "I know, and I am not fond of it either. I'm not suggesting you ask Jon to do anything. I am only suggesting you tell him the truth about the warning. After that, what he does with the information is up to him. He should at least hear the warning, right? He deserves the truth."

Rillen reached over and set a hand on Megan's still-damp shoulder. "No matter what, you should see him. Leave or stay, undo your coming or not, you are friends. Be a friend to Jon."

Aylun puzzled over the first part of the protector's remark. What could she be referring to when she said, "leave or stay"? Still, Rillen was right, so he nodded. "Do not dwell on what to say to Jon. Give him the warning, then give him a chance to say all that he wants to say. The rest will come."

Megan considered for a moment, then she gave a tiny nod. "Okay, fine. Let's find Jon."

Aylun glanced at Rillen, then leaned toward Megan and lowered his voice, though it seemed likely the protector could catch every word. "Do you have a white spire stone?"

Rillen appeared surprised by the question and stared at Megan, paying a little too much attention to her reply.

Megan left a long pause before answering. "Yes. I remember seeing it."

Rillen's eyes flew wide. "What? How many do you have that you need to spend that much time thinking about it?"

Megan paused again. "Um … all of them? I think."

Rillen gave a long whistle. "*All* of them?"

"Yeah, a couple dozen, I suppose. I didn't count."

"Didn't count? There aren't even that many spires."

"So I've been told."

Rillen lowered her voice and leaned closer to Megan. "A bit of advice. Don't let word of that spread to anyone, not even Jon."

Aylun swung up onto Juzhi's back. "We should head back to the spire. It should not be a problem to make it to Shirdon before nightfall."

Rillen nodded. "Let's go."

With that, Aylun took the lead. They wound their way down the broad road back to the seldom-used path and the spire in the woods. Birds sang through the trees, and leaves rustled in the breeze. They drew a sharp contrast to his mood. Every step became a struggle to manage his dismay.

This was his burden to bear. It was the only way to undo all that he had done to her from the start. It would erase his shameful abduction of her, her terror and trauma in Katapa, and her abject misery after finding Jon and learning of his marriage. A marriage that never would have happened had he allowed Megan to stay at Jon's side. It was the only way to ensure her return to happiness.

He would find Jon and convince him. Then, he would help find the means for Megan to visit herself in the past, and he would protect and escort her until it was well and done. Then, everything would return to its proper place, and he would never even know that any of this had happened.

The memory of her dismissal from the council still burned in Kayleen's memory. They claimed it would be temporary but took everything from her. All they left her was the Window of Rhina, the device she used to relay reports and orders to and from Dellia. Then they dangled the council leader position in front of her like a carrot to a horse. Intending to use it as leverage, to extort her into using the device to persuade Dellia to bring Jon in.

Before Garris had gone on this mission, she had hurried to the stable to give him his half of the window. It had the appearance of a pair of simple polished metal bars, but in reality, it was a rare artifact, many centuries old, that would allow her to communicate with him while he remained in the field. As acting council leader in Jon's absence, she had ample reason to keep in touch with him. As the protector accompanying Jon, no one would question Garris as her point of contact.

In truth, it was all a pretext. The councils, both old and new, were upset that Jon had left at such a critical time and showed no interest whatsoever in the details of his outing, which made her insistence on giving Garris the window purely personal. She had done so because she knew him, she trusted him, but most of all because his was the face she wanted to see. Even more, she was worried and needed reassurance that he was okay.

So here she sat, in her small room carved from the mountain, staring at his face through the shimmering curtain floating above the bar. The device sat on the same small table before the same window that Garris had come through when he tumbled back into her life.

Being the experienced protector he was, he had given his usual efficient, thorough, and dispassionate account of the horrifying turn of events at the lighthouse.

She had played her part too, striving to be the unshakable leader who took even the worst news with contemplative calm.

The trap at the lighthouse was expected, so it wasn't much of a challenge to take in stride. However, she struggled to keep her composure upon hearing the Dead of Night had left Saranik and was headed down a chasm toward the rest of Talus. It hadn't moved in centuries, and the idea of Garris so close to something so dangerous was hard to stomach. It was all she could do to keep a straight face and not betray her hysteria by ordering him to come home that instant.

What had shocked her was Jon's perceptiveness in intuiting the purpose of the lighthouses. Just as surprising was that he had recognized they'd been sabotaged and figured out how they worked well enough to repair one of them. His performance was at odds with the abysmal impression he had given at their first meeting. He could destroy a horde of the dead and defeat the council, yet he was afraid of a few simple decisions.

The fact that Garris had captured the man who had trapped them only to let him escape was unfortunate, as was the arrival of Saneya. However, what was far more disturbing was the rumor she bore. It could undermine Jon's influence as a leader. This little trip of Garris's had turned into quite a volatile predicament.

Even more concerning was that the new council leader and his two protectors were perched in front of a vast cloud of death. What good was it to contend with this disturbing rumor only to wind up with the man at its center deceased?

Her attention snapped back to the present, and Kayleen realized she had been toying with the long blue crystal Garris had given her—the one that always hung from a thin, silver thread around her neck.

For his part, having finished his report, Garris seemed anxious to end their conversation. It was disheartening. If only he would be as eager to talk to her as she was to talk to him. Despite his apparent rush, many troubling issues still clouded her mind. So she stared at him through the shimmering curtain as she composed her line of questions. "Excellent work, getting the lighthouse working."

He gave an efficient bow of his head.

"But we still have no idea who is behind the sabotage and what their aim is. And you lost the only man we knew was directly involved."

He remained calm. "We had a clear choice. We could either watch him and risk the darkness rolling over the lighthouse or leave him unconscious and fix it."

"I didn't mean it as criticism. You did the right thing, but can you get him back? Can you track him?"

"Now that's downright insulting, Kayleen. Of course I can."

"Then that's your priority … um, if Jon approves."

Garris nodded.

"Was there nothing unusual about the items they used for the sabotage, nothing we could use to track them down?"

"The chests and tarp were nothing special, but I already mentioned the chains were unusual."

"In what way?"

"They were made of a lightweight metal that showed no signs of corrosion. It was like nothing I've seen before."

Kayleen smiled and motioned to the men standing off to her side. Grekor, Nikosh, and Pedrus dutifully gathered behind her, on the other side of the bed.

It was the first time she had let Garris see the three of them, and he groaned. "Oh for …" He stared at Kayleen. "Don't tell me you actually asked for their help." He looked at Grekor. "No offense."

She peered over her shoulder as the burly soldier smiled and shrugged.

She decided to ignore the comment. "Grekor, I'll need you to see if you I can locate the one who forged those chains. They are unique, and the sabotage required multiple sets. See if you can find a smith who recalls making them."

Grekor nodded.

Nikosh elbowed him.

Grekor cleared his throat. "Um, yes, ma'am."

She turned her gaze to the man next to him. "Pedrus, keep looking for any information on Ahmet's supposed illness. There has to be a way to find out if he really was sick or if this was a murder made to look like a suicide. We must know."

He gave a respectful bow. "Yes, Madam First Advocate."

She turned her gaze to the last of the men. "Nikosh,

outstanding work locating Ruepo's house. If not for you, Jon wouldn't have been there to stop the Dead of Night."

The man beamed.

"Now, I want you to see if you can figure out where this rumor about Jon came from. I don't like it. It seems deliberate—to undermine people's faith in him. See what you can find out."

He simply gave a bow of acknowledgment and smiled at her.

Garris cleared his throat and spoke in that gruff authoritative voice he put on to impress or intimidate. From his tone, she suspected he intended to do both. "I have an order for you three."

Surprised, she turned with her underlings, waiting to find out what would come out of Garris's mouth.

His voice became even more demanding. "You lunkheads make sure Kayleen stays safe, you got it?"

Kayleen froze. She could certainly handle herself, yet for him to be so concerned about her welfare made her heart leap.

She stared as Garris continued to command her three allies. "Know where she is at all times. Check in on her. Not too obvious, mind you. Don't let on that you're watching her. And if there's trouble, you better be there to protect her. If anything happens to her, I'll make sure the same happens to you guys three times over. Are we clear?"

As if he couldn't end their conversation fast enough, Garris slashed his hand through the rippling image. The shimmering curtain in front of her turned into colored droplets that evaporated as they pelted the surface of her small table.

She rose and turned to face the men still standing shoulder to shoulder. "Well, get to it."

They rushed from the room, but Kayleen remained motionless, confused and bothered by the exchange with Garris. Without her willing it, her hand went back to fingering the long blue crystal around her neck. He had expressed a baffling level of passion for her welfare, yet couldn't wait to terminate their discussion. It was more than just proof he wanted to escape some supposed apparition of his past. It was proof that deep down somewhere in that old and scarred heart of his, he might care about her, much more than he was letting on.

She sank into her chair, thinking about it, recalling that evening a few weeks earlier when he'd crawled through her window. His anger and venom then seemed a stark contrast to his heartfelt words of minutes ago.

A chill breeze blew through the window as a knock came on her door. Without thinking, Kayleen rose and headed for it, expecting to find one of her three miscreants had come back for clarification of their orders. She let go of the blue crystal and calmed herself. When she pulled the door open, she almost stumbled backward at the sight that greeted her. It was Rillen, but with her stood a tall, muscular Elorian man and an Elorian woman with red hair.

"Megan?" Kayleen stepped up to her and lifted a lock of her ginger hair. Here stood a woman who held a great deal of sway with Jon, but perhaps of greater importance was that she was a good friend to him. As the man's representative, it was only suitable that she treat his friends with every bit of the same care, fondness, and respect that he would. She smiled. "I'm so relieved to see you."

Megan looked up at her with surprise. "You know me?"

"There aren't any other red-haired Elorians, so of course I recognize you."

There was a self-conscious quality to Megan's quiet response. "Where I come from, people dye their hair, so everyone just assumes I do too."

Kayleen eyed Rillen. "Thank you so much for bringing her to us."

Rillen bowed, and Kayleen motioned for them to enter.

The three passed through, and Kayleen guided Megan over to the small bed, sitting her down on it as she faced her. She motioned to the man to sit beside her, and Rillen stood at attention next to the pair.

Kayleen turned to Megan, but no sooner had the man seated himself than he spoke. "Ma'am, I am Aylun. We came seeking Jon. We have urgent news he must hear as soon as possible."

She looked at Rillen. "Is this true?"

The protector bowed her head. "Yes, it is true."

Kayleen considered for a moment. It was vital she earn their trust as quickly as possible. First impressions were critical, and giving Megan the information she sought was the best way to demonstrate she was willing to be open with her. She wanted to address her comments to Megan, but it seemed as if, for whatever reason, the three wanted Aylun to speak for them. So, in the best interests of diplomacy, she indulged them and turned her gaze to him. "An urgent matter arose in Talus, south of Nydri. He is there with Garris and Dellia." She leaned closer to him. "Is this matter one that I can help with?"

He shook his head, then left a pause. It was the type of pause she commonly saw when one was choosing one's words with care. "We have reason to believe Megan's removal from Jon's side may have dire consequences and seek to bring her to him with all haste."

The man was being crafty with his words, giving away only what he must, and he showed every sign of being practiced at it. It seemed doubtful she would get anything from him that did not serve his ends.

Still, she had to try. "As one in charge in Jon's absence, may I ask as to the nature of these dire consequences?"

Aylun looked her straight in the eye. "It is a matter between Jon and Megan. It involves their fate, and it would be inappropriate for me to reveal it to you before informing him."

She nodded. He was a circumspect one, and diplomatic, and nothing he had said was wrong. It would not do for news of a problem involving Jon and Megan to reach Jon's ears before Megan herself had a chance to deliver it to him. She could not fault Aylun's manner or his approach. So, she decided that, given all the other matters before her, she did not need to take on one that appeared to be well in hand.

Kayleen met Megan's gaze. A week or so ago, Jon had mentioned his plan to wait a week to see if she appeared on her own, and, if not, Dellia or Garris would go find her. Since that time, she had been making arrangements for Megan's eventual arrival. Kayleen smiled. "I have prepared a house for you."

The woman seemed startled. "For me?"

"Of course. You are important to Jon, and that makes you important to me." Kayleen smiled. "It is a permanent residence and yours to use whenever it pleases you, for as long as it pleases you. I have arranged for its upkeep and a small stipend for you. It is near Shirdon, where you can get food and drink, and it has a small stable of its own, so you may come and go at your leisure." She turned her attention to Rillen. "By coincidence, it is near your place. You can escort Megan and Aylun there, and they can set out for the mountains due south of Nydri at their pleasure."

Rillen bowed. "Is it that place near the spire?"

Kayleen nodded.

"Then I'll guide them. And there's one more favor I must ask. Let me escort them to Jon. I feel obliged to protect Megan."

Kayleen nodded. "That is an excellent idea. I would appreciate you lending her your protection. It is probably best for you to go with them anyway. Trouble is brewing, and your assistance may be needed."

"May I ask the nature of this trouble?"

Kayleen hesitated as she weighed the pros and cons. Their goal was to meet Jon, not to help with the Dead of Night. Moreover, what little she could describe of the threat wouldn't prepare the three of them for any eventual encounter. It would only alarm Megan over a situation beyond her control. With no upside to telling them and only downsides, Kayleen chose her words with care. "It is an evolving situation, and any information I give you might be out of date by the time you get there. For now, the Talesh are in charge, with Jon, Dellia, and Garris there for support. It would be best to have them fully brief you when you arrive."

Rillen paused for a moment. "This trouble, it's serious enough to warrant the presence of three protectors?"

Kayleen smiled. "Yes. It is a potential threat to all of Talus." Without further elaboration, she rose to see them out.

As Aylun stood, his head came up above hers, and from her angle, a sudden familiarity hit her. She had seen him before. Her mind raced back to a sketchbook Leanna had kept during her days visiting the Augury. It contained drawings she made of people and things she had encountered within its walls. Leanna kept it as if her life depended on no one seeing its contents, but one day Kayleen had come across it unguarded and paged through it. Several of the more memorable sketches were of a young man. It was fifteen years ago, but Aylun bore a striking resemblance to a fifteen-year-older version of that teenager.

She stopped and turned to face Aylun. "Have you seen my sister Leanna before? She had a sketchbook with a picture that looked just like you."

Aylun smiled. "I may have met her a once or twice." He said no more, nor did Kayleen ask. It was confirmation enough. He was from the Augury. The entire conversation with him took on a sudden seriousness far beyond what she had assumed.

Kayleen set her curiosity aside as she escorted her visitors to the door and saw them out. Then she returned to her chair and slumped down into it.

Alone with her thoughts, she let the gravity of all that had been told to her sink in. A trap had been laid for Garris by a man who had been trying to kill him for fifteen years. That trap involved letting loose the Dead of Night. It had worked, too. It had set it on the move, and if not for one damaged lighthouse, it could have obliterated all of Talus, maybe even all of Meerdon. Rumors that Jon was responsible appeared out of nowhere, and now this visit. A man who was most likely connected to the Augury arrived bearing a warning of dire consequences from Megan's not being with Jon—a situation she and the council had no small part in creating.

AYLUN

Her fingers moved to toy with the long blue crystal again. As alarming as all of that was, what concerned her most was that Garris was standing next to the man who was at the center of all of it. If things went badly, it was impossible to see how he could avoid being right in the path of the blowback.

Chapter Twenty-Six

REUNION AND DISSOLUTION

For two days, Dellia had put up with the insufferable idleness. She had gotten past her frustration enough to stop blaming Jon. In fact, true to his word, he had brought her to Saneya's spacious tent, and she stood by while he gave it his best. He argued doggedly, making one exceptional point after another, striving to persuade her to let Dellia work with her fellow Talesh—not as a protector, but as one of their own.

Throughout it all, Saneya remained intransigent, refusing to let any of them help in even the most superficial ways. Eventually, the woman grew irate and threw Jon out of her tent. Then she ordered Prian to set a guard to stop him from going near her again. So, Dellia sat around, growing more frustrated by the moment as she heard of Talesh soldiers tracking the saboteur, only to give up when his trail entered a small village. If it were she or Garris, they would have persisted until they found the man.

Weary patrols came, and fresh ones went. Eager reinforcements arrived. Scouts were dispatched to the Dead of Night and guards set up at the lighthouse while she paced and kicked at the grass and fretted. Rickety carts loaded with flamestones, both large and small, were delivered. Fires for them were built, and units were set up to collect wood and maintain them—all of it while she could only sit by and watch.

Throughout it all, civil words between her and Jon were increasingly rare, and she found it a constant battle not to lash out at him as an outlet for her fear and frustration. Then again, perhaps it wasn't fear or frustration, but how galling it was to see him and Garris so unconcerned about the risk to her homeland. In fact, the pair didn't seem to mind their idleness at all.

With ample free time, Garris held several training sessions for Jon each day while she watched and fidgeted. Not that anyone had prohibited her from participating in them. It was just that they were focusing on trivial matters while the fate of her home realm hung in the balance. So, she sat on the cool grass in the warm sun and watched as her anxiety mounted.

As for the state of his training, Jon was abysmal, as might be expected of an adult who hadn't held a weapon his whole life. How does that happen? Did his world have no war or crime? Garris kept the exercises varied, with a distinct emphasis on drills and basics, which was a shrewd approach with one who had never held a weapon his entire life.

As had become the custom, this particular session occurred outside their tent, its brown canvas stretching out behind them, making an exceptional backdrop against which to view their unfolding antics. Jon used a thick green stick with its bark torn away as a practice sword, holding it out in front of him to defend himself. Garris held one of his own with its tip to Jon's.

The warrior would move, and Jon was supposed to react and counter the blow. Instead, he was too slow and simply got whacked with a heavy stick over and over and over. To his credit, he winced a lot but never got frustrated or angry or even discouraged.

On the other hand, Dellia was finding it difficult to stay still, much less hold her tongue. After a particularly nasty hit that was bound to leave a welt, she couldn't contain her disapproval and sprang to her feet. "I appreciate what you're trying to do, Garris, but his foundation in awareness is too weak. He simply can't handle what you're trying to teach. Instead, you're just thrashing my husband."

Garris grinned. "I know. It's fun, isn't it?"

Dellia glowered.

He sent her a solemn look. "Okay, then why don't you demonstrate awareness for us?"

"What good would that do?"

"Humor me."

Dellia threw up her hands and marched across the lawn to her old, worn pack. She shoved its contents around until she found a large rough sack, which she snatched up, then strode back to Jon. "Give me your practice weapon." She kept her tone demanding, and he complied with the silent respect of a pupil to his instructor. After tossing the bag into his hands, she snapped into a fighting stance and thrust out the stick, touching its tip to Garris's. "All right, put the bag over my head."

Jon sent her a quizzical look. "What?"

She gave him an impatient stare and waited.

He glanced down at the bag in his hands, then up at her. "Is this some kind of a trick or something?"

This time, Dellia spoke with a great deal more emphasis. "No. Put the bag over my head."

"You mean, so you can't see?"

She gave an exasperated sigh and nodded.

With gentle care, he slid it over her head.

Unable to see, and the odor of old burlap heavy in her nostrils, Dellia calmed her anxiety and frustration and focused all her attention on her remaining senses. It took longer than usual to reach a relaxed and alert state. Then she called out, "I'm ready."

Nothing happened for a while. Then, Dellia caught the rustle of Garris's heavy pants. Something in her senses told her he was thrusting for her heart.

She knocked his stick away.

Then came an unexpected rush of air and the sound of leather armor stretching and binding against skin. She sensed movement from above. His stick was coming down on her head.

Dellia hit it away, but it was only the first of a flurry of attempted blows. She stopped thinking, stopped directing her actions, and let her instincts and reflexes take over. Sounds, smells, and the texture of the air assaulted her senses as whack after whack came in rapid succession. She parried, blocked, and countered every move. Then she sensed an opening. She had dodged a blow, causing him to overextend himself. So, she sent a lightning jab to his chest and was rewarded with a loud grunt.

She yanked the coarse bag off her head and squinted at Jon through the bright light of day. "Tell me, how did I do that with my eyes covered?"

He gawked and blinked. "I have no idea. You never missed a beat. You even knew when to strike back. It was a trick, wasn't it?"

She shook her head.

"Then it had to be some kind of gift, right?"

"No. Nothing so exotic. It's training. It's heightened senses combined with honed reflexes. I can teach you." Dellia glanced at Garris. "I mean, I wouldn't want to step on Garris's toes. He can keep teaching you the same as he always has, but I can teach you awareness. If Garris doesn't mind." She glanced again at the warrior.

He shrugged. "Be my guest. I never put much effort into awareness training."

She bowed to him. "Because you didn't need to. You're a natural at it."

"Sure. I've been tested. It's true, I'm naturally good at it, but because I never put any effort into it, I never got much better. So, I can't do anything like what you just did."

Dellia turned back to Jon. "The reason you couldn't stop a single one of Garris's blows is because you're watching his weapon."

He sent her a questioning stare. "What else would I do?"

"Watch his weapon, sure, but realize it's the last thing to move. So, don't only watch his weapon, watch Garris. When he strikes, he has to move. He may lean on his forward foot, glance at a part of your body, or tense a shoulder. Those tiny movements are signals betraying his blows. They tell you what he is going to do before he does it, sometimes even before he consciously knows what he's planning to do."

"Okay, but what does that have to do with what you just did?"

Dellia handed him back his practice stick. "Everything. You have to train your mind and senses. It starts with just paying attention. You learn to watch every tiny movement your opponent makes. Then, after a while, your mind simply expands on its own. You begin to see things, to simply know what he's going to do, even though you aren't quite sure what's tipping you off. You learn to read your opponent's body. That's the first stage."

"Then what's the second stage?"

"Expanding your awareness to include everything around you. So, you do things like switching to two opponents, then three. After a while, your mind expands again to pay attention to all the things going on around you, and you learn to react instinctively."

"Like with the spiders in the Recluse Tower. You just seemed to know when they were going to jump."

Gratified that he showed such a quick grasp of the subject, Dellia smiled. "Exactly. From there, you work on weaning away your dependence on eyesight, so you heighten your other senses even more. You begin to simply know what is happening around you."

"Like the invisible demon in the temple."

She nodded. "I can teach you while Garris continues your other training. Try what I described with Garris. Don't focus only on his weapon. Watch him, too, and pay attention to the tiny movements that give him away."

She went back to sitting in the grass off to the side as Jon did the exercise again, with Garris whacking him over and over. His performance wasn't much better, but every once in a while, he countered a blow. It showed he did have a slight grasp of what he needed to do. It was a start.

Seeming pleased with his paltry successes, Jon kept Garris occupied long after the large warrior suggested stopping. She could see why Garris liked to teach him. As a student, Jon was dogged in his thirst to learn. Their session went on until the soldiers around them became impossible to ignore. They were stopping and staring to the east.

Dellia turned around. And across the vast grassy expanse, five riders were approaching. Under the shadow of a passing puffy white cloud, precise details were difficult to make out. After a while, two of the riders peeled off. One headed around them while the other returned along the path they had come. She watched for a time until the cloud drifted past them and the shadow moved on across the grassy expanse.

In the brightness of sunlight, it became clear the two who had veered off were Prian's soldiers, acting as escorts for three other riders. One of the horses was recognizable right away as Rillen's red stallion, Laal. The other two riders were atop a pair of spotted horses. They were a man and a woman, and the woman had ginger hair that matched the mane of her horse.

It only took a moment for a mix of emotions to hit her. The red-haired woman was Megan. Dellia brought herself up taller and steeled herself. The woman her husband once loved had arrived.

Megan awoke to the melody of songbirds echoing through the pine forest, and the aroma of fresh-baked bread wafting through every room. It was the morning after they had met with Kayleen, and it took a moment for the mental cobwebs to clear enough for Megan to realize they were in the house the woman had arranged for them.

The rustic log cabin was on the small side, but nicely appointed. It contained a beautiful kitchen complete with dining table and chairs. The beds were sturdy, soft, and warm, and it was adorned with a smattering of tasteful paintings and statues, every one of them appropriate to the home and its secluded woodland setting.

It turned out Rillen had brought the food from the bustling Shirdon Market, several minutes' walk south. Their repast consisted of still-warm bread and something that seemed like oatmeal, only with a satisfying, chewy texture. It was hearty and filling, but nowhere near as intriguing as the dishes of Mundus.

Afterward, they readied their horses in the adjacent small stable and set off to the spire, only a short ride to the north. Traveling by spire was fun, as always, and the red stone sent them to another spire in a small clearing that Aylun explained was in the Illis Woods, near the Talus Plains.

The ride across the flat expanse was boring enough, and Megan whiled away the time by trying to find shapes in the puffy clouds that drifted across the soft blue sky. This part of the grassland was a little more plush, with fewer trees than on their trip to Katapa. Far off to the left, sweeping mountains always graced the view. They were beautiful, but she had seen them close up, and they didn't hold fond memories.

Rillen seemed familiar with the area, and after a very long day's journey, she led them to a small building sitting alone on the plains. Its walls of heavy fieldstone gave it a rustic air that contrasted with its cozy furnishings. Together they gave the place the feel of an ancient bed and breakfast. They ate at the establishment, slept, and had their early meal before heading off again cross-country.

It wasn't very many hours before they encountered a pair of somber Talus soldiers. The two recognized Rillen right off, and she informed them she was here to bring her friends to Jon. At once, they escorted all three farther east but also a bit south, angling toward the mountains, which continued to grow larger as they thudded across the verdant terrain. Having a protector with them had turned out to be a pretty handy thing. It brought them knowledge of the area and instant credibility with everyone they met.

After a short ride, a neat and orderly encampment came into view. And with it, Megan's excitement grew. She was finally going to see Jon again. That excitement was tempered with the reality that she didn't really know who this council leader who'd married a protector was, but it wasn't the Jon she knew; it wasn't the same man who, weeks earlier, had hidden in his office to avoid telling people he was going to turn down a promotion.

Soon, their escorts pulled up closer to Rillen and pointed to a man and two others in front of a small brown tent. They said something about that being Jon and eyed Rillen, appearing to seek acknowledgment. It was hard to tell over such a distance, but the three appeared to be a woman sitting with her back to them watching a rather large brute with a stick repeatedly beating a third figure, who must be Jon. It was something she might have wanted to do from time to time, but this just seemed mean.

As soon as Rillen acknowledged it was Jon, their pair of escorts veered off. One circled around the camp to report their arrival to their leader, and the other headed back the way they had come. A short time later, the brute became recognizable as Garris and the woman as Dellia. They were engaged in what looked like some kind of sadistic practice session.

Megan's anxiety rose as Rillen led the way closer to the camp and to Jon. What would she say? What should she do?

The moment Jon spotted her, all activity came to a halt, and Dellia rose to her feet. He stood gawking as they rode up, his two companions unmoving at his side, apparently waiting to see what would happen.

As she swung down off of Yuki, Jon followed her with a steady gaze. "Megan?" Though he spoke, he didn't move, acting hesitant and unsure, as if he didn't know quite what else to do or say.

Megan remained still beside Yuki, uncertain herself what the moment would bring. Under normal circumstances, she would have rushed to Jon and given him a big hug, but awareness of Aylun standing right at her side made that seem somehow awkward and inappropriate. To do nothing seemed wrong, too, so she settled on the least demonstrative thing she could imagine. She strolled across the yard and straight up to Jon as she kept an eye on Dellia, unsure how she would react. Then, with a minimal show of emotion, she gave him a quick hug and stepped back.

Dellia lurched forward and flung her arms around Megan, embracing her with the enthusiasm of an old, cherished friend. "I'm so sorry I didn't come to get you myself. Are you okay?" She stepped back and looked Megan over. Her concern, as always, didn't seem the slightest bit artificial.

Megan smiled. "I'm fine." She pointed to her companion. "Aylun has taken good care of me, and Rillen has too. She's my new best friend."

Dellia glanced over at Rillen with a surprised expression. Then she turned her gaze back to Megan, her concern still evident.

Megan hesitated, unsure what to do in the face of such an outpouring of affection from a virtual stranger, especially one who could sense she was self-conscious. "It's just, a lot has happened, and I feel a bit awkward."

Dellia nodded. "That's understandable."

Jon finally spoke up. "I've been worried about you. Where have you been?" His concern was as genuine as always.

"Katapa and Lanessa, apparently," Garris chimed in as he leaned on his practice stick. His relaxed, informal tone and manner drew a sharp contrast to the tension of the moment. "Anyone that can go there and come back alive has my deepest respect." He straightened and gave a generous bow to Megan, then to Aylun.

With Garris acting more relaxed than anyone else, Megan started to feel a bit more at ease and smiled again, meeting his informal tone with her own. "It was a nightmare."

"I can imagine." He smiled. "In the Verod camp, you said you were on the trail of something super important, that it could turn out to be nothing, or it could change everything. Did you find what you were after?"

She faltered as she recalled their encounter. She had been in the process of fleeing and had just made up whatever story she needed to extricate herself from a horrible situation. She lowered her head, staring at the well-trodden grass. "Oh, that. Well, to tell you the truth, I kinda made that—"

"Yes. We found what we sought." Aylun rushed to cover for her. "We were after a message from Wistra—a warning she described in one of her journals, the one we retrieved from Lanessa. It said that Megan should never have been taken from Jon."

Megan looked away, her gaze following a distant guard as he walked down the neat rows of tents. She hadn't expected her news to come out so soon or to be blurted out before a gathering of pensive onlookers. Nothing Aylun had said was wrong, and she was grateful to him for taking the lead in a situation that still seemed quite strained. Yet, his announcement had made the mood more awkward than ever.

Jon looked baffled, eyeing Aylun. "Taken from Jon? But it was you who took her."

Afraid this might turn into a discussion of Aylun's abduction of her and not wanting to subject him to an even more embarrassing inquisition, Megan decided to clarify. "You don't understand. He took me because he was worried someone might hurt you or me. He was worried about her." Megan pointed to Dellia.

Dellia's expression turned to one of shock. "Me?"

Not feeling particularly comfortable being overly critical of Jon's wife, Megan gave a careful explanation: "Yes. We knew about the prophecy. We knew you were a protector sent by a lying council. We also knew about your gift. It was obvious Jon didn't know any of that. We were afraid that if he found out, you might hurt him or at least take him back to Shirdon, where he'd never be heard from again."

Dellia balked. "Me? Hurt Jon?" She shook her head. "I was never going to hurt Jon."

Aylun stepped up in front of Dellia, wedging himself between her and Megan. "Really? I saw you in the oracle's message. Braye ordered it, and you stabbed Jon in the back. He bled out at your feet. Are you saying that was a lie? Are you saying she made that up? Are you saying that if the council gave you a direct order to kill the one who was to end civilization, you wouldn't have followed that order?"

Dellia stammered at his all-too-direct accusations. "Well, I ... I ..."

Jon stiffened and stared at Dellia in utter shock. "You would have killed me?"

She reached out to set her hand on Jon's arm.

He pulled it away.

She let her hand drop to her side. "I never got an order to kill you. I was only supposed to find out if the prophecy was about you."

"But if you *had* gotten an order …"

She remained silent.

"Really? You don't answer?" Jon looked her in the eyes. "Okay, then what if they ordered you just to bring me in. Would you have hauled me off to be locked in a cell, never to be heard from again?"

Dellia hesitated, drawing out her reluctant response. "I'm … I'm a soldier, Jon. I have a duty. I follow orders."

Jon seemed crestfallen, but Aylun interrupted, thrusting out the leather-bound tome they had found in the hidden city. "All of that is in the past. It is irrelevant now. We found the warning from Wistra. It says that Megan cannot be separated from Jon. If she is, he will eliminate the council so he can be with Dellia. It says the council is essential to the future of us all. It says if the council is dismantled, the consequences will be far worse than if Jon had never come to our world."

Jon gazed at him in confusion. "But that's the opposite of what her message to me said. You saw it."

Aylun's rebuttal was blunt and matter of fact. "I did, and I think you are wrong. Her message never mentioned you marrying Dellia or confronting the council. It said you would become a great leader, nothing more. This warning says she saw you working with the council."

Silence fell as Megan watched her friend's face. She knew that look well. It was the one he wore whenever she brought up whatever haunted his past. It was the look he had when he thought he had wronged someone.

She was about to say something to soften the blow when Dellia glanced over at the white tower barely visible in the distance. "The rumor."

Aylun stepped back and eyed Dellia sideways. "What rumor?"

"That Jon caused the Dead of Night to be on the move. That he damaged the lighthouse."

Aylun breathed the deep breath of someone making up their mind. He eyed first Garris, then Jon, then Dellia, and when he spoke, his words were simple, clear, and forceful. "The warning from Wistra says if Jon brings down the council, there will be only one way to set things right, only one way to save any part of humanity, and that is for Megan to undo Jon's coming to this world."

Jon stood with an expression of complete puzzlement. "Undo my coming? How could Megan undo our coming to this world?"

She stepped up to Jon, endeavoring to speak in a calm and rational tone. "Before we came to this world, I got a visit from my future self."

Jon boggled and shook his head in confusion. "A visit from the future?"

"Yes."

"That ... that can't be true. I mean, if it's true, then why didn't you say anything?"

Megan kept her gaze steady. It would be absurd here, in front of everyone, to go into the reasons she hadn't told him. So, she kept it simple. "It's all in the past now. It doesn't matter why, but I had good reasons. The thing is, it seems likely it was a visit from my future self in *this* world. If there's a way to visit myself in the past, I can use it to warn myself before the accident in the lab. I can make sure it never happens."

Jon gawked at her. "On Earth, you got a visit from your future self in *this* world?"

She nodded.

"But that's not possible."

Megan straightened in surprise. "Look around you, Jon. I can move things with my mind. Dellia can sense emotions. Her mother can open portals. What do you mean it's not possible?"

696

There was a determined tone in Jon's voice. "On this world, sure. I think it works on a different set of rules than Earth, a different set of physical laws, so stuff like that can happen here, but it can't happen on Earth. The physical laws of Earth are well established and well proven, and they prohibit it."

"Jon, it happened. Believe it."

His determination seemed to turn to distress. "I can't. I can't accept that there's a way to visit yourself in the past on Earth. Einstein's theory of general relativity says that time travel to the past can't happen the way you're saying. Think about it. On Earth, has that theory, ever, even once, been proven wrong on the scale you're talking …." Jon froze. He stayed that way for a second, then his eyes widened as his gaze rose to the sky. "Oh no."

Dellia's gaze whipped over, and there was a look of deep concern on her face. "What? What is it?"

Without another word, he whirled around, raced back to his tent, then ducked through the flap and out of view.

Guilt stabbed at Megan. She had expected the news wouldn't be well received, but she hadn't been prepared for this.

Dellia didn't follow Jon. She stepped up to Aylun, meeting his bluntness with equal force. "I don't believe you."

Megan interceded, striving to bring the confrontational tone down a little. "You can sense if I'm telling the truth, right?"

Dellia nodded.

"We did find a warning from Wistra. It does say what Aylun said."

Dellia brought herself up taller. "That only proves you believe it to be true. It doesn't make it true."

Aylun spoke up. "I can spot Wistra's work. The warning is genuine. It is from her. It says we must undo Jon's coming to this world. There is no doubt."

Dellia remained straight and unflinching. "You're wrong. Jon is my one true love. He has to be with me. All you've proven is that the deception is good enough to fool you."

She glared at Megan. "There's something wrong with Jon, and I don't know what. I need to go talk to him. So, if you'll excuse me." She bowed her head, then spun around and marched back toward the tent into which he'd disappeared.

Concern overwhelmed Megan. Jon's reaction was much stranger than she'd expected. Yes, something was wrong, and a compulsion tugged at her to go and see for herself. It's what she always would have done throughout their ten-year history, but things were different now. So, she yelled out to Dellia as she marched away. "Something's wrong?"

The protector stopped in her tracks and, without turning, addressed Megan over her shoulder. "Yeah. Someone just told him he has to give up his wife. Would *you* be okay?" She surged forward and followed Jon, disappearing inside the tent.

Megan's guilt grew out of control.

Then she noticed Garris. He seemed unaffected by the tension. He eyed Aylun and tilted his head. "Well, that was awkward and spectacular all at the same time." He sent Megan a warm smile. "You hungry? We have food."

Megan faced Aylun. "I don't like it, Aylun."

He set a reassuring hand on her shoulder. "It had to be done. Now, give them some time to adjust."

She turned her gaze back to the tent. It was obvious it was their tent. Guilt clawed at her, and she wanted to find out what the problem was, but it was a place for Jon and Dellia and not one into which she could intrude. With nothing more she could do about the mess she'd made, Megan looked back to Aylun and nodded.

Jon gawked at Megan, unable to accept the very concept. "On Earth, you got a visit from your future self in *this* world?"

She nodded.

"But that's not possible."

Megan remained resolute. "Look around you, Jon. I can move things with my mind. Dellia can sense emotions. Her mother can open portals. What do you mean it's not possible?"

He stood frozen for a moment, desperate to grasp at any line of argument he could find to refute what Megan was saying. It couldn't be true. He couldn't allow it to be true. Because if it was, he might lose Dellia. "On this world, sure. I think it works on a different set of rules than Earth, a different set of physical laws, so stuff like that can happen here, but it can't happen on Earth. The physical laws of Earth are well established and well proven, and they prohibit it."

Megan remained adamant. "Jon, it happened. Believe it."

His mind raced, still trying to summon any line of reasoning that might debunk her claim. Not a day had passed when he hadn't spent a long time mulling over the myriad violations of physical laws that happened with alarming frequency in this impossible world. Summoning bolts of lightning out of nothing, visiting the past, even his own gift—they were all impossible. After countless hours, the only theory he could summon was that the physical laws here had to be different from those of Earth. Megan had to be wrong. She just had to.

His breath began to come faster. "I can't. I can't accept that there's a way to visit yourself in the past on Earth. Einstein's theory of general relativity says that time travel to the past can't happen the way you're saying. Think about it. On Earth, has that theory, ever, even once, been proven wrong on the scale you're talking …"

Then it hit him: the dream. Three days ago, or was it two, he had dreamed of that moment in the oracle room when Wistra had caught his gaze. It was so vivid, and his every instinct was telling him she was watching him. She was watching her prophecy play out from seven hundred years ago. Either his impression was wrong, or she was time traveling.

Then, he recalled the platform Wistra stood on and the symbol below her. It was a ruby-red circle inside a triangle with five golden lines radiating out. He had noticed the same symbol on the Shirdon

Spire, only in pure white. Then there was the stone she'd picked up. That stone had ended the vision. It was translucent, with swirls of sparkling ruby and gold. Not only was it the same size as Dellia's spire stone, but it was also imbued with the exact same colors as the symbol.

All of a sudden, he knew with unerring certainty: his theory was absolutely wrong, and Megan was right. She had visited herself in the past, and he knew exactly how she'd done it. He knew how to undo their coming to this world.

His gaze rose to the clear blue sky, scattered with puffy wisps of white, as the sudden realization drove a dagger through his beating heart. "Oh no." A knot of anxiety wound its way around his insides and tightened. Too stunned and distraught to contemplate what he knew would come next, his mind went numb. Incapable of dealing with any more talk, he whirled around and bolted for their tent.

Dellia called out from behind him. "What? What is it?"

Jon ducked through the flap and lowered himself down into the grass inside, huddling there in the quiet shade with his arms wrapped around his knees. He hunkered there in the warmth of their tent, unthinking, as the shadow of a patrolling soldier passed across the sunlit sheet of brown canvas.

As if out of nowhere, anger savaged him. This wasn't fair. He had done so many things that were so hard for him. He had pretended to be strong as he convinced the leaders of the three realms to help him. He had talked the ruling council into relinquishing power. He had agreed to be council leader, even though it was worse than any fear he had ever imagined. Packs of Blood Wolves, armies of the dead, demons, torturers, and kidnappers—he had faced them all. And for what?

His anger turned to desperation as he realized what Dellia's answer would be. He had seen it. She had stabbed him in the back because Braye had ordered it. What Megan was suggesting wasn't even killing someone. Not only that, but Dellia herself had told him what she would do. He had heard it in her own words. She would choose her duty over family, and her duty would be to undo their meeting because it might save lives.

The rustling of the tent flap drew his attention to his wife, stepping through. She hurried over and huddled down next to him, enfolding him in her arms. "What is it? What's wrong?"

Desperation seeping out of every pore, Jon peered into her face, and his pleading words rushed out on their own. "I'll try harder. I'll do everything Kayleen asks. I'll save the protectors. I'll do anything. Just don't ask me to never have met you."

For a few seconds, Dellia stared in shock. Then her eyes widened. "You know, don't you? You know how Megan can visit herself in the past. You know how to undo your coming to this world?"

Jon froze. He wanted to lie. He wanted to deny it, to tell her no, he had no idea, but he couldn't. Not just because it would be wrong but because she would know he was lying. He gave a small, slow nod. "Remember the room in Kanlu, up along Kita Pass, the oracle room, where we first saw the message from Wistra?"

Dellia nodded. "The oracle room."

"When the message was over, she looked at me. I mean, really, actually looked at me."

She seemed puzzled.

Of course she didn't understand. "You talked about awareness before. Well, it's one thing for someone to look your way. It's another when your eyes meet. It's something in their gaze or their facial expression or their reaction, something below your level of awareness that tells you that you are looking into each other's eyes."

"And you felt that with Wistra?"

"Yes."

"And you think she was watching you from seven hundred years ago?"

"Yeah. There was a symbol on the platform"—Jon pointed to the ground—"exactly like the one on the spires and a stone exactly like a spire stone, clear with swirls of red and gold. If you had that stone and touched it to the symbol on the platform, I think it would let you visit a time in the future, and I'll bet it can take you back to visit yourself in the past."

Dellia remained quiet for a time, holding him close as she stared down at the green carpet of grass upon which they were both squatting.

He lowered his voice. "Don't tell them, Dellia. Please?"

She looked up at him, seeming as upset and hurt as he was. "Jon, this involves the fate of all of Talus. I don't think we can simply—"

"Please. Not now, at least." He gazed deep into her eyes, searching for some small sign of sympathy or acquiescence. "I'll figure something out. Just give me time. Okay?"

She closed her eyes. "Okay, okay. For now."

The awful knot of panic in his stomach eased as she held him. He just needed to find an alternative to undoing his coming, and everything would be okay. They stayed huddled together like that for some time, as his tangle of anxiety eased even more.

After a while, Dellia rose to her feet and offered her hand. "Come on, you have guests, and they're going to wonder."

Jon looked up at her, still searching her eyes for any clue to what she might be thinking. He nodded and took her hand. She helped him up, and he followed her outside.

Megan, Aylun, Rillen, and Garris were gathered around a few rickety wooden crates shoved together to create a makeshift table. They appeared to be talking and enjoying themselves. The jovial ambiance seemed terribly wrong given how near he was to losing Dellia. Not to mention the guilt that nagged at him for keeping what he knew from Megan.

He pulled himself together, putting the whole subject as far out of his mind as he could. He trailed Dellia over to the group and sat next to her on the cool bed of green. Before him lay the remaining carcasses of a couple of roasted giant birds. It looked like an oversized turkey perhaps, but leaner and gamier smelling. He paid little attention as Garris waved a giant, half-eaten drumstick and gave the assemblage his own unique interpretation of their time together. He joked and poked fun at every part of their journey, from completing the medallion right through to Jon becoming council leader and marrying Dellia.

When he finished and the table grew quiet, Garris waved the half-eaten drumstick at Jon and smiled. "Did the talk of undoing your meeting Dellia spook you that much? You had to run off and hide?"

Jon sent him as sincere a smile as he could muster. "Yes."

Garris set down his drumstick and smiled back. "Not very council-leadery of you."

Jon put away his smile, and his words were only half sarcastic. "I'd explain the depth of my love to you, but it'd be like describing a painting to a blind man."

Garris's grin broadened. "Not bad. I got no comeback."

Megan leaned toward Jon as she eyed Garris. "I see you've made some dysfunctional friendships while I was gone." She nodded to the big man.

Garris chuckled, and Dellia choked on her mouthful of meat. Rillen responded by throwing her arm around Megan. "You and I are going to be best friends."

Aylun rolled his eyes and motioned to Rillen and Megan. "Adi, help me. Riding with these two is a mountain of knives and a sea of fire."

He got blank stares all around the makeshift table.

"It means a dangerous situation. It means I never know what crazy, life-threatening things they'll drag me into next."

There were nods of understanding all around, except Megan, who glared at him. "Oh, really?"

Aylun glared back. "Yes, really. I seem to recall it was you who personally threatened to pulverize me if I did not take you to Lanessa."

"Oh, well. I might have been a little peeved."

"A *little* peeved? If throwing massive fallen trees at me is your idea of being a '*little* peeved,' I'm afraid to find out what happens when you really get angry."

Jon laughed. " 'A mountain of knives and a sea of fire.' I like that."

Megan shook her hunk of meat at Jon. "You shut up. You're supposed to be on my side."

Dellia sent Jon an oversized smile. "I just love the warmth and camaraderie when friends reunite."

Garris laughed.

It was cut short by yelling across the camp. Jon's gaze turned to the tower, and a short time later, several riders flew out of the camp toward it, their steeds thundering across the plains. The distant sound of shouts and clanking from that direction rose above the thudding of hooves, but it was too far off to make out any details. He tried to snag a soldier running by.

Dellia was faster and more determined. She ran up and grabbed the man by the arm.

Jon raced up to the pair in time to catch Dellia grilling the poor fellow. "What's happening?"

"There's been an attack on the tower. Something came out of the dark or the mountains near it. It's bad." The soldier turned and raced away.

Dellia moved to follow him, then halted as a familiar look of intense frustration overcame her. She let out a short screech of exasperation and slammed her foot down. "People could die. I could save lives, but I'm stuck here being useless."

Sympathy for her frustration moved him, and Jon stepped up to her side.

She glared at him, her face red with anger. Then, she turned and stormed away into their tent behind him.

Deeming it best not to follow and let her vent her frustration on him, Jon moved a handful of steps closer to the tower and squinted, trying to discern what was going on. He remained like that for a long while, until another soldier came by from the direction of the tower. He caught the frenzied woman by the arm. "Any news?"

"It's not the Dead of Night. It's some kind of giant insect things coming out of the mountains. We are holding it off, whatever it is, but there's already been one casualty. It seems like they're targeting the tower and aren't at all sensitive to the light. So maybe they're working with the Dead of Night or helping it or something. If the lighthouse falls …." The frantic soldier raced away.

Jon glanced at the tent to see if Dellia had overheard the last remark. She was standing in the entry, and her expression told him she had at least heard the worst part. He moved to placate her, but she glared and marched away again with an angry stiffness to her steps.

Jon returned to watching the tower for what seemed like an eternity. Then, weary and wounded soldiers began straggling back to the camp. As they passed, Jon studied their blank faces, their gashes and scrapes, and their bloodstained clothes, trying to figure out what had just taken place. Then, he caught a few fragments of their conversations. It was enough to be certain that the attack was over and the lighthouse still functioning. The Dead of Night hadn't moved.

A quiet rustling of grass came from behind him, and Dellia stepped up to his side. "I'm sorry, Jon."

His heart fell as he knew in an instant what she meant. He looked her in the face, pleading with everything he had. "We can fight this. There are other ways."

She lowered her head. "No. I told Megan and Aylun everything: the oracle room, the symbol, the red and gold spire stone, everything. Megan has the stone. She believes she can do it."

He shook his head. "Dellia, no."

Her answer was flat with a hint of sadness. "Can't you see, Jon? We have a duty. This isn't the time for your selfishness."

"But what if—"

"No. They are leaving in a few minutes, and I am going with them to ensure their safety. You can do whatever you want."

He watched in disbelief as she turned and headed for their tent. She had given up on him. He had lost Dellia, and even if they somehow got out of this without undoing his coming, their relationship would never survive. It would never be the same. The thing he feared most had happened. His marriage to Dellia was over.

Chapter Twenty-Seven

TO BE UNDONE

Despite the warm, sunny day and cloud-strewn sky, an awful gloom crowded around Megan as they plodded across the verdant plains, headed back the way they had come. Her mind jumped between second-guesses: about the prophecy, about what she had done to Jon, and about returning Aylun to his life of post-traumatic self-torment. She couldn't shake the feeling that something wasn't right, something didn't fit, but she couldn't tell if it was just how wrong it felt to hurt Aylun and Jon so badly.

Rillen had wanted to come along, but Garris pointed out the idiocy of three protectors escorting two people on a reasonably safe trip to Kanlu. He also fired off a sarcastic remark about the tower being under attack and that if the situation started careening downhill, he and Rillen would be needed more in the camp than with Megan and Aylun. A pair, he added, who had survived Katapa and Lanessa on their own. That appeared to settle the matter.

After that, Dellia seemed to take over. She insisted they use her mother's home as a place to spend the night, since it lay at a convenient halfway point between the camp and the spire. Despite her apparent eagerness to get this over with, she also assured them it would take until well after nightfall to get there. Her plan was to stay for whatever remained of the night. Then, with Megan's spire stone and an early start, they could reach Kanlu by sundown of the next day.

So, she and Aylun left the camp behind, with Dellia in front, acting as their guide. Having grown up in the area, she was the most familiar with the terrain. Aylun protected their rear, which left Megan in the middle.

For the first couple hours, her second-guesses were spent fretting about leaving Jon out of the decision to stop them from coming to this world. That, and leaving him behind. Especially when their mission was to undo meeting his wife. Both seemed like things he ought to have some kind of say in, but somewhere along the way, this had become as much Dellia's mission as Aylun's, and her and Jon's opinions seemed to have become afterthoughts.

It wasn't very many hours, though, before Jon trotted up behind them. Well, sort of behind them. His attempt to follow had led him way too far north, so he came in at a sharp angle behind Aylun. He stayed in the rear for a little while, until Aylun dropped farther back, leaving her and Jon in the middle. His arrival couldn't have gone unnoticed, but Dellia never even glanced his way.

After many hours, with the sun freshly set, the sky a dark blue, and multicolored fireflies whirling up out of the fields, her concern for Jon became too much. Most disturbing was the way Dellia had ignored him from start to finish. It wasn't right.

Megan pulled back on Yuki's reins to drop her back next to her longtime friend. Not wanting to broach a touchy subject right off the bat, she asked about something more mundane. "Have you noticed how everyone here speaks English?"

Jon seemed in a complete daze, but her words nudged him out of it enough for him to send her a blank stare. "Huh? Did you say something?"

"The people of this world can't possibly speak the same language we do, yet they appear to understand and speak perfect English … only I can't tell if it's Mandarin or English."

Still in a daze, Jon nodded. "Oh, that."

Surprised that he took it with such nonchalance, Megan said, "Yeah, what's the deal?"

"In Isla's lair, after—" He stopped himself and sent her a tentative look. "Isla, the dragon."

"Do you mean Islong?"

He shrugged. "The dragon, Isla, Islong—whatever you want to call her. Do you remember the light that passed over us and the burning sensation?"

"Yeah, I remember feeling different somehow. I even wondered about it."

"I think that's when it happened. She changed us, gave us something she called the Gift of Understanding."

Megan boggled. "She called … are you saying you had a conversation with the dragon?"

He nodded.

She pondered the concept for a while, but it only led to more questions. "But Aylun and Rillen use idioms and expression like 'beat around the bush,' 'hit the hay,' or 'ticked off' that are peculiar to our culture, and they appear to understand ones I use even though they shouldn't. Then, there are other times one of us doesn't understand the other at all. How does that make sense?"

"I don't know." There was a note of weariness in Jon's soft voice. "It's called the Gift of Understanding. Maybe it works on the basis of intent, so they understand our meaning and we understand theirs. Maybe it's not perfect and not everything gets translated. How would I know?"

Megan huffed. "You're supposed to be the science guy. If it works off the intent behind our words, then you're saying it understands our thoughts. What science would make that even remotely possible?"

Jon heaved an even wearier sigh. "Why are you asking questions you know I can't answer? What difference would the answer make anyway? Would it change the fact that after tomorrow I'll never see Dellia again?"

He was brushing her off because he was in no mood to chat. So, she hung her head and let the subject drop, even as she considered what he'd told her. If the dragon had changed them, it might explain why she could read the sign outside Katapa and why she seemed to know what the wolves were doing. If it worked the way Jon suggested, then this Gift of Understanding might go far beyond simple spoken language. It might apply to written language, too, and even to the way animals communicate with one another through body language. Anyway, it was clear that now was not the time for chats about the nature of the universe.

They plodded along awhile more, side by side, as Jon's dazed and far-off look returned. After what seemed like a suitable interval, Megan mustered enough courage to ask what was really on her mind. She leaned over and spoke in hushed tones. "I don't get it. What do you see in her anyway?" She motioned with her head to Dellia's outline, jostling in the saddle against the dark sky and endless fields of swirling fireflies.

Once again, Jon regarded her with that vacant expression. "I'm sorry, what did you say?"

She nodded, then spoke in a quiet enough voice to avoid being overheard above the thud of hooves against the plush grass. "Dellia came to us. We never asked her. She volunteered the information. She told us you knew how to undo our coming. She gave us every detail. The way she came without you, and the way she acted, it was obvious she was doing it against your wishes. How could she do that? How could she give you up so easily? It was like the pain she might cause you was irrelevant."

The tormented expression on Jon's face was awful to watch. He really did love Dellia like nothing she'd ever seen before. He lowered his head. "You don't understand."

"Enlighten me."

"It was her duty."

"So what?"

Jon fell silent.

Megan let out a hushed sigh. She hadn't intended to hurt him more than she already had, so she tried again. "Okay, okay. I'm sorry for criticizing the woman you love. I just don't really understand what's so great about her."

He shrugged. "Who knows? Anything I say would be an excuse. It would just be things I like about her. It's not like I wouldn't love her if she wasn't as beautiful or courageous or understanding."

Megan pulled away but kept her voice down. "Understanding? She gave you up in a heartbeat."

He sent her a flat stare. "I find your concern and your search for understanding ironic after what you said to me in the lab."

His verbal jab hit her in the gut. He was right, of course, so she reached over and set a hand on his arm. "I'm sorry. That was all a lie."

He sat up tall and straight in the saddle and stared at her motionless for a while as Enna moved beneath him. "What?"

"None of what I said in the lab before the accident was the truth."

He studied her with an expression of deep puzzlement. "Why would you do that?"

"I told myself to." Jon seemed confused. "When I got the visit from the future, she told me you were going to ask me out. I didn't want to turn you down, but she told me I had to."

He paused as if mulling it over. "I don't believe it."

"It happened, Jon. Believe it."

"No, that's not what I mean. I believe you had a visit from your future self. You might even buy into everything she said, but you're not the obedient-little-girl type. You're not one to just do as you're told. You had to have your own reasons for turning me down, so why did you do it?"

Megan pondered for a moment, trying to put her ambivalence into words. "To be honest, I'm not really sure anymore. At one point, I desperately wanted you to ask me out again. That's the honest truth. But I also had good reasons to turn you down. It might be comforting to think those reasons were stronger, but if I'm being honest, I think I was just afraid."

"Afraid?" He boggled. "Afraid of what? Am I some big ogre to be afraid of?"

"No. It's not that kind of fear. It's not fear of you. Look, you've asked me out dozens of times, and I always told myself all kinds of reasons to say no, but I think it all really comes down to fear it would go bad—fear that things might not work out."

He became quiet for a while, staring at the dapple gray of his horse's neck. "I'm not really sure I'm following you. What's the point in bringing all this up now?"

"My point is ... what I'm saying is, when I visit myself in the past, I will tell myself not to let that fear rule me anymore. I will make sure I go out with you."

His tone became cynical and biting. "It took being sent to another world to get up enough courage to go out with me. I'm so touched."

"I'm telling you I wanted to be with you, but I was afraid, and you twist it around with that sarcastic attitude?"

"Sorry." Jon fell silent for a time, seeming to consider what she'd said. "So, you're saying you're going to visit yourself in the past and tell yourself to go out with me. ... Why do I feel like that's the plot from *Back To The Future* or something?"

Megan giggled. "I know, right?"

His aspect turned serious again. "I appreciate what you're saying, but I can't recall feeling any more miserable than I do right now. I'm not really in the mood to think about you and me, much less talk about it. Just do what you want to do. Don't worry about me."

She nodded.

Jon shot her a quick glance. "And don't sacrifice yourself because you feel bad for me, okay?"

Startled by the notion, Megan stared. "You think I said all that because I feel sorry for you?"

He didn't answer.

"You know you're kind of being a jerk."

"I know. I'm sorry. You haven't done anything wrong."

Megan caught his eye. "It's that bad?"

712

He eyed her with an expression that was as serious as any she'd seen from him. "Yes, it's that bad."

"Then should I stop here? I could refuse to go back and undo our coming. Nobody could make me. It would be over, and things could go back to normal."

Jon shook his head. "It's never going to go back to normal."

"Why not?"

"Because it's done. You can stop what you plan to do, but it won't take back what Dellia did, and it won't change the reasons she did it."

"A little while ago, you were defending her."

"Just because I understand her doesn't mean I can just forget it like it never happened. Or pretend it won't happen again."

She considered his assertion for a while. "Then what do you want?"

"I just want to get this over with, and then I won't have to remember all the bad stuff that happened."

Megan shrugged. "Suit yourself."

She urged Yuki ahead, and they returned to the four of them riding in loose single file. Jon's decision not to stop this trip had eased her guilt a little. She may have been instrumental in creating the conditions that resulted in Jon and Dellia's breakup, but she had offered him a chance to back out, and he refused to take it. And although he hadn't said it in so many words, the reason he had given meant that on some level, Jon knew the breakup had always been inevitable.

Aylun spent a quiet day protecting the rear, which amounted to keeping a lazy watch out for intruders. The only one of which was Jon. He came bearing a somber look and a downturned face and was greeted only by a brief exchange of nods as Aylun let the man take his place in front of him.

The rest of the day dragged by with painful slowness born of their awkward situation. The sun crawled across the cloudy blue sky, a blazing sunset passed, and fireflies of amber, emerald, and fuchsia appeared, then dwindled. In all that time, Dellia never looked back, not a single time. Not even a fleeting glance, and not even when Jon caught up with them. It was difficult to fathom what was going through that woman's head.

For a while earlier, Megan had dropped back and spoken to Jon, the two riding side by side as they waded through the swirling, multi-colored dots of light. Aylun viewed their exchange with heightened interest, and as much as it gave him intense discomfort to admit it, they looked good together. There was a casual familiarity and camaraderie between them that shone through, even at a terrible time like this. So, even though it was uncomfortable to watch them together, it also set his heart at ease. He was doing the right thing.

Their chat reminded him of one other thing. He needed Jon's help. So he occupied his mind, trying to devise a pretext to talk to him alone.

Not long after the fireflies had disappeared into the night, a home appeared before them, a mere dark outline against the millions of stars winding their way across the black sky. It was accompanied by two other buildings. One appeared to be a low stable, and the other a main house behind a second smaller building. Both were built of carved stone, and like so many in this part of the world, they possessed larger than normal chimneys, which jutted into the winding swath of stars, like the outline of dark towers rising above the flat expanse.

Dellia led them to the squat stable, set off from the main house. She dismounted with her head down, and as he and the others swung off their mounts, it was hard not to notice that she never looked at Jon.

She did, however, glance at Megan. "It seems my mother is away. I imagine she is attending an emergency session of the Ephori. Since you are the key to this endeavor, I would be more at ease if you stayed with me in my old room where I can protect you. I'll settle you in, then tend to the horses myself. Just leave them here. The two men can

714

stay in the guesthouse." She motioned to the smaller building set off from the main house.

The crestfallen look on Jon's face was painful to behold. Not only had Dellia ignored him again, but she had arranged not to spend her last night with him. She had even referred to him as one of "the two men," like her husband was an irrelevant tagalong. Sympathetic to the poor fellow's plight, Aylun strolled up and patted him on the back. "Let us go. I will build us a nice fire, and we can warm up a bit."

Jon gave a pitiful nod and followed off to the guesthouse as Aylun held his flamestone high to light the path. Inside stood a massive fireplace of stone, separating two simple beds shoved against the opposite walls of the room. Each was kept company by its own table and dresser.

Jon strolled to one of the two beds, his motions automatic, betraying that he'd been here before and knew which one was his. He tossed his bag on the floor next to the small dresser, then shuffled over to a simple wooden cupboard. It creaked as he opened it. From inside, he retrieved a neat stack of bedding that he tossed onto the opposite bed. As Aylun began to make it, Jon returned and gathered another set of bedding. Then, he followed suit, the two of them working in silence.

No sooner had he finished than Jon threw himself onto the bed, staring up at the deep shadows of the ceiling timbers. Aylun took his flamestone outside, leaving his roommate in total darkness. He dug through a stack of wood on the side of the building and pulled out a few choice logs and some kindling. Upon hauling them back inside, he constructed a good-sized fire that appeared meager in the massive fireplace. Then, he lit it with a flint he always carried.

Jon never moved throughout the whole process, even as the flame spread, turning to a crackling fire that sent a comforting warmth across the room. At a particularly loud pop, he winced and shut his eyes. His pitiful expression made it easy to guess what had caused the reaction: the place contained memories of Dellia and their time together. The cracks and pops of the fire were a reminder of those times that soon would never have occurred.

Aylun lay down on the bed across the room and laced his fingers under his head. The need to find a pretext to talk to Jon alone had taken care of itself when Dellia suggested they room together. Now all he needed was an opening to discuss the topic he wanted. It seemed wrong to blurt out his request, so he glanced over at him. "I am truly sorry about all this."

Jon closed his eyes. "You didn't seem very sorry before."

Aylun paused. His undiplomatic approach at the encampment had been deliberate, so he'd deserved the rebuke. He nodded to himself. "Well, I am sorry if I seemed that way. This is difficult for me, too, but it needed to be said, and it would not be right to equivocate."

Jon let out a quiet snort. "Equivocate? You mean, show a little sensitivity to other people's feelings."

"I suppose I was needlessly blunt, and for that, too, I am sorry."

Jon finally glanced over at him. "You seem to be sorry about a lot of things."

"You have no idea."

Jon's face took on a puzzled expression. "What does that mean? And what do you mean, hard for you, too? How is this hard for you?"

Aylun held his tongue for a while, not sure if he should make things worse by dragging his own dilemma into an already grim situation. Then he realized it would make a stronger case for the favor he needed to ask, so he tried to explain. "I love Megan."

Jon rolled over on his side and stared. "What did you say?"

"I have feelings for Megan."

"Then how can you do this?"

"Because it is what she wants. It is what she has always wanted. She wants to be with you, but she created a misunderstanding, and all she has thought about since I met her is getting back to you so she can clear it up. How can I not help her when it is what she needs to be happy?"

716

The bed creaked as Jon rolled onto his back and stared at the ceiling again. "What about my feelings?"

Aylun kept his voice matter of fact. "I don't know you."

Jon turned quiet.

Sensing he was done talking, Aylun decided there would be no better time to ask for his favor. He sat up and scooted to the edge of the bed, facing Jon. "I didn't tell you all this to sway you or impress you or soften the blow of what has to happen."

Jon remained flat and unmoving, the firelight casting his silhouette against the softly lit sheet of stone behind him. "Then why?"

"Because I need a favor, and I want you to understand why I am asking."

Jon turned his head and stared. "A favor? From me?"

Aylun gave a crisp nod. "Yes. I cannot be there when Megan undoes your coming."

"Can't be there? What do you mean?"

Aylun suddenly realized how unfair his favor was. "I want to slip away before you reach the place, but I do not want Megan to know. I do not want to distract her."

"Oh, I get it. You don't want to watch the person you care about throw you away, but you expect me and Dellia to watch as our marriage is discarded like rotten trash."

"You are not wrong." Aylun gave a bow of acknowledgment. "But there is another reason—another journal—and I intend to retrieve it. If something goes wrong and things cannot be undone, it may be our last chance to set things right. My partner Yaolin and I went to retrieve it. I even had it in my hands, but she died, and I lost it. Now, I need to go find it again."

Jon rolled his eyes. "Oh great, more prophecies. Just what I need. What will they predict next, that I am destined to make the sun explode?"

Aylun drew a long breath, trying to ignore Jon's bitter and sarcastic attitude. "Look, this will be your last chance to say goodbye to Dellia. Megan will be busy visiting herself in the past. Do you really want some strange guy watching you as you say your last words to your wife?"

Jon seemed stunned at the notion. This time, his silence became protracted, and his face possessed the conflicted look of a man that was only now coming to terms with how he wanted to leave things with the woman he loved. He eyed Aylun. "You're right. I don't want it to end like this, but she won't even look at me anymore."

"Because she wronged you, and she knows it."

"Then what do I do?"

"How can I tell you the words to say to the one who knows you the best? That is for you to decide."

Another silence ensued, equally as protracted as the last. Then Jon sat up and turned, perching himself at the edge of the bed. "I'm sorry. I haven't been in a good mood."

Aylun gave a deep and respectful bow. "That is understandable."

Jon drew a deep breath and brought himself up taller. The flicker of the fire danced in his eyes as he peered straight into Aylun's. "You helped, guided, and looked after Megan when she needed it the most. For that, you deserve my respect and my gratitude. We both care about her, and for that, too, I am grateful. So, I will do what you ask. And not just out of appreciation, but also out of understanding. I know what it is to give up the one you love. So, leave it to me. When the time comes, I will make some excuse while you slip away. It is the least I can do for the one who has helped and protected my friend through so much."

Aylun stared. It was the first time he'd heard Jon speak from the heart, and it took him by surprise. In those few simple lines, he began to see the potential leader in which Wistra had placed so much faith. And as he did, troubling questions began to bubble in the back of his mind.

Dellia kept replaying the moment over and over in her head, trying to understand what had happened. Jon's panic and pitiful pleading were heartrending when he figured out how Megan could visit herself in the past. The way he begged her not to undo their coming had told her in an instant that he had figured out how. She could feel his panic with him. He was terrified of losing her, and she had meant it with her whole heart when she promised him she wouldn't tell anyone.

Then the fighting started, and it was on her home soil, a day's ride from the house where she'd grown up. That those flower-filled fields of her youth might succumb to utter darkness was horrifying to her. The people she grew up with, the citizens of Egina she had seen every week, the soldiers she had sweated and trained with: all obliterated. Desperate to do anything to save her people, she found Megan and asked if she really could undo Jon's coming.

It made no sense. She'd never believed Jon caused the Dead of Night to move or that damaging the lighthouse was a deliberate act. Even if both were true, it would be a big leap to assume either had anything to do with the warning Aylun brought them. Even if Jon had never come to this world, the threat to Talus might still exist. Yet, in that instant, it had all seemed so simple and clear. Wistra said she and Jon being together was a mistake, that it would lead to disaster. Her people were facing a disaster, and that made it her duty to do something about it. She could never be her father and choose Jon over her people.

It was so illogical. The lighthouse and warning might not be related in any way. Yet, at the time, it had been such a simple calculus. Undo Jon's coming, save her people. So, she found Megan and asked again if it was possible to undo Jon's coming. Aylun handed her the old and faded warning, and it was all there in black and aged yellow. As she read it for herself, the words hit her with tremendous impact. They were proof that she and Jon were a mistake, a thing that should never have been allowed to happen.

So she blurted out all that Jon had told her. Megan strolled to her pack and rummaged for a while, then returned and said she had the stone they needed. Without batting an eyelash or a single thought for Jon, she volunteered to guide them to the place where they'd seen the prophecy, to the oracle room. She had made sure they would undo Jon's coming to this world. She had made sure she would never meet her husband.

Only as Aylun and Megan hurried off to ready their horses for the trip had the reality hit her. She had stayed true to her convictions. She hadn't been her father. She had chosen her duty over Jon. Only it was nothing like what she had imagined. It wasn't noble or good or courageous. It was ugly and dirty and cowardly. She once argued with Garris that what her father had done in Githeo by choosing his family over his duty was wrong. And she had been so sure of herself. So, why then did what she had just done feel so much worse than what her father had done. She had given up her husband without a care for how she was hurting him.

Unable to look Jon in the eye, she had told him it was over and even chided him, calling him selfish when he begged her to give him time to find another way. Shocked and numb from the experience, she'd left without even looking back. Only later, when another set of hoofbeats raced up behind them, did she sense he was there.

Her husband, who had done nothing to deserve this, had chased after her. He had chosen to be with her, even after all she had done. Her struggle with this decision had made her gift nearly abandon her, yet she sensed his grief with ease. His presence became a constant reminder of how much pain she was causing to the one she loved. She wanted to tell him to go back, that she wasn't worth it, but she couldn't break his heart further.

So, time dragged on with agonizing slowness. The day seemed interminable as the sun crept across the sky, the heavens grew dark, and the fireflies came and went. Throughout it all, her heartache grew. This was so much worse than the Chaldean Desert when she'd agreed to turn him over to the council. At least then, she could tell herself that she would be an advocate for him, that she would protect him, even though she knew she was powerless to stop the council from doing anything they wanted. This time, she had conspired to end it all. He would be gone, irretrievable. Not even a memory would remain.

Now, finally alone in the stable, having fed the horses and extinguished her lantern, Dellia leaned her head against Ulka's sturdy muzzle and let her tears fall. With her sunstone in the room by Megan, she remained in the dark, feeling broken and wretched. She had always been proud of the way she put her position as a protector above everything else. Yet, it had led her here, alone and friendless, sobbing in the shadows because she had sacrificed her husband on the altar of her duty.

After a time, when it seemed as if her absence would become conspicuous, she pulled herself together and wiped away her tears. Then, she crept across the yard, through the darkened kitchen, and down the narrow hall to her room. No sooner had she lain down on the floor and set her sunstone next to her than Megan slid out of her bed and lay down on the floor by her side. Her face lit by the daylight of the sunstone, Megan set her elbows on the floor and cradled her chin in her palms.

She stayed there for a brief time, studying Dellia like she was some kind of bug under glass. "How do you do it?"

Too dead inside to exchange more than a few words, Dellia continued to stare at the old wooden beams of the ceiling. "Do what?"

"Give up the one you love as if it were the easiest thing in the world."

"You think it was easy?"

"Yes. You made it look effortless."

Megan's words were like a sword carving up the pieces of her already shattered heart. It was tempting to deny it, to say how hard it had been, but how could she when everything Megan had said was true? It seemed effortless because she had done it without a single care for the consequences. How could she object when she had been so careless with the heart Jon entrusted to her?

Tears wanted to come, but Dellia held them back with her frustration and bitterness. "What about you? You don't seem all that worried about what you're doing to Jon."

"He won't remember."

"He does right now. Do you know what he's going through? Do you have any idea?"

Megan didn't respond, and a sudden realization came to Dellia. Throughout this entire ordeal, there had been something off in Megan's reaction. Dellia turned her head and stared at the face that was peering into hers. "For that matter, why aren't you more jealous?"

Megan startled. "What?"

"The thought of you and Jon together makes me crazy. I can hardly stand that he cares about you at all. Why aren't you more jealous of *me*?"

Megan perked up, seeming indignant. "I am too jealous."

"No, you aren't. You're more concerned about Aylun than you are about Jon."

"I am not. I'm equally concerned."

Dellia scoffed. "Are you trying to lie to me or to yourself?"

Megan huffed.

Dellia sat up and peered down at her. "How can you ask me how I did this when you did the same? So, tell me, how did *you* do it?"

Megan seemed surprised and sat up, facing Dellia. "When did I do the same?"

"In the Illis Woods. You made him leave you behind. I tried to get him to reconsider because you were both hurting, but you were very convincing with your lie about not wanting to be with him."

Megan barked back, "I did it because I was in fear for his life. It gave me time to find proof the prophecy was a lie, so I could protect him. How about you? Did you do this to protect him?"

"No. I panicked. I felt powerless. This whole time, my own people haven't let me lift a finger to help hold back the darkness. When the fighting started, it seemed like something I could do to help stop this."

"So, you did it because you were bored?"

722

AYLUN

The characterization was a complete trivialization of her agony, and Dellia fired back, "No. I did it because Wistra said it had to be done, and that made it my duty."

"Duty, shmooty. You gave up your family on the off chance it might help a bunch of people you don't even know."

"You don't understand."

"You're right. I don't understand. You act all strong and self-assured, but you gave up on the one you love without a fight."

"I did it because of a warning you brought me, a warning from the greatest oracle who ever lived. If you didn't believe in it, then why did you bring it to us?"

Megan shook her head. "No. You did it because you were more afraid of some future that might not happen than you were about the heart you were trampling."

At the precipice of breaking down, Dellia lowered her gaze. "Can we not do this now? I can't do this."

Megan seemed to react with an odd sympathy. She pulled herself over and threw an arm around Dellia. "Okay, okay. I'm sorry. We both know what we're doing has to be done. I guess I'm just feeling crappy about it and taking it out on you."

Dellia kept her head down, avoiding Megan's gaze. "No, I'm a horrible wife. I've done nothing but hurt Jon."

"That can't be true."

"Every day, I find new ways to make him miserable."

"If he's so unhappy, then why did he chase after you."

"Because he's a fool."

Megan hesitated, then lowered her voice. "No argument there." Then she smiled, seeming eager to cheer Dellia up. "Look, he chased after you because he's in love with you; otherwise, he wouldn't have asked you to marry him."

"He didn't. I asked him."

Megan's eyes widened. "Whoa. I couldn't even get up the courage to say yes when he asked me out."

Dellia sniffled. "You're just afraid."

"I know." There was a moment of conspicuous silence, then Megan spoke to herself. "But what am I afraid of?"

"You carry scars. Everyone does. Yours run deeper than most. You share that with Jon."

Megan seemed deep in thought. Then, for a second time, she spoke, half to herself. "You're right. But still, what am I afraid of?"

Dellia could tell it wasn't a real question, so she didn't answer.

Megan fell silent for a time, still seeming preoccupied. Then, she gazed at Dellia with a look of sympathy. "There's something I need to ask you, and I need you to give me an honest answer."

Dellia breathed a slow, deep breath and nodded. "Okay."

"Aylun will do whatever I say. That's our deal. If I tell him to stop here, if I tell him I won't undo Jon's coming, he will honor my decision. So, I need to know if this is still what you want?"

For a long time, Dellia stared at her little table below the shuttered window, the one with the inlay of a galloping horse. Her mind wandered from the warning she'd read to the lighthouse and the Dead of Night and then to Jon's refusal to shoulder any responsibility. After a time, she nodded. "Yes. Wistra said our being together is a mistake, and when I look at it calmly and rationally, it makes perfect sense. I don't think this Dead of Night incident had anything to do with him, but it made me realize something."

A flush of shame darkened her mood even further, and Dellia lowered her head as she uttered the difficult words. "Jon is no leader." She kept her gaze on the pattern of the blanket she was lying on. "He has such incredible potential, so I believe that someday, with your help, he might become one. But that's not possible anymore because of me. And if he keeps going the way he has, I can see how he could endanger everyone in the three realms. Already the protectors might be dismantled. That alone will endanger people, and Jon refuses to do anything about it."

She stared straight into Megan's eyes. "So yes, everything I read in that warning is in agreement with what I know to be the absolute truth, and that means we have to do this. We have to undo his coming."

Megan gave a single, solemn nod. "To tell you the truth, my heart hasn't been at ease about this, but now that I know that you and Aylun and Jon are all in complete agreement, I will do what we've set out to do."

Dellia froze as the remaining pieces of her shattered heart disappeared into a pit of nothingness as deep as the Dead of Night. Jon was in agreement? Her husband, who loved her enough to take on every leader in the three realms, had agreed to undo his meeting her. He had given up on her.

It was late in the day, and long shadows followed the soldiers as they weaved in and out of the pine trees below, combing the rocks for evidence. This was the second mangled body Kayleen had needed to cope with in recent days.

The cliffs at the edge of the ramp from Shirdon to the plateau were steep, and accidents here were rare but not unheard of. Like Shir Keep, the steady incline had been carved from the rock of the mountain. It was a back entrance to the plateau for delivery of goods and people. Its architects made it broad enough for many carts and soldiers to come and go at the same time. Plus, it had a knee-high lip at its edge, making it hard to simply slip off. Still, the barrier wasn't high enough to protect a rider falling from a horse or a passenger tumbling out of a carriage. So, it was not the accident itself that gave her pause but the coincidences that surrounded it.

This was the second gruesome death by falling in a few days. The plateau was a place where many lived and worked, and it hosted its share of sightseers, merchants, and visitors. Even so, falling deaths were rare. It was often years between them. Two of them happening within days of each other seemed suspicious on its own. That they occurred so close to a change in leadership made them worrisome.

She pulled her gaze from the activity below as the clomp of feet drew her attention. She glanced over and spotted Pedrus, strolling down the ramp as casual as could be, headed past her. Kayleen stared down again and monitored him out of the corner of her eye.

When a sound came from below, the large fellow glanced over and did a double take. Then he stopped and cocked his head. His movements were exaggerated and his acting a little over the top, but to the casual observer, it would pass. With an expression of intense curiosity, he strolled to the edge. He stopped a short distance to her left and peered down at the moving shadows below. For a while, he remained there, watching the soldiers clamber over giant boulders and peer into dark cracks and crevices, searching for any evidence of what had happened.

After a while, Pedrus spoke in a quiet voice. "I heard about this in the barracks. Figured I should come take a look."

Kayleen kept her gaze below, trying to play into his imitation of an interested passerby. "Good thinking. You made that look pretty casual."

"I try."

He continued to speak without glancing over at her. "Who's the poor fellow?"

"We don't know yet. The face is badly damaged, but it's a man with short white hair."

His tone turned cynical. "Probably another sick guy putting himself out of his misery, don't you suppose?"

"If you mean the same kind of death as Ahmet, that would be my guess as well. Have you made any progress finding out if he was sick?"

Pedrus paused, squinting at the movement below as if it were his sole focus. His acting was improving. "That depends on what you consider progress." He gave a very subtle nod toward Shirdon. "I asked around everywhere I could think to ask, including every physician and herbalist in town. Many people had seen him. Not a single one saw any sign he was sick. I'm figuring if he had some fatal illness, at least one person would've heard or seen something."

She heaved a sigh. "So, now we have a second death from falling."

"It gets worse. I heard about this from some of the guys at the barracks. More than a few grumbled that this kind of thing wouldn't have happened under the old council."

Kayleen tried not to betray her concern. "I suppose that's to be expected, but it's troubling, even so. Keep an eye on that for me. I want to know what soldiers are saying at the barracks."

"Are you asking me to spy on my comrades in arms?"

She smiled to herself. "Yes, but I'm more interested in the higher-ups. A soldier or two is nothing. If commanders start griping, it could get serious. And the higher up, the more serious."

He straightened his collar and pulled the wrinkles out of his shirt. "Understood, ma'am."

The clomping of hooves against stone drew Kayleen's attention to a soldier leading a massive brown mare up from below.

Staring one last time down the cliffside, Pedrus shook his head in a reasonable imitation of disillusionment and pulled away from the wall. Then he clasped his hands behind his back and continued his stroll down the ramp, passing only a few feet from the massive beast.

As her minion continued away, the soldier led the horse up to Kayleen, then stopped in front of her. "We found her below, ma'am. Some of the fellas recognized her as Chiyun's horse."

The name matched a man with short white hair, and in an instant, Kayleen tensed up. Ahmet had been a well-known friend and adviser to the Erdish members of the new council. Chiyun was a respected elder who advised the Elorian members of the council.

It was all becoming too coincidental. If you included the darkness threatening Talus and the rumor that Jon was behind it, all three realms now had reasons for discontent. It was feeling more and more like these deaths had a purpose. One that would not spell good things for Jon.

Chapter Twenty-Eight

DAYS OF FUTURE PAST

A hazy silken sheet of white clouds lay draped over the crystal sky, turning the sun into an indistinct white blur. Standing on the platform of the Illis Woods spire, Jon shielded his eyes as he stared up at it, centered in the giant white teeth arcing high above. He was weary, despondent, and not even sure why he was here anymore, except that if this was the end for him and Dellia, it was the place he had to be.

The sound of rustling of vegetation underfoot carried across the round stone slab, riddled with symbols and runes. Megan had stopped to retrieve her spire stone and, with it now clutched in hand, was wading through the long grasses and vibrant flowers as she neared the spire.

Jon returned his gaze to Dellia. She was ignoring him. So far, this day had been an echo of the last. She had ridden in front, never glancing back at him as she led the way from her mother's home to the Illis Woods, then to the spire. In some ways, it was worse than yesterday. She seemed even more upset, and her avoidance not at all subtle. It was gut wrenching to become a sudden stranger to one who had been the reason for everything he'd done.

When Megan passed onto the platform, a crackling came from above. It mingled with the melody of songbirds and swishing of grass in the midday wind. A shimmering circle painted with dull gray clouds appeared above, where the tips of the three arching teeth neared one another. It obscured the sun, leaving the platform in hazy shadow.

With a quiet click, Megan touched the stone to a symbol on one of the polished ivory monoliths. The circular curtain fell, slowly at first, then faster, growing larger to fill the space between the teeth. The instant it passed over them, they were standing on a new platform amid the wooded hills of Elore.

They switched leads, with Dellia in the back while Aylun led the way down an almost indiscernible path. No longer did Jon have to bear the snubbing Dellia had been so devout in doling out. Only now, he found himself doing the same. Afraid to look back at her, he kept his focus ahead rather than find out what cold disdain might greet him. His own reluctance gave him a better understanding of Dellia. Perhaps she wasn't snubbing him after all. Maybe it was as Aylun had said: she was afraid to meet his eyes for fear of what she might find there.

In time, the overgrown path led to another broader and more well-traveled road. That one emptied into yet another at the shore of Kinshai Lake. The view of the shoreline was familiar, with its quaint houses and single-sailed boats. Yet, the waves lapping the sandy beach seemed much colder and darker beneath the heavy sheet of gray cloud cover.

As the day dragged on, the sky grew darker, and the outskirts of a city appeared ahead, bordering the lake. Aylun led the way to a stable there, where they boarded their horses.

The broad, late-day street was bustling with activity as Dellia took over, leading them ever closer to the end of it all. The thrum of quarreling children, haggling customers, and animated conversations only served to amplify the apocalyptic mood of the group. No longer confined to following Dellia, Jon managed to gather the courage to step up to her side. She glanced over but was quick to return her attention ahead. As they strolled past busy strangers, he spoke softly to her. "If this is the end, can we at least not end it as strangers?"

She kept her gaze down at her feet, stepping along the cobblestones. "What difference does it make? In a little while, you and

I will never have happened. Why force ourselves to pretend everything is fine?"

He tried to catch her eye. "I'm not pretending. To me, every moment between us matters."

For a fleeting few seconds, Dellia appeared shaken. Hope flared that his sincerity might have moved her, but it was short lived. She soon recovered and sent him a flat stare. "Can you not do that? Can you not act like it's all okay? Can you yell at me or hit me or threaten me?" She lowered her head again. "Or at least not agree to this?"

He turned his own gaze downward, too, wondering when he had agreed to this. It didn't matter. There was so much he wanted to say, but he reminded himself this wasn't about what had already happened. It was about how he wanted it to end.

He kept his tone soft and his words gentle. "I never agreed to this." Jon shook his head. "I never had a chance. It was your decision, and you never gave me the smallest opportunity to discuss it. So maybe I could get angry about that and yell and rant, but it wouldn't change anything. And to be honest, I just don't have the will to quarrel with you in the last few seconds we have together."

She finally sent him more than a fleeting glance. "What do you want from me, Jon?"

He became quiet for a while. It was apparent Dellia wasn't in the mood to talk and, in fact, was determined to avoid him until it was over.

While he was considering what more to say. Dellia pulled ahead, keeping a brisk pace.

He tried to find openings to step up to her side again, but she always seemed to sense him approaching and evaded him before he could get out a single word.

So it went, down the streets and along the peaceful riverside and serene plazas. Then came the vast expanse of lush grass and tranquil ponds that was Kianlong Square. It was where he and Dellia had been at odds with one another. She must have sensed his discomfort because she sped ahead as if a quick crossing of the neat and well-maintained expanse might hold back the memory.

They hurried up Kita Pass, a pathway that wound upward through the mountainside, and he grew out of breath, trying to keep pace with her determined stride. Although it was nothing compared to the nerve-shattering ordeal of the last time he was here.

They reached the plateau overlooking the park, and Jon stared down at the peaceful scene below, recalling the moment he had seen Dellia fighting her way toward him. He turned his attention to the alcove with the circular platform that looked like a mixed-up version of the spires. The three teeth were still there, jutting down from the ceiling over the circular slab of stone, but the sight struck him as odd.

Then it dawned on him. The shimmering black sphere he had made appear between the teeth was missing. He turned his attention to the table full of slots next to it, the one they had found last time they were here. Even now, he found its resemblance to the laser table in his lab shocking. It was obvious that it was just another part of Wistra's twisted plan. She must have somehow foreseen it in his lab and duplicated it here. Yet, it still surprised him.

Last time he had been here, he was being chased. With time running out, it had been Garris who made him realize the resemblance. So, he had taken the stack of black polished plates from the corner and jammed them in slots to match the position of the mirrors on the laser table in his lab. The result had been the appearance of a dark spherical portal, not unlike a smoother and less undulating version of the one that had appeared in his lab. Oddly, the plates were no longer where he had left them when he was last here, but stacked in the corner, where they'd started. And since the slabs were no longer in their proper slots, the portal was no longer there.

Then another, more contentious thought occurred to him. Without him here to put the mirrors where they belonged, they would never be able to enter the chamber. In fact, the power to stop this expedition was in his hands right now. If he refused to help, they wouldn't know how to get the dark plates back in their proper places, and they'd never be able to enter.

Jon hesitated. Dellia hadn't bothered to ask him before telling Megan how to visit herself in the past. Why should he help them now to do something he'd never agreed with?

He was considering the notion when Megan sent him an I-told-you-so stare and pointed to the table. "See? Your theory was already blown to bits, and you never saw it. If the physical laws of this world are different from those of Earth like you said, then how do you account for someone on this world knowing what your laser table on Earth looked like?"

Jon froze. She was right, of course. Earth's physical laws would apply to him and the table and his lab. Those laws would prevent someone from spying on him from another world. But the last time he'd been here, he had been so distracted by his pursuit, he had no chance to make the connection.

Megan stepped up and grabbed the stack of shiny black plates from the corner. Removing the slabs uncovered a hole, and a blue beam shot out of it to the first slot on the table. She jammed the slabs into the exact places each mirror would be on the laser table. The bright blue beam ricocheted here and there, from plate to plate, then shot out and into a hole at the base of the platform. He had forgotten: Megan had assembled the table more times than he had.

No sooner had the dark sphere materialized between the teeth than Dellia strutted through.

Jon eyed Aylun. Now was the time to make good on his promise to give him a chance to leave without Megan noticing. He pointed to the table. "You stay here. Make sure no one removes these." He brushed a finger along one of the black plates. "We wouldn't want someone to take them while we're in there and trap us." He sent Aylun a subtle wink, hoping he would understand the gesture. The whole thing was utter nonsense. There was no one around to take the plates, and he had no idea what would happen if they did.

He turned his attention to Megan and paused, waiting to see if she would object. She glanced at him, then at Aylun. Her gaze lingered on the man for a moment as a peculiar hesitancy came over her. Jon waited through a long pause as Megan seemed to do some kind of mental deliberation. Then, her expression fell, and she seemed to accept the arrangement with reluctance.

The moment he was satisfied he had given Aylun his chance to leave unnoticed, Jon raced after Dellia into the black sphere. He stumbled into the dim light of the cavernous corridor. She was already partway down the smooth dark hallway, and the glass-ball torches that lined the walls were lighting up as she neared each pair. He hurried after, with Megan appearing almost at once behind him.

He had forgotten how odd the air felt and smelled in this place. As he hustled to catch up, the amethyst daggers that clung to the ceiling sparkled with the reflected light of the glowing spheres on the wall. Dellia shot through a narrow passage, and he dove after her into the large hall with the circular platform in the center. It was where he had first heard Wistra's prophecy. It was where it would all end.

Then, for a second time in only a few minutes, the peculiarity of the scene struck him. Shards of amethyst should have coated the floor from when Garris shattered one of the stalactites by making it fall on the platform, but someone or something had swept them away. He turned his gaze to the ceiling, and it appeared as if all the stalactites were still there. No one had cleaned them up. They were back where they had started. In fact, the room looked as it had when he first entered it, except for one detail. Last time there had been a pedestal and box that held the black leaf of his medallion, but now, they were nowhere to be seen.

He shook his head, trying to bring to mind some explanation for the unexpected state of the room. Perhaps this place existed in a different time, and the events he remembered from the past hadn't yet happened here. Or, even better, it might exist outside of time, and that's how you could use it to visit yourself in the past or future. None of those explanations made sense in any scientific way. In fact, the whole thing was an utter contradiction.

The puzzle couldn't hold his curiosity. None of his questions and theories mattered anymore. So, he turned his attention back to the only thing in the room of any importance.

Unable to flee him further, Dellia halted before the raised circular stone slab where the images of his prophecy had appeared.

He stepped up to her side and tried to peer into her eyes, but she kept them focused ahead. "You asked what I want from you. It's this." Jon took her hand into his and stood close to her.

Then, as if a dam had burst, silent tears flowed down her face. Her gaze turned to him, her eyes filled with regret and longing. She threw her arms around him, leaning on him for support. "I'm so sorry, Jon. I don't want this. I don't want it to end."

Her pleading tugged at his already broken heart. He pulled her even closer as tears began to stream down his own face. He stayed in her warm embrace as Megan's faltering footsteps passed them, headed for the platform. All the while, Dellia kept repeating, "I'm so sorry," in a quieter and quieter voice.

The footsteps halted, and Jon glanced over. Megan stood peering at them from the platform's edge. She continued to stare for a moment as she took a deep breath. Then she set both hands on the edge.

It wouldn't be long now, so he squeezed Dellia tight and whispered, "I love you."

She squeezed back.

With no small number of misgivings, Megan watched Dellia and Jon embracing. Then she turned and hauled herself up onto the round stone platform. Above her, translucent amethyst stalactites dangled from the ceiling, much more imposing now that they loomed so close to her head.

They were her own sword of Damocles. Their massive size and hard, jagged tips were like the weight of the mission she was about to complete, ready to cut right through her and Jon, and even an entire world, if she faltered or failed in reaching her goal.

As she fished through her pouch of spire stones, it occurred to her she'd miss having them, traveling here and there, crossing vast distances in the blink of an eye. On Earth, that kind of power didn't exist. She glanced down at the symbol on the center of the platform. It was just as Dellia had described it, a replica of those on the spires. An etched triangle, with a ruby circle in the center and five golden lines radiating out from it, like the rays of a setting sun.

The simile seemed somehow appropriate. This was the end of the road, the end of this long day, both for her and for Jon. No more strange beasts. No more gut-wrenching escapes. … No more thrill of moving things with her mind.

For a fleeting moment, it all seemed so odd, like one of those overused television time paradoxes. Aylun had stated with great authority that nature abhorred a paradox. Yet, what was this if not a quintessential example of a time paradox? It was two moments in time that contradicted each other, that couldn't exist together. If she was successful, she and Jon would never have come to this world. So how could she be here now, on this platform, preparing to visit herself in the past?

If she was successful, then what of her existence here and now? Would this version of her with great power, the version that had met a Greek goddess, cease to exist? Would she even remember having been here? To remember or to forget, which would be worse?

She shook her head, banishing the thoughts. Of course she wouldn't remember. She would have undone it. Besides, the whole topic was too much like one of those geeky sci-fi things she never cared for.

Anxious to have it over with, Megan reached into the pouch and snatched the small translucent marble with flashes of ruby and gold swirled throughout it. She stared into it, caught for a moment by its complexity and beauty. The subtle shades of color were a perfect match for those of the symbol. She reached down, ready to touch it to the center of the ruby circle, and a familiar feeling grabbed hold of her, halting her inches above it.

No, that wasn't right. It hadn't suddenly grabbed her. That feeling had been here all along, simmering in the background where she could willfully ignore it. It had just roared higher now, thumbing its nose at her attempts to suppress it, nagging at her, telling her to stop and rethink what she was about to do. It was the feeling that she stood on a railway platform watching the last train destined for home leave without her.

That feeling had disappeared for a while as she wallowed in her misery in Mundus, but it had crept back with Aylun's return and followed her all the way here from the Vault of Time. The image of Aylun walking away from her at the Verod camp came back with it, and she realized it was about him. Even back then, she didn't want him to disappear out of her life. Back then, she had told herself Jon was her home. But the very fact she needed to remind herself meant she was questioning it, that she didn't fully believe it. She was trying to convince herself of something she knew wasn't true.

She shoved it out of her mind. It didn't matter. They all knew the reasons this needed to be done, and once it was over, she would be back home with Jon. That was the plan. It was why they had come all the way here in the first place. To stop now, when her goal was so close, would be sheer madness.

She brought forth the memory of her small room and the night she had received the visit from her future self. Then Megan closed the last few inches and touched the stone to the symbol on the platform. As she did, she caught a glimpse of Jon and Dellia. He was holding her so close, and it struck her as wrong somehow. It wasn't jealousy or remorse. It was the same feeling she remembered from before, the impression of a puzzle with two sets of pieces that could never fit together, a puzzle she couldn't solve.

She straightened. It was probably just her emotions running away with her, the excitement of being so close to her goal. ... Yeah, the excitement. She pulled herself together as time beyond the platform seemed to slow to a stop, and a bright mist enveloped her. With it came a flurry of emotions as varied as the colorful swirls gathering around her: guilt, confusion, doubt. Before she could sort through the tumult, the mist came together and solidified.

All of a sudden, she was standing in the corner of her own bedroom back on Earth. Pinpoints of bright light emanated from her body, dancing and whirling across the familiar soft-peach walls of her cozy room. Her past self was in bed, asleep.

Megan watched for a moment as the lights played across the huge blooms that crowded the plum-bough wall hanging above the woman's head. She had always loved that wall hanging. Yet, looking at herself in bed, it seemed like it wasn't really her. This girl was so innocent. She knew nothing of the current Megan, what she had learned and what she had been through.

Deep sympathy struck her at the plight that faced that sleeping woman. She drew a deep breath. It was that plight she was here to forestall. She had come to prevent that future from ever scarring her. The sleeping woman's eyes cracked open, and she stared for a moment, then clamped them shut.

Megan put a smile on her face as she gathered her resolve. She had to be strong. This needed to be done.

The confused woman in the bed bolted up on her elbows, the covers falling as she blinked and squinted down at the brilliant flashes darting across the quilted pattern on their surface.

So, Megan waited with patience as the woman's sleepiness and disorientation cleared. Then her gaze flew upward, and her dark eyes caught Megan's. Confusion clouded the familiar face—her own face. The woman gasped and pulled the covers closer around her. Her disheveled hair fell around her shoulders as she shook her head in a futile attempt to scatter away the confounding scene.

AYLUN

Megan tilted her head in sympathy as she recalled how startled she had been that night and all the terrible things that followed: the accident in the lab, her abduction, and the trip through Katapa and Lanessa. Gathering her courage, she broadened her smile and waved. "Don't be afraid. It's just me." Then, she realized how confusing that statement might be. "Um, future me." Well, that wasn't any better. "Or I guess it's future you."

The woman seemed stunned, staring with her mouth half-open. Then, in a quiet voice, she spoke to herself. "I'm asleep. I have to be asleep."

The denial set off a cascade of memories. Tomorrow that same woman would convince herself this moment wasn't real and even go about her day as if nothing had happened. Then, when Aylun abducted her, she'd convince herself a whole new world wasn't real. She would even argue with him about it.

Megan rolled her eyes. "You know, you really have to work on this whole denial thing. It doesn't suit us at all."

"No. This is impossible." The woman shook her head again. Then it seemed as if she had an epiphany. "All right … answer me this. Wha—"

"Tuesday," Megan blurted out as she recalled the day she had placed in her mind to test herself. Then she realized the foolishness of the very concept. If the woman before her were dreaming, the test would be part of the dream and therefore irrelevant. She kept her gaze steady. "And how exactly does that prove this isn't a dream?"

"Whoa …" The woman stared down at her hand, then back at the image. "Wait. How do I know—"

"I'm really you. Hmm, let me think." The memories started to come back. It hadn't been that long ago. She had said … "Oh. Right. You go to the King Chi every Friday for lunch. Somehow you always wind up with that hot and sour soup you dislike. Last week it was particularly awful. You thought it was burning the skin off your tongue."

The woman let out a dismissive grunt. "That doesn't prove anything. Everyone knows King Chi's hot and sour soup tastes like battery acid."

"I know, right? What do they put in that stuff, furniture stripper?"

"Hey, that's what I was going to say."

Caught up in the moment, Megan giggled. Then it came back to her, what this woman would face in the coming days. In fact, the very reason she was here now was to stop that future from happening, yet something was tugging at her. A desire to stay, or maybe that feeling that this wasn't right.

Megan returned her gaze to the woman.

She was giving her a slow nod. "Okay. So, maybe you *are* me. So what?"

Megan stared at the light drifting across the peach wall behind the woman and hesitated, held back by a flurry of emotions pulling her in every direction. Still, she had come here for a purpose, so she forged ahead. "There's something I need you to do."

The woman appeared to be alarmed and leaned forward. "Why? What's wrong?"

"Nothing, now. It's just … tomorrow, in the lab, Jon is going to ask you out."

The woman's face lit up, and she sat up straighter in bed. "Really?" Then her expression morphed into a puzzled sort of frown. "Wait, you visited me from the future to talk about a date?"

The question caught her off guard. "What? No. … Well, yes. Kinda? … Hey, it's complicated." She set her hands on her hips and stared. "Besides, that's not the point." She sighed and relaxed, letting her arms fall to her sides. "Look, I don't have time to explain. It's just … the thing is …"

She froze, stopped yet again by that feeling. Only it had grown so much stronger now. It was that sense of watching the last train bound for home leaving without her, and she knew she felt this way because this wasn't what she wanted. Perhaps at one time, this

740

moment of returning home had been everything she hoped for, everything she was about, but not anymore. What she really wanted was to stay with him, with Aylun. Once before, she watched him walk out of her life, and she didn't want to see him vanish again.

She looked at the sleepy woman in front of her, and the very idea of returning to that time and that person no longer appealed to her in any way. And despite what he had said, it wasn't what Jon wanted, either. He had given up on Dellia, but he still cared about her.

Megan took another glance through the hazy dark image back at Jon and Dellia behind her. Frozen like an exhibit at a wax museum, they were clinging to one another, tears streaming down both their faces as they shared one last embrace. Dellia was right. The sight of it didn't make her jealous, not a little bit, not even an ounce. Instead, a pang of sadness struck her at the idea of tearing them apart. She was hurting her best friend. How could she take away the one thing that mattered to him more than his life?

The sight of them together brought back another memory. This time of the warning in the Vault of Time. It said Jon would be a great leader, but if he and Megan became separated, he would fall for a protector, and for her, he would topple the ruling council. That prediction had come true, but it also made no sense. Almost without thinking, she mouthed the words she had uttered when she first read it. "Like a puzzle with two sets of pieces that could never fit together."

Suddenly she knew beyond any doubt—this was wrong. Not morally, not ethically, but logically wrong. It was utterly twisted and self-contradictory. The full reason still eluded her, but she was sure now. This was wrong for her, wrong for Jon, and tragically wrong for this world.

Megan faced the woman again, this time recalling the exact shocking words she had said to herself. "I need you to turn him down."

Her poor past self slumped back down in the bed. "What?"

Sympathy struck. Sympathy for the woman whose world she was shattering, for all the things she was going to put that poor girl through. She tilted her head. "And you need to be emphatic."

The woman slumped even more. "You mean, like, really turn him down hard?"

Megan nodded. "Yes."

"I can't do that. He'll be crushed."

Yeah, Megan thought, *he was. He was devastated, and it was hard, but one day, not long from now, it will be what he wants, too.* She gave a slight nod. "I know, but you have to. The next day, you can take it back. You can tell him anything you want. You can say I made you do it, but you have to do this."

"But why?"

Megan paused. From what she remembered, the end of this visit was approaching, and there was no way she could convey in those few fleeting seconds all that she needed to say. There was no time to convince her past self that although Jon is the one she wants now, there would come a time when she longs more deeply for someone else. How could she express that there will be a man who only thinks of her well-being, a man who yearns for her with his whole heart but wants her to find happiness even more? What words would make her understand that she will meet a man who loves her so much he would give up his peace of mind and even his life to help her be with the one she wants?

She looked her past self straight in the eye. "Sometimes, to get what you want, you have to give it up."

Pain and sorrow flashed across the woman's face. Her head fell, and she stared down at her covers. "How can I take you seriously when you sound like a fortune cookie?"

"Megan, I know you, every thought, every feeling, and I know how hard this is—but this is important."

"But you're asking me to—"

"I know what I'm asking." Megan looked away as she recalled how difficult it had been to reject Jon and how scary and traumatic it had been to be thrust into a strange world and torn from his side. A sympathetic sadness racked her again over what she was going to put this poor girl through. "I've lived through it. ... Trust me. I know."

The woman's gaze flittered across the room, searching for another answer. "But to do it so cruelly. How can I hurt him like that?"

Megan shook her head. "You've hurt him dozens of times already. Every time you rejected him." The woman lowered her head even further, but Megan kept her gaze fixed on her. "Promise me you'll do this."

"But I've waited so long, and I ... I ..." She continued to stare at the covers as tears welled in her eyes. "I love him."

Megan's eyes teared up, too, as she gazed upon the pitiful woman's face. She cocked her head in sympathy and couldn't keep the quiver out of her voice. "I know." She lowered her head, and as the scene drifted back into mist, she repeated, "I know."

The colored swirls dissipated, and she was back again on the platform in the oracle room. She had changed nothing. Megan turned around. Time began to move again as she staggered to the edge and dropped off of it.

Dellia turned from Jon and looked up at her with a puzzled expression.

Megan shook her head. "I can't do it."

Alarm spread across Dellia's tear-streaked face. "What's wrong?"

Megan stared. The poor woman had put herself through a nightmare to do this. Unsure how to begin, she struggled out her first words. "This." She waved a hand across the entire chamber, motioning to all its dark rock walls, smooth round platform, and amethyst stalactites. "This whole thing, it's wrong."

Disbelief clouded Dellia's face. "I thought we agreed."

"No. No." Megan shook her head again as she began to pace across the worn gray stone floor. "Something doesn't make sense. It doesn't add up. I can't put my finger on it, but it's thoroughly messed up."

Dellia's confusion only deepened. "I don't understand. 'Messed up'?"

Megan stared down at her feet and nodded her head as the bits of knowledge began to organize themselves. "Yeah. Yeah. Just give me a minute, and I'll figure it out."

She recalled Garris at the table waving a roasted leg of some giant bird in his hand as he told of everything that had happened to Jon. Her gaze snapped to Dellia as she stopped in front of her. "Think about it. Someone knew Jon by name. Knew exactly where he'd be and when." Megan grabbed Dellia by her arm, staring into her face as the thoughts and words began to flow. "They recorded a message for him on a rare medallion, then broke it up and hid the pieces. They put them in custom-made boxes and hid them in hard-to-reach places that would put him through a massive ordeal to find them."

Jon stood next to Dellia, nodding even as he seemed stunned. "That's right."

Megan let go of Dellia's arm, and her enthusiastic gaze shot over to Jon. "And they gave what's left to a dragon. Think about that, a *dragon*. Not only that, but they talked her into sending Jon on a mission." She intensified her gaze on him. "Is it easy to talk Islong into a thing like that?"

He shook his head. "Isla? No way. She'd hate it."

When she turned her attention back to Dellia, she seemed a bit intrigued, so Megan forged ahead. "Think of all that effort they went through."

Dellia nodded once, seeming to struggle to get the point. "That's ... that's true."

This time, Megan grabbed both of her arms and came closer to her face. "But why? Why go through all that unless you need him to do something extremely important. And why would a dragon agree unless that something was important to her, too?"

Jon nodded again. "She implied her survival depended on it."

"Exactly."

Megan stepped back and stared at Dellia. "If you went through all that, how can it make any sense that doing nothing is an alternative. How could never coming here be better?"

Jon stared, adding bewilderment to his stunned expression. "I thought Dellia and me getting together made things worse."

Megan gave an emphatic shake of her head. "No, don't you see? It's the exact opposite. Because it means Wistra would have gone through that massive effort when there wasn't the slightest chance Jon would stay in this world."

Dellia stared with a blank expression, not seeing her point in the slightest. "Why would there be no chance of him staying?"

Intense satisfaction grabbed ahold of Megan as she finally understood, and with it came a rock-hard certainty. What she had been about to do would have been catastrophic. She smiled at Dellia. "Don't you see? You're the key to the whole prophecy. To all of them, in fact. To all the journals and warnings and prophecies. None of them makes an ounce of sense without you."

Dellia's bafflement only seemed to grow.

Megan had to make her case ironclad, and she had to make sure Dellia understood. So much depended on her. She turned her gaze back to Jon. "Look, would you have stayed in this world if not for Dellia?"

Jon shook his head, perhaps sensing the thrust of her argument. "No. No power on any world would have made me stay."

"You're sure of that?"

"Absolutely sure."

"Beyond any doubt?"

"I was leaving. The only reason I stayed was Dellia. So yeah, not even the slightest speck of doubt."

She gave a series of rapid nods and turned her attention back to Dellia. "Right. All the prophecies—the message from the medallion, the journal from Lanessa, the warning from the old Vault of Time—they all said the same thing, that Jon was destined to be this great leader. They all agree on that. But how can he become a great leader unless he stays here, unless he stays for you?"

She stared straight into Dellia's eyes. "Without you, he doesn't stay in this world, so he isn't here to lead anyone." She glanced at each of them again as a glimmer of realization appeared in their eyes.

She brought her gaze back to a dazed Dellia. "The warning I found said I had to stay with him, so he doesn't fall for you. But if he doesn't fall for you, he leaves and never becomes a leader. Don't you get it? The warning is logically inconsistent. It doesn't make any sense. It contradicts itself. It could only have been written by someone who didn't have the slightest clue why Jon stayed." When neither Jon nor Dellia reacted, Megan enunciated each word with care. "It's a deception. It has to be a lie."

Now on a roll, she began again to pace across the dark, smooth floor as the logic of it all flowed with casual ease. "Other things don't make sense either. Like, why keep a journal in the bottom drawer of a dresser?" She pointed to Dellia. "You keep them in the top drawer where it's handy. Unless you've planted it there in an old dresser where the top drawers are frozen shut from age."

Megan snapped her fingers and pointed to Jon as she strolled past. "And the dragonflies. The ones on the cover of the journal and warning were crude outlines, not like the ones on the chest and wall in Lanessa. They were beautiful and perfect. And then there's the message in that journal. The one where Wistra warns of tampering with Jon's path."

Dellia's gaze intensified. "What about it?"

"Don't you see?" Megan paused in front of them and let her gaze drift from Jon to Dellia. "The most powerful oracle that ever lived could foresee that someone would tamper with her carefully laid path. Yet, she couldn't see, or even guess, who, what, where, when, how, or why it was tampered with?"

Dellia stammered, "Yeah, that … that seems unlikely."

"Or foresee that Jon and I would be separated?"

746

Jon stared into space as the gears seemed to begin turning in his head. "That's true, too."

With the dawn of understanding lighting up his face, Megan kept her eyes focused there. "Or see in advance that her carefully prepared warning left in the Vault of Time would be forgotten, sabotaged, or misplaced?"

Even though Jon had no knowledge of her trip to the old Vault of Time, he nodded. "If that's true, it does seem far-fetched."

"Aylun said that oracles see every detail of the future with perfect clarity. Yet, they can't see events arranged by a more powerful oracle. It's how nature avoids a paradox."

He shrugged. "Okay, if you say so."

"That would mean the kind of tampering the message warned of could only be done by an oracle more powerful than Wistra."

Dellia stared as she, too, began to come around. "But there has never been an oracle more powerful."

Megan smiled as she nodded again. "Exactly."

Jon's focus snapped over to her. "What about a *group* of oracles?"

Megan and Dellia both responded at the same time, "No."

Dellia eyed Jon as she spoke. "It's one of the rules of all gifts. They don't add. They conflict. A group can only ever be as powerful as its most gifted member. A group of oracles could never see any more than its best oracle. And the others would only muddle their vision."

"There's only one explanation that fits." Megan walked straight up to Dellia. "I've been set up. The path that was tampered with is not Jon's but mine. The journal in the lost city of Lanessa, the warning in the old Vault of Time, they always struck me as fishy, as wrong somehow."

She struggled, trying to explain how the deception could have been pulled off. Then, all at once, it hit her, and she snapped her fingers again. "There were spires near both places. If you had a spire stone, you could go there, you could plant fakes, right? You could have near-perfect forgeries made and plant them to get me to do this." Megan pointed to the round stone platform. "To undo the prophecy."

Dellia seemed to understand, yet there remained an inner conflict in her eyes. "I don't know."

Jon cocked his head. "Then why not stop it? If she's so powerful, why didn't Wistra warn you?"

Megan nodded. It was a fair point, so she eyed him. "Because she didn't need to. Oracles don't act unless they have to, and maybe she knew I'd figure out the deception. Or maybe the visit from my future self was necessary. Maybe it distracted me and helped cause the accident in the lab."

"I don't know. It all sounds like a bunch of speculation."

He was wrong. Sure, some of what she'd said was speculation, but at its core was one indisputable fact. "No." Megan gave a slow shake of her head. "I'm certain. The journal from Lanessa and warning from the Vault of Time are wrong. They both presume you'd stay even without Dellia, and that's impossible. Someone doesn't want you around. And they went through tremendous trouble to see you gone."

"But what about ..." Dellia sent Jon a fleeting glance as she trailed off. She turned her gaze back to Megan. "How can I believe you, whe—"

"I don't need you to believe me." Megan crossed her arms and stood taller. "I'm certain. It's done."

"But you can't simply—"

"I don't need your permission. I don't answer to you or the council or these stupid three realms. I answer only to what I know is true and right." She moved closer to Dellia, standing toe to toe with her, determined to be firm and stand her ground. "What I do know is that you need to come to grips with reality. You and Jon were meant to be together. You are supposed to stop an apocalypse, and this"—she waved all around her at the oracle room—"is nothing but one giant distraction designed to undermine you."

Dellia staggered back and stood reeling. "And I played right into their hands."

Jon leaned his head back and stared at the crystalline amethyst daggers that riddled the high ceiling. After a moment, he gave a slight shake of his head. "We're so doomed." He appeared unsteady, perhaps from the shock of it all, and lowered himself to sit on the smooth floor, staring at its dark surface.

"No." Megan crouched before him and set a hand on each shoulder. "I don't accept that."

He raised his head, his questioning gaze meeting hers. "The darkness will kill us all."

She shrugged. "Then you'll stop it."

He scoffed. "You are so delusional."

She smiled and punched his shoulder. "Come on. Where is all this negativity coming from? This isn't you, Jon."

A smile spread across his face, and for a moment, they were back to their old selves: Jon afraid and uncertain and she, a best friend, lending him her support.

Megan smiled. "Wistra said you would be a great leader, and there's not the tiniest speck of doubt in my mind that you will be amazing. You're brave and kind and compassionate and articulate and the smartest person I've ever known." She pointed to Dellia. "And you have some pretty brave and astonishing people by your side. If anyone can figure out how to stop this darkness, it's you guys." She stood and thrust out her hand to help Jon up. "Now stop being such a downer and go fix this."

He took her hand and rose to his feet.

Megan glanced around the large cavern and spoke with a deliberate note of cheerfulness in her voice. She needed to break the gloom and doom mood of these two. "Now, let's go get Aylun."

Jon hesitated. "Um, well, he may have asked me to arrange for him to leave while you were busy." He motioned to the platform.

She froze as mild alarm spread within her. "What? Where did he go?"

749

He lowered his head, acting sheepish. "He said he was going to find another one of Wistra's missing journals."

Her mild alarm exploded into full blown panic. Not only was Aylun gone, but he was headed back to the one place he insisted, even under the penalty of death, he would never go again. She peered at Jon. "Do you know what you've done. Do you have even the slightest idea where that journal is?"

"Well, he seemed—"

"You can be so stupid sometimes. That journal is in the Dead of Night. He went there twice before to get it, and he's just foolish enough to do it again."

Jon's astonishment became profound. "He survived in the Dead of Night?"

"For many days."

Megan raced out of the room and down the hall. Footsteps from a stunned Jon and Dellia dragged after her as she dove through the narrow passage into the dim light of the hall. Glowing glass torches raced by as she hurried back to the outside. Panic tried to take over, but she kept it at bay. Jon could be wrong. He was only relaying what Aylun had told him, and there was still a chance that it might not be what Aylun had done. She had to find out for herself.

Chapter Twenty-Nine

TILL THE TRUTH COMES OUT

Kayleen strutted down the streets of Shirdon, past its well-cared-for shops and homes. She turned at the apothecary with its neat jars of exotic herbs, roots, and flowers on display in its front window. The market would be busy and full of people who might take note of her presence, so she passed two streets west of it. Once the rumble of the shoppers was behind her, she headed south, toward the edge of town and Aetna Smithery. It was the largest and most well-known smith in the area and the home of Yann.

This was part of an arrangement she had come to with her three lackeys. After the last time Pedrus approached her, she contacted Grekor, proposing a new method of conveying messages. If anyone had anything they wished to report, they were to leave a small, leather bag with a note far back under a designated, out-of-the-way bench in Shir Courtyard gardens. It had to be dropped off well before late afternoon, and she would pick it up in the early evening.

Messages were to be kept short and cryptic. If the bag was empty, it would mean to meet at the designated time and place: dusk on the porch of Ruepo's home. The message could alter the time or place. This time, it only had a name, Yann. With no alternative time, she had interpreted it to mean she should seek out the smith at dusk at his house.

Kayleen rounded the corner, and Yann's workshop came into view on a porch at the near side of a large home. It had all the customary equipment you'd expect at a smith's shop: a giant bellows aimed at an enormous forge full of still-glowing embers, and next to it a huge anvil. Within arm's reach stood a rack of hammers, tongs, and other tools, with a shiny metal-topped table and a large grinding wheel resting nearby.

The shop stood empty now, but smoke from the forge still curled above it into the cool evening air. Kayleen strolled onto his sturdy front porch and was greeted by a pair of dark blue eyes peeking through a cracked door. They were set in a ruddy face topped with a flurry of light-blond hair, and his expression betrayed an eagerness for her arrival. A hand covered with heavy calluses popped through the slit and gave a couple of quick motions for her to come inside.

As she stepped up to it, the door jerked open, and she passed through into the interior of a rather expensive stone home with a well-built floor of smooth wooden planks. The unique odor of smoke, coal dust, and hot iron drifted on the air from a leather apron hung near the door. She had spotted Yann before, around town. He wasn't a large fellow, but his arms were massive and bulging and his shoulders broad beneath his simple tunic.

"Councilwoman." His manner always came across as solemn and even-tempered, yet casual. As if all those years of dealing with customers had taken all the sharp edges off his personality. He bowed, then ushered her to a large table made of dark, fine-grained wood. It had a gorgeous finish and was adorned with an artful engraving of a running horse.

Although Yann did the best business of any smith in Shirdon, the home and table seemed beyond the means of even the most well-to-do smith. He motioned her to sit, and after she had, he came to rest across the table, sitting upright, his hands folded on the smooth surface. "It's an honor, ma'am. That soldier fellow talked to me earlier and told me to expect you, but I have to admit, I was pretty sure he was pulling a prank on me. But here you are." He motioned to her.

"Here I am." Kayleen smiled, eager to hear what Grekor had unearthed. "I assume you have some news regarding a set of chains you made?"

AYLUN

The man squirmed a bit. He seemed about to speak, then stopped and leaned forward as if sharing a confidence. "Well, here's the thing. I've never actually seen any chains like those ones he described, but I do have a story he seemed mighty interested in. I was told to tell it to you."

Not sure if this venture would pan out after all, Kayleen leaned back in her chair and relaxed, feigning more interest than the situation now warranted. "Then I am excited to hear it."

"Well, my family didn't come from Shirdon. Now I suppose that's not a surprise. Most folks around here had families that came from somewhere else. My kin were all smiths, back eleven generations. We used to serve the village of Vathys, along the shores of the Altic Ocean in northwestern Talus."

She smiled, trying to set the man at ease. "Really? So how long has your family been in Shirdon?"

He puffed out his chest. "Three generations: my grandfather, my father, and me. My great-grandfather moved here seventy years ago. See, that's all part of the story, the story of how we came to be the greatest smiths in Shirdon."

Kayleen sat up in her chair and set her hands on the table, mimicking the man's posture. "Seventy years ago?"

"Yup. See, my great-grandfather used to tell a story about a man who came to him back in Vathys, He asked him to make five sets of these chains out of this strange metal. Ruewhen was his name, I believe."

Her interest soared. The name sounded like a possible relative of Ruepo, and she repeated, "Ruewhen?"

Yann nodded. "He supplied the metal, and my grandfather never figured out what it was or how it was made. It was different, lightweight-like, and it never rusted. The links required a special technique to forge, and each chain had to be sixty steps long. It took months to make one, what with all the other work he was doing, you understand. The full set took him all of three years to finish."

She hesitated, struck by the curiosity of it. "Those sound like they could be the chains, but you seem to be saying your grandfather made them in Vathys over seventy years ago?"

He gave a vigorous nod. "And he was paid a fortune in pure gold. Enough to move to Shirdon and set up the best-equipped smithy in the entire area."

Now lost in thought, Kayleen didn't respond.

Seeing her reaction, Yann's expression deflated. "That soldier fellow didn't seem to think much of my story either." She glanced up, and Yann's eyes met hers. "At least he didn't exactly seem interested until he saw that." He pointed to a small frame on the wall with a shiny gold metal piece in it. "It's the first coin my great-grandfather was paid for the chains. He kept it as a reminder of how he came to be able to move to Shirdon."

She rose and strolled over to the ancient-looking frame. She froze as she saw the golden coin enshrined in it. It seemed bigger than the one Garris had given her. She fished in her pocket and found it. The light glinted off it as she held it up next to the one in the frame. Other than its size, the image stamped on the one on the wall was identical, down to the last detail. In a sudden burst, it all came together. This was much bigger than she had suspected.

She turned to the man. "You have to promise to never mention my visit, or the soldier's, to anyone—not a friend, not a relative. Do you understand?"

The man nodded, seeming duly impressed.

Kayleen marched to the door and turned to face the man. "I must take my leave, but you have been tremendously helpful. I won't forget that. Now, remember, tell no one."

She scurried out the door and back down the street, not paying attention to the homes and shops as she passed them by. Her head was swimming with this new piece of the puzzle.

She wanted to keep as much information as possible to herself, but now she needed help. So she headed through town, up the long stairway to the plateau, across it to the keep, then straight for Braye's quarters.

She barged in without knocking.

AYLUN

He looked up from his table, and his gaze remained on her as she stormed across his bearskin rug. "From your expression, it would seem you've learned something."

Kayleen halted in front of him. "Yes, and it changes everything. I assume you've heard what happened at the Southern Lighthouses?"

Braye leaned back in his chair. "Only what I've gathered on the street: that the Dead of Night is on the move, that Jon is rumored to have been responsible, that the lighthouses were sabotaged, and that Jon damaged one trying to put it back in working order."

She nodded. "That is essentially correct. Except for the part about Jon being responsible for the Dead of Night being on the move. That has no basis in fact." She stepped closer and lowered her voice. "What you don't know is what I learned just now—that the chains used in the lighthouse sabotage were forged over seventy years ago in Vathys, along the northeast shore of Talus."

Braye's eyes seemed drawn to the village, a mere dot on the map of Meerdon painted across half of his wall. His gaze remained on that small spot along the coast while he stroked the salt-and-pepper stubble of his chin. Then he rose and strolled over to it. He glanced at her. "And you're sure these particular chains were the ones forged over seventy years ago? And that they were made with this purpose in mind?"

She shook her head. "The length and rare material sound similar, and they were paid for with a unique kind of coin. The same kind of coins we found with the map that sent us to the lighthouses. Even so, there's no way to be certain."

He stroked his chin some more, as his gaze remained fixed on the map. "You admit they might not be the same chains. So why the concern?"

"Suppose for a moment that they were the exact ones."

Braye halted his stroking and lowered his head. "It would suggest a plan seventy years in the making, one as long as a normal lifespan."

"Which then raises the question: why set your plan in motion now?"

His head rose, and his gaze drifted over to Kayleen. "Because this is a time of political chaos. Which would mean that they had extraordinary patience, or ..."

"Or they knew what was coming."

Braye seemed startled by the idea. "Surely you don't think this is the Augury's doing."

"That kind of patience is something I might expect from a group like the Augury. However, another fact makes me think otherwise. We tripped onto this information while investigating attempts on Garris's life that stretch back through his entire exile."

"Surely they can't be related. A seventy-year-old plot to eliminate Garris is absurd."

"I agree. It's nonsense. Unless ..."

Braye kept his gaze steady as his curiosity appeared to grow. "Unless what?"

"Unless Garris was never the goal." Kayleen sent him a piercing stare. "Think about it. We are in a time of unprecedented political change."

His gaze hardened. "Which you helped facilitate."

"Granted. But regardless of how it came about, who is at the center of the changes in the council?"

"Jon."

"A fact of which you may not be aware is that Garris was instrumental in bringing about that change. Had he not appeared, Jon would have never caught up to Dellia, never let Megan go, and never gone with Dellia. In fact, he might still be lost somewhere in the Illis Woods while Megan sat in our prison."

"But if you kill Garris before he meets Jon, the Otherworlder remains lost in the forest, and there is no period of political chaos."

Kayleen shook her head. "Not necessarily. He might be lost in the forest. He might not. All we know is that events would not have played out in the same way. Remember, the Otherworlder was predicted to bring about a new age. That doesn't happen without political upheaval. The truth is, Garris was pivotal in things unfolding as they have, and only Wistra knew what would have happened without him."

"I'm struggling to see your point."

"My point is that Garris is one of Jon's pillars of support. He's a stabilizing force. Take him away and the political situation may very well become far more unstable."

Braye paused, making it obvious he was beginning to see the thrust of her concern. Yet there remained a skeptical glint in his eyes. "You've made two suppositions now. First, that the chains used were forged seventy years ago for this purpose, and second, that knowledge of the future must be involved."

"Then let me add a third supposition. The rumor you mentioned, the one that claimed Jon damaged the lighthouse, it reached Talus before Jon had even arrived there." Kayleen paused to let the implication percolate in Braye's mind. "If we suppose it must be related, then does a rumor that started before the central event of that rumor had taken place not speak to a knowledge of future events?"

He stroked his chin some more and turned back to his map of Meerdon. "I want to object, but I can't find any fault in your logic. It would seem that the rumor is either a colossal coincidence, or knowledge of the future must be involved in its origin."

She left a deliberate pause. "Then let me add a fourth supposition."

He eyed her once again. "A fourth?"

"Yes. Suppose the two recent falling deaths are part of this as well."

His expression darkened, and he went quiet for a while. "Oh, I don't like that."

"Exactly."

He stroked his chin some more. "Taken as a whole, they look like an attempt to throw a fledgling government into chaos."

"And it's working. Soldiers in the military are already grumbling about the deaths. How long before they start blaming Jon?"

757

Braye took a step toward her, and he didn't hide the look of disdain on his face. "I'll be honest. I couldn't care less about Jon or his inane experiment, but I won't stand by and let some outsider take all of us down with him."

Kayleen strolled over to his much too ornate desk and sat upright in his overstuffed chair. "For right now, there's too much supposition. We need to gain some certainty."

"I assume that's why you're here. You didn't come looking for a heart-to-heart. You want me to use my contacts to find out what I can."

"Yes. I can only learn so much from three soldiers stationed in Shirdon. It was my hope that you might cast a broader net. I thought you might be able to get us closer to finding the source of the rumor and figure out who might have wanted Ahmet and Chiyun dead."

"Oh, is that all?"

She kept her tone serious. "No. I also would like to know as much as you can find out about Ruepo. He is at the center of the attempts on Garris's life and the Dead of Night moving. He had to come from somewhere. He has to be known somewhere."

Braye heaved a sigh. "All right. I'll do what I can."

Kayleen rose from the chair and headed out of the room. "Good. You have a lot to do, so I won't distract you any further." She stepped out the door and hurried down the hallway, headed back to her chambers.

It was done. Taking Braye into her confidence was a risk. She might be handing an adversary just the opening they needed to do some real damage, but what could she do? The size of the threat was growing. Someone with a plan seventy years in the making was determined to throw Jon's new government into chaos. And it was impossible to imagine a single reason to do so that wouldn't be disastrous for her and Jon.

Garris stared down the alley at Rillen, racing toward the man they'd just spent two and a half days tracking. He lay unmoving on the ground. That lone was cause enough for alarm, but the more concerning sign was the blood flowing down his red-stained clothes and pooling near his stomach. This wasn't going well.

The current catastrophe began the moment Jon left to chase down Dellia. It was then that his current partner in crime, Rillen, had come to him. She insisted they go on an illicit hunt for the man responsible for sabotaging the lighthouses. Her eyes held a mischievous glint as she said things like, "When the cat's away, the mice will play." It made it hard not to suspect she was merely bored and looking for something exciting to do.

It didn't matter because her plan was precisely what he'd intended to do all along. In fact, it was the real reason he'd argued his way into staying behind. So, he'd feigned reluctance as he let her talk him into it.

As soon as Jon had vanished on the horizon to the east, he and Rillen put on a little show for the benefit of the camp. In a rather loud voice, she insisted they should go after Jon, saying they'd forgotten to tell him critical news from Kayleen's last message.

He argued back that it was useless claptrap to Jon and, therefore, a mere distraction. It soon turned into a shouting match, with Rillen calling him a variety of creative names. They included such gems as "appallingly indolent," "self-infatuated," and, his personal favorite, "puffin-brain," whatever the heck that was supposed to mean.

As per their prearranged script, Garris eventually relented. Not wanting to rouse suspicions, they headed off without even packing up or speaking to anyone. Which also meant he'd left the Window of Rhina in his tent, which was unfortunate. It meant they'd be out of touch with Kayleen until they returned to camp.

Once he and Rillen had traveled out of sight to the east, they circled around in a broad arc, avoiding the detection of patrols, and headed west toward the modest town of Zagra. Their circuitous route wasted half a day, but it was better than wasting half a day sitting on their butts, watching others work and fight.

They arrived in the modest town after sundown, when most residents were home for the evening. With few people out on the streets to question, they stayed the night at a rustic local inn and started their search early the following day.

They scoured the town, asking for a man who looked like the one Garris had picked up near the tower. Unfortunately, their description of a sturdy, bald-headed man with a scraggly blond beard was a bit too generic. It fit several people, forcing them to run down a number of unproductive leads.

They stayed another night at the inn and began again in the morning. Almost immediately, they encountered someone who had spotted him the afternoon before, leaving town to the west. So, they traveled to the next town and started all over again, asking around.

This time it turned out to be a complete bust, and they were about to leave when Rillen became desperate enough to start asking clusters of playing kids. She wandered the streets, going from group to group until she found some who said they'd just seen him with a group of people, going into an alley at the west end of town.

A few minutes later, and here they were, staring into the dark recesses of a dirty alley at a limp body bleeding into the dirt. Rillen reached it before Garris and rolled the man over on his back. He was conscious, looking up with intense pain written on his face and a desperate pleading in his eyes. "Help me," he eked out. His breath shuddered as he clutched his stomach with his blood-drenched hands, though they weren't doing much to stanch the bleeding.

Rillen removed the man's hands, then put pressure on the wound herself. The act elicited moans of agony that faded as he neared unconsciousness. Garris rifled through his pack and found a few strips of cloth as she kept pressure on the injury.

He folded one into a large pad and held it over the wound. The other he wrapped around the man's body, bandaging the long, grisly slit. It had the ugly, jagged look of an injury made by twisting the blade before pulling it out—a surefire way to maximize damage. From the location and appearance of the wound and the size of the pool of blood, the man's prospects didn't look good.

The poor fellow struggled against the pain as he looked up at Garris. He managed to force out a few words between winces. "When they found out you'd caught me at … at the tower, they stabbed me. I think they'd have finished the job if … if you hadn't come along."

Garris finished the bandaging and tied it tight, causing a grimace and a tormented cry from the grievously injured man. Rillen took one arm and Garris the other. As they prepared to lift him, the man reached up and grabbed Rillen's hand on his shoulder.

His grip slid under his blood-soaked fingers as he stared at her with eyes wide. "I didn't know."

Rillen granted him a sympathetic nod. "It's all right."

The man flinched. "The Dead of Night. I didn't know."

Garris set a hand on the man's shoulder. "Know what?"

The man looked over at him, his face pale and his breathing labored. "Their leader, a … a woman named Ruahn, told her men … when the council falls …." The man winced, then held still for a while. "When the council falls, she'll capture the Otherworlder and … and send him to stop it."

"When the council falls?"

The man gave a tiny nod.

The words "when the council falls" continued to rattle around in Garris's brain, repeating over and over. He shoved the thought from his mind and leaned closer. "Stop what? The Dead of Night?"

The man gave an even smaller nod.

"Did she say how?"

Garris moved still closer, putting his ear to the man's mouth.

The sound of a group of horses clomping past on the street outside the alley almost drowned out the man's voice as he leaned toward Garris's ear. "She said … you need to find the heart of—" He coughed and sputtered out more words, but they were impossible to make out. "… It's in a temple … in Saranik. Find it there. … Burn it."

The man slumped in Rillen's arms.

With startling haste, she checked his pulse. "It's weak, too weak." She shook her head. "He's not going to make it."

They carried the limp body, one of them on each arm, as they raced through the streets. As they did, Garris's mind kept going back to that single phrase, "when the council falls." His tension mounted with each step. A lump formed in his throat, and his mouth ran dry as he realized it could only mean one thing: Kayleen was in grave danger, and there was no way to warn her.

He peered at Rillen. "I have to get to Kayleen."

She looked over at him. "No, we have to catch this Ruahn woman."

His anxiety grew at her insistence. Any plan to topple the council had to play out in Shirdon, not out here with Ruahn. He shook his head. "How, we have no description of her? We could be looking right at her and not know it. Besides, Kayleen is in trouble. I'm not going after some woman we may not catch and leave Kayleen to possibly die."

"It's two days' ride to Shirdon at best, and that's if you hardly sleep."

"I won't leave her to die. I can't."

Rillen's acquiescence had an odd abruptness to it. "In that case, the camp is almost on the way, and it's a little more than a day from here. You could use the Window of Rhina to warn her, then go to Shirdon, if you must."

He nodded as they stopped at a building with the sign for a doctor. A man and a woman raced out and took over, hauling their bleeding patient inside. Before they even made it to the door, Garris had spun around and was sprinting down the street, toward the stable, with Rillen following just behind. Kayleen's life might very well depend on how quickly he made it back to the encampment.

Standing in the oracle room, it took a moment for the magnitude of her own recklessness to hit Dellia. She looked over at Megan, who had just explained in detail how they had been duped. "And I played right into their hands." Her mind in a daze, Dellia stumbled backward and stood for a moment, reeling. She wanted to rebel against the idea, but that impulse made her feel so much worse.

Megan was right. Without her, Jon would have never stayed in this world. If he never stayed in this world, then he would never have become a great leader, as the prophecy predicted. That meant, beyond all doubt, the warning they had brought her couldn't be right. It was a lie. There was no fault in Megan's reasoning.

Dellia stood there, dumbstruck by the obviousness of it all. Yet, she didn't want to accept it because if she did, it would mean she had damaged her union with Jon for nothing. Not only that, but it meant she had believed such an outrageous lie about him with all her heart. And she had done so with shocking ease.

Jon's head tilted back, and his blue eyes fixed on the ceiling as he shook his head. "We're so doomed." He dropped down to sit on the smooth black floor, his face a blank as he stared ahead.

Megan squatted in front of him, her expression resolute. She set a hand on each of his shoulders as she peered into his face. "No. I don't accept that."

Dellia froze, shocked by the contrast of her own lack of faith against Megan's unquestioning belief in her friend.

Jon's gaze rose to meet Megan's. "The darkness will kill us all."

She gave a casual shrug. "Then you'll stop it."

He scoffed. "You are so delusional." Despite his reaction, and despite Dellia's gift being crippled by conflict and guilt, she could sense Megan's encouragement lifting his spirits.

Megan smiled and punched Jon in the shoulder. "Come on. Where is all this negativity coming from? This isn't you, Jon."

Even in his distraught state, Jon broke out in a smile.

Megan smiled back. "Wistra said you would be a great leader, and there's not the tiniest speck of doubt in my mind that you will be amazing. You're brave and kind and compassionate and articulate and the smartest person I have ever known."

Jon's resolve grew as Dellia watched, and she felt more and more wretched with each word of reassurance that came from

Megan's mouth. She pointed to Dellia. "And you have some pretty brave and astonishing people by your side. If anyone can figure out how to stop this darkness, it's you guys." She rose to her feet and gave Jon a hand in getting up. "Now stop being such a downer and let's go fix this." She glanced around. "Let's go find Aylun."

Dellia stopped following their conversation. Every word of encouragement Megan uttered was like a new slice of her soul being carved away. Jon *was* brave and kind and everything else Megan saw in him, so why had it been so easy to believe he would doom them all?

Eventually, Megan raced out of the room, eager to find Aylun. A dazed Jon trudged after. Heartsick at what she had done and not sure what to do anymore, Dellia trailed behind him. They wandered down the dark hall and passed back into the shimmering black ball through which they had entered. Megan was on the other side, searching the area for Aylun. Jon turned and stared at the table Megan had assembled to get them inside. He puzzled over it, and Dellia gave it her attention too.

It seemed strange. The polished black plates Megan had placed with such care were no longer where she'd put them. They were stacked in the corner where they'd started from. Yet, who would have been here to move them?

Jon puzzled for a moment, then mumbled, "That's odd. I feel like I'm staring at Schrödinger's cat. It's like the table and oracle room exist in two different states at the same time. Their original state and one where we've changed them." He studied the table for a moment more, then shrugged it off as if the puzzle held no interest for him. Then he raised his head, gazing off to the darkening sky in the west. "Are we staying in Kanlu for the night?"

Megan's search for Aylun had expanded to scanning Kianlong Park below. At Jon's question, she tore her eyes from the scene and glanced down. Her gaze followed some unknown line from her hand back to the path that had led them here. It lingered for a moment, then a crestfallen expression came to her face as she seemed to give up and stood by, waiting for Dellia's answer.

Dellia pulled herself out of her gloom enough to nod and begin leading the way. They threaded down the path, across the now-abandoned Kianlong park, and along the street, passing the dark shops of the more prosperous quarters of the city. As her feet carried her automatically toward one of the better inns in town, her thoughts turned to an even darker prospect. She had no idea how to *be* anymore.

Moments ago, she had assumed every aspect of her current world would go away, and she would be back to her life as a protector, unaware of Jon or anything that had happened with him. Now, in the aftermath, she didn't know who she was or how to be with Jon. No longer was she that carefree, single protector. She was a wife, yet she had done things that made her unworthy of considering herself one.

They checked into a quiet yet plush inn, with one room for her and Jon and a separate one for Megan. In silence, they huddled around a cozy dining table, picking at a delicious meal for which none of them seemed to have the slightest appetite. Then, they retired to their modest rooms.

Dellia lay in the soft, but unfamiliar, bed next to Jon. He seemed to need her, so she snuggled close to him under the covers, even as the gulf between them made it awkward to utter a single syllable. What would she even say to him? How do you tell someone, "I'm sorry I used your trust in me to stab you in the back, I'm sorry I almost undid our marriage, I'm sorry I thought you might end the world"?

Still, she had to try, so she gave voice to the simplest sentiment she could think to express. "I'm so sorry, Jon. I know I keep saying that, but I really am."

He kept his back to her. "I'm sorry too." His voice was quiet and flat, and she paused, unsure what he meant.

"What have you done to be sorry about?"

There was a long moment of hesitation. Then came Jon's response, with no hint of anger or sarcasm. It was simply tired and joyless. "I'm sorry I let you down. I'm sorry for dragging you into this whole ill-fated relationship. I'm sorry I didn't just go home so you wouldn't have to go through all this."

She tried to hide her alarm. "Go home? What about the prophecy? What about my *world*?"

Jon let out a soft and weary sigh. "The prophecy. Of course. That's what matters to you right now."

She descended into an even deeper shame. Her husband had just said their relationship was ill-fated, and her first concern wasn't for him or their marriage, but the prophecy.

Before she could correct her misstep, he continued. "And why even bring that up now. Surely you can't claim you still believe in the prophecy."

Shocked that he would think that way, Dellia raised her head and tried to peer around at his face. "I believe it."

"Then why would you even consider undoing my coming to this world?"

"Because of the warning. Don't you see? Now that Megan figured out it's a lie, it changes everything."

There came another protracted pause before Jon responded. "No. Nothing has changed. I'm still me. You are still you. All the problems that led us to that oracle room still exist."

"The warning brought us to the oracle room. It changed."

"I know you want to think that, and maybe that's comforting to you. But I know you, Dellia. When you believe in something, you believe with your whole heart, and nothing will sway you. If you were truly certain about us ... about me, nothing would have made you believe that warning."

Her alarm grew as she saw the blinding truth of his words. Still, the warning had started this all, so she tried again. "Without that warning ..." She trailed off, not sure how to finish what she was saying without confirming everything Jon thought.

As she struggled for the right words, he finished her thought for her. "If not for that warning, you would still believe we aren't right for one another, that I'm not right for this world."

Dellia fell silent as she tried to conjure a reason why he had to be wrong. Yet, he wasn't exactly wrong. In her conversation with Megan of the day before, she had said he was no leader and that he would get people killed. None of the reasons she said that had changed. So why then did it feel like everything had changed when Jon was right? Nothing had really changed for him, or for her, or for her world?

In the long pause that followed, Jon finally turned his head enough to see her with one eye. "I'm tired, Dellia, and I hurt, and the last few days have been really hard. I thought everything would be over, and instead, we have this long trip back to the lighthouse ahead of us. I have a lot to think through, even though I'm not even sure what to think anymore. Could we just not talk about this now? Can we just get some sleep?"

His plea was as heartfelt as his sorrow at saying it, and she held back her objections and pleadings. Then she sensed it, a touch of anxiety in his heart, as if he was afraid she would press the issue when he didn't want to speak his thoughts. It was all wrong. Jon never seemed hesitant to speak his true mind.

Then she realized the most important part of what hadn't changed was that she loved him and was desperate not to lose him. She had let a lie blind her, and for that, her remorse could not be more profound. But she still felt the same way about him, even with everything that had happened.

She wanted to say so. Because to her, it was important. But Jon wanted silence, and she owed him that. He hadn't run from her. In fact, he had come after her, and his warmth lay next to her now. He even seemed to want to be here, to touch her. That was enough for now. As long as that didn't change, there would be time to talk about it later. So, exhausted, she let her despondency overtake her and fell into a deep sleep.

It turned out the awkwardness and silence of that evening had been only a tiny preview of what lay ahead. Uncertainty and gloom enshrouded Dellia as she led them back the way they had come. They traveled in quiet along the bright shores of Kinshai Lake, then to the overgrown spire in the forest. Dellia used her red spire stone to deliver them back to the flower-filled clearing at the edge of the Illis Woods. Then she led them out of the trees and across the long plains to her mother's home.

With his silence, the gulf between her and Jon seemed to grow. There was so much more she needed to say, but she never found a good moment to bring it up. Even if she had found a time, what words could express what she was feeling? How could she say, "I know I turned against you, but I still love you? I know I wanted to undo our marriage, but you're still the one I long to be with? I may have thought you might end the world, but I never stopped believing in your heart"? How could she make him understand when the words didn't even make sense to her?

She asked Megan several times where Aylun was going, and she kept saying she didn't know exactly. Yet she always emanated an odd certainty that they were headed in the right direction. Most of the time, Megan seemed deep in thought, as if working out some vexing puzzle. Jon was even more distracted and growing more distant as he became more preoccupied.

When they arrived at her mother's home, Jon said he needed time alone to think and elected to sleep in the guesthouse, assuming she and Megan would once more share a room. His rejection hurt, but she reminded herself that two days ago, at this same house, it was she who had elected not to share her room with him. What she had done over the past days was a far more permanent and painful rejection of him.

Before they divided up, Megan blocked them both and sent them a solemn look. "I think there's something you should know, because it has to do with what you're up against."

In the cool dark air of evening, with crickets chirping and gentle movement of tired horses in the stable, Dellia and Jon stared at her, waiting for her to continue.

"There's a reason it took me so long to figure out mine was the path that was tampered with. It's because, from what I know, it's impossible. How could someone plant a journal in Lanessa and a warning in a hidden city and know I'd find them? And, even if they did, why wouldn't Wistra have foreseen it and stopped them?"

Jon scrunched his face. "I'm confused. It sounds like you're saying all that stuff you said back in the oracle room is impossible."

"No. I'm saying it *seemed* impossible. At least I thought so. Until I realized I'd seen what might make it possible. I'd seen the Eye of Syvis."

Overwrought and overtired, Jon groaned. "Oh man, not Syvis again. The Stone of Syvis had me in spasms of pain for half a day."

Concern clouded Dellia's face as she regarded Megan. "What's the Eye of Syvis?"

Megan shrugged. "I don't know. But it has to do with oracles, and the thing is, I saw it on a woman. A woman who met us at the Mundus Spire when we used it to escape Lanessa. A woman who had to have known we would arrive there before we knew we would be there."

Jon still appeared baffled. "Back up a minute here. So you met a woman who must have foreseen where you would be, and she had this Eye of Syvis. Okay, I get that, but if you don't know what it does, how can you know it made the impossible possible?"

"I know it has to do with oracles and that it is powerful. What if it bends the rules of prophecy? What if it allowed someone to alter Wistra's plan? Normally, that would be impossible because she would have foreseen it and stopped it. But as soon as you allow for oracles who don't follow the rules, whose actions can remain hidden from the Augury and from other oracles, it starts to make sense."

His aspect darkened. "So you think there are rogue oracles out there messing with us?"

Dellia nodded and lowered her head as the sad truth of it fully struck her. "No, she's right. That's how you start a rumor about damage to the lighthouse that hasn't happened yet."

Megan went on. "Pretaj mentioned a group called the Mirhal."

Jon startled. "Pretaj? You met Pretaj?"

"Yes, I spent a couple weeks in his library, but that's not the point."

"Sorry. The Mirhal—what about them?"

"They're considered a myth, a group of oracles outside the Augury. But, what if they're real? What if they have the Eye of Syvis and used it? Not to interfere directly with Wistra's plan but to use me to undo it after the fact."

Dellia looked up at Megan. "To what end?"

She shrugged again. "I don't know. But if I'm right, you're up against people who know exactly what you're going to do next. How do you fight that?"

Jon seemed deep in thought as he spoke half to himself. "You do something completely out of character, something no one would ever expect."

Dellia watched as he got that expression he had when he was spinning some crazy plot. It was the same one he'd had when figuring out his plan to confront the council. She wanted to ask what he was thinking, but before she could get past her own awkwardness, he'd turned away and wandered off toward the guesthouse.

Unable to resolve anything, she turned to tending the horses, as she had done last time she was here. Except where two days ago she had been in shock over what she had done, now she was racked by guilt and worry. It seemed more and more like she had destroyed her own happiness, that she had lost Jon for good.

After she finished, she spent a long while sitting in the darkness and quiet, feeling too alone and miserable to face anyone or anything. For stretches of time, silent tears fell, as images came of betraying Jon's trust, of scolding him for being selfish, of refusing to even acknowledge his existence, and all the ways she had mistreated him these last days. By the time she made it back to the room, Megan was asleep on the floor.

So as not to disturb her, Dellia crept into bed and spent a long wakeful time trying to keep at bay all the concerns that plagued her. Not the least of which was the look she had seen on Jon's face. What if he was planning something? What if it involved going home? What if it required dangerous and insane things? But most of all, what if it didn't involve her? What if she wasn't in his plans at all anymore?

After an almost sleepless night filled with ceaseless fretting, she awoke in the dark, fixed a meager meal, then prepared the horses while Megan and Jon ate. As dawn was beginning to light the sky, they led their horses out for the day's ride. A light cool breeze blew as they prepared to mount.

Before they could, Megan stopped them again and pointed to the southwest, toward the silhouette of dark mountains. "Aylun is that way. I can't go with you anymore. I have to follow him."

Jon became more animated than in days. "Into the Dead of Night?"

She nodded. "Yes. If he's in danger, I need to be at his side."

"Are you out of your mind?"

"No." She smiled. "Scared, yeah." She shook her head. "Out of my mind? No. I can do this."

He stared, seeming shocked. "And he means that much to you?"

Megan smiled. "I know. It's funny, isn't it, but yes. He only ever thinks of my happiness. It's time I thought about his."

Dellia drew a deep breath. "Are you certain?"

Megan gave her a playful punch in the shoulder. "You guys, I am not some weakling. I can take care of myself. Remember what I did to Jon? I threw him into a tree, and that was a minor accident. If I want, I can do some truly serious damage."

Dellia looked down at the familiar grassy yard. Aylun had talked about Megan throwing giant logs at him. Perhaps she really could take care of herself.

When she glanced up again, Jon was still staring at his friend with an expression of incredulity. "But it's dark in there. It's almost like it eats light. How will you see?"

Megan fished in her pocket and produced a round glass ball. In the near darkness, it glowed with a color that was not the daylight of sunstones or the warm fire of flamestones but an ethereal golden hue that defied description. It lit her mesmerized face as she held it in front of her where all of them could see. "I have an aetherstone. It puts out quite a bit of light."

Fascinated, Dellia reached out to touch its smooth golden surface. "I've never heard of an aetherstone. Where did you get it?"

"Athene gave it to me."

Shocked, Dellia took an unconscious step backward. "Athene? *The* Athene? The goddess Athene?"

Megan nodded.

"That's absurd. She's a myth."

She thrust the aetherstone closer to Dellia's face. "The proof is right in front of you."

Jon's expression turned to one of realization. "That's the woman you sent to tell me you were okay, wasn't it?"

Megan seemed to get more excited. "So she actually visited you?"

"In my dreams, yeah. Or in my unconscious state, I guess. She showed me you heading to Lanessa." Jon boggled for a moment longer. "A goddess? And you just now mentioned it?"

"Well, it wasn't the part of the trip that left the biggest impression."

Dellia's mind refused to accept it. "You've both met Athene?"

"It would seem so."

Megan eyed Jon. "I think we know her as Athena. She was quite helpful. I met her in her temple in Katapa."

"I suppose if dragons are real, it shouldn't be a shock that Greek gods are real."

"She said they aren't really gods. She said they are human, like us, but I'm not really sure what that means." Her face took on a thoughtful expression, as she stared at her aetherstone and brought it still closer to her bright eyes. "At the time, I thought she gave me this to light my way in the tunnels below Katapa, but maybe she knew all along that I was headed to the Dead of Night."

Jon stared at the stone. "How do you charge it up?"

"It never needs charging."

Dellia finally snapped out of her surprise and blurted out, "I can't let you go near the mountains unescorted." Then it occurred to her she had spoken without any thought for Jon … again. She looked at him. "I mean, *we* can't let you go so near the mountains without our protection. Right, Jon?"

He nodded. "Of course. We'll stay with you as long as we can, but then we *really* need to get back to the lighthouse."

Dellia stared for a moment. His insistence seemed a little too strong to write off as a random impulse or concern for Garris. There was a reason he wanted to be at the lighthouse, some kind of plan, but she still hesitated to ask about it. It didn't seem like she had the right anymore.

Megan took the lead this time, insisting she knew which path Aylun had taken. They angled toward the mountains, the rocky blue peaks rolling by, ever more prominent against the billowy white clouds that drifted above them. The foothills, at first too small to make out, became wavering green mounds that rippled out from their base. Shadows of the puffy clouds wandered across their rounded surface while the wind blew waves through their grasses.

Their brief discussion may have eased the tension a bit, but as soon as he was on horseback again, Jon became as distant as ever. Perhaps even more so, since he now seemed deep in thought. Dellia fretted, not wanting to ask what he was thinking about and not even sure she wanted to know.

Just before midday, they arrived at the entrances of a set of dark caves. Megan dismounted, and Dellia and Jon followed her lead.

Megan pointed to the caves. "He went through there. So, this is where we part." She stepped up to Jon and gave him a long hug. Then she faced Dellia and handed her a set of reins. "Take care of Yuki for me. She has seen me through so much. Don't let any harm come to her."

Dellia began to nod but was interrupted when Megan threw her arms around her in another long and strong hug. She pulled back and eyed her. "You're special. You know that, right?"

The unexpected praise caught Dellia off guard. It was utterly at odds with how she felt right now, so all she did was stare.

"I've known Jon for ten years. No matter what encouragement I gave, no matter how supportive I was, I couldn't even talk him into leading a meeting." Megan smiled. "For you, he became leader of the ruling council. It still blows my mind every time I think about it. I know things are strained between you now, and that's my fault. For that—"

"No, my actions were my own." Dellia shook her head. "You are not to blame, not for any of it. In fact, you deserve gratitude and praise for helping us avoid a huge mistake."

Megan nodded. "That was the past. And I know it was only a day ago, but you need to get beyond it. You need to be of one mind. Jon needs you. Be there for him. He's worth it."

Dellia glanced at Jon, who stood there looking away, acting as if he hadn't heard a single word. She bowed to Megan but couldn't assemble a decent response. How could she be there for Jon when he acted as if he didn't want her anymore?

As she looked into Megan's face for what could be the last time, the Great Oracle's words about her came to mind. She held her gaze steady. "There's one more thing you should know. Tsaoshi, the Great Oracle, once told me you had a fate that might be more important than mine, or Garris's, or Jon's. He can see the future, and he thought you might be more important than all of us."

Megan stifled a laugh. "Well, that's ridiculous."

Dellia maintained her solemn demeanor. "You know I have the Gift of the Heart, right?"

"Yeah. You can sense feelings. Kind of hard to forget."

"When Tsaoshi told me that, he wasn't joking. He was deadly serious."

Megan waved it off. "That just means he was delusional."

"The head of the Augury, delusional?"

Megan seemed to startle. "Oh, he's the head of the Augury?"

Dellia nodded.

"Well, I still don't believe it." Megan stepped back and sent a fond gaze to Jon, then Dellia. "Make me one last promise. Each of you protect the other. I don't want to return and find anything happened to either of you, okay?" Megan fished in her pocket and retrieved her aetherstone. She held it in her hand as she turned and walked away.

Dellia called out to her as she neared the cave, "Be careful. Be sure you do come back. And bring Aylun with you."

Megan waved one last time and disappeared into the cave. All that remained was a bright golden light bobbing and swerving as it grew more distant in the darkness.

Now alone with Jon, the distance between them gained a whole new sharpness. Not knowing what else to say or do, Dellia faced Jon and tried to hide her fear and sadness. "Back to the lighthouse?"

"Yeah, I think we're needed there, even if Saneya doesn't see it."

The comment once again gave her pause. It wasn't anything Jon said but the way he said it. She had heard that tone before, when he was devising a plan to topple the council. In fact, he had used it when evading her questions about what he was planning. The compulsion hit her again to ask him if he was up to something, but he was even more likely to evade the question now than he had been back then. Besides, she feared the answer he might give as much as she feared his plans might no longer include her.

Instead, Dellia swung up onto Ulka and set a course to come up slightly to the northeast of the lighthouse. It wouldn't be wise to arouse suspicions of "meddling" by making it look like they were coming from the darkness.

In the time that ensued, her mind wandered from the events of the past few days to Jon's assertion that they were needed at the lighthouse, to Megan's goodbye. Megan was right. Yet what could she do? She and Jon needed to be of one mind, but she had shown him she couldn't be trusted and damaged his belief in them. Why would he reveal anything to her now?

It was late afternoon by the time they neared the camp. Their time alone together was slipping away, and along with it, any chance to find out what he intended to do next. She was about to look back and ask, when the distant sounds of yelling, swords clanging, and chilling screeches came from the direction they were headed.

Dellia was turning to tell Jon she suspected the camp might be under attack when Enna bolted past, carrying him straight for the noise. She urged Ulka faster and pulled on Yuki's reins, and they both surged up beside Jon. By his actions, he seemed intent on doing something about the attack, but she no longer had any idea what he might have in mind.

Chapter Thirty

DON'T LET IT SHOW

All the way back from the oracle room, Jon kept hearing Megan's refrains repeating in his head. She'd insisted that his negativity wasn't like him, that he would be a great leader someday, and that he could fix this. Clearly, they were all her over-faith in him talking. There was no fixing this—not the threat to Talus and not his relationship with Dellia.

Ulka's hoof-falls resounded ahead of him as he lifted his gaze. It made his heart hurt to look upon her beautiful face, scanning the vast pastoral plains. The woman he loved with his whole heart was still there, a torturous reminder that love didn't conquer all. If anything, the last few days had been a vivid illustration of that one agonizing truth. He and Dellia had never been of one mind and never could be.

For a fleeting moment, he had considered leaving the Illis Woods spire for Isla and the way home, but it would be unconscionable to leave the woman he loved and her people in this dire situation. Megan was half right about that one thing. Even if he was doomed to failure, he had to try to fix this.

Over time, despite his efforts to keep his mind on track, it kept being drawn back to the impossible state of the oracle room. When they left the first time, after hearing Wistra's prophecy, the room had been in a chaotic state. A stalactite had fallen and shattered, and the floor had been strewn with its fragments. All of that, and more, had changed between the first visit and this last one. It was as if gremlins had come and reassembled the stalactite and put it back in place. Only, that was a ridiculous and fanciful explanation.

It reminded him of the "many worlds" hypothesis of quantum physics, where an infinite number of alternate realities exist where particles could be in differing states. It had always struck him as the wishful thinking of overactive imaginations rather than a serious attempt to explain the nature of reality. It conjured into existence entire unprovable universes just to explain certain observed behaviors of particles that didn't fit into current accepted theory.

Now, after what he'd seen in that oracle chamber, it seemed far more credible. If there were a veil between realities and if energy could be transferred between realities, it could explain how he summoned lightning out of nothing. It hadn't come from nowhere. It had come from another reality. If portals could pass between different realities, it could explain how the oracle chamber could be in two different states. Because he hadn't visited the exact same oracle room—he had passed into the same room in two different realities.

Still, it didn't matter. In the end, the nature of the oracle room was only a distraction. Understanding it wouldn't help him in the here and now. So, while many topics had consumed his thoughts since the oracle room, the one that had tortured him the most was his attempt to understand the Dead of Night and devise a way to thwart it. It was imperative that he prevent the Mirhal's schemes and his mistakes from heaping unending shame on Dellia. He couldn't allow himself to become a repeat of her father at Githeo.

Jon's gaze remained on Dellia as his mind drifted. Then a distant screech brought his focus back to the present. It was followed by the clanging of metal and bellowing of soldiers, and it was coming from right in front of them. The yelling was too far away to make out a single word, but, in a flash, it became clear: the camp was under attack.

His heart began to race, thumping in his ears as he urged Enna forward. She sprang to a gallop, her hooves pounding the grassy ground as she flew by Dellia, Ulka, and Yuki.

Without a pause, hoof-falls broke into a gallop behind him. They gained on him as the camp became a dot along the horizon.

Dellia surged up to his side, the two flying across the flat grassland and toward the disturbance ahead.

He glanced over and shouted to her, "I need a weapon! Not yours."

She understood his request. Without raising an eyebrow, she reached into her saddlebag, pulled out a whip, and held it up for him to take.

He stared at the thing. He'd had no idea his wife carried a whip.

She heaved in the saddle, her hand jogging as she thrust it out for him to take. "It's Rillen's. She lent it to me so I could learn it."

With the horse bounding beneath him, Jon reached for it, fumbling with unsteadiness. After a few tries, he grabbed it and tried to trigger his gift. He had never seen Rillen with it, so he concentrated on the whip itself. Time seemed to stall out in the world around him, with Dellia's hair blowing behind her and the horses galloping in slow motion. Even the activity in the camp ahead came to a crawl, then stopped.

Enna, Ulka, and Yuki remained frozen midstride as they dimmed, and a shimmering scene appeared around him, overlaid on top of the real world. He rolled time backward until he spotted Rillen in some kind of arena, taunting Dellia with the whip. He focused on her and the whip, and in a flash, a feeling of mastery came over him. He knew, beyond doubt, he could wreak havoc with this thing in his hand.

As the world sped up again, he smiled at Dellia. "Let's go teach those things what their blood looks like."

She stared, slack-jawed. "Adi, help us. You sound like Rillen."

Jon smiled and kicked again, surging ahead.

The camp was the embodiment of chaos. Far off toward the towering rock cliffs, the lighthouse still stood, shedding its warm light on the chasm entrance. Emerald-green creatures, ten feet long or more, were skirting it. On multijointed legs, they skittered out from the mountains and darted across the flat plains. They had the appearance of insects—like enormous praying mantises. Only they had flat, half-human faces that stared with eerie black eyes. They scurried, dodged, and leaped on the six legs along their body but could rear up on four and use needle-sharp pincers in front to slash or stab.

Moving with unnatural speed, they dove in and out and swerved away from every attack, and they screeched and chittered at one another as if speaking some ancient insect language. They shot forward, not in a chaotic mess as might be expected of a mass of scattering beasts, but with determined purpose, heading straight for the soldiers of the camp.

Some part of him, perhaps the part that knew how to use this whip, was sure this was a coordinated attack. As they thundered closer, Jon scanned the encampment. While he'd been gone, it had grown larger, perhaps more than double the size. Here and there, soldiers shouted to one another as they sprinted down the neat rows of tents toward the open area nearest the lighthouse and the swarm descending upon it.

Then he spotted Garris and Rillen galloping toward the bedlam from the opposite side. The two protectors were headed straight for another new arrival, Sirra, his mother-in-law, at the far end of the conflict. She was unmistakable, with the same rich brown hair and slender frame as Dellia.

On the near side stood Saneya, with one of the massive, green insect things racing toward her. With Garris and Rillen helping Sirra, Jon focused on the creature headed for Saneya, charging it on a collision course. To his own surprise, he let out a loud whoop as he neared. The thing looked back at him as he flicked the whip. As if by magic, it coiled out and wrapped around the beast's narrow neck, still some distance in front of Saneya.

He slung the handle end around his arm and pulled back on Enna's reins. She came to a stuttering stop, and the entire weight of the creature hurtled forward, pulling back against the whip around its neck. With a violent snap and painful jerk on his arm, the whip yanked the beast around and twisted it to the ground.

Saneya leaped on its neck and rammed a sword through its head. It went limp.

Jon let the whip go slack, and it uncoiled from the neck. He brought Enna around and let fly with another unintended scream as he charged the largest group of creatures headed for a group of soldiers. With a flick of his wrist, he unleashed the whip again as he pulled sideways on the reins, bringing Enna alongside the lead creature. The whip coiled out around the front leg, and with a quick yank, he pulled the creature's foot out from under it as Enna's rear slammed into its body.

Off-balance and unable to recover, the creature tumbled at high speed, rolling sideways across the grass. Not able to stop in time, the beasts following it slammed into the careening body. With a chorus of screeches and terrible crunching, they merged into a chaotic jumbled mass. Limbs broke, heads snapped, then soldiers dove into the heap, beheading and impaling until nothing moved.

Jon glanced around and spotted Dellia, some distance away. Three of the beasts were converging on her, two of them in front while a not-quite-dead third dragged itself toward her back. If she didn't notice it, the one behind her would impale her.

His heart leaped into his throat as he urged Enna to a gallop, heading straight for Dellia.

He veered toward the narrowing gap between a creature approaching a group of soldiers, trying to squeeze through before it closed in on them. Suddenly the thing leaped forward and landed in front of Jon, blocking his path. It crouched low.

He let the whip unwind again, and with a crack, it snapped inches from the near side of the crouching beast's head. Enna leaped over the lowered front end as the thing twisted around to face the noise, but Jon was no longer there. Then a pair of soldiers impaled it in the chest while it remained distracted.

Now almost upon Dellia, the creature behind her raised a pincer to her exposed back. Jon cracked the whip. The strips of leather at the tip snapped in the beast's eye, and it splattered, sending viscous goop spraying. The creature screeched and flailed its head as

Jon flew off of his horse. He came down on his feet with his back to Dellia, facing the half-blind creature. The whip lashed out again, and the other eye exploded in another spray of slimy, clear liquid.

Blinded, the creature writhed as it jabbed at the air with its needle-sharp pincer.

Jon slammed the hard handle of the whip into the creature's flat green face with a satisfying crunch. Then, as it aimed for him, Jon ducked under it. On all fours, he scurried through, then leaped onto its back. He swung the heavy end of the whip around the creature's neck and yanked back with all his strength until he got a gratifying snap as its neck broke.

The beast dropped to the ground, with Jon still perched on its back. He began to slip off. While he was still off-balance, a startling screech bellowed out from his right side. His gaze whipped around to spot one of the creatures, with its pincer headed straight at his chest. His heart stopped.

Dellia came out of nowhere and dove in front of the green needle, blocking it with her stomach. Time seemed to slow down again as if he'd willed it. A horrible grunt of pain rang in his ears as the tip of the blood-drenched pincer hit her, then stabbed through and poked well out of her back.

Everything became surreal. Red blood flowed down her brown leather armor. A horse slammed into the creature. Two women leaped on it and stabbed it in the side. The pincer yanked free, leaving a bloody hole in Dellia's back.

She began to fall backward.

Jon leaped for her and caught her body, cradling it in his arms.

Her limp head fell, facing downward as blood poured out of the torn flesh of her back.

In a flash, he was back in his high school classroom, holding the body of his stepsister, staring down at her bullet-riddled body. She was still alive as her weak voice squeaked out for him to help her, but he could only stare. Her warm blood flowed out onto his hands, and there was nothing he could do to stop it.

AYLUN

Jon looked up, and the bodies of his classmates were strewn across the room. One of them was moaning in pain, and their blood was spattered across the walls and floor. A scream met his ears and snapped him back to the present.

Still in shock, he stared out at the bloody field. Soldiers were fighting here and there with a dozen bodies scattered across the red-stained grass. His gaze snapped down to his wife's body in his arms. In desperation, he pressed his hand over the jagged hole, trying to stanch the bleeding, but the wound went clear through. It was no use.

A cold horror froze his soul as he stared downward. This couldn't be happening. Not to Dellia. It couldn't end like this. Not like this. He had treated the most precious thing in his life so terribly. If only he hadn't refused to protect her. If only he had done something. If he had just done anything, maybe she wouldn't be lying here like this.

Tears streamed down his face as he hugged her close to him. He stayed that way as the fighting went on and on as his weeping turned into heaving sobs. Then he let go and pulled back. Afraid to look, he lifted her head and supported it as he peered into her eyes.

It wasn't Dellia. It was Brita. She looked up at him and let out a pair of pitiful coughs. Then she smiled, and he could barely make out her voice above the clanging of swords and moaning of the wounded. "I did good, didn't I?"

An even stronger round of tears threatened to let loose, but he needed to be strong. He forced them back and stared into the eyes of the woman who had saved his life. With his hand still pressed on the wound, the pulse of her warm blood was flowing out between his clenched fingers.

He smiled back and nodded. "You saved my life, cousin. Dellia will be so proud of you."

Her smile broadened, then she coughed again.

Jon sniffled as the tears wouldn't be stopped.

A pair of soldiers raced up to Brita's side. They knelt next to her and gently moved his blood-drenched hand. With care, they set her head on the grass, then one of them put their own pressure on the wound.

He stood and stumbled back, staring down at her, then at the two soldiers—a man and a woman. "You have to save her."

The woman looked up at him with sorrowful eyes and gave her head a small shake.

Jon stepped back again in shock. She wasn't going to make it. Brita was a relative of his. A few days ago, she said she had been looking forward to meeting him, and now she was going to die? He surveyed the bodies lying on the field, and sudden remorse racked him.

In an instant, he was back in that classroom again, staring at the bodies of his classmates, friends, and family who had died because he took charge.

Then he was back on the bloody battlefield, staring at the bodies of the fallen. Only this time, he hadn't taken charge. He had done everything right. He hadn't made a single decision. He hadn't even been here, and still, it turned out like this. Yet it seemed as if he was just as responsible. Not because of what he had done, but because of what he hadn't done.

His chest tightened, and his breathing grew labored as his mind rebelled, unable to resolve the incongruity of the two situations: one where he had caused deaths because he took charge and the other where he had caused deaths because he hadn't.

The sound of heavy feet pounding the ground pulled him out of his daze. He looked up as a massive, sickly-green creature with four muscular arms followed the last of the insect-like beasts. It seemed like it was herding them toward the camp. As it flew into view, its form became recognizable. It was just like that wretched demon from the Mundus catacombs.

It stared at Jon with bulging red eyes, its ugly skin covered with heavy, dark veins. A set of familiar scratch marks ran down the left side of its grotesque face, and, in an instant, it was clear: this had to be the exact same demon who had taunted them in the Mundus Temple.

It let loose with a deep, resonant laugh that bellowed across the field of wounded.

Eyes turned toward it, staring in shock.

It pointed, and its voice boomed out across the plains, tents, and fires. It was a familiar voice. "Behold your great leader, crying like a baby."

Garris called out from the side as he advanced on it. "Don't listen to it. It's a Bahkaana. It has the Gift of Deception. It spins lie upon lie."

Jon froze as he struggled with how to silence the beast. What Garris had revealed wasn't the worst of it; he had seen that firsthand in the Mundus temple. Somehow the creature seemed to know every detail of their lives, their hopes and their fears, and it used these. It spouted a toxic web of truths and half-truths designed to mislead anyone within earshot. He glanced around. A few of the soldiers were still fighting, but those who weren't were tending to the wounded or staring in stupefaction. He snatched the whip from the dirt and began storming toward the beast.

The demon smiled as it turned its attention to Garris. "You know full well I can only tell the truth."

"Half-truths," Garris shouted back.

"Oh, then should I tell the half-truth that you are planning to abandon your family because you can't handle Leanna's death." It put on an ugly, toothy smile with oversized canines. "Or should I tell the whole truth? Should I tell them what really happened to her?"

Garris's face turned red with anger. "Shut up."

It dismissed him with a wave of one of its four huge hands. "You're right. You are of no consequence."

His face flush with anger, Jon cracked the whip and slowed as he closed in on the beast.

The demon's gaze whipped over to him, and it pointed. "Let's talk about your so-called leader. Every day he cringes in Shirdon, paralyzed by fear. He plays the part of one who would be the leader of the ruling council, while he plots ways to get out of being responsible for a single thing." It laughed. "The leaders of the three realms, his friends, every human life in this world put their faith in him, and he couldn't even honor them by trying to lead."

It laughed again, a twisted, mocking sound that rose from its bowels. "He doesn't believe he's the Otherworlder. He knows he can't lead. He is so sure of it he was willing to disappear."

Dellia moved out to flank the demon on the opposite side from Garris. Her movement caught the monstrosity's attention, and it turned its bulging red eyes to her. "Ask his witch wife. She thought so too." It waved one of its four muscular arms as if presenting her to the crowd. "Do you know where she went? Of course you do. She went to get rid of her husband for good. But do you know why?" It laughed again, deep and unrestrained. "Because she was certain he was going to be the death of every one of you." It waved a pair of massive hands across the soldiers, still standing stunned and mute. Then it tilted its head back and let out another long, bellowing laugh.

As Jon stood amid the bloody bodies of his wife's people, it became all too clear: the demon was right. He hadn't even tried to save them, and the proof was all around him.

His thoughts flew back again to that classroom. Two bloody scenes of death, one in the past and the other here and now. His mind reeled and his breathing became labored as he tried once again to reconcile the two opposite situations. Pain shot through his head, and he clamped his hands down on it, trying to make sense of the impossible dichotomy. Memories forced their way back: of Kayleen's exasperation as she told him *"Look, leaders make decisions,"* of Dellia shouting *"If you're so determined to be useless, then why are you even here,"* and of the demon mocking him for plotting *"ways to get out of being responsible for a single thing."*

Then, in a sudden burst, it struck him, and he stumbled back as his whole concept of the world shifted out from under him. He had been mistaken his entire adult life. Not a little mistaken, but in a huge, glaring way. His stepmother had been wrong. His whole stepfamily had been wrong. Half his life had been wasted in believing them when they called him a curse. How many times had they told him he was a menace and that he'd killed his stepsister because he took charge?

In that classroom, all those years ago, he hadn't been at fault because he took control of the situation. He had been at fault because his plan had been to do nothing.

He had refused to listen to his classmates. They had wanted to escape, and they were right. A few steps away from the door stood a stairway that led down to a fire exit. If he'd listened to them, they would have been outside the building and safe in minutes. Instead, he convinced them to shelter in place and wait for someone else to save them. He had convinced them to do nothing while armed shooters were headed straight for them.

He had done it again with his wife. When the protectors were in the crosshairs, he refused to act, and it had shattered his marriage. Now he had done it a third time here. When a crisis threatened everyone, he had been more than happy to step back and let Saneya and others deal with the danger. He had played the fool and done nothing.

Each time there had been a crisis, and each time he had failed because he had chosen inaction when it had been within his power to do something about it. He looked back at the body of his young cousin-in-law. She was going to die because he had done nothing to stop it.

No longer.

Jon took off again toward the demon and unleashed the whip. It snaked out, and with a crack, cut a gash in the brute's face and stopped it mid-bellow. The mark healed itself as a shimmering liquid curtain appeared, mostly hidden behind the monstrosity. Uncertain what was happening, Jon halted in his tracks.

The demon brought its glaring red eyes to bear on him as signs of movement came from behind it. Someone or something had just passed through the portal. Unable to see what it was, Jon looked to Dellia, and she stiffened. His heart began to race again, hammering in his ears. Something that alarmed Dellia was behind that demon.

Suddenly flames leaped at the beast's feet. It let out a pained roar as the fire spread up its legs and body until it became a raging inferno. Jon remained frozen as the hideous monster let out a last anguished wail, then vanished, leaving someone standing there, no longer hidden behind the beast.

With her head down, only her short silver hair showed, and yet the sight rang a disturbing alarm bell. She held out something dark, slick, and sickly in her outstretched hand, aimed at where the demon had stood. As he stared at the thing, it pulsed in her hand as if it were alive.

The portal still shimmered behind her as she raised her head, revealing Idria's thin face and pale-blue eyes. Panic welled within him as he recalled what happened the last time they had encountered her. She and Braye had been council members together, yet she had stabbed the man and twisted the knife as if he were nothing to her. With his blood spilling onto the swirling-marble floor, she had produced the Stone of Syvis and thrust it high between her gore-covered fingers. Her icy words still gave him the shivers as he recalled her accusing him of being an "insect" and of "ignorant meddling." Worst of all—she'd wielded the power of that smooth dark stone to destroy his friends, one at a time. Though he had no idea the true extent of her power, he knew, almost by instinct, that the threat she posed to him and all he held dear could not be underestimated.

Dellia and Garris bolted toward her.

Idria held up a hand, and in a crisp voice called out, "Stop, and I won't kill you."

It didn't slow the two, and Garris raised his sword.

Alarmed, Jon shouted, "Freeze!"

His two protectors halted in their tracks.

He rushed to speak. "Can't you see what's in her hand? Have you forgotten the last time? She killed Braye and turned you guys to dust."

Idria smiled and lowered her arm with the shiny greenish mass still clutched in her hand. "Smart. I *could* kill them, but I won't. I came with a proposal."

Jon stood taller. "I won't listen to a proposal from a woman who killed three people as if their lives were nothing."

She shot him a disapproving glare. "Last time, I warned you. I told you that you have no idea what forces you are trifling with. ... and look." She waved her hand as if presenting the dead and wounded, then did so again, motioning to the lighthouse and darkness beyond. "Here are the consequences."

Guilt racked him at the truth of her words, yet he stood resolute. "Or maybe you orchestrated all this so you could blame me."

Idria let out a high-pitched laugh. "You're still a menace. You have no idea what's going on, or you wouldn't even think of blaming me."

"Did you come here to hurl insults?"

"No, I came with a bargain. Join us. You are a mere child with immense power, a power that makes you a danger to all. Join us. Learn to harness that power, and together we can stop the Dead of Night and bring order to Meerdon."

Jon stood taller. "If you are so powerful, then stop the Dead of Night yourself. No one here will stand in your way."

Idria's face twisted in anger. "Syvis is not some servant to go around cleaning up your messes. You are the cause of this. Fix it yourself, or join us, and together we can accomplish great things."

He could barely recall the seductive allure of Syvis's power, but he did remember that it was not benevolent. It was fueled by hatred. Not blind hatred, but hatred of disorder and chaos. The details were lost to him now, along with the power of the stone, but one impression remained. The order Syvis craved could only be brought about through death and destruction and the shattering of souls.

Jon shook his head. "I will never join you."

Idria smiled. "Never? Such a strong word." She eyed Dellia and smiled. "How about if we take your wife? Then we'll see if you remain so arrogant."

Dellia stood taller. "Just try to take me."

Idria donned a knowing kind of smile that was deeply disconcerting. "Oh, you will be ours." She seemed so confident, and the idea was horrifying. The portal behind her still shimmered in the sunlight as her gaze turned back to Jon, and her smirk broadened. "Yes. Try to fix this mess you've made. You will fail, and we will be here to take advantage of the aftermath. If by some miracle you succeed, then we will see if you still refuse to join us when we have your wife in our grasp." Idria turned and bolted back through the portal.

Dellia sprinted after.

Jon shouted, "Dellia, no!"

She looked at him, and for a split second, she hesitated.

Beyond the shimmering curtain, two people appeared in gray robes with violet trim. One on either side of Idria, they grabbed her arms and held on.

Dellia turned back to the portal and leaped, but in the delay it had become unstable, and she only passed through a colored mist drifting on the wind. She sprang to her feet and whirled around with a look of intense frustration. "Why did you stop me?"

Anger consumed Jon at the sheer negligence of what she had just attempted. "She threatens to take you away, and you decide to help her by following her alone to who knows where?"

Dellia's face turned red with anger. "It was my choice."

Jon noticed that all eyes were now on them. "Really? Your choice? Then your choice would be completely irresponsible. What happens when she comes back and makes me choose between you and my duty to the three realms?"

She seemed to grow even more irate. "Your duty? Since when have you been serious in your desire to serve the three realms? The demon was right. You never believed you were a leader, so stop throwing around words like 'duty' when you have no idea what they really mean."

Unwilling to engage in more pointless insults, Jon whirled around and marched away. He'd realized it was over when Dellia decided to undo his coming to this world. For a brief time, on the way back from Kanlu, he had wondered about asking her for help in a plan to thwart the darkness. He knew it was a bad idea, but if this exchange had made one thing crystal clear, it was that Dellia's presence would only make the impossible so much harder.

He had spent every minute of the return trip trying to figure out how to redeem himself. How to remove the shame he had brought to the woman he loved. That was still his goal. But the deaths here had given him a new purpose, even as they crystallized his plan. He knew now, beyond all doubt, that he had to act. If it was within his power to protect these people, he had to try. He had to put an end to the darkness, but if he was to succeed, he would have to do it alone. There was no way he could do it with Dellia harping on how wrong he was about every move he made.

Jon charged back to their tent. In his pack, he found the pen and inkwell he'd brought along for jotting down thoughts as he studied Kayleen's notes. He took a sheet of paper and scrawled out, "Goodbye, Dellia."

The reflex not to act on impulse brought him to a stop. He drew a calming breath and recalled Aylun's words at Sirra's home. They were just as true now as they had been then. This wasn't about what had happened. It was about how he wanted to leave things with Dellia.

He crumpled up the sheet and tossed it aside. Then he grabbed a fresh one and sat for a while, calming himself, as he considered with care what he would write in his farewell note to his wife.

Dellia's anger and frustration seethed as she watched Jon walk away. Then it hit her. What was she doing? She was frustrated with herself and upset at the situation with these Mirhal, and she was terrified for Jon, but she wasn't actually angry with him. So why was she yelling at him? She had wronged him so badly, and here she was, venting her fear and frustration on him again.

Then her mother caught her eye, marching toward Dellia with that grim look she had when she was upset with her. Usually, it was her mother's disappointment she hated the most, but things were too messed up with Jon now for her to even care.

Part of her frustration was over Jon keeping her in the dark about what he intended to do, and it was imperative she find out. Except now, her angry outburst had made a difficult situation impossible. Then she remembered Garris. He was her best hope. Perhaps he could find out what Jon might be planning and even convince him not to do anything dangerous.

She tore her eyes from her mother's approach and looked over to where Garris had been standing, then she scanned the camp and found him disappearing into his tent. Dellia took off toward him, but her mother charged across the grass and stopped in front of her, blocking her way.

She glared as she spoke in a quiet voice. "What in Adi's name do you think you're doing?"

Dellia tried to step around her. "My job."

Sirra dodged in front of her again, only this time she raised her voice, not hiding her ire at all. "Oh, is it your job to humiliate your husband? You say Jon doesn't understand his duty. What about you? You have a duty to Jon, not just as his wife, but as your leader. From the spectacle you just put on, it's clear you don't have the slightest idea what that means."

"I don't have time for this. I think he's planning something dangerous, and I have to find out what." She began to sidestep her mother again.

An iron grip seized her arm and jerked her to a stop. "Dangerous, like instigating an expedition to undo meeting your husband?"

"'Instigating'?" she repeated. It seemed like a bit too strong a word. Then she recalled it had been she who had sought out Megan and told her everything. Her mom was right. She was the one who had forced the issue and led the expedition to stop her husband from coming to this world.

Her frustration grew, and she became aware of many eyes watching her. She lowered her voice. "Can we not talk about this here? It's private, between Jon and me."

Sirra raised her voice even louder. "Private? Is that why I can ask anyone in this camp, and they'll tell me all about how you left to undo your marriage?"

Dellia stared for a moment in mortification. Everyone was talking about it?

Her mother stepped closer. "Do you have any idea why Saneya refused to let the three of you do a single thing? It's because she sensed how distrustful and afraid you were of what Jon might do."

Dellia froze in shock. "She didn't say that, did she?"

"Yes. A big part of why you've been told to stand down is that she doesn't trust the people you don't trust, and she won't put her faith in a team that can't work together."

Dellia moved even closer and lowered her voice again. "Can you not speak so loudly? People are watching."

"Oh really? How about if I make certain everyone can hear me." Sirra bellowed as if addressing a crowd, making sure every corner of the encampment could hear, "I wish I could go back and undo giving birth to such an unsympathetic, untrusting, sharp-tongued wife as you! I don't want a daughter who can't appreciate her family."

Even those who hadn't already been watching turned their gazes toward her, and Dellia froze in embarrassment. In a whisper, she eked out, "Mom?"

Her mother finally lowered her voice. "Don't 'Mom' me. How does it feel?"

"You don't mean it, do you?"

"Oh really? Does your husband think you meant it?"

"What was I supposed to do? Talus was at risk."

A look of dismay clouded her mother's face. "So you really do have no faith in him?"

"It's not a question of faith."

"It's *exactly* a question of faith." Sirra's grip on her arm tightened, and her gaze could have burned a hole in Dellia's head. "I told you before that Jon is not the leader he needs to be, and that whether he becomes one or not depends on you. You refused to listen. You were so sure you were right. Well, how has your approach worked out for you now? Because of you, is Jon closer to being the leader we need today or further away? Is he fighting against you as well as Saneya and the darkness?"

"He was going to do nothing to stop the end of the protectors."

"So what? What did you do to try to understand him? How did you try to give him the courage to face his decision? How did you convince him that keeping the protectors was the right thing to do? How did you support him?"

Not able to give her mom an answer that would not lead to further public humiliation, Dellia stood mute.

Sirra shook her head. "Listen well, Dellia. You may be right that he should have supported the protectors, although I'm not at all sure you are. But be honest with yourself. What was in your heart—his welfare and his success, or your selfish concerns? Did you tear him down with cruel words or try to build him up so he wasn't afraid to make the right choice? Did you help him or hurt him?"

Dellia remained mute, ashamed to tell her mother what had really happened, because it was so much worse than just a few cruel words.

Sirra's disappointment hung thick in the air as she waved her daughter off. "Go find my son-in-law. The sight of you makes my heart sick. I don't want to be reminded of what I just saw."

Shaken by her mother's words, Dellia headed off toward Garris's tent. Sirra was right. What she had said to Jon was cruel and hurtful. So why was she treating the one she loved this way? Why was she so angry and frustrated? She had spent most of the trip back becoming more and more frantic about what Jon was planning and how dangerous it might be. Why then had she yelled at him? Why had she made things so much worse?

AYLUN

As she neared the entrance to Garris's tent, he burst out of it, nearly colliding with her. He brushed by in a frantic hurry, headed for his horse. Panic struck as she realized he was leaving. If Garris left, so would her last chance to find out what Jon was up to and stop him.

Garris held himself in check as his anger demanded he bash the hideous grin off of Idria's face. He peered at the grotesque thing in her hand. It was like a rotted, disembodied organ, and even though it sat motionless now, it had pulsed when she held it out. A voice inside told him to kill her now and take the thing while he had the element of surprise, but he couldn't. Jon had told him to stand down, and he was right. Venting his frustration on her might be satisfying, but that thing in her hand had vanquished a demon. It was far too dangerous.

Idria tore her eyes from Jon, spun, and bolted through the portal behind her. Impatience nagged at Garris, but he kept his feet planted as Dellia took off after her.

Perpetual worry had driven him back to the camp as fast as he could ride. Rillen seemed as anxious to return as he was, and they made excellent time, only to come upon this unholy mess. He couldn't very well leave brave men and women to die while he ran off and talked to Kayleen. And he couldn't stand back while the Bahkaana shouted lie after lie. Then came Idria. When it rains, it pours.

Two people jumped into view on the other side of the portal. They would have been nearly invisible in their gray robes if not for the violet trim outlining their movements. They each grabbed one of Idria's arms and held on as the water-like portal turned to mist.

As Dellia leaped, it disappeared and so did any threat from Idria. Without pausing for a beat, Garris whirled around and raced across the well-trodden grass to his tent. The flap slapped open as he flew inside. The Window of Rhina sat near the top of his pack, so he yanked out the smooth metal rod, which was about the length of a forearm. He slapped it down on top of the worn canvas of his pack, and with a soft breath, exhaled on the smooth metal surface. The breath seemed to be drawn into the length of metal, then released again.

He sat on the grass before it and drummed his fingers as the mist grew and formed and thickened above the bar. Soon, it became a shimmering curtain with the inside of Kayleen's chambers reflected on its surface.

No sooner had the image taken form than Kayleen appeared, seeming as disconcerted as he was. "Where have you been? I've been trying to reach you for four days." She had an uncanny ability to remain calm in the most catastrophic of circumstances. That she was already in this overwrought state was not a good sign.

He hurried to answer her question. "We found the man who sabotaged the lighthouses. Unfortunately, the ones that sent him got to him first, and he's dead. Before he died, he told us what he'd overheard from them. A woman named Ruahn claimed they could stop the darkness, but they plan to hold off until the council falls."

Kayleen froze, staring at him, yet he read far less skepticism in her face than expected. Had she not understood?

Garris forced the words out as fast as he could. "Did you hear me? They plan to topple the council."

She leaned closer, her breaths seeming to come faster. "That's what I've been afraid of. I'm hearing news from multiple places, including my three miscreants. It seems the rumors about Jon are being taken seriously by some in the military. There's a lot of discontent. I'm afraid if this keeps up, we're headed for a coup."

He pounded his fist against the ground. "Then get out of there, now."

She gave a rapid shake of her head. "No. I can't. Every revolution throughout history has ended with the death of old leadership and its supporters. That's you, Dellia, Jon, my uncle Edan, your mother, Eejha. We have to stop it, but they've been planning this for over seventy years. I think it's a group of people who can see the future. How do we stop them? How do we stop people who know what we're going to do?"

"That's it! No more messing around. I'm coming to get you."

Her reaction seemed akin to mild panic. "No. I think they've been trying to kill you for fifteen years because they foresaw that you would one day help Jon. They'll anticipate you coming here to help me. They'll kill you. You have to stay. You have to do something to end the threat of the darkness. If you don't, it won't matter whether you come home or not. We'll all be dead. We'll be hunted down and executed."

"All I'm hearing from you is a stinking pile of guesses. You're in danger. That's not a guess. I'm coming to get you."

Her voice became commanding. "No. That's an order. Stay and help Jon." She leaned closer. "Didn't you hear me?" An indistinct figure flashed through the door behind Kayleen as she enunciated with care. "You have to end the threat of the Dead of—"

A thud came from just out of view. Kayleen's eyes rolled back in her head, and she fell forward. Her blond hair hit the watery curtain above the bar, and it disintegrated, leaving colored droplets falling onto his pack, only to disappear.

Garris flew to his feet and spun around.

Rillen was standing in the doorway watching him. She stepped forward. "Don't worry, it might—"

Garris grunted. There was no time for this. He shoved her aside and flew through the tent flap, almost colliding with Dellia as she passed. His feet thudded against the grass as he stormed around the tent, headed for Kyri. If he rode hard, he might reach Shirdon in a little less than two days. His anxiety soared. That was way too long. Anything could happen to her in the meantime.

He flinched as Dellia called out from right behind him. "What are you doing?" She sounded frantic.

He whirled around. "Kayleen is in trouble."

She pointed to the chasm. "What about the darkness?"

Rillen strutted up to her side, gawking like a spectator at a flogging.

He kept his focus on Dellia. "I want to help, I do, but this is Kayleen."

She grabbed his arm and pointed again to the darkness. "What about Talus?"

He wrenched himself free. "What about them?"

Her pleading contained an unusual note of urgency. "I understand you want to protect Kayleen, and I do too. But if this thing gets through, it won't stop at Talus. The entire three realms will be at risk."

Garris straightened. "And what have the three realms ever done for me? They threw me out."

"That was a corrupt council, not the people—innocent people, Garris. How can you ignore that?"

"This is Kayleen. I've known her my whole life. Our fathers died in the same battle. We grew up together."

She seemed to become even more frantic and blurted out, "It's Jon. I'm worried about him. I think he's up to something."

He stared. "So what?"

She looked at him with desperation in her eyes. "What if it's incredibly stupid and dangerous, and he needs to be talked out of it?"

He gawked. "So what if he does?"

"He knows you. He trusts you. He'll listen to you."

"You're his *wife*."

"I don't think that will hold much sway with him anymore."

Garris let out an exasperated sigh and spun around. This was idiotic. She had stabbed Jon in the back and tried to get rid of him, and *now* she was worried about him? His boots thudded against the ground as he finished the distance to Kyri.

He put one foot on the stirrup, but Dellia's distraught voice begged him from behind. "Send Rillen. We need you. Jon needs you."

He stopped, but kept his back to her.

She tried again, sounding even more overwrought. "Send Rillen. My mother can open a portal. If we do that, Kayleen will have help at her side in a flash."

Garris wheeled around to face Dellia. "Then have your mother open a portal for *me*."

"No." She shook her head. "You vow to help Jon. I get my mom to send Rillen to help Kayleen. That's the deal. It's not negotiable."

Rillen eyed him with sincerity. "Trust me, I can protect Kayleen."

He hesitated. Having help now would be better than two days from now, so he stepped closer. "I need your word."

Rillen nodded.

He clenched his teeth, then glared at her. "You remember in Kanlu when you broke me out of jail?"

Dellia's eyes widened in surprise, but she kept silent.

"You left a trail of incapacitated bodies."

Rillen gave a quick nod again.

Garris loomed closer, putting on his most menacing manner as he bellowed his demand in her face, "You be just as ruthless to anyone who gets in your way! More ruthless! If anyone tries to harm Kayleen, you rip their guts out. You find her, you rescue her, and you protect her with your life. And if anyone tries to stop you, you tear them limb from limb! Do you understand me?"

Rillen smiled and tilted her head. "Aw, that's so romantic."

Dellia's eyes widened even more. "Rillen!"

She huffed. "Oh, fine. You have my word."

Garris hesitated. How could he leave Kayleen's protection to this flighty young girl? He had worked with her these last few days, and she had proven more than competent, but this was Kayleen. How could he live with himself if something happened to her after he'd left her safety in the hands of a relative stranger?

Then Kayleen's orders came back to him. She had told him, in no uncertain terms, not to come. Her reasoning was sound, and she was counting on him to do his part, to remove the threat of the darkness. Anxiety and frustration pulled him in two different directions until he couldn't take it anymore.

He let out a groan as he relented and motioned to Sirra standing partway across the camp. "Then go," he shouted.

All three took off, headed for her at a near run.

As they approached, Dellia yelled out to her mother, "Kayleen is in trouble. Open a portal to my house. Rillen is going to help her."

It was a good idea. Sirra would remember the place so she could open a portal, and, from there, Rillen could reach Kayleen in less time than it had taken to argue about it.

Without the slightest hesitation, Sirra closed her eyes and stretched out her palm. A mist formed in front of it. They reached her and stopped as the haze continued to grow and deepen.

Rillen looked at Garris with an expression as serious as he'd ever seen on her. "Don't worry. I know a hundred ways to kill a man, and if I have to, I'll use every one of them to protect her."

Relieved at her determination, Garris gave a quiet scoff. "Now who's being romantic?"

Dellia shook her head and muttered, "You guys are just disturbing."

The mist came together into a shimmering curtain, with Dellia's house at the edge of the plateau just beyond. Uncertainty yanked at him again. This was stupid. Kayleen needed him, and he needed to be there. He took a step forward, but Dellia grabbed his arm with an unrelenting grip and jerked him to a stop.

Rillen stepped through.

Sirra lowered her arm, and Rillen took off toward the keep as the mist dissipated.

As the colored droplets drifted off in the breeze, Dellia released his arm. His frustration and anxiety stronger than ever, he turned and stepped up into her face. "You better hope this works!"

He stormed off toward his tent, grinding his teeth. Kayleen was in danger, and he was powerless. The only thing left to him now was to try the Window of Rhina one last time and pray he could get through to her.

Dellia hesitated to follow, and her anxiety grew as she watched Garris march off toward his tent. Her need was urgent, but he was far too upset now to entrust with such a delicate request. It was impossible to envision a frustrated and furious Garris using the subtlety and tact needed to ferret out what Jon was planning and talk some sense into him.

Besides, after all the time wasted arguing with Garris, it was more worrisome that she hadn't seen Jon in a while. Her gaze darted across the camp as a sudden compulsion took hold. She had to find out where he was and what he was doing. Garris could wait. She stopped her random glances and made a methodical scan of the entire encampment, but he was nowhere in sight.

She ran to their tent and plowed through the flap. Jon wasn't inside. As she turned to leave, a sheet of paper caught her eye. It rested on her worn pack, and there was handwriting on it. It only took her a moment to realize it had to be a note, and the only person who would have left that note was Jon.

Her anxiety exploded. She rushed to it and began to read.

I love you, Dellia, and I know you love me, but I worry that this entire scheme Megan talked about is aimed at smearing me. The rumor that I let the Dead of Night loose speaks of the Mirhal's determination to make me into an evil demon. They want the people to hate me so much they'll get rid of me. I know how much your duty means to you, and I know how much it hurt you when your father didn't do his at Githeo. So, now it's my turn to do mine. I intend to try to stop the darkness. Please, I beg you, don't follow me. I don't want you caught up in this. It's the only way to keep my reputation and my actions from bringing you the kind of shame your father did at Githeo.

She turned over the page.

So do me one last favor. Don't give anyone a chance to hurt you because of me. If people say I'm to blame for all of this, tell them you were wrong to marry me. Tell them you never really knew me. Everyone knows you left to undo my coming to this world. They already think we're at odds with one another. So all I'm asking is that you continue to let them think what they will. That means no matter what horrible things they might say about me, don't defend me. No matter how angry it makes you, keep it inside of you. Don't show the slightest concern or sympathy for me, and no matter how hard it might get or how much it hurts to hear what they say, don't let it show.

She dropped the sheet of paper, and it fluttered down to the grass.

Chapter Thirty-One

BACK TO DARKNESS

In need of a weapon that excelled at cutting rather than thrusting, Aylun stopped in Kanlu only long enough to buy a shiny new katana at a local smith. It was arguably one of the finest swords from one of the best smiths in the known world, with a heft and balance that lent it a seductive feel in his hand.

Then, at a breakneck pace, he and Juzhi headed back to the Kinshai Lake spire and used the red stone he'd pilfered from Megan to travel back to the Illis Woods. He pushed westward, riding hard to a small town just west of Egina. There, he found a stable that sold assorted equestrian equipment. He purchased a long strip of goatskin leather and a pair of hefty, barbed hooks, which he tied to the end. The whole contraption he wound around his waist as a sash.

After a bit of haggling, he doled out a modest sum for stabling Juzhi and an excessive amount for an escort to the mountains who would return his steed to the stable. He got a paltry few hours of sleep, then met with his leathery-skinned and grizzled guide at dawn. With precious few words between them, they headed to the hazy white mountains. The man was the silent type but reliable, keeping a sharp eye on their surroundings and issuing concise warnings of every threat, no matter how remote.

As the morning wore on, the vast carpet of green before them grew narrow, and the mountains towered high above it into the cloud-dotted sky. Along with the soaring peaks came apprehension. Not just about this undertaking, but what could have happened back in that oracle room. Neither were things he could change, so he shoved them to the back of his mind.

Upon arriving at the dark maw in the towering rock wall, Aylun said goodbye to his precious mount and watched as his stalwart guide hurried away with Juzhi. As they disappeared from view, he dove into the cavern with his flamestone seated in a holder on his belt.

His footsteps echoed through the dark as he wound his way along the twisty passage, carrying with him a heightened sense of this mission's importance. Since he continued to exist in this world, he had to assume that, for whatever reason, Megan had failed. Which meant the journal he sought, the one he and Yaolin had once held in their hands, might provide crucial information needed to navigate the current crisis in Talus. Even the chest he and Yaolin had left behind in Wistra's cabin might hold something of use, though the lock seemed unpickable. So, by the warm yellow light of his stone, Aylun drove deeper and deeper into the bowels of the mountain, then worked his way back outward again toward the other side.

After what he estimated to be half a day, he found his way out of the cavern and into the cursed land of death and darkness. As he left the entrance behind, he kept his step light, his breathing shallow, and his awareness focused on every slight sound or movement. Nothing but blackness met his eyes, save for the warm yellow light of his flamestone brightening the dirt just around him. He weaved around rocks and logs and the dried-up remains of old trees, heading farther and farther into the heart of this black void.

The safety of the cave now well behind him, Aylun finally made his way to a landmark he knew, a fixture by which he could navigate: the edge of a cobblestone road. He turned right and tread down it farther, skirting the edge of the mountains, or so he recalled from maps he'd studied.

The road led on and on, as all around him remained wrapped in perfect silence. With no sun, moon, or stars to guide his way, the usual methods of navigation were useless. Instead, he used a network of roads along with the signposts, houses, and other landmarks he passed along the way. Fortunately, four prior trips through the same thick darkness had lent the area a smidgen of familiarity.

After a while, the road curved left, heading away from the mountains and farther into the heart of the darkness. It wasn't long before a warbling met his ears, followed by the click and scrape of claws against stone. Time passed, and more and varied sounds gathered outside the paltry range of his light. The only way to gauge distance was by sound and echo since his eyes couldn't see far in this dark cloud that seemed to swallow the light of his flamestone.

A low rumble like the rasping growl of a massive cat neared, so he unwound his new leather sash with the hefty hooks at the end. Then he began whipping it in a circle over his head, the leather whistling through the air.

The noise drew the creature in with a skittering that raced toward him from the left. His best hope for survival was to make sure not a single creature that came near escaped and brought reinforcements. So, he let go, and the barbed metal flew toward the sound. The hook sank into something, and it let loose with a pitiful yowl.

He held tight and spun, and the leather strip wound around his waist, reeling in whatever abomination he had snagged. His feet slid from the pull, and he yanked out his katana.

A dark shape writhed and kicked as it hit the light, and it let out a grating screech that sounded like intense pain.

He spun the katana around him and slashed at what appeared to be a neck, just below the source of the screech. The blade hit something heavy. Fetid blood spattered, and the sound and furious movement came to a sudden halt, followed by an all-consuming blaze and sparkling waterfall of glowing cinders.

Then, the thing was gone. Not even the tiniest piece remained as Aylun's hook fell to the ground with a clank. The disturbance drew in two more creatures. One he reeled in like the first, and the other he caught escaping and brought its wretched existence to an end.

So the rest of his day went as he followed the reverse of the path he had treaded only a few weeks earlier. Darkness reigned as all manner of chittering, hissing, howls, pattering, scraping, scratching, and myriad other noises appeared and disappeared around him. They issued from in front, behind, and from every side. Any that came close, he snagged or killed by surprise. The resulting commotion almost always drew in more creatures, ending in a flurry of death, flame, and spark.

With no ability to tell time, he continued until the sounds grew thick, the heightened alertness frayed his nerves, and he feared his flamestone would give out. Only then did he stop at the next cabin he found, thankful that he had made good progress with only a few minor injuries.

After hauling in several armloads of firewood from a well-desiccated pile on the side of the home, he closed the shutters and doors and shut himself in. Unnerving sounds gathered in the darkness beyond the meager four walls, with skittering, clacking, and thudding. He was surrounded, and it was only a matter of time before they found him and got in.

He built a small, crackling fire, and when its flame masked the light of his flamestone, he found an area of the floor that had caved in, crumbled away by age and dryness. With care to remain as quiet as possible, he pulled away small pieces to enlarge the opening and slid through into the crawl space below the floorboards.

Lit by the glow of his flamestone, dark shapes swirled at the edges of the home. An open area lay along the back wall, so he pulled himself along on his stomach until he reached it. Without a sound, Aylun slipped out his katana and pulled himself up along the wall. With light, silent steps, he crept around to where the shapes were gathered.

Then he leaped into the center of the crowd. Dark shadows swirled around him, sparkling embers scattered, and flaming bodies lit the darkness as he kicked, slashed, punched, and stabbed in an adrenaline-fueled flurry. As he cleared the last few, one of them raced away. He chased after, sprinting through a forest of long-dead trees. As he gained on it, he swung the hook out to grab the creature. It sank in, eliciting a sharp cry, and he hauled the slick, black blob over a branch and cut it in two while it dangled there, screeching and writhing.

Then, with quiet steps, he returned to the house, put his flame-stone in the fire, and spread out a blanket as a bed. All was peaceful. All was quiet, except for the pop and crackle of the fire. Sitting by its warmth, he bathed in gratitude at having survived the first day … or something approximating a day. He had remained unnoticed by any still-living beast and made it through quite a few encounters unharmed. But this was the easy part.

Experience told him the closer he got to his goal, the more frequent and deadlier the encounters would become. Along with them would come a greater likelihood he would get noticed and overwhelmed. As time went on, it would only become more critical to stay alert, and alertness required sleep.

So, he laid his head down and let a restless few hours of sleep take him. And as the last bits of consciousness gave way to slumber, a sense of accomplishment and peace came over him. He had brought himself one day closer to protecting that which he valued the most in the world, and it made him feel just a bit closer to her, to Megan.

Dellia continued the stare into space long after the paper hit the grass. Every word Jon had written was like a mirror of the things she had said to him, but twisted around in ways she could never have imagined. She'd never asked him to commit suicide to protect her honor, yet she could see how he had gotten that out of what she'd said about her father. More than that, everyone appeared to know she had tried to undo ever having met him, so what he described might work. If she did the ridiculous things he suggested, the public perception of him would no longer affect her. It was logical, no matter how stupid it was.

For a moment, she stood, stunned that her actions had driven him down a path of such incredible recklessness. Then it dawned on her how determined he sounded in his note. He had given up on her. He had given up on life, and she might not be able to talk him out of it. The idea of him dying because of her words and deeds clawed at her insides.

Seized by a desperate need to get to him, Dellia flew out of the tent and began running up and down the rows of brown canvas. She raced up to every soldier she spotted and asked if they'd seen any sign of Jon. A dozen or more passed before she stopped at a woman tending a fire with several firestones in it. At her hysterical questioning, the woman blurted out that Jon had come to her, taken a pack full of stones, and marched off toward the lighthouse.

Shocked that he was actually going to do what he said, Dellia dashed across the long stretch of plains to the lighthouse. Blinded by the light through the open entrance, she squinted as she flew up to one of the guards posted there and asked if he'd seen Jon.

The guard's description of his determined expression and rigid gait made her anxiety explode. Then he volunteered that he'd seen him a while ago, and he figured Jon would be most of the way to the chasm by now.

Her heart sinking with each stride, Dellia tore off, sprinting toward the warm yellow beam from the lighthouse and the darkness beyond. An eternity passed, accompanied only by the thumping of her own footsteps and the sound of her labored breath. Her heart pounded, and her body grew weary, and still, she pushed on until the wall of light towered high above her and the dark nothingness beyond stretched up to blot out the sky.

Then she spotted Jon, moving at a rapid pace. She stormed up to him, her breath heaving as she walked briskly at his side.

He glanced over and startled, but soon recovered and began to ignore her.

When her breathing had grown less frantic, she glared at him. "So you're running away again. You promised we wouldn't do that anymore. Do promises mean nothing to you?"

Jon never slowed, but he winced and closed his eyes as if her words had caused a physical wound. Then he sped up, shortening the time she had to talk him out of it.

Alarmed at his reaction, Dellia hustled up alongside him again. "So that's it? One little bump in the road, and you flee like a scared child?"

He threw her a hurt glance, and as he faced forward again, he scoffed. " 'Little bump'?"

She stared for a moment as they both consumed the precious few steps between them and the dark cloud. It towered there beyond the light at the chasm entrance, threatening to swallow Jon if she couldn't talk some sense into him. This wouldn't do.

Dellia grabbed his arm and jerked him to a stop. "Don't do that. Don't hide away what you're thinking from me. I can tell you're hurt, so stop running and talk to me."

Unable to avoid her any longer, Jon turned to face her. Then came his voice, flat and matter of fact. "How can you stand there now so angry at me for running away, when a couple of days ago you were ready to throw me out of your life?"

She stared. "That's so unfair."

"Really? Do you even remember what you said when you asked me to marry you?" He shook his head. "You told me it was forever. You made me believe we would never be apart. You vowed to work it out with me, no matter what. But it was a lie. A few weeks later, you decided on your own to undo your ever having met me."

Her panic and anger began to crack, and she fought back the tears threatening to come to her eyes. "The fate of every soul in the three realms was at stake. You, me, Garris, Kayleen—we could all die. What was I supposed to do? What would you have done?"

With the mountainside rising behind him, Jon gazed at her with a soft and faraway expression, and his voice came out quiet and sad. "I'm selfish, Dellia. I would have done anything. I was ready to move heaven and earth, to take on the darkness and more, to defeat every single demon, every horror on this world, for the chance to be with you."

She faltered, shocked at the strength and sincerity in his few simple words and how much it matched the conviction she saw in his heart. "Do you think it was easy for me to see you disappear? Do you know how much it hurt?" She shook her head. "The only way I could bear it was to tell myself that when it was done, I'd never know you existed." She motioned to the dark, billowing wall filling their entire view. "This is so much worse. How do you think I could live through each day knowing I killed my one true love?" She began to choke up and stomped her foot. "How could you want to do that to me?"

Jon lowered his head, and his voice remained soft and solemn as he stared at the plush green carpet below. "It wasn't me who did this to you. It was you who gave up on me. And I don't blame you. I understand why, I do, but it still really hurts, you know?"

"What do you mean? What hurts?"

"To know I'm not the most important thing in your life."

Stunned, Dellia stared. "What? How can you say that?"

"I was willing to march into the fires of hell if you were by my side, and it just really hurts, you know, to realize I'll never be as important as your job and your duty."

"Don't say that."

"I wish I could be noble and brave, like you. I wish I had the heart to give you up for the three realms, but it's like you said, I'm selfish and weak and a coward."

Dellia stood aghast. She wanted to deny it, to say she never said he was selfish or weak or a coward, but her memory argued otherwise. She realized with profound sadness that she'd been saying it over and over for days.

Half in a daze, she gazed into his anguished eyes. "Oh, Adi. Is that how I make you feel?"

"No, it's reality. I'm so far below you, Dellia. Everything I come near I screw up. I get people killed. Your cousin Brita died protecting me. I held her dying body in my arms. I'm not the person you deserve. I'm not a person anyone deserves."

"That's not true."

810

"You said it yourself. I'm insecure and afraid. Just look around you." Jon thrust his arm out, pointing back toward the encampment. "Those were your people, lying dead on the ground. I'm supposed to be their leader, but I did nothing to stop this, not a single thing. Their blood is on my hands." He shook his head. "I'm nothing more than a scared child pretending to be something I'm not. I'm a menace to every life in the three realms."

"I didn't mean it like that."

"It doesn't matter what you meant. It's true."

Jon looked up at her, tears running down his cheeks. "I love you, Dellia, and there is nothing I'd like more than to pretend this whole mess didn't exit and go live happily with you. But I can't, because it's too late. I've already brought you too much shame and disappointment. I didn't fight for the protectors. I didn't defend your people. I didn't preserve what was important to you. I've driven you away, and I'll do it again and again and again. So all I can do now is try to help you do your duty, and that means going into that"—he pointed to the dark void—"and trying to stop it."

Dellia stared at him in disbelief. "Without me?"

Jon looked at her with a hurt expression. "Your being there … It just reminds me of how much of a mess I've made of things. It reminds me of what I could have had and how much I've let you down." He lowered his head. "It's too hard."

Jon turned away and began to walk toward the darkness again as Dellia stood in shock. So many of the things he'd said were words that had come from her own mouth, but it wasn't at all what she really thought of him. Most of the time, it was her own fear and frustration talking.

Each time she lashed out at him, she sensed the hurt in his heart grow, and his fear heighten. Every time she made him more hurt and afraid, it fueled her own fear and anxiety, so she lashed out more and more. It became a vicious cycle that pushed Jon further and further away and made her even more frantic. And now he feared being with her because she would make him feel like an even bigger failure. All she could do was stand aside while he went off to kill himself.

Her tears began to flow. "No, please. I don't want this. I don't want it. I want to take it all back. Please don't leave me."

At Dellia's pleading, Jon spun around to face her. The light from the lighthouse made his gentle face glow and the look of sympathy in his eyes soft.

Dellia stared at him with the dark cloud filling the view behind him, and her panic welled. "This is my fault. You were right. My mom was right. I should have believed in you."

Jon took a step toward her. "Since when have I given you even the slightest reason to believe in me?"

"No, no. I should have believed in you even when you gave me no reason to, even when you didn't believe in yourself. Instead, I chose fear over faith. I chose anger over understanding. I haven't been a good wife. I don't know how to do this. It's so much harder than I thought."

He began to stride across the plush grass toward her.

She placed her hands together in front of her, any semblance of pride vanishing as she pleaded, "Jon, don't do this. I'm begging you. Come back with me. We can talk about thi—"

He wrapped his arms around her and held her tight. "You are everything to me, Dellia, more important than life itself, but we're way beyond the point where talking is going to fix things."

"No. No. Just come back with me. Be my husband. The one who was ready to slay every demon on Thera for me, the one who took on the entire three realms to be with me."

Jon pulled back, and dismay filled his voice. "That person never existed. It was a fantasy, a dream. It wasn't really me. The real me only ever let you down and brought you humiliation. The real me is the one who drove you away. The real me is the one who got your cousin killed and got you mixed up in all of this."

Dellia shook her head. "No, you're wrong. I was there in Kanlu. I saw you defeat an entire army of the dead. I saw you save Mundus from a Blood Wolf attack. I was there at the top of the lighthouse when the darkness was coming, and you found a way out." She put a hand on his chest. "This isn't you talking. It's me. It's my fear. Ever since you became council leader and talked about stopping an invasion, I've been terrified. So every time I got frustrated, I took it out on you. Every time you showed weakness, I got angry because I know that isn't you. I let my fear undermine my faith in you."

"Don't have faith in me. That's how you got dragged into this whole mess."

"No. Come back with me. Be the man who gave up his world for me. Whatever you decide, whatever you must do, I will believe in you. I will have faith in you. All I ask is that you give me one more chance to stand by your side."

"I wasn't running away. I never wanted to be away from you, not even for a second, but this is the only way to make this right, the only way to bring some honor to you."

She shook her head. "Can't you see, I don't care about my honor. I care about you."

"I wish I could believe you. I really wish I could, but even if I did, it wouldn't change the fact the darkness is out there, and I have to do something to try to stop it."

"Then come back with me. Face the people who came here to fight this thing with you, and tell them what's in your heart. Let them know what you intend to do. You owe them that. Afterward, do what you must, but don't run away. Face it head-on, and be the person I know you are. All I ask is that you let *me* decide where I'm willing to follow you."

Jon stood frozen, and she sensed his indecision, pulling him in two different directions. For what seemed like an eternity, he studied her with forlorn eyes that hurt her soul. "Do you really mean it? You're not just saying all this because you're scared. You really mean everything you just said?"

Dellia wrapped her arms around him, pulled him close, and whispered, "With all my heart."

They stayed that way for a moment, Jon's reluctance beginning to wane and Dellia not wanting to let him go for fear that he would turn away. Then he stepped back and gazed into her eyes. "After everything that's happened, I don't see how we can just go back to the way we were."

"We can't." She smiled at him. "But maybe, if we're both willing to try, we can become something better."

At her gentle words of encouragement, his hesitancy drifted away, and he nodded. "Okay, okay."

"Really?"

Jon smiled back. "Yeah." He turned and took her hand. Then they lowered their heads against the brilliant beam from the lighthouse and headed back toward the encampment. Now, as they strolled side by side, a sense of both relief and dread began to fill her. They had reached a better understanding, and the sense of relief at Jon still being by her side was profound, yet she hadn't put a stop to his suicidal plan to enter the Dead of Night. Still, she had vowed to stand by him, and as frightening as the prospect was, it was also beautiful, because, for the first time since they'd met, she felt like they were acting together as a team.

As she struggled toward consciousness, Kayleen became aware of a sharp pain boring through the back of her skull. Still in a groggy haze, she tried to reach up and rub the spot, but her arms wouldn't move, and her shoulders ached. Voices, at first mere random sounds drifting on the air, began to organize themselves in her mind.

A man spoke from her right. "We could lay her out on the bed and have some fun first."

Fear ignited as she recognized the sound of her own feet dragging across the marble floor. Her arms wouldn't move because two men had ahold of them and were hauling her by her armpits. Then came another voice on the left. "Knock it off, and help me get her over the table."

Her panic washed away the grogginess, and she recognized the swirled-marble floor. This was her own room.

The first man spoke again. "We could take the necklace. It looks valuable."

Then the man from her left: "No. Absolutely not. She always wears it. This has to look like suicide, not a robbery."

She tried to lift her head, and the pain sharpened, shooting down her neck. The grip on her arms tightened. She brought her head up enough to spy her window ahead, and in an instant, the reality of her situation hit home and panic took over.

She was being dragged by her arms toward her table and the open window beyond. Images of Ahmet and Chiyun's bodies flashed in her mind. She saw her own body crashing to the rocks below, then lying in a mangled, bloody heap. What if she didn't die right away? What if she lay there, a mass of shattered bones and ruptured flesh?

Out of control, she began to thrash and yell, but one of the two men cranked her right arm behind her back with a stabbing pain. He shoved it farther up her back, lighting her elbow on fire and making it seem as if her shoulder would pop out of its socket at any moment.

The one on the right grumbled, "What about the table?"

"I already said, throw her over it. We'll move it later."

They heaved.

Her chest flew across the table's smooth surface, and her head banged against the edge of the window opening as it went partway through. The world began to swim. Her vision turned dark, and the grasp on her left arm loosened as they thrust her farther out over the table.

She wrenched her hand free and grabbed ahold of the man's clothes, then pulled herself back in. He yanked himself away, and her hand flew to the window frame. Her head slid back out the window. With one arm still behind her back, her free hand thrashed, trying to get some kind of grip on the smooth marble opening.

The man grabbed one of her legs and shoved.

Her entire chest drove through the opening, and she shrieked as the mountainside and cliffs below came into view.

The grip on her arm disappeared, and the man clamped down on her other leg.

Both her hands now free, she scratched and clawed at the opening. Her fingernails scraped against the unforgiving marble, trying to hold back the inevitable.

The man on the right bellowed, "On three. One ... two ..."

A thunk came from either side that sounded like heads banging against the wall. The grip on her legs released, and the sound of bodies hitting the ground came from the left and right as she began to plummet out the window.

A hand grabbed her ankle and tugged, and she was all but dangling over the jagged rocks far below. A woman's grunt met her ears as she slid farther down. Then came Rillen's voice. "Hang on. I can't get a good grip from across this table."

Kayleen's body slid farther down with a jolt as all her weight fell over the edge, and she was hanging by the grip on her ankle. Little by little, the fingers began to slip.

Footsteps raced across the floor, then two large hands grabbed her feet and yanked her up and in.

The force pulling her ankles inward caused her body to swing out. Then, like a pendulum, it swung back again, and her forehead smacked against the outside wall. The cliffs and trees below disappeared into darkness, and the world spun. One of the big hands regripped her leg, and her body jolted upward. Her chin hit the unyielding window frame as powerful arms dragged her through the opening. She slid across the smooth table and crumpled down onto the floor.

Dazed and panting, she lay there as Rillen's face stared into hers. The woman reached up with catlike movements and slipped the abalone hairpin out of her hair. Her blond locks fell around her shoulders, and her head remained unmoving as her gaze darted in the direction of the man behind her, then back again. She tightened her grip, and her shoulders tensed as she raised the sharp, pointed end in front of her chest.

Kayleen looked where Rillen had glanced, and Grekor came into focus, standing right behind her.

The protector sprang to her feet and spun around, raising the hairpin to stab him in the throat. Grekor brought up his arm to block her, but Rillen merely dropped the hairpin to her other hand near his groin.

Kayleen shouted, "Rillen, stop!"

Rillen froze.

Kayleen motioned to Grekor. "He's with me."

Rillen relaxed and mumbled, "I was just going to immobilize him."

Grekor, who seemed unfazed by the affair, put his arm down. "Is she okay?"

Rillen squatted again and peered at Kayleen's hair.

A warm trickle ran down Kayleen's cheek, and she reached up and brushed it away. The back of her hand came away red, and it hurt like she'd been hit with a hammer.

Rillen continued to scrutinize her skull. "These wounds look nasty. Are you okay?"

Kayleen managed to nod, but pain seared the back of her skull. Her vision blurred again, and her voice came out slurred. "I'm just a little woozy."

The protector set a hand on Kayleen's head and peered into her eyes, examining them. "Garris sent me."

Grekor looked down at the young protector. "You looked like you needed help. Good thing Garris had us keep an eye on her."

Kayleen was only somewhat aware of Rillen looking up at Grekor's face. "You did well."

The soldier glanced at the two unconscious bodies on either side. "You want me to throw them out the window?"

Her mind still mired in pain and panic, Kayleen only stared.

Rillen didn't respond, so Grekor nodded and strolled over to one of the bodies, picked it up, and began to ferry it to the open window.

Kayleen snapped out of her daze. "Wait."

The burly fellow halted and stared at her, innocent surprise on his face as he cradled the man in his arms.

Kayleen motioned. "Put him down. We need to think this through."

She turned her attention to Rillen. "You were just going to sit there while he threw people out the window?"

She shrugged. "It's not my call. Besides, it's exactly what they were going to do to you."

Grekor nodded. "Garris told us to protect you. If we kill these two—"

"They'll just send more." Kayleen shook her head.

Rillen stood, crossed her arms, and scanned the room. "Okay. I'll handle this. We need to stash these two thugs here." She motioned to the remaining body. "If they go missing, whoever sent them will be left wondering what happened. It will take time for them to sort it out." She looked up at Grekor. "You, help ..."

"Grekor." Kayleen motioned to the big warrior. "His name is Grekor."

Rillen nodded. "Okay, handsome, you help me with the bodies, okay?"

A huge grin broke out on the bulky soldier's face. "Sure thing."

"I'll tie them up, and you help me put them where no one will ever find them." Rillen sent a becoming smile at him. "Then what do you say you and I find a place to stash Kayleen where nobody can find her? Somewhere she can recover."

Grekor bowed. "Yes ma'am, Rillen, ma'am."

Kayleen spoke up. "Garris and I used to break into this place all the time. I know a couple spots that no one else knows about."

Rillen grinned. "Perfect." She strolled over to the man Grekor had just set down and began to remove the leather strip that served as his belt.

Now feeling more alert, Kayleen used the time to explain. "There are passages between all the rooms of the keep to let air flow through. Most are hidden behind furniture or in corners. Like this dresser here." She pointed to a simple set of drawers standing against the wall. "Behind it is a small passage."

Rillen nodded as she proceeded to tie the man's hands together with the belt.

Kayleen pulled herself up to sit more upright. "Farther in, there are large storage rooms … massive caverns really, with food and supplies and a catch basin for water. There are many larger passages in and out of them. Some lead down to other caves, and some of those lead to more passages that go down to the base of the mountain."

Grekor hoisted the body over his shoulder and stood watching.

Rillen pulled her sunstone out of her pocket. "Where can we find one of these storage caves?"

Kayleen pointed. "One is just down this corridor. My room is a bit isolated. It's the last room on the hall and a ways from the room before it."

Grekor butted in. "Which makes it a pretty good place for murder."

Kayleen ignored him. "If you keep going down the hall past where the torches stop, it leads down to one of the storage areas."

"Does that storage area have passages that lead to one of those caves you mentioned?"

Kayleen nodded.

"Does anyone ever go to that storage area?"

"Once a day, in the morning, to patrol it and make sure the food and supplies are intact."

"Perfect." Rillen looked at the door, then back at Kayleen. "New plan. How about we all go together to that storage areas? Grekor will carry that fellow"—she pointed to the limp body dangling from his shoulder—"and I'll scout out the path and help you along. He and I can come back for the second body, then from there, we can stash these guys and get you down to one of those caves deeper in."

819

Kayleen set a hand on Rillen's steady but small shoulder. "Solid plan. Now I see why we have protectors."

As Rillen helped her up, she peered into Kayleen's face. "Should we find a dead body that looks like you and throw it out the window?"

Kayleen started as she tried to steady herself on her feet. "You would desecrate the body of someone's loved one like that?"

Rillen shrugged, then slipped her arm under Kayleen's and around her back to hold her up. "It might make the people who are after you think you're dead and give up."

"The Mirhal. Yeah, it might." Kayleen studied Rillen's face. It showed far less reaction to the mention of a mythological group of oracles than she expected. She noted this and continued to explain. "It will also make the council, the military, and the people think I'm dead. And a dead leader is almost certain to throw any government into chaos."

Rillen helped her to the door and leaned her against the wall, so she could poke her head out and peer in each direction. As she pulled her head back in and slid her arm around Kayleen to lend her support, she lowered her voice. "Then what's the plan? If you go missing, wouldn't it have a similar effect?"

Her mind seeming clearer, Kayleen considered the question as they ventured into the hallway. She was right, but the bigger concern right now was what the Mirhal would do. The sound of their shuffling feet remained muted as they hurried down past the last torch. Rillen's sunstone lit the way through the dark hall as they kept going around and down.

Confirmation of her death would cause the Mirhal to move sooner rather than later. Evidence of her survival would cause them to be more cautious and send others to find and kill her. Which reaction was better depended on what she intended to do.

When they were far enough to avoid being heard, Kayleen eyed Rillen. "How about we spread a rumor that there was an attempt on my life, and I've gone into hiding?"

Grekor sent her a peculiar look. "But … that's the truth."

Rillen considered the idea. "And they'll come after you again."

Kayleen smiled. "Yes, but what if we add our own little twist? We add that the story seems fishy because if it's true, why haven't I contacted anyone?"

Rillen's expression said she appreciated the idea. "So, we spread the truth and cast doubt on it at the same time."

"Yes. It will confuse things and leave the Mirhal guessing. Am I in hiding, or am I dead?"

All of them fell silent, digesting the idea. Then the three reached the vast cavern. Rows of chests and crates were stacked all across the floor, and a slight medley of odors hung in the air, with notes of flour, vegetables, dried fruits, and aromatic spices. The temperature remained much cooler down this deep, acting to preserve the cache of supplies.

Grekor tossed the trussed-up brute in a heap on the floor as Rillen set Kayleen down, seating her against the wall. The protector stood and bowed to her. "We'll be right back. Hang on, and we'll get everything settled."

"Bring me a heavy blanket when you return." Kayleen nodded, and Rillen returned the gesture. Then she and Grekor hurried off around the corner, leaving Kayleen alone in a cavern so enormous, the light of Rillen's sunstone disappeared into its vastness.

Darkness descended as their shuffling footsteps disappeared down the hallway. Kayleen leaned her head back against the cool rock wall and closed her eyes. She had survived an assassination attempt, and the person most responsible for her survival was Garris. Even after she ordered him to stay away, he had sent Rillen to stop the killer, and it was he who had demanded that Grekor and his crew keep watch over her.

He had also discovered the Mirhal were behind this—and the idea that this was the plan of a mythical group of oracles fit everything she'd discovered far too well to be untrue. Without the help Garris had sent, she would be lying shattered at the bottom of a cliff.

Without him, the Mirhal's plan would have succeeded, and they would make sure everyone she cared about died too. If they died, Jon would die with them or be driven out of Meerdon, the prophecy would fail, and the invasion he was supposed to stop would kill every living soul.

As she sat in the cool cavern in utter darkness, it all became clear. Even if the Mirhal could see the future, even if they could fore- see what she was going to do, the consequences of failure were too high to entertain thoughts of defeat. She had Rillen and her three miscreants to aid her, and among the five of them and Braye, they had to find a way to stop these Mirhal, once and for all.

Chapter Thirty-Two

SOME OTHER TIME

Megan moved quickly through the caves, where all was cool, dark, and quiet. The path below her reflected the light of her aetherstone, as if many feet had polished it smooth in ages past. That notion triggered another—one that had stuck with her since the oracle room. Whether it was the Mirhal or the Augury or Wistra herself, it seemed as if her and Aylun's lives had ceased to be their own. It was as if someone were looking inside her mind, scrutinizing her every thought and feeling, then using them for their own purposes. They had all become pawns in a war that spanned realms and centuries, a conflict between powerful people in some other place, somewhere, in some other time.

The very idea turned her stomach. Her choices were her own, and she would never relinquish them. She'd experienced an abundance of manipulation and disrespect for other people's decisions in her own family. It was more than enough to convince her she would never let herself become the tool of another person, no matter how well-intentioned they may be. Her life was her own and not anyone else's.

Aylun, too, had suffered enough as a sacrificial chess piece in the Red Queen's game of oracles and prophecies. It was for her now to make sure his life was his own, which made it even more imperative that she reach him, help him, and protect him.

Megan arrived at the cave's exit and halted at the perfect quiet and vast stretch of thick darkness before her. It seemed heavier than that in the cave. Light from her aetherstone seemed not to carry as far, and it was like she was back in her childhood, locked in her father's cramped closet because she had annoyed him. Only this time, she was shutting *herself* in. Who knew what monsters might lurk in this closet?

She had been so confident when she told Jon and Dellia she could defend herself, but now, as she faced the unknown, her certainty melted away. The dark metal and jade ring had become her guide now, so she glanced down and concentrated. The silvery thread darted forward toward the middle of the vast blackness. She hesitated. It was still possible to go back. Aylun would never know she'd run away in fear. Yes, that was it. This was stupid. She should go back.

Megan tried to turn around, but her legs wouldn't obey. It had never been her way to run from things. More than that, Aylun was out there somewhere, all by himself, and she couldn't let him face this place alone, a place that had given him years of crippling anxiety and night terrors. So, she crept out into the infinite darkness, steering by the golden light of her aetherstone and the ethereal thread that showed her the way.

After a short while, she found a dusky cobblestone road, and the wispy silver strand aimed down it to the right. No sound came, beyond that of her own footsteps, as she trod its length for an hour or more. Then a sharp pain struck her ankle. She jerked her leg away and looked down.

A pitch-black snake hissed as it headed for her other leg. Or at least it looked and moved like a snake, but upon closer scrutiny it was more like a slithering absence of anything. She jumped back to avoid it, and her aetherstone tumbled from her hand. It landed on the back of the dark serpent with a thud, and the abhorrent thing exploded in a shower of sparkling light.

Then she spotted it: a sickly black ink creeping up the veins of her leg from the bite. In a panic, she tried to wipe it off, but it lay buried beneath her skin. With inexorable slowness, the dark stain spread out from the veins to engulf the entire area, and her leg began to tingle, then go numb. A horrible dread filled her, and she went stiff as she realized if it reached her heart, it could kill her.

Dark threads began to slither out of the darkness on every side—more snakes, many of them smaller ones. Then a hideous image came to her: what if the first bite paralyzed so the smaller ones could consume her alive. Her stomach convulsed at the image of her laying on the ground, unable to move as they gnawed away chunks of her flesh.

Her gaze flittered all around, searching for something to save her. Yet they kept coming, hissing as they drew closer. She quelled her panic and banished her imaginings. Now was not a time to lose control. As her mind cleared, inspiration struck. She snatched up her aetherstone. If it had killed the snake, maybe it would destroy the poison.

Megan slammed the glowing orb down on top of the largest and darkest vein, and a fierce burning sensation shot out from it, as she stifled a cry. It was imperative she remain quiet. In a second, the burning vanished. So she rolled the stone down the black track on her leg toward the bite. Screams wanted to escape her again from the anguish of a blowtorch searing her skin.

Clenching her teeth, she rolled it all around the pitch-black area. The torture followed its path, like a red-hot coal digging into her skin. Then it eased as the darkness disappeared. Her stone's golden light hit the bite mark with a crippling jolt of agony, and she stifled yet another shriek.

Woozy from the pain, she put out a hand to steady herself. The dark world began to reel and slip away as the slithering threads neared her leg. She fought her way back to lucidity. If she succumbed now, they would reach her, and she would die. She thrust out her palm with the aetherstone resting on it, then used her gift to float it over the slithering lengths of black.

An immense sense of satisfaction came over her as each one disintegrated in a gratifying shower of fire and spark. Megan kept it flying around her in circles, wider and wider, until, at last, not a single sign of them remained.

Shaken, her leg shocked from the pain, and her heart still hammering in her chest, she sat for a while until the need to move compelled her to her feet. She redoubled her pace, paying much closer attention to every bit of movement and sound around her.

Soon, warbling squawks, sharp chittering, and cries that resembled those of a wounded bird arose from far out around her, sending shivers down her spine. Hours passed with her nerves on end and the sounds threatening to close in, but they never did. They remained at the distant periphery, a constant reminder of how deadly this place could be.

No other encounter came, and finally, the ring with the dashed jade line led her to the doorway of a modest cabin constructed of dried-out logs. She slid inside and eased the door closed behind her. The faint odor of burning wood met her nostrils. Then a glow from the fireplace caught her eye, and she raced to it. A few last red embers lay in drifts of white ash. Someone had been here and built a fire, and the only someone she could imagine was Aylun. If he'd stayed here, he must have deemed it safe.

So, exhausted, Megan huddled by the warmth of the embers for a while before finding a small cubby to hunker down in. She curled herself into its comforting recesses, cringing in her self-imposed dark closet. Sounds kept jangling her nerves and sending her heart pounding until, at last, her mind, spent from the long stretch of vigilance and anxiety, could no longer hold back sleep.

As she drifted away, images of Aylun filtered into her dreams. They were in the warmth of their Mundus home, and he smiled as he burst through the door, toting bundles of treasures for breakfast. Their sweet aroma filled the air as he laid them out on the table, and in her half-dreaming state, it came to her. It had never been the warm house or the sumptuous food or even the serene ambiance that made this such a treasured memory, but the man with whom she'd shared them.

It was with no small degree of shell shock that Jon strolled back toward the camp, hand in hand with Dellia. Her comforting refrains still whispered in his mind: that her criticism had just been her fear and frustration talking, that she hadn't meant it, that she would try harder. It had been both heartfelt and touching, and in so many ways it made him feel even less worthy of her.

As they passed the guards at the lighthouse entrance, that sense of unworthiness weighed on him. She had been unabashed in her apology, but he had done little to reassure her. As soon as they were out of earshot of the guards stationed outside the door, he looked over at her walking next to him again. "I'm sorry, Dellia."

She sent him a look of puzzlement and concern.

He halted and let go of her hand as he faced her. "This all started when I refused to save the protectors. I want you to know I realize that, and I want you to know how much I regret it."

She lowered her head. "We both made mistakes."

"No, this was no little mistake. I should have fought for something so close to your heart. You shouldn't even have had to ask. I want you to be able to count on me to protect what's important to you, but I failed."

She nodded and took his hand, leading him back again toward the camp. "It's no secret I think the protectors should be kept. I think they are vital to the safety of the people. But I don't think I was as upset that you didn't want to defend them as I was that you didn't stand behind me. You didn't have my back, and for that, I forgive you."

Jon gazed at her as she strolled across the plains next to him. It was a breathtaking sight—her beautiful face with the line of white-capped mountains stretching out behind it, far into the hazy distance. "Then we're agreed, we keep the protectors?"

She seemed to ponder the question. "No, we're not. I appreciate that you want to keep them to protect me, but now that you say it like that, I don't think whether they are kept or not should depend on me being the wife of the council leader. I want you to consider it carefully, weigh all the consequences, and come to your own decision."

He shrugged. "I have thought about it. On the way to the oracle room, I spent a lot of time trying to figure out where I went wrong, but it was pointless. It was all founded on a faulty assumption. It was based on the belief that my being in charge would lead to disaster."

Dellia seemed startled by the remark. She studied him for a while, and as she did, he couldn't escape the feeling she was leaning on her gift again, trying to see if he was being sincere in what he was saying. "And you don't believe that anymore?"

"No, I don't." He looked over and smiled as he captured her gaze. "What happened in the camp made me realize some things, and when I look at it through new eyes, it seems pretty obvious."

"What's obvious?"

"The answer to whether to disband the protectors. I was just too blinded by fear of making the decision to see it."

"Then what's your answer?"

Jon drew a deep breath. "If this whole lighthouse incident proves one thing, it's the need for the protectors. Erden and Elore shouldn't be at the mercy of Talus to fight this thing. Talus wouldn't like it either if there were a threat like this in Erden, and they had to sit back and do nothing except hope the Erdish people were capable of stopping it from spreading. All three realms need a common defense they can trust to deal with common enemies, and the protectors are a crucial part of that."

"Is that your decision?"

He became silent for a while as he mulled it over yet again, rethinking it. Then a sense of relief washed over him as he reaffirmed his decision. "Yes, fighting to keep the protectors is the right thing to do."

"I'm glad."

"That I'm going to try to save the protectors?"

Dellia stopped and eyed Jon. "No, that you were smart enough to figure out I was right all along." She sent him a coquettish smile.

He shook his head and threw his arm over her shoulder. "I guess I walked right into that one, didn't I?"

AYLUN

As the outlines of the camp grew clearer, Dellia's mood seemed to brighten, yet what began to percolate in his veins was a noxious stew of anxiety, skepticism, and foreboding.

It was hard to escape a lifetime of feeling as if his actions were bound to doom people. The sense of foreboding hounded him, the sense that he had just had a momentary lapse of judgment in agreeing to let Dellia follow him into the Dead of Night. One that would drag her, and everyone else he cared about, into a repeat of his stepsister and that long-ago classroom. Yet, he was committed now. He had told Dellia he would try to act more like a leader, and this is what that decision looked like when he put it into practice.

Even as he was committed, there remained the thorny problem of explaining what he planned to do. He had promised to address the camp and let them know what he intended, but how do you describe a plan of such absurdity without seeming like a deranged madman? Perhaps he *was* a deranged madman for even contemplating it. It was difficult to believe that Dellia would choose, of her own free will, to follow him in such an ill-conceived course of action. Or that if she did it wouldn't result in more chaos and death. Yet he had to try. He had to give her the benefit of the doubt.

As they passed the guards patrolling the edge of the camp, Jon steeled himself. He still wasn't any less afraid, but he had resolved to conquer his fear, and now, he had to convert that resolution into action. So, he walked down the rows of the tents, horses, and piles of ash that had once been campfires.

He stopped at the makeshift table where they had eaten and laughed and talked a few days earlier. The hodgepodge of crates still lay there, so he snatched one up, and Dellia followed as he hauled it back to the front of the camp. He dropped it a couple dozen feet in front of Saneya's spacious tent, and it came to rest with a thud and rattle.

His anxiety at taking this step gripped him, and he glanced at Dellia. "I want you to do something for me."

"Name it."

"What I'm determined to do may very well be the most danger-ous, reckless, and stupid thing I've ever done, by far."

She only nodded.

"So, I want you to think really hard about whether you want to follow me this time. I don't like putting you in this kind of danger."

She seemed about to respond, but before she could, and before he could talk himself out of it, Jon climbed atop the crate and yelled as loudly as he could. "The demon was right."

From his higher perch, it was easy to spot the eyes turning toward him. Heads popped out of tents, and soldiers stopped to watch. Saneya and Prian appeared too, around the side of a tent.

Jon waited until all eyes were on him, then repeated, "The demon was right. I didn't believe I was a real leader, so I never acted like one. I huddled in Shirdon like that thing said, afraid to make decisions, afraid to lead." He gazed down at Dellia next to him. "Dellia has been trying so hard to tell me not to be a coward, not to deny who I am, and I refused to listen. I remained steadfast until she felt she had to take drastic steps to prevent my inaction from hurting her people."

As silent onlookers continued to gather, Jon paused and sent his gaze across the crowd. "For my cowardice, I am sorry. When I became council leader, it was a promise to you to do my best, and I never even tried. For breaking that promise, I am also deeply sorry."

He paused, scanning the faces. "But, as usual, the demon only told half the truth. You see, I believe now, as I always have, that Talus is best governed by the Talesh. You, like all people, deserve to decide your own fate and not to have it dictated for you from afar."

His speech was met with a smattering of approving nods.

He pointed to Saneya, now working her way up to the front of the crowd. "Those you elect to the Ephori are wise beyond my paltry years. They know what's best for your people in a way that none of us in Shirdon ever could, least of all me." Jon left a pause as the nods spread. "But I have come before you now to tell you that the time for me to sit still is over."

830

As the words left his mouth, his chest tightened, and a sudden nausea set in. His whole body rebelled, trying to tell him this was wrong, that it would only lead to more blood on his hands. Yet, he had come to understand it was only his years of guilt and fear talking, so he brought back to mind the image of Brita, lying in his arms, her still-warm body bleeding out into the grass. A splitting pain shot through his head, and he reminded himself he couldn't let more people perish because he did nothing.

Saneya stopped in front of him, seeming perplexed. There was no doubt she sensed his turmoil. So, he focused on her, shoving out all that negativity that Megan had insisted wasn't like him. He locked eyes with her. "I believe the Dead of Night is alive. It acts with purpose, like a living thing, and I believe that, like all living things, it can be killed." He left a pause as he returned his gaze to the crowd, scanning them to meet as many eyes as possible. "I intend to go into it and destroy it."

A man in the crowd shouted out, "Destroy it? How?"

"I'll be honest. I have no idea. All I have is faith that I will find a way." The nods stopped, and shocked expressions appeared, so Jon barged ahead. "As soldiers, you know that every living thing has weak spots, places where one well-aimed blow will kill it. I intend to find a weak spot and exploit it. I intend to kill the Dead of Night."

No sooner had the declaration left his lips than Dellia turned and marched away. He followed her with his eyes for a few seconds as she weaved through the crowd and across the grounds. It seemed as though she had decided not to follow him after all. Relief spread. If he was back to himself alone taking this risk, then he needn't worry about the ones closest to him. This was for the best. As much as he could use her help, he couldn't handle it if she got hurt because he'd dragged her along. It saved him from seeing his hubris harm her.

In the protracted pause, Saneya called out from in front of him, "You agreed to stand down, to cease your meddling in this matter. Are you announcing that you are going back on your word?"

Jon turned his gaze to her as a few hushed comments came from the back. She possessed the same gift as Dellia. No doubt, she sensed his apprehension and was testing him. He needed to show her he meant it, so he kept his focus on her. "See it however you want, but let me ask you this: do you care more about who is in charge, or do you want to see this threat to the lives of our people eliminated?"

Again, all eyes turned to Saneya. "I care that you do not go riling up the darkness. I care that your interference does not make things worse."

Jon returned her verbal jab with a disapproving scowl. He made a point of raising his voice even more. "Worse? Wake up, Saneya. Our people are dying. I held my cousin in my arms as she breathed her last. You're not fighting to win here. You're fighting not to lose ground. Is that your idea of a strategy? Let our people keep dying until the darkness has taken our best, and we fall? My plan is to take the fight to this blight, to make it pay for the lives it has taken."

Muttered comments grew in number and intensity.

Saneya took a step toward Jon. "Moments ago you said we Ephori know what's best for Talus. By acting against the darkness, are you not taking back your own words as soon as you spoke them?"

The crowd grew quiet once more. Saneya was testing him again, but this was an easy test to pass. Jon brought himself up taller. "No. Because this isn't about Talus anymore. The Talesh are more my people than any in this world. What you are doing here is wise and necessary. So I will not hamper you in any way. But it's not enough, and make no mistake, this thing will not stop with you. It will go on to Erden and Elore. As council leader, I must speak for them because they are not here to speak for themselves. I must act for them because they are not here to act. It is they I am here to protect as much as it is Talus."

"And how many of *my* warriors will you take with you on a suicide mission to protect Erden and Elore?"

A rather muscular warrior in the back shouted out, "Brita was my friend. I will go with you to avenge her death!" From the passion in his voice, this man sounded like more than a mere friend.

Jon looked over at him. "No, my friend. I share your loss, and I appreciate the offer more than you know. Your faith in me is greater than I deserve, but Talus needs you here, to hold this line." He turned his gaze to Saneya. "I will not take any of your people. I need to work quickly and draw little attention. So, I don't want your help. I intend to do this alone."

Looks of disbelief spread as the hushed discussions resumed.

Jon startled as a crate thudded against the ground beside him. He looked over as Dellia mounted it and stared out over the crowd. "I must correct my husband. *We* intend to do this alone." She took his hand into her own, and at her gentle touch, the tightness in his chest eased, and his nausea dissipated. "If Jon says he will go into the Dead of Night and destroy it, I believe he will. In this goal, we are of one mind, and I *will not* let him go alone."

In a sudden burst, the comments turned into a persistent rumble of approval.

Jon glanced at her determined face, and his fear that this decision would hurt her somehow seemed distant now.

Garris stepped up to Jon's side and spoke out loud and clear. "Oh no you don't. You talked me into staying here when Kayleen was in danger. Now, you're stuck with me. Besides, this is what she ordered me to do."

Jon leaned closer and whispered to Garris above the mutterings of the crowd. "Aren't you supposed to work for me?"

Garris whispered back, "Sure, why not? If that makes you happy, keep telling yourself that."

"Thanks." Jon suppressed a chuckle. Then uncertainty took hold, and he eyed Garris, unsure whether he was being sardonic or really meant it.

Garris grunted back, then added, "Besides, you need me. I have some clue where to go and how to kill it."

"Really?"

Garris didn't answer. He just glared at Saneya and raised his voice again so all the fighters assembled could hear every word. "Since we were sidelined on your orders, I assume we won't be missed if we go handle this problem for you." He bowed his head.

Perhaps sensing the tide of sentiment going against her, Saneya bowed back. "If you wish, you three may go. But you go alone. Not one of my people will I allow to accompany you."

Sirra stepped up to her daughter's side. "You don't speak for all of us, Saneya. If things go wrong, they'll need a means of escape. No matter how deep or what trouble they encounter, I can open a portal and get them back to safety. I believe in my son-in-law. If anyone can defeat this thing, he can. I'm going with him and my daughter, and I will not be stopped by you or anyone else."

The murmur turned to a rumble of discussion. It appeared the decision of one of the Ephori held a great deal of weight.

Saneya peered at Dellia and raised her voice above the crowd. "A few days ago, you were ready to see your husband gone from this world. Now you trust him?"

Silence fell again as all eyes turned to Dellia.

She kept her head up, but lowered her gaze. "I believed in lies." She looked back up at the crowd. "This rumor you have all heard, that Jon is responsible for this darkness, is an obvious deception." She paused. "We did not let the darkness loose, the sabotage to the lighthouses did that, and Jon put a stop to it. We believe both were part of a plan by the Mirhal to cast doubt on my husband."

A louder murmur spread at the mention of the Mirhal.

Dellia forged ahead. "The same people planted false predictions that said it was a mistake for me to meet Jon and for us to marry." She hung her head. "To my eternal shame, I believed them." She paused as she raised her head and eyed the crowd with a look of fierce determination. "I once told Jon serving him was my duty, but I turned it into a lie when I went against him. He has forgiven me, but I learned something. Lies exist. Treachery exists. The truth is deceptively hard to discern, so it is impossible to know what is best for everyone."

She brought herself up tall and proud. "I choose now to place my trust in the man I know rather than in the rumors and vague predictions that swirl around him. Jon is what is best for this land. So, I say again, with a new understanding of what it means, that my duty is to Jon. My duty is to him because he will do what is best for the people, and my duty is to him because he is the one person who can save us. I urge all of you to do as I have done and trust in Jon."

This time, the roar of discussion was accompanied by almost universal nods of approval

Saneya gave a satisfied sort of smile. "Good. That is what I wanted to hear. Based on your assurances, I will provide all the flamestones and provisions I can spare, and you four may begin as soon as you are rested and able."

She turned to Prian. The commander surveyed the crowd of leather and sweat, now numbering over a hundred, and shooed them away. "What are you all standing around for? You're here to protect Talus. Get back to work."

The response was almost instantaneous, and people drifted away.

Jon stood for a moment, a bit stunned. It was as if he'd fallen into an alternate reality. Saneya hadn't refused to let him go and was, in fact, supplying provisions. Dellia had agreed to go with him, and her support was unconditional. She had even made a public apology. Even Garris and Sirra had signed up for this madness.

Saneya stepped up to the crate that had served as his podium. "You can't be serious. Your plan can't be as simple as to stroll in there and hope you figure out how to stop this thing."

Jon paused. There was no hiding how feeble his plan was, but he had to try. He drew a deep breath and stepped down in front of her. "I have a few ideas. The Dead of Night is not a mindless force. It moves and acts like a living thing. It is made up of many distinct creatures, but they act together with a single purpose. Something must direct that purpose. Whatever that is, it would be protected, like a hive of bees or a colony of ants where the queen is near the center. Whatever controls the Dead of Night would be somewhere near the center of Saranik. So, we go there, to the darkest spot, and kill it."

He waited to see if everyone would buy it. After all, what fool would? Much of what he said was wild speculation, and it would be hard to miss that.

During the ensuing silence, Garris stepped up to Saneya. "The disgraced ex-protector can perhaps give a better answer." Now intrigued, Jon watched as Garris spoke. "Rillen and I caught the man who sabotaged the lighthouses. With his dying breath, he said he regretted it, and he seemed pretty sincere. So, I trust what he said." With a brief pause he met Saneya's gaze. "He claimed a woman named Ruahn sent him. He overheard her say the Dead of Night can be stopped. So, I think Jon is right about that. I couldn't make out every word, but he told me what Ruahn said about her plan to stop it. She said you have to find the heart. If that means the heart of the Dead of Night, it would agree with what Jon just said. She said it's in a temple. We have to find it there and burn it."

Saneya appeared thoughtful for a moment. "There were a lot of temples near the center of Saranik. You can't just wander into every one of them until you find what you're looking for."

Jon peered down at the grass as he pondered the new information. Then he looked back up at Garris. "So, this Ruahn person was planning to go herself to stop it?"

The big warrior seemed flustered and avoided his gaze. "Um, well, she was planning to capture you and send you to do it."

His head came up, and he stared. "Me?"

Garris nodded. "Yeah, that seemed to be the drift."

"How did she plan to capture me with two protectors around?"

Garris brought his gaze to bear on Jon. "They plan to take over the council. It's a pretty safe bet that the rumor about you is a part of their plan."

Thrown by the idea, Jon reeled. If that was the Mirhal's true goal, it explained a lot. Still, it seemed odd to send *him*, of all people. "Okay, but why would I do what they ask?"

Garris shot him an exasperated look. "To save Talus?" When Jon didn't answer, he continued. "Look, let's face it, you're a pushover. I can think of a dozen ways to force you to do what I want."

Jon stared in disbelief. "Really? A pushover?"

Dellia nodded. "Agreed. All they'd have to do is capture me and threaten me, and you'd do whatever they asked."

Flustered, Jon half mumbled. "Oh. Well, that sounds disturbingly plausible." He shivered at the thought. "But what doesn't sound plausible is that they'd just shove me into the chasm and expect me to survive for several days, much less find this temple and kill the heart." He considered the idea for a moment. "It doesn't fit. They're much shrewder than that. It hasn't been their way to leave anything to chance, and expecting me to make it to the center of Saranik on my own is taking a huge risk. They'd have a more surefire way to reach the temple."

The light of sudden revelation crossed Dellia's face. "Spires. The Mirhal seem to like spires."

Jon nodded. "They used them to plant fakes to mislead Megan." He turned his gaze to Saneya. "Was there a spire in Saranik?"

A smug look settled onto her face. "Yes, in the capital city, Carpoli."

"Is it near the center?"

She nodded. "Of course. It's a little closer to the rest of Talus but very near the center."

"Are there spire stones for it?"

Garris scoffed. "Obviously. Who would build a spire without them. But it's unlikely we'll find one."

Saneya considered the question more carefully. "He's right. After the Dead of Night came, the Saranik spire was useless. The spire stones lost all value and disappeared. Even if one was still around, it would be difficult to find."

Garris grumbled, "There's no point in even discussing it. If we had one, it would be great, but we don't, and we don't have time to hunt for a long-lost spire stone. We have to stop the darkness before Ruahn and her people use this whole mess to take down the council."

"So, we're back to walking in through the chasm." Jon glanced at the lighthouse. "Except, now we might know where we're headed: a temple in Carpoli that's near a spire."

Saneya motioned to her tent. "I carry maps. I believe I might have one of Saranik before the fall."

The five of them filed over to Saneya's generous tent and ducked inside. After a period of rummaging, she came back with an ancient-looking roll of paper. She took it over to a table at the back of her tent that already had a map of the lighthouse area unrolled on its surface. She lifted the two weights at one end and set them on the left edge of the map of Saranik. It crackled, and a musty odor filled the air as she rolled it out and repositioned the other two weights to hold it flat.

Jon peered down at the aged map. Surrounded by what appeared to be massive mountains, the land in the center had the shape of the deformed right hand of a four-fingered monster. Towns were spread out everywhere, connected by roads and rivers. A slight bit to the north and west of the center lay Carpoli.

He pointed at a symbol next to it. It was a round platform with three teeth that curved up over it. "This has to be it." A sense of encouragement filled him as his plan began to solidify. He pulled his gaze from the map and turned to Dellia. "I need to memorize this map."

Saneya spoke up. "You can take it with you."

Jon bowed his head to her. "I still have to commit it to memory. We can't be squinting at maps in the dark. I have to know my way around." He turned to Dellia again. "Can you and Garris get us ready? Gather as many flamestones as Saneya will grant us. The longer they've been in a fire, the better." He glanced around the room as he spoke. "We also need a way to burn it, so we'll need some flaming arrows." He spotted a nearby lantern. "And a waterskin filled with oil, the kind you use for lanterns. No—make that two or three, in case one breaks. Pack them up with some food, firewood, and bandages. We'll get some sleep, then ride to the darkness early and enter it on foot."

Dellia nodded. "Of course." She sent him a knowing look and a smile. "Don't stay up too late. You need sleep too. I'll see you when we're done, and we can get a quick nap before we head out."

"A nap, huh?"

She nodded as she blushed, then spun around, and she and Garris flew out of the tent with Saneya following.

Alone with Sirra, awkwardness and guilt descended upon him, and he didn't know quite what to say.

She sought his gaze. "What is it? What's wrong?"

The words wouldn't come at first. Then, in a weak voice, Jon forced them out. "Brita, your sister's daughter, I killed her."

His mother-in-law's reaction was abrupt and instantaneous. Her expression clouded, and she fell silent. Then, she shuffled over to a chair at the side of the map table and slumped down into it. For a while, she remained there, looking out across the tent. Then her voice came out soft and sad. "You didn't kill her."

Jon lowered his gaze, unsure of what to say. She was obviously grieving, and he didn't know how to ease her pain. When the silence became awkward, he let the words he most wanted to say come out. "She died because she was protecting me."

Sirra looked up at him. "It was her choice."

"But I didn't do anything to stop it."

She stood again and peered into his face. "Jon, don't cheapen my niece's sacrifice like this."

His gaze drifted up to hers. "What?"

"She wouldn't want you to wallow in guilt and self-recrimination. She thought you were stronger than that. Don't make her wrong. Be the person she saw in you, the one worth giving her life for."

Jon remained quiet for a time as the disturbing notion of people dying for his sake ate away at him. Then his concern became too much, and he had to give it voice. "What if I get you killed too? I don't want any more people around me to die. I don't like taking you with me."

She tilted her head. "Why were you near Brita in the first place?" Her intonation was not so much that of a question or accusation, but of prodding. It was as if she had seen it and already knew the answer but wanted him to say it. He obliged. "One of those things was going to kill her."

Sirra stared straight into his eyes with a gaze that was both stern and sympathetic. "Then would it have been her fault if you died protecting her?"

He stood motionless for a moment as he considered the question. Sirra was trying to say he held himself to a different standard than he did Brita, and she was right. But knowing that changed nothing. It didn't ease his guilt in the slightest. He nodded. "I understand what you're saying, I do, but it doesn't stop me from feeling like it's my fault."

She gave a sad sort of smile. "It's not bad that you feel responsible for her death. For better or worse, you have accepted being a leader now. You must find a way to deal with this kind of thing. You can't let grief over Brita's death blind you to the other lives still in your hands."

He lowered his head. "What if I can't?"

"Then start small and realize that Dellia, Garris, and I are following you because we believe in what you're doing. If any of us gets hurt or dies, it's not for you. It's for a cause we believe in."

He struggled for a while, trying to imagine Sirra or Dellia dying and seeing it as Sirra suggested, but the image only made him sick to his stomach and caused his head to ache. Still, what she said made sense, so he nodded. "I'll try."

"That's all anyone can expect of you." She smiled, then stepped around him and toward the door.

Jon set a hand on her shoulder as she passed. "Just don't get hurt, okay?"

She set her hand on his. "You too."

Sirra strolled across the tent and ducked through the flap, disappearing into the night and leaving Jon alone in the quiet walls of brown canvas. He bent over the table, studying the map. After a while, he stopped and closed his eyes, recalling what he'd seen. Then he tried envisioning what it might look like from the ground at different angles. He had little time, and he had no photographic memory, yet he needed to memorize every mountain, road, town, river, and bridge. It might be the only way to get them to the temple.

Dellia eased herself down from Ulka, eyes fixed on the massive, billowing cloud of black that loomed before them, filling the entire view. It was still night, still dark out. The sun had not yet risen above the mountains on their left, but the light from behind them was as bright as the sunniest of middays. The air was stifling too in the beam from the lighthouse. It sent waves of heat rippling up from the rocks and cobbles between them and the wall of darkness. The Dead of Night hung in the air just beyond, keeping its distance, as if it knew to stay away from the deadly lighthouse rays.

Trepidation filled her as she watched it. She knew what she was here to do, what she must do, but the sight of the darkness so close made her want to flee. It was an instinctive reaction, like the compulsion to step back from the edge of a cliff or recoiling from a snake. Alarm bells rang out in her mind, telling her to protect herself, to keep away.

Jon swung down from Enna, his shoes crunching against the road next to her. He peered at her, standing in the barely tolerable swath of heat and light. For a moment, he turned his attention to the dark and imposing cloud. The Dead of Night stretched across the width of the chasm, obscuring the path and rising above it to block out much of the sky.

Dellia turned to their escorts, avoiding looking directly up into the blinding circle of light at the top of the lighthouse tower. The man at the front was one she recalled from her distant past when she would visit Egina. He was her age, with short brown hair, dark eyes, and a square jaw, and his armor was covered with bronze studs.

She peered up into his face, which always seemed more stern than his personality, and handed him Enna's reins. "Alekus, I am entrusting Ulka to you now. Please take care of him and Enna and the others. Get them away from the Dead of Night and out of this heat and light. Return them to camp as quickly as you can, okay?"

He granted her a solemn nod, and all four escorts turned and trotted away, leading the mounts behind them.

Dellia gathered her courage and turned to face Jon. "You know I have to do this alone, right?"

He hesitated, seeming unsure what she meant. Then disbelief clouded his face. "What? I know nothing of the kind."

She stepped closer. "I trained to fight without relying on my eyes. You know I can fight in the dark, right?"

"Sure, but I—"

She took his hand. "No 'but.' I've thought this through. Of the three of us, I am best able to handle this, so I am the first who should go. If you or Garris go with me, it will only make it harder and more dangerous for me because I won't just have to protect myself. I'll have to protect you."

Garris stepped up to Dellia. "Now wait a minute here ..."

Sirra set a hand on his shoulder. "You know she's right."

Garris grumbled but stepped back.

"I don't want her to do this alone any more than you do, but she's right. It is the correct strategy, and she's the one best suited to implement it."

Dellia took Jon's other hand. "You were planning to go in alone. I'm better trained and more experienced. You know in your heart this is the best way forward."

He nodded. "I know, but let me do it in your place. I can use my gift to take your fighting ability. You've seen me do it before. I can fight as well as you can. Let me do this instead of you."

"No. You told me why that isn't the best choice, remember?" She locked eyes with him. "You can take my skill, but ..."

842

"... I can't take your wisdom in using it," Jon finished the phrase with her.

Garris scoffed. "Oh, so now you're stealing my lines?"

Jon lowered his head. "I don't like it."

Dellia let go of Jon's hands and faced the darkness. "Let your thoughts and prayers be with me. That's all I need."

She sensed Jon's apprehension intensifying, then his heart seemed to harden. "Okay, but you better succeed. And know that if you don't come back, it won't stop me from following you. If you die, I die. So don't you dare fail."

She nodded and stepped toward the black cloud.

He shouted from behind her. "That's an order."

Dellia smiled as she continued forward. He was beginning to sound like a leader. As sweet and adorable as his threat was, it was not an idle one. He would follow her, so she dared not fail.

The wall of darkness grew as she neared it, billowing out toward her like an enormous hand ready to grab hold of her and pull her in. Yet, she was entering of her own free will.

With only a few steps remaining, she stopped and drew her sword and dagger. With one in each hand, ready at her sides, she faced the cloud of blackness. She closed her eyes and took a deep, calming breath as she drew on her other senses. Cries from deep within and the minute movements of air registered to her heightened awareness.

She took several cautious steps forward. The heat of the outside vanished, the air grew cold, and she knew she had entered the darkness. With slow, silent footfalls, she went deeper. The more she quieted her mind, the more she became aware of countless sounds approaching her, from above, in front, left and right. She waded farther in, and the noises weaved their way around her, a swirling wall of growls, screeches, and sickening cries echoing through the darkness. She opened her eyes, and nothing changed. All was pitch-black.

Then they came, a violent wave descending upon her all at once. She readied her weapons, planted her feet, and waited. She felt the wind of something huge diving at her, and she let herself go. Her weapons whooshed through the air, almost as if by their own volition. Her sword struck something. A screech resounded near her ear, and a swath of fire and sparkling light shot across the darkness.

She stabbed at a noise over her head. A cry came as her blade pierced something. Pinpoints of light rained down from above, but she had already stabbed another and another.

The pace quickened. She was surrounded now, so she pushed on, moving on instinct and reflex alone. Slashing and lunging where her senses told her to be. Wailing, rasps, and roars came from everywhere. Sheets of flame and glowing embers pelted her from every direction and crashed down all around her.

In their light, she could see the sea of dark shapes weaving in and out of each other, closing in, wave upon wave that never seemed to end. Her resolve began to crumble. They were inexhaustible. She stood under a grinding wheel, and it would wear her down until she collapsed and they tore her to shreds.

Then Jon's voice came to her, reminding her Jon would not hesitate to follow. If she died, he died.

Dellia gathered her strength and redoubled her efforts, fighting with all her skill in the hope the assault would soon ease, but it only intensified, coming faster, a fury of black forms encircling her in a deadly dance.

She heard herself gasp as a sharp claw raked across her arm. She slashed it in two in a shower of light. Warm blood trickled down her arm, and she hardened her resolve, fighting still harder and faster. Her breathing became labored, and her body reacted on its own as the onslaught refused to ease.

Then, she cried out as a sharp stabbing pierced her leg. Dellia lunged at the body with both blades, and it burst into a burning pyre, throwing off bright cinders that flew past her in a storm. She pushed through her fatigue, her muscles growing weaker and her breathing more labored, but she couldn't give up. If she died, Jon died.

More quickly now, matching the pace of the torrent of shadow and light bearing down on her, she stabbed and slashed, pierced and tore with everything she had. Time wore her down, her legs grew weak, and her arms began to fail, and still, the onslaught refused to abate.

Her senses flooded with more than she could handle, her mind went blank. She *became* the sword and the dagger, all movement and death, as she drew on strength that seemed to come out of nowhere. Her stance grew wobbly and her blows ineffective, and still she would not yield. If she died, Jon died, so she forced herself on.

Showers of flame and glittering light poured down, piercing the inky darkness. Shapes flew at her. Cries roared, and the blood from the wound on her arm made the dagger slick in her hand.

By the light of a dozen deaths, she spotted a massive form bearing down on her. Her sword lurched in one bone-shattering jolt as it struck the enormous thing. Her mind failing and her blows feeble, she resorted to speed, stabbing it over and over at a frantic pace, dodging, whirling, and thrusting.

A deafening roar rattled her chest, and a sudden spray of pin-point lights, like a thousand pricks of lightning, ripped through the darkness, and she fell.

More flashes of glittering light, dozens of showers, broke out all around, one after the other. Dellia tried to drag herself up, but it was no use. The bursts gave way to darkness as her vision grew dim.

All of a sudden, every bit of motion ceased as she lapsed into unconsciousness.

Fists clenched, Jon lurched toward the rolling wall of darkness, but an iron grip held him back. Garris's voice accompanied it. "Steady."

Jon tried to heed Garris's urging, but he couldn't. She was in there. Inside, with the bloodcurdling roars and shrieks. He had heard her cry of pain. She was hurt, yet it went on and on. He began to thrash, trying to break free.

Then Sirra's calming voice met his ears. "Be still, Jon."

He stopped his tugging and looked back at his mother-in-law.

She met his gaze. "If she were dead, the sounds would cease."

He calmed himself. She was right.

Sirra's voice remained steady and soothing. "Remember this feeling. Whenever you send someone into peril, there will be a loved one in fear for their life, like you are now."

"But what if she can't handle it?"

"Faith, Jon. Have faith."

He turned back toward the darkness, his muscles sore from squeezing his fists as he held himself back and waited. The sound intensified, growing louder, until after a long while, there came one last loud roar, and all fell silent. The black cloud began to recede. Jon trailed it as it drifted farther and farther back.

Then it revealed her body, in a heap on the ground with her sword and dagger lying at her side. His heart went cold. Had it killed her? Was the darkness showing him her dead body? Was it mocking him? Had his decisions once again murdered the one he cared about?

As Jon raced up to her, a tiny movement of her hand caught his eye. It was just a slight twitch of her fingers, but it meant she wasn't dead yet. He dropped beside her, the cobblestones painful and cold against his knees. Her eyes were open and staring at his hand. Relief flooded him as she brought herself up, then collapsed.

He thrust his arm under and around her so she wouldn't fall all the way to the pavement.

She lifted her hand and grabbed his shoulder. It was warm and wet where blood was running down from a long gash on her arm. Nausea punched him in the gut. Her blood was smeared on his neck and shoulder. He scanned the rest of her and only found one other injury, a nasty puncture on her leg. "Are you okay?"

She nodded.

He pointed to the wound on her arm. "This needs to be treated."

Dellia shook her head. "Not now. The darkness is leaving." She pointed, and Jon followed her finger to the dark wave rolling backward down the chasm, leaving them a broad path to walk down.

He turned his gaze back to Dellia. "But your wounds?"

"Can be treated when we rest."

Jon helped her pull herself up, but her legs seemed to wobble beneath her. He put his arm around her and held her up, helping her walk. She stumbled at first, and they made slow progress down the Saranik Road, trailing the darkness. It pulled farther and farther away until it was out of sight beyond the twists and turns of the chasm. Dellia recovered to a degree, but at times she still struggled to remain steady on her feet.

After a while, their escorts returned with their horse.

Jon looked up at them. "You came back."

Alekus smiled. "We stopped at the lighthouse. When we saw the darkness moving off, we thought you could move faster on horseback."

"I appreciate it, but it was dangerous. We still don't know if this is some kind of trap, a ploy to draw us in."

Alekus's smile turned to a flat stare. "We'll risk it."

The Talesh could be a bit testy when you impugned their intelligence or bravery. He had just done both. Obviously, Alekus knew it was dangerous, and he was willing to take the risk. Jon sent him a generous smile and bowed his head. "Your aid is greatly appreciated."

He helped Dellia over to Ulka and assisted in her attempt to mount, but she was weaker than expected and didn't make it. She fell back down and lost her balance, tipping over backward.

Jon dove forward and thrust out his arm to scoop her up. She landed on it with her hands clutching his shoulders and her gaze on his eyes. He peered down at her face, her soft brown hair draped over his arm. She seemed more innocent and vulnerable than he had ever seen. Their eyes locked, and for a moment, all the bickering, awkwardness, and disappointment of the past few days disappeared into her beautiful face.

Then Alekus called out from behind him. "I can help your wife mount if you're not up to it."

Jon pulled her up and let her catch her balance. Then he turned to face Alekus. The man had a huge grin, so he indulged his jealousy, responding with his own flat stare. "I'll manage."

This time, he helped Dellia mount with ease. When all were ready, they began down the chasm again, but the darkness was nowhere in sight. Unease rode with them. Now that he'd said it, the awareness this might be a trap haunted him.

As Jon fretted, the sky brightened, the air warmed, and the road became bright and clear. With the morning almost spent and the first lighthouse now miles behind them, they encountered a subtle and familiar widening of the towering rock walls. They were nearing the second lighthouse. Then, around a turn, it appeared again, the wall of billowing darkness, holding steady, neither charging at them nor receding.

Jon scrutinized it, trying to reason out its purpose. Its retreat wasn't accidental. Dellia had hurt it, killed parts of it, and it needed to pull back, or more of it would die. Even so, it had stopped short of retreating beyond this second lighthouse. The most probable reason seemed to be that if it went beyond it, they could repair the light-house. If that happened, it would lose ground it might never get back.

As he pondered the situation, a disturbing possibility struck him. A trap made the most sense. It had lured them deep into the chasm, as close as possible to the second lighthouse, in order to sur-round and trap them. And if he was right, it would only be a matter of time before this trap was sprung.

Now feeling a sense of urgency, Jon turned to Dellia. "Garris and I will handle it this time. You get the horses and your mother out of here."

She seemed shocked. "We've already had this discussion. I fight. You wait."

Jon and Garris swung down off their mounts, then he peered up at his wife. "No, we had a different discussion. One where you weren't already exhausted." He strolled toward her, and as he did, the darkness began to crawl down the chasm toward them.

She crossed her arms and sat taller in the saddle. "I can handle it."

"We can't risk it."

She stared at him with fiery anger in her eyes.

He shot back, speaking with all the urgency he felt. "If the Dead of Night loses here, it loses the chasm and any chance of invading Talus. It's do or die for it. I think that's why it hit you so hard. It knows the stakes. You weakened it. Now we have to finish the job and reclaim the second lighthouse. If we do, it's game over for invading Talus."

"All the more reason I should be fighting."

"No, Garris and I are fresh. You are not. We fight. You rest. That's an order."

She hesitated.

It didn't feel right pulling rank on Dellia, but she had to know he was also making sense. "Now, give me your dagger." Jon stopped in front of her and reached out his hand.

He jumped as Garris slapped the hilt of a sword into it. "Remember this from the Recluse Tower."

Jon turned his attention to the unexpected weapon in his hand. It was the same one Garris had handed him in the Recluse Tower. He had used his gift to visit the sword's owner in the past and acquire his skill. Flashes came to him of that vision and fifteen years of the strange lizard man using it to spar with Garris. He was as big as Garris, with dark scales shining in the bright sun, his arms and tail a blur as he pummeled him with blows. Elt, Garris had called him, his only companion during his exile. Jon nodded. "From the lizard man?"

"Yeah. We do the same. We fight back to back, right?"

Jon nodded as he fished in his pack. He found two large flame-stones and nets and tossed one set to Garris.

Dellia balked, seeming even more unsettled at the idea of him fighting. "I've seen Jon in practice. He can't handle it."

Garris grinned. "But you never saw him in the Recluse Tower. He *can* handle it ... or rather, *we* can. Trust me. We've got this."

The darkness was getting very near now, so Jon barked out his last orders to Dellia, hoping it would settle the matter. "Move till you can't see the darkness and wait. If you see it coming down the chasm again, pull back. Keep pulling back until it retreats. Wait at least three times as long as you spent fighting it, then find us. With luck, we'll be fixing the second lighthouse by then."

Her face twisted into a frustrated sort of grimace.

Jon glanced at the darkness, now almost upon them. "You are our best fighter for this, but you already did your part. There will be days ahead before we reach our goal. We can't lose you or have you get injured even worse, or we'll never make it. I've made a command decision. Our best hope is to save you for the tougher fights, and my gut says this isn't one of them. Now go."

Sirra set a hand on her daughter's shoulder and gently tugged as she motioned with her head, urging her to back away from the darkness.

Dellia leaned forward, her look still angry as she resisted her mother. "Remember what you told me. It goes double for you. I will kill this thing with or without you. If you die, I die. So don't you dare fail."

Jon gave a crisp nod before Dellia turned, and she, Sirra, and their escorts galloped away. He tightened his grip on the sword and eyed Garris. "You ready?"

He and Garris stepped back away from the advancing wall of black as they tied the flamestones in nets at their waists. No sooner had they stopped and put their backs to one another than the darkness passed over them. The sun disappeared, and the air grew cooler.

Jon concentrated on the sword, and it took longer and more effort than usual to trigger his gift, but after one last push, time slowed, then stopped. He spun the image backward, watching the sword's existence in rewind. Images raced by of Garris eating, hunting, training, and living with this Elt in a small cabin atop a mountain sized column of rock. Well into Garris's fifteen years of exile he found a moment when the lizard man appeared to be in rare form. His scales glistened in the early morning sun as he outmaneuvered Garris, assaulting him with a hail of blows. He stopped the image at that moment and acquired Elt's fighting skill.

A sudden confidence, perhaps even an arrogance, surged through him. He began to actually pity the darkness for what it would suffer at his hands. Either this feeling was a new aspect of his gift or one he hadn't noticed before. His eyesight suddenly improved too, and he could see quite a distance into the darkness. Everything turned to shades of green. The daylight side had an almost unnatural emerald glow that darkened to nearly black farther in. Painted in lighter shades stood the indistinct form of the lighthouse a few hundred feet away with the chasm walls rising up on either side of it.

When time began to flow again, he whipped the sword around him with a flourish, testing its heft and balance. He straightened and waited.

In a mere few moments, he spotted them. Waves of dark shapes whipped down the chasm and around the lighthouse, filling the breadth between the walls of rock. He called over his shoulder to Garris. "This Elt friend of yours has quite good night vision. I see them."

As the emerald glow of the daylight side deepened, dark green shadows flew by and out around them, encircling them. Spinning like a hurricane with him and Garris in the eye. Little by little, they closed in until they were a mass of shapes flying in and out of each other. They hit the warm light of their flamestones, and Jon barked out a few last words to Garris. "There's a sea of them all around us. Brace yourself. Incoming in three ... two ... one."

Garris heaved, sparks flew, and Jon whirled into action. An ocean of creatures descended upon them. As the front edge of the storm hit, he let the lizard man's reflexes take over, directing his action, hacking and slashing at a pace beyond any he could have imagined. Bodies fell, whole or in pieces, as soon as they dared come in range of his blade. His weapon blurred in an indistinct flurry as the area around them became ablaze with disintegrating bodies. A shimmering circle of glowing ash whirled into the air above until it disappeared into the green haze of his night vision.

Their movement and the darkness made their forms hard to discern, but out of the swarms came distinct shapes: twisted arms, razor-sharp claws, and grotesque heads with mouths brimming with jagged teeth. They were not amorphous. It was just as he'd suspected when he first watched them perish in the lighthouse beam. They were individual entities, though the movement and darkness made them blur together into a swirling mass.

He forced himself to fight harder. Yet even as he pushed himself to his limits, the only way he could keep up with the fury of the attack was with Garris standing at his back, heaving and thrusting with a pace not much less than his own. How Dellia had survived alone in the midst of such an onslaught was beyond imagining. The first wave slowed, but the next was on its heels, writhing around them, a sea of indistinct, dark shapes punctuated by spindly limbs, huge razor-tipped paws, and hideous faces.

Then another movement caught his eye. Far in the distance, something massive towered above the sea of moving shapes. It approached slowly, arcing in on them. It was an instant reminder of the Blood Wolves and their careful, circling approach. Then it dawned on him: this massive creature wasn't behaving like the rest. Whereas the swarm of smaller forms were attacking straight on, the larger one's approach was cautious. Its behavior was different, independent of the others. Like a swarm of bees, the creatures that lived in this dark cloud acted together, betraying a unified purpose. Yet their individual reactions and attacks said they each possessed a separate intelligence.

Another wave almost upon them, Jon called out, "More in three … two … one." His arms aching from exertion, he let loose with another flurry of blows, striking in every direction as the full brunt of this new wave fell upon them. From behind him came Garris's breathing, as labored as his own. Then his voice joined it, rasping out, "We can't keep this up forever."

AYLUN

With the words still ringing in his ears, something slashed Jon's leg with a jolt of pain, and he began to lose balance. The lizard man's reflexes took over again, and he righted himself, then cleared his mind and let his enhanced skills and instincts push him harder. Time seemed to drag. His body was near exhaustion when the second wave began to wane, yet a third was right behind it. Then a panic-inducing thought struck him. What if the creatures were inexhaustible? What if they were being created out of the darkness itself? He calmed as he rejected the idea. Dellia had survived, she had killed enough to make it retreat. They weren't infinite.

He called out, "Another wave in three … two … one." He pushed through his exhaustion. His blows were weaker and his speed pushed to the limits, but his blade flew around him. Its shining metal glinted in the inferno of bodies that crumbled and burned as they threw off sparkling trails of cinders.

Then he caught sight of the enormous dark form as it lunged up in front of him, its waist near his face. It raised a deformed paw tipped with long razor claws. His heart almost stopped as he leaped and slashed downward with his blade. It caught on what seemed to be its slick dark stomach in a misaimed and shallow blow.

A deafening roar rattled his chest and the thing lurched back. Its cautious approach and the leap forward, combined with its quick withdrawal, created an instant impression of a wounded predator. It held there, biding its time, waiting for an opening as the third wave waned and the moving dark shapes around them began to thin out.

In a sudden burst the monstrosity lunged again. This time Jon was ready, and his blow well aimed. It took off the end of what seemed like the creature's arm. The severed part fell in a blaze as a screech rang through the black cloud. Everything came to a halt, as all the dark shapes pulled back in a sudden jolt, retreating the way they'd come. They flew out around the lighthouse, twisting and winding their way into the distance. That instant clarified an impression already lurking in his mind: They all retreated like a single wounded predator the moment he inflicted a grievous wound on the giant creature. They acted independent of one another, but they were also tied together. The retreat of the largest led to the retreat of them all.

Brandishing his sword, Garris took a few stumbling steps toward the fleeing shapes, but Jon yelled, "What are you doing? They're retreating."

He turned to face Jon and doubled over, his breathing heavy and hard. "Sorry, caught up in the moment."

With fascination, Jon watched the fleeing wall of deep green as it grew smaller behind the lighthouse. A blinding light hit as sunlight washed the area around them. Through squinting eyes, he watched the dark cloud retreat with the same speed as the shapes. It was as if it was generated by them. It left a distinct impression that the creatures were doing what should be impossible. They were emanating a black cloud that was the Dead of Night itself. They were throwing off a region of space that absorbed light.

Jon slumped onto the ground, his breath heaving as he closed his eyes. As he sat there, out of breath, with every muscle spent, another impression came to him, one not grounded in any observation or fact. The smaller shapes followed the larger one. This thing had a hierarchy. It had a structure, and that reinforced his earlier inference. Hierarchy meant a pyramid with one creature at the top. That meant it had a single organizing intelligence. It had a "heart," as it were. With that realization Jon's hope grew to near certainty that he was right. If they killed whatever was at the top of the pyramid, it would almost certainly stop the whole thing.

Dellia waited with excruciating patience as the sound of restless movements came from Alekus, his three fellow soldiers, and their mounts behind her. The sounds only heightened her anxiety.

Jon was right, of course, but she hated being commanded to stand down again. Doing nothing had never been her strong suit, least of all now when the stakes were so high. Still, it was an order, so she tried her best to ignore the familiar frustration clawing at her.

What wasn't as familiar was her fear. Jon was out there in the darkness somewhere fighting the Dead of Night without her. Of that she was sure. Garris had radiated an absolute certainty when he said he and Jon could handle it. Yet she found little comfort in that with his life on the line. Still, she had no choice now, so she waited.

The darkness hadn't followed them far, and she was practiced at taking orders, so she had done as Jon demanded and stepped back while he put himself in harm's way. Her sense of time inside the Dead of Night had been imperfect, so she counted on her mother to gauge the duration of this wait. Dellia stole frequent glances at her, and though she presented a calm exterior, her mother's apprehension almost matched her own.

After what seemed like way too long, Sirra finally okayed them to return. When they rounded the same bend where the darkness had first stopped, all that met their eyes was the sparkling white wall of the lighthouse with Jon and Garris resting against it. The order to keep herself in check no longer in force, Dellia took off toward them at a gallop. A cool wind whipped around her as Ulka's hooves thundered down the chasm.

The two stood as she flew off of her mount. Jon's pants were ripped below the knee and soaked with blood around the tear. Garris bore a few minor scratches but seemed almost unharmed.

Jon smiled at her as she stepped up to him, then she threw herself at him and hugged him. His body warm against hers, he spoke softly in her ear. "It didn't last as long as your fight, and I could see everything, but it was still intense."

She pulled back and crouched to peer at the hole in his pants and the leg beneath. Usually, she was levelheaded about injuries, but this was Jon, and the sight made her stomach twist. "That'll need tending."

He nodded, then simply seemed to take over, addressing their escorts first. "Alekus, can you and your men help us repair the lighthouse?" He faced Sirra. "I need you to make a kind of mask to block the light. I'll show you how."

Sirra nodded.

Dellia watched as they hurried off. It was the first time she'd seen Jon take charge of a group. He had a soft-spoken and casual style, but at the same time, his expectant tone left no doubt his words were orders. The combination made taking charge look as natural to him as breathing.

Having been assigned to take it easy, Dellia wandered into the lighthouse and helped by dispensing tips as their escorts worked. Three of them put sunstones back in the holders at the edge of the stairs. As they did, the burliest of their helpers clattered up and down the steps behind them, hauling chests of sunstones.

With more experience and more people, it went much faster than last time. When all the sunstones were in place, Dellia returned outside. Her mother and Jon were finishing a pair of masks with pinpoint eye holes made from spare bandaging. Dellia took one and handed the other to Garris, and they climbed to the top of the tower.

With the chains already gone from their prior escape, they only had to remove the tarp and throw it over the edge. As it fluttered down the glistening tower wall, the inside became awash in a blinding light. They tied on their masks, and Dellia followed Garris as he raced down, avoiding the brilliant beam winding up the inside of the stairway. His heavy footsteps echoed through the tower as the air grew hotter and hotter.

At last, they flew out into the open, and Dellia yanked off her mask. She stood for a while, staring off at the straight stretch of towering rock walls, admiring the soft, yellow beam flooding its entire width.

It was just after midday and they were already weary when they set off again, headed farther in. After a long afternoon's ride, they found the third lighthouse, in the open, near the final stretch of the chasm. With the day fading and the light inside the tower growing dim, they repaired it too.

Once it was throwing off its warm rays, Jon ordered their escorts to return to the encampment and make a full report to Prian.

He also directed them to take all the horses, insisting it would put everyone at risk to take them into the Dead of Night. It wasn't a pleasant thought, being on foot in the dark, but he was right, of course. She had barely managed to survive her encounter with the Dead of Night when all she needed to protect was herself. If she'd had to protect the front, rear, and both sides of Ulka from dozens of simultaneous attacks, they would have both perished.

With a crisp nod, Alekus took his leave with his men, leading all the horses behind them. Afterward, Dellia rested as Jon spent a while engaged in some mysterious tinkering with a few flamestones near the tower entrance. Then he showed them that the flamestones glowed much more brightly when placed inside the tower, close to the beam. So they put all of theirs at the base of the steps near the first sunstone in the hope that the blinding light inside might make them stay brighter for longer.

Now permanently on foot, Dellia and the other three settled at the tower's white stone base to rest, eat, and recover for the night. No fire was necessary. The light and warmth of the lighthouse made a generous substitute, so they camped on the side opposite the entryway.

Before long, Sirra hugged Jon. She thanked him and commended his leadership and decisions making, then headed off to sleep.

Garris said little, other than warning Dellia once again that she better hope Kayleen was okay. It was an idle threat and completely unnecessary since Dellia's guilt at keeping him from Kayleen still nagged her. Then, he scolded Jon, saying he'd better make sure all of this was worth it, or he would face some unknown consequences. His theatrics done, Garris strolled over to his bedroll, dumped himself onto it, and soon fell asleep.

Jon found their medical supplies, filled a bowl with water, and used a moistened cloth to clean Dellia's leg wound, insisting that his wasn't anywhere near as bad, so hers needed attention first. As he worked, her awkwardness grew. What should she say? She had been pretty angry with him earlier, and the guilt of her poor treatment of him for the last week still hounded her.

While she wallowed in her awkwardness, Jon spoke to her in a gentle voice. "I miss you, Dellia."

Her heart melted at his soft-spoken words, and she lowered her head. After what she'd done, she still didn't quite feel worthy of such overt words of kindness. Still, no matter how she felt, he was trying, and her guilt would only make things more difficult between them. Tears came to her eyes as Dellia returned his quiet refrain, "I miss you, too." She sniffled, and her gaze returned to Jon's face. "Just so you know, I hated being ordered around, and"—she winced as he brushed the rough cloth across her puncture wound—"I got pretty mad a couple of times, but now that I'm calmer and able to see things with a level head, I have to admit, all of your decisions were good ones. I don't think I've ever been more proud of you than I am right now."

Jon finished his cleaning and began to wrap her leg with a soft strip of cloth. He looked up at her. "I feel like I didn't really do anything worth being proud of. So much of the time, I'm just hanging on by a thread. I mean, I've made no secret that I don't like being in charge. To have anyone's life in my hands, especially yours, makes me incredibly nervous."

"I know. I felt it, but it didn't show." Dellia smiled. "You were decisive, and you never appeared the slightest bit nervous or unsure."

He seemed puzzled. "Is that important?"

"Of course it is. No one wants to follow a wishy-washy leader into battle. In fact, it's a sure way to get your troops killed. When you lack confidence, your troops lack confidence, and won't fight as fearlessly."

He nodded. "Well, I'm just trying my best to not make dumb mistakes."

She smiled at him again.

He finished, and it was her turn, so she dipped a clean wad of cloth in a fresh bowl of water and began washing around his leg wound.

The conversation seemed to wane, then all of a sudden, Jon spoke. "Tomorrow, we all enter the Dead of Night. After it lost the second lighthouse, I think it knew the chasm was lost, so it abandoned the third lighthouse. It's also possible it wants us to think we're winning. It could be drawing us in where it can fight us on its own ground."

She gave the conversation half of her attention as she blotted the dark, dried blood away from the edge of his gash. "That sounds ominous."

"It is. And I know Sirra said she can get us out of there no matter how deep in we are, but you saw what it was like in there. If we're caught in the open, would one of her portals really get us out?"

Dellia never paused. "No way. I was surrounded, there was nowhere to move."

"My thoughts exactly. And even if we happened to be in a sheltered spot, it's still a huge risk. Each person through the portal is one less to protect the group, and the last one through is at serious risk of being overwhelmed before they can escape."

"Agreed."

Jon hesitated. "Not to mention losing ground."

"What do you mean?"

"How much do you know about your mom's gift? Can she just make a portal to anywhere she's been?"

Dellia shook her head. "No, if its somewhere familiar enough for her to picture it in her head, sure, but otherwise, she has to study a place. She has to make a mental image she can recall later."

"Right. So, she can't just pop us right back to where we were. Even if she could, we might land in the middle of a swarm of those things."

Dellia hid her annoyance. "So, are you saying my mom will be useless in there? That we shouldn't even take her?"

"No, she could save all our lives, but we have to be smart. I need a plan for how best to use her gift."

She was about to ask what kind of plan he had in mind when Jon spoke again. "Which brings me to an important question I need to ask."

His solemn tone made her take notice, and she stopped and looked into his eyes. "Then ask."

"The darkness could afford to lose the chasm." He pointed down past the lighthouse, where the darkness had retreated. "It can't afford to lose Saranik. It has been its home since it took it from Talus hundreds of years ago, and it can't afford to lose its homeland. The longer we keep going straight for the center of Saranik, the more obvious it will become that we are headed toward its most vulnerable point. Which means, the closer we get to its heart, the more determined and desperate we can expect it to become. So, the question is, what would you do if you wanted to defeat us and we were invading your territory in such an obvious way?"

"You mean if I were in its shoes?"

Jon nodded.

Dellia returned to her cleansing of his wound as she considered for a moment, but it wasn't a tough question. "I'd follow you, track you from a distance, draw you in until you had no chance of retreat. I'd wait for you to get complacent. Then I'd ambush you at a point where I had a decisive strategic advantage."

"That's good. I like that. Now, if I can just come up with a few ways to use that against it …"

"Like what?"

"Well, for one, we don't let ourselves get complacent. Other than that, I'm not sure yet."

She had finished her cleaning and was ready to bind the wound, but she halted with bandage in hand, eyeing his face. "Why is it every time I ask you what you're planning, you get evasive?"

"Evasive? I'm not trying to be evasive. I just don't know yet."

"How can that be? You always have a plan. You're just not saying what it is."

"What you're asking is a little like asking someone their strategy to win a chess game. There are too many possible moves to give a simple answer. All anyone can do is think ahead and devise responses to each move your opponent might make."

Dellia puzzled. "What kind of game is … chest?"

"Chess, not chest." Jon motioned to the ground between them. "It's played on a board with sixty-four squares and pieces like knights and pawns and rooks that each move differently."

The references only deepened Dellia's puzzlement. Elore had a board game where one opponent used white stones and the other black to surround each other and take over their pieces, but the game Jon described was difficult to envision.

He seemed to sense her confusion. "It's just a strategy game." He sighed. "Okay, bad example." He paused for a while. "Look, there's an old saying I once heard. It basically says that no plan survives first contact with the enemy. That's even more true when you don't know what the enemy is even like."

She paused, thinking about the concept. It was true. In every fight, once your opponent figured out what you were doing, they adapted, forcing you to adapt. It was just one of the reasons she liked sparring with Rillen. She was a constant stream of surprises, forcing Dellia to think on her feet and be flexible. In fact, if anyone asked her how she planned to win a sparring match against Rillen, she couldn't tell them because she had no idea what to expect. In many ways, it was the same kind of question she had just asked Jon.

Dellia nodded. "There's truth in that. Things never quite go as expected."

"If you want to know why I can never tell you what I'm planning, that's the reason. It's because I can only try to anticipate a bunch of different scenarios. I won't know what to do until I see what it's like in there."

She smirked. "Is that the real reason, or are you trying to be mysterious?"

"No, I'm serious, and the thing I fear the most is that all my ideas will add up to nothing." He looked at her with a solemn expression. "When it comes down to it, there's only one plan I'm absolutely certain of, and that's you. You are my best plan."

She looked up from her work. "What does that mean?"

"It means when everything is falling to pieces, I can count on you to hold it together. If there's a way to accomplish our mission, you won't stop until you find it. When all hope is lost, you'll find a way out."

She nodded.

After they finished cleaning and bandaging their wounds, she and Jon went to their bedrolls and lay down next to Sirra. Jon fell asleep right away while she lay next to him, waiting for slumber to take her. She glanced over at the lighthouse sending bright rays across the chasm from its doorway.

What they had done today was a monumental achievement. They had repelled the darkness all the way back to Saranik and repaired the remaining two lighthouses. The Dead of Night was no longer on the doorstep of Talus. It was where it had been for hundreds of years. But it had not been easy. She had almost died in that first encounter, and this was only the periphery.

Jon's question of earlier this evening came to mind. The strategy she described would work. If the Dead of Night drew them in, so they had nowhere to retreat, surrounded them, then attacked where it had a clear advantage, it would certainly prevail. If it really was aware of them and had a plan like that, how could they hope to reach the temple?

With that question came doubt and fear and the impulse to wake Jon and talk him out of this. It was impossible to see how they would stay alive in the heart of this madness. They had countered the damage the Mirhal caused, so why were they even considering carrying out their original plan.

Dellia rolled onto her side and reached out a hand to wake him. Then she froze as their frantic discussion came to mind—when she had talked Jon out of going into the Dead of Night alone. She had said many things, and she had believed them with her whole heart. The most important was that she promised to have faith in him. At the time, the words had come so easily, yet here she was, ready to wake him with her doubts and fears.

A calm came over her as, in that moment, she realized what it meant to have faith. Dellia lay back down and closed her eyes. Jon had said she was his best plan, that when all else failed, he trusted her to find a way to save them. He had faith in her. Now it was her turn. He intended to enter the Dead of Night, and she would follow him. Not begrudgingly, with doubt and fear in her heart, but with faith that no matter what happened, he would keep them alive long enough to get to the temple and put an end to the darkness.

Chapter Thirty-Three

INTO THE HEART

Uncertainty and self-doubt enshrouded Jon as he crouched on the long road through eternal darkness. He had led the four of them here, to the Dead of Night, where even the slightest misstep could spell a gruesome end for them all. He held his flamestone high and, by its warm light, examined the dark cobbles. With his bare fingers, he brushed away the ancient debris from their cold, hard surface. He placed his palm on the dry rock, worn smooth in ages past, and concentrated on the road itself.

Once again, time slowed around him. His companions came to a halt, standing still, their wary faces staring into the thick, chill blackness that always surrounded them. An ethereal version of the dark world appeared, overlaid on the current field of nothingness. He turned time backward through centuries of ceaseless darkness where little moved until, at last, a warm light broke through. At that moment, he stopped and stood, admiring the bright translucent world visible above the perpetual black.

On his right, towering mountains reached for the cloud-filled sky. A muscle-bound rider meandered down the long road toward him. Beyond him, to the left, lay a lake, glistening in the morning sun, and beyond that, on its shores, stood a quaint village, perhaps a mile away. Its people were mere ants at this distance, as they squatted on the shore washing clothes.

He studied the scene, trying to relate the lake, village, and tallest peak on the right to his recollection of the map. If he was right, they were a third of the way to their goal, though much of that was sheer guesswork. Even if he knew the precise distance, it was impossible to gauge their pace. Time had lost all meaning when they entered this land of never-ending night, but if his weariness and aching body were any indications, they had made it a third of the way in one very long day.

He relaxed, and time began to flow again. In an instant, he was yanked back to his crouching position, where he had started. He stood, but before he could explain what he'd seen, Sirra asked, "What are you doing?"

"I'm using my gift to visit the past." Jon pointed to the cobblestones. "I don't know how it works, but it's like the entire history of these bricks is stored in some way. By touching them, I can see that history. I can go back and take skills, abilities, or gifts from those who have been in contact with them. Right now, I'm not using it to take abilities but to view the landscape here at a time before the darkness came."

Sirra gaped at him. "You can see this land before the Dead of Night? You're kidding, right?" She turned to Dellia. "He's kidding, right?"

Her daughter shook her head. "No, that's his serious face."

Garris chimed in, "I've seen him take your gift twice to get us out of a fix, but it seems he can't take it a third time."

Jon smiled at Sirra. "You want proof? There was a lake ahead, along the left side of this road, and on the far shore, a village."

Though still shocked, she seemed to accept it, so they began again down the long road through unceasing darkness. The air seemed thick with the black fog that only let them see a handful of feet around them. They moved with swift, quiet steps, following the edge of the road. Beyond it, here and there, stood the remains of what must have once been thriving trees. Most had been reduced to jagged, broken-off trunks, their sharp, dry peaks jutting into the air. A few still supported heavy, barren branches, mere remnants of what were once living, growing architectures.

866

While Garris kept an ear open behind them, Dellia, with her heightened senses, led the way, tense and alert to every cry or growl, but they were rare. All around lay in ominous silence, broken only by their footsteps along the stones of the ancient road. Jon endeavored to remain calm and keep his mind clear, but events seemed to be playing out a little too much as Dellia had strategized. They were meeting no resistance, as if the Dead of Night wanted them to go deeper, to be drawn in, only to pounce on them when it knew it could win, and they had no hope of escape.

Though Jon kept a sharp eye out, no lake appeared. Instead, the road passed a gradual slope on the left that might have been the bottom of a long-dried-up body of water. Perhaps the darkness altered the weather in ways he couldn't fathom. Not that he could fathom much anymore, with no clue what physical laws shaped and governed this place.

The sunken ground was followed almost at once by buildings on their right. Many were just paltry remnants of fallen walls and timbers, but a number of stone structures remained, some seeming intact.

Jon stopped at the first that appeared sound, then eyed Dellia. He kept his voice to a whisper, aware that it might carry a long way in this barren landscape. "Sirra and I will go in and memorize the room. That way, she can open a portal to it later if needed. Dellia, can you keep watch at the entrance?"

Sirra spoke up. "You all seem tired. Aren't you afraid we'll miss something from fatigue? Shouldn't we rest?"

Jon shook his head. "Every moment we're in here is a huge risk. We can't afford to dally in such a dangerous place. We move until we have to stop."

No sound came from Dellia or Garris, and Sirra didn't object, but just slid through the cracked door. Jon followed and scanned the dark interior. The shutters were all closed and locked, and as best as he could see in the ineffectual light, the building was sound. Its four heavy stone walls were still whole and solid, and rugged beams spanned their tops, supporting a substantial roof. It seemed as if it would provide adequate protection against conventional attacks. Who knew what unnatural things might assail them were they to find themselves holed up in this modest space.

Jon fretted, anxious to keep moving as Sirra spent a long time studying the small fireplace. As soon as she announced she had finished, they returned outside, closed the door, and hurried on. Jon stopped at the other end of town, and after a brief search, they found another undamaged stone building. Once inside, he closed and locked the shutters as Sirra committed the place to memory.

They moved on again, leaving the village behind at a brisk pace. Jon remained wary. He was way outside his carefully cultivated bubble of inaction. It was that same practiced state of avoidance, nurtured over a lifetime, that had always protected him. Now he was trying to break free, but the feeling of impending doom was stifling. With each step, the ominous silence became more unnerving, and his sense of foreboding grew.

Unsure how many times he could use Garris's sword to acquire a prior owner's lizard sight, he had clung to the idea of saving his gift, hoping to gain the ability when needed most. Only a few minutes outside of town, that resolve crumbled, and the entire day's worth of anxiety caught up with him in a single rush.

He glanced at Garris and spoke in a hushed voice. "Do you still have Elt's sword?"

Garris kept scanning his pitch-black surroundings as he replied, "You've already used it twice. I thought that was the limit."

"It's not his swordsmanship I intend to take. Someone else might have owned that sword before Elt, another lizard man. I want his night vision."

Garris smiled, even as he continued to survey the nothingness. "I like it." With great care, he slid the weapon out and presented the grip to Jon.

He took it and concentrated, and his gift kicked in right away. Sure enough, when he rolled time back further, he found another owner. He considered stopping there. After all, he only needed the lizard's night vision, but then a cleverer course of action occurred to him. Taking Elt's swordsmanship also seemed to confer the lizard's sight, which seemed logical since you'd be a better swordsman at night with expanded vision. Since he could use both, why not find the lizard man most comfortable with the weapon. So, he went still further back through two more owners.

Then he found it, another lizard man who appeared to be at complete ease with the weapon, as if it were an extension of his being. Jon tried taking his skill with the sword, and it seemed to work. For a brief moment, he wondered why he couldn't use Dellia's ring even a second time, but this was the third time he had used the same item to acquire someone's swordsmanship.

Perhaps what he intended to do played a role. How the physics of intent made any sense was impossible to see. Thoughts were insubstantial. They were only shifting neural patterns, so how could they influence physical behaviors? However, Megan had blown to bits his theory of how this world worked. Not to mention the idea that a different set of physical laws constrained Earth. Absent any plausible theory about the rules governing this or any other world, he couldn't rule out the concept that his intent played a role. But that would have to be an experiment for another time.

As the world sped up again, suddenly he could see. The world around him gained a new and strange visibility. It was still dark and the entire landscape painted in shades of deep green, but he could see things out for a mile or more. It couldn't be ordinary visible light, so perhaps he was seeing heat or some other portion of the spectrum that was invisible to humans.

Their hurried walk continued, and he leaned over toward Garris and whispered, "It worked. I can—"

Then Jon noticed it with unnatural clarity, a shifting mass of creatures way out in the distance. They moved and spread as if they were a single unit and keeping its distance from them. As he watched the purposefulness of their collective movement, it connected with a deeper impression from the day before. He had seen, close up, that the creatures that lived within the Dead of Night moved and acted independent of one another. Yet, at a distance it became clear, once again, that some singular intelligence directed their collective behavior. The perception only served to reenforce Garris's report that the thing had a heart and could be killed by attacking it.

Yet, the way the shifting cloud of creatures seemed to keep its distance had another, more ominous implication. Such deliberate avoidance meant the darkness had to be aware of their presence, yet it was moving away rather than attacking. That meant Dellia was almost certainly right. This whole setup had to be a trap, and the darkness was waiting for the best time to spring it on them.

His face snapped forward, but he kept his eyes on the distant shifting shapes. For some reason, their movement seemed to jump out at him in a way it never would have with his normal sight. He knew, deep down, that it would be a strategic mistake to give away that he saw them. Once they knew, they'd adapt, and he'd never spot the next attack coming. So, he hurried up behind Dellia and set a hand on each shoulder.

He leaned up to her ear and whispered in the quietest voice he could manage, "We're in trouble, so we're going to put on an act."

Her expression never changed. She remained alert and attentive and moved ahead as if he'd said nothing.

"I'm going to argue we return and rest. You argue we should press onward. I need to win this argument."

At once, Dellia halted and swung around. In a quiet but irate voice, she barked, "That's ridiculous. We just got started. I'm not tired. Garris isn't tired." She eyed Garris. "You're not tired, are you?"

Garris seemed puzzled at the sudden fuss. "Um, no."

Jon raised his voice a little above hers. "We need to be careful. Why push ourselves when we could rest at that village back there?"

She raised her voice too, playing along as if she had read his mind. "We'll never get anywhere with you being paranoid like that. Be a man for a change."

He raised his voice to a yell. "Paranoid? It's better than being a reckless, obstinate fool. I say we turn back and—"

The shapes began to move faster and spread out along the vast horizon. Then Jon noticed more movement as other clusters began to appear.

Dellia did too. She swung around, facing one of several groups now pouring out of the cracks and shadows to fill the landscape around them. She froze. "I hear something."

Jon shouted, "Run! Back to the village."

Dellia bolted, and they all followed.

Jon glanced around, trying to pretend he was searching but not finding anything. He counted seven groups almost all the way around them. In a short time, they would be surrounded.

Dellia was surging ahead, so he shouted out, "Keep together. Don't get lost in the dark."

She shouted behind her to the rest of the group, "Hurry, they're getting closer."

Then Jon noticed the sky. His focus had been on the terrain around them, but a dark cloud of shifting green shapes was rolling out across the heavens, and it was coming faster than the ones on the ground. Still trying to hide the fact that he could see them, Jon shouted out, "Flapping. I hear wings. Watch out for an attack from above." He set a hand on Sirra's back and guided her ahead of him. "Stay between us. We'll protect you."

A hundred feet or more remained when it descended on them: a tornado of ragged wings, jagged claws, and clacking beaks whirling down from the sky. They dove and banked, soared and turned, making it impossible to catch sight of individual shapes in the winding, green mass.

Dellia and Garris flew into action, their blades flying to meet each threat. Jon followed as the fluttering torrent fell upon them, blanketing them like a sandstorm until it blotted out everything. A glittering hurricane of flame and spark whirled in circles around them as flying creatures perished the moment they were within reach of a blade.

Jon wielded the weapon with confidence born of his acquired skill and reflexes. He slashed and jabbed, barely keeping the snatching claws and clacking beaks from overwhelming them.

He shifted his focus to protecting Sirra as she hunkered down and covered her head.

Corpses crumbled apart around them in a sparkling rain of glowing ash that lit up the entire area as the cobbles raced by beneath.

Still fighting as he ran, Jon brandished his sword with one hand as he unslung his pack of a dozen flamestones with the other and yanked the top open. Warm light poured out, drenching the descending storm of flapping horrors. He donned it again, this time backwards with the opening pouring light out in front of him.

Almost at once, the pace of the attack eased. Though it wasn't stopping the torrent of shapes, they didn't like the light. Then, through the new gaps in the whirlwind of talons and featherless bodies, Jon spotted it: a fluid, shifting wall of ground-borne creatures surging down the path toward them. And it would be impossible to reach the doorway to the building in time.

Dellia heard it before she saw it. Amid the sound of her own frenzied movement, the whooshing of her blade, and the chorus of flapping and screeches came a new sound, the wailing cries of countless creatures pouring across the ground toward them.

She raised her voice. "We have to move." She pushed harder, fighting at a frantic pace, throwing more weight behind each blow. "Can you bring the light up here?"

Jon pushed up next to her. The sack of flamestones was slung over both shoulders with the opening in front, sending a blazing light bursting from his chest.

For a fleeting moment, she spotted it, a closed wooden door a dozen steps away. Then it vanished behind a swarm of indistinct dark forms.

Jon called out, "I see the door."

Dellia yelled back, "What if they can pass right through doors and walls?"

"The only reason the lighthouse could stop them was they can't pass through solid things like the cliff walls or the ground."

She could feel the jolt as the swimming mass of dark bodies hit. Jagged claws raked her arm. A deformed skull jumped out of the darkness to slam into her head, and dizziness struck. Her movement took on a panicked pace as she struggled to remain lucid. She couldn't go down. Not now. Not like at the Recluse Tower.

Jon must have noticed because he moved up beside her, the deadliness of his weapons matching her own. The blazing fallen flew past, throwing off sheets of glittering light, their sundered bodies becoming a morbid, sparking torrent that lit the perpetual dark.

As they neared the entry to the house, Garris called out to her. "I'll take the right side of the door. You take the left and use the door as a shield."

Pushed from behind, Sirra shoved up between them, then Garris surged past, each heavy blow slicing through the wall of creatures as if they were paper. He slammed into the unforgiving stone on the far side of the closed door. His blade was aglow with the reflected shower of light as he cut down the flood of bodies the moment they reached him.

Her dizziness now easing, Dellia yanked the door partway open and shoved her mother through the crack. With Garris protecting her back, she set her shoulder to the sturdy wood trying to open the door further, but the hammering of creatures against it caused her feet to skid across the ground.

Jon leaped to her side, protecting her with his blade. Then he flung his weight against the door and yelled, "Go inside! Protect Mom."

Without thought, she complied, her years of following orders overriding all independent judgment. She dove through and whipped around to face the door, only to see Jon fling it wide.

He yelled again, this time to Garris, "On three, I'll dive behind you to the inside. You back up and hold the doorway." He nodded, and Jon started his count. "One ... two ... three." He flew behind Garris, then the big fellow lurched backward to just inside the doorway, forcing the sea of creatures through the narrow passage in their struggle to reach them.

He began felling shadows with powerful blows as they poured through the passage. A wash of flame and cinders obscured their view out the door as sheets of pinprick light flew around Garris. They rained down across the room, scattering over the floor, only to consume themselves into nothingness.

Alarmed, Dellia called out, "What do you think you're doing? Why didn't you close the door and block them out?"

Garris bellowed over his shoulder, "Yeah, what kind of lame-brained plan is this? We should be getting out of here."

Jon remained adamant. "Not yet. We can take turns holding the doorway."

A dull thud rose above the wailing shrieks as creatures hit the stone wall and heavy shutters.

Garris shouted above it, "What's the point?"

"To kill as many as we can. To bloody its nose."

Garris seemed incredulous. "Bloody its nose? They'll be tons more still out there. It won't make any difference."

"It'll make an impression."

Garris grumbled, "Fine. Then let's make an impression." He redoubled his efforts, his whole body behind each blow. His blade became a shredder, decimating the dark bodies flooding through the opening, sending a storm of blazing remains pouring around him in a constant wail of screeches and cries of pain.

The thuds against the wall came faster and faster until they merged into a long, muffled roar.

Jon took over for Garris, then when he grew tired, Dellia took over for him. As she slashed and stabbed, the urgency to get them all out of this cursed place gnawed at her until she couldn't stand it any longer. She had to get Jon to see reason.

As soon as Garris took over for her, Dellia stepped up to Jon, her breath heaving. "This is a reckless strategy. Sooner or later, we're going to make a mistake, and someone will get badly hurt. And for what? I don't know what strategic advantage you hope to gain."

She sensed his anxiety mushroom, but then he steeled himself. Her concern was justified, of course, and every moment Jon insisted they stay risked lives.

He nodded. "I know, but something tells me that every one of these we kill now is one less that can spot us and one less it can throw at us later."

"Are you so sure it's worth someone getting hurt?"

As if on cue, a grunt came from Garris, and a spray of blood spattered Jon's face. His hand flew up, smearing the thick red liquid across his cheek in a futile attempt to brush it away.

Dellia shifted her focus to the big guy, and he had a nasty-looking gash on his shoulder.

He bellowed, "It's nothing! I'm fine!"

She sensed Jon's tension soaring higher, and the need to escape tugged at her with even more urgency. She sent Jon a flat stare. "There will be a sea of them left to spot us or attack us later. This won't make any difference."

"Look, you said it yourself. Your troops being confident is important. Well, that means the reverse is true. Demoralizing your enemy is just as important. By taking this stand here, we'll kill many of them, eroding their confidence just a little. Maybe enough to save us next time."

She wanted to argue, to tell him this thing was probably mindless and incapable of being intimidated. Every fiber of her being was telling her to talk some sense into him so they could get out of here, but she couldn't. This was his mission. It was a burden Jon had taken upon himself. She had volunteered to go with him to support him, but now, she was dangerously close to undermining his confidence, so she held her tongue.

Jon shouted out, "I'll take over for Garris. Sirra, bandage his shoulder."

He shoved Garris out of the way and carved his way farther into the mass of dark bodies crowding the doorway.

She decided to drop it, but her unease kept nagging at her as the roar of screeching and the rumble of thuds grated on her nerves. They kept taking turns, but each round became shorter as their fatigue grew. At first, wounds were few, but before long, Sirra was tending their injuries nonstop.

They were growing weary and getting hurt. Jon's anxiety continued to mount with each round and each new batch of fresh cuts and bruises.

It was Jon who was at the door when the wall around him began to shake and heave. Chunks of mortar rattled loose and fell, leaving trails of dust that hung in the air. It was about to come down on top of him.

Dellia was readying herself to jump up and push him out of the way when a much louder hail of thuds came from above.

Confusion reigned for a moment as she stared up at the ceiling. Then the rafters let out a loud creak, and it dawned on her. The flying creatures were diving into the roof and piling up. Soon it would collapse under their weight.

She was about to say something when Jon shouted, "Sirra, can you open a portal to your home?"

She yelled back, "Good idea."

"You go first, then Garris, then Dellia. I'll keep holding the door and go last."

Dellia couldn't keep the alarm from her voice. "What if they overwhelm you? What if they're faster than you. What if you don't make it?"

"I'll make it."

Jon never looked back, his movement a frenetic dance as body upon body outside the open doorway perished in a blazing pyre.

AYLUN

Sirra raised her palm, and a mist formed in the corner closet while flashes of glowing pinpricks scattered across the floor below it. It came together into a portal with Dellia's childhood home reflected, quiet and serene, on its fluid surface.

The rumble of thuds against the walls and roof grew louder, followed by a jarring thunk from above. The rafter creaked, then groaned, as Sirra and Garris dove through the portal.

A sudden crack came as a corner of the ceiling bent, then it dropped halfway to the floor and bounced. At the edge of the feeble light, shapes of darkness fell into the crack. Their contorted black wings and claws flailed as they screeched, trying to break free. Yet, every moment, more and more became wedged in the jagged opening between the ceiling and wall.

Dellia called out, "You have five heartbeats. If you don't follow, I'll have my mother send me back here." She watched for a fleeting moment as Jon made one last push.

She dove through headfirst and landed in the warm air and soft grass of her mother's front yard.

A mixture of cries, screams, pounding, creaks, and groans came from beyond the portal, and it carried on for what seemed like forever, though it was probably only a matter of moments.

Then a large section of roof collapsed, and dust shot out of the portal. The nerve-shattering medley of screeches, wails, and desperate cries grew in intensity.

The urgency to reach him overpowered her, and she lurched for the shimmering scene, almost colliding with Jon as he plunged out onto the cool, green grass.

He coughed as he rose to his feet.

A loud crash resounded, and more dust billowed through the portal. Then the image shattered as the shimmering curtain turned to mist. With it, the crashes, rumble of thuds, and grating screeches came to a halt, leaving only the chirping of crickets and croaking of frogs. A few remaining fireflies drifted above the fields around them as Dellia stood, recovering.

Jon turned to the weary group. "Is everyone okay?"

Her vision in one eye had been blurry since the blow to her head, but with the other, Dellia surveyed the bloody assemblage. They were a hodgepodge of scrapes, gashes, and punctures, Garris's worse than the others. The scratches on her own face and arms smarted, and blood was caked in her hair. Her mother seemed unharmed, but her face held a traumatized look.

Garris scanned them with her, then snorted. "Given the insanity you just put us through, we're all just dandy."

Jon gave a thoughtful nod. "I'll tend Dellia's wounds. She can bandage mine, and Sirra, can you see what you can do with Garris."

She nodded.

"Then we rest. I'll go back once I get a little sleep. If you all still want to take part in this madness, I would welcome you. But I have to admit, after what we just went through, I don't like our chances."

Dellia offered to let Garris stay in her room, and she would stay with Jon in the guesthouse. He agreed, and the two groups dragged themselves off to their respective quarters.

Later, she was lying down with her head over a basin of water as Jon washed the blood out of her hair. She kept her focus on the ceiling as his fingers massaged her scalp with a firm but gentle touch. "Jon, where you go, I go, but I have to ask, why are we even there? We restored the lighthouses. The Dead of Night is contained. Isn't that enough?"

He shook his head. "No, if the Mirhal take over, we're all dead."

"But we counteracted the rumor. Shouldn't that be enough to stop the Mirhal?"

Jon seemed to consider the question as he continued his tender kneading. "Do we know for sure they can be stopped? What if it's already gone too far? What if the damage the rumor did to our reputations is too great?"

Dellia hesitated. Nothing Jon said was wrong, yet it still had a wrong feel to it.

As she struggled for a response, he tried again. "Think of it this way. If we stop after repairing the lighthouses, it could make things worse. It will look like we only responded to the rumor. So, the Mirhal will just spread more rumors, saying it's proof I let the Dead of Night loose. They'll claim I only fixed it to cover up the damage I caused. Things have gone too far."

He was making sense, but even so, what he was attempting was unthinkable. That they could make it to the heart of this thing and kill it seemed impossible. "If we die, the Mirhal win."

"And if the Mirhal win, we die."

He was right, but it still didn't make what he was doing any less ludicrous. "How does what we're doing make more sense than fixing the lighthouses and going back to Shirdon to stop them?"

"That was my first impulse, which means they'll anticipate it. They can predict us. They'll be there to stop us wherever we go. If they seize control, returning would most likely be an immediate death sentence. It would be the end of you, me, your mom, the protectors, everything."

Dellia paused to consider his assertion. Confronting the Mirhal in Shirdon was a predictable strategy. One any clever strategist would have no trouble countering, much less an oracle who could foresee the exact details of their every action.

While she pondered, Jon kept going. "Look, since we left Shirdon, we have been used and manipulated. We have been playing the game the Mirhal set up for us." His deft fingers avoided her wound as they continued to rub away her pain and anxiety.

She peered up into his eyes. "And most of that is my fault for not believing in you."

"Which is my fault for giving you no reason to believe in me." Jon smiled. "Look, it's enough that you're here to do this with me now."

She averted her gaze, feeling even more ashamed in the face of his kindhearted sentiment.

He forged ahead. "I figure we can never win a game where oracles make the rules. The way you beat them is to not play their game. I want to force them to play *our* game."

"*Our* game?"

"Yes. We have to do something completely unexpected and shocking. We have to take their own lies and turn them upside down. We can't just confront them. We have to expose them, crush them, and humiliate them. Defeating the Dead of Night is how we begin to do all that. The instant we succeed, the rumor will be forgotten, and all the people will talk about is how we ended a threat to Talus that had hung over them for hundreds of years. All people will remember is that we reclaimed land that was lost eons ago. That's how we defeat the Mirhal."

Dellia recalled Jon's statement to her on their first day of marriage. She eyed him again. "What about this invasion? If we die, who stops it?"

He drew a deep breath as he began to squeeze the water out of her hair. "I'll be honest with you. I don't see how we can stop an invasion any more than you can see how we stop the Dead of Night. It's ridiculous. The invasion I saw was far bigger and more deadly than what we faced today." He set a hand on her arm. "You want to prove to me we can stop the invasion, then help me kill the Dead of Night."

It was impossible not to admire his courage and persuasiveness, and she nodded. "Okay, but answer me one question."

He grabbed a towel and squeezed her hair with it as he peered at her with concerned eyes.

She studied his emotions with her gift as she scrutinized his face. "Do you really believe we can defeat the Dead of Night?"

Jon halted and seemed to consider her question for a long while, then drew a deep breath. "When I think about it rationally, what we have to go on isn't much: just a few secondhand words from an unreliable source that Garris may or may not have heard correctly. It seems insane. Or it would be, if not for the fact that it agrees with my own strong impressions. All along, my gut has been telling me there must be a central organizing intelligence, that it is mortal, and that it can be destroyed. Now, maybe that's just my own wishful thinking. But perhaps it's more. Perhaps it's some kind of residual effect of the temporary insight I gained from the Stone of Syvis; I don't know. What I do know is everything I've seen points to my gut feeling being right."

Dellia nodded. "But first, we have to make it to that temple."

Jon continued his gentle squeezing of water from her hair. "By my figuring, we've already made it a third of the way. We have the ability to see our enemy. That's an advantage of which it is unaware. And we have your mother to get us out if things go bad. I think we have a chance."

Dellia peered straight into his eyes. "You sound confident, but I'm sensing a lot of uncertainty and fear, and it worries me."

"I know." He reached down and embraced her. "I wish I could be confident, but I'm used to dealing in provable facts, and I have none here. The bottom line is, my head keeps telling me yes, there must be a way to reach it and kill it. And my heart wants to believe I can find it. But there's still a part of me that is terrified that one of you will get hurt. I don't think I could handle that."

With that, she let the subject drop. It was enough of an answer. Jon believed with all his being that they could do the impossible, and she couldn't fault him for being afraid. The prospect of her or Garris or her mother getting hurt was more frightening to him than it was to her.

She had played her part in things becoming as bad as they were. Their plight was all the more desperate because she went to undo Jon's coming to this world. It was a harsh lesson to find out she had been used as a tool to hurt him and betray the people, all because she placed faith in rumors and lies rather than trust in the man she knew. Supporting him now in what he was attempting was the right thing to do. It was the price she must pay for her prior lack of faith.

Later, as they lay down to get a few hours rest, Dellia wrapped her arm around him and snuggled close, basking in his affection for her. As she did, for the first time, it hit home how close they were to losing each other. Sure, she had always known what Jon was attempting was beyond risky, but the idea of what it might be like after he was gone was not one she had ever let herself entertain.

With that realization came a new understanding of her monumental foolishness. She had always imagined herself to be fearless, and when it came to facing a foe, she was. But with Jon came a new kind of fear, one she couldn't handle. It was one thing to stand toe to toe with death and never flinch, but it was an altogether different thing when death was peering into the face of the one you loved.

She had let that fear drive a wedge between her and Jon, as if by venting her anger and frustration, she might cause him to turn away from his mortal fate, but it had done the opposite. It had pushed him away and left him vulnerable when he needed her the most. And with that realization, she resolved that tomorrow, whatever came, no matter how dangerous or chaotic it got, they would face their fate together, and for him, she would not flinch again.

Aylun's breath rasped as he leaned his head back against the stone wall of the cliffs. He closed his eyes as trails of sweat streamed down his face. His chest tightened, and a crushing heaviness stole his breath as the echoes of her screams repeated in his head. This was the place where he had argued with Yaolin. It was where they'd spoken their final words. It was the last place he'd seen her before she died.

He turned his focus to his uneven breathing, shutting out all thought. As he quieted his mind, the screams crept back to the recesses. He stayed that way for a while, until he was calmer. Then, he returned his thoughts to the mission that had led to her death.

It had been Yaolin's desire to undertake the search for the journal. She had come here because she sought answers she believed could save many lives. Her purpose had been noble and one she deemed worth her life. It was now his mission, his purpose. As long as he held to that truth and embraced her goal, her death, no matter how gruesome, would never be in vain.

AYLUN

Aylun glanced again at the crumbled-away edge of the bridge above, then at the sheer rock walls that disappeared into darkness out on either side. The site of their terminal encounter seemed a fitting place to begin his final push to reach the journal. That he would ever find it still seemed unlikely, which also made this a fitting place to start what might be his last stand.

A sudden shame fell upon him. This was for Megan. He couldn't entertain thoughts of defeat. He glanced over at the gash down half of his left arm. Bloody and deep, it ran from his shoulder down past his elbow, making it a constant source of pain. To divert his focus, he closed his eyes and summoned peaceful memories of sharing breakfast with Megan and her excitement at exploring the hidden city.

When he rested like this, the throbbing of his wound eased, at least until he moved his arm again. Then the sharpness of the pain was excruciating. At those times, he was forced to rely on his right arm, making the risk of further injury even greater.

It had become like this when he lost the leather strip and hook he'd used as a weapon. The barb had sunk into something so big, he couldn't hang on to the goatskin cord. So, like a fool, he'd wrapped it around his arm. Instead of the leather strap slipping through his grasp, it dragged him through the woods. Not only did he get banged up pretty good, but he had been hauled smack into the midst of another group of shadow creatures. There, he was forced to untether his arm while he defended himself.

He'd managed to eliminate all of them but drew another of the enormous beasts, and in the melee that followed, he'd earned the nasty gash on his arm. He prevailed but then lost countless hours nursing a fresh and agonizing wound as he searched in the dark until he found the road again. Now, he was reduced to using his bladed staff and katana. It was effective but forced him into close combat with only one good arm where the risk of injury was greatest.

Aylun brought himself back to the moment. It was mandatory he keep moving. If he allowed himself to be swarmed again in his present state, it would be the end for him. So, he hauled himself to his feet and wandered along the base of cliffs until he discovered a climb shallow enough to manage with one arm. Once he reached the top, he followed the upper cliff's edge back to the road.

The permanent darkness muted the light of his flamestone, only allowing him to see the road's edge and a little beyond. His goal was just shy of Wistra's cabins, less than a half day away. All vegetation in this forsaken place had perished centuries ago in the unyielding dark where it seemed to never rain. Not even mushrooms survived here. All that remained were the jagged, long-desiccated trunks of ancient trees.

The road began to climb up the mountainside, a sign his goal was even closer now. He recalled running down it to escape the smoke and flames of Yaolin's fire and the airborne horde it unleashed. The drop-off at the road's edge might have given him vertigo if he could see its depths, but darkness devoured the view, leaving only his imagination to fuel his caution.

Distance and direction were difficult to gauge in this never-ending blackness, but Aylun plodded up the road until right before what he estimated to be the location of the last of Yaolin's cries. He had reached his goal, so now came the tricky part. She had spotted the enormous nests of the flying beasts. They rested on top of the massive ledges jutting from the cliffside and reminded her of the ones made of saliva that were a treasured ingredient in bird's nest soup.

Now, his task would be to search them, and there was no way to do that without drawing the attention of the things that nested in them. The last time those abominations had spotted him and Yaolin, it had led to a swarm chasing them in an all-out flight for their lives. It was in that moment that the seeds of her death had taken root. Today's intrusion might trigger a repeat of that incident, but he had to try. After all, a sailor could not expect to reach their destination without leaving the shore.

In order to search the nests, he needed a light he could dangle over the cliff's edge. He was rigging the flamestone to the end of a section of rope when the sudden roar of countless wings surrounded him. It issued forth from every side, as if all at once a vast ocean of beasts had taken flight.

Aylun dropped the flamestone, unslung his weapon, and rolled onto his back. Blades sprang from the weapon's tips and the two halves clicked into place as he brought them together across his chest and twisted Squawks and cries pierced the roar of the fluttering all around him.

In a sudden rush, dark outlines shot past. They sped through the space above his face, then dove out over the cliffs. Eyes wide, he lay on his back, clutching his weapon in panicked anticipation of his certain demise. Yet it didn't come.

More and more appeared, and many of the black shapes stared down at him as they raced past. They followed him with dark, red eyes and vicious retracted claws as they soared only a couple of arms' lengths above his face.

He held his breath and waited. They saw him. How could they not? Yet every single one of them ignored him. What could draw such intense interest that every last one of them would leave him unmolested?

He stayed on his back, frozen by fear as the flapping shapes blurred together and the rumble of beating wings went on and on. Then, as suddenly as the noise had started, the trailing edge of the flock rushed past, and the medley of flapping and cries receded.

His heart still hammering in his chest, Aylun rolled to his feet and stood for a while, facing the cliff's edge as the noise faded into the dark and foreboding distance. He stayed that way until all that remained was a silence as thick as the darkness.

Then he ventured to the cliff's edge and leaned over it. Fortune had handed him a chance to search the cliffside nests in peace. So, he lowered the rope, dangling the flamestone above the jagged rock surface, scanning for any sign of Yaolin's remains or the journal.

In the ensuing half day, or so he estimated, he traveled up along the cliff's edge. He found an alarming number of massive nests and even a few wet-looking, featherless young ones. They yawned their jagged beaks up at him in a fruitless quest for food, but he found no sign of the journal or Yaolin's remains.

When he became worried his flamestone would lose its light, he sought out the ancient stone house where they had recovered Wistra's journal. For a mountain home, it was rather spacious, with a generous open fireplace. Yet, despite its size, it possessed a simple and serene ambiance. Little doubt remained that it was where the Greatest of Oracles had once lived.

It was tricky to find in the darkness, but once he had, he carried wood into the house using his wounded arm and built a small fire. Discouraged and in pain, he hunkered next to it, trying to warm his aching bones. With time, his mind fell blank, drifting in a haze born of intense fatigue, both mental and physical.

It was then, as Aylun stared at the fire flickering around his flamestone, that they came back. At first a quiet rumble below his awareness, cawing and screeches soon rose above it. It continued unrelenting, the squawks growing louder until outside the cabin, there roared a sea of wings flapping. It seemed a safe bet they were returning for him.

He was lying awake, fearful and drained of all strength, when his eyes fell on the metal trunk he and Yaolin had left behind when they found the journal. She had wanted to pick the lock, but it became apparent this was impossible when she'd expended ten times the effort she usually required. Not one to give up without a fight, she then insisted they take it with them. In the end, they were forced to abandon it when they discovered it had been built into the stone floor at the foot of the bed and was therefore unmovable.

When they brushed away the dust that lay thick upon its lid, they uncovered a gorgeous dragonfly inlaid diagonally across its surface. It was further evidence that the chest had once belonged to Wistra, but whatever lay inside, she was determined it not be taken by him or Yaolin. Who knew what valuable insights it might contain? If only he had brought Megan's dragon key, perhaps he could unearth those secrets now.

He tore his eyes from it. There was no point in dwelling on what might have been. He returned his attention to the noise outside as it settled to an occasional plaintive cry.

After a time, weariness won out. His last thoughts as he drifted off were that he was now alone, trapped, and wounded, a raccoon up a tree with the hounds circling below. He had no way to escape this snare, much less finish his search and find the journal. Even if he could, his wound was only going to get worse, and it seemed impossible now that he would make it out of here before he succumbed to it.

Still, he must. Megan needed his help. So, no matter how dire things might become, he needed to finish this one last task. He must not fail her.

Garris braced himself as the rough wet cloth ground against his bloody, raw flesh. He distracted himself by focusing on his burning concern over the fate of Kayleen. It had been fifteen years since he had been in a similar situation. He was stuck on a mission with no idea what had happened to her, or, for that matter, what might be happening to her right now.

Sirra pulled back from the wound and glowered at it for a moment. She dunked the cloth in her bowl of cool water and wrung it out again, then heaved an exasperated sigh. "You know as well as I do you have no business going back out there."

He glanced down at Sirra's face. Her forehead was wrinkled in concentration, her focus intense, as she dabbed the skin around one of the three gaping wounds on his shoulders and arms. He peered down at the bowl of water, now dark red with his blood. "You're right, but not because I'm hurt."

She looked up at him.

"Kayleen is my business, and every bone in my body is telling me she's in trouble—that I have to go to Shirdon and get her out of there." He drew a long, deep breath. "But I made a bargain."

"A bargain?" Sirra nodded. "Is your honor worth her life?" She seemed to ponder her own question for a moment. "Is it worth your life?"

Garris scoffed. "No. My honor isn't worth the putrid garbage you throw to the dogs." He peered down at the large wirehaired canine lying in a heap at Sirra's side. "No offense, Tilla." He returned his gaze to Sirra. "Rillen is with her. Whatever happened was done and over with a day ago. She's either safe with the protector or …" He couldn't bring himself to utter the word. "Or she's beyond my help. The only reason for me to go there now would be to satisfy my own insecurity."

She scowled. "It's not insecurity to worry about someone you care about."

Garris let out a low grunt. "However you want to say it. The fact remains that me being there won't change anything. It would only satisfy my own need to know she's safe."

She continued to work with rapt attention, and it wasn't until she began to wrap a bandage around his chest and shoulder that she spoke again. "So you actually intend to go back and do more fighting in this condition?"

Garris drew another deep breath. "Yes, Kayleen ordered me to do this, and as much as it drives me crazy to admit it, she's right. We have to stop the Dead of Night, or we may all wind up fugitives or dead."

She looked up at him. "These wounds of yours are serious. If you keep this up, you could jeopardize everything and everyone."

"I'm not crippled yet. It'll be fine."

Sirra sighed. "You're a grown man. I can't very well call you pigheaded, stupid, or reckless."

He chuckled. "Thank you for not calling me pigheaded, stupid, or reckless."

She stifled a laugh.

There was very little further discussion and many a disapproving stare as she finished and dumped the bloody water out the window. Then she asked for his flamestone so she could put it in the fireplace. After she'd taken it, she bid him an efficient good night. For a long while, he lay alone and in pain as his weariness battled with his concern for Kayleen, until eventually, fatigue won.

It wasn't long before Sirra awakened him. He could tell by the stinging of his eyes and the darkness beyond the window that it was still night out. Mired in worry, tired from lack of sleep, and sore and aching from the ordeal of the day before, Garris dragged himself out of bed.

When he arrived in the kitchen, his flamestone lay on the table next to a small bowl of porridge and a piece of stale bread. With no one to share his repast, he ate alone in the dark and quiet. The isolation was more than fine. To avoid a fuss being made over his physical state, he would have had to pretend he was okay, and putting up an act like that was taxing.

The servings were on the meager side, which showed Sirra's wisdom. A heavy meal would bloat them and slow them down, and too little would leave them lethargic. Here, the portions were just right.

Afterward, struggling to hide his pain and stiffness, he strode out to the lawn where everyone had gathered for the day's journey. Sirra opened a portal and brought them back to the permanent darkness and the small stone home at the other end of the town from where they'd left.

Garris watched with confusion as Jon used his gift again on Elt's sword. It wasn't hard to understand why he was doing it. He wanted the lizard sight so he could scout out the area.

What puzzled him was that this was the fourth time the man had used his gift with the same sword: once in the Recluse Tower, once before the battle at the second lighthouse, and this made the second time in the Dead of Night. Yet, he couldn't seem to use Dellia's ring even twice. Unable to make sense of the differing situations, Garris focused instead on keeping a sharp ear open for trouble.

Throughout the day, travel was torturous. Even worse, he was a useless fifth wheel. Dellia was adept at fighting without her eyes, and with his lizard sight, Jon now saw well in this lightless place. By comparison, he was blind and distracted by concern for Kayleen, not to mention, the pain of his wounds throbbed with each step.

Getting around had been arduous enough the day before when all he could see was the edge of the road and an occasional bridge, crossroad, sign, or walkway. For this outing, Jon decided to stay off of the road, hoping it would keep them out of sight. It made sense but rendered Garris a useless tagalong with no idea where they were. The only thing that kept them from becoming utterly lost was Jon and his enhanced vision.

They made good time, despite the disconcerting way he led them here and there, traversing stump forests, hiking across barren fields, and winding through long-abandoned cities. He claimed it was working and that they hadn't been spotted by things only he could see.

Throughout it all, Garris persevered. At first, his hopes for this venture were tempered, at best, but as time dragged on and everyone grew weary from strain and fatigue, his hopes rekindled. They had to be well past halfway, none of them was in dire shape, and the city they were in was more expansive than any so far. Best of all, throughout the entire day, Jon and Dellia had neither seen nor heard a sign of anything.

Then as they were crossing a plaza and heading for another alley, he spotted it off to the side: a pitch-black, chest-high mound lying on the ground beneath the overhang of a building.

With as little sound as possible, he hurried up to Jon and set a hand on his shoulder a mere dozen steps from the dark pile. He signaled to Dellia to stop and slipped out his sword as she did the same.

Jon remained frozen, peering at the black heap on the stone walkway as it expanded and contracted. It was breathing.

Garris stepped between Jon and the thing and motioned him to return the way they had come.

Dellia hurried past her mother and out ahead, leading the retreat.

Jon followed.

Garris was about to join them when a massive head slid out from under a wing far enough for a closed eye to appear. The lid snapped open, revealing a dark red iris. He and the beast stared at one another for a moment, frozen by uncertainty.

Then a huge set of featherless wings unfurled. The whole beast was larger than any of the last ones they'd encountered. It flapped, lifting a massive body into the air in a cloud of dust. It shot forward, and a needle-sharp claw as long as Garris's forearm reached for his side.

He dodged away but was too slow, and it sank into the flesh at the edge of his waist with a stabbing jolt. He tried to bring the sword down on the leg, but the beast let loose with another powerful flap that blasted dried dirt and dust from the ground and sent it all around them. Agony ripped through Garris's side as the beast shot overhead and its claw tore free, leaving a bloody gash in his side where the skin used to be.

Sirra ducked as the now-airborne creature soared above her. The monstrosity dropped onto her back and pushed off again with huge claws, sending her flying into the ground with holes along her back.

Sirra's head cracked against the cobbles, and she fell limp.

A shrill shriek rang through the darkness.

Dizzy and reeling from the pain, Garris ducked low to checked Sirra's breathing. Blood was trickling down her forehead. It looked bad, but then again, head injuries usually did. He peered up at Dellia. "Your mother is alive. She has a head wound, and she's unconscious."

Jon was staring up into the black sky. "We need to move. I think that shriek was a call for reinforcements."

The warning was pointless. Garris was already moving. He grabbed one of Sirra's arms as Dellia lifted the other. Pain tore at his side with every step, and Sirra's feet scraped against the cobblestones as they hauled her into the alley.

They set her against the wall, and Dellia kept her focus on her mother as Garris raised an ear to the black sky.

Above them, the flapping grew distant, then a screech came, then another. The sound of beating wings multiplied, turning into a persistent rumble. As the chaos of fluttering grew closer, it hit him. They were trapped in a narrow alley, their only means of escape lay unconscious, and they were about to be under siege. He looked to his two partners, and Jon stood above him, scanning the sky.

Dellia was still checking her mother over, then her head shot up, and she peered out of the alley. "Do you hear that?" She looked at Garris, and in the warm light of the flamestones, her face paled. "Oh, Adi! Can you fight like that?"

Without looking at the wound, he could tell it was bad. The pain was enough to dispel all doubt. Even so, Garris glanced down to where she was looking, and his side was laid open. A large rip had left a chunk of skin dangling loose and the muscle beneath showing through.

He steeled himself. "I have to. I'll manage." He winced as he stood, then looked up as a flurry of countless wings came from above. The sound was deeper than before, betraying that these flying things were also larger than in the last encounter. If they were the size of the one that had torn open his side, they'd be unable to fly into the narrow space of an alley.

Another sound blended with the squawks and flapping, a repeated clacking from above. He didn't need to see it to know. It was the sound of countless claws landing on the roofs on either side. It was followed by scraping, then, all at once, slick, black faces appeared out of the darkness—faces of beasts crawling down the walls with beaks lunging at him.

A rush of wings and squawks came from the end of the alley, only an arm's length in front of Dellia. In an instant, she whirled into motion, stabbing and slashing at the sheet of black forms whipping by her. They were close enough to reach her, to claw and peck at her. She couldn't hold them off for long before they tore her to shreds.

Grimacing through his pain, Garris joined her, hacking at the faces climbing toward them from above.

A storm of embers and sparks showered down as Jon crouched to examine Sirra. It was a smart move. She was their escape plan, and getting her back to consciousness might be the only way to save them now.

Then the low rumble of myriad feet came from the other direction. Somewhere in the heavy darkness, a wave of things was coming, but he couldn't see the end of the alley, much less what was headed their way. Even if he could, he dared not take his attention from the creatures above to fend them off.

Garris shouted over his shoulder as he cut through face after face climbing down, the severed bits falling like burning comets with glittering trails of ember and ash. "Any bright ideas on how to get us out of this?" He glanced down at Jon. The man remained crouched before Sirra with the dazed look of a trapped animal.

Overwhelmed by the speed with which things had spiraled out of control, Jon stared at his mother-in-law, propped against the wall and unmoving. His anxiety shot up. He had no miracle cure to get her back to consciousness, and she was their way out of this jam. Without her portals, the onslaught would wear them down until they perished in a gruesome flurry of claws and teeth. His gift was of no use either, since he had barely been able to acquire her ability to create portals a second time, and a third seemed impossible.

Garris's voice snapped him out of it. "Any bright ideas on how to get us out of here?"

With a speed born of anxiety, Jon checked her eyes. The pupils seemed to respond to light, and they weren't dilated. An abundance of medical television shows had taught him this meant her brain was probably okay. He pressed his fingers into her neck—her pulse remained regular and strong. Then he turned his attention to the gash on her head. The blood coating her face made his stomach turn but didn't seem life-threatening.

Still, she wasn't opening any portals anytime soon. Jon looked up at Dellia, fighting with all her speed and skill against the furious wave of shadow-beasts crowding the alley entrance. They were larger than the ones they'd last encountered, with longer winding arms and larger razor claws. His anxiety crept up again. This situation was more deadly than the last. He yelled to her, "I think your mom will be okay."

Garris shouted down to him again. "I said, any bright ideas on how to get us out of this?"

Jon looked over at him. "I'm thinking."

Above the chaotic clamor, Garris yelled back, "What about you use that gift of yours on Sirra's dagger and make us a portal out of here?"

"I tried. I can't do it more than twice."

"Why? You've used Elt's sword four times now."

The question struck him all at once. Garris was right. It didn't make any sense. Why could he use Elt's sword over and over but not Dellia's ring or Sirra's dagger?

He stared ahead in confusion as blades whistled through the air and thudded and clanged against flesh and claw. Then the difference hit him. When he used Elt's sword, he didn't know what he was looking for, so he concentrated on the weapon itself. When he used Dellia's ring, he brought to mind the portal she'd opened in her yard. In one case, he had no particular skill or ability in mind. In the other, he had focused on acquiring Sirra's gift.

A pained grunt came from Garris, along with the thud of a sword striking flesh.

Jon looked over as a flaming body plummeted down at his side, landing with a startling thud, then consuming itself in a whirling flurry of cinders. He ignored it and reached for Sirra's dagger.

She groaned and stirred, but her eyes remained shut.

He wrapped his fingers around the grip and concentrated on the dagger itself. Time slowed. The sparkling rain of severed pieces slowed with it. Wings soaring overhead came to a crawl, and the swinging of Dellia's blade through the sheet of beaks and claws ground to a stop. Her face held a fierce look of determination as she stood there, frozen midblow.

A shimmering scene appeared, overlaid on the darkness. It was the image of moments ago as the creature took flight. Jon spun time backward to the gray dawn before the Recluse Tower and Sirra opening a portal to it in her yard. He focused on the shimmering curtain itself, but the image only melted away, and time began to speed up again. He had failed.

Still, it seemed closer than he'd gotten in the past. In determination and terror, his heart racing in his ears, he concentrated and stopped time from resuming. When the world had frozen again, he turned back time to the same event and focused harder. The image began to slip away, so he focused still harder, trying to summon every detail of the memory. The scene flashed and jittered as if it wanted to flitter away, but he forced it back in one final push, and this time, it stayed. He had taken her gift a third time.

As time resumed, he looked up at Garris. "It worked. I can open a portal and get us out of here."

Garris cut two creatures in half with a single blow. As a sparkling avalanche of their crumbling remains pelted him from above, he scowled at Jon over his shoulder. "We're not abandoning this mission."

"I'm sending Sirra back to camp for medical help." He looked to Dellia to see her reaction.

In a flurry of motion, she hacked and stabbed. A wildfire of burning parts and swirling embers whipped around her as she shouted to him, "We're pinned down. We all leave, or we all die."

Garris bellowed back. "You can leave. I won't."

Jon yelled, "I have an idea. Can either of you get me one of those creatures ... alive?"

Dellia shouted, "What?"

"Can either of you—"

"I heard you. I just ..." She heaved forward with a grunt and stabbed one of the flying beasts in the neck.

It flailed, and sharp claws raked her arm as she yanked it around by her sword. She groaned in pain as she flung it to the ground and jabbed her weapon into the dirt, pinning the huge beast by its throat as it thrashed.

The instant it was down, Dellia turned back to her struggle, and a spray of warmth showered Jon's face.

He wiped it away and peered up at Dellia. There was now a second gash on her arm with blood flowing down it.

He tore his gaze from his wounded wife and focused on the creature. It was the first time he'd seen an individual beast close up. As he peered at it, the difficulty in making out individual creatures became clear. The beast emanated a smokey darkness that distorted and blurred its form. Nearly as long as Dellia was tall, the half-bird, half-bat, writhed there, flailing its slick, featherless wings and snapping its long, sharp beak in every direction with furious intensity. Just as it clacked shut, Jon reached out and grabbed it midair. It squirmed and wriggled in his grasp, and it took all his strength to hold it still and shut as he concentrated on the beast itself—and then time slowed.

Still half-hysterical from seeing her injured, he glanced at Dellia.

She stood all alone, with only her dagger against a raging wall of creatures careening past the end of the alley. Her blade swung out into it, slashing body after body, her movements becoming slower and slower.

Sharp claws raked another deep cut in her leg as her dagger came down, sundering the beast. Blood sprayed from her wound in slow-motion, then froze in the air. Even the sound waves of her frustrated groan rippled out from her as she stood still, then dimmed.

AYLUN

Disorientation hit him as a shimmering aerial world blinked into existence, rolling over the current frozen one. A sudden dive downward jarred his stomach as the land neared, then fell away as he swooped back up.

He was viewing the land from above, and it wasn't dark like before. So these creatures could see in this endless blackness, and he was viewing it as the beast saw it.

He rolled time backward, searching and searching. Long stretches of barren landscape, dotted with towns, roads, rivers, and villages, flew by beneath. They went on and on until, at last, he spied it from above: at the edge of a sprawling city lay a massive spire, its ivory teeth arching up below him as he banked and dove past it.

He froze the image and searched the area. Near it stood a temple. Like the icon on the map, it was a round stone structure, perhaps two hundred feet across and ringed by enormous fluted columns. This was their goal.

He scanned the nearby area and found what looked like an ancient Greek coliseum across a plaza to the east of the temple. The abandoned stone structure had an open center with bleachers on four sides, protecting it from view. It was the perfect spot to escape to and hide.

He let time resume.

With all the haste he could muster, he yanked Dellia's blade down, severing the pinned beast's throat.

The dead body disintegrated in a flaming fury, shooting off burning particles in every direction.

He called Dellia's name and tossed her the weapon, hilt first.

She reached back as she stabbed and slashed, and without looking, she snatched the grip midair. A weapon now in each hand, she whipped them out into the torrent of beasts spinning by. She heaved, slashed, and lunged.

Jon stretched out his palm, picturing the camp near the lighthouse. A shimmering curtain formed in front of him.

Through the glittering waterfall of decaying remains, he spied a patrolling soldier, walking the perimeter, with rows of tents behind him.

He shouted, "I'm sending Sirra back to the camp! They can help her. You should go with her, Dellia. She's your mother. Garris and I will finish this."

She never paused. "I stay with you."

The patrolling soldier stopped, turned toward the watery curtain, and stared as Jon lifted Sirra up by one arm.

With fire and embers on every side, he heaved her forward. She groaned but didn't open her eyes as he shoved her through the portal headfirst.

A clang rang out, and the head of a beast plummeted from Garris's sword. Flames consumed it, and ash whirled up as it fell past the portal, obscuring his view.

Through the sparks, he caught sight of Sirra, falling on her side in the grass as the soldier raced toward her.

He let the shimmering curtain fall apart, then a blast of glowing particles from Dellia's blade obliterated the remaining mist.

He shouted to her, "A soldier on patrol was nearby. She'll get help right away."

Screeches and roars resounded near his head, and a sparkling deluge pelted Jon as he stretched out his palm again. A dark mist gathered into another portal.

A new creature plunged past his head, landing on the dirt as Garris heaved his sword down and cleaved it in two in a roar of fire and cinders.

As the image solidified, the green-tinged bleachers of the coliseum rippled on its surface.

Jon shouted, "I have our escape ready. When I say 'now,' it'll mean I'm already going through the portal. Garris, you follow, then Dellia, as fast as you can. Got it?" Without waiting for a response, he yelled, "Now!" and dove through.

He dodged out of the way, and Garris appeared almost at once. The massive fellow rolled and lay there on his side, unmoving, as Dellia came through.

A sharp beak followed by red eyes in a slick dark head dove after Dellia as she hit the ground.

Jon grabbed Garris's sword and brought it up, sheering off the head in a flurry of blazing decay. He let the portal dissolve, and the mist blew away in the backwash.

The cacophony came to a sudden halt, replaced by a thick darkness and perfect quiet that was unnerving.

A groan broke the silence as Garris pulled himself up on one knee. Blood coated half his body.

Jon rose to his feet. They were at the center of the coliseum. No creatures knew where they'd gone, so now was their chance to seek a quiet place to recover, but it all hinged on remaining unnoticed.

Adrenaline still fueling his haste, he scanned the area. Almost at once, he found a hallway to the west, leaving the center. It led in the direction where he'd seen the temple.

He grabbed one of Garris's arms and slung it over his shoulder. Dellia took the other, and their labored breath echoed across the coliseum grounds as they hurried the bulky fellow to the hallway.

Partway down lay a heavy wooden door. Jon heaved it open, and they piled through. He shouldered it shut. Their footsteps resounded through the dark and twisting halls as they wound their way along them to a back room.

He lowered Garris onto the hard stone floor, with his back resting against the wall.

Dellia slid down to sit beside him.

Jon stood up and stepped back, taking in the scene of Garris and Dellia, side by side, propped up against the sheet of cold, dark stone. He froze, standing motionless, surveying them as a slow dripping of water came from a puddle in the far corner of the room.

Garris was a bloody mess. Wounds from yesterday had reopened and were mingled with fresh ones from today. It was stomach-turning to even look at the gash in his side, and all his fighting had only torn it wider. He could barely walk.

Jon's wife was covered in slashes and scrapes. Her beautiful face was raked with claw marks and smeared with blood. She put on a brave front, trying to hide it, but there was no mistaking that she was in terrible shape.

He looked down at the blood on his hands and clothes, their blood, his wife's blood. His head rose, and a familiar dread filled him as he took in the horrific scene. It was like his stepsister and Brita all over again.

In a quiet voice, he spoke to himself. "What have I done?" He staggered, stunned by the bloody state he'd forced his friends into. "This is all my fault. I'm so sorry, Dellia. I'm so sorry. I didn't mean it. Forgive me, please."

She didn't move, her eyes fixed ahead. "What are you apologizing for?" She forced a smile. "You've done nothing wrong."

"Are you kidding me? Look at you. Your beautiful face is a mess. I did that. I scarred you. I'm a terrible person."

Dellia looked at him, and her smile broadened, no longer seeming forced. "You think my face is beautiful?"

"That's not the point. You're in terrible shape. Garris can hardly stand."

The man sat up straighter. "What are you talking about? It's just a flesh wound."

Jon's panic grew. They were in no shape to fight, yet they were quarreling with him. He pointed to the raw muscle showing through the gash in Garris's side. "A flesh wound? You're one giant flesh wound."

Dellia spoke softly. "Nobody made us come. We came of our own free will."

Now in a panic, Jon hurried over to stand at her side. "No. This has gone too far. I have to open a portal while I still can. You guys have to go back." He raised his palm and pictured the camp at the lighthouse. "That's an order."

Garris scoffed.

A soft, warm hand rested on Jon's wrist. It didn't so much pull on him as the weight of it dragged his arm down. He glanced at Dellia, and a smile still graced her marred face.

She shook her head and, in a quiet voice, said, "No, Jon."

He stared for a moment.

Then her hand slid away into her lap, but she kept her eyes on him. "I've never been more proud of you than I am right now."

"What crazy person would be proud of *this*?" He motioned to their beaten, bedraggled, and bloody bodies.

She glanced at herself and Garris, then brought her blue gaze back to rest on his. "You're trying to save people. You're trying to save *my* people." She leaned her head against his leg, letting it take her weight as she wrapped her arm around it and gave it a weak hug. "I know you're afraid, and I know how hard it is for you to see us hurt. I feel it with you. But I also know you can do this."

A strange calm came over him at her praise.

She tugged on his pant leg.

He leaned back against the wall and slid down to sit at her side.

She tilted her head and rested it on his shoulder. "Megan was right. You got us this far. If anyone can get us the rest of the way, it's you. How much farther do we have to go?"

Too shocked to respond any other way, Jon spoke in a quiet monotone. "I used my gift on that flying thing you caught for me. I could see what it saw from the air. I searched its past until I saw the layout of this colosseum thing we're in and everything around it." He pointed to the west. "There's a plaza at the end of the hallway. The temple is on the other side."

Dellia seemed surprised. "It's that close?"

Jon nodded. "A few hundred steps."

Her relief showed in her scratched and sweaty face. "See, we're almost done. We can't quit now. Live or die, we finish this, okay? One heart, one mind—you and me."

Jon looked around Dellia at Garris, searching for some sign of disagreement. The warrior glanced at him, then his eyes flittered away. "What she said. We're almost there. You can't wimp out now."

Dellia squelched a giggle, then elbowed Garris. He groaned, and she stifled another laugh at his reaction. "I never used the word *wimp*."

Garris grunted. "Sure. He's a fine upstanding young man of unparalleled bravery who wanted to chicken out when we've almost reached our goal."

Still in shock, Jon shook his head. "This isn't funny, you guys."

Garris's voice took on a serious note. "We're willing to see this through to the end. To give it everything we have, even our lives. That's our decision. What's yours?"

He eyed Garris for several drawn-out seconds as the dripping of water echoed across the room. "I'll bandage your wound."

Dellia didn't quite suppress another laugh. "I've seen you do it. *I'll* bandage his wound."

His alarm only increased at their cavalier attitude. "Come on, guys. I'm worried about you. I'm kind of freaking out here, and you make fun of me?"

Garris sent him a solemn look. "What else am I supposed to do? Cry with you? If you freak out every time we get hurt, it's going to get real tedious, real fast. We don't have time or energy to coddle you right now. We need you on top of this. We need you focused. So pull your head out of this mopey, blame-yourself crap it's stuck in and figure out what we do next."

At Garris's chastising, his panic vanished. The warrior was right. They were counting on him, and having a meltdown and blaming himself wasn't what they needed. They weren't going to stop, which meant he couldn't stop, nor could he give them anything less than his best.

With a sigh, he scooted over to sit in front of Garris. "I'll bandage your wounds. Dellia, you rest."

He unslung his pack and rummaged through it, pushing the waterskins Dellia had filled with oil out of the way. They had made it here intact, which meant his plan to burn the thing still had a chance. At the bottom of his pack, he found some bandaging. With no small effort, he quelled his revulsion and began to examine Garris's many wounds. He eyed the big fellow. "There's no way I can get you into fighting shape, but I'll get you as close as I can."

Garris gave a quick nod. "Good. Now stop yapping and get it done."

Jon set to work. The pool of water in the corner would be clean enough to cleanse the area around the wounds, but that wasn't the hard part. It would be a monumental job to bind their wounds so fighting wouldn't reopen them, if it could even be done. His friend and his wife were hurt and counting on him. So, he leaned closer, reexamining the most gaping of Garris's wounds.

Chapter Thirty-Four

THE PRECIPICE

Reclining in the cold dampness of her cave, Kayleen stretched out her hand, and Rillen placed the small leather pouch on her palm. These past few days, the protector had been her eyes and ears, her legs, and her voice. The young woman was her only contact with the outside world. So she had kept her busy with a constant stream of tasks. Rillen had brought comforts and provisions, ferried messages, and even spied when needed, and she had facilitated a continuous flow of information. All of it while going through great pains to ensure not a soul knew a protector was back in Shirdon.

Despite Rillen's assistance, as well as that of Braye and her three miscreants, the political landscape had become unnavigable. The council members appointed by the three realms were up in arms. Rillen had brought word from Braye that, cut off from leadership, they felt discarded. There was even talk of doing away with any kind of ruling council. Among the military leaders, discontent was rampant. With no one to guide the ship, they had begun to steer things on their own and weren't far from taking power themselves.

On top of it all, ill ease with Jon was mounting among the people, a situation that was always hard to turn around. Rumors swirled that Kayleen was dead, and that Jon, Dellia, and Garris had left the lighthouses and abandoned their people at a time when the Dead of Night threatened the land. Each rumor contained a kernel of truth, which made it all the more believable.

Kayleen looked down at the small leather bag in her palm. Before the protector's arrival, it had been used to convey messages. She tilted her head in puzzlement. "Why did you bring this to me?"

Rillen motioned to the pouch. "Look inside."

Kayleen opened the drawstring and peered down into the soft leather interior. It was empty, which signaled that Grekor wanted a meeting at Ruepo's house at dusk. It made no sense. She looked up at the protector. "You've been in regular contact with Grekor, right?"

She brought herself up to attention. "Yes. As ordered. In fact, I met with him early this morning."

"He helped relocate me here. So, he knows I'm alive and in hiding, and he was the one to suggest passing messages through you."

"Exactly."

Kayleen puzzled some more. "Then why would he feel the need to meet me face-to-face?"

"I don't know. I couldn't figure it out either. That's why I brought it to you."

"You did the right thing."

Still at attention, Rillen straightened even more. "Maybe he doesn't trust me to pass messages anymore. Maybe he's heard some rumor about me."

Kayleen gave a slow nod to the young protector. "Perhaps." Grekor knew she was in hiding, so why ask her to go out and risk exposing herself? What message could be so sensitive he had to avoid passing it through Rillen or so important it was worth the risk? Could the military be moving to seize power? Could Braye have ordered her three miscreants to move against her? Could news have arrived of Garris or Jon? If it had, would it be something horrible she wouldn't want to hear? At the notion, her hand flew to the long blue crystal dangling from a silver thread that always hung from her neck.

She discarded her guessing game. The possibilities were too numerous. Kayleen took a breath of dank, clammy air and glanced around the dark stone walls of her cramped and inhospitable cave. "It

906

doesn't matter. His reasons for wanting a face-to-face meeting are irrelevant. If he has important news, I can't afford to ignore it. I have to meet him."

Rillen seemed somewhat alarmed. "What if you're seen? What if it's a trap? It could put your life in danger. I could go find Grekor now and ask what he wants?"

Even as she shared Rillen's concern, her resolve hardened. "No. There's no time, and if he was willing to tell you, he'd have already done it. I have to go."

"Then send me in first, or at least let me accompany you."

She paused. Rillen's insistence was unusual. Up to this point, she had only done what was asked without offering her own suggestion or opinion. Kayleen nodded. "Okay, but you remain out of sight. Nobody sees you. Got it?"

Rillen grinned. "Oh, I like it."

With their course of action decided, the two set off. The sound of their movements echoed through the labyrinth of caves and dark passages as Kayleen, with her sunstone in hand, led the way down. After a while, they exited into the deep forest, not far from the spire.

Pine needles crunched underfoot as they made their way through the heart of the towering pines to Ruepo's log cabin. They arrived to a fiery sunset, with the wooded world becoming a pattern of deep darkness and long shadows. Having been stuck in a dark cave for the last few days, she reveled in the odor of pine-scented air and the warmth of the red sun.

Rillen hung back, out of sight, as Kayleen held her sunstone high and tiptoed up the steps. To all appearances, no one was home. Even so, she kept her footsteps light and quiet as she neared the door. If the message was genuine, Grekor would be inside. If not, she would need all the stealth she could muster.

She crept through the front door. Sunlight from her stone reached the timber walls and closed shutters of the lavish space yet left the corners and cubbies in deep shadow. The shattered remains of the bookshelf were still scattered across the floor, exactly as she and

Garris had left them. Behind them, the doorway to the cave led down into darkness.

Kayleen glanced around as she took several cautious steps inside. When she turned her head, a man sitting in silence behind the ornate desk startled her.

It wasn't Grekor, Nikosh, or Pedrus, or anyone else she recognized, for that matter. The stranger's long hair, short beard, and thick mustache were well groomed in an attempt to lend his angular Elorian face a more imposing look. He eyed her with a self-important air that was so overblown it might have been comical if not for the crossbow in his hand aimed right at her chest.

His chair creaked as he leaned farther back into the shadows, keeping the weapon steady as he studied her. Then she noticed his finger. It rested on the trigger where the slightest twitch, sneeze, or tremor would send an arrow through her heart. She froze, trying to gauge what kind of situation this was.

Before she could ask, he spoke. "You seem confused. So let me remove all confusion. I am Ruepo, the man you've been looking for."

Kayleen stopped breathing. The man who appeared to have no qualms about putting all of Talus at risk now had her in his sights. Then a question arose in her mind. He had tried to have her killed once. So why was he waiting to pull the trigger now? What did he want that only she could supply? Then a more alarming realization entered her mind. Whatever Ruepo wanted, as soon as he got it, she'd be dead. She couldn't simply wait for him to ask. She had to figure it out before she made a misstep and gave him whatever answers he had summoned her for.

Kayleen remained still, striving to appear calm and composed. "If you can see the future, then why bother meeting me? What could you want from me that you don't already know?" She put on a warm smile. "Except you can't see everything, can you?"

It was a calculated bluff, and he responded with the slightest tinge of anxiety, an almost indiscernible widening of his eyes. Then it was gone. It was as close to confirmation as she would get.

He puffed out his chest. "I didn't come here to exchange pointless banter. I came to avoid bloodshed. I came to offer you a chance to surrender."

Kayleen folded her arms in front of her. It was a simple act, quite common in ordinary conversation, but it protected her heart just a little. "And why would I do that?"

"Garris isn't coming back. Neither are Jon or Dellia. You have never sought power for yourself. Give it up now, and I will let you and those you care about walk away, alive."

She drew a deep breath. "On what basis would I accept your word? Have you killed the three of them, or are you admitting you can see the future, and in that future, they don't return?"

Ruepo took a while to answer, eyeing her with cold calculation in the quiet and near darkness of his home. "All right, I admit, I can see the future. It's how I knew you were looking for me. It's how I knew about your scheme for passing messages, and it's how I knew you'd come here."

When he made the last assertion, it came with a scant look of apprehension, an almost imperceptible shifting of his eyes to avoid her gaze. It was a reaction she'd seen many times. It meant the last part of what he said was a bluff. He hadn't known that she was going to come here.

All of a sudden, the situation gained a lot more clarity. He could see the future. He'd shown no sign of lying when he said so, and it was an admission she'd maneuvered him into making. But things weren't going the way he foresaw. He had sent men to kill her, and when they didn't return, he began to question his vision of the future. If her guess was right, he hadn't summoned her here just to find out if she was still alive. He had summoned her because he was in the dark. He had no idea what she'd been doing.

With that realization the situation suddenly seemed even more dangerous. The man may not have known she was alive, but now that he did, he'd want to rectify that. What's more, he was in the dark as to

909

what she'd been doing, and he would have no qualms about using any means to force the information out of her.

It was imperative she stall for time. Kayleen feigned shock as she nodded. "You're right. I have no desire for power, but I was entrusted with a responsibility to protect the people. I can't pass that responsibility to someone else unless I know they will rule better than I would."

Ruepo seemed annoyed. "It's obvious, isn't it? It's not me ruling. It's the Mirhal, a collective of oracles that has existed for centuries. Look what we have accomplished with you and your ruling council. We have orchestrated events such that you are on the verge of being overthrown. Think what we could accomplish if we set our minds to more constructive goals. With our ability to see the future, we could end crime and conflict before it begins. We could store food and water before a drought or famine arises. We can stop disease before it spreads. We will create a world free from strife."

The conversation took a sudden familiar turn. It was a subject she and Braye had debated over and over throughout their fifteen-year rivalry. It was the seductive cry of the power hungry. Just give me enough power, and I will create peace and prosperity. But power given was always power taken. So, it always became the peace of the subjugated and the prosperity of the well-cared-for slave.

She wanted to point out the many fallacies of his vision of a perfect world where oracles rule, but what would be the point? In all her years, she had never been able to convince Braye. Not to mention, the idea was to delay, not bring a fanatic over to her side.

She gave a thoughtful nod. "I know you have good intentions, but power corrupts. The Mirhal may start out benevolent but will turn into a band of corrupt leaders who make the people suffer so they can enjoy lavish lives."

"Lavish lives? Isn't that what the council does now? You live in your keep with ample food, water, and medicine, while ..." Ruepo seemed to come to his senses. "You have no intention of handing power to me. You're stalling." He raised the crossbow, putting her heart in its sights once again.

She rushed out her answer as quickly as she could. "Wait. You claim Garris, Jon, and Dellia aren't coming back? Then you should be in no hurry. Two days. Give me two days, and if they haven't returned by then you will have proven your ability. I'll surrender to you unconditionally."

He kept the weapon steady. "Another stall for time?"

Kayleen shook her head. "No. If they don't return, the things I have striven to protect will be gone. I will have no reason to serve, and even if I wanted to, I doubt I could manage to retain my position. Your plan will have succeeded. I will have no choice but to let you take control."

Every word she had said was true. Ruepo must have known it since he appeared to give her request serious consideration. He leaned forward and set down the crossbow. Then he laced his fingers together on the surface of the desk and closed his eyes. A look of serenity and concentration came over him. It was almost certain that he was probing the future to find out if he could trust her.

He remained motionless and calm for a while as the hoot of an owl echoed through the forest outside. Kayleen slipped off her shoes and crept backward toward the door. If he was peeking into the future, he might see Rillen, and things would get very messy, very fast.

Suddenly Ruepo's eyes flew wide as he grabbed the crossbow. The chair sailed backward, landing with a clatter as he shot to his feet. He leveled the weapon at her heart again. "What's going on here? What have you done?" He seemed torn for a moment, with more than a little alarm on his face. Then his eyes rested on the shattered remains of the bookcase and the passage behind it. He strutted toward it as he motioned with his crossbow. "You're coming with me."

Confused, Kayleen hesitated. He appeared to be even more in the dark than she'd thought. One thing seemed certain: the only reason he'd risk taking her with him was to find out what he couldn't foresee. Which meant she couldn't allow it, because that course led to torture and death.

He bellowed, "You have until three! One ..."

She glanced around.

He raised his voice. "Two ..."

A bang came from behind her as the door flew wide and cracked against the wall. A body slammed into her back, jarring her and sending her toward the floor.

The crossbow twanged, and Ruepo bolted.

She plummeted as the arrow whistled toward her.

It came to an abrupt stop.

He vanished into the doorway behind him.

She hit the hard wooden floor and rolled over.

Rillen was quicker. She was halfway to her feet with the arrow in her bloody hand. She'd caught it, but the sharp tip had sliced open her palm in the process. In a flash, Rillen tossed the arrow aside and flew across the room, disappearing into the darkness of the stairway.

Kayleen rose and checked herself over, then hurried after. Debris from the shattered bookcase clattered as she raced through it and down the stairs. As she hit the last step, a light appeared. The protector was holding a sunstone in her hand as she surveyed the room.

Silence fell, and confusion reigned. Ruepo was nowhere in sight. Rillen raced to the ornate desk. Furniture scraped against the floor as the protector shoved things around, searching for any means of escape. Kayleen joined her, walking the periphery as she examined walls, shelves, paintings, and furniture. They both arrived at the map at the same time and looked down at the bookcase below it. The protector tugged on it, but no matter how hard she pulled, it refused to budge even the smallest amount.

Then the image came back of Garris tearing apart the bookcase upstairs. Kayleen pointed to the stairs. "This room was behind the bookcase above."

Rillen nodded and tried pulling out a few books, then sped up until she was spilling handfuls onto the rough stone floor. She arrived at one that wouldn't pull out. When she tugged at the top, it rotated down with a click. With both arms, she heaved on the bookcase again. Without a sound, it pulled out the span of a few fingers, then jerked to a stop with a clank. She thrust her sunstone above the opening, and the light through the crack revealed a latch, holding it shut.

Kayleen looked over at Rillen. "He must have prepared this as an escape route. I'll bet he left the bookcase open so he could dive through. He must have had a light source inside, grabbed it, and latched the thing shut, so no one could follow."

Rillen nodded. "Makes sense. I doubt it's worth trying to follow him. He'd be prepared for that. By the time we find where the passage comes out, he'll be long gone and difficult to track in the dark. If he's smart, he'll head to the spire where we can't follow him at all."

Kayleen considered the possibility. "No. He won't use the spire. He'd have to use the same one to get back here, and he knows we could post a guard to catch him on his return. But you're right. There's no point in following him. He'll head into town, where it's impossible to track him. He'll move in the dark without being seen and have a well-prepared hiding place. Tomorrow, we should do a full-scale search of the town."

"No. We shouldn't." Rillen gave a thoughtful nod. "He's a distraction. Whatever the Mirhal's plan, it will have a contingency for Ruepo being caught. It will carry on without him. In fact, he may *want* us to chase him. It would waste our time in a fruitless pursuit while the Mirhal's plan moves forward. What you need to do now is focus on countering his plan, not on him."

Kayleen eyed Rillen. "My, aren't you a surprise? You avoid offering the slightest advice for days, and now you insist we ignore our one surefire lead."

Rillen didn't react and even seemed a bit contrite.

Kayleen smiled. "I think you're absolutely right. There are only five of us and limited time. We need to get ahead of them, not chase after them."

She headed for the way out and motioned Rillen to follow. They had much to accomplish, and it seemed they had only a day or two to get it done.

It had been a much quieter couple of days than Megan had expected. From the way Aylun had talked, she'd been prepared to spend every moment battling her way to him. Instead, it seemed more like the eye of a hurricane or the still water in the wake of a ship. If Jon were here, he might go on about turbulence and Kelvin wake patterns, but nobody really understood those. Yet the analogy seemed apt. Aylun was literally killing everything in his path, and she was benefiting from the vacuum he created.

There had been only a handful of encounters with the creatures in the last two days, but only one had sent her heart hammering. A massive, dark, catlike form had bounded toward her, its rasping breath and scraping claws approaching at an alarming speed. Without thinking, she'd thrust out her palm and, in a storm of wind, flung the thing away with her gift. With a deep oomph, it shot from the ground and sailed through the air, almost disappearing into the blackness.

With a sudden grunt of pain, it had jerked to a stop and plummeted onto the jagged remains of a shattered tree trunk. The sharp peaks plunged through the beast's chest, and it exploded in a firestorm of flame, embers, and sparks. A second later, the quiet clank of metal against stone echoed through the dark terrain.

She stared for a moment, her heart still pounding as she puzzled over the confounding series of events. When she investigated, she discovered the clank came from a barbed hook falling onto some rocks. She picked it up, and a leather cord attached to it snapped taut. When she followed it back, she found it wedged in the ragged crotch of another tree trunk.

The hook must have been lodged in the creature, and when she flung it backward, the leather strip caught in the crotch of the tree. It

914

yanked the beast to a stop in midair, and then the thing fell on top of a tree trunk and impaled itself.

By the golden light of her aetherstone, she dislodged the leather strip and stared at the glistening barbed hook. Outside of the houses at the roadside where she'd spent her first night, it was the first sign of human existence she had seen in two days of wandering this dark path. Then it occurred to her—it might have belonged to Aylun. That might explain how such an odd creation wound up lodged in a huge beast.

She wrapped it around her waist like a sash, then looked down and caressed the smooth leather strip. "Just hold on, Aylun. Don't get hurt, okay? I'm coming."

It had been a day since then, and she'd only had minor scuffles that ended as soon as they started. Megan stopped under the crumbling remains of an ancient bridge, where the wispy silver thread from her ring took a sharp turn to the right along the base of a cliff. She leaned her head back against the sheer rock wall and stared up into the rich darkness. If anything remained of the bridge it would offer pitiful protection. Yet, it was still comforting in this vast, impenetrable blackness, where she was always exposed and on alert.

She turned her gaze downward and focused on her dark metallic ring with the dashed jade line. A silvery thread leaped from it, and she followed it into the dark. The shimmering trail led along the base of the wall, then up it, and back along its upper edge to the road again. She traveled through an intersection with an illegible road sign, and a while later, the road began to climb.

After an hour or two of trudging up the steady incline, she looked down at the leather sash, and, as had become her ritual now, she caressed it. "Next time, go to a flatter place. It's no fun if it's all uphill."

She looked up and froze at a far distant shriek on her left echoing through the darkness. It was followed almost at once by the roar of countless wings taking flight somewhere ahead. She stared into the heavy darkness, waiting for it to become louder, to head her way, but it never did.

Her tension mounted. Had Aylun caused this? What if he was under attack? Then it dawned on her. She had been walking straight toward some vast collection of flying monstrosities and never even guessed it. Her feet remained frozen to the ground, refusing to move as the roar of far-off wings raced past, then grew distant.

Upon checking her ring again, the thread led her farther down the same road, straight toward the spot where the noise had originated. Aylun lay dead ahead, somewhere in the middle of the uproar. Megan redoubled her pace, not paying attention anymore to the climb or her own exhaustion. If he had been in the center of that mess, he might need help, and he might need it now.

The road carried on and on in its never-ending climb. Still, she had to find the last place Aylun had been. She stopped again to check her ring. With the sound of her own feet against the road no longer masking it, the far-off clang of metal met her ears. She raised her head, held her breath, and listened.

Again it came, clang after clang, ringing through the endless night. In an instant, she recognized the rhythmic cadence. It was the same metallic clatter she'd heard in the tunnels beneath Katapa. It was the sound Aylun had made when battling the beasts lining the hallway.

It was him. Aylun was ahead. He was in a fight, and from the frantic pace of his blows, it sounded serious. She broke into a sprint, her feet propelling her faster and faster down her silvery thread into the endless dark. The metallic clatter grew louder and more determined as she raced past the porch of a stone cabin and farther and farther up a hill.

Then, before she could make him out, she spotted his light. His flamestone was flying all over, circling, lurching left and right, bobbing up and down. It glinted off a set of three ivory teeth, like those of the spire, only much smaller.

Megan's head jogged as she ran, disrupting her vision and rendering details indistinct. She squinted through the darkness until, suddenly, she spotted his outline, yet it was still impossible to make out the dark shapes around him. His weapon kept slamming into some mass hidden in the darkness. Then it came into view: an enormous black claw large enough to encircle him, flashing down from somewhere high in the black fog.

A pair of clanks echoed out as he whirled around and each of the blades struck the claw. He ducked, then spun as he lashed out at something above. Then Megan spotted them, a pair of enormous flying beasts flapping as they clawed and snapped at him.

Aylun was in serious trouble. The spire teeth arched up over him, surrounding him, protecting him. If not for them, he would never be able to evade the claws, wings, and talons in the creatures' relentless assault. As she raced toward him, the size of the beast in front of him became evident. It was too tall for the light of his flamestone to reach its head, if it even had one.

She circled around, so Aylun wasn't in her path, then brought herself to a stop a couple dozen feet from him. She jabbed out with her palm, putting all her panic into her gift. A shock wave struck the massive dark form as a barrage of wind almost blasted Megan off her feet.

The force hurled the heavy monstrosity up into the darkness, where it disappeared into the black void. A deep, angry roar rattled her chest as she slapped the flying creatures and sent them tumbling through the air.

She waited for the thud of the massive beast hitting the ground, but it never came. Instead, the fierce roar grew distant.

Without a pause, the pair of flying creatures righted themselves and dove after the enormous dark monstrosity, disappearing into the ground.

Aylun whipped around to face her with a look of panic. "Get out of here. Hide!"

Megan stood her ground and yelled, "No!"

"There's no time to argue. Run!"

She strode forward. "Then stop arguing."

917

A blast of air hit the platform, billowing Aylun's hair and clothes and sending dirt and dust all around.

She halted as a wind from the flapping of the huge dark forms battered him. He swung around to face them, and now that she was closer to it, the platform on which he stood became familiar. Aylun was in the center of a miniature version of a spire, and it was perched at the edge of a precipice.

With painstaking slowness, the dark flying shapes rose beyond Aylun. In a flash, it all became clear. She had thrown the enormous beast off a cliff, one she couldn't see in the darkness, and the two flying ones were now hauling it back up.

Megan mumbled to herself, "Oh, no you don't."

She reached out with two hands, ensnaring each of the flying creatures with her gift. In a sudden violent jerk, she yanked them upward in a tornado of wind.

Their claws tore free from the massive beast, spraying blood and hauling chunks of black flesh with them.

The enormous creature roared as it plunged downward again, its cries growing more distant with each second.

With a blast of wind, she hurled the two flying things forward. Their bones crackled as she smashed them into the teeth of the mini-spire, and they fell limp to the ground.

She raced toward Aylun.

They didn't disintegrate, and one of the flying things began to crawl toward him, using talons at the joints of its wings to drag itself forward. A trail of black blood stained the ground behind it as the roar grew ever more distant.

She reached him and stopped a couple feet from his turned back.

The distant bellowing ended in a crash that echoed across the landscape below.

She covered her eyes as, one after the other, the two beasts before her exploded in a burst of flame, then disintegrated in a whirl-wind of cinders.

AYLUN

Aylun startled at each, then stared at the cliff's edge. After a moment, he began to turn but stopped himself and scanned the surrounding darkness. "I think it's okay."

She flung her arms around him and pulled him close. "You dum—"

He gasped and his whole body spasmed then shivered.

She pulled back as she realized her hug had caused him pain. She studied his scratched face. It made her heart hurt to see him so banged up. "Are you all right?"

He stared with wide eyes. "You came after me?"

She nodded.

"Why?" Aylun stood frozen, his complexion pale and shocked. "My friends died here. My sister pleaded for my help while they killed her right in front of me." He choked up as he pointed down the path. "Yaolin died just over there. She called out for me over and over as they tore her to pieces." He had to pause for a moment to compose himself. "Do you have any idea what it would do to me if something like that happened to you? I'd die on the spot. I'd throw myself off that cliff." He pointed behind him.

Megan stood peering up at his traumatized expression.

He seemed almost too stunned to talk as his eyes became wet and glassy. "Why would you do that? Why would you come after me?"

"Because you left me. Don't leave me again."

Then she noticed it. The darkness was easing. All around her, more and more distant objects were becoming visible, at first just the dried tree trunks farther out and a wider swath of the cliff's edge.

Aylun's gaze remained fixed on her, and he tilted his head. "What?"

"Don't leave me." She pleaded and scolded at the same time. "And don't you ever do something this dangerous again without me."

He remained dumbstruck and unmoving as the world around them continued to brighten, and more of the cliff's edge, path, and mountainside became visible.

He finally pulled himself together enough to speak again. "What about the warning? What about Jon?"

"The warning was wrong. It was a fake, a lie." She smiled. "And you were wrong, too."

His face awash with confusion, Aylun repeated her phrase. "I was wrong? About what? The prophecy?"

"No." She gave her head a scant shake.

"Then what?"

"It hasn't been Jon for a while now."

His glassy eyes grew bright with surprise.

Megan peered into them, seeing for the first time the true adoration reflected there. "It's you I want to be with, Aylun." She leaned closer. "Can you make me a vow?"

"You want *me* to make *you* a vow?"

It was nearing the lightness of dawn as she nodded.

He gave a nod of his own. "Name it."

"Stay by my side. Be with me."

"Is this real? Am I in a feverish delirium? Am I unconscious? Did I die just now, and this is the afterlife?"

"No. This is me doing something I've never done before with any man—telling you my true feelings." She set a hand on his cheek. "I love you, Aylun."

He seemed to come out of his fugue state, and a sudden eagerness took hold of him. "Of course. I'll stay by your side for as long as you want me."

She closed her eyes against the growing light and leaned forward to kiss him. As their lips met, a sudden warmth and brilliance surrounded them, but she kept her eyes clamped shut. She stayed that way for a long while, her lips pressed to his as the new sun drenched them in its comforting rays.

She pulled back, and they both squinted as they turned to face the new light, bathing a desolate wilderness that hadn't seen the sun for centuries.

The spire stood at the edge of a precipice. Behind it, darkness still smothered the land below as far as the eye could see in every direction. It lay there, a billowing black fog consuming every road, village, farm, and forest. Far out behind it, rising above the peaks of distant blue mountains, a brilliant rose-colored sun was heralding the start of a new day.

The death of the massive creature must have ended the darkness here, but only in the immediate vicinity. They watched the sun for a while, even as it stung her eyes, its warmth a welcome relief after days of unyielding darkness.

Aylun grabbed her wrist and pulled her along as she squinted against the brightness. "Let's get back to the house."

Megan let him lead her off the hill, the patter of their feet the only sound echoing down the sunlit path. A pair of plaintive squawks carried up from the dark blanket far below as they flew around a bend. They mounted the porch of a stone home, and the door creaked as he shoved it open and hauled her inside. Another round of squawks came as he pushed it shut, leaving only the warm light of dawn peeking through cracks in the closed shutters to illuminate the interior.

When he turned back to her, she flung her arms around his neck and kissed him again. She lingered there for a while, reveling in the surprising warmth of his body pressed to hers.

Then she pulled back and grinned. "You're mine now. There's no taking it back."

"Yours?" Aylun returned her smile. "Does that mean you're *mine*?"

She gave a crisp nod, and her grin broadened. "Yes, and don't you forget it. You're responsible for me now. So don't you ever go running off on your own again to do dangerous things."

"I love you." A genuine pleasure sparkled in his eyes as he uttered the phrase.

Megan stepped back and scrutinized him. His shoulders and right arm were covered in scratches and gashes, and his left one was a blood-soaked mess of bandages. It was shocking he hadn't cried out in pain when she hugged him. She sent him a stern glare. "You lied to me. You're not okay."

In need of a place to take care of his arm, she turned her attention to the interior of the home. It was spacious, and despite its stone walls and openness, it somehow projected a homey ambiance. She led him over to a soft, wide bed and seated him where a narrow beam of light fell on his left side.

The bandage on his arm had become torn, and the wrapping was clumsy, no doubt because he had tried to wrap it with one hand. He remained motionless as Megan unwound the blood-soaked shreds of fabric to get a good look. The sight of the wound made her stomach do flip-flops. It was deep, too deep and long, running from his shoulder past his elbow. Her nausea grew as she examined it. It was a wonder Aylun could still function, and her every touch made him wince or draw a sharp breath. She couldn't take her eyes from it. "This is horrible. If you don't take care of it, it will become infected, turn septic, and you could lose your arm or maybe even your life."

He looked down. "I wasn't thinking about me. I was thinking about you."

She sent him another sharp glare. "From now on, thinking about yourself *is* thinking about me. It makes me sick to imagine you out there fighting with a wound this serious."

He kept his head lowered and nodded like a child before an irate parent.

Her father came to mind and his berating of his children. Megan softened her tone. "I'm sorry. I'm just upset. You can't do that, okay? You can't get hurt trying to protect me. When you hurt, I hurt."

He nodded again, more eagerly this time, and a smile broke on his face. His bedroll still lay on the rough stone floor, a sign that he'd spent the night here. She led him over to it and set him down, then pulled his arm out, so it rested over the stone floor.

For the next long while, she worked on his wound, pouring water over it and cleaning around it to wincing and pained expressions. Stitching it shut would be the wise thing to do, but she hadn't the materials to do so or the heart to see him in such agony. So, when it looked clean enough, she wrapped it tight to keep it closed.

Then she lay Aylun down and reclined next to him, holding the hand of his good arm. Now at rest, her exhaustion began to weigh on her. She slid closer and set her head on his warm shoulder.

He barely opened his eyes, and in a half-groggy tone, he spoke to her. "Is this real? Are you really holding my hand?"

Megan smiled. "Shush. You need rest."

At her gentle chiding, he quieted, and she lay with him, both contented and terrified. Despite their surroundings and her concern for his condition, part of her was at ease. She had found something she'd been missing from her life. Someone to share her heart and soul with, and that warm feeling of belonging suffused her. But she was also terrified, and not just because he was seriously wounded. She had never let herself get this close to any man, and the idea frightened her to her core.

Yet, more than all of that, she had taken a step she had never taken before, and excitement filled her as she faced all the terrible and wonderful things the future might hold.

Jon fidgeted and paced in the dark and quiet of the back room, trying not to disturb his sleeping companions. He eyed Dellia and Garris as the unrelenting dripping of water into the corner puddle grated on his nerves. They needed rest, and he wanted them to get it. Yet, it had been hours, and any time now, the ability to create portals he'd borrowed from Sirra would fade. It had never been a part of any of his earlier-imagined plans, but it had now become a crucial part of all of them. Because, when it disappeared, so would any surefire chance of escaping possible failure in their run at the heart of the Dead of Night.

Once that gift was gone, it would take a mad dash to the spire and Dellia's red spire stone to get them out. If the last couple of days had taught him anything, it was that once a swarm came, moving any distance at all could become nearly impossible.

Still, the success of the mission was paramount and that depended on Garris and Dellia being in fighting shape, so he needed to wait to the very last moment. As he agonized over precious minutes slipping away, Garris stirred. His eyes opened, and he peeked up at Jon. Then he spoke in a low weary grumble. "The longer we sit here, the harder it will be later." His eyes opened wider. "So, what's the plan?"

Jon pondered the best way to explain. "I still have the waterskins filled with oil. They made it here intact. First, we'll have to find this heart of this Dead of Night thing. Then, we'll use the waterskins. I'll open the top of one and squeeze it, spraying the thing with oil, then you'll shoot a flaming arrow to light it on fire."

Garris stretched his stiff shoulder and arm. "Just like that? We just find the heart of the Dead of Night?" He shook his head. "How? We don't even know what it looks like."

"I don't know, some kind of creature, maybe? I think we'll know it when we see it."

"So the fate of Talus rests on killing this thing and we don't even know what we're trying to kill." Garris sent him a stare of skepticism. "And that's just one problem. You know this plan of yours can go wrong in a hundred other ways."

"Like what?"

Garris sighed. "Is the temple big?"

"Yeah."

"What if the thing is too far away to spray with oil? Do we just stand there and wait while it charges down on us?"

Jon shook his head. "No. The Mirhal expected me to burn it, so perhaps it will react to the flame like an allergy or something. Maybe it will burn even without the oil. Maybe all we need is just a flaming arrow."

"Are you out of your mind? Are you actually proposing we try to kill a thing that destroyed a quarter of Talus with a single flaming arrow?"

Jon hesitated. "Okay ... if the thing is too far away, how about I throw the waterskin and you shoot an arrow at it?" Garris just stared, seeming confused. "You know, it'll explode and spray oil everywhere?"

Garris grumbled, "An arrow won't explode a waterskin. It won't even spray oil. It will just make a hole for the oil to leak out."

Jon pondered for a moment. "What if I open it and hold the top shut while I throw it. Will the arrow spray the oil out then?"

Garris paused. "Maybe. Possibly. Okay, that might work, but still ..."

Dellia's eyes cracked open, and she eyed them both with a pained and weary expression.

Garris's movements appeared stiff and sore as he pulled himself to sit straighter. "Look, what if it's not just one thing in that temple? What if the temple is full of creatures?" When Jon didn't respond, he elaborated. "You do realize, archers don't usually stand in the thick of a fight, right?"

"And?"

"Are you seriously asking me to light an arrow and shoot it at some unknown thing while under the kind of attack we just went through?"

"So, you don't think you can do it?"

Garris gave a frustrated sort of grunt. "What if I don't have a clear shot? What if one of you is in trouble and needs help? What if this thing is too far away to throw a waterskin full of oil at it?"

Jon shrugged. "Okay, so, we may have to improvise."

Garris became even more irate. "So, your real plan is to come up with a plan in the middle of the battle of our lives, is that it?"

Jon threw up his hands. "You're right. I knew this plan was stupid. This proves it. I should open a portal, and we can just get out of here."

Garris went quiet for a time, his disapproving stare unrelenting as the staccato of water drops echoed through the room. Then he huffed, and all sarcasm disappeared, only to be replaced by frustration. "You know what? I take it back. I'm excited about this plan. I think it's a great plan. Let's go shoot that thing with little flaming arrows."

Dellia sent Garris a flat stare. "What is your problem? You've gone into other situations with far less. You went straight to the Southern Lighthouses when you knew it was a trap and had no idea what you were walking into."

Garris let out a quieter grumble. "Because this time, Kayleen's life is on the line. If we fail, the council falls and the Mirhal will kill her."

Dellia shoved her face into his, but there remained a quiet and controlled quality to her voice. "Look at what we've already done. Nobody has ever made it this far. Nobody has even come close. Are we walking into the unknown? Sure, but you knew that from the very start, so stop whining. We're here, we know how to kill it, and we have a solid plan, so we have to try."

Garris grunted. His quiver and pack scraped against the ground as he pulled them over to him, the sound reverberating through the room and down the hall. He yanked out some bandaging and a flint, which he pocketed. From his quiver, he retrieved four arrows and placed them in a neat row at his side. With stiff, pained movements, he started to wrap the arrowheads with cloth.

He nodded to a heavy burned-out torch lurking in the shadows. "We'll need that to light the arrows."

Jon had let his mind wander as he stared at Garris, but the request brought his attention back to the moment. He retrieved the torch and passed it to Dellia. She wrapped it in cloth while Jon retrieved a pair of waterskins filled with oil. When Garris had finished, he produced a tin of rendered fat. Then they all three smeared it into the fabric around the torches and arrows.

With their preparations completed, Garris staggered to his feet with another quiet grunt of pain. Jon helped Dellia up, and by the warm glow of their flamestones, they started their final push.

Dragging and scraping sounds carried through the cramped, dark space as Jon helped Garris shamble through rooms and corridors to the door. A sharp clacking reverberated down the hall as Garris struck the flint. He lit the torch, and it let out a quiet fluttering as he handed it to Dellia. Then he loaded one of the prepared arrows into his crossbow as Jon eased the door open.

They slipped out into the hallway. Garris's steps became light and quiet. Jon glanced over to see how he was doing, and there was a grimace on his face, as if the effort were causing him pain. They reached the end of the corridor, and it opened up to a pitch-black paved area.

They paused, and all three braced themselves. An eerie quiet settled around them. Then, with a motion forward from Dellia and a quick nod from Garris, they broke into a run. The torch fluttered as they sprinted away.

Almost at once, darkness swallowed the passage behind them, and all around them lay a thick blackness as they scurried across the paved expanse. No other sound met their ears, only the quiet patter of their own footfalls and the flutter of flame as the endless torchlit cobbles flew by beneath.

A fluted column jumped out of the dark, then the temple appeared behind it. They dodged to the right and raced down the curved wall. From pillar to pillar, they ran around the outside until a massive columned doorway appeared, leading to the pitch-black center of the temple. They darted left and flew through the entry and into the pitch-black interior.

No sooner had they left the doorway behind than an ethereal golden light burst forth, filling the massive circular hall. It seemed to radiate from an enormous statue of a woman. On the far side of the temple, it towered thirty feet or more, and the glow had the same golden quality he'd seen in Megan's aetherstone.

Jon pointed and whispered, "That's Athene."

The gentle radiance shimmered off of a pool of crystal water behind the statue, sending reflected light dancing across the walls. They slowed, and all became quiet except for the flutter of the torch and the soft rustle of their movement as they crept across the vast hall.

All three shot glances around the round room. The massive curved walls were ringed on the inside by enormous fluted columns, but no living thing appeared.

Jon whispered, "Do you guys see anything?"

The only response was from Garris, signaling him to keep quiet.

Jon watched his companions for a moment, their faces a study in concentration as their gazes darted here and there. He joined them, scanning for anything that might be the heart of the Dead of Night, but there was nothing.

Tension prickled the atmosphere, and Jon found himself holding his breath as the three beaten and bloody intruders approached the enormous statue. Nothing moved, nothing showed as they came to a stop at its feet.

They stood there for a time scrutinizing their surroundings, then Dellia's arm flew up, and she pointed. "There."

He followed her finger and squinted, trying to make out what looked like a dark spot on the wall, obscured in the shadow of a column. He jumped as it scurried out from behind the pillar. It stopped, and a lizard-shaped void stood out, clinging to the stone wall like some kind of black gecko.

They froze, and Jon whispered. "It's too far away to throw this thing." He nodded to the waterskin full of oil in his hands. "Just use an arrow."

With measured care, Dellia brought the fluttering flame of the torch closer to Garris's leg.

Slowly, he moved the cloth-wrapped arrowhead into the flame. It caught, and he whipped the weapon up to his shoulder. With a twang, the arrow flew. It whistled across the chamber and hit the dark form dead center.

The black lizard fell and writhed, then burst into flames. The fire consumed it until all that remained were embers drifting through the air.

Jon stood for a moment, not sure what to make of it. "Did we just kill the heart of the—"

A deep, resonant moan rumbled the pillars of the building. It rattled Jon's chest and echoed through the hall.

His gaze shot upward toward its source. The entire vast ceiling, a couple hundred feet across, was a sheet of sickly black with stalactites strewn across it.

An enormous mouth full of jagged black teeth opened in the center. The stalactites around it began to descend, becoming longer and thicker at the same time.

Then it dawned on him: they weren't stalactites, they were tentacles, dozens of them, and they were attached to an enormous thing that covered the entire ceiling. What's more, it was way too high up to throw anything and reach it.

He called out, "I think we found the heart. We need another arrow. Now!"

Garris gave out a quiet groan as he pulled back the bowstring, then started to load it. "One little flaming arrow is not going to kill *that* thing."

Jon glanced around as the irregular mouth of the monstrosity continued to open and sprout new teeth until it was large enough to fit several people at once. Then it hit him. "A portal. I'll open a portal. Dellia can throw the waterskin through. Then you shoot an arrow after it." He tossed Dellia one of his waterskins full of oil. She caught it in her free hand as he stretched out his palm.

He glanced overhead, but there weren't many spots without tentacles where he could locate the other end of the portal. Then he spotted one. A mist formed before his hand as the other end appeared high above, just below the creature's massive mouth.

Garris lit the arrow on Dellia's fluttering torch and took aim at the gathering black mist.

She dropped her torch on the cold hard marble with a clatter, then uncorked the waterskin. She squeezed the end shut and readied herself for the throw.

929

The mist solidified into a shimmering curtain, and on its surface rippled the view out of the other end of the portal, the massive maw of the monstrosity. On one water-like edge there appeared rows of huge black teeth, sharp and menacing, and in the center the soft inside of the mouth.

Dellia hurled the waterskin, and oil splashed from the end and through the portal.

Garris's arrow sprang forth, rocketing through the shimmering curtain to hit the waterskin just as it reached the inside surface of the mouth.

Oil splattered and flames raced from the arrow, turning the whole side of the beast's mouth into a sheet of flames.

A deafening rumble echoed out as tentacles began to writhe in pain, whipping through the air overhead with frightening speed.

Jon ducked away from them as he tossed the second waterskin to Dellia. "Again." The portal turned to dark droplets drifting on the air as he stretched out his hand a second time. This time, the other end of the portal formed at the edge of the beast, in an area with no tentacles.

Dellia dodged wriggling black arms as she uncorked the second waterskin and squeezed the end. As soon as the portal solidified, she threw.

Garris made another perfect shot that sent oil and fire splashing across the beast's slick dark skin.

With a pained and angry roar, a tentacle reached back up into the flames and yanked the arrow free. The slimy appendage curled back and whipped it down into the pool of water, where it extinguished with a hiss. The flames never spread, even as all the sharp-tipped tentacles ceased their flailing and began to descend again. They hadn't lit the thing on fire. In fact, it didn't appear as if it *could* be set afire.

Dellia drew her sword and dagger and whirled into action, covering herself and Garris as he knelt to load the last of his arrows. Her two blades whistled through the air, lopping off tentacles as fast as they reached her.

Almost at once, the black stumps reshaped themselves into sharp tips, their forms seeming to change at will. The severed ends fell around them, bursting into flame. A fiery downpour hit the floor, and sparks and ash whipped up around them as they consumed themselves.

Garris finished loading his last arrow and jammed the tip into the fluttering torch on the cold marble floor.

Jon spun, trying to lop off tentacles as fast as he could while Garris whipped the crossbow to his shoulder and fired.

The arrow shot upward, but a tentacle batted it away, and it plunged down into the water.

Another deafening moan rattled the temple as Garris yanked out his sword and began staving off the dark arms grabbing for him.

Jon shouted, "This isn't working. I'm getting us out of here." No objections came, so he raised his hand, and pictured the encampment. A black mist began to form before his palm.

Dellia struggled to protect herself and Jon at the same time as the dark cloud deepened and began to solidify.

No longer able to defend himself, a tentacle flew straight toward Jon's face.

Dellia lunged out with her dagger, severing it right before it pierced his skull. Her sword whooshed down from above Jon's head. A thunk came from behind him, and a second chunk of something fell on his back.

She teetered, off-balance from protecting him, as another tentacle punched through Dellia's shoulder and out the other side.

It yanked her into the air as she shrieked in pain.

In a panic Jon, abandoned his portal and grabbed Dellia's leg. The mist dissipated as he pulled down with all his weight, but it didn't even slow her.

Garris leaped from the ground, grabbed her arm, and yanked himself high into the air. With a tremendous heave, he swung his blade down and severed the slick dark tentacle embedded in her shoulder.

They all fell. Garris landed hardest with his side torn wide open from the effort and blood gushing from it.

Off-kilter, Dellia came down on one leg. With Jon's entire weight on it, she slammed into the unforgiving marble floor. The leg bent at an unnatural angle and cracked with another screech of pain. The tentacle in her shoulder exploded in a shower of sparks, leaving singed flesh around the hole.

Jon had tried hard to hold it together, but his panic raged out of control, and his stomach rebelled as he took frantic swings at the dark snakelike arms reaching out for his disabled friends.

Dellia swung her sword, protecting herself as she tried to drag herself up on her unbroken leg. Instead, she fell back down, and cried in agony and frustration as her leg bent farther.

With a dozen tentacles descending toward them, Jon glanced around, his gaze darting in every direction, searching for anything that might get them out of this disaster. Then it fell on the glowing, golden statue. He lunged out and set a hand on one of the enormous luminous sandals and concentrated.

Dellia shrieked, "Jon, no!"

He ignored her. He knew taking a god's power was an unimaginable risk. The power of Syvis had nearly crippled him, but he couldn't let Dellia die, so he slowed time until it came to a standstill. His bloody friends, their swords flying through sheets of cinders, and the snakelike tentacles reaching down all stood in unnatural stillness, then the world became dim.

He removed his hand and rose to his feet as a shimmering darkness sprang up across the glowing world. He rolled time back, searching for an era before Saranik had succumbed to darkness. Further and further he pushed through ages past until light came to the temple. He had found it. A time before the Dead of Night. Visitors in ancient Greek garb visited the statue and strolled the temple's vast floor. Jon stared, studying the scene as night and day flashed, and time moved further and further back.

His feet grew tired from standing and his eyes bleary, and still, he searched, hoping against hope, to find something, anything, to help them. Then, at last, he caught movement. The head of the statue had turned to look at a man. It was a slight shift but quite definite. Athene must have been looking through its eyes. He stopped time there and focused on the turned head. He had to have her power. It would be the only way now to save them.

Time resumed, and it was as if his mind exploded. Past and present, knowledge and power flooded his consciousness. Visions poured into his head of worlds both infinite and infinitesimal, the formless and formidable, forces of chaos and order, kindness and evil, and the vast creative force that infused it all.

Suddenly he became aware of everything happening in the world all at once. It was night at the encampment and Saneya was under attack, while Sirra recovered in a tent. Ruahn was back in Shirdon with Ruepo and the other Mirhal, and they were readying to march on Shir Keep. Megan was nearby, in a mountain home, nursing Aylun and his fatal wound.

Then he saw through Athene's silvery eyes how her group discovered portals near Athens in ancient Greece. Some traveled through them to this world, Thera, to settle here. From there, they discovered places that conferred eternal youth. Other places gave indestructible bodies, and still others granted immense power that only their enhanced bodies could handle. One of these places they named Olympus and settled there.

Her fondness for humankind compelled Athene, and she eventually sought out other travelers who, like her, had found portals that brought them to new worlds. One such group came from Sparta of ancient Earth to settle on Meerdon. From far Olympus, she and her kind watched over this struggling new nation-state. With a restrained hand, they helped and guided them as they established a shard of that ancient militaristic culture here in Talus and waged war upon war against Erden and Elore.

Before the vision could finish, a sudden searing pain and pressure slammed into him. It crushed him under its immense weight until he cried out. His own consciousness began to slip away. If it did, they would all die, so he forced his way back to lucidity. As the pain ate away at his soul, Jon glanced up at the statue, and in one last gamble, he pleaded, "Athene, save us."

All went black.

In a sudden burst, he was standing on a beach with blinding light pouring down on bleached sands. The sound of crashing waves filled the salt air. Cool water spilled over his bare feet. Then it flowed back out, washing the sand from under his toes. A brisk breeze blew back the hair of the woman standing before him.

Jon blinked a few times in the bright midday sun. "What just happened?"

Athene smiled. "I saved you, as you petitioned."

He squinted and glanced around at the low wall of rock and dirt that bordered the beach. Beyond it lay lush fields of waving grasses strewn with flowers of golden yellow and bright tangerine. Flowering trees dotted the landscape. He looked down at his tanned arms, now unscathed, then brought his gaze back to her. "Where am I?"

"Elysium, of course."

Then the fresh memory forced its way back, the gruesome scene of his companions' broken and bloody bodies, and his panic returned. "What about Dellia and Garris? You have to send me back."

Athene's smile faded. "I'm afraid you can never go back. You took a power not meant for a mere mortal body such as yours. If I send you back, it will soon kill you."

Jon blanched as boundless guilt fell upon him. His legs became weak, and he staggered. He had done it. He had actually done it. He had killed Dellia and Garris.

Chapter Thirty-Five

ELYSIUM

Megan awoke for a second time and waited for sleep to take her, but it would not come again. She slipped her hand out of Aylun's and lifted her head from his shoulder. The sun still peeked through the slits in the closed shutters, casting soft, narrow beams across the room and telling her the darkness had not yet returned.

She propped herself up on her elbow and peered down at his handsome sleeping face. He looked so peaceful, but he was hurt and needed to recover. She checked his forehead. A hand made a crude thermometer, but as best she could tell, he didn't have a fever. Unwilling to wake him from needed rest, she pulled herself up and glanced around the room.

At the foot of the bed lay a chest with a dragonfly inlay across the surface. A warm beam of sunlight glistened off of its pattern of ebony, jade, and ivory. It was gorgeous, and she'd seen that dragonfly before. It meant the chest had once belonged to Wistra and contained secrets for her to unearth. Only, would they be secrets she wanted to find?

Megan crept over and ran her fingertips across its smooth surface. Curiosity got the best of her, and she retrieved her dragon key. It was a perfect fit for the keyhole. When she turned it, the lock clicked as it unlatched. Afraid the noise might wake him, she froze and glanced at Aylun. He stirred, then settled again.

The lid gave a soft creak as she raised it, and she froze again with it halfway open. Her gaze returned to Aylun, and he turned his head and moaned but remained asleep. She peered down into the

935

chest—all that lay inside were a few handwritten pages. With care, she lifted the yellowing stack. She brought out her aetherstone and held it up, letting its golden rays rain down on the crisp pages.

As she read the first words, she gasped.

Aylun stirred again, and this time, his eyes cracked open. He glanced up at her with a sleepy gaze, and his voice came out lazy and hoarse. "What is it?"

She carried the sheets with her as she crept across the room and slid down against the wall to sit at his side. "It's from the chest." She motioned to it. "It's a letter ... to *me*."

A look of surprise came over his face, and with his good arm, he scooted himself back to sit up against the wall at her side. "What does it say?"

She lifted the papers to a comfortable height for reading and held the aetherstone at her shoulder, so its golden light illuminated the ancient pages.

> *Hello, Megan. I am the humble oracle you know as Wistra. Let me begin with an apology. I am sorry for your abduction and my part in allowing it to happen. Let me also beg your forgiveness for allowing the Mirhal to play their cruel game at your expense when I could have stopped it.*

Megan halted. The statement implied Wistra knew all about the Mirhal, which seemed to cast doubt on her theory that the Eye of Syvis had hidden them from her.

In the few seconds of silence, Aylun spoke. "The Mirhal?"

She looked over. His face warmed her soul, and she couldn't help but smile at him. "Yeah. Remember that ugly eye thing Ruahn had? When I was in Pretaj's library, I saw a drawing of it in a book. It called it the Eye of Syvis. Since the Mirhal were supposed to have it, I guessed Ruahn might be one of them. This letter would seem to say I was right."

AYLUN

Still sleepy, he scratched his head for a second. "Huh, Ruahn part of the Mirhal." He motioned to the page. "What about them?"

Megan returned her attention to the letter.

> *Don't be surprised. The Eye of Syvis did hide the Mirhal from me, but it also left traces. You see, in the first version of my plan, you left Isla's lair with Jon and helped him evade capture in the Illis Woods. However, that branch of the tree led to your death in the Recluse Tower. I couldn't allow that to happen. Yet, because of the eye's interference, that fate was a mirage and unchangeable. I tried hundreds of alterations to your path, but no matter what I attempted, you always wound up dying in the tower as Jon watched. In the hope its power might help me understand why I couldn't change you fate, I obtained the Eye of Syvis. With it, I could see the Mirhal's entire plan with clarity.*

She halted again and let the stack fall in her lap. They crinkled as she peered at Aylun's face, lit by the warm light of her aetherstone. "Is that even possible?"

He shrugged. "I suppose." Then he froze, and a look of realization filled his face. "When I think about it, I took the Dead of Night mission because of something Ruahn told me. She implied Yaolin was planning to go without me. I'm sure she did that on purpose. She wanted me to go. It was a part of her plan. So, from that point on, the Mirhal's plan was in motion, and my original fate would appear unchangeable."

He paused again, and a more profound look of realization crossed his face. "If not for that, I would have been nowhere near Isla's cave when you came out of it. As soon as we met, you would become a part of the Mirhal's plan, too, and your real fate would have changed. My abduction of you would have been unseeable by Wistra.

She would have only seen the original fate where you never met me, and to her, it would seem as if that fate were unalterable."

Megan mused, "That doesn't seem consistent with the rules of prophecy. No matter what led Wistra to obtain the eye and figure out the Mirhal's plan, it should have also hidden enough of that plan from her so she couldn't change it."

"You have a point, but we are not dealing with the normal rules of prophecy anymore. The Eye of Syvis changed the rules, so who knows what could happen?"

It was a valid argument, and she considered the idea for a while before resuming her reading.

> Once I understood their existence and intent, my strategy was simple. Aylun would call it "deceiving the heavens to cross the sea." I would say it more plainly: my aim was to make them believe I remained ignorant of their plan and let it play out until the last moment. Yet my antidote was with you the whole time. You see, I used the Eye of Syvis to devise a plan of my own, a foil to the Mirhal's scheming. I founded a second group of Shou, outside the Augury, a group nobody knew about or could foresee. Their descendants are Rillen and her kind. Because they originated with the eye, they cannot be predicted by anyone but me.

Megan glanced over at Aylun. "I always thought there was something off about the way Rillen avoided offering her opinions."

He nodded, his eyes still sleepy. "When I questioned her at the hidden city, she said she was acting on some sort of orders—vague ones, like a Great Oracle would give. And she admitted she was not sure why she was doing what she was doing. At the time, it reminded me of how Tsaoshi would give orders to the Shou."

Megan nodded, then returned to her reading.

Now, I come to you for a different purpose. Once already, I have visited Jon to give him a choice. Now, I write to you to do the same. Your understanding of chaos theory is both right and wrong. I was born in a future where even the young among us know that a butterfly flapping its wings in Brazil cannot cause a hurricane in Texas. They understand that the weather is created by forces of vast power: the energy of the sun, the rotation and angle of the Earth, and the gravitational pull of suns, moons, and planets. By comparison, the power of a butterfly's wings is insignificant.

She shuffled the first page to the back of the stack and resumed from the top of the next.

Oracles can predict the future precisely because it is shaped by forces of similar power. Surrounded by the Hordes, held back by tyrannical elements, and protected and threatened by unimaginable powers, Meerdon sits at the center of a convergence of terrible forces. These same forces make its future nearly impossible to alter. Yet, I have tried to do so. An invasion is coming, and Dellia's fate had always been to face it alone. No alteration I envisioned ever managed to change this one simple fate. At least not until I discovered Jon.

Megan glanced over at Aylun in surprise. His face held a contemplative look. She returned her attention to the page.

He is the only answer. It must be so because he fears to rule, and because of that, he will set people free. And a free people unified behind a struggle to preserve that freedom is a power equal to any in the universe. He is also Dellia's one true love, and it was my plan that together they would rally a free people to face an overwhelming invasion and ensure some portion of humankind survives.

Pages rustled again as Megan buried the top page and read on.

Still, I am no being of great power like Isla or Athene. I am but a simple woman, no different from you. Just because I was never able to find a way to save all of humankind, or to prevent Jon, Dellia, and Garris from dying in the attempt, does not mean that a path does not exist. Just as no slave is ever truly prosperous and no cage so opulent that the prisoner does not yearn to be free, no power of oracles can control the future without creating a cage of apathy and despair. So, I give you the one thing that is our only hope: free will. I set you free, Megan.

She sat up straighter.

Aylun eyed her. "What?"

She glared at him. "I'm not some caged animal to be set free. I decide my fate, nobody else."

He remained sleepy and his voice soft. "I think she is merely saying she will not try to manipulate you. Read on, and her meaning will become clear."

Megan huffed, then returned her attention to Wistra's note.

In the Carpoli Temple down below, Jon, Dellia, and Garris struggle against the darkness in a fight to save this land. My heartfelt hope is that you leave them behind and go live happily, for none of this is of your making. But there exists a harder path. One I dare not urge you to choose. Be my champion. Be the one who defies fate, the one whose future cannot be seen or toyed with. Be the one who protects Jon and Dellia, even now, as they fight for their lives. Be their eyes and ears, and their counsel, and perhaps together you can find a way out of this crisis that my elaborate meddling never could.

Megan stopped and let out a long breath as she tilted her head back, staring up at the ceiling.

Aylun looked over at her. "What now?"

"I don't even want to keep reading,"

"Why not?"

"It's making me upset. Be her champion? More like be her toy."

He sighed. "Just finish it. Then, whatever you decide, I will support you."

Megan shot him an annoyed stare, then shuffled the top page to the bottom.

If you decide to choose this path, find Ruahn, and take the Eye of Syvis from her. It is a thing of immense power. With it, you will be unseen to even the strongest of prophetic gifts, even to mine. Keep the spire stones, for they will allow you to travel freely and evade pursuit. Keep also this home as a hiding spot. It is remote and not a place of which anyone knows. Rillen has delivered a note to Tsaoshi telling of your importance, and he will make the resources of the Augury available to you. Lastly, Rillen is my right arm in your time. I give her to you now.

In giving you this message and this choice, I have created a paradox. A place into which no oracle can see. By taking the Eye of Syvis, you will become a variable that no being can predict. It is an act of faith and of trust. Because I can no longer see your path, I can no longer guide you into ever more elaborate cages designed to enslave your will. I have placed my faith in you and Aylun, and in Jon, Dellia, Garris, and Kayleen. I have brought you together, and now I set you free. From this point on, all I can do is trust the future to all of you and hope that you can bring about what my coercion never could: a safe, free, and prosperous Meerdon.

Megan finished, and the papers crinkled as she clutched them in her lap. Frustration seethed within her. "This isn't fair."

Aylun peered at her with curious eyes. "What is it that is not fair?"

"My life is my own. It is not a plaything for Wistra or anyone else. I am nobody's 'champion' but my own, and I will not be manipulated into being her pawn, no matter how high the stakes might be."

He remained calm. "Even if Jon's life is one of those stakes?"

"He made his choices. The responsibility for his actions falls on his shoulders, not mine."

"Then what do you want to do?"

A sudden lightness came to her heart as Megan turned her gaze to him. "Come with me, Aylun. There's nothing keeping you in this world. Leave it behind and go back with me to my world."

He became even more solemn. "Is that your choice? Will you do as Wistra said? Will you leave all this behind and go live happily?"

His words only increased her ire. "Do you really believe that? Do you really think it was her heartfelt wish that I leave? That's ridiculous." She scoffed. "If she really believed I'd leave, then why did she later say she placed her faith in me? Why did she say she trusted the future of Meerdon to me? I'll tell you why. She said it because she's sure I'll stay. So, no, I'm not going to play her game. And I refuse to let my life become a sacrifice to some cause that has nothing to do with me."

Aylun smiled, and his words were soft. "Why does it sound like you're trying to convince yourself and not me?"

She glared at him.

He bowed his head. "Okay, okay. Where you go, I go. If you wish to return to your world, then there is no other place I would rather be."

His gentle voice and kind words touched her but did little to ease her frustration. For far too many years, she had played the role her tyrannical father had scripted for her. Her mother and sister died trying to live the life he forced upon them. There was no way she would let herself become a pawn in someone else's cosmic battle of good and evil. Her life was her own, nobody else's.

In a flash, Dellia's agony vanished, and she was on a white-sand beach. Jon stood some distance ahead of her, staring at a silver-eyed woman who had the same appearance as the temple statue. It had to be Athene.

Confused by the jarring disappearance of the pain from her broken leg and hole in her shoulder, Dellia peered down at her arms and body. They were uninjured. In fact, they were flawless. Even scars that had been with her for many years had vanished.

The squawk of a seagull drew her attention back to her environs. She glanced around at the beach and ridge that bordered it. The sun was bright, and, inland, the fields of green grass and colorful flowers rustled as they swayed in a brisk breeze.

Jon's voice brought her focus back to the beach. "Where am I?"

The woman replied with nonchalance, "Elysium, of course."

943

Dellia boggled. Elysium was a myth. For a moment her mind refused to reconcile the legend with her current reality. Then the note of desperation in her husband's utterances banished her disbelief. "What about Dellia and Garris? You have to send me back."

The woman's smile turned to an expression of sympathy. "I'm afraid you can never go back. You took a power not meant for a mere mortal body such as yours. If I send you back, it will soon kill you."

Jon lost his balance as Dellia sensed his guilt overwhelming him. She wanted to run to him and comfort him, but her feet were frozen by shock and despair. He could never go back. She and Garris were too far gone to make it without him, which meant *she* could never go back.

Jon lowered his gaze, and a crippling remorse fueled his soft-spoken words. "I failed them."

Thoughts of defeat flew from her mind, and Dellia shook her head. He hadn't failed her. She wanted to say something to ease his hurt, but Athene spoke first. "How did you fail? You are still alive."

He sounded even more defeated. "I would rather have died than leave them like this. Why did you bring only me when I asked you to save us all? Please, I beg you, send me back. If I die, so be it."

Dellia's heart went out to him, banishing her despair. He would rather die than leave her behind. Tears welled in her eyes as she stepped along the soft, wet sand toward Jon's side.

Athene smiled a broad smile. "I didn't bring only you." She pointed.

He turned, and relief lit up his face.

She finished the distance to him and slipped her arm around his. In confusion, she searched his face. "What's happening? Is that Athene?"

It appeared he needed more than her arm because he threw both of his around her and hung on as if she might slip away. "Thank ... Athene, you're safe. I thought I'd lost you." He let go and bowed his head to the woman. "Yes, this is Athene."

"The goddess Athene?" She granted her a deep bow of her own.

"Yes. I asked her to save us, and she brought us here to Elysium."

Dellia addressed her with reverence. "Please don't think I am ungrateful, but if we're here, where is Garris?"

Athene sent her a soft gaze. "That is a difficult question to answer. You see, you are all still back in my temple. Your bodies lie there, under my protection. No harm will come to them. They cannot die, nor will they age. I have taken the essence of what makes each of you unique, and I have brought it here and given it corporeal form, so you may all live here in peace."

"Please, goddess, if you took Garris, where is he?"

Athene stood admiring Jon and Dellia for a moment as the waves rumbling onto the beach spread out behind her. "Time moves differently in Elysium. A minute in Meerdon is two hours here. I did not take you all at once, but one at a time. It took you longer than Jon, and Garris will be here soon. You will all find abundant food, water, and shelter. The bodies I gave you will not grow sick nor age, so you can live here in peace for as long as you like."

Shocked, Dellia stammered as she addressed Athene. "But ... but my people."

There was sympathy in the goddess's silver eyes. "The price you paid is enough. It is no longer your fight."

Jon seemed just as flustered. "I don't understand. We did everything Garris said. Why did we fail?"

Athene sent him a soft look of sympathy. "Your plan never had a chance of working. What Garris overheard was only part of the Mirhal's plan."

"Then what were we missing?"

"It was never the heart of the Dead of Night you needed to find. It was the Heart of Syvis. You've seen it. And you've seen what it can do. Idria had it in her hand. She used it to banish the Bahkaana, the four-armed demon who attacked your encampment. With it you could have done the same to that abomination in my temple. You could have banished it in a blaze of fire."

Dellia could sense Jon's shame and regret. "So, all of this was just a huge mistake?"

Athene only smiled. "You see, even if I send you back, you won't be able to defeat that thing."

He hesitated, then lowered his head. "I thought you might help us get rid of the darkness."

"I dare not."

Dellia didn't hide her surprise. "Why? You are a goddess."

"No, I'm not." For a fleeting moment, Athene gazed out across the vast panorama of waves rolling onto the shore. The stiff breeze tossed back her hair as she motioned to the white sands a short distance inland along the beach. "Come, both of you, and sit, and I will tell you what I can."

They moved back to drier ground and sat in the warm sun, one on each side of Athene. They faced the waves rolling onto the shore as seagulls swooped and dove into the surf.

Athene stared ahead, her gaze becoming far away. "We were once many: Aphrodite, Poseidon, Hera, Zeus, Demeter, Phoebus, Dionysus, and so many others. We left Earth behind, just as you have, and eventually found places that conferred immortality and great power. But we were foolish. We set ourselves up as gods, and like people do when freed from the consequences of their actions, we became capable of great cruelty as well as great arrogance."

Dellia peered at Athene. Her gift worked on the goddess, and it told of her profound sadness. "You are so alone. How can you bear it?"

She seemed surprised, but instead of letting it show, a smile graced her face. "It is my lot, but it is good to speak to you two."

"But, if the gods are real, where are they? Why must you be alone?"

"We are few now, and scattered." Athene glanced over at Dellia. "You see, there is a balance in nature, just as there is a balance within us as people. Our desire for comfort and control constantly battles with our need for closeness and the touch of our own kind. People are at their best when those passions are in balance. So it is in nature.

Order and chaos, light and dark, good and evil—if they become unbalanced, catastrophe follows. We who pretended to be gods abused our power and upset the balance. We paid with our lives."

"I don't understand. What could kill a god?"

Athene shook her head. "We are not gods. There are places and things of much greater power than that which I wield. Isla is not even a god, yet she would have little trouble killing me. Some of her kind can kill with a thought. If I upset the balance, if I help too much, I will surely die, just as so many of us already have."

Silence rested upon them for a while, then Jon spoke, and the deep sorrow and concern in his heart matched those in his voice. "So we really have lost."

Sympathy graced Athene's face once again. "Many a brave soul would not count this as a loss. You are still alive."

Dellia lowered her head in sorrow. "But we can never go back?"

"That is not cause for despair. Count yourself lucky." Athene motioned to their idyllic surroundings. "Most never get a chance to live a life free from the struggle for existence."

Athene stayed for a long while, staring in silence at the sea as gulls soared along the shore and plunged into the brine to retrieve fish. She drew a deep breath and stood to face Dellia and Jon. "It has been long since I enjoyed the company of others, but I dare not stay longer. I have interfered enough by bringing you here."

She eyed each of them in turn, her gaze settling finally on Dellia. "You and Jon are two sides of a coin. You are both brave and compassionate. But you have a strength of will that Jon needs if he is to face what he must do. And Jon has the insight and wisdom to see the way forward that you do not. In that way, you each balance the other. You must learn from each other. You must lean on one another and find that balance. Only then will you be able to see this through to the end."

Dellia stared, baffled by her remarks. What good was Jon's insight to see the way forward or her strength of will if they were forever stuck in this place?

947

Athene disappeared in the blink of an eye, leaving a wisp of golden mist drifting down the beach in the brisk midday breeze. Gulls cried, flying fish skated across the water, and the surf roared as the mist drifted away. With it, so did the amazement of meeting Athene and the wonder of this place. All that remained was Dellia's worry and remorse.

When they were wounded, Jon had wanted to get them out of that hellish place. She had helped convince him to stay. Because of her, they were stranded here, and she would never see her mother again. More than that, she had left the people she'd vowed to protect at the mercy of the Dead of Night, and she would never speak to them again or learn of their fate.

Perhaps sensing her sorrow, Jon scooted over and pulled her close. "I'm so sorry, Dellia. I needed to do something, but it always turns out like this."

She looked over at him. "Don't say that. You have nothing to be sorry for. This was you and me together, live or die. And so we did. We decided together, we failed together, and we will face the consequences together."

His deep concern was etched on his features as he stared at her. "But you're so sad. How can I bear to see you like this?"

She peered into his eyes. "I need to be sad now. It is how I mourn those I have lost and honor those who have lost me. Be with me. Comfort me and be patient. Show me kindness, and give me time, okay? You may not think it's much, but it is everything to me now."

Jon kissed her forehead and nodded.

Aylun strutted down the sunny dirt path for the seventh time in this new day. What had begun as a desire to get him up and around, to aid in his recovery, had turned strange. He and Megan had started out strolling the barren area around the small stone home. Once in a while, she would stop and stare down into the black, billowing fog that suffocated the land below. At some point during the sunlit morning, their strolls had led to Megan's proclamation that they were leaving.

This was followed by numerous trips from the stone home to the small spire. Each time, she would stop and stare at the rune-covered platform and ivory teeth, perched at the edge of the precipice. She stood for a while peering at it with a line of towering mountains stretching far off behind it into the misty distance. Then she'd twirl around and storm away.

With each trip up to the thing, her expression became more tense, and her anxious energy built until it saturated the air. With each pass, she would insist they were going home, and each time, he half expected her to use the red spire stone she clutched in her hand. Yet she kept strolling up the path to it, studying it, then marching back down again, seeming angrier than the last time.

As they turned and headed back toward the cabin, Aylun felt obliged to mention it. "For someone who has made up their mind to go back to their home world, you seem a bit hesitant."

Megan snapped around to face him and barked back, "Hesitant? I am not."

He countered her note of defiance with a calming voice. "Then why have we gone to the spire seven times but have not yet left. Soon it will be too late in the day to get to Isla's lair by sundown."

"Well ... I'm ... I'm worried."

"About what?"

Megan glared at him. "I know what you're thinking, but it's not Jon. It's Yuki I'm worried about."

"Jon?"

"I just said it's not Jon. Why do you keep mentioning him?"

"Sorry. So, it is Yuki you are concerned about."

"Of course, who else?"

Aylun nodded. "Well, she will be fine. In fact, she is probably better off than Jon."

"Jon?" Megan huffed and resumed her march down the hard-packed dirt path. "There you go, bringing him up again. Did I mention Jon? No, I didn't. So why are *you* mentioning him?" She adopted a sour look and crinkled up her nose. "He made his choices, and they have nothing to do with me. If he wants to take on the entire darkness, well, that's just super for him." She mumbled to herself, "Big shot, Otherworlder idiot. I don't even know why we're talking about Jon."

As they approached the stone home again, Aylun hurried in front of her and walked backward as he set a hand on each shoulder. "Come here." He guided her over the broad stone front steps and sat her down. Perhaps if she talked about leaving, it would help her think through her choices. So he eyed her with a steady gaze. "Tell me about your life, you know, back on your world."

Megan seemed thrown by the sudden change of topic. "It ... It was okay, I suppose. I worked in a basement as a lab assistant to Jon."

Aylun smiled. "Did you like it?"

"Sometimes. There were lots of reports to write and papers to file and other boring stuff, but I tried to do the best job I could."

"So, it was rewarding? You looked forward to each day?"

She shook her head. "It doesn't matter. My job was going away."

"Going away?"

"Yeah, the higher-ups were killing the project Jon and I were working on."

Some of her words were foreign to him, but he understood enough to get the general idea. He spoke slowly as he mulled over what he'd heard. "So, you have no job. What about your family? What about friends?"

Megan looked down. "You know I have no family. In some ways, Jon *is* my family, and I left all my friends behind to go work with him."

"So, you have no friends or family and no job. Remind me again why you're so eager to get back to your world?"

950

She became indignant and sent him a scorching stare. "Because it was the life I chose."

"But will it still be the life you want without Jon?"

She appeared to mull over the question but didn't seem to know how to answer. So Aylun tried another tactic. He took her hand. "How do you feel about all the good you have done here?"

Megan yanked her hand away. "What is this? Why are you trying to convince me to stay?"

"I am not."

"Yes, you are."

"No, I am trying to get you to think about it and not simply reject the idea because it was not yours."

Megan's gaze went from irate to fierce. "Is that what you think? I'm rejecting it out of stubbornness?"

He paused. From extensive experience, he knew, beyond doubt, that from this point on, he had to choose each word with great care. Aylun spoke in a soft and measured tone. "Is there any answer to that question that will not get me in more trouble?"

Her anger seemed to ease, and she crossed her arms. "It's good that you know you're in trouble."

He left a pause and watched for her anger to abate a bit more. Then he tried yet another tack. Aylun lowered his head and spoke softly. "Have you ever had to leave someone behind who was in trouble?"

The question seemed to shock Megan. "You mean like Yuki, right?"

He decided it was best not to bring up Jon. "Of course."

Her concern seemed to grow. "You mean, like if Yuki was in the Carpoli Temple below, engaged in a life-and-death struggle with a darkness that threatened this whole land?"

Surprised that Yuki had somehow become Jon in this conversation, Aylun nodded.

"That would be terrible. Yuki is my best friend."

"I thought Jon was your best friend."

"There you go mentioning that name again."

"Okay, aside from Yuki, is he not your best friend?"

"He was until his stupid oracle put me in this stupid position."

A sudden sadness nipped at him. He was well aware of Megan and Jon's history, but even so, his jealousy compelled him to ask, "Do you think there might ever come a time when I might be your best friend?"

Megan snorted. "Not the way this conversation is going, buster."

Aylun gave up. He had tried to help her think through the problem, but perhaps what she really needed was just a shoulder to lean on. He put his arm around her and pulled her close. "I know. It is hard."

She put her head on his arm and pouted. "It's not fair."

"Impossible choices never are."

She stayed that way for a time, with her ginger hair draped across his shoulder. Then she sighed and pulled herself up. She rested her elbows on her knees, interlaced her fingers, and set her chin on them.

For another long while, Megan stared out past the jagged stumps of former trees to the cliff's edge and the distant blue mountains rising above the roiling blanket of black. "You know, I always wanted to do something exciting like kickboxing or race-car driving, and this last week has been way beyond any of that. I've seen amazing places and done incredible things, but they were also the most terrifying days of my life."

"I know. I was there."

"She's asking me to solve a problem she couldn't solve in her lifetime, and she sounds way smarter than me."

"I don't think Wistra is smarter than you. She has just had more time to meditate on it all."

Megan peered at him. "Aren't you afraid? I saw the invasion in Wistra's message. This is life and death, and it's scary. If I don't find the answer she believes I can, then we all die." She looked straight into his eyes. "We all die, Aylun."

He granted her a nod as he considered her statement. She was right, but she was also wrong. He smiled. "I think you are looking at this backward."

"How so?"

"Jon, Dellia, and Garris saw the same message you did. They saw the invasion, and they have made their choice. The path they are on is one where they are destined to die, and they know it. It is the natural order of events now. You have a choice. You can stay out of it and let them die, or you can choose to be a part of it and maybe save their lives."

"By doing crazy, insane, risky things."

Aylun smiled. "It does seem to be your specialty."

Megan grew upset again. "You don't get it, do you? On my world, we'd be safe. Here, we'll end up doing things that might get us killed."

"Then I will protect you. I will make sure no harm comes to you."

"That's worse, because if you're with me, I might have to watch *you* die." She eyed him with sorrowful eyes. "That's not okay, Aylun."

The remembrance of the aftermath of Yaolin's death hit him like a sledgehammer, and Aylun lowered his head. "I know that fear well. I never want you to go through that." There came a moment of silence. "Then it is decided. We go back to your world."

Megan became incensed. "And leave Jon behind?"

"I thought we weren't talking about Jon. You mean leave Yuki behind."

"No. Yuki is fine. We're talking about Jon now. Keep up."

"What about being the master of your own fate? Do you still feel as if you are being manipulated into all of this?"

"Yeah, but if I look at it objectively, Wistra didn't create this situation. So, she isn't really the one giving me these choices. She's explaining them to me. If I choose to leave because I don't like her asking me to be her champion, in some ways, I'm still allowing myself to be manipulated. The only way to avoid being manipulated is to disregard what Wistra might want and make my own choice." She sent Aylun a hard stare. "But if I choose to do this, I do it *my* way and for *my* reasons."

He bowed his head. "You have obviously thought this through, and I trust you. So, whatever you decide, I will follow."

An expression of resolve filled Megan's face, and she eyed him again. "Can you get us to the Carpoli Temple?"

"Does that mean we are staying?"

Her temper still seemed short. "Do I have to say everything in actual words?"

He smiled. It was apparent she had made up her mind a while ago and just needed to make peace with it. So, he rose and motioned to the front door. "Let's check inside. Something tells me Wistra would not have asked this of you without leaving clues as to where you should go."

Megan nodded. She joined him, and they did a cursory search of the kitchen with its black stove, the main room with its small plum-wood table under the window, and the nightstand near the bed. Their efforts having unearthed nothing, Aylun stopped and glanced around. He considered checking more elaborate hiding places but rejected the idea. It wouldn't be in an obvious place, but any note for Megan wouldn't be an ordeal to find either.

His eyes came to rest on the chest with the dragonfly lid, now partway open. He hurried over to it in the hope that Megan might have missed something. When he looked inside, it was empty. He stared for a moment as his mind whirred. Then, he noticed the underside of the lid. He flipped it farther open, then eyed Megan. "Over here."

She came to his side and looked down over his shoulder at a map of Saranik painted on the underside of the lid. Along the mountains at the northern border lay a symbol—a detailed drawing that resembled the stone home they were now in and next to it a miniature spire. Farther south, near the center of Saranik, was a circular temple with a mark next to it, and the map's legend named it the Carpoli Temple. Overlapping its top edge sat a symbol that looked like a full sized spire, and the legend showed a fuchsia dot next to its map marker.

Megan fished in her pouch of spire stones. She found one and held it up to the map. The brilliant pink was a near-perfect match for the stone. "Okay. We have a stone for that spire, and it appears to lie due north of the temple."

Aylun gave a contemplative nod. "When we arrive at any spire, we are always facing the exact same direction as when we left."

She pointed. "So, according to this map, if we face south before we use the spire stone, we will be facing right at the temple when we arrive."

He drew a deep breath and sent Megan his most sincere look. "We should go now."

She looked down at his wound. "But your arm?"

"Won't heal anytime soon, and Jon and his friends can't wait that long."

"But, Aylun …"

"I got all the way here with only one good arm. I'll manage."

She seemed torn, but he simply turned and, with one hand, slipped his harness over his shoulders. He picked up each end of his bladed staff and slid it into the holder on his back. Then he set his flamestone in a net and tied it to his belt.

Megan relented and joined him, checking for her dragon key and bag of spire stones. Then she produced her aetherstone and tied it in a net to her waist. She drew a deep breath, and with her fuchsia stone in hand, they exited the house and climbed the path back up to the spire at the precipice.

As they stepped onto its small platform, a shimmering curtain of black appeared above them where the teeth were closest. Aylun studied the landscape below and around them, getting his bearings. He took Megan's shoulders and guided her around to face south.

He stepped up to her side and smiled. "You ready?"

She nodded and gave a sharp affirmative, "Hmm."

Then she placed her fuchsia spire stone against the symbol on the small spire. The curtain above fell, and, in the blink of an eye, they were plunged into darkness. The only thing visible in the small circle of light around them were the ancient symbols on the spire platform below their feet. All was quiet.

Aylun glanced over as Megan pocketed her spire stone. He took her hand into his and whispered in her ear. "Let's go."

Side by side, they hurried straight in the direction they'd been facing, their footsteps soft against the stone of the platform. The smooth ivory surface of one of the massive spire teeth appeared out of the black. They dodged around it to continue on. The enormous monolith disappeared behind them, leaving nothing but the surrounding darkness.

Cobbles flew by beneath, then a sudden, sharp screech rang out from above. Aylun's gaze shot up. A sudden stabbing pain shot through his bad shoulder as a giant claw ripped through his flesh to punch out the other side.

A tremendous flapping of wings blew dust and debris into the air all around them. Aylun reeled in agony then lurched upward, his feet leaving the ground. Megan's hand jerked out of his grasp, and the ground dropped away. With another powerful flap, the cobbles disappeared below him. Her face stared up as it fell away, only to be swallowed by the darkness. Another forceful flap yanked him higher, setting his shoulder afire with pain as his consciousness slipped away.

Kayleen looked up as footsteps raced into the small cave that had served as her hideaway for the last several days. Rillen stood before her in the dim light, out of breath and appearing distressed. "It's happening."

Kayleen lowered her head, peering down at her quilt spread out on the rock floor. "Any word of Garris, Dellia, or Jon?"

Rillen knelt before her. "No, same as before. The last anyone heard of them, they were entering the Dead of Night."

"The lighthouses are fixed, right? And they are holding back the darkness?"

Rillen nodded. "Yes. At least we have that going for us."

Kayleen strived to pull herself together. "What should I expect?"

Rillen hesitated, as if it was painful to give voice to the answer. "Grekor says there are three commanders and a contingent of soldiers, along with Ruepo, his daughter Ruahn, and several other Mirhal. They will arrive shortly to demand surrender of the council."

"Any idea what their conditions for surrender might be?"

Rillen delayed again, then lowered her head and spoke in a quiet voice. "Nikosh overheard the commanders discussing among themselves. Surrender is to be unconditional. You and all the old council members are to be handed over with no questions asked."

"Handed over? No questions asked? I guess we know what that means."

"Pedrus reported rumors that they will execute you on the spot for betraying the people."

Kayleen stood and straightened her clothes. She looked down at her blue crystal pendant and spoke to it in a hushed voice. "You always wanted to be a big hero, Garris. Well, I'm pretty scared now. So, if you ever wanted to save me, now would be a good time." She lifted the ancient crystal to her lips and kissed it. Then she raised her head, squared her shoulders, and looked straight ahead. "Okay. Let's go surrender."

Rillen nodded, and, for the last time, Kayleen led the way out of the cramped cave.

Dellia dried herself off, then slipped on her new chiton, looking in the mirror to adjust it to fit just right. Here on Elysium, clothes always appeared in her wardrobe whenever she got the yearning for something new to taunt Jon with. This one was perfect. It was soft and smooth and revealed all the right parts, while hiding just enough to make him crazy. And if there was one thing she reveled in more than anything else, it was driving Jon mad with desire for her.

He had left to let her "bathe in peace," he said, and there was a fair dollop of truth in that. It was difficult to get any actual bathing done when Jon was around. However, it was also true that he had a solitary side and seemed to need time alone. She didn't mind indulging it, but this time he had been gone for too long, and she missed him.

So, she scurried out of the house and raced across the field laden with flowers in shades of golden yellow and brilliant orange to find him at the cliff's edge, staring out across the sea. She stopped before she reached him and smiled for a while, admiring his gentle face. Then she clasped her hands behind her back and strolled up to him, acting as casual as she could manage.

Jon looked up, and in an instant, she felt the lust for her burning within him.

She glanced down at her new clothes. "You always have the same reaction to this old thing."

"Me?" He smiled.

She sent him a stern look. "There'll be no ravishing this time." She sat down at his side and snuggled in as close as she could.

He kissed her cheek. "The ravishing can wait till we get home."

"Liar," Dellia mumbled to herself, and Jon chuckled. She caressed his cheek, and at her touch, his love for her ignited, burning as bright as the midday sun. Her appetite for that feeling seemed as boundless as her love for him. She relished the moment, staring out at the red sun as it inched its way down the horizon.

Then she sensed that feeling again, and she moved still closer. "What's wrong?"

He smiled at her. "Do you ever think about home?"

"This is our home."

"I mean Talus, your mother, our people?"

She sensed his concern for them. "It's only been a few weeks."

"It's been seventeen weeks and two days. Athene said time moves faster for them. A minute there is two hours here, so it's only been a day there."

His worry and remorse were as strong and real as hers had been at first. In fact, it was an odd sort of role reversal. The first days they stayed here, she'd been angry and upset, and she fretted over her mother and Kayleen not knowing their fate. Athene was nowhere to be found and never reappeared, so she yelled and subjected Jon and Garris to endless pestering about possible ways to get back to their world. When it became clear it could never be, sorrow and guilt set in, and she was inconsolable for days.

In those distant times, Jon had nurtured her with boundless care and patience until one day her inner conflict eased, and she felt the intensity of his love and concern. It was then that she resolved to bring him the same care he had bestowed upon her. Every day since then was different yet perfect. The weather changed but always suited her mood in every detail. Or perhaps this place influenced her mood to match the weather. She was never hot or cold, at least not until she yearned for Jon's warmth near her, and every day she basked in their love for each other.

By contrast, Jon had taken to this place right away. As happy as a lark, he planted a garden and tended it with care, though it wasn't necessary. The sweetest of fruit hung in abundance from nearly every tree, and they never grew hungry or thirsty and so never needed to eat or drink. At times, when they got a craving for some particular delicacy, it simply showed up in their cupboard.

He insisted she teach him awareness, and he took to it with vigor, making something approximating decent progress. They sparred every day. Quite often now, he could intuit her moves before she made them, and every time, she sensed his joy at his accomplishment. From time to time, he even cleaned the house, though it never seemed to need it.

In their abundant free time, they went for long walks in an almost endless variety of nearby settings. They strolled grassy flatlands, rolling hills, wooded shorelines near waterfalls spilling into crystal pools, and even high rocky pathways overlooking forested valleys. They talked and enjoyed the scenery, from the beauty of a delicate flower to the majesty of a crimson sunrise. He was so in love with her and thoroughly content, but as time wore on, a tinge of regret and worry began to cloud his mood.

Garris was another matter. He enjoyed the place but never seemed to acclimate. A veil of longing surrounded him, an echo of when they had first met. Over time, she had come to understand him better and realized he was lonely. He missed his family. He missed Kayleen. For many days at a time, he would disappear into the mountains to fish and hunt. When he hauled his catch back, he seemed amiable enough—eating, drinking, and laughing with them—but that longing never vanished. Perhaps she and Jon were a reminder of what he'd left behind, because a day or two later, he would disappear again, not to be seen for many days.

Dellia looked at Jon now, his face so close to hers. Somehow it wasn't surprising that he knew to the day how long they had been here.

She smiled at him. "Seventeen weeks and two days?"

He nodded.

She shook her head. "It's not enough. I want seventeen cen-turies with you. You would do that for me, right?" Her soft words wiped away all his worry and remorse. She set a gentle hand on each shoulder and nudged him backward. "Lie with me."

He reclined on the soft grass, and she nestled in next to him. She pulled out his arm and rested her head on his shoulder, and for a while, they stared upward, watching the puffs of white tinged with crimson drift across an azure sky. "I know it's hard, and you worry about them. You feel responsible. My gift is stronger than ever. I feel it with you, and it makes me sad to see you like this."

Jon drew a deep breath of clean, fresh air. "Do you really never think about them?"

She paused, then glanced over at his sweet face. "I think about them every day, but I've made peace with the fact I gave it everything I had, even my life. What's left of me back in that temple is proof of that. If I were to go back and survive, I'd probably wind up crippled and scarred for life. We've paid enough of a price, Jon. When I think of my mom or Kayleen, it's no longer regret or worry I feel, but longing for them and fondness for the memories they gave me."

There was a long pause. "I wish it were that easy."

Dellia lifted her head and set a gentle hand against his cheek. "Then let me be your shoulder to lean on. Let me console you and help you forget. I feel all your wounds and weaknesses, and I love them. They are part of what makes you the person you are. We have forever now. Day by day, let me heal them with you."

Jon rolled over on top of Dellia, his weight pressed against her as his adoring eyes stared into hers. "How did I ever get to be so lucky?"

She smiled and returned his gaze for a while.

Then his longing for her grew.

"Oh no." With care, she rolled him off of her and set him back down on the long, emerald grass. "This is how it always starts."

Jon gazed upward again. "What? Can't I just look at my perfect wife for a few minutes?"

She lay her head back on his shoulder and turned it away, so he couldn't see her smile. "You don't think I know what's on your mind?"

He mumbled, "I swear, you do this on purpose."

Dellia put on a solemn expression and turned her head, gazing upward with him. "Just enjoy the day with me. Let's watch the sunset together. Who knows? If it's perfect enough, maybe I'll be the one doing the ravishing tonight."

"Is that a promise?"

"I said maybe." She smiled again, despite herself. Her heart had already promised, but she wanted to enjoy the moment for now. The warm sun bathed them with its comforting rays, and a soft breeze rustled the long grasses. It was perfect.

961

She understood all the intricate reasons for Jon's remorse. Perhaps the strongest was that he was in charge and had failed. He didn't blame himself. He seemed to have gotten beyond that, but the failure had left him with a sense of incompleteness. There would never be a way for him to resolve it, but she had time.

It might take years or even decades, but his remorse would fade, and with care, she could heal his heart. After all, they had a lifetime or more in this most perfect of places. Dellia smiled at the notion and snuggled closer, and her fingertips began to caress his chest.

Chapter Thirty-Six

WITHIN THE HEART

Megan stood on the platform of the plateau mini-spire, her anxiety rising as she scanned the billowing darkness below. She raised her head to the shimmering curtain of black above. The sight sent a chill down her spine. The curtain above was a portal and that very blackness that smothered the land below was visible on its surface. In a few moments it would fall over them, and she and Aylun would be plunged back into the Dead of Night. His hands startled her as they rested on her shoulders, guiding her around to face south, the direction of the temple.

She looked over to catch him step up to her side and smile. "You ready?"

The thought of being thrust into darkness again gave her fresh shivers, but she ignored her trepidation and gave a crisp nod with a sharp, "Hmm."

She raised a sweaty palm and touched her fuchsia spire stone against the symbol on the small spire. In an instant, the shimmering circle fell and its darkness consumed them whole. All that remained visible was her and Aylun and the soft glow of their stones lighting the rune-covered platform below them.

She slipped the spire stone into her pocket and Aylun took her hand. His soft voice calmed her as it whispered in her ear, "Let's go."

Still trying to master her fear, Megan clung to the hand in hers as she raced across the flat spire platform. She glanced over at Aylun next to her, taking comfort in the calm look of concentration on his face. His strength was her strength now, and she drew on it as their footsteps and quick breaths echoed through the unseeable expanse.

Already on edge, she startled as the massive ivory spire tooth jumped out of the darkness. She squeezed the hand in hers and pulled.

Moving as one, he dodged left with her.

They dropped off of the platform and raced onward until the spire tooth disappeared into the black fog. Then darkness reigned, and the only thing that could be seen was a small circle of cobblestones flying by beneath their feet.

The sudden screech of some flying beast startled her as it broke the silence. From the sound, it was enormous and loomed close, right above and behind her. Megan wrenched her head back and stared upward, but all that met her eyes was utter darkness.

A sickening grunt of pain came from the man next to her. She spun toward him as a gigantic claw punched through Aylun's wounded shoulder in a spray of blood. He reeled, then lurched from the ground. She stood paralyzed as he shot skyward, his face growing dim in the light of her aetherstone. Then it disappeared, and all that remained was a faint dot of light that vanished into the darkness.

Desperation took over, and she reached up into the black heavens with her gift. In a torrent of wind, she yanked something huge back down. It let out a frantic screech as a pair of claws appeared with Aylun in one of them. Megan reached higher this time and got a fresh grasp on what she hoped would be its body. She pushed harder. Wind blasted her as the massive form raced downward under the force of her gift.

Aylun came down with it, crashing into the pavement and slamming his head into the stones. The massive flying abomination, with its slick hairless body, razor claws, and enormous wings, came down next to him. Dust and debris blasted out from under the creature as it struck the stones of the pavement with a ground-shaking thud and loud crunch. She pushed down still harder, and an even louder cracking came. Then the body disintegrated in an inferno that sent blazing particles spiraling into the darkness.

When it was gone, Aylun lay there, unmoving. Heart racing, Megan hurried over to him. She crouched down and placed two fingers on his neck, checking his pulse. It beat strong and steady, but blood was flowing out onto the cobblestones from a huge gash on his the right side of this forehead. Alone and hunkering in the dark, she gave his body a shake, but he remained limp and lifeless.

In a frenzy, she turned her gaze back toward the spire. It was her only hope now. She rose to her feet, but her legs refused to move. Something in the back of her mind, a voice she had come to trust, an awareness beyond thought and reason, told her that along that path lay Aylun's death.

Megan hesitated as the low sounds of creatures stirred in the blackness on every side. She spun around, facing the temple as frustration welled within her. Her head tilted back, and she belted out a scream that came from the depths of her anguish. It echoed into the endless night, coming and coming, unstoppable, pouring out all her torment and fear.

As it ended, a fiery rage took over, holding back her terror and keeping her legs steady beneath her. She lowered her head, lifted Aylun's ankle with her gift, and dragged his limp body across the cobbles toward the temple. Mutterings replaced her scream, flowing out of her unbidden as Megan marched ahead in a shocked sort of trance.

"Oh, this is just perfect. Stupid idiot, Aylun. 'I'll protect you. I can get you to the temple. No problem. I won't let any harm come to you. I'm a gorgeous, hunky man with sinewy muscles and elite martial arts skills that will be *totally useless* when you really need them.'"

The low whoosh that betrayed massive wings flew down from her left.

Too overwrought to think straight, she didn't even look. With her gift, she reached out, scooped up the thing, and flung it forward. A blast of wind hit her as it rocketed overhead and then down onto the pavement.

It struck with a ferocious crackle of bones splintering. A bonfire shot upward, sending fiery pricks of light arcing through the darkness, illuminating the whole area.

Her chest tightened as she spotted it. Some enormous dark form was bounding down the street toward her.

The roar of two more sets of giant flapping wings came down at her from either side, and she froze, her heart hammering. Aylun's leg slipped from her grasp. Megan reached out with a hand on either side and felt her gift take hold of the flying beasts. She yanked them forward and down in front of her with a shriek and the shrill whistling of the creatures whipping through the air. A roar of wind rushed past her ears as they slammed into the dark creature ahead in an explosion that sent glittering trails shooting into the black void.

The new light revealed more massive creatures pouring around buildings and across the plaza toward her. The sight reignited her terror, but she held it back, letting her rage take over again.

With her gift, she took hold of Aylun's ankle for a second time and started lugging him toward the temple as her muttering seemed to come out of nowhere. "And you, Jon, with your big fat brain and all your stupid schemes, where are you now? Big shot, Otherworlder, idiot. Nowhere, that's where. You and your stupid prophecy, and your lamebrained oracle, expecting me to become some ridiculous champion."

A chorus of cries and claws against stone came from every side, closing in on her. She dropped Aylun's ankle and screamed, "That's it! I've had it!"

She shoved out a palm on either side and spun as she pushed outward with her gift. A whirlwind whistled in her ears as she slapped creatures back, midstep. A circle of bodies sailed through the air into those behind them with grunts, thuds, and cries of pain. Bones cracked and limbs shattered as broken bodies ate themselves in fire and plumes of embers. The flames whipped around her, caught up in the whirlwind, turning into a dervish of spark and ash.

When it eased, Megan grabbed Aylun's ankle again and marched on, huffing and grimacing. And still, the words flowed from her, louder and louder, until they turned into shouting. "You just try it again. I dare you, try to hurt one hair on Aylun's head. If you even think about it, I'll turn the city into a raging inferno of your bodies!"

She slapped a swath of creatures headed toward her, dashing them into a nearby wall. They perished in a barrage of sparking fireworks. A hurricane blew around her as she dragged Aylun. She scooped, slapped, and smashed any sound that came at her.

Her pace grew frantic as her fury began to crack, and abject fear threatened to overwhelm her. In the wake of her gift, dark slick creatures shot into the air only to slam into walls, cobblestones, pillars, roofs, and each other in a ceaseless storm of fiery explosions. They burst all around her, their falling bodies bombarding the plaza until it resembled a battlefield. Then the pillars of the temple appeared. Creatures came, and she threw them into the night, smashed them to the ground, or tossed them to the top of the roofs. Her muttering ceased as her fear took over, and the supply of incendiary creatures slowed, then stopped, and all grew dark again.

Her angry breath echoed through the quiet darkness as Megan followed the curved wall. She moved column to column, until the entryway to the pitch-black interior appeared. As she passed through its pillars, an ethereal light sprang from the statue of Athene across the vast circular hall. It illuminated the pillars lining the walls and reflected off of the pool of water behind it, sending shimmers across their curved stone surfaces.

Megan halted, staring at the three battered and bloody bodies lying on the ground near the statue's sandaled feet. It took a second to make them out in their mangled state, but when she did, the urge to retch hit her all at once. She pushed it down, dragging Aylun step by step up to the shattered bodies of Jon, Garris, and Dellia.

Her heart seemed to stop. They appeared dead. Garris was a mass of ripped skin, torn flesh, and blood. Dellia had a hole in her shoulder where no hole should be, and her leg was bent where no leg should ever be bent. The urge to throw up returned as she spotted the broken and jagged shard of bone poking through her skin. Jon was beaten up and bloody, but in the best shape of the three. As she surveyed their bodies it struck her that something wasn't right. Then she noticed the blood from their wounds. It was fresh, and there was a lot of it, but it wasn't flowing like it should. It was as if it were frozen. In fact, they seemed like they were alive but somehow suspended in time, as if the entire scene were a three-dimensional photograph.

She looked back at the trail of blood leading through the entry to where she'd dragged Aylun. All her friends, all who might be able to save her, would be better off if they remained unconscious.

A deep, resonant moan shook the pillars of the temple. It echoed through the hall and vibrated the floor beneath her until she had to steady herself. Then she caught it, reflected in the rippling waters of the pool behind the statue, a mass of tentacles descending toward her. She looked up as sharp tips reached downward, threatening to engulf her in a sea of winding black arms. "Just super."

Megan dropped to her knees and peered up at the face of the statue. "Save me, Athene."

A sudden bright light caused her to squint. Through her half-closed eyes, she stared at the figure before her. Warm sunshine beat down upon the woman and the white sandy beach that stretched out behind her as far as the eye could see. Though no longer giant in stature, Athene radiated a regal bearing. Cool waves caressed Megan's feet as the goddess's calming voice came to her. "There is little I can do to help you."

Still in shock, Megan stared at the woman as she pleaded, "Please. Anything."

"What if I sent you home, back to Earth?"

It hadn't been long ago that returning home had been her plan, yet it seemed repugnant to her now, and Megan recoiled. "To Earth?"

"Yes. I always liked Wistra. She had a contagious serenity and compassion about her, and she spent her life helping others. Yet, as much as I may have respected her, this is her plan for your life, not the one you made for yourself."

At the idea, desperation took hold of her. "I can't just leave them there—Aylun, Jon, Garris, Dellia. Now that I've seen them, I couldn't live with myself if I didn't at least try to save them."

"Even if that thing in the temple kills you?"

The thought terrified, and her head didn't want to move, but she forced a nod.

"Then perhaps you are worthy, after all. You may keep the aetherstone, and the key, and the rings are for you and Aylun now. I have a feeling you may need them."

"Then you'll help?"

Athene peered out at the waves rolling up on the shore, and for a moment it seemed as if the weight of the world rested on her shoulders. Then she looked back at Megan and sighed. "I cannot. You must help yourself."

Megan's fear and frustration reached the breaking point. "If you're just going to let them die, then what's the use in keeping your stupid baubles?"

Athene only smiled. "What I can do for you is tell you three things. First, as you suspect, Jon, Dellia, Garris, and Aylun are all very much alive. In fact, the two lovebirds are over there." The goddess pointed at a distant pair strolling hand in hand through the long, waving grasses near the beach.

As the man passed a yellow flower, he plucked it from the field and handed it to the woman. She snatched an orange one and did the same to him, but when he reached for it, she yanked it away and added it to her own. The man tilted his head back, and the faint sound of Jon's laughter drifted across the idyllic landscape. A moment later, it was followed by an unfamiliar sound. It was Dellia, and she was giggling.

Megan kept her gaze on them. "If they're over there, then what's in the temple?"

"What you see over there is the essence of their consciousness given physical form." Athene returned her gaze to Megan. "I have preserved their real bodies. That's what you saw in the temple."

"Can you send them back to help me?"

The silver-eyed goddess sent her a soft look of sympathy. "Garris is gravely wounded. Dellia can hardly stand, and Jon used his gift to take my power. It is not a thing any normal human body can contain. If he goes back, the strain will kill him in a handful of seconds."

Megan's heart fell. It was hopeless.

Athene smiled at her. "Take heart. All is not lost. Which brings me to the second thing I can tell you. It is in your power to bring them back to the temple."

"Me? How?"

"The moment their bodies are whole and able to fight, I will send them back to help you."

Megan stared. "I don't understand. I don't have a secret gift that can heal people. How am I supposed to make them whole and able to fight?"

Athene's smile broadened. "That is the third thing I can tell you. Everything you need is in that temple. You like puzzles. I have faith in you. You'll figure it out."

"How am I supposed to figure it out? You have to give me more."

"I have interfered in your affairs enough. It is unlikely we will meet again. You can pray to me if you like, but I won't answer. Goodbye, Megan. Be the heroine I know you are."

Athene strolled up to her and gave her a firm hug.

Before she let go, Megan found herself standing back in the golden light of the temple, with her four wounded friends lying at her feet. She dared not look up because those dark tentacles would already be reaching down toward her. Then she realized, why not?

She raised her head and reached up with her gift to grab a tentacle from the writhing mass. With a blast of wind, she stabbed its sharp tip into the snakelike limb nearest to it. She grabbed another and another, piercing one tentacle with another until the wriggling arms recoiled, and the beast let out another deep, resonant moan.

In the lull, Megan glanced around as she spoke to herself. "Heal them. Make them whole. Heal them. Make them whole." She peered at one body after another, scanning their clothing and wounds. The compulsion to vomit came back, but she kept it at bay by focusing on the puzzle at hand. Athene said there was a way to heal them. All she needed to do was to figure it out. Her gaze rested on Aylun, and Megan repeated, "Heal them. Make them whole."

Then a memory burst forth. In the den of thieves below Katapa, he *had* been healed. Aylun had been wounded in the stampede through the city. Before he entered the temple there, she had noticed a gash in his leg. Not as nasty as the one now on Garris's side, but quite real and severe enough to cause a pronounced limp. In fact, it was serious enough that it had caused him to fall behind as they raced across the pavilion to the temple entrance.

Later, when she examined him in the den of thieves, his pants were still torn from the injury, but the wound beneath had vanished. He had even mentioned that he'd injured it in an alley and found it odd that he was unharmed. With Athene's insistence that everything she needed was in this temple, it became clear. There was no mistake. Something in that Katapa Temple had completely healed his wound. Whatever that was, it had to exist in this temple too.

Megan glanced around as she repeated the line to herself "Everything you need is in the temple." Her eyes met the pool of water, and a gasp escaped as she spotted it. Reflected on its surface was the ceiling, coated in the purest of black. A ragged, deformed cavity had formed in the middle with countless tentacles around it, snaking down toward her. Then, as she stared at the ripples, it hit her. Aylun had been wet when he entered the den of thieves. She'd assumed it was sweat, but what if …

She scooped up Jon's body with her gift and tossed it over the lip of the pool. It landed with a loud splash, and he disappeared below the surface.

Unable to defend herself and watch at the same time, she turned her attention above. Now staring directly at the ceiling, what she had seen reflected in the waves of the pool became clear. The hole in the middle was a mouth ringed with jagged, black teeth, and the tentacles were growing in size and number. No doubt their goal was to impale her with their sharp tips and snatch her upward where they could feed her to that hideous mouth. Using her gift, she began to throw tentacles back upward, stabbing them into each other and the enormous body and mouth of the beast.

A sudden splashing came from the pool. Her gaze whipped over, and Jon was standing. He appeared to be unscathed, and his face held a stunned expression, as water dripped from his hair and ran down his torn clothes. The blood had washed away in the pool, and not a single scratch showed on his skin. Athene had been true to her word. She had sent him back the moment he was whole and able to fight. But yanking him out of Elysium appeared to have left him disoriented.

He stared ahead for a moment, then his eyes fell on his wife's battered body. "Dellia!" He raced to the edge of the pool.

Some instinct within her rebelled at the idea of him leaving the water, and Megan shouted, "Jon, no!"

He leaped over the lip and took two steps before crashing to the floor, unmoving.

For a moment, his collapse shocked her. Something had told her Jon needed to stay in the pool, but she was too flustered to work out why. Then the answer came to her. He had been sent back because the pool had healed his physical wounds, but Athene's power wasn't an illness or injury, so it remained. He still had it, and he needed the healing power of the pool to continuously mend the damage it was causing. Without that, he would lapse back into unconsciousness, followed, no doubt, by death. She had solved the riddle, but she had made things worse, and now she had mere seconds to save Jon's life.

Still flinging tentacles back upward and stabbing them into each other, Megan scanned the three remaining bodies for a split second. Garris—he was big. He could carry the others to the pool. She grabbed his leg and yanked upward in a blast of wind.

He sailed from the ground, over the edge, and into the pool, landing with a much larger splash than Jon. A moment later, he shot upright and stood there, his broad, muscular chest and golden skin smooth and unscathed.

Megan yelled, "Get Jon back into the pool. Quick! If he stays out too long, he'll die." She kept her attention on the beast above as the tentacles closed in on her. They were too many now to fight one at a time, and the abomination seemed to be making more and more.

With a quickness that surprised her, Garris leaped out of the pool. He threw Jon over one shoulder and Dellia over the other, then raced back to the edge and tossed them in. Without the slightest delay, he drew his sword, whipped around, and began hacking his way toward Aylun.

Moments later, Jon and Dellia splashed up out of the water. The protector's wounds were gone, and she stood there, whole and healed, yet appearing as disoriented as Jon.

Tentacle pieces fell in flaming chunks behind him as Garris finished the distance to Aylun. He hoisted the man up under one arm and rushed him back to the pool. A few seconds later, Aylun splashed up, standing in the pool with his arm and head injuries gone.

Jon peered at Megan, still seeming a bit dazed. "Megan, get yourself into the pool."

She shook her head as tentacles stabbed at her from every direction. "I can't. There are too many."

One banged into her head, and she began to fall. Her vision blurred as Jon started to splash his way toward her.

Dellia lunged out, grabbed his arm, and shouted, "No!"

Megan recovered and returned all her focus above, using her gift to throw and grab as she rushed out the words. "Stay in the pool.

You still have Athene's power. You need the continuous healing of the water to combat the damage it causes, or you'll die."

Dellia dragged him back from the edge. "You heard her. If you leave the pool, Athene's power will kill you."

Jon turned to his friends and bellowed, "Guys, get her into the water, now!"

Garris was first to react. He plowed through the water, his wake rippling across the surface. His sword whipped through the air, hacking black chunks off the limbs that snaked down upon her.

Suddenly Megan's feet flew out from under her as Garris scooped her up in his arms. She continued to throw back the winding black arms as he hauled her to the pool. He tossed her like a sack of flour and the world spun as she flew over the edge. She tumbled into the water and floundered there until she caught her footing, then splashed up.

Jon shouted out to her, "If this is a healing pool, then we can't die if we're in here, right?"

Garris shouted as he slashed across the water to Megan's side, "Those tentacles will have no problem removing us from this pool."

Jon glanced at Megan as he heaved wild swings at the things reaching for him. "Aetherstone, now!"

At first, his demand seemed rude, given the circumstances. Then, all of a sudden, it clicked. Megan snatched the golden orb out of the net at her waist and tossed it to him.

Jon caught it. A look of concentration crossed his drenched face, and the aetherstone glowed brighter.

The creature's maw above issued a deep moaned that rumbled through the temple.

The look of concentration faded to a wince of pain, and the stone dimmed. Jon shouted, "Garris, Aylun, who can throw the farthest?"

Garris sent a glance to Aylun. "I shoot things. Aylun can throw it."

Jon tossed the aetherstone to him, and he snatched it from the air with ease.

Jon shouted again, "Megan, if Aylun throws that thing at the beast, can you shove it the rest of the way up into the body?"

She smiled as she fended off wriggling tentacles accosting her. "I can shove a lot more than that tiny thing through it."

"Then do it."

Dellia's two blades whipped through the air around Aylun as he paused, and a look of calm focus filled his face. With a quick dodge to the side, he wound his arm back and threw.

The aetherstone raced upward. Tentacles reached for it and hit it, but they recoiled as if the thing had wounded them.

Megan stood firm and stretched out her hand above her, aiming at the glowing orb.

Garris came to her side, his sword whooshing through the air near her head, protecting her. Bits of tentacle fell past her, bursting into flame or erupting into a flurry of cinders and ash as she focused on her gift.

Jon splashed over and set his back to her, staring upward past her hand at the aetherstone.

Dellia followed him and joined Garris in protecting the pair. Their blades whistled around her as Megan pushed against the stone. A whirlwind surrounded her, whipping up the water. Mist and spray mingled with the fire and air winding around her.

Aylun waded over to join Dellia and Garris, as his bladed staff ends stabbed and slashed tentacles reaching for him.

All three set their backs to Megan and Jon, forming a circle of flying metal around the pair. Wind and water blasted them as their blades cut through the spray above and around her. They lopped off the snaking dark arms at a furious pace, their weapons becoming shredders dismembering anything within reach.

The dark severed pieces fell around them, disintegrating in fire and spark as they plunged downward. The ash, embers, and smaller pieces mixed with the whirling water, turning it into a tornado of mist, spray, and fire.

Megan pushed harder and higher. In growing numbers, the tentacles that surrounded the horrid mouth pulled away from them. They began to reach for the rising aetherstone, trying to block it as it grew brighter and brighter. They sizzled as they came near, and steam burst forth where they touched it.

She pushed still harder, forcing it through the tangled mass of writhing black limbs. The higher she shoved it, the brighter it became and the stronger the whirlwind.

The slick, black appendages recoiled, then shattered in glittering showers of fire and light upon nearing the blistering ball of light. A moan of pain boomed out, louder, longer, and deeper than before, shaking the pillars of the temple. Dust and debris rained down around them, then got caught up in the flaming waterspout.

It became too bright to see, and Megan stretched out her hand, shielded her eyes from the light.

Jon's head remained tilted back behind her, and from the angle it seemed as if his gaze was fixed on the light.

Still, she forced her aetherstone higher. It passed through the mouth, and as she met resistance, the whirlwind around her intensified, becoming a hurricane of water, fire, and debris. She took a quick glance around her, and Dellia, Garris, and Aylun were squinting through the barrage of spark and rain. Their metal flew, their blades whipping through the wall of water and fire.

The aetherstone hit something hard, and Megan pushed with all her might. The light became blinding even through her shielded eyes. Her feet slid across the wet marble bottom of the pool. Then the blazing orb lurched upward, and a deafening explosion rocked them. It rumbled through the ground, sending rolling waves across the water of the pool.

She peeked through her fingers as sheets of fire and gleaming embers rained down around her, sizzling and hissing as they hit the pool's surface. A loud slap came from behind her, and she spotted her golden, glowing aetherstone. It had fallen into Jon's hand.

AYLUN

When the rain of fire eased, Megan dropped her hand and peered upward. The massive black behemoth was gone, leaving only pieces of ash falling below the bright marble ceiling. She glanced at the four surrounding her. Jon stood tall. From what she had seen he never flinched, much less blocked his face or closed his eyes. One by one, the others unblocked their view and stared upward, watching the curtains of flaming remains drift down and hiss as they hit the pool.

A flash caught her eye, and Megan turned her gaze to the temple entrance. Beyond its pillars, more and more of the stone walkway became visible. Then the cobblestones farther out appeared. A flash broke the darkness beyond, then another and another, and she pointed. "The darkness, it's disappearing."

She leaped over the lip of the pool and raced to the temple entrance. Water dripped from her hair as a soaking-wet Aylun stepped up to her side. They watched together as glittering flashes burst out here and there, piercing the darkness. Screams and cries of pain accompanied them as sparks showered down on the ruins.

The darkness was receding, and with it, more and more of the cityscape became visible. The Dead of Night was dying. Not all at once, but one creature at a time. The fate of the beasts in the darkness was tied to the behemoth in the temple. Without it, the darkness faded, and in the light, they were burning.

Megan glanced around her, and everyone but Jon was standing with her, watching. Her friends, her new family—they were all whole and free from scars or wounds or even blemishes.

Sunlight burst out above, sending its warming rays down on their sopping-wet bodies. It lit the wall of darkness racing backward, beyond the fringes of the ruins. More and more of the landscape became visible as the screeches grew more distant, and the flashes of light and fire multiplied.

The far-off screams and pained wailings rang through the majestic ruins of the city. They came from every direction as blast after blast lit the billowing black cloud like a never-ending fireworks display.

Then the enormity of it hit her. They had just banished the Dead of Night. They destroyed a plague that had consumed this land for hundreds of years. The others continued to watch the flashes spread all along the vast black horizon.

Megan turned and strolled back to Jon. He had the broadest of smiles on his face. She met his warm gaze. "How did you come up with all that stuff so fast?"

He shrugged. "On the way back from the oracle room, I had a lot of time to think about the lighthouses and how their flamestones worked. I dreamed up all kinds of crazy, unworkable ways to kill that thing. Then when I saw you near the statue of Athene, I thought of your aetherstone, and it just clicked. I knew what to do." He motioned to her with his head. "How did you make it here alone? How did you figure out the pool was the key to saving us all?"

Now it was her turn to shrug. "In Katapa, Aylun got a big gash on his leg, and then it just seemed to disappear after he'd been in the temple pool. Later, I treated his wounds with that water, and they healed faster than they should have. It just took me a minute, you know, to figure out the common denominator."

She glanced at the door, and beyond it, the constant flashes in the cloud of darkness grew ever more distant. As she returned her gaze to Jon, she smiled. "I wish you could see it."

He smiled back. "I have Athene's power. You think I can't see it?" Then his smile faded. "Is my wife okay?"

Megan let her smile fade as well. "Don't worry. I will never let anything happen to her."

Jon seemed touched by that. Then he looked at the group huddled at the entrance. He drew a deep breath and thrust out her the aetherstone for her to take. "I'm stuck here. So, could you take that abundance of confidence and go help protect what's important to Garris. The Mirhal are in Shirdon, and they're headed for Kayleen. She's about to face them alone. I don't know if you can get there and find her in time, but try."

She cocked her head. "How do you know?"

978

"Athene's power. In my mind's eye, I see it happening. Help her, please."

Megan took the aetherstone and nodded. This was her role now. She was the oracles' champion. She had to protect what was important to Jon and to Meerdon. More than that, she needed the Eye of Syvis, and something below her awareness, something in the part of her mind that loved to unravel puzzles, was sure it would be in Shirdon with the Mirhal. She took a step back as she eyed Jon. "I have to take the Eye of Syvis. It's there too, right?"

He smiled and nodded. "Yes, it's with Ruahn. But then, you already know that." He motioned for her to hurry.

She left Jon and strolled back toward the door. As she reached Garris, she slapped him on his broad back and looked up into his face. "This isn't over yet, big guy. Kayleen is in trouble. We need to get to her, fast."

He gave a crisp nod as Megan shoved her way through and rounded the corner out of the temple.

Aylun and Garris hurried up to either side of her, the three walking abreast.

Dellia remained at the entrance, seeming torn.

Megan peered back over her shoulder and called out, "You too, Dellia. Jon isn't going anywhere. He can take care of himself."

Dellia hesitated awhile longer. Then she gave a nod to Jon inside the temple, turned, and raced after.

Megan fished in her pocket and found her bag of spire stones. She retrieved the white one and clutched it in her hand as she and her three companions strutted toward the spire.

Kayleen halted in the dark hallway before the entrance to the audience hall. It was the largest room in the keep, larger even than the council chamber. The Mirhal's demand to meet here seemed a strong political move. She would be alone and exposed in a large space, facing a dozen or more adversaries.

Rillen stood by her side, and her voice brought Kayleen's attention back to the protector. "It's not too late. I could still approach the military leaders and order them to put a stop to this."

"No." Kayleen shook her head. "It is too late. Jon's image has been tainted, and they've been cut off from council leadership for far too long. We no longer know what the military leaders are thinking. Even if you could convince them the order came from me, we don't know how they'd react. It would make a volatile situation even more unpredictable."

Silence fell again, and she peered out the entry at the long white hall. It lay empty now, in foreboding silence. It was the perfect setting if their goal was to intimidate her, but she could not afford to let them intimidate her.

She tore her gaze from it and faced Rillen. "No matter how this turns out, I want to thank you for these past few days. You gave me a lot of your strength. For that, I am grateful."

Rillen appeared surprised. "But I'm going with you."

Kayleen shook her head again. "No. They're bringing a bunch of soldiers and a contingent of supporters. It's a display of force. Meeting that force with more force is not how you win political battles. It has always been my way to have my strength come from the truth I speak, not from the weapons with which I surround myself."

"But to be out there alone and vulnerable ..."

"When facing an opponent who has overwhelming numbers, it is always best to avoid the threat of violence. I don't want you hurt, and I don't want to be caught in a fight with nervous soldiers."

Rillen glanced out at the empty hall beyond the door. Then she opened her robe to show a harness with a couple dozen throwing daggers. "If this leads to violence, I will protect you. More than a few of them will go down."

Kayleen smiled. "From those little things?"

Rillen smiled back. "Have you ever seen someone get a dagger in the throat? It's messy and fast."

"Okay. That makes me feel better, but stay out of sight. No one must spot you, got it?"

Rillen nodded, and Kayleen turned and headed into the chamber. Alone in the vast space, her soft footsteps echoed through the hall as she walked to its center. A lump formed in her throat as she scanned the empty room. Like every room in the keep, it was carved out of solid marble. The floor and walls were swirled a creamy white, with a row of black pillars along either side, reaching up for the high ceiling several stories above. At the center of the floor sat an inlay, two huge overlapping rings of black marble. Kayleen stopped and waited at the center of the nearest ring.

Almost at once, soldiers began filing into the hall along either side, their clatter echoing through the chamber. There were far more than she'd expected, and among the first two dozen were many faces she recognized as members of the Shirdon military. Armed with long, gleaming swords, they marched the length of the hall and lined up at attention in front of the row of dark pillars on either side.

When the row spanned half the length of the hall, a second group came. They were black-leather-clad Elorians, another two dozen of them, carrying crossbows loaded with arrows. None of them was recognizable to her. As each one stopped, he or she turned and took up their position in front of the pillars. With grim, unreadable expressions, they raised their weapons and leveled them at Kayleen.

As the last clattered in, the lump in her throat grew. On each side of her now stood a row of two dozen armed soldiers. The half behind her were all Shirdon militia, while those in sight were Elorian mercenaries with two dozen crossbows aimed at her.

As she gathered her courage, a group of seven somber Elorians strolled into the hall, led by Ruepo and a woman Kayleen didn't recognize. She bore a resemblance to the man, and it seemed likely she was his daughter, Ruahn. If her guess was right, the remaining group were all members of the Mirhal.

Then, behind them appeared another two Elorians, hauling a beaten and bedraggled-looking Idria along. With each clutching an arm, they yanked her down the shiny marble hall. The pair wore dark robes with violet trim, and the sight was incomprehensible. What were the Mirhal doing with a former council member who was somehow related to Syvis?

Their footsteps resounded through the chamber, growing closer until they came to a halt some distance in front of her. Ruepo and the woman kept advancing until they were standing at the center of the other of the two dark rings.

Ruepo glanced over at the woman. "You see, Ruahn, she came alone, as you predicted. She thinks she can talk her way out of this." He turned his gaze to Kayleen. "Jon, Dellia, and your precious Garris have not come back, as we foretold. Are you ready to hand over power as promised?"

She held back her fear and sent him a gracious smile. "You can't be so foolish as to consider a promise binding when you extracted it at the point of a crossbow."

The man eyed Ruahn again. "See, again, it is as you foretold. She never intended to honor her bargain."

Kayleen scanned the hall, eyeing the row of grim, black-clad mercenaries on either side. All in all, she had two dozen crossbows aimed at her chest. "I'm honored, and more than a little shocked, that you think you need forty-eight armed warriors to handle one lowly first advocate. Did your vision of the future tell you forty-seven wouldn't be enough?"

Ruahn stepped forward. "Don't be flippant. We both know why I brought these soldiers. It's to show you we have the support of your military."

"Ah. So, you have the support of the Shirdon military?" Kayleen faked a thoughtful nod. "Is that why you brought two dozen Mirhal soldiers of your own? Your confidence is breathtaking to behold."

Ruahn seemed surprised by the impudence of her remark but soon regained her arrogant demeanor. "Your quick tongue and delay tactics don't amuse me. It will gain you nothing to argue over logistic details of no importance. We have control of your military. That's all you need to know."

Kayleen smiled. "Do you? Are you certain?"

The query seemed to throw Ruahn. She seemed startled at the words and uncertain how to respond. Her reaction told Kayleen all she needed to know. The woman wasn't at all confident in her ability to see the future.

Ruahn's temper grew short. "We are not here to negotiate. We are here to accept your surrender."

"And then kill me and everyone I care about. Why would I not oppose you to the last?"

"Then you should be pleading for your life, not fighting us. You know as well as I do, you have no choice but to surrender."

She kept her gaze rock steady. "Oh, really. Then tell me, am I going to surrender?"

Ruahn seemed shocked again. "Stop playing games."

"It's not a game. You claim to be fit to rule because you can see the future. Yet you are uncertain whether you have the support of my military, and you don't know if I'll surrender or not. Can you or can you not see the future?" She left a pause for dramatic effect, then stepped closer. "Admit it. Things have gone wrong with your plan. Your ability to see the future isn't perfect. Events aren't playing out as you foresaw." Kayleen inched even farther forward. "The very reason you consider yourself fit to rule is invalid."

Ruahn stood taller. "We do not need to be perfect. We only need to be better. My father told you the reasons why we can rule better than you. But you will not listen. You are the evil one here. You would let your people die to crime and war, famine and disease, when we can predict these things and stop them."

As she studied Ruahn's face, movement came from behind the woman. New figures crept into the council chamber. Garris and Dellia slipped to the right, and Megan and Aylun to the left.

Kayleen kept her expression unchanged. Hoping to distract and make a strong point, she raised her voice, so all in the room could hear. "You claim you can predict catastrophe and stop it, but that's a lie. You can't even predict *me*. You can't even stop me."

Ruahn seemed surprised once again. "Words will not get you out of this."

The new arrivals started taking out the Elorian soldiers one at a time. Garris slammed the butt of a sword into the first one's head. With silent movements, Dellia caught the falling body and dragged it back behind the row of pillars.

With much greater subtlety, Aylun grabbed the crossbow of the first mercenary as he put him in a choke hold. Then he waited for a few moments until the soldier passed out, before dragging him out of sight.

Kayleen kept her gaze ahead, trying not to give away her relief. "If you don't believe me, prove me wrong. Tell me, what does your gift say about me? What rumor have I spread about the Mirhal?"

For the first time, Ruahn seemed truly shaken. "You're bluffing. What rumor?"

"The truth. It's always the best rumor."

"What truth?"

Kayleen sensed the tide of debate turning. She had the woman worried, and she needed to stall, so she smiled and gazed for a while, remaining mute.

Ruahn raised her arm high in the air.

In response, all the remaining crossbow-wielding mercenaries shouldered their weapons and aimed them directly at Kayleen.

Ruahn glared. "I asked a question. What truth?"

Quelling her alarm, Kayleen lowered her voice. By now, everyone in the hall had to be curious, and she wanted their absolute attention. "Several rumors, actually. That the Mirhal are real and dangerous. That they set the Dead of Night loose and sabotaged the lighthouses on purpose. That they did it so they could spread a rumor and blame it on Jon. That they were so afraid of him, they laid a trap and tried to send him home. That they aren't to be trusted because they put every life in Meerdon at risk for their blind ambition."

984

AYLUN

Ruahn lowered her arm. The soldiers lowered their crossbows as the stunned woman stared. "You couldn't have done all that."

Her friends on either side had brought down half the black-clad mercenaries, so Kayleen raised her voice again, hoping to cover any sound. "You think I can't spread rumors like you did? Why? Because I should be dead? Because you foresaw my death? Well, you were wrong. By now, every one of those rumors has reached all the major cities in Meerdon and every soul in the Shirdon military. Even if you take control, you will never keep it. You will be overthrown by the people you misled because by now, they all know the truth. They know who you are and what you were willing to do for the sake of power."

"Enough of your bluffing." Ruahn snapped her arm high into the air again, and the four remaining black-clad mercenaries raised their crossbows and put Kayleen in their sights.

Aylun grabbed one crossbow and put its owner in a choke hold. At the same time, he flung out a strip of leather with a hook at the end. It wrapped around the second crossbow. He yanked it over to him and snatched it out of the air. As the mercenary fell, Aylun raised the crossbow and set his sights on the remaining black-clad warrior.

Garris and Dellia each yanked a crossbow out of a surprised soldier's hands, then turned them on their backs.

With their moves no longer silent, Ruahn spotted the protectors on either side. She looked to the remaining soldiers, all of them Shirdon militia, but they didn't move. They were standing down as Kayleen had hoped. Word had reached her through her miscreants that the truth spreading in the military had led them to question supporting the Mirhal. With no guidance from her, the best she had hoped for was that they would choose not to act against her. It appeared they had made their decision.

When no soldiers moved, Ruahn glared and slipped a long curved dagger with a dark metal handle out from under her clothes. She lunged, and the tip of her blade headed for Kayleen's chest.

A loud clank reverberated through the hall as a glint of metal slammed into it, bashing the blade out of Ruahn's hand. Kayleen followed the noise as the weapon and a throwing dagger clattered across the smooth marble floor.

Ruahn yanked her hand away.

Footsteps stormed toward her. Kayleen's gaze flew over to spot Megan with her arm outstretched and palm facing Ruahn as she marched right at her.

Out of the corner of her eye, she caught a sudden jerk and blast of air as the woman disappeared.

Kayleen's gaze whipped around to watch Ruahn sail through the air, across the room, past Garris, and between two of the black pillars. She slammed into the white swirls of the wall, banging her face against the hard marble. With a short stagger, she crumpled into a dazed heap, leaving two red splotches of blood on the wall.

Megan strode passed a stunned Ruepo. He lunged out for her, but she remained focused on Ruahn as she thrust out a palm. In a blast of air, he and half his contingent went flying backward, landing on their rears and sliding across the floor.

Among them were Idria and the two holding her. The former council member sprang to her feet, thrust out her palm, and a mist formed in front of it. With her free hand, she reached into the robe of one of the men and grabbed something dark and sickly, then sprang for the mist just as it solidified into a shimmering curtain. No sooner was she gone than the portal turned back into droplets floating on the air.

Megan finished the distance to Ruahn and stomped up in front of her. She grabbed Ruahn's foot, and wind whirled around her as she dragged the dazed woman back out beyond the pillars. The whirlwind intensified as she dropped the foot and used her gift to lift the woman's limp body off the ground without touching it.

Ruahn stared with the frightened look of a cornered animal as blood trickled down her forehead and lip.

986

With her free hand, Megan reached into Ruahn's robe and yanked out the Eye of Syvis. She pulled the chain over Ruahn's head and held up the disgusting disembodied eye, displaying its heavy red veins and indigo iris for all to see. "This is mine now."

She lowered her arms, and Ruahn collapsed into a heap on the swirls of cream-colored marble. Megan shouted, "Does anyone here disagree?"

She sent a fierce gaze across the room. One of the Mirhal started to step forward, and Megan raised her palm toward him.

He halted, but Ruepo rose to his feet and shouted, "No! It belongs to the Mirhal. It has been ours for hundreds of years."

Still holding up the Eye of Syvis with one hand, Megan reached out with the other as if she were grabbing him from across the room. Kayleen watched slack-jawed as a whirlwind whipped around Megan, and Ruepo's feet left the floor. He drifted higher and higher into the hall until his head hit the high marble ceiling, forcing him to bend his neck.

Megan glared at him and shouted as the air whistled around her, tousling her hair and billowing her clothes. "It was Wistra's before it was yours. She gave it to me. So … I repeat. Does anyone disagree?"

Ruepo's face turned red with anger. "No. I will not let you intimidate me. By rights—"

Suddenly he was tumbling downward. A scream escaped him, and he flailed as he plummeted toward the shiny marble floor. He jerked to a stop, his head floating a mere foot above its unforgiving surface. His breath, short and sharp, echoed through the chamber as he started to rise again.

A dervish of air whirled around Megan. "Your daughter is next, old man." She slipped the chain of the eye around her wrist and reached out her other hand. Ruahn's battered body began to rise along with Ruepo's.

As they both drifted higher, Ruepo stared wide-eyed as Ruahn started to thrash and cry out in a pitiful panicked wailing. As they approached the ceiling, his resolve seemed to crumble, and he blurted out, "Take it! I have no objection."

The pair drifted back down as Ruahn's whimpering echoed through the chamber. The wind ceased as Megan set them on the floor. For a second time, she sent her gaze across the soldiers and Mirhal in the room. She thrust the eye up high for all to see. "Good. I'll ask one last time. The Eye of Syvis is mine now. Does anyone object?"

All fell silent, the only sound the sighs of relief from the Mirhal and Ruahn's weeping as Megan waited. After a protracted pause, she bellowed, "No. No further objections? Good!" She gave a crisp nod and strolled back toward Kayleen.

A bit alarmed that the erratic woman who liked to toss people around like they were rag dolls was now headed toward her, Kayleen glanced at Garris and Dellia. The two were still anchored to their spots, each with a crossbow to the back of a black-leather-clad mercenary. They both seemed unconcerned.

Her voice brought Kayleen's focus back to Megan, who was still strolling toward her. "And one last thing." She pointed to the contingent of Mirhal. "These bozos used this"—she held up the eye—"to threaten all of Meerdon and smear my friends. Jon, Dellia, Aylun, Garris, and I destroyed the Dead of Night to stop them. It is gone now, and we reclaimed the land it took."

Kayleen's anxiety rose as the ginger-haired woman from another world stopped at her side and sent another fiery gaze across the room. "I warn you all now, so spread the word: You want to disagree with my friends, that's fine. You want to argue with us and debate, no problem." She threw an arm around Kayleen's shoulder and pulled her close like they had been friends their whole lives. Her gaze turned wicked as she scanned the room and barked out, "But you come at us sideways with schemes and lies, and what we did to the Dead of Night will seem like child's play compared to what I'll do to you."

Megan slipped the chain around her neck and tucked the eye into her clothes. She removed her arm, leaned over to Kayleen, and whispered in her ear. "Too much?"

AYLUN

Kayleen leaned over and whispered back, "No. You were magnanimous yet terrifying. It was perfect."

Megan stepped back and smiled at Kayleen, then she bowed to her and spoke in a loud voice. "I'm done now. You may continue."

Kayleen stood frozen by the display of raw power.

Aylun stepped up to Megan's side, and his calm gaze rested on Ruepo. "For centuries, the Augury has shunned rule. You know that, and you know full well the reasons why."

Ruepo answered, his voice as calm as Aylun's. "I do."

"Then why?"

Ruepo shook his head. "We do not all wish to be pawns of the Augury."

"Then you should have gone and lived your life in peace. You had a choice. Don't use your gift to alter events of significance and the Augury will not bother you."

"But we could save lives. If only the Augury could see that we oracles make the superior rulers."

Aylun shook his head. "You would turn people into slaves serving the Mirhal. You would arrest the innocent before they commit crimes. You would force people to go hungry as they store food and water, and you would kill the diseased to stop its spread."

"For the good of all."

"No, because you would never accept it for yourself. You would shout injustice to be arrested for a crime you never committed. You would be outraged to sweat and toil to reap an abundant harvest only to have it taken from you and watch your family go hungry. You would fight tooth and nail to stop Ruahn from being killed because she was sick." He stepped closer to the man. "Every life is precious. Every life is valuable, but you deem your life and your freedom more valuable than that of others. That is your sin. That is why you are unfit to rule."

More Shirdon soldiers poured into the room.

Kayleen tore her eyes from Aylun and motioned to the Mirhal contingent. "Haul them away and lock them up. They will stand trial for high treason, as will all those who aided them." She scanned the two dozen Shirdon soldiers still at attention. "Those who stood down here and refused to oppose me will be rewarded."

The soldiers already in the room hesitated for a moment, then one after the other, they joined the new arrivals. They scurried over to Ruepo and his gang and escorted them away. Others took the black-leather-clad mercenaries and lugged their unconscious bodies out of the hall.

As soon as a soldier hauled away his target, Garris set his crossbow on the ground and headed for Kayleen.

Dellia flung hers aside and raced over with Garris. She pushed ahead of him and stepped up to Megan. "I have to get back to Jon." The speed and sharpness of her statement elicited puzzled expressions and stunned silence from all assembled. Dellia didn't wait before repeating her plea. "Please. We left him in that temple all alone. Do you have a way to get back to him?"

Megan eyed her for a brief time. Then she scanned the group with a self-conscious look and turned away. It was clear she was hiding something, but not well. After a few moments, she spun back, and in her small hand lay a fuchsia stone. It resembled a spire stone but was of a color Kayleen had never seen on a spire stone before. Perhaps her possession of such an unheard-of rarity was what she was hiding. Megan held it out for Dellia to see. "This will get us to the Saranik spire. Let's go make sure he's okay." She motioned to Aylun, and they both moved to walk away.

Dellia stepped up in front of them, blocking their way, and an even stronger pleading came. "I want to be alone with him."

Megan stared, seeming puzzled.

Dellia's insistence grew. "I need to be alone with him." The strength of her desperation and urgency were a new and puzzling wrinkle in her personality.

Megan's expression softened. "Of course, I'll catch up with you later and get the stone back."

Dellia snatched the fuchsia stone from Megan's hand as if she were poisoned and it the antidote. She gave a quick bow of her head and sprinted away.

Garris stepped up to Kayleen and set his strong hand on her shoulder. "Are you okay?"

At his unusual and gentle concern, she let her guard fall and stared up at his face. "No. I'm not. I thought you weren't going to make it back. I thought that even if I stopped the Mirhal, they'd kill me because it would be smarter than leaving me alive."

Suddenly she was in his arms, and he was patting her back with a soft touch. He whispered in her ear, "I'm sorry. I worried about you every minute."

"Really?" She stepped back and gazed into his eyes.

"Yeah, but it's a long story, and you look tired. I'll take you home. Rest, and then I'll tell you about it over breakfast." He glanced at Rillen, Megan, and Aylun. "Join us if you can. I have quite a few questions about what just happened, and we can exchange stories. We'll be at my mother Eejha's place. Rillen knows the way."

He took Kayleen's hand and led her toward the keep exit. She peered up at his face as she walked at his side. "Are you really coming home?"

"Yes, Kayleen."

"But … I've been stuck in a cave for days, and I'm famished. Can we eat something before we rest?"

"Of course, Kayleen."

She hesitated for a brief time, then added, "And you won't run away like last time?"

He smirked. "Whatever you say, Kayleen."

She leaned her head on his muscular arm. He was teasing her, of course, but there was no hint of sarcasm or humor in his voice, only a note of sincerity and gentle concern. As they walked the keep's halls, out of it, and down the streets to her home, that note of gentle concern remained.

That day, long ago, when he had carried an injured young girl home, she had seen her first glimpse of the Garris who could be concerned and caring. That version of him had made appearances from time to time until the day he decided to join the protectors. From that day until this, she had waited for the return of the man who took care of her, who worried about her, whose concern warmed her soul. He was back now, walking beside her, and somehow, she knew he would never leave her again.

Chapter Thirty-Seven

THE FINAL DEAL

Alone in the warm, crystal waters of the temple pool, Jon sat and worried over Dellia. In need of distraction, he focused on trying to make sense of his own tangled thoughts, of the insights that had come with the power of Athene. Visions of places he had never visited and bits of information he had never learned flashed through his mind in a chaotic jumble.

He had only taken one biology class in high school. Yet one of those passing thoughts allowed him to explain, in detail, how the cells and DNA were in a perpetual state of accumulating damage and repairing it. Histones accumulated aberrant methylation patterns that are inherited when the cell divides. The immune system can repair such damage and remove faulty cells, but that ability diminishes with age. Just as growth and maturation are governed by the switching on and off of genes, aging is as well. As people grow older, certain genes get switched off, eventually leading to mitochondrial dysfunction, dwindling supplies of somatic stem cells, and a weakening of the immune system. Thus, the balance shifts toward more damage than repair.

A picture came to him of the place Athene and her kind had visited to make a permanent change to their DNA to forever shift the balance, to eliminate damage and speed repair. For a fleeting moment, he knew where they had gained their perpetual youth, and he could describe the intricate biological mechanisms by which it worked.

Then the knowledge vanished, replaced by other thoughts and other images. In his mind's eye, there appeared a place that had conveyed the ability to bypass the veil and tap into vast power that one could control with a thought. Yet, crippling pain debilitated him every time he tried to dwell too long on one of those passing bits of knowledge. So, he let them go. It was pointless to try to hang onto them anyway. No matter how hard he tried, they would fade along with that power, until all that remained were vague impressions.

So, Jon lowered his head and closed his eyes, focusing instead on the serene isolation and peaceful lapping of water against the side of the pool. Just when his borrowed power and knowledge began to fade, and the idea of Dellia out there without him grew too sorrowful to bear, footsteps came as if bidden by his desire. They echoed through the chamber, and he looked up to see Dellia racing across the marble floor toward him.

Eager for her touch, he moved closer along the pool's edge, sitting with his arms open. As she reached him, she threw herself into his embrace and flung her arms around him, clinging with a tightness that surprised. Her hand pressed him to her chest, and her fingers pulled across his back as if she couldn't get him close enough.

He couldn't see her face, but there were tears in her voice. "I missed you."

She hadn't been gone for more than a couple hours, and yet her greeting was as if they'd been apart for weeks. Then it dawned on him, and sadness shot through him. To be thrust out of Elysium in such a sudden and jolting way had been a shock, but to Dellia, it seemed, the loss was deeper and more profound.

He ran his fingers through the hair on the back of her head and held it close. "I love you more than life itself. You know that, right?" Her head nodded in his hand, and her cheek brushed against his. "I'm here whenever you need me."

Then he felt her body's gentle heaving against his chest as she clung to him as if her life depended on it. She was crying, and he understood what she was going through. She had lost Shangri-la, and there was no going back.

After a while, her voice came, small and pleading. "I don't like this world, Jon. I want to go home."

It hurt his heart to see her like this. Even more so because he shared some of what she was going through. So, he continued to hold her, lending her every bit of support he could. "I'll be with you every minute, every second. We'll take it one day at a time, okay?"

She pulled back and cupped his face in her hands. "But you'll be busy with council business. I'll never see you."

Jon smiled and shook his head. "I have Kayleen, and I think we just earned as much rest as we want."

He knew his reassurances were not the truth. They came not from the rational part of him, but from the part that wished with all his heart for them to be true. Dellia sat with him, the golden glow of the statue framing her beautiful face as they talked and consoled each other.

After a long while, which seemed all too short in Dellia's company, the knowledge he had gained when he used his gift to take Athene's power faded. With her power gone, he knew he could leave the pool without pain. So they left the temple behind and strolled the streets of a city that harbored only their two souls. In that way, it was as if they were back in Elysium, alone together. When the sun had drifted below the distant mountaintops, and the light dimmed, they found a place to rest.

They stayed that night in a small stone home near the temple. Jon gathered wood from a pile outside and made a fire. The logs were far too dry and burned with unexpected ferocity. Jon and Dellia scooted back and kept their distance as flames billowed in the fireplace. The mishap brought a small smile to Dellia's face, and for a while, she teased him and laughed at his fire-building skills. They talked by the roaring flames, and she stayed close. Apart from a mild desperation to be near him, to always be touching, she seemed herself for a time.

The next day, beneath drab gray skies, they were the first to tour the remains of a city that hadn't seen human visitors in centuries. The buildings, though ancient, had held up well. Beyond them, in every direction, desolate flat lands spread out to enormous white-capped peaks that scraped the cloud-filled skies.

He and Dellia held hands and guessed at the nature of each shop and house. For a while, it even devolved into wild speculation as to the appearance and disposition of each shop's owners. In the evening, they sat together on the steps of an ancient monument, and as they watched the sunset, the clatter of distant horses came up from behind them.

They rose and strolled out to meet a pair of scouts led by Sirra. Dellia smiled at her mother's arrival and again when she spotted Ulka and Enna with them. Wetness came to her eyes as Sirra dismounted. Then she raced up to her mother and flew into her arms.

After a long hug, Sirra pulled back and looked at her daughter. "What's wrong?"

Sensing it best to avoid delving into the details here, in the middle of the street, Jon spoke first. "I'll tell you everything later. Just know that Dellia hasn't seen you for over four months."

As expected, Sirra seemed shocked. "Four months? But it's only been—"

"Four *months*," he insisted, as he sent her a nod of affirmation and a stare that she seemed to understand meant now was not the time to talk about this.

They found a larger home with a generous fireplace, and beside roaring flames, they sat and talked. They told Sirra of their confrontation with the heart of the darkness and of Kayleen's showdown with the Mirhal. From there, the conversation veered into matters both trivial and profound, until Dellia decided to go to bed. She implored Jon not to stay up too late, and he told her he understood.

Once Dellia disappeared into the bedroom, Sirra turned to him. "What's going on, Jon? What happened to my daughter?"

He drew a deep breath. "We spent over four months in Elysium."

Sirra sat straighter, and her eyes widened in surprise. After a few seconds, she asked, "Elysium? *The* Elysium?"

"Yes. It's real, and Dellia and I were there." A long pause followed, accompanied by a look of disbelief. He didn't wait for Sirra to give voice to her incredulity. "It was only a day here but four months there. She never wanted for food or water or clothing. She took to it like a madwoman. We were inseparable, and Dellia was so happy every moment, happier than anyone I've ever seen."

Sirra closed her eyes and lowered her head. "She was kicked out of heaven."

Jon clarified. "She misses her home there. She's homesick."

"How can I help?"

He laced his fingers in his lap and leaned closer. "She's already worried that council business will take me away from her, and I don't blame her. It's hard for me now to be apart from her, but there are things I must do."

She sent him a surprised look. "It's that bad?"

"Yes. For Dellia, even more so. It was different for her. She made her peace with leaving this world behind, but I always wanted closure. I wanted a chance to come back and honor everyone's faith in me. I wanted the three realms to be as free as they can be and Shirdon to be a force that helps them work together for their common benefit."

Sirra smiled. "It seems like you've thought this through, and I appreciate your vision."

Jon set a hand on Sirra's and peered into her eyes. "I will try to involve Dellia as much as I can in council decisions. That will keep her near me. And I'll use Kayleen to stand in for me in the less complicated matters. That will give me more time with Dellia. But it would be helpful if you were there with us. It would mean a lot to Dellia if you could be there for her when I can't. Not to mention, I could use your support and advice on political matters."

Sirra sat back and sent him a stern look. "Are you asking for my help in consoling my daughter or for the support of one of the Ephori in political issues?"

Jon considered her question. "I'm asking for your help as one who cares about Dellia and wants to see her and her people preserve the things they cherish."

She smiled, making it apparent her earlier displeasure was an act she put on to test him. "Well said, Jon. If you can argue like that in front of the council, it will be hard for them to deny you any reasonable request." She lowered her head for a second, appearing to give his suggestion serious thought. "All right. I can tell the Ephori I am going to stay in Shirdon for a couple of weeks to support the new council members from Talus and to whisper in your ear. As long as you don't mind me using you for *my* political aims."

Relief spread through him. "I really appreciate this."

She sent him another solemn look. "One more thing, and it's not a request. Tilla will be coming with me."

Jon smiled. The idea of bringing her dog was a stroke of genius. Nothing would brighten Dellia's mood more than having the things she loved around her. He gave a crisp nod. "Perfect."

Sirra shot him a dour expression. "Now, off to bed with you. Don't let my daughter lack for the comfort of you being near her."

Jon rose and gave Sirra a long hug. "I love you ... Mom."

It seemed like a bit too strong an expression and an overstepping of boundaries, yet Sirra's smile broadened. "I love you too." There was a genuine fondness in her tone, then her smile went flat. "Now go." She shooed him away, but as he turned to head back to the bedroom and Dellia, he caught the smile returning to Sirra's face.

Garris stood in the backyard of his childhood home, gazing at the rose-colored clouds and crimson sun peeking above the tall wooden fence. During his months in Elysium, he had witnessed a hundred sunrises like it. When they entered the Dead of Night, it was with the expectation he would return within days to learn of Kayleen's fate. Instead, he had spent months away from everything he knew, worrying about the gut-wrenching ending of their last talk.

AYLUN

The only distraction from his constant brooding had been his fleeting visits with Jon and Dellia. Each time, Jon would remind him it hadn't yet been a day for her in Meerdon, and she was probably fine. But it was a hollow claim, and his reassurances cold comfort. The man hadn't seen the violent interruption of their last exchange, and he had no way of knowing what happened after it. So Garris had only smiled and nodded.

The familiar and comforting bustle of his mother behind him broke his trance, and he tore his eyes from the morning sun and the graying wood of the old fence. He drew a deep breath, savoring the aroma of his mother's home cooking. It brought back a flood of fond memories from his childhood, and he glanced over his shoulder at her.

Eejha was in abundant good cheer as she ferried savory dishes from the kitchen to the terrace. She arranged the items on the rough surface of the round stone table as she eyed the wooden gate, watching for visitors. She had been somewhat shocked that he had invited guests home for breakfast, but she now waited with eagerness for their arrival. In truth, despite his months of near isolation, he wasn't up to guests, yet he had invited them anyway. He wanted the distraction.

The creak of a door drew his attention across the yard to Edan's larger home of wood and stone. It was where Kayleen had always lived. She closed the door behind her and strolled across the grassy yard with a familiar half-awake look on her face. When their eyes met, she smiled and hurried over. She opened her mouth and was about to speak when Megan and Aylun appeared at the gate.

Garris nodded to Kayleen, then marched over to the woman who had saved them in the temple, greeting her with a deep bow. As Aylun stepped up to him, Garris gave him a brief hug and clapped him on his back.

Rillen arrived as they were exchanging greetings, and Kayleen welcomed her like an old friend. When Garris went to say hello, he leaned forward and whispered in Rillen's ear, "I am in your debt."

Rillen whispered back, "I only did what I should."

He pulled back and eyed her. "If you ever need anything, just ask."

He returned his attention to Kayleen, and the look of surprise on her face made it clear she had heard every word of the exchange and understood it was about her.

With his hand on her back, he guided Kayleen over to the table, then he seated her on one of the wooden stools in front of it. He crowded in on the seat next to her, leaving room for his mother on the other side of him. Megan, Aylun, and Rillen took up seats across from the three.

Eejha kept the food coming, and the company was good. They took turns relating their stories. Megan and Aylun told of her abduction and trip through Katapa to Lanessa and Mundus. Garris described the discovery of the sabotaged lighthouses, while Rillen took everyone through the story of finding the man who had done it. At the end, Megan explained how she wound up lugging Aylun to the temple and reviving them all.

When the eating was done, and Aylun was helping Eejha clear the table, Garris decided he had dragged his feet enough. He had made a fool of himself with Eejha and Kayleen—now it was time to do it again, but with an apology. He leaned away from Kayleen and turned his head, seeking her gaze.

She froze, seeming flustered when she spotted his eyes upon her. Then she stopped herself and returned his gaze, unflinching. She was like that, always greeting the unexpected with an unshakable calm.

He bowed his head to her. "I am deeply sorry, Kayleen."

She seemed stunned. "What?"

"When I saw you get hurt, all I could think about was getting back to you so I could find out if you were okay. It made me realize something."

His expression of concern seemed to put her even more on edge. "What's that?"

"It made me realize I'm an idiot."

Her tension melted away, and she smiled. First Eejha then Aylun stopped at the doorway, surveying the scene. There was a strong note of sympathy in Kayleen's response. "Oh, Garris. I've known that since we were little."

Megan had been drinking from her glass, and she choked and sprayed water all over her leftover food. She covered her mouth. "Sorry." Her eyes darted between Garris and Kayleen. "Carry on."

Garris sucked up his pride and did as Megan suggested. "Last time I was in this yard, I made a big spectacle of myself, saying I wasn't going to stay here in Shirdon."

Kayleen's sympathy turned to a flat stare. "Yes, I remember, and I don't think the term idiot quite covers it. You were an ungrateful, self-centered, coldhearted jackass."

Garris stared for a moment. "It's hard to believe you use that mouth to sway politicians and diplomats."

She scoffed. "Since when have you *ever* cared about diplomacy."

He nodded. "Fair enough. I was ungrateful, self-centered, and coldhearted. I'm sorry about that."

Megan leaned over her plate, watching them as if they were gladiators and she was viewing their death match. "You forgot jackass."

He suppressed a laugh. "Okay, I was a jackass, and I'm sorry about that too, but I had my reasons."

Kayleen sent him a questioning gaze. "I'm used to you abandoning me, but what possible reason could you have to abandon your mother?"

Garris considered the question. The answer was why he had wanted the distraction of company. He didn't want to go into all the details behind his reluctance to stay. "I've done things, Kayleen, things I haven't let myself face. Things that make it almost impossible for me to face you and Mother."

"What could be so horrible?"

"This is not the time or place to go into all of that. It is an occasion to celebrate making it out of that darkness alive. And a chance for me to apologize to you and Mother." He eyed Kayleen first, then his mother. "In time, I will tell you everything."

Eejha took a step toward him. "Does that mean you're staying?"

"Yes, Mother. It was wrong of me to decide on my own to leave without telling you the whole reason why. Besides, this business with the Mirhal convinced me Kayleen needs me here with her."

A huge smile broke across Kayleen's face.

Flustered by her obvious satisfaction at his capitulation, he tried to backtrack on his display of concern. "And for that matter, Jon needs looking after too. And he'll get Dellia into scrapes that she can't handle alone." He motioned to Aylun, then Megan. "And don't even get me started on this pair. They willingly go into places like Katapa and Lanessa and take midnight strolls in the Dead of Night. There's no way they won't need help."

Megan shot him a big grin. "Remind me again, who saved whom in that temple?"

Rillen leaned over the table. "Yeah, the way you're all puffed up now, I'm a little unclear on that?"

Garris bowed his head. "All right. All right. You've made your point."

Rillen eyed him. "I have to admit you were a lot of help when I went after the guy who sabotaged the lighthouse."

"Hey, who helped who?"

Megan leaned closer to Rillen. "If you liked that, you should try stealing horses with this guy." With her thumb, she pointed at Aylun next to her. "He's a pro."

Garris leaned back, and with the taste of his mom's sumptuous cooking still in his mouth and its aroma drifting on the air, he let the conversation take its course. It was good to be home, gathered with everyone around the table where he'd eaten thousands of meals with his mother, Leanna, and Kayleen. It was good to have resolved to stay here with her and his mother. He felt as if a burden had been lifted from his shoulders. Yet, it was only a moment of respite in a sea of discomfort he had yet to cross. What had left him disquieted wasn't merely the discussion he still needed to have with his mother and Kayleen. It was also the feeling he had just made a decision of monumental foolishness.

Jon had told him how this all ends. It ends with his death, and only a fool would stand still while death raced toward them. Only a fool would let himself be taken from the ones who loved him. Then again, perhaps he was a fool for even thinking that way.

He had never believed in this prophecy nonsense. It almost always took you to places that bore no resemblance to what you had imagined. All that was certain was that his decision had led him back to his mother and Kayleen, and for the first time since he had left to become a protector, it felt like he was home.

The atmosphere remained tense, and his mouth dry and pasty from anxiety, as Jon leaned over the dark marble council table. He rested his palms on its cool surface and scanned the nine faces peering at him across its polished expanse. "So that's my proposal. That is the measure I'm asking you to now vote on." He raised his gaze to the torchlit council chamber beyond.

He had worked hard with Dellia and Kayleen to develop a set of laws that preserved the independence of the three realms while also making the best possible use of the military and protectors. Even so, his presentation to the council had racked his nerves. His apprehension wasn't due to lack of confidence, nor was it because he was unaccustomed to public speaking. It was because it just felt wrong.

He may have accepted the role of council leader, but that didn't ease the sensation of playing with fire. It still seemed like this would all somehow blow up in everyone's faces and leave him shouldering the blame. Still, he had accepted that this was his role now. It was what he must do. So, he strived to quell his anxiety and feign unflinching confidence as he faced the council members.

Iolus, one of the two Talus representatives on the new council, seemed eager to speak. He was the only member who wore leather armor and bracers to council meetings. It somehow seemed fitting because, despite his happy-go-lucky nature, he never backed down from a fight. Like the leaders in the Ephori, he spoke with a strength of conviction that was difficult to resist. He seemed even more self-assured in public view, where he appeared to revel in putting people on the spot.

He leaned forward across the table, and his light brown eyes rested on Jon. "Did you bring your wife and mother-in-law with you to impress us with your display of support?"

Jon chuckled.

Iolus seemed to take offense, or at least he put on a good show of it. "Did I say something funny?"

"Yes. You know Sirra. The idea that she would be here if she didn't believe in what I was proposing is laughable. And as for Dellia, I asked her to come for your benefit, to answer your questions."

That seemed to silence Iolus, but Makira, the other Talesh council member, became intrigued. Her light blue eyes and fiery hair matched her outspoken and skeptical nature. She sported a sly sort of smile and spoke in a soft voice that could turn strong and commanding in the blink of an eye. "Good. Then I'll ask her directly, because if she can't explain her duties under these new rules of yours, how can any of us accept them?"

Jon smiled and gave a crisp nod. "Fair enough."

Her green eyes rested on Dellia. "So, under your husband's proposed rules, could you simply take over our military, leaving its leaders to sit by and watch?"

Nervous that Dellia might not be up to their grilling, he interceded to remind them of the rules he had just explained. "As I said, protectors always have the first say in any situation, and their decisions are based solely on whether there is a threat to the other two realms."

Makira seemed annoyed, and her voice gained a sudden sharp and disapproving edge that resounded through the large marble hall. "I didn't ask you. I asked Dellia."

1004

Dellia stepped forward. Perhaps only he was aware of it, but it was a bit too easy for her to seem dispassionate. Not because she wasn't passionate about the subject, but because, since their return, it had been hard for her to show interest in anything outside of him and her daily routine. Still, she maintained her poise and presented herself with an informal ease that conveyed her deep understanding of her new role.

"As you all know, Garris, Jon, and I discovered the sabotage of the lighthouses. Since it might have set loose the Dead of Night, it became a threat not only to Talus but to Erden and Elore. Under the new rules, a threat to the other two realms would obligate Garris and me to take charge and represent the interests of Erden and Elore in the matter."

Jon studied the Erdish and Elorian representatives, who met Dellia's simple illustration with approving nods. Using the southern lighthouse incident as an illustration while it was still fresh in their minds was a stroke of brilliance. It appeared to have gone a long way toward swaying them. Of course, there was no need to convince the old council members, Ceree and Braye. They already supported his proposal. Not that it mattered. This issue was about the extent of the new council's power—so while the old members could debate, the only votes that counted were those of the representatives of the three realms.

Jon's gaze fell on Makira. She had a self-satisfied expression as she leaned back in her chair. "So, your answer is yes, you would take over our Talesh military?"

"No. While the rules might allow it, I would be foolish to let myself get bogged down in managing a military force. It would be to everyone's advantage to leave the existing military structure in place and work with Saneya in handling the situation. In fact, that will always be the case. Protectors are trained to work alone, not lead soldiers. It will always be more effective to work with military and political leadership rather than try to take their place."

Fraysha, one of the two Erdish members of the new council, had a familiar "gotcha" glint in her eye. She loved poking holes in every proposal, and it appeared that something in this one intrigued her. Her long, tightly braided black hair fell around her shoulders, and her lavish golden jewelry tinkled as she leaned forward. "What if you and Garris didn't agree on whether the threat might affect Erden or Elore?"

Dellia put on a smile that almost appeared genuine. "That would never happen. Protectors are trained to work together as a team and to respect the experience and wisdom of our elders. We think alike, and that means we seldom disagree. And if on a rare occasion we couldn't agree, I would always defer to Garris's judgment as one who has more years of experience than me."

"What if Jon told you to stay out of it?"

"I work for the council. Jon is council leader. His orders are law." Dellia eyed him, then leaned over the table and lowered her voice as if to keep what she was saying a secret from him. "However, since I'm his wife, he might find it a bit uncomfortable to disagree with me too much."

There were a number of appreciative chuckles around the table. Jon smiled. It was a crafty response. The hardest-to-sway members might trust Dellia more than him.

Iolus leaned forward again, his reflection dark on the shiny surface of the table. "What if Saneya refused to cooperate?"

Dellia answered with her same casual ease. "I would remind her she can send a message to the council, and they can order me as they please. If she wanted, I would be happy to send it on her behalf." She stood taller and left a slight pause. "My only aim is to serve. I have no ambitions to govern or command. The issue of who calls the shots in resolving a matter is of little concern to me. My only desire is to be of as much help as possible in resolving it."

Jon decided it would be a good time to restate the rules. The more times he repeated them, the more familiar they became and the better the chance the council would accept them. He leaned over the table again, feeling its cool surface under his palms.

"Remember, the protector gets the first say in any situation, but the council *always* gets the final say. If the council members from Talus could convince those from either Erden or Elore that there was no threat to them, they would only need one more vote to get the protector to stand down. If a protector were to keep going against the wishes of the council, it would take all nine council members to dismiss them permanently."

Makira shot Jon another "gotcha" look. "By requiring all nine members to dismiss a protector, you are setting the judgment of one lone council member above that of the rightful rulers of all three realms. How can you justify that?"

Jon paused. It was a good question because it gave him a chance to set out his most persuasive argument. He nodded. "Because they exist to act on your behalf. Remember, the council recruits, screens, trains, and supports protectors at great expense. We teach them to be the first and last line of defense in the most dire circumstances. They are the eyes, ears, mouth, and right arm of this council."

He scanned the faces across the table as he let his argument gather weight. "That means they are *your* eyes, your ears, your mouth, and your right arm. Gouging out our eyes, plugging our ears, and cutting off our right arm is not something we should do lightly. It should only be done when we all agree it must be done."

Jon faced the council again. To interject himself further into this matter would soon become counterproductive. So, it was time to sum up. He smiled, trying to be affable even as he struggled to keep from shaking. "I have tried to devise a set of rules that preserves the sovereignty of all three realms while also making no compromise in providing for their common defense. This measure is the answer. When the next crisis arises in Erden or Elore, the protectors can respond with lightning quickness to make sure Talus is not left to the mercy of another realm's judgment or capabilities."

He eyed them all one last time. "You know my vote. Now it is time for you to choose. Will you leave the safety of your people to the leaders of the other two realms, or do you want the protectors there to act in your interests? You decide."

He turned and marched away, heading past the torchlit columns and displays of ancient artifacts. Dellia and Sirra followed, their footsteps echoing through the chamber. He never glanced back at Kayleen, who remained at the table to vote on his behalf.

Leaving now, before the vote, would be seen as a show of confidence. At least, that's what Kayleen had advised. He had said what he needed to, and those who agreed with his proposal would carry on and argue for it. His continued presence would only make him seem desperate to convince everyone that the rules he had put forward were the right path.

As soon as he passed into the hall, Jon leaned against the wall and heaved a deep sigh of relief. "I hope they bought all that."

No response came from Sirra or Dellia.

He knew he wasn't up to this kind of thing, and their silence proved it. He straightened and sought Dellia's gaze. "I'm sorry. I wish I could have been more persuasive."

She slipped her arms around him in a firm hug. "You were perfect."

When she let go, Sirra gave him a strong hug of her own. "Don't worry, I've been at this a long time, and you held your own. I know Iolus and Makira, and despite the way they acted, I am confident you won them over." She pulled back and looked at Dellia, then Jon. "I want to sit in on the rest of the meeting so I can fill you in later. You two go back home. Tilla will be waiting."

Jon smiled, then took Dellia's hand, and they strolled back down the polished, torchlit halls. Her mood had improved each day since they had come back from Elysium, and it had helped a lot to have Sirra and Tilla around, but her greatest need was for his support. It worried him to see her like this, but he also felt a level of closeness to her he had never felt before. She was truly a part of him now in every way. His hope was that she would return to her old self, but at the same time, they would preserve the closeness they now shared.

They exited the keep and headed down the street for their home on the plateau. Dellia remained somber and quiet. After a time, she looked over at him in the warm sunshine, and a broad smile lit up her face. "Thank you for that."

He glanced at her, looked away, then glanced again. And as he did, he couldn't stop a huge grin from creeping across his face. He was a little schoolboy who had just been praised by his favorite teacher. He looked down at his feet, stepping along the cobbles. "I only did what I should."

Dellia kept staring. "You know you're easy, right? One smile, and it makes you so happy."

Jon gazed up into her face. "One smile from *you*."

At that, she sped up, and there seemed to be a new bounce in her step. For the moment, life seemed perfect. He had come up with the best possible proposal, drafted it with Kayleen, and presented it as best he could. He had done what he needed to do.

Now it was finished, Dellia was at his side, and they were headed back home where the big, wirehaired Tilla awaited them with her ever-buoyant personality. Later, they would eat and laugh, and when they grew tired, he would sleep next to his beautiful wife. Well, if Tilla didn't decide to sleep between them, that is.

Jon peered up at the white clouds drifting across the azure sky, then he turned his gaze to Dellia. "We've earned a break. Let's go get Tilla and do something fun."

She nodded. "I have a place I want to take you." She grabbed his hand, and they hurried back to their small home on the plateau and the simple pleasures he loved so much.

Dellia burst through the door of her familiar home, and the gray-haired Tilla bounded over and made her exuberant greeting. Afterward, she plopped down on the floor, a large pile of wiry fur that watched with eager brown eyes, scrutinizing Dellia's every move as she readied herself. When done, she put Tilla on a leash and waited at the door. Jon soon came and opened the door for them, then followed them out onto the cobblestone street. He was so eager to spend time with her, as always, which was one thing that hadn't changed, and she hoped it never would.

As she led him down the familiar streets past strolling residents, it was striking how drab and colorless it all seemed now. The only thing that had made the last few days bearable was Jon. He was still here and still as much in love with her as ever. He and his devotion had become the one stable thing in her life, the one constant she could count on.

They turned onto the winding stone pathways of Shir Courtyard, and few words passed between them. Few were needed. They passed a familiar patch of tall grass, and she led the way around a wall of deep pink blooms, whose sweet perfume saturated the air. Just beyond lay the pool with flowers of bright orange and yellow at its edge. As they strolled its border, she watched the colorful fish dart in and out of the butter-yellow water lilies that drifted on its crystal surface.

She stopped near the spot where she had proposed to Jon. It was a bittersweet memory, in part because of how mistaken she had been back then, and she wanted to tell him that. She wanted a new understanding. So, she found a patch of thick grass at the water's edge and they sat down, with Jon on one side and Tilla in a heap on the other.

She faced him. "I'm trying, Jon, but everything here is so dull."

"I know." He sent her an earnest stare. "Would it help to go back to training the young protectors? Maybe just watch? I know you. It wouldn't be long before you'd have to step in and help."

She shook her head. "Give me time. I'll get there. But I appreciate you worrying for me."

Silence fell for a while.

Then, with the vibrant flowers all around and the lilies floating on the cool waters beside her, she took his hands into hers. "I was wrong, Jon."

A look of concern filled his face. "Don't say that."

She hurried to explain. "No, I was. I said marriage was about being determined to make it work with you, but in my heart, I was never willing to give up a single thing I wanted for myself in order to be with you. I treated you like ... like a second-class, part-time husband, someone I could leave behind to go do what I really wanted. Then I expected you to be there for me when I was done. It was cruel and unfair."

"No." He shook his head. "Being a protector was what gave your life meaning and purpose."

In shame, she lowered her head. "You're a person, Jon. You're more important than things. You're more important than a job. You give my life meaning. You give me purpose."

He responded with the determination of a man trying to cheer up the woman he loved. "But you wanted to serve the people, to protect them. There's nothing wrong with that."

"It's true. There is nothing wrong with that. But my heart was in the wrong place. Megan once said that I was willing to give you up for a bunch of people I didn't even know. She was right."

Even as she sensed that he was touched by her words, his desperation to ease her guilt remained. "But this world needs people who will fight to protect people they don't know."

"You're right. But you were also right to be hurt that I didn't put you first." He had a bewildered look, so she rushed to explain. "It would have been different if being a protector was something we both wanted for me, but I never asked you what you wanted. It would be different if I were a protector to protect you and what was important to you, but that was never my reason. My reasons were selfish."

His desperation turned to alarm. "Don't say that. You're not a selfish person, and it hurts to see you look at yourself that way."

"I *am* selfish. Do you know how hurt I would have been if you decided on your own to leave me alone for long stretches of time to go do a job? Do you know how lonely I would have been, how left out I would have felt?"

Jon shook his head. "Don't beat yourself up over those things. They don't matter anymore. It's enough that you're here with me now."

She lowered her gaze again, feeling a fresh wave of shame as she recalled her proposal. "The worst part is that I was wrong from the very start. I said marriage was about being determined to make it work with you, but what that meant to me was getting you to accept a life where I would go and do what I wanted without you. That's not what marriage is about. It's so much simpler than that. It's about love."

Jon sent her another puzzled look, so she rushed again to explain. "I was striving for all these things I thought were so important. I was willing to leave you out of big chunks of my life for them. And the saddest, most foolish part of all is that none of those things would have lasted." She looked into his eyes and set her hand on his. "Jobs don't last. You and me—we last. Love lasts. At least it can if we put each other first in our hearts. I guess what I'm saying is that our time in Elysium made me realize something. Long after I've grown too old to be a protector, I still want to be with you."

She let her gaze fall again, and Jon remained quiet for a time, in that way he had when he was digesting what he'd heard. He petted Tilla's rough hair with long gentle strokes, then looked up at Dellia. "But you still want to be a protector, right?"

She smiled. He was still trying, but he didn't need to. Her gaze rose from the soft, green grass to meet his. "I want to be your protector. I'll go where you decide."

"You mean, you want to be *our* protector. You'll go where *we* decide."

Dellia nodded. Having forged a new understanding, her mind turned to another topic that had weighed heavily on her these last days. She had just given up an eternal life with the one she loved for an existence that would be cut short by the coming invasion. Jon had been given a vision of her death amid the same kind of misery the Dead of Night had brought. A ray of optimism in her otherwise short and bleak future was what she yearned for now. She needed a future worth fighting for, a light she could seek at the end of this dark and bleak tunnel. So, she held Jon's gaze as she summoned the strength to make her absurd request. "But right now, I need strength." She sent him a soft, pleading look. "Strength to face what's to come. So, promise me something."

He smiled back at her. "Anything."

"Promise me if there's any way to get us back to Elysium someday, you'll find it."

A stunned silence fell as Jon stared at her with a shocked expression. "Wow. Your faith in me is way overblown."

"I know what I'm asking is ridiculous, but don't dismiss it like that. It would really help me get through this to have hope that one day, when all this is over, we might return to that life."

He went quiet for a time, and she could almost see the ideas bubbling in his brain. Then she sensed him give up and let out a small laugh. "Sure, why not? If I can do something as absurd as stopping an invasion, why can't I find a way to get us back to Elysium?"

Disappointment stung Dellia. "Now you're making fun of me."

His smile broadened. "That's the most amusing part. I'm not making fun of you at all. I swear, I'm agreeing with you. I want it as much as you do."

He meant what he said with his whole heart. She had misread him. Jon hadn't given up. He had given in. Suddenly everything seemed brighter. "You promise?"

"Yes, and even if it's the most ridiculous promise I've ever made, it's also the most heartfelt. I loved our life there as much as you did."

She muttered, "Liar."

"No, I did. And I promise, when we have done what we must do here in this world, we will find our way back to Elysium."

The cloud of gloom over Dellia seemed to lift, and the world brightened. He was beside her now. Tilla's head lay in her lap, and they were in this beautiful place. It was the spot where she had proposed to him and he to her, and now it was the place where they had reached a new understanding.

They would stay here and enjoy the peaceful beauty for a while, and when they returned home, her mother's smiling face would greet her. She had all the things she loved around her, and now she had the most important thing of all: hope for the future.

Megan stared out past the marble columns at the steady rain falling on the ruins of Carpoli. This was Saranik, a land, it appeared, that had not seen rainfall for hundreds of years. Lightning flashed through thick gray skies, followed by a chest-rattling boom. It echoed on and on, rumbling across the landscape beyond the crumbling remains of the ancient city.

Behind her, Yuki let out a quiet nicker, and Megan glanced back at her spotted face, placid and beautiful. Behind Yuki lay the Carpoli Temple entrance, and within, the golden glow of the statue of Athene.

Aylun crept up to Megan, unnoticed. She startled as she almost bumped into him, standing close by her side.

He pulled his gaze from the storm and glanced over at her. "So, what is next for you?"

She smiled back. "You. You're next."

He cocked his head. "What do you mean?"

"When I was following you in the Dead of Night, I had a lot of time to reflect on myself."

"And what did you learn?"

"That I'm afraid. That I've been afraid since I left home." Megan drew a deep breath. "Did you know I've never had a boyfriend?" She shook her head. "Oh, I went out a lot and danced and had a good time with friends, but I used Jon as an excuse to avoid getting close to anyone. I guess I told myself he was the one, and in some ways, he was. Yet, I always kept him at a distance. Despite so many chances, I never once accepted him."

Aylun nodded, but a tinge of jealousy showed on his face, and a slight crispness came to his voice. "I see."

1014

She ignored it. What she had to say was important. "Oh, I told myself all kinds of excuses. I just wanted to have fun. He was too serious. We were too different. He wasn't part of the plan. I didn't want to lose who I was. Being more than friends could ruin our relationship."

He nodded, and again, there was a stiffness in his manner.

Lightning crackled nearby, and the thunder thumped her chest again, then rumbled outward over the land, echoing far into the rain-obscured distance.

Megan smiled at him, trying to set him at ease. "But the truth is they were all excuses. When you love someone, I mean *really* love someone, all of those things that seemed so important become trivial. None of it matters. I love you, Aylun. I really love you, and with you, I don't want excuses."

The brittleness in his manner seemed to melt away, and Aylun smiled back.

She hurried to speak again. "But I'm still afraid. Afraid that it will turn out like my mom and dad. At one time, they loved each other too. I think what drew me to Jon was that he was the opposite of my dad, but even with him being so different, I still couldn't bring myself to get too close to him. With you, it's so much harder."

His countenance fell. "I see."

"No, you don't. You terrify me, Aylun. I love you so much, but we started out so badly, and I can't help thinking you might go back to being that man. It would be like my father and mother all over again."

His disposition remained dour. "I suppose I earned that. I deserve it."

"So, what I'm saying is, don't leave me. Please, be patient with me. Stay by my side. I know how important it is to you for me to commit to you, but I just can't right now. So, give me some time to get over my fear?"

He nodded and glanced out at the gray blanket of rain obscuring the crumbling remains of the vast city. Then he looked down at the wet slab of rock beneath his feet. "You already know my answer."

She peered up into his dark eyes. "I do?"

Aylun met her gaze with a solemn look. "You are everything to me: my savior, my friend, my companion, my partner. In my heart, there is you and only you." She smiled as he continued to stare with those earnest eyes. "There is no point in me vowing to commit to you because it is already done. My heart belongs to you until the world is old, the heavens are desolate, the seas run dry, and the rocks crumble. So, all I can do is show you my heart and wait until you are ready to trust it."

His confession, delivered with such profound conviction, made her heart flutter. When she recovered the power of speech, all she could manage were a few paltry words. "So, we're still together, right, you and me?"

"Of course." Aylun remained quiet for a time. "In that case, what is next for *us*?"

Megan considered the question. "Rillen, I guess. Wistra said she is a part of this and to use her. But …"

"But what?"

"You are forbidden to get along with her. You understand?"

He seemed surprised. "Oh. It's like that, is it?"

"Actually, forget that. I want you to myself for a while." She paused for a second as she tried to picture where they might go and what they might do together. As she did, her mind naturally turned to the many loose ends that had nagged at her these past few days. She stared out across the vast city before her. "Besides, there's a part of Jon's story that bothers me."

"Are you talking about his abduction and torture?"

Megan stared in surprise. "You noticed that too? I can't figure out who took him and why they were so determined to find me. That's a mystery we definitely need to unravel, but no, not now."

"Then what?"

"Syvis is a bigger problem. Idria banished a demon. One that posed a threat to everyone, including Jon. Yet, at the same time, she threatened him with taking Dellia, which isn't some benevolent act. I

1016

don't get it. What motivates her? Why does she want his power? What would she do with it?" Megan set her hand on the grotesque eye tucked into her clothing. "And to be honest, it bothers me that I'm carrying around the Eye of Syvis when I don't really know what it is. I think we need answers, and we need them before Idria tries to make good on her threat to take Dellia."

Aylun nodded agreement.

Above the soft patter of the rain came another quiet nicker from behind her. Megan glanced back at Yuki standing there waiting. She leaned her head on Aylun's shoulder and stared out at the rain that had not fallen for hundreds of years.

She drew a deep breath, cool and fresh from the storm. It was done. She had told Aylun of her apprehension, and he hadn't flinched. He was still here. They were still together, with the air cleared between them. She had taken a new step.

Soon she and Aylun would leave this place to find answers. She would take another new step, another path she had never traveled before. That step could be one of unfathomable proportions, and it might take them to many dark and dangerous places. The prospect terrified but also excited her.

Lightning crackled through the flat gray skies, and thunder rumbled out across the temple walls, so Megan clung to Aylun's arm. She didn't need his protection, but she so much wanted it. Distant flashes lit up the ruins, one after another, as excitement filled her, and her mind turned once again to all the terrible and wonderful things the future might hold.